Without You

Without You

SUE LANGFORD

iUniverse, Inc.
Bloomington

Without You

iUniverse books may be ordered through booksellers or by contacting:

iUniverse
1663 Liberty Drive
Bloomington, IN 47403
www.iuniverse.com
1-800-Authors (1-800-288-4677)

ISBN: 978-1-4697-8831-9 (sc)
ISBN: 978-1-4697-8832-6 (e)

Library of Congress Control Number: 2012903392

Printed in the United States of America

iUniverse rev. date: 02/16/2012

To the ones who believed, and encouraged.
For Charlene, Leanne, Kaila and my family
and all those who knew this day would come.
Thank you for being my strength.
I wouldn't know what to do without you . . . .

ACKNOWLEDGEMENTS

Firstly, I wanted to thank my family for always believing in me and encouraging me to follow my dreams. For my parents who showed me that love can last forever, and in turn gave me the inspiration to write love stories where true love prevails.

For my friends who always believed in me and helped me write from my heart. Thank you for making me write through the tears and the pain. Thank you for being a sounding board, an advice giver, the voice of reason, or the distraction I needed to get through writer's block. Thank you to Leanne for helping me with all the little things, and being a slap of reality when I desperately needed one. For being the one who was there in good and bad, and who never let me doubt myself. I believe in you too. To my friend Kaila, who recently reminded me that writing has been a dream since childhood. You always will be like a sister to me. Love you guys.

For my friend Charlene who showed me that being strong isn't always a bad thing. You know I'll be you're rock whenever you need me. Love you.

To those who inspired me, gave me a hug when needed, were a shoulder to cry on or a sounding board when I had no idea what to do, thank you for being who you are. Don't ever change.

I want to thank all the bands who played every song that I listened to while writing this. You know who you are. For one specific one in particular, I will be your fan for life, Playboy bunny hat and all.

And thank you to each and every one of you who are buying this book. Thank you for being part of making my dream come true.

CHAPTER 1

"I have to find her Ryan," Joe said. "You realize the lobby is filled with girls trying to get your attention," Brad said. "There's something about her. I have to find her," Joe said. "And just how are you gonna pull that off," Ryan asked. "I told her to come up," Joe said. "Her and half the blonds in town," Brad joked. "What was her name," Joe asked. "Ava," Ryan said.

A few years later . . . .

"What do you mean you broke up?" Rose asked. "He showed up with coffee, dropped the bomb, then left. It's like he was going through a damn McDonald's drive thru. I'll have one break up to go please," Ava replied. "Are you kidding me? Just like that?" "Tell me again why I wasted my time."

After another breakup, every girl needs her friends. Ava Ross was definitely no stranger to heartbreak. She was always the one to comfort everyone in their times of need, but now it was hers. Her boyfriend of three years had walked out. Not even a warning sign as to what was going to happen, she was in shock. It was time for another girl night, and she refused to be designated driver.

Ava Ross stood around five foot seven, long blonde hair and piercing blue eyes. She worked out, she ate right, she did everything right. She always dressed to impress, even at the gym. She looked perfect from the outside, but right now, she fell a heck of a lot short of perfect. She had a tendency to fall for the bad boy, then try to heal him into a good man. She was almost too caring, too warm. She wore her heart on her sleeve with everyone, but this time, it had burned off and formed what felt like a lump in her throat.

"Ava, you didn't waste your time. You'll never regret being with him. That's what you told me when I broke up with what's his name." "Only thing I regret is not taking off the blinders when it came to him. I thought he'd changed, Rose. I thought he'd grown a heart. I thought for once it would work out."

Rose Shaw wasn't a stranger to heartbreak either. Instead, she'd opted to be more like the guys. Dump them before they dump her, use them like the ones before used her. She was one strong woman. She was around the same height as Ava, and they both took care of themselves, but Rose was very different than Ava. She had a presence around people that always put them at ease and had the guys staring. Her long dark hair and hazel eyes were her strong suit. The fact that she knew just how to work every curve was what made her irresistible. Deep down, she wanted one man all to herself, but there was no way she'd ever admit it to Ava, or any of her other friends for that matter.

"Ava, you need to get out of the house. Pack a bag for a few days. We're going away." "Where the heck are we gonna go Rose?" "Let me figure it out. There has to be a million last minute deals online." Ava did just that. She turned on her Aces CD, and started packing.

Ava thought back to a few years ago when she'd actually met the band—and that conversation she'd had with Joe Morgan.

She'd been nervous for weeks and had every song memorized by the time she got into the lineup. Her heart was racing, her palms were sweaty and the drink she'd had at dinner with Rose was kicking in. She finally walked in and was less than 5 feet from Joe Morgan. He was only the guitarist in the band, but she'd been dreaming about him forever.

Joe Morgan was every woman's dream. He stood almost 5 foot 10, had the brown hair and the killer blue eyes that women wished they could practically swim in. He was enticing enough to have half the fans drooling over him, and took advantage of that fact. It was a well-known fact that he had girlfriends in every town, and Ava was sure that Buffalo was no different.

Her turn finally came and she was face to face with him. "And you are," he asked. "Ava." "Nice to meet you," Joe said. "You too. You are so much better looking in person," she joked. "Okay, I like her," Joe joked. Ryan and Brad, the other two members of the band, just smirked. "You have to share," Ryan teased. "Nope," Joe joked. She got her picture done with them, then went to leave. "Ava, can you stay here for a moment," the manager said. "Sure," she replied not knowing what was going on. Once the meet and greet was finished, Joe walked towards her. "So, about what you said," he teased. "Well, you are Joe," Ava replied. "What are you doing after the show?" "Going back to my hotel with my friend Rose." "Why don't you come hang out with us at the hotel a while." "You do realize I'm not a groupie right," Ava asked. "We could have fun," he said. "I bet," Ava replied.

"We could talk and get to know each other." "Okay," Ava replied. He wrote down the suite number on her hand and kissed her. He walked her back to security and she went to her seat while Joe headed on stage.

She'd made it to the hotel that night and saw more than one girl with the same number on a card, or their hand. She wasn't about to be just another notch on the bedpost. She wanted him to remember her. Instead of making her way through the gaggle of women, she went back to her hotel and headed to bed.

She couldn't help but smile at that. Being hit on by Joe Morgan of all people? She shook her head, trying to knock her brain back to reality.

Ava packed her Aces CD away in her suitcase with a grin ear to ear. She had two full suitcases packed by the time Rose called her back. "Two round-trip tickets. Five day trip. You owe me $800." "Fine. Where the hell are we going anyway?" "Jamaica. The resort is in Rio Bueno. It's really nice, plus we got a discount on the flight with the air miles." "Great." "We're leaving in 5 hours. Finish packing. I'll be there in an hour or so to pick you up."

The girls left for the airport, excited about getting away from all the drama, but even more excited to be away from work. They made it through security then sat down, waiting for the boarding call. Ava looked around, checking out the guys in the terminal, then one caught her eye. He looked up, staring right at her. He grabbed his bags and walked towards her.

"Boarding for flight to Montego Bay." Ava got up. The man looked over and smiled. Ava smiled back. "You are supposed to be getting vacation man. Not home man," Rose teased. Ava went to grab her bag and he was directly in front of her. "Hi," he said. "Hi." "You're going to Montego Bay too?" Ava nodded. "Maybe we'll bump into each other." "Maybe," Ava replied. They boarded and Ava grabbed her seat. Rose was seated right in front of her. The guy boarded and looked over, then looked down at his ticket. "I promise I'm not stalking you. I guess our seats are together." Ava laughed. "Have a seat then. I'm Ava by the way." "James." She went to shake his hand and he kissed her hand instead. She couldn't help but smile.

He chatted Ava up a good portion of the flight. "You sure you don't have a man? Who could possibly pass you up?" "Thanks for the compliment, but I'm definitely single." "Not for long pretty lady." "You think so do you?" He nodded. Ava smiled. "So where are you two ladies staying?" Ava told him about the resort. "Seriously? My buddy and I are staying in the same place?" "Okay. Now that's stalking." "Booked an Oceanside suite." "So did we," Rose said. Ava laughed. "So, what are you doing for dinner tonight?" "Unpacking,"

Ava replied. The movie came on and she tried ignoring him the rest of the flight. Another relationship was the last thing she needed.

The plane finally landed. They headed to the resort, then got checked in. Oddly enough, Ava and James were a few doors down from each other. Around dinner, Ava and Rose headed to the restaurant and James invited himself to the table and sat down with Ava and Rose.

Rose started feeling like a third-wheel at dinner and went over to the bar, noticing a guy she thought was handsome. She flirted her way into a free drink or two, then noticed Ava and James heading out. Ava walked over to her. "Meet you in the room. I'm going for a walk," Ava said. "Your shadow coming with you," Rose teased. "My stalker? Probably," she teased. Rose hugged her and Ava left. James was right behind her.

"You gonna follow me all night," Ava asked. "No, just something I wanted to do." "Which is?" She looked over at him and he kissed her. Tingles shot right to the tips of her toes. "Been wanting to do that since I saw you at the airport." He kissed her again. "What are you doing tomorrow morning?" "Morning run." "You're on vacation." "Exactly what Rose said, but I'm doing it anyway." "Then I'll meet you for a run." "You don't have to." He pulled her into his arms and kissed her again. "Yeah I do." "I should get back," Ava said. He grabbed her hand and they walked back to the room. He kissed her again as they got closer to the room. "So when was your last girlfriend?" Ava asked trying to distract him from laying another kiss on her. "A few months ago. Why?" "Just asking." "I'm not the player type." "Good to know." They got to the door and he leaned her against it, kissing her again. "We should get some sleep," Ava said trying to break away from him. He kissed her again. Tingles all over. "Sweet dreams beautiful." "You too," Ava replied. He kissed the tip of her nose, then went down to his room. Ava went into her room and locked the door.

Ava went and slipped into her pajamas. She laughed. There was no way she was jumping into another relationship. She knew exactly what Rose would say to her. "We're on vacation. It's a vacation fling. Just go for it." It wasn't enough. The man was more than fine. She thought about it then realized that she had to stop over-analyzing things. Whatever happened on vacation was staying on this island. Sort of like the Las Vegas saying 'What happens in Vegas stays in Vegas.' If only it were that simple.

Rose walked in a few hours later, laughing, then fell into the other bed. "So how's hottie from the airport?" "Fine. He's okay. I just honestly don't need another guy around right now," Ava said. "So where'd you two disappear to?" "Went for a walk on the beach." "And?" "Nothing. We talked and walked." "Thought we were here to escape from guys?" "We are. How's the guy you met at the bar?" "Met a few actually. One of them asked me on a boat ride in the morning if you're up for it." "Going for a run, then vegging on the beach. I need the down time," Ava said. "I'll meet you back here for lunch then." Ava nodded. "If not, I'll come find you two on the beach," Rose joked. They fell asleep and Ava was still wondering about James. There was no way he didn't have some chick on the side or something. He had bad boy written all over him.

The next morning, Ava woke up and slipped her iPod on to head out for her run. She got changed, then headed to the beach. She walked right past James' room. As she was about to start her stretches, James showed up. "What time did you leave?" "8." "You do realize vacation means sleeping in?" Ava laughed. "Need help with the stretches," James asked. "Think I can handle it," Ava said. She wasn't about to give in to the flirting. They headed off a little while later and she was at least 5 feet ahead of him the entire run. He was breaking a sweat just trying to keep up with her. "You're good," he said when they finally made it back to the resort. "Thanks," Ava replied. "How long have you been a runner?" "A month or two. Just run to clear my head." "What did you need to clear this morning?" "Just a million questions that I don't need to answer." "Yes I do like you, if that clears one question out of the way." Ava laughed. "Thanks, but that wasn't one." "Yes I think you're hot," James joked. Ava laughed. "Okay. Give me a hint as to what's going on in that brain of yours lady," James said. "Just wondering why you have no girlfriend or anything." "I want the spark that never goes away," James said. Ava almost laughed. He was beginning to sound like a Harlequin novel. "You realize it takes work to make relationships like that." "Hell yeah, but if I don't want to kiss the lady every minute of the day, there's no point to dating her right?" "Really?" He nodded. The guy had an ego. "You ready to head to the beach for a swim," he asked hoping that she'd say yes to the nude beach. "I'm going to shower first. I'll meet you down there." It was dropping a hint on deaf ears. "I'll come meet you at your room." They walked back and Ava went and changed. He grabbed a quick shower, then threw on his bathing suit and went down to get her. He knocked and got no answer. He left and headed down to the beach and saw her walking through the pathway. "Ava," James said.

She turned to face him. He wrapped his arms around her, pulling her in close and kissed her. She broke the kiss and walked out towards the beach. Ava found a spot in the middle of all the people, hoping that he'd take the hint. Instead, he grabbed her hand and found a spot away from the rest of the crowd. He grabbed her sun lotion from her bag and rubbed it on her back for her, noticing that with one pull, the top would be off. "Don't you even think it," Ava said. "Think what?" "I know what you're thinking. The suit isn't coming off that easily." He just looked over at her. "Would you stop?" "Stop what?" "Eyeing me like I'm dinner." He laughed, but she had read his mind to a tee.

After a few hours of him flirting, he talked her into a dip in the water. They joked around, splashing each other, then he dove under water. Next thing she knew he picked her up and walked out as far as he could. "Let go." He kissed her. They were both up to their necks in the water. He wanted her so bad he could taste it, and at least she wouldn't be able to tell. He finally went to let go and she tried to swim away. Instead, he pulled her back to him and kissed her again. "I'm gonna say something totally ridiculous, but I need to know," James said. "Okay," Ava replied. "I don't wanna share." "Meaning what?" He kissed her again. "Meaning I want you." "Getting a little ahead of yourself," Ava said. "Can't help it." "James, it's flattering, but I . . ." He kissed her again. "James." She pushed him away and made her way back to the shore. She walked through the hot sand back to her chair. An attendant came walking out. "Ava Ross?" Ava raised her hand. The attendant walked towards her and handed her a note:

Met a guy. We're doing lunch. Meet you at dinner. Bring sexy.

Ava laughed and thanked the attendant. "What's so funny," James asked. "She met a guy on the boat cruise this morning." "That means I get you to myself this afternoon." "I have to get some writing done." The guy was past annoying. There was just no way that she was spending her relaxing vacation with a guy she couldn't stand. "No. You're on vacation woman. No work permitted." "And just how are you thinking that you're going to stop me?" "Don't you tempt me." Ava leaned back in her chair. The guy wasn't taking a hint at all. "Bet you I could talk you into not working." "Just how were you thinking that was going to happen?" He grabbed her bag, and her hand and led her back towards the hotel. "Can I have my bag back," Ava asked. The minute he got to the private pathway, he picked her up and kissed her. "Down." He shook his head. He walked towards the sliding door to his room. "James." He sat her down on the bed in his room. "What are we doing in here?" "Talking you into doing something other than work," he teased. He leaned towards her, leaning her back onto the bed. "I need to go," Ava said. She brushed him off and went to her room.

Ava got some writing done, then got changed for dinner. She was about to leave when there was a knock at the door. She opened it and was face to face with James. "And what do you want?" "Give you one hint," he teased. "I'm meeting Rose for dinner. I have to go," Ava said. "Company?" There was no way that two days in a row he was inviting himself to dinner. "Sort of a girl's night," Ava said. "I'll walk you down then," he said hoping he could talk her into another walk.

Ava walked in and Rose walked over to her hand in hand with the mystery man she'd met. "James, this is Greg," Rose said. "Nice to meet you," James replied. "You joining us for dinner," Rose asked trying to get Ava to relax a bit. "Sure," he replied sitting down right beside Ava. They all chatted through dinner, then had a coffee and went for a walk on the beach. Everything was fine until James tried untying the neckpiece of Ava's dress. It turned into tag down the beach. Ava had finally had it. The guy was driving her nuts. "I have to get some sleep tonight," Ava said excusing herself from the walk. "I'll walk you . . ." "Thanks but no thanks," Ava said brushing James off again.

The next morning, Ava slept in a bit, then left for her run. She came back and saw James sitting with Rose on the patio. "How was the run," Rose asked. "Good." Ava went inside, putting her iPod in her bag. She grabbed a bathing suit and her shorts, then hopped into the shower. She got changed, threw on a little lotion, then came out. She went to grab her laptop and James walked into the room. "I have to get some writing done." "You're on vacation. You need to get a suntan and a drink." Ava logged into her laptop. He knew there was no point in fighting with her. He went and sat back on the patio with Rose.

An hour or so later, Rose came in and shut the door behind her. "Are you blind woman?" "Rose, I'm not doing this. I'm not meeting some random guy on vacation and spending my vacation trying to flirt with him. I told you that I'm done with the idiot guys." "Look at him. The man is fine. He's been talking my ear off about you for an hour and a half." "Not happening," Ava said. "Stubborn," Rose said. "You go have fun. I'm relaxing my own way," Ava replied.

Rose finally talked Ava into going to the beach. "Leave the laptop," Rose begged. "Fine," Ava replied. They went down and Rose sat down in the chaise's beside James. "Was wondering when you two would make it down here," he said. "Had to wait for the workaholic to take a break," Rose teased. Ava just shook her head and sat down.

After an hour or two of sun, Ava headed to the water to cool off. Rose nudged James. He headed straight to Ava. "James, I get what you're trying to do alright?" "What are you so afraid of," he asked. "I'm not the vacation fling type James." She swam out a little further and he followed her. He finally caught up to her and pulled her to him. He kissed her with a toe-curling kiss that girls only see in the sappy chick flicks. "You know how much I want you right now?" "I told you . . ." He kissed her again. "James." "Who said it has to be a vacation fling?" "You are nuts," Ava said. She broke away from him and tried swimming off but he pulled her back to him. "I mean it," he said. He never was one for putting off the inevitable. She knew exactly what Rose would tell her. There was no way she was doing it. No way was she giving into a random guy on vacation.

She thought back to that chance she'd had when she met Joe Morgan. If she'd just had the guts to go through with it back then . . . .

"Promise you won't regret it," James said. She gave in. She figured once he'd got his way, he'd walk off like all the other men she'd dated . . . . or at least she hoped he would. She made her excuse to Rose, and James walked back to the rooms with her. A half-hour later, clothes were flying in his room. It was intense, passionate, mind numbing sex. She knew she'd regret it tomorrow. This totally wasn't her. She got up after and got dressed. "Where are you going?" "Meeting Rose for lunch." "Company," he asked. "I guess," Ava replied. She went back to her room and showered and changed. She came out and James was waiting in the hall. He slid his hand in hers and walked down with her.

They walked into the restaurant and Rose was chatting up a man at the bar. Ava laughed. James looked and saw his buddy Jake. Part of him knew exactly what was going to happen next. "Long time no see," Jake said as he got up and gave James a guy hug. James shook his head. Jake smirked. Rose was in for a heartbreak and James could predict just when it was gonna happen. They had a drink or two, then Ava headed back to the room to relax, and Rose and Jake took off for a walk.

"So you live out our way too," Rose asked. "Just moved back." Rose chatted Jake up, and the more they talked, the more she liked him.

Jake Madden was a lean, muscular guy that had every head turning. Both him and James looked like they walked out of GQ, and Jake could sweet talk a girl into almost anything. He was cool, smooth and handsome. Dark hair and green eyes, he was around six foot two and built like an athlete. He'd been working with a law firm in New York, then decided the big city wasn't his style anymore and was offered a partnership at James' law firm. Jake had a perfect smile, the perfect body. Almost everything was perfect. The man had women all over him. He preferred it that way, and Rose was always up for the challenge of turning a bad boy into a puppy dog.

"So what are you two up to tonight," Jake asked. "Dinner. Might try talking Ava into going to the club for some dancing. Why do you ask," Rose asked. "Was gonna see if you wanted to come to dinner with me, but since you have plans," Jake said. "Depends on where we were going," Rose said. "The five star restaurant," Jake said. It was a sure fire way to get exactly what he wanted that night . . . or so he thought. "Sure," Rose replied. "Meet you at 5," he said. "Room 136." He kissed Rose. 'This is gonna be fun to see him turn into a puppy dog,' Rose thought to herself. What Jake was thinking was a little more x-rated. He walked Rose back to the room, kissed her, then headed to his room.

CHAPTER 2

Ava got more writing done. She had dinner in her room alone, hoping that she'd managed to shake James. Part of her wondered if she'd done the right thing. She couldn't take any of it back now. She slid the Aces CD into her laptop and plugged in her earphones. She thought back again to the night she'd met Joe. It fueled her writing enough to have a full-fledged writing marathon for a few hours. Around 10, she slid her earphones off. She had a shower, then relaxed. She had to be right about James. It was a stupid vacation fling and nothing else. After this, she'd probably never see him again. She left and headed out for a walk along the beach, making sure to bring her iPod fully loaded with every Aces song there was.

Jake walked Rose back to her room after their dinner alone. Rose had spent the entire dinner attempting to convince him that he was gonna fall for her. She teased, taunted and flirted her way back to the room. One kiss that he wouldn't let her out of had her convinced she was right. "Think that's going to change my mind?" Rose nodded. "Don't know me that well Rose. You sure?" She kissed him again. "You know you're still wrong." Rose laughed and opened the door to her room, walked inside and slid her dress off, then turned to face him. The light glow of the bedside lamp drew attention to her curves. Jake looked towards her. "What's wrong Jake? Cat got your tongue?" "You are messing with the wrong man." "Just getting changed for bed." "If you're trying to tempt me, it's not gonna work." She slid off her g-string and flipped it at him. He looked over and saw her sliding on a satin and lace teddy. "You aren't interested, you can always leave," Rose said. She grabbed some lotion then rubbed it on her legs. He moved towards her, stopping to watch every move. "Jake." "What?" "Can you turn the light off for me?" He flipped the light off then walked over towards her. She slid over in the bed as she heard the sound of him pulling his shirt and jeans off, and his boxers, sliding into bed behind her naked.

He leaned his body against her, pulling her to him and sliding the teddy off. "Admit I was right," Rose teased. "You weren't." "The fact that you're so turned on you're radiating heat means what?" "Means you're a really good tease." "Or you could just admit I'm right."

He nibbled into her shoulder. "Admit it," Rose joked. "Would you stop?" "I can get up and walk out. You on the other hand . . ." She heard a wrapper of some sort then his hand slid over her hip and between her legs. "Partially right." They had sex. It was intense, and passionate, and took every ounce of energy they both had left.

They were tangled among the blankets and bed sheet, then fell asleep. Rose knew she was right and so did he, but there was no way his ego was letting her know. He woke up a half hour later and disappeared.

The next morning, Ava took off for her run. She had a feeling that Rose was going to need the extra sleep. An hour and a half later, she came back and saw Rose and Jake on the patio talking. "Morning," Ava said. "Was wondering where you disappeared to," Rose said. "I'll be out of your way in a minute or two," Ava said. She went in, showered, then slid her swimsuit on with her shorts. "Have you seen James today," Jake asked. "No," Ava replied. "He was looking for you this morning," Jake said. Ava shook it off, then went and grabbed breakfast and headed to the beach.

Rose went back to the discussion they'd had the night before. "Fine. You're right." "About time," Rose teased. "Still, I'm not a relationship guy." "Other than the fact that you're a liar." "Really?" Rose nodded. "And why would you think that Rose?" "Because you're here. Didn't want me to think bad of you." "Didn't have other plans." She kissed him again and he was horny in seconds. "What were you saying?" He picked her up and carried her back to the bed.

Ava relaxed by the water and saw James a few minutes later. "And where'd you disappear to last night," James asked. "Was writing." "You seen Jake around anywhere?" "He's with Rose." "I need to talk to him before he does something stupid," James said. "Like what," Ava asked. "The man is a playboy. He has a girlfriend at home." "Your point? This is a vacation. It's like the old phrase . . . what happens in Vegas." That's what Ava knew Rose would say. Maybe she was wrong about him and Jake, but she had to get rid of James somehow. "You think that about us too?" Ava nodded. "And now?" "James, it was a mistake." "A few more days and you won't want to lose me for a second." "Think pretty highly of yourself." Ava sipped her mango pineapple smoothie. "You won't Ava. You're gonna miss me the second we're apart." Ava finished her smoothie, then her breakfast. The man was a piece of work that she wished she could just wash away. He headed back to his room, leaving Ava to her sunshine.

An hour or two later, there was no sign of Rose. Ava headed back to the room. "What the hell do you mean? I'm on bloody vacation. I'm not coming home tomorrow." James was in the middle of a fight on the phone and Ava was pretty glad she'd walked away from him.

There was something about him that didn't sit right with her. When she walked in, Rose and Jake were both gone. She logged into her laptop and turned her iPod on, turning the music up. After two hours, and a battery charge of her iPod, She took her earphones out, then showered and made an appointment for a massage. It's exactly what she needed. She slid her room key into her pocket, then headed down to the spa. "Ava," James said as she walked past him. She kept going. "Why are you ignoring me?" "Go home James." She kept walking and went right into her appointment.

An hour and a half later, she left and went back to her room. The minute she walked past his door, he opened the door and pulled her inside. "What," Ava asked. "I'm not going until the end of the damn vacation." "Go." He kissed her, leaning her against the door. "You're not getting rid of me that easily," James said. "You need to go, then just go." Ava tried to push him away and he wouldn't let her. "I'm not going anywhere. I conference called them and told them it could wait." "James, if you need to go, then go." "I know what I need." "And what in the world would that be?" He kissed her again. He undid her robe. "I'm going back to my room to get work done." "No. We're going to the beach." "I'm not in the mood for the beach." He dropped the robe to the floor. "Have another idea." Ava pushed him away and walked down to her room, slipping her robe back on. He followed her. "Stop," James pleaded. Ava walked into her room. "We're going," James said. Ava went to grab her laptop and he pulled it out of her hands, putting it on the bed. He grabbed her bikini, handing it to her and took her plug for her laptop.

Ava changed, left a note for Rose, then he finally got her on the beach. He put a little sunscreen on her, then kissed her. "When are you going back," he asked. "End of the week." She put her head down on the sand pillow she'd made and relaxed. After a few hours of sun, and what seemed to be a pretty nice tan, Ava got re-dressed and they headed back to the room. "So what do you feel like tonight?" "Going to bed." "Okay. Want some company?" Ava had just about had it with him. What she wanted was to be rid of him. He walked her back to the room. "Seriously," James said. "Answer is no." "See you tomorrow then," James said. He wasn't about to give up on her. Ava walked into her room and he saw Jake with Rose.

"Afternoon." Rose almost jumped and Jake acted like it was his mom walking in on him. "Where'd you two disappear to," Ava asked. "The nude beach. What were you two up to," Jake asked. "Went down to the normal beach," Ava replied. James knocked at the door. "You seen Jake," James asked. Jake got up. "What you needing bud," Jake asked. James motioned for him to follow him and they went back to James' room.

"What the hell are you doing? You promised her that you wouldn't cheat and that's the first damn thing you do." "I kinda like her," Jake said. "You are dating one of my oldest and dearest friends who's practically like my little sister. Jake, stop acting like an ass." "I talked to her this morning. I broke it off." "Because of this? Jake, you promised her." "And, I kinda like Rose." "And you can never stick to one person. The second there's any tidbit of a problem, you run. Great. Now I have more mess to clean up." "I cared about her, but there was no way it was gonna work. We weren't sexually compatible. She wasn't enough." "Nobody ever will be," James said.

"So," Rose asked. "So nothing. At least one of the two of us is thinking clearly. I know damn well the minute I get home this is over. That's why there's no point in getting all fucking excited." "Why do you always short change yourself? You know he likes you. The man hasn't been away from you the entire trip." "And?" "Do I need to slap some sense into your head?" "Nope. The McDonalds moment is playing loud and clear." They got changed and headed down to dinner alone.

They were on their third drink when James and Jake showed up. "You disappeared on me," Jake said. Rose kissed him. James looked over at Ava. It was getting almost ridiculous to Ava. She couldn't manage to keep a damn boyfriend at home, but this one was like a leech that wouldn't back off. They sat down to dinner and as soon as they were done, Ava headed out and walked down the beach alone. Was she scared to be in a relationship again? Maybe she should give James a chance. It was all too confusing. Part of her remembered what Rose had told her the last time they were away. "Things happen for a reason Ava. Just go with it." She hoped she wouldn't regret it.

Ava walked back to her room. "Ava," James said as she walked past him. She kept walking. He grabbed her hand. "What," she replied. "What's wrong?" "Doesn't matter." She went to pull away from him and he lifted her chin so her eyes would meet his. "I'm not just around for this vacation. When we get back, I still want to be there." "Just call it what it is." "I think I'm in love with you." Ava looked at him. "What?" "I've known you for how many days?" He kissed her. Ava went to turn and go to her room and he pulled her into his arms. "James, there is no way that you could be in love with someone you barely even know." "Yeah there is." He kissed her and pulled her close. His heart was racing. He picked her up in his arms, pulling her legs around his waist and carried her to his room and straight to his bed.

He leaned her back onto it, undoing her dress. "James, this is ridiculous." He kissed her until she was out of breath, then kissed down her torso. "This isn't happening James." Ava walked out.

Rose was with Jake in his suite for the next two days. Breakfast, lunch and dinner, they were alone. They talked, got to know each other, watched movies and had mind-blowing sex. "Rose, I have to come clean about something. When we first met, I had a girl. I broke it off, but I was with her before I left." "Why did you break up?" "We were compatible in every way but in bed. I need the whole package." "And?" "Happier with you than I've been in a year." Rose finally knew why Ava hadn't wanted to get close to James. It was vacation sex . . . . or at least she thought it was.

The next morning, Ava woke up headed out to the beach for her run. She had less than 24 hours left for the vacation. Tomorrow before dinner the fantasy was over, and reality was back on the menu.

She got changed and went out to the beach, avoiding James and his room altogether. That night, she made a reservation for one. She had wine, dinner, then went to her room and went to bed. She packed her things and Rose's, then went down to the front lobby and checked out. "There's a note here for you." The front desk person handed her the note:

Come see me before you go. Please.—James

Ava threw it away. "The shuttle will be another hour and a half. I'll keep the bags up here for you." Ava nodded. She went back out to the beach for an hour, then saw James walking towards her. "Ava, where are you going?" "My flight's leaving in 3 hours." "You're not going home already." She nodded. "You were going to leave without even saying goodbye?" "After that stunt?" "I'm sorry. We got caught up in the middle of things." "Don't start." "Ava, please. Don't go." "I'm going home. As soon as Rose gets her ass down here, we're leaving." "You're running off." "No. I'm running back to my life." "I'll call you when I get home." "Why James? What's the point?" "Don't start this again." "Your friend is at reception and the shuttle is here," the concierge said. "Thanks," Ava replied. She got up and walked towards the lobby. He grabbed her hand and pulled her to him and kissed her. "I'll call you when I get back." "I didn't give you my number." Ava went to walk off and he grabbed her hand again. "Please." Ava wrote it down and handed it to him hoping he'd never use it. She walked off and left for the airport.

Ava and Rose got on their flight. "Tell me again why you switched it to an earlier flight," Rose asked. "Because you told him what flight we were on tomorrow. I need to get back to real life Rose." "He told you he was in love with you and you take off?" "Darn right." An hour or two later, they were headed home. Rose dropped Ava off, and Ava walked into the house and saw reality. The boyfriend from hell had finally left, and left a mess behind. She checked through her things, and nothing was missing. He'd left her a note:

Some guy named James called. Nice to know it took you a split second to find a replacement.

She laughed, then threw the note away. She unpacked, threw in her laundry and sat down to relax and have dinner. Her phone rang ten minutes later.

"Ava?" "Who is this?" "Don't be mad. Please." "James." "I'm getting on a plane home. Meet me at the airport." "No." "Ava, I know you're mad." "I'm not mad. I just think it's a little messed up that you're trying to make more of it than it was James. It was a vacation. That's all." "Not for me. Just meet me." "James." "I'll be landing in 2 hours. I'll tell you when I get there." "Tell me what?" "Just be there." He hung up. Figures. The moment she finally gets peace and quiet and a guy messes it up.

Two hours later, she was at the terminal. He got off the plane, bags in hand and walked towards her. "You came," James said. "What did you have to tell me that was so damn important?" He dropped his bags, pulled her to him and kissed her. It wasn't just one of those quick hello kisses either. It was a nobody else is in the room, we might as well do it here type of kisses. He finally put her down. "Fine. You missed me." "Let's go before I do something illegal," he teased. He grabbed his bags and they headed out to her car. "What did you have to tell me?" "That I want you in my life." "Friends. Fine." He put his things in the trunk, then grabbed her keys. "What?" "Not just friends Ava." "What are you talking about? We got carried away on vacation. That's all it was James." "You're wrong and you know it." "So what was it then?" "If you don't know, I'm going to have to make sure you figure it out." "Which means what oh puzzle master?" "You're coming to my place for a few hours," James said. "I have things to get done at home." He hopped in the driver's seat. Ava got in and they left.

They pulled into his driveway an hour later. "Seriously," Ava asked. He parked and grabbed his bags, then opened her door. "James, you are kidding right?" He grabbed her hand, then walked to the front door, unlocking it and heading inside. "There's no bloody way." "No way what?" He flipped the light on at the front door, then went through his mail. "Drink," he asked. "I guess," Ava replied. He went into the kitchen and grabbed them each a beer from the fridge. He popped the lids off and handed her one. "James, really. All it was, was two people getting carried away on vacation." "Not to me Ava." "James, this is ridiculous." "I'm here because of you. I came back because I want to spend the last week of my vacation with you." "You should have stayed." "Why? All I was doing was wishing you were there." "You're really going overboard James." "Tell me one thing then." "What's that?" "Why did you show up?" "Because I didn't want you to be stranded." "How very girl scout of you. Real reason Ava." "Because I wondered what you wanted to tell me." "Because you actually do care, even if it has only been a week." "James, it was sex. That's all it was." He slid the beer from her hand. "What?" He pulled her to her feet and led her into the dining room. "What?" He grabbed the remote for his stereo and turned it on. "Come here," he said. He led her up the steps to the second floor. All she heard was her favorite Aces song on the stereo.

"What are you up to?" The music played quietly on the speakers in the master bedroom. He lit a few candles, then asked Ava to dance. "This is crazy." He kissed her. "Why is your heart racing again if it was just sex Ava?" "Fine. We were attracted to each other. That doesn't mean . . . ." He kissed her again, and she was swept away. He picked her up, then carried her to the bed, leaning her onto it. "James, we shouldn't." He ignored her and kissed her again, this time not letting her up for air. Her sweater and jeans hit the floor alongside his in minutes. He reached for his bedside drawer for a condom, then made love to Ava. This was pure, passionate, intense, romantic, and almost perfect sex. To him, it was a chance to make her see what he did. To her, it was a reminder that vacations don't last forever. She regretted it the minute she did it.

They laid on the bed, as he pulled her into his arms. "I didn't just come back because I was horny Ava. I missed you. I couldn't figure it out, then it hit me. I want to be with you. Can't you just understand that?" "I could have if we'd met some other way, but this was just a vacation fling James." "You wouldn't have been with me if we'd met some other way?" "Meaning what?" "Meaning we met at the airport, not there. We talked for the first time on the plane. The second I saw you at the airport I wanted to walk over and kiss you. That's not a damn fling." "You are so darn determined aren't you?" "Even if it takes me every day of the rest of my life." "You sound like a Hallmark card." He kissed her again. "You'll see just how determined," he thought to himself, plotting out just what he'd have to do. There was no way he was letting go. Everything he'd wanted was staring him in the face, and he was going to hold on for dear life if it killed him in the process.

Ava got up an hour or so later, once she heard him fall dead asleep, then got dressed. "Where are you going?" "Home." "Nope." "I'll talk to you in the morning." "It is morning." "Go back to sleep James." He got up, then walked over to her and picked her up, pulling off the bra and g-string she'd just managed to slip on. "I have to go home." He kissed her and leaned her back onto the bed. "James, I have to go." "You don't have to do anything." He kissed her again, then made love to her. Just the fact that she was even trying to make it difficult for him had him turned on. She wasn't sure if she wanted him, but there was no way she was letting him win.

There really was nothing she could have done. The man was unbelievable. Still, the thoughts ran through her mind of her last boyfriend, who in his fast-food kind of way, dumped her like last night's garbage. She was never getting hurt like that again, not if she could stop it.

A few hours later, Ava woke up and his arms were tight around her. She tried to sneak away and he pulled her back to him. "I can't stay here all day James." "I know." "Am I allowed to get up?" "On one condition." "What's that?" "You come back tonight." "You really are getting carried away aren't you?" "Either that or you don't leave." "Nice ultimatum." "We'll go for a run, then you can decide." "I don't have my stuff here." "Then we'll go to your place and get some of your stuff." "James, you do realize I have a life here?" "And you needed another week of vacation, so here it is." "Then after this week, no more crazy shit right?" "Meaning?" "No more relationship talk?" "I'll bet you." "Bet what James?" "By the end of this week, you're going to realize that you don't want to be without me either." "And what's the bet?" "If I'm right, then we stay together. You're my girl, I'm your man." "And if you're wrong?" "I won't be, but if I am, then I just get to regularly taunt you into bed." She had to laugh. There was no way he was winning. "Fine," she said. Ava got up and went to get dressed. "I'm going home." He walked into the master bath and turned on the hot water for a shower. "Coming," he asked. "No," Ava replied. She finished getting dressed. I'm coming to get you tonight then." "I can drive myself." "I know. This way, you're all mine," he said.

Ava finally headed home, then got a few things done and sat down to do some writing. After a few hours, flowers showed up. She knew who they were from. She put them in water, then got more writing done before she started getting ready for the date with James. She threw a few things into a bag for that night, then finished doing her hair and makeup. He showed up right on time. "Ready," he asked. "Where are we going?" "I'm not telling." "James, seriously." He grabbed her bag, and her hand, and headed for the car. They hopped in. "Just tell me." He pulled her into his lap and kissed her. "Trust me." "Not even a hint?" He kissed her again and they left.

CHAPTER 3

They pulled into his place. He ran in and dropped her bag off, then hopped back in the car. "We're going out?" "Some friends of mine are doing a concert." "Who are these friends?" "You know them, or at least heard of them." "Then tell me." He shook his head. They headed towards a hotel. They pulled in and walked in and went right up the elevator. "Seriously. Who?" He pulled her to him and kissed her. The doors to the elevator opened and they headed down the hall. "Just give me one hint." He knocked on the presidential suite.

His friend opened the door. "Hey James. What's up bud?" Ava thought she was seeing things. "Good. This is her. Ava, this is Ryan." "Nice to meet you. He's been talking my ear off about you for the past week. Nice to put a face to the name," Ryan said. "Nice to meet you too." He introduced her to the two other guys in the group. "This is Joe and Brad." "That I knew," Ava replied. "She is definitely more beautiful than you said," Joe said. "Thanks," Ava replied. "We're just practicing before the concert tomorrow night. You two are coming right," Brad asked. "That was the plan," James said. "I have the tickets at will call for you. We doing dinner before," Brad asked. "Sure," James said. "Good." They spent the evening with the guys singing and cracking jokes. "So what's your favorite song," Joe asked as he talked to Ava. "Like Me." "Told ya," Joe teased. "That and You Are," Ava said. "We'll do them for you at the concert," Joe said. "Thanks," Ava said still in shock that she was sitting with them.

After a few more hours, and dinner, they headed home. "Why didn't you tell me," Ava asked. "They said to surprise you." "Impressive. I'll give you that." "Just thought you'd want to meet them. They're good guys." "That they are." "So does this mean I get you all to myself again tomorrow might?" "You do realize that it's not the people you know that are going to win me over." "You aren't the shallow type Ava." "Nice to know someone notices." "The fact that we're front row and have backstage and VIP access doesn't impress you at all." "It impresses me, but I could have got those tickets myself." "Wouldn't be half as much fun without you." He turned on his CD player and one of their songs came on.

"And this is You going out to Ava and James." They pulled into his driveway and he pulled her into his lap. He kissed her, holding her close, then sang the line from the song. "The only thing I can't live without is you." "Showoff," Ava teased. He kissed her again. Once the song was done, they headed inside.

"Come sit outside with me." "I still can't believe you didn't tell me," Ava said. "Full of surprises." "That you definitely are." He kissed her and leaned her onto the chaise. "Figured out what this place was missing," James said. "What's that," Ava asked. "You." "Really," Ava said sarcastically. "Missed having someone to share it with." "How could you not have someone to share it with?" "Nobody was ever right. Never wanted to be with someone so much. This place was always my hideaway." "The bat cave," she joked. He nodded. "Now it feels like home." He kissed her. They curled up and stared out at the stars.

It started getting a little chilly and they headed inside. He took her hand and led her up the steps. "You're really that determined to win me over aren't you?" He kissed her, pulling her into his arms. "More than you know Ava," he said. "Why," she asked. "Butterflies." She smiled. "Really?" He nodded and kissed her again. He just wanted her in his arms for as long as he could have her. Tomorrow didn't matter to him.

He leaned her onto the bed and made love to her. Something was different this time. He had a week left to convince her to stay. How was he supposed to do that? He kissed her like it was their last kiss. Made love to her like there was no tomorrow. He didn't want to let go for a second. She was like a bad drug habit, that he wasn't about to give up. There was no way he was ever letting go, whether he convinced her or not.

They curled up on the bed, him holding her close. "You know you're never gonna want to leave." "You keep talking a good game," Ava teased. "No game. You won't." A grin came across her face. "Convinced you even a little bit," James asked "A little." He nibbled her neck, then her ear. "If I convince you, you know that you are going to be the happiest woman in the world." "We'll see." "I know I'm right Ava." He pulled her on top of him and curled up on the bed with her. "Why are you so convinced that you're right?" "Because the day I met you, I wanted you. The first time we kissed, I never wanted to let you go." "It's called a crush," Ava said knowing that this wasn't going to last. He lifted her chin and his eyes met hers. "There's another name for it Ava." He kissed her. She fell asleep in his arms. He looked at her, smiled and fell asleep.

The next morning, he woke up and she was still curled up with him. "Morning," Ava said. "You're awake?" "Was too comfy to move." He smiled. "Good. Get used to it Ava," he said as he held her close. They curled back up together. "You don't really have to go anywhere today right?" "I have to get some writing done," Ava said convinced that she needed to leave. "So nothing too pressing?" "I have two chapters left to write before Wednesday." "Good thing you have some inspiration then." Ava laughed and he kissed her again. "I'm not staying in bed with you all day." "Okay then. Pool it is," he teased. Ava went to hop out of the bed and he pulled her back, tackling her back onto the bed. "Let go," Ava said. He kissed her and pulled her on top of him. "You know how crazy you are?" He nodded and kissed her again, rolling her over onto her back. "What is going on in that crazy head of yours," Ava asked. "You haven't figured it out yet?" "It's barely even been a week and a half James." He kissed her again. "Could be right if you just admit that you feel the same way Ava." "You know how crazy it sounds?" He kissed her again and held her tight. "Pool," he said. "What?" He got up, pulling her to her feet, handed her a swimsuit he'd bought her, then went downstairs. He grabbed his from the clean laundry while she changed into hers and then headed out to the pool.

He dove in and Ava walked out, sitting down on the edge. He swam over to her, then lifted himself up just enough to reach her lips for a kiss. He grabbed her and pulled her in with him. He pulled her into his arms. "Now this is what I call vacation." "One-track mind and all," Ava teased. He kissed her again. "Always." They swam a while, then splashed around before he had her pinned into the wall of the pool. "Do you want to stay here today," he asked. "I need my laptop and something to wear tonight. I have to get some things from home." He kissed her again. She was determined to get out of there, especially if she was going to be face to face with Joe.

They hopped out, then had breakfast, and headed back to Ava's to pick up some clothes for a few days. She walked past her phone and Ava saw that there were messages.

"Ava, it's Kevin. I need to talk to you as soon as possible. I know you're mad, but just call me okay."

"Where did you go? I've been trying to call you for two days. Did you know that Jake and James came back? Call me," Rose said. Ava laughed.

"It's Derrick. Call me."

Ava deleted the messages, then went upstairs to pack. "Who's Kevin," James asked. "My ex-boyfriend." "The reason you were in Jamaica?" Ava nodded. "You aren't actually going to call right?" "Just to see what he wanted. That's all.' Ava made the call to him while she was packing.

"What did you want Kevin?" "I messed up." "Meaning?" "I miss you." "You only miss me because you know you can't win me back. You made it crystal clear just how much you actually care." "Who's James?" "A guy I met." "That where you've been?" "Does it matter? I'm not your girlfriend anymore, remember?" "I love you." "Funny ass way of showing it. I have to go. I have a concert to go to." Ava hung up. Then Derrick called. "What's up?" "Where the hell did you disappear to?" "Staying with a friend for a few days." "So who's James?" "Doesn't matter Derrick." "You met a guy on vacation didn't you?" "I'll talk to you later." "Only you could turn vacation bootie into a boyfriend." "Funny." "He's there? You let him in the house? Now I know you want him." "I'll talk to you later." "Have fun in the love shack," Derrick said. Ava hung up, then finished packing. "Just a friend," James asked a little worried to hear the answer. Ava nodded. He wrapped his arms around her waist. "So a friend can do this?" He said kissing her neck and unbuttoning her sweater. "James, you wanted me to pack." He nibbled her ear. His hands cupped her breasts under her bra. "James," Ava said. He kissed her neck again, then went for her jeans. "Enough," Ava said. She walked him downstairs and sat him in front of the sports channel so she could get changed.

She had a long hot shower, did her hair and makeup, then spent a half hour trying to pick out the right outfit. She had to find the right outfit to turn Joe's head. Who knew when she'd get a chance like this again. James was a distraction. There was no way they were ever getting serious and once he understood that, she'd be free of him for good. She packed a few things, then came downstairs and they headed back to his place. He threw her bag in the back and they pulled out of the driveway. "What time are we supposed to be there," Ava asked more excited than ever. "An hour and a half." He kissed her at the stop light. They got to his place, he changed, then they left.

"About time you two showed up," Joe said as they came into the lounge. "Got sidetracked," James joked. "I bet you did. You look beautiful Ava," Joe said. "Where's Ryan?" "Talking to his soon to be ex-wife." James wandered over and grabbed a drink for Ava and himself then talked to Brad. "So how long have you two known each other," Joe asked. "A few weeks," Ava replied. "And he's trying this hard to impress you already? Nice." Ava smirked. "Don't know how he managed to talk you into dating him. Definitely a lucky man," Joe said flirting away. "You got that right," James said sitting down with Ava. They had dinner with the guys, then went and found their seats. "Front row," Ava asked. "They didn't have a choice," James teased.

Once the concert was finished, they went back to say goodbye to the guys. "Have a good night Ava," Joe said. She gave him a hug goodbye and they left. "So," James said. "Was a good show," Ava replied. "Still haven't figured it out yet have you?" "Figured out what James?" He smiled and held her hand the rest of the way home.

They pulled in and went inside. "What am I supposed to be figuring out," Ava asked. "Why I don't want to be without you." "First guess would be obsessed," Ava said. He laughed and linked his fingers with hers, slowly backing her into the wall of the front entryway. "Second guess?" "Determined to win what you know you won't," Ava replied. "That too," he teased. "What's the third guess," he asked as he kissed her neck. "Your hormones have taken over your brain." He kissed her again. "Ava," he said. He kissed her, then picked her up and carried her to the sofa in the TV room. "Why's it too soon? Not allowed to? There some rule I don't know about," James asked. "The one that says not to rush into something or you'll get hurt." "Throw that rule out. Need a recount.," James said. He kissed her and leaned her onto the sofa. "Funny." "You aren't going to get hurt and either am I Ava. And just so you know, I'm never letting you go." "You may say that now James." He kissed her. "Will every day if you need me to." He pulled his shirt off, throwing it to the floor. "Sweet, but no." "Ava, I know it hasn't been that long. It had me freaked out when you left the resort. Fact is, I didn't feel better until I was with you. It scared me, but it was worth it. I don't want to be without you." "What are you saying?" "Stay here. Move in with me." "You're hilarious." "You'll never have to sleep alone. You get free reign of the house." "I have my own house," Ava said realizing that he'd just passed into crazy territory. He kissed her. "Stay." "You know how ridiculous this is?"

His phone went off at 2am. "Hello?" "James, I need to talk to you." "Do you realize what time it is?" "Yeah. I wouldn't have called you this late if it wasn't important." He hung up and slipped out of the bed, pulling on his jeans and sweater, then went downstairs. "What did you need Robin?" He noticed her bags behind her. "Oh hell no. You and Kev get into a fight and you think I'm hiding you out?" "Could be like old times James." "Not with my girlfriend here." "Since when?" "Doesn't matter Robin. You aren't staying here." "You like her that much?" "I love her. You aren't barging in to screw it up either." "James, seriously." "Seriously. You can crash at the hotel like other people." "Fine," Robin said as she walked off and left.

He came back up to the bed and Ava wasn't there. He went out to the balcony and realized she'd seen it all. "What are you doing out here at this time of night," James asked. "Question is, why would your phone go off at 2am, then someone show up at your house at this time of night?" "It's my buddy's girlfriend. They're in another fight and normally, I would have let her crash in the spare room, but you're here. I would rather have the house to ourselves." "And just what was she suggesting?" "Meaning what?" "Like old times?" Ava walked back into the bedroom and went to grab her things. "Ava, I made one mistake a long time ago when they split up. Since then, she kept bringing it up. I have no intention . . ." She pulled on her sweater. "You aren't going." She pulled her jeans on. She'd had enough. She knew it was her one chance to finally walk away. "Ava," he said. "I'm going home." "You realize you're over-reacting." She went to grab her phone. "Just stay." "James, if that's any indication . . ." He kissed her. "That was way before us Ava. I don't want anyone else." "And if I wasn't here?" "Don't do this." "Just like I thought," Ava replied grabbing her phone and charger. "Don't go Ava." "I don't deal with people who play with people's feelings James. Not my style." "I'm not the same guy I was back then." "Heard that before too." "Would you stop?" She walked towards the bedroom door. "I love you." She kept walking.

She got home, had a hot shower and leaned into her bed. She was so done with James. Fact is, she couldn't stop thinking about Joe. The man was even better looking than before. She fell asleep dreaming of what would have happened if she'd stayed that night. It was one of the only things she regretted.

The next morning, Ava went for her jog with the Aces tunes cranked. As she was turning the corner to head home, she saw James' car in her driveway. She went in the back way and managed to get into the house undetected. He wasn't about to leave. She showered then got her writing done for the day. Her phone rang right around 4.

"And where did you disappear to," Rose asked. "Trying to get James to back off. I gave him a chance Rose. It's just not gonna work." "Then you wouldn't want to meet up for dinner with Jake and I." "Tell me you didn't Rose." "Bumped into him." "I bet you did," Ava teased. "Just meet us at Rock's." "If he brings James . . ." "I know," Rose said. "What time?" "5:30," Rose replied. "If I have to bring pepper spray," Ava joked. "See you tonight." They hung up and Ava went back to her writing.

Ava headed to the restaurant and James was sitting on the bench outside. "Should've known," Ava said. "Ava, please," James said. "I'm not doing this James. I don't know what language you need to hear it in. I'm not dating you and I don't want to," Ava said. "Not allowed to try and convince you?" "No," Ava said walking past him into the restaurant. He followed her. They sat down to dinner and there was so much tension in the air, you could cut it with a knife. After James pawing at her all the way through dinner, Ava went outside for some air, and Rose followed her.

"What's wrong," Rose asked. "He's driving me nuts. Every time I turn around, he's in my face trying to talk me into dating him. This is crazy and you know it Rose." "He likes you. That's all there is to it." "The feeling's far from mutual." "So where did you two disappear to the other night?" "Aces concert." Rose laughed. "What?" "Still can't believe you bailed on Joe Morgan of all people," Rose said. "Don't remind me." "At least he's trying to impress you," Rose joked. "Not worth the energy," Ava said. "I'll see if I can get Jake to talk to him," Rose said. She hugged Ava and headed back inside. A little while later, Jake stormed out of the restaurant and walked over towards Ava.

"Hey Jake." "What the hell did you do to him," Jake asked. "Meaning what?" "All I know is you better be prepared. He's freaking unpredictable." "Meaning," Ava asked. "You have him tripping over himself. You could talk him into damn near anything." "Oh really," Ava asked. "You did it at the resort. I had him set for a guy trip and he blew me off for you. Either you're that good in bed, or you did something mind-blowing." Ava walked off. She went back into the restaurant and grabbed her purse and pashmina and walked out.

James came after her. "Where are you going?" "Home," Ava replied. "Ava, don't go," James said. "What is going on with you two," she asked. "Me and Jake?" She nodded. "Long story. Don't go." "James, we're never going to be boyfriend and girlfriend. Just call it what it was." "If that's all it was than why am I falling for you?" "Are you kidding me? James, snap out of your dream world. I'm not your soul mate, and I am not ever gonna be your girlfriend." "Ava, just give us a chance." She rolled her eyes. "What makes me so irresistible James? You could find another girlfriend anywhere."

"Every girlfriend I've had never worked. They never made me feel secure in the relationship. I never got the butterflies and the excitement. It was a damn chore. I was only dating hoping that everyone would stop asking why I wasn't married yet, then I stopped dating altogether. I realized that a relationship is supposed to be butterflies in the stomach, the craving to be with someone. When we met, there was a connection. I got butterflies every morning until I saw you and all I wanted to do was kiss you. Everyone can think I'm nuts, but the fact is, I'm seeing things clearer than I did. The priorities changed. Being with you is the best thing that ever happened to me. That good enough reason for you?" He walked back into the restaurant and sat down at the bar. Ava headed home.

An hour or so later, Ava was immersed in her writing. James had driven her nuts all night and she needed to get the tension out. She turned on her favorite radio station and got a little writing done. She'd just turned the music off when she heard her phone ringing. "Rose," Ava asked. "Can I crash over at your place," Rose asked. "What's wrong?" "Ava." "Okay," she replied and Rose hung up.

Rose pulled in and turned her car off. "What happened," Ava asked walking outside to meet her. "I don't want to talk about it. He's being a royal ass." Ava let her in. She went and made tea. "I didn't want to interrupt you," Rose said. "It's fine." Ava handed her a cup of tea. "Just tell me." "He made some comment about how women can sleep with men and take over their lives. Then he said that no woman is ever getting control of him and tried to force himself on me." Ava had enough. "I'll deal with it," Ava said.

After dealing with bad boyfriends most of her life, Ava had enough self-defence moves to kick anyone's butt. "Where are you going," Rose asked. "Give him a piece of my mind. What's the address?" "Ava." "Address," Ava asked. "You're not going alone." "Fine." Ava sent a text to her personal trainer friend to meet her at Jake's. A half hour later, she was at his doorstep with backup.

"Jake, open up." He opened the door and saw how pissed off Ava was. "Little miss pissed off is all angry. What happened?" Ava slapped him, as his face went almost purple. "You ever go near her again, I will kick your damn ass myself." "And she's feisty." Ava was about to slap him again when her buddy held her back. "We're talking right now Jake. Sit your fucking ass down on your fake leather sofa."

"What?" "Ever heard the term no means no," Ava asked. "She liked it." Her friend walked her to the door and dealt with Jake himself. 10 minutes later he came out. "Go home," her friend said. "What happened," Ava asked. "Let's just say he's gonna be crying to his momma in a second."

CHAPTER 4

Ava got back and headed inside to hear Rose talking to someone. She looked over and it was James. "Seriously? You have to be freaking kidding me," Ava said. "Needed to talk to you," James said. "Think you've said more than enough James," Ava replied. She walked into the kitchen and he followed her.

"Ava." "What?" "Why can't you just give me a chance," James asked. "Because the whole idea was crazy James. We have nothing in common. There's no way that we're ever gonna work," Ava said. "And if I told you that I was in love with you?" He was talking a new form of crazy. "You need to get your head checked," Ava said. "Then this wouldn't make a difference," he said sliding a small velvet box in front of her. "Buying my attention isn't gonna . . . ." He opened it. A princess cut diamond ring. "Now I know you're crazy," Ava said. She handed it back to him. "Marry me," James asked. "No," Ava replied. She walked towards the front door and practically kicked him out.

"What was that all about," Rose asked. "The crazy man talking crazy," Ava said. "You feeling any better?" "A little. Carrie called. She wants us to go out for her birthday tomorrow night." "Where," Ava asked. "Dare." Ava laughed. "Of course that's where she wants to go.

Dare was the only male strip club in the entire city. The men were hot, but as far as Ava was concerned, they only talked to you when you had money or something they wanted. Ava was right for the most part, but it was Carrie's birthday.

They caught a few hours of sleep and Rose headed home in the morning. Around 7:30 that night, Ava picked Rose up and they headed off to meet Carrie.

Carrie Jones was one of Ava's best friends. They'd known each other since Ava moved into town. Carrie was around five foot six, blond hair and green eyes. She had curves, and worked out religiously with Ava. Both of them were in search of the perfect guy. Carrie still was trying to figure out her "type" but they all knew that Carrie's type was tall, dark, handsome and rich.

They headed in and grabbed a table, then the entertainment began. There was guy after guy, doing their thing on stage. Ava looked up and saw someone she thought she knew. He looked towards her and smiled. Ava went and grabbed another drink, then was about to head back to the table, when the man came up behind her. "What the heck are you doing here," Andrew asked. "Carrie's birthday. Since when did you start doing this?" "A few months. Needed the extra money. Finally bought a house." "That's great. I'm just going to head back to the table." "You hanging around a while?" "We'll see." Ava went and sat back down then almost laughed. Carrie went back to hitting on the strippers and Ava grabbed her another drink. "Ava," Andrew said. "What?" He motioned for her to come closer. "What?" He kissed her. "Andrew," Ava said pushing him away. "Figured I'd take the chance. You know how long I had a crush on you?" "I can just about guess," Ava said. He leaned her against the wall and kissed her again. Again she pushed him away. "One night won't kill you." She walked over to the bar and ordered an ice water. "Come on Ava," Andrew said, as Ava replied by dumping the ice water down his jeans. She brought Carrie her drink, then left.

She went to go outside and saw James' car. She walked towards it and saw the back seat windows steamed up. She saw the door open and James stepped out. A woman left out the other side. "Nice." He turned and saw Ava. She got in her car and left. A half-hour later, she was home. She turned her phone off, turned off all the lights, and locked the car into the garage. She had a hot bath, then went to bed. She was glad that she hadn't said yes to that ring. He was just like all the other guys.

The next morning, she did her writing in bed. She made coffee, then took her breakfast and full cup of coffee to bed with her. She left the phone off. She finished the last chapters, made the revisions and edits, then made lunch and chilled upstairs. She showered, then went to the mall to go shopping. After a few hours, and a few hundred dollars, she headed home. James was sitting on her front step. She walked around him, went inside and locked the door behind her. "Ava," he said. "Go home or you're trespassing." "Ava," he said. "Go home." She went upstairs and put her things away, then made her dinner. "Please," he said. She went to the door. "Get off my front step. Go the hell home. Leave me the hell alone James." She went back in and locked the door.

An hour or so later, he was still there. "Can't take a hint or what?" "I need to talk to you." "You aren't coming in here." "Ava, please." "Leave." She went back in and went to close the door, when he stuck his foot in it. "What?" "I'm not leaving until you talk to me." "Then you can wait until you're 90." She pushed him away and locked the door. She went inside, poured herself a drink, then went onto the patio. She heard his car pull out a half-hour later.

Ava went to sleep, tossing and turning all night. She finally turned her phone back on. It was full of messages from him, then one from Andrew. "I know you're mad, but still, call me." Ava deleted it, and all the I'm sorry messages from James. The next day, she got up and went for her run, then came home and spent the day cleaning. Her phone didn't ring all day. Rose finally called close to dinner. "What are you up to tonight," Rose asked. "Single life," Ava teased. "See you in a couple then," Rose replied hanging up.

Rose showed with a bottle of vodka, and two bottles of orange juice. "Nice." "Goes with the famous mango chicken I could smell all the way here." "Funny." They sat down with a pile of chick flicks, had dinner and one too many drinks, then fell asleep on the sofa. A few hours later, she heard a knock on the door. She got up. "Ava," James said. "You don't sleep do you?" "I can't." "Answer is still no James." She closed the door, locking it, then turned the lights out and went upstairs to her bed.

The next morning, the two ladies got up, went for a walk/run then went shopping. "I still can't believe you said no," Rose said They shopped a while, then headed back to the house, which by now had 4 dozen roses on the front step. Ava walked past them and went inside. "The man's trying." "Pointless." They went in and had dinner, then relaxed and got caught up on their TV shows. Ava went up to go to bed and James was on her front step. "You don't get it do you," Ava asked walking outside. "Get off my porch." "Please." Ava went to walk back in and he grabbed her arm. "Let go." "No. Not until you talk to me." "I'm done James. Was fun while it lasted. Have a nice life." She tried to break free of him. He grabbed her other arm. "Let go." He pinned her to the wall. "Nothing happened." "Take your hands off me James. It's done." She finally managed to break free and went inside, locking him out. She went upstairs and showered. She came out and Rose was on the edge of her bed. "You okay," Rose asked. "I'm fine." Rose looked and saw a small bruise on her arm.

She grabbed her phone and called Jacob. He was a friend from years ago who turned into a personal security guard. She told him the situation. "On my way. She go to the hospital?" "She won't." "He still there?" "Not that I noticed." "Be there in ten." He hung up. Ava slid on her sweater and leggings, then went downstairs and made tea. Ten minutes later, Jacob was at the house. "Long time no see," he said as Rose answered the door. "She's not going to do anything," Rose said. "She wants him gone, I'll make it happen. She wants a break, it's done." "Quit talking about me like I'm not here," Ava said. "Well?" "He asked me to marry him and I said no. I told him it's done and he's being an ass." "I'll take care of it. Grab a pencil and roll it over the bruise. It'll be gone in the morning." He left and went to deal with the James situation.

The next morning, Ava got up to her phone ringing. "What?" "Ava," James said. "What part of screw off don't you get?" "Just give us a chance," James asked. "Stay the hell away from me," Ava replied hanging up.

"Ava, Jacob's here," Rose said. Ava came downstairs sliding her robe on. "And good morning to you too." "Looked into that James guy for you," Jacob said. Ava poured herself some coffee, then went into her office. "Your opinion?" "He's not exactly an angel. The guy was a major player in the day. There's only one woman he was in a long-term relationship with, and she left him for one of his friends." "That explains things." "He also has one hell of a jealous streak." "No shit Sherlock." "I gotta say though, he's a cool guy." "Figures you'd say that." "He hasn't had a girlfriend in 2 years. Nada. The only girl that he's dated was you," Jacob said. "Not sure if that's a good or a bad thing." "It's an I don't know thing," he said. Ava walked out and went upstairs, then came down 20 minutes later and left.

Ava slid her shoes off and walked along the beach. The weather was getting cooler. The summer was ending. There was no way that she wanted to go through any more crap. She needed a break from guys period. She walked, then turned and headed back towards her car. She got back and saw James. "Give me a damn break. Are you stalking me now?" "Ava, please." "Can't just screw off and leave me alone can you?" Ava got in her car. "Don't go." "Move." He got in the car with her. "What part of go away . . ." He kissed her. He pulled her into his lap and held her close. "Let me go." He kissed her again, then tried to grab the car keys. He had them in his hand. "Let go." "You aren't going. We need to talk." Ava went to grab her keys and saw him get out of the car with them in his hand.

"At least lock the damn doors." Ava slid her shoes off and walked down the beach. "Give me back the keys." "Not until we talk this out." "Touch me and I break something." "You mad about me being at that bar?" "No. James, I told you before there was no point to this. I'm not marrying you. Whatever this was is over." "Why can't you just give it a chance?" "Because I'm not attracted to you like that James. What's done is done. Stop showing up at my house, following me around and begging me to take you back. It isn't happening," Ava said getting in her car. Her phone went off a minute later.

"Ava?" "Speaking." "It's Joe. How are you?" "Good. How did you get this number?" "Long story. We're doing a concert tomorrow. You going to come?" "I guess." "I'll leave the passes and the tickets at the gate for you." "Sounds good." "I'll get Ty to pick you up." "Who's that?" "One of our security guys. I'll give you a ride back after." "I'll see you tomorrow then." He hung up. Her heart was racing. "Who was that," James asked. "None of your damn business." "Please," James begged. She started the car and left.

The next day, she got up, went and got her hair and nails done, then bought something to wear to the concert. The car showed and she left.

CHAPTER 5

Ava grabbed the tickets and followed Ty. "Was wondering where you were," Joe said. "Hey yourself," Ava said. "Clean up good." "Thanks," Ava said. "So how's James?" "Don't know." "Oooh." "Long story." "Then I don't have to worry." "About what?" He kissed her. When he let her up for air, his hands slid down the back of the mini dress to her backside. "I thought . . . ." "Thought wrong. So I have an idea." "What's that," Ava asked. "You're a writer right?" Ava nodded. "You can write almost anywhere right?" "I guess. Why?" "Come with us for a week or two. We have a few days off between concerts. We can hang out at my place." "I can't just disappear." He kissed her again. "Can't talk you into it?" "One week. That's it." Joe kissed her again. He went and grabbed them each a beer and handed one to her. "Out of all the girls . . ." "Don't start. Yeah the girls like me, but there's only one reason why most of them even talk to me. You talk to me like I'm just like everyone else." "Because you are." "That's what I liked about you," Joe said. "So how are the concerts going," Ava asked trying to change the topic. "Best one was when you were there." She smirked. Joe kissed her. "We have to do sound check," Ryan said sticking his head in. "Cool. Coming," Joe asked as he got up and grabbed Ava's hand. He kissed her before he went on stage. She thought back to that day where he'd asked her to come meet him. She wasn't giving up the second chance.

Once sound check was done, they had dinner then Ava relaxed while the guys had the meet and greet. Once it was finished, Joe came in and kissed Ava, then relaxed with her before he had to go on. "So where's James," Brad asked. "We broke up." "Guess it's Joe's lucky day," Brad teased. Ava smiled. "If this is too weird for you guys," Ava said. "He's been talking about you ever since he met you Ava. He's been trying to figure out who you were for years. Maybe now he'll finally shut up," Ryan said. They joked around. They got changed to go on and left Joe alone with Ava. He kissed her. "Well beautiful. I'll see you after the concert right?" "I have to pack." He couldn't help the grin that came ear to ear. "I'll come with you." Ava nodded. He kissed her, leaning her into the wall. "I swear you could make me hate performing." "Why's that?" "I know what I'd rather be doing." Ava smirked. He kissed her again. "Joe." He kissed her one last time then headed out, and Ava was escorted out to her seat.

She sat down and thought about his proposal. One week wasn't going to hurt anyone, but he was the ultimate ladies man. Was it even a good idea?

The guys walked out on stage and every chance he had, Joe was walking over towards Ava. Once the concert was done, Ty walked Ava backstage. Girls were clammering to get backstage, and Ava got back to the lounge just in time. "How was the concert," Joe asked. "Way to make it obvious," Ava joked. He kissed her. "Let's get out of here." Ava nodded and they headed off towards her place.

They pulled in and headed inside. Rose was out cold on the sofa. Ava went upstairs and packed up enough stuff for a week. Joe came up behind her. "Something I can help you with?" "Not even gonna say it," Ava joked. She zipped up the bag, then threw in two pairs of shoes, her iPod and her laptop and charger. "Ready," he asked. "Have to tell Rose where I'm going." He kissed her. "We should go." He kissed her again and they headed downstairs. Ava quietly slipped over to Rose. "Where the hell did you go?" "Long story. Stay here this week. I'll call you when I can." "Where are you going?" She saw someone walk towards the door. "I'll be back. I'll call you in the morning." She left. Rose looked out the window. "There's no fucking way." Joe turned and waved goodbye and Rose's mouth dropped to the floor.

They left and headed to his hotel. "So where are you playing tomorrow night," Ava asked. "New York City. We're leaving first thing tomorrow." "Okay then." They pulled in and made their way upstairs to the room.

They walked in and there were lit candles all around. Champagne was in an ice bucket with two glasses. "I'll give you credit, this is beautiful," Ava said. He put her bag in the bedroom. "Kinda needed to unwind after the concert." "With candlelight and champagne? Nice." He kissed her. "Come sit." She slid her heels off and they sat down by the gas fireplace. "Still can't believe that James was that stupid to lose you." "Can we not talk about him?" "No problem here. So tell me about what you're writing." "Just finished one. Starting a new one this week." "What's it about?" "Not sure yet. Thinking something along the lines of girl meets boy, boy is famous, girl falls for boy, they break up then realize they were meant to be." "Sounds good. Let me know if you need any help." Ava smiled. "I seriously have to be the luckiest guy right now." "Really," Ava asked as he handed her a glass of champagne. "You're here, after New York I have three days to chill with you, and you are staying with me. Couldn't ask for anything more." "I bet," Ava teased. He kissed her, sliding the champagne glass from her hand.

In minutes, she was in his arms on the sofa. One kiss after the other, and she was at his mercy. "I could so get hooked on this," he said. Ava smiled. A half-hour later, he was sliding her dress off and his shirt was on the floor. He kissed down her neck, then her arm. Oddly enough, this seemed better, more safe and calmer than anything else. Not even the vacation topped this. "Ava," he said. She looked at him with that smirk that drove him nuts. "Come with me." "Where?" He took her hand and led her to the bedroom. The hotel really did think of everything. Rose petals were on the bed. He kissed her again and leaned her onto the bed. "You know how soft your skin is?" "Take good care of what's mine," Ava said. He kissed her again. Her dress dropped to the floor and he kicked his jeans off. It felt like it was going on forever. The kissing, the sex, more kissing. "I still can't believe you said yes," Joe said. They curled up together under the covers. "Why wouldn't I?" He kissed her again. Finally, they fell asleep, still entangled with each other.

The next morning, she woke up and he was singing in the shower. She almost had to pinch herself. She slid on his shirt and followed the scent of the coffee, pouring herself a cup. He came out a few minutes later, then saw her sitting on the sofa with coffee. He walked out and kissed her. "Morning to you too," Ava said. "Nice shirt," he said. She smirked. "So what time are we leaving," Ava asked. "A half-hour." He kissed her again. He took a sip of her coffee, then finished the cup. "Coffee thief," she joked. He kissed her and picked her up, carrying her towards the bed. "I thought we had to get ready?" He kissed her again and slid the shirt off her. They did it again, then had a quick shower before they left.

Ava made a quick call to Rose before the plane left. "How in the hell did you manage that?" "What?" "I know who you're with Ava. Where the hell are you going?" "New York City, then back to Tennessee." "Never been there." "Me either." "Just don't go up and disappearing on me okay?" "No prob. Any problems at the house?" "He showed last night after you left. I told him you were away." "And?" "He didn't believe me. He went and checked upstairs and saw your stuff gone, then was crying upstairs." "He did leave right?" "Yeah. He's really upset." "Good. I have to go. Talk to you later." Ava hung up. Fine. She felt a little bad for the guy, but not enough to stop and ruin the moment. She looked over at Joe and her heart started racing again. If this was a dream, she didn't want to wake up.

The plane landed a while later, and they headed to the hotel. "If you don't want to go tonight," Joe said. "Wouldn't miss it." He kissed her. "Good. Wouldn't be half as much fun without you." He kissed her again. "What time do you have to be there?" "Two hours." "Did you want to go out for a bit," Ava asked. He kissed her and walked her backwards to the bed. "You really don't have to go tonight," Joe said. "Who's going to be there that you don't want me to see?" "Nobody, just saying." "I'll be there. When you're finished, if you do well, you might get a surprise," Ava said. "And what surprise is that?" "You'll have to wait and see." "You know I'm not the most patient person." "You can wait," Ava replied. He kissed her again and slid her sweater off.

A while later, Joe and Ava left for sound check. After, they had something to eat, then went back to the hotel and got changed. "Tell me you aren't wearing that," Joe teased. "Too distracting?" She laughed. She knew there was a reason she'd bought that little black dress. He walked over towards her and pulled her to him. "Tempting is a better word." He kissed her, then attempted to undo her jeans. "We have to be there in a half-hour." "And," he teased undoing the zipper. "Go get ready." He kissed her neck, then picked her up and carried her to the bed. "Are you seriously trying to be late?" He kissed her and slid the shirt off. "They can wait." They did it again before they left. "Are you trying to get me in trouble," Ava asked. "Never. Just enjoying every second I can before the concert," he teased. They finished getting changed, then headed to the venue. They were hand and hand all the way inside. "About time buddy," Ryan teased. "Funny. You're always the late one Ryan," Joe replied. Ava said good luck to the guys and headed out to her seats.

"So where are you," Rose asked. "The concert. Front row." "And?" "And what?" "Don't tell me you demanded your own room?" "Nope." "James is gonna freak when he finds out." "That's nice. Rose. He knows we're done." "Ava? You aren't that person." "I'm living my life Rose. He lost his chance. He doesn't get to win another one." Security came down and handed her a rose. She smirked. "What?" "Sending me flowers via security," Ava said as she gushed over the gesture. "Go enjoy. See you next weekend," Rose said hanging up. Ava sat through the concert, then was whisked backstage at the end. Joe walked over to her and kissed her in front of everyone. "Now where we off to," Ava asked. "Home."

That night, they got in late, and headed to his house. "It's beautiful," Ava said. He showed her around, making sure the last stop was the master bedroom. "So, what do you think?" "It's a beautiful house." He wrapped his arms around her and walked her back towards the bed. "Where are we going?" He kissed her and picked her up, then they both fell onto the bed. "Thought you should lay down." "Really? Good call." He kissed her again. "You know you're a bad influence." "And why is that," Ava asked as he slid her shirt off. "Make me want to stay in bed with you all day." "I suggested going out," Ava teased. "Too tempted to kiss you every second." "There should be medication for that." They laughed. "What do you feel like doing tomorrow," Joe asked. "Could show me around." "That's a possibility." "I know you have things to do around here." "Shopping. That's about it for now." "Okay." "Still can't believe I get you all to myself for three days straight." "Whatever are we going to do with all that time?" He kissed her again and within minutes were curled up under the covers making love.

The next morning Rose got up and went to go to work when she saw James. "She's not home." "Where did she go?" "She was meeting with the art director and going for a photo shoot for the book cover." "You're full of it. Where is she?" "Tennessee." "Who the hell does she know there?" "A few of our girlfriends," she replied trying to cover her butt. "Who is she with Rose? She never said anything about anyone there." "A friend of hers. They were here the other night." "What's his name?" "James, Josie is one of our buddies. She moved there years ago." "When did she leave?" "Three days ago." "The same night as the concert." "What concert," Rose asked trying to play dumb. He glared at her. "She saw that band that you took her to see," Rose said knowing she had stuck her foot in her mouth. He walked off. "Where are you going?" "I know where they'll be this weekend." "So?" "So I'm winning her back." "You won't win James." "I have to do something." "You already did enough James." "Just tell me she isn't with Joe." "She went with our friend that we knew. They're at her house there." "You sure?" Rose nodded. "If she calls, tell her I need to talk to her." He finally left. Not ten minutes later, Rose called Ava's phone.

———

"Babe, phone," Joe said. Ava kissed him and ignored the phone. "Like your thinkin' today." He kissed her and pulled her into his arms. He was way too happy for this to be right. He had Ava, the fame of being with the guys, and everything he'd ever wanted. Something was bound to happen. He curled up with her until they both finally decided to get up. They showered and got dressed, then headed off to grab groceries.

He was singing in the car which literally had Ava giggling. "What?" "You're as bad as I am." "What?" "Singing into the steering wheel." "Bet you could sing like an angel." "Why thanks for the vote of confidence. Maybe you'll hear it sometime." They parked, then he pulled her into his lap and kissed her. "Sing." "Tonight." He kissed her again and they went into the store.

———

James tried to get as much work done as he could, then would go home and do a super intense workout to knock himself out. After three days, he needed to find her. He searched through whatever info he could find. There was nothing. There was one charge from Victoria's secret in Memphis, but that's all.

———

After three days of fun, laughing, sex, teasing and taunting, Ava felt like a million bucks. "You promised," Joe said on the Thursday night. "You play and I'll sing," Ava said. He did and she belted out her version of the song. "Damn." "What?" "You know you sing it better than Ryan?!" "Don't let him hear you say it." Joe kissed her. "So many hidden talents. First you can cook like a damn chef, then this, and everything else the past few days." They both giggled. "Well gee. Does that mean I get the job," Ava joked. He kissed her. "We have a month left." "Of the tour?" He nodded. "And," Ava asked. "I have an idea." "What's the idea?" "Stay." "Here?" He nodded. "I'm home 4 nights of 7 next week." "I have a house there Joe." "So you go home for the 3 days I'm away and we rack up the long distance?" Ava smiled. "That a yes," Joe asked. "Depends." "On what?" "Why you're asking." "So we don't have to fly all over the place. We can be together and have no drama, no stress. Just you and me and this huge house." "I can't just move in." "Yeah you can. At least I know you'd be okay here. James wouldn't be able to come after you." "You think I can't take care of myself," Ava asked. "I know you can. Would rather that you have backup to hold you back from kicking his butt." Ava smirked. "I'll tell you after the concert Sunday," Ava said. He kissed her. For once he was happy to have one woman in his life. One woman that he loved being with.

She didn't want to make a huge mistake, but overthinking it wasn't going to help her either. He was a better man than anyone else she'd dated. She still worried, but for some reason the worries almost melted away with Joe. True, it was ridiculous, but it was a chance her gut told her to take.

James called Rose. "She back," he asked. "Nope. She's not coming back until Monday." "You talk to her at least?" "Yep." "And?" "She changed the topic every time your name got brought up." "Where in Tennessee is she?" "Don't even think it James." "Why?" "I wouldn't push this. She's not about to let you back in her life." "I just need to get her alone so we can talk it out." "She met someone James." He hung up.

After two more concerts, they curled up at the hotel. "We'll get your stuff tomorrow and take it to the house." "I didn't answer Joe." "I know. Wishful thinking on my part." "Keep hoping." He pulled her into his arms. "When?" "When what?" "You're killing me with suspense," Joe said. "I will on one condition." "Anything." "Answer me one question." "Okay." "Not that I haven't loved the past week, and love being with you, but why?" "I need normal in my life. The flash and the fame and all of it sucks without someone to share it with. I want someone who grounds me. Someone who makes life off the stage normal. I come home and I curl up with you and I'm not the guitarist from the group. I'm just plain and simple me. I have the woman I want right in my arms, and if she'll have me, I'll make her a happy woman." "What are you trying to say?" "This is the first time in years that I can finally relax. You're here. I have someone with me that I love being with. I just don't want to lose that." Ava looked at him as he kissed her again. "I know what Rose is going to say," Ava joked. There was something about him. Instead of worrying anymore, Ava took the chance. Worse came to worse, she had a new city to explore.

—————

"What the hell do you mean you're moving," Rose asked. "I'll still be back every few weeks to visit." "You don't know anyone there but him, and he's gone half the time." "It's either that, or here by myself fighting with James and everyone else. I'd rather be there," Ava replied. "You know you're crazy right?" Ava smirked. "He's gonna lose it." "Here's my idea," Ava said. "What?" "You stay here. If things don't work, I come back. You can't afford a house anyway. Just no trashing the place or any orgies." "Funny. Can I just move into the guest room?" Ava nodded. "It's all yours, and if anything changes, I'll tell you. Plus, you can always stay out there with me every once in a while." "Holy shit," Rose said. "I know," Ava replied with a smile ear to ear. "No, I mean he's outside," Rose said. Joe walked towards the front door.

"Hey beautiful," Joe said as he came inside. "Hey yourself," Ava replied. He kissed her. "You remember Rose?" "Nice meeting you again," Joe said. Rose was still in shock. "You better take good care of her. She's pretty important to me." "To me too," Joe said. Ava grabbed her other suitcase from downstairs, then went up and started packing. "Surprised you got it all packed in 3 suitcases," Joe said as he walked upstairs a half hour later. "I told you there wasn't that much." He kissed her. "What are we going to do with all this extra time," Ava joked. He had her shirt off in 2 minutes and was going for her jeans when she heard Rose coming upstairs. "Ava, door," Rose said. He kissed her stomach. "I have to." He kissed her hip. "Busy," Ava said. No way was she letting someone get in the middle of this. "Might want to answer it," Rose replied. He kissed her again, and Ava got up and went downstairs, slipping her shirt back on.

"It's only you. Turn around and go," Ava said the minute she saw James. "I need to talk to you." "That's nice. Goodbye." "I need you." "Go," Ava said desperately trying to get rid of him. "Ava," he said. "I'm packing. I don't have time for this crap." "Where are you going?" "Moving for a few months." "That wasn't an answer," James said determined to find out where she was going. "And I don't have to answer your questions. Goodbye." Ava kicked him out the door, locked it, then went back upstairs. She walked into her room and Joe locked the door behind her.

Joe kissed her then slid the shirt off. "Back to where we were," he said. He picked her up and carried her back to the bed, leaning her down and kissing her stomach. "I could so get used to this," he said. "Get used to what," Ava asked. "Having you in my arms all the time." She smiled and he undid her jeans. He nibbled her hip, which somehow had her hot as hell. He moved up and kissed her as she peeled his shirt off. They made love, then curled up on her bed.

"We're staying tonight right?" Joe kissed her. "Whatever you want beautiful. We can go in the morning." Ava nodded. "I have an idea for dinner," Joe said. "What's that?" "That seafood place. The one you said was your favorite. One last time." "Sounds good," Ava replied. They left the house, pulled into the restaurant and headed down to the private dining room part of the restaurant.

Once dinner was finished, they went out for a walk on the beach. "Can see why you love it," Joe said. "Rose is staying at the house, so whenever we come back, we have somewhere." "Sounds perfect. Plus it's a great house." "My first place strangely enough. Bought it with my first writing bonus." "It's all you isn't it," Joe asked. Ava nodded. "See, that's what my place is missing." "What?" "You," he teased. Ava smiled. "You just haven't been there long enough." "Three years this spring," Joe said. "You've been on tour." "Once this tour is done, we're taking a few months off. Then I finally can relax a bit." "You have to admit though, having all the girls drooling over you has to have its perks." "Only perk was meeting you." "Well played hand," she joked. He pulled her into his arms and kissed her. A few minutes later, he saw camera flashes. They left as fast as possible and headed back to her place. He made a call and booked the flight home for that night. The last thing he needed was the paparazzi spilling this all over the news.

—————

"You can't just take off. We didn't even get a chance to get everyone together to say goodbye," Rose said. "I'll be back next week." "You sure about the house?" Ava nodded. She said goodbye to Rose and left with Joe. "You'll see baby. You'll love it," Joe said. "Being with you or being there?" He kissed her. They headed out to the runway and got settled on the plane.

Rose headed back to the house. The courier showed to pick up the last two boxes Ava had packed with her necessities. Right behind him was James. "What are you doing here," Rose asked. "Where is she?" "Gone. She moved." "What?" "She moved to Tennessee." "Stop talking crazy," James said. "Her flight is taking off any minute." "What gate?"

"I still can't believe you talked me into this," Ava said. "You'll see. It's nice and quiet, so you can get your writing done, plus, Brad's wife isn't that far away. You'd love her." "What about Ryan's wife?" "Their divorce was final last week." "He alright?" "Not really. He's taking it really hard." "It takes time, that's all," Ava said. "Was thinking of taking him out one night or dinner or something." "I'll make dinner. Let me know when." "Babe, you don't have to go to all that trouble." "Have nothing but time. Just let me know when." He kissed her and wrapped his arm around her. "Seriously, I think he'd love it," Joe said. "So long as he doesn't bring James as his date, it's all good." He kissed her again. This felt so right. For once Ava wasn't worried. There wasn't a regret in sight. For Joe, he was happy the girlfriend search was over.

Joe and Ava landed and grabbed their things, then headed through the press to get to the car. "It's like this all the time isn't it," Ava asked. "After that camera man saw us tonight, probably a safe bet that it will be on the news or something tomorrow," Joe said. He kissed her as they got in. They headed off to his place, and walked in to a party. "Hey you two," Ryan said walking over. "So this is why we had to leave tonight," Ava teased. Joe kissed her. "Just wanted to give a big welcome to you is all Ava," Ryan said. Brad came over and introduced his wife and kids, and a few of the other neighborhood people came to say hi. "We've heard so much about you," Brad's wife said. "I bet you have," Ava replied. Joe kissed her then went to talk to Ryan. "I know you didn't get much chance to say goodbye to your friend's there. We're happy you're here. We needed some fresh meat," Danielle said. "Happy to oblige I think," Ava said. "Just nice to meet new people. It's a quiet neighborhood." "Quiet's definitely good." "Joe told us you were a writer. So what do you write?" "Romance." "Now we definitely have to talk," Danielle said.

By the end of the night, Ava's face hurt from smiling. Everyone finally left, and it was just her and Joe. "Probably not the best timing," he joked. "Now, I'm just plain tired." "I have an idea." He ran off and Ava cleaned up. About ten minutes later, he came downstairs. "What," she asked seeing the look on his face. He picked her up and carried her upstairs to the master bath. There were candles, a bubble bath, and music. "Much better," Ava said. "Hop in. I'll grab us a drink." She motioned for him to come closer. She kissed him. He had her backed into the counter in 5 minutes flat. She slid her sweater off, then her jeans. "Drinks." He kissed her again, then ran downstairs. She grabbed her lingerie from the suitcase, and put her jeans and sweater aside, then slid into the tub. This was heaven.

He came back upstairs and walked in with a towel wrapped around him and slid into the tub with her, handing her a cold beer. "How did you know," she joked. "We needed this. Long ass day." He pulled her into his arms and cuddled with her in the tub. "You know, this is a pretty great tub," Joe said. "You never used it?" "Until today, no." "Why?" "Never had anyone to share it with." "Never had the time?" He kissed her. "Never wanted to until now." "Sweet talker." He nibbled her ear and his hands slid down her torso. "Tell me no more parties this week," Ava begged. He kissed her. "Sunday." "Your birthday." "Don't want to do a big thing either. Just you and me." "The guys are going to want to do something Joe." "Seriously, prefer just you and me. We can go do dinner or something." "I'll work on it. You just relax."

They leaned back into the water and talked and relaxed until the water went cool, then slid out, blew the candles out and curled up together in the bed. "I seriously have to be lucky or something," Joe said. "Why is that," Ava asked. "You." "It's definitely luck," Ava teased. "I mean, who would've thought I'd be here with you?" He kissed her. "Minute I met you," he said. His arms curled around her. "You knew way back then?" "I knew things were going to definitely change." "Really?" He kissed her and he made love to her.

From the satin sheets, and candlelight, to the perfect music, it was amazing. He made her feel so beautiful, so sexy and so wanted that she couldn't imagine wanting anything more. They fell asleep in each other's arms, and for once, she wasn't worried about anything. She wasn't worrying about what was going to happen tomorrow. She'd finally taken a chance and she was happier than she had been in a long while.

The next morning Ava got up with an odd feeling. They were still curled up together when she woke. "Morning beautiful." "Morning handsome." "I had an idea last night," Joe said. "Tell me you slept." "I slept. Woke up at 7 and watched you sleeping," he teased. "Seriously," Ava said. He kissed her. "What's the idea?" "Just had an idea for a song. Got it all down, then came back to bed." "What's the song called?" "Love letter." Ava smirked. "You know I get to hear it first." He kissed her. "I emailed it to Ryan last night." "How much sleep did you actually get?" "4 or 5 hours." She kissed him then went to get up. "Where are you going?" "You'll see," Ava said. She got up and slid on the satin teddy that was still on the counter. She went downstairs, made coffee and orange juice, and omelets. She came upstairs and he was sleeping. Ava put the tray at the bottom of the bed. She slid back into bed with him and within seconds he was awake. "Where did you go?" Ava looked over towards the tray. "So that's what took you so long." He kissed her again. Within minutes, the satin teddy was on the floor, and they were making love. They had breakfast in bed, talking for what felt like hours, then his phone started ringing. He was tempted to ignore it. "Answer it. It could be Ryan." He kissed her. Ava grabbed it.

"Hi Ryan." "Hey Ava. Is he around?" "He's right here. One sec." She muted it and handed the phone to him. He kissed her stomach, then her hip. She unmuted the phone. "Can he give you a shout back in a few?" "You two enjoy. Tell him to call me before 5." "He'll give you a shout back in a half-hour. He's just working on something." "I bet. Talk to you later hun." Ava hung up as he was about to tip the teasing into overdrive. "I can't believe you,"

Ava said. He was like a magnet to the one spot that drove her over the edge. "What were you saying," he asked as he nibbled and licked. "Joe." When her legs started to shake, he made his way back up her torso and kissed her. "Ava, I think I might be addicted." "To what," she asked as his hands pulled her legs around him. "To this," he said as they curled up together. Round two that morning. Every time was more mind-blowing than the last. "We can't spend all day in bed," Ava said. "You have a point." "We should get groceries or something." He kissed her shoulder. "Groceries it is."

The rest of the day, they ran errands, then came home and had dinner. They curled up by the fireplace and he sang the song he'd written for her. "Did you call Ryan back?" He picked up the phone and called him. "Just played it for her," Joe said. They chatted a while, and Ava went on her laptop and started trying to plan out what to do for his birthday. By the time he got back over to her, she had the laptop away. "What were you up to," Joe asked. "Just checking email." "Ryan's popping by to work on the song. He wants to perform it this weekend." "Oh really?" "That alright," he asked. Ava nodded and kissed him. "I promise I'm coming to bed before 2." "I'll hold you to that." "Was hoping you'd say that," he said. He kissed her and pulled her into his lap. "When is he coming by?" "An hour." "Really." He kissed her then picked her up and carried her upstairs to their bed.

———

"What do you mean I can't get a flight until tomorrow?" "I'm sorry. The flights are booked solid." James booked the flight, opting to be on call for another one. He had to get there before he lost her altogether.

———

Ava curled up in bed with Joe after making love again. "What do you want for your birthday?" "Already have it." "Cute, but seriously." "You." He kissed her and pulled her close. "You already have me." "Never letting you go either." He kissed her. She heard the doorbell. Joe kissed her, then got up, pulling on his jeans and went downstairs. Ava's phone went off. The second she saw James' name come across the screen, her heart jumped. Joe came back upstairs and grabbed his shirt. "What," he asked as he saw the look on her face. "Nothing," Ava said. He walked over to her and kissed her. "I'll be back up in a little bit." She kissed him, then he went downstairs.

James called her back a few minutes later. "What do you want James?" "So you did move." "Yeah. What do you want?" "Where are you?" "Doesn't matter." "I know you don't just move that far away from everyone unless there's a reason." "There is. I like it here." "Where are you staying?" "Gated community outside Nashville." "You bought a place?"

"No. I'm staying with a friend." "Who?" "What do you want James?" "Come home." "I am home." "I miss you." "The feeling isn't mutual." "Ava." "I'm staying. I don't want you here James." "Who is he?" "None of your business." Ava hung up. She had to admit she was more than happy to be rid of James, especially now.

Joe came back up a while later and Ava was doing her writing. "Thought you'd be sleeping," Joe joked. "Got inspired after hearing you two singing downstairs." "How you doing on it?" "Just finished the third chapter." She turned the laptop off and put it away. "Not even one peek," Joe asked. Ava shook her head. She snuggled up to him. "Ryan said hi." "He doing any better?" "A little. The song gave him something to concentrate on." She wrapped her leg around him. "Missed you too," he joked. He kissed her. "I want to ask you something," he said. In the past it had always been a bad start to conversations. Something told her that this time would be different. "What's that?" "How do you feel about kids?" "Love them." "Do you want kids?" "Of course." "With me?" "What are you getting at Joe?" "Nothing. Brain is in over-drive." "Answer is yes." "Really?" "I definitely would," Ava said. "Even though I'm on tour a lot?" "And when the touring is done, you can be superdad." "Really?" "You already said once that you were off for a few months, and home a good part of the week. Why not?" He kissed her. "What brought all this on anyway," Ava asked. "Nothing." "Liar." "Was just thinking about it is all."

The next morning, Ava woke up to her phone ringing. She looked at the number and pressed ignore. It was too early in the morning for another fight with James. Joe pulled her close. She curled back up with him. "So what do we feel like doing today?" "Sleeping." "I have to leave tomorrow." "I know." "Do you want to come with us," Joe asked. "I could." He kissed her. "There's something I have to ask you." "What's that," Ava asked as she yawned and snuggled in closer. "You and James are over right?" "Definitely." "So I don't have to worry about losing you?" "Never." "Promise?" "What is all of this about?" "Nothing," Joe said trying to cover his butt. "You're so full of it." "Just talking to Ryan had me a little freaked out." "Stop worrying. I'm not going anywhere." He kissed her and held her in his arms. "Why do I get the feeling like you're going to spring something on me," Ava asked. He kissed her then leaned her onto her back. "Think I'm seriously falling for you," Joe said. It was music to Ava's ears. "Good." He kissed her and made love to her.

———◦◦◦◦◦◦———

James had 24 hours left before his flight left. He had to think of a grand gesture that would throw her enough to win her back. Something popped into his head, and he went with it. Come hell or high water, he was winning her back.

———◦◦◦◦◦◦———

After a relaxing day, Ava and Joe curled up by the fireplace. "This is the best part of this house." "What's that," Ava asked. "Curling up by the fireplace and having someone to curl up with." She smiled and kissed him. "I almost don't want to go." "You need to." "I know, I just don't want to be that far apart." "What are you hinting at?" He grabbed his phone and made a call. "One extra ticket, plus the all access for the concert and front row," he said as he talked to management. Ava smiled. He got off the phone a little while later then kissed her. "Both?" He nodded. "Can't stand to be away can you?" "Without you? Probably wouldn't even sleep," Joe said. He kissed her as she straddled him. "Really?" He kissed her again and leaned her onto the soft rug. "Don't want to be without you anymore." "You got me." He made love to her by the fireplace. Sparks were flying, and not just in the fireplace.

CHAPTER 6

The next day, Ava packed up for the weekend, and Joe got his things together for the two shows that weekend. They left that afternoon.

James' flight landed and he grabbed a rental car and headed for the hotel. He had it narrowed down to two areas. After he settled in, he headed off to the first of the two. "I'll have to check and see if they will authorize you," the security officer said. There was no answer. "Sorry sir. They're not available. You'll have to leave." Now he knew. That had to be where she was. He left, determined to find her.

Another day of sound check, interviews, meet and greets and concerts passed them by. She was just happy they'd be home for his birthday. While he was doing sound check on the last night, she went to the mall for a little bit of last minute shopping. She came back and had the bags hidden in her suitcase. After a quick clothing change, she headed straight to the concert. Was perfect timing. They were almost finished the meet and greet before dinner. He left as soon as he could and came into the change room. "Where'd you disappear to," Joe asked. "Errand to run." "What are you up to beautiful?" "Birthday surprises." He kissed her. "I told you what I wanted," Joe said. "I know. Got you something else anyway." He kissed her again. They had dinner with Brad and Ryan then watched the opening acts, then Joe begged her to stay backstage. "Why?" "No reason," he teased. He kissed her, then went to start the show. She sat side stage through the concert. When it came to singing the new song he'd written, he motioned for her to come. She shook her head.

"This is a new song our buddy Joe wrote. It's dedicated to his lady. Yes, he's taken now ladies," Ryan said. The audience didn't seem too happy. Ryan walked over, grabbing her hand and led Ava on stage. They sang the song for her, then Joe kissed her and she headed off stage. She shook her head with a grin ear to ear. They finished up the concert, then Joe walked down to the dressing room with her. "Had to do it," he teased. He kissed her. They all packed up then left to head back to the hotel. "I still can't believe you did that," Ava said. "Ryan wanted to do it." "You two are trouble." He kissed her. "And you love it." He kissed her again and they got changed for bed.

The next day, they got up and it was another full day of rehearsal, sound check, then interviews. "So we heard that last night you played a new song. Can you tell us about it," an interviewer asked. "Sort of came to me one night. The next day, Ryan added in his vocals and Brad added in a little piano and bass and there you go." "We heard that you wrote it for your girlfriend." "That I did." "So who is she?" "She's a writer. Let's just say it was love at first sight." "Really?" He nodded. "So, sorry for all the ladies out there, but I'm a one-woman man. She has my heart." Joe looked over at Ava. "Can you sing a little of it for us guys," the reporter asked. They sang it, then finished the interview. Joe walked over to Ava and kissed her once they were off camera. "Had to right?" He kissed her again, smirked, then they all headed off for dinner.

That night, after the concert, the four of them headed home. Ava fell asleep with her head on Joe's shoulder. "So what are we doing for your birthday tomorrow," Ryan asked. "Dinner." "And?" "We'll go out somewhere," Joe said. "You sure?" "I don't want a party this year." "Okay," Brad said. "What?" "She has your heart," Ryan teased. "She does." "Tell me you aren't going to do what I think you are," Brad said. "In my pocket." "Seriously," Ryan asked. Joe nodded and smiled. "What are you two gabbing about now," Ava asked. "Nothing. He's just making fun of the comment during the interview," Joe replied. Ava smirked. "You got him hooked you know," Ryan said. "That I do know." Joe kissed Ava, then got up to check on something. "So what time tomorrow," Ryan asked. "Seven. I'm taking him to dinner. He thinks it's just us," Ava replied. "Cool." "Don't know how you managed to plan all of it," Ava said. "Connections," Brad replied. Joe came back over and sat down. "We're landing in a half-hour," he said. "What are you up to smiley," Ava asked as Joe came back with a grin ear to ear. "Nothing." They chatted the rest of the way home, and Brad had a cat nap. "We're home buddy," Joe said as they landed. "Finally," Brad said as he winked at Ava.

Joe and Ava finally came home and went straight to bed. "Finally," Joe said laying on the bed. Ava got ready for bed and slid on the black satin and lace teddy she'd bought on her mini shopping spree. She came into the bedroom and Joe's mouth dropped. "Whoa." "What?" "So that's where you went." She smirked. "You realize that it's after midnight?" "Happy Birthday baby," Ava said. "Now that's the present I wanted," Joe said. He pulled her to him. He kissed her, slowly sliding the teddy off, then made love to her. The perfect start to his birthday.

The next morning, Ava got up and Joe's fingers were linked with hers and his arms were around her. "Happy Birthday again," Ava said. "Morning," he replied. He wouldn't let her hand go. "What?" He kissed her, pulling her towards him. "Remember what I said yesterday during that interview?" Ava nodded. "I meant it." "Meaning?" "I love you." "I love you too." "Good. Now look at your hand." There was a ring. It was the perfect ring. "What the?" "That's what I wanted for my birthday." "Joe." "Marry me." "You're crazy." "In love with you. Say yes." He leaned her onto her back and kissed her. "If you can handle me being on tour, and still love me, then I'm yours forever." "And if I miss you?" "Then you can come with us." He kissed her again. "Yes," Ava said. He kissed her and made love to her. Now she really needed to pinch herself. Was this really happening?

That night, Ava and Joe went to the restaurant for dinner. They had a quiet dinner, then headed back to the house. "We have to stop at Ryan's," Joe said. "Okay," Ava replied knowing full well that the party was there. They headed inside and he saw his parents. "What are you two . . ." Everyone yelled surprise. "This is why you were so sneaky," Joe said. Ryan nodded. Ava walked around and chatted with everyone. Joe pulled his mom and dad aside. "Something I wanted to tell you," he said as he held Ava's hand. "Tell me you're snatching her up," his dad commented. He nodded with a smile ear to ear. "I was kidding," his dad said. "I'm not. We're engaged." His mom hugged Ava. "Welcome to the family baby," his mom said. "Thanks. I'm so glad you two could come tonight," Ava said. "You planned this?" Ava nodded. "Ryan's idea to have it here." "Sneaky," Joe said. He kissed Ava. "Joe. One song," Ryan asked. Joe kissed Ava again then went to sing with Ryan. "This is for Joe and Ava. Congrats you two." They sang one of Ava's favorite songs . . . . 'Like Me'. "Just so everyone knows, my good friend Joe and his girlfriend Ava are engaged as of this morning," Ryan said. Everyone cheered and congratulated them. Once everyone started to head home, Ava and Joe left. They made plans for dinner the next night with his parents. They went to walk out and Ava could have sworn she saw James.

They hopped in the car and headed back to his place. They were about to pull in when Ava saw James. "I knew it," Ava said. "What," Joe asked. She rolled the window down. "I need to talk to you," James said. "Tomorrow," Ava replied. "Now." They pulled in to go past the gate. "You okay," Joe asked. She nodded. "I thought I saw him at the party." "Want me to take care of it," Joe asked. Ava shook her head. He parked and she talked to James.

"First off, why the hell are you here James," Ava asked. "Trying to talk you into going home." "I am home." "You know what I mean Ava." "If that's what you were here for, you can go home." "This why you came here?" She nodded. She went to brush her hair off her face and he saw the ring. "What's that," James asked. "James, you should go," Joe said as he hopped out of the car. "You asked her to marry you," James asked. "And she said yes,"

Joe said wrapping his arm around Ava's shoulders. "You stole my girl." "Back to being a piece of property. Go home James," Ava said. Joe and Ava went back and got in the car and went to the house.

"You know he's not going away," Joe said. "Don't really care. He can stay out there for a month if he wants. Not changing my mind for a second." He kissed her. "You should call your parents and tell them." "Probably a good idea," Ava said. She kissed him. He carried her upstairs to bed. "Still can't believe you were behind the party." "Who do you think I was talking to at dinner?" "Seriously," he asked. Ava nodded. "How am I going to thank you," he teased. He kissed her and slid the zipper down of her dress. Joe had the dress on the floor in minutes, and his shirt and jeans beside it a few minutes later. "Have an idea," he teased. "What's that?" He flipped her over his shoulder and ran downstairs and jumped into the pool. They splashed around for a while, and joked around. He finally got her pinned to the edge of the pool. "I love you," he said. "I love you too." "I can't wait to marry you." "Me either." He kissed her and they did it in the pool. They curled up on the chaise with a towel after. "What if we went off to a beach somewhere just us and did it," Joe asked. "You sure you don't want anyone there? I think your mom and dad would want to be there, the guys." "Really small then." Ava nodded. "Before Christmas." Ava agreed. "I'd do it tonight if we could," Joe said. "Why don't we just practice the honeymoon part," she joked. He kissed her. "Now there's an idea."

The next morning, they got up and called her parents. "Have a surprise for you," Ava said. "What's that?" "I'm getting married." "Congratulations." "In a month or so." "Let us know the date," her dad said. "Once we figure that out, I will." "We heard about you and Joe Morgan. It was on that station you used to love," her dad said. Joe smiled. "That's who the interview was with?" He nodded. They talked a while longer and they made reservations to come out. After the long phone call, Joe and Ava curled up together on the sofa.

He kissed her. "I still can't believe all of this is happening," Ava said. He kissed her again. "Get used to it. There's a lot more surprises where that came from." Ava smiled. "Can't wait." Ava grabbed something from under the sofa. "What's this," Joe asked. "Your birthday present. Didn't manage to get out of bed long enough to give it to you yesterday," Ava teased. He kissed her again then went to slide her sweater off. "Present first."

He opened the box and saw the bracelet. "Baby. This is beautiful." "Look on the back." He saw the engraving:

Forever—Ava

Joe smiled and put it on. "It's perfect." "Had a feeling you were going to love it." He kissed her and noticed something else in the box. He pulled out a shirt that he fell in love with the minute he felt it. "Where the hell did you find this?" "Thought you'd like it." He kissed her. "This is unbelievable." "Ryan told me about that one." He slid his shirt off and tried the new one on. "Perfect." Fit him like a glove. He slid it off, then pulled her back into his arms. "You spoil me you know." Ava nodded and kissed him. "What am I gonna do with you?" "I'm sure you can think of something," Ava teased. He held her close. "I love you." "I love you too." He kissed her and they curled up on the sofa.

The next day, he got packed for two more shows. "You sure you don't want to come?" "I should go and see the girls," Ava said. "Come Saturday night." "You can't wait that long can you," she joked. Joe shook his head. "We have the rest of our lives," Ava said. "Not enough time," he replied. He kissed her and pulled her to him. "Won't be the same without you there Ava." "Then Saturday will be even better," she replied. He kissed her again. "What time does your flight leave?" "7am." "I'll go to the airport with you," Ava said. He nodded. The rest of the day, they relaxed together. He made the best of every minute. Ava packed her things for the weekend, then they curled up in bed. "Stealing my shirt already," Joe asked. "Smells like you." "See, you miss me already," Joe joked. "Why wouldn't I?" He kissed her, then slid his shirt off and pulled her into bed with him.

The next morning, Ava got up and took Joe to the airport. The press was all over them. He handed her the plane ticket to head home, and the other one to meet him on the Saturday. "You sure I can't change your mind about going?" Ava shook her head. Joe kissed her, picking her up in his arms. "You're going to miss the flight," Ava said. He kissed her again, then ran for the gate. Ava parked the car then headed to her flight home.

⸎

"Hey stranger," Rose said picking her up from the airport. "Hey yourself. How's the house?" "Good. James has lost his damn mind, but the house is fine." They pulled in a while later and went inside. "So, I need your help with something," Ava said. "What?" "Need to find a dress." "For what?" Ava showed her the ring. "No bloody way," Rose said. Ava nodded. "We need to find a dress for you too. We're getting married either at the house or at the beach in Malibu." "Holy crap." "So, you gonna help me?" Rose hugged Ava. "When?" "A month." "What date?" "18th of October." "Shit. That's cutting it kinda close," Rose said. "Hence why we have a lot of work to do. Oh, and we're going to the concert tomorrow night." "We?" "You and me."

They left and went dress shopping. Ava finally found a wedding dress that had Rose in tears. "It's beautiful." Ava bought it then found a maid of honor dress for Rose. The best

46

part was there were no alterations needed. They left with their dresses in hand and headed to lunch. Ava hid the dresses in her trunk.

After lunch, they headed back to the house to go through invitations. Ava had one picked out within a few minutes. She sent it to Joe and he agreed. She got the code for them and put in an order. Now all they needed were the flowers, the minister, the location and the reception. They went through a pile of locations and had one picked out, or at least narrowed down to the top two. She called to ask about them, putting them on hold until her and Joe had made a decision. After a full day, Ava and Rose had dinner together at the house. "I still can't believe you two are getting married." "It feels right," Ava said. "You know James is going to freak out." "Don't really give two hoots," Ava joked. A few minutes later, James was at the front door.

"What," Ava asked. "I need to talk to you," James said. "We're busy." "Now." He grabbed her arm pulling her towards him. "What do you want?" "You're seriously marrying Joe?" "Date's been set." "You can't." "Why? I love him James. That's why I'm marrying him." "You can't just leave." "Already did." "Ava, you can't just walk away from me." "Yeah I can James. Watch." She slammed the door and locked it behind her.

The next morning, Ava and Rose woke up and packed, then left to meet Joe and the boys.

The press was all over Joe when she finally made it to the venue with Rose. "So we heard that you're engaged. When did this happen?" "My birthday. Was a little surprise for her. It's kind of funny how priorities change." "So when's the big day?" "We're keeping it private. I'm sure you guys understand." "Well, congratulations to both of you then." "Thanks." "So what's this we hear about a new song?" "Wrote it for her actually."

Ava showed just as they were starting to ask him about the wedding. Joe looked over and smiled. The guys finished up the interview with the new song, then Joe walked over to Ava. "Hey beautiful." "Hey yourself sexy," Ava replied. Joe picked Ava up, pulling her close. He kissed her with a kiss that could have melted an iceberg. "I missed you," he said. "Missed you too." He kissed her again. Joe finally put her down. "You remember Rose right?" "I'm glad you could come," Joe said. "Wouldn't have missed it for the world," Rose replied with a grin ear to ear. "Rose, this is Ryan and Brad," Ava said. "Nice to meet you," Rose said as Ryan kissed Rose's hand. Both the guys were smirking. "What," Ava asked. "Nothing," Brad said. "Spill it," Ava said. "This is the single friend right," Ryan asked. "Yes I am actually," Rose said. "We'll be over here," Ryan joked as he left and showed Rose around. "He missed you bad," Brad said. "I bet. How did it go," Ava asked. "Not as good as when you're here," Joe said. "You're lying, but nice try." "It went good. A few girls tried to get backstage, but he stopped them before they tried anything," Brad replied. "Oh really?" "Security stopped them." Brad walked off laughing. Ava showed him the invites. "So, two ideas for the ceremony," Ava said. "Booked it. A villa in Cabo." "Seriously?" "Everyone can stay there then we go on our honeymoon. It's a vacation for everyone," Joe said. Ava agreed after she saw the information. "Booked it for 3 days." "Seriously?" "All we have to do is call and send them a picture of the flowers and the menu for dinner. Everything else is done." "Guess it's a good thing I got the dress yesterday then." Joe picked Ava up kissing her. "You realize you're stuck with me forever." Ava nodded. "Not sharing either," Ava replied. He kissed her then finally put her down. They headed out to have something to eat and the guys got to know Rose a bit. "So where did you two decide on for the wedding," Rose asked. "Cabo," Joe said. "The one I told you about," Brad asked. Joe nodded. "You realize that place is like paradise," Brad replied. "Good," Joe replied. Ryan smiled. "I could tell him his foot was falling off and he'd still be smiling around her," Ryan teased. "You have a point there," Rose replied. "It's kind of nice seeing him so happy though," Brad said. "They're both lucky," Rose replied. "Very true," Ryan said looking right at Rose.

Once dinner was done, the guys had sound check and then went to get changed. "Tell me you aren't wearing the red dress," Joe asked. "Black top with the jeans." "Damn." "What," Ava asked. "Guys, I might be tripping over my feet tonight," Joe joked. "What else is new," Ryan replied. Ava got changed, then came back and sat with him. "Seriously, you aren't allowed to go out there like that," Joe said. "Why?" He kissed Ava and pulled her into his lap. "I have a bodyguard," Ava joked. "You sure you two don't want to watch it from the side of the stage?" "Whichever you want." "You're coming up for that song though," Joe said. Ava nodded. He kissed her again. "Which color are we doing tonight," Ryan asked. "Black and blue," Joe replied. "Nice. Color co-ordinated and all," Brad teased. Joe threw a towel at him. "I love you," Joe said as he kissed Ava. "I love you too." "One more month," he said. "I know." "Not soon enough," Joe replied. "Meaning what," Ava asked. "Vegas." Ava laughed. "Seriously." "You have to be joking." He kissed her. "We can go tonight," Joe said. "You drank the wrong kool-aid," Ava said. He laughed. "Seriously." "Tonight?" He nodded. "Right after the concert. We're like a half-hour from there." "You are going bonkers," Ava said. "Think about it." "Okay, but I still say you're crazy." He kissed her and nibbled her neck, then her shoulder. "Joe, 5 minutes. Quit molesting her and let her get her seat," Ryan said. Joe laughed. Ava went out and found Rose, then went to their seats.

Just like he planned, Joe pulled Ava on stage when they played the song. It was the last one of the night before they left. When the guys came off stage, Joe told the guys they were going on a road trip. "Where," Brad asked. "Top secret road trip. You'll see when we get there," Joe replied. "I did want to get home," Brad said. "Trust me," Joe replied. Her stomach started flipping. Butterflies was an understatement. They pulled up and Ava gave him a look. "What," Joe asked. "I know you're all excited about it." "If you want to wait," Joe said. They went and had a drink, and a little something to eat, then Joe excused himself and Ava. "Where are you two going?" "Wanted to show her something," Joe said.

CHAPTER 7

Joe and Ava came back a half-hour later. "Where did you two disappear to," Brad asked. "Went for a walk for a bit." "I was almost thinking that you two went to one of those wedding chapel places," Ryan teased. "We're planning a wedding. Why would we do that," Ava asked as he slipped the wedding bands off their fingers. "Why do you two look guilty then," Rose asked. "We were just talking." "Right. Can we get on the plane and head home now," Brad asked. Joe nodded.

An hour or so later, they were home. "Here's the guest room," Joe said showing Rose around the house. "This is bigger than Ava's master suite at home," Rose said. "Bathroom is through there." "Nice." Ava and Joe went into the bedroom and he locked them in, sliding the wedding bands out of his pocket and onto their fingers. "He would have killed us," Joe teased. "Why?" "He wants to sing at the wedding. If we did it without them . . . you mean Rose wouldn't have been pissed," Joe asked. "True. You have a point there." He kissed Ava, walking her backwards to the bed. "What?" "Sort of like a honeymoon." Within minutes, she had his shirt off, and her clothes on the ground. "I have an idea," Joe said. "What's that?" He kissed Ava, then picked her up carrying her to the shower. The steam from the hot water filled the room. They made love in the shower, on the counter, the edge of the tub, then crawled into bed for round 3. "Still don't know how you have all this energy after the concert," Ava said. "Energizer batteries," Joe joked. They curled up together and fell asleep with their legs entwined.

The next morning, Rose woke up and headed downstairs. She made coffee, then made herself some breakfast. It was one hell of a house. She realized why Ava felt so at home there. It wasn't the granite counters and gourmet kitchen. It wasn't the killer view and massive pool, and it wasn't the things inside the house. She'd never seen Ava this happy. Even with her old boyfriend, who she claimed to love, she'd never been this over the top happy. Rose's phone rang as she was closing the door to sit outside. "Who's this?" "It's Ryan. They up yet?" "Something tells me they are, but they're not if you know what I mean," Rose said. "What are you doing this morning?" "Probably wedding stuff, but until she's up . . ." "Come for a walk," Ryan asked.

Ava finally managed to get out of bed, slid the ring off, hiding it in the jewelry box, then showered and got dressed. "Come back to bed," Joe said. "Rose is here. I can't just leave her downstairs." He grabbed her hand and pulled her back to the bed. He kissed her neck, then slid her tank top off. "You are determined aren't you?" Joe kissed her again. "I don't get to seduce my wife every day you know," he replied. He kissed her again, pulling her skirt off. "Never going to make it out of bed are we?" He slid her g-string off, then went for her bra and pulled her back in under the covers with him. "We have to get up at some point." Joe kissed her again and leaned his body against hers. The man turned her on with one kiss. "Well Mrs. Morgan, what did you want to do today," Joe asked. "Be with you." "You got it." "Why is it so quiet in the house," Ava asked. "She must have gone out." "With who? She doesn't know anyone else but the guys," Ava said. Joe giggled. "What?" "If she's out with him, I will seriously laugh." "No way." "I know he likes her." He kissed Ava. "Ryan," Ava asked. "So since we have the place to ourselves . . ." His head disappeared under the blankets.

———

"Something tells me they were up to something last night," Ryan said. "They wouldn't have done that without one of us there," Rose said "He was talking about it yesterday." "Seriously?" "That he didn't want to wait that long. That Vegas would be faster." "What's the rush anyway?" "When you find it, you hold on with both hands," Ryan said. He knew all too well what it was like. "I mean how do you really know it's going to be forever?" "I thought I knew once. I was wrong, but damn it felt right," Ryan said. "You don't really think they got hitched?" "It's funny that we worry about those two isn't it," Ryan asked. "It's like I'm her mom or something," Rose said. "At some point, you let them make their own decisions good or bad." "What do you think about them," Rose asked. "I've never really seen him happy like that. They complement each other in every way, and what's better is that her work and his work click. I do know that she said she wished you were closer. That you two are almost like sisters." "Pretty close to. You and Joe are practically family." "Like a big brother," Ryan said. The two of them talked. The more they talked, the more Rose understood why Ava loved being here. The guys were completely different, and she was realizing more and more that Ryan was totally her type. She thought about it. "Nah. Could never happen," she thought.

———

Finally, Ava and Joe came downstairs and had breakfast. They were curled up in their swimsuits by the pool when Rose and Ryan came in. "Told you so," Joe teased. "I see you two finally got out of bed," Rose teased. "Was tired," Ava said. Rose smirked. "So where were the two of you," Joe asked Ryan. "We went for a coffee. You have one heck of a friend here Ava," Ryan said trying to change the topic. "That I do." "So, is it okay with you two if I kidnap Rose for the rest of the day," Ryan asked. Joe smirked. "I have a few wedding things to do today anyway," Ava said. "Goodie," Joe joked. "We'll see you at dinner," Ava said. Rose went up to change, and Ryan was outside with Ava and Joe. "I know you two are up to something," Ryan said. "Like what," Joe asked. "Did you two go to that chapel last night?" "No. We went and walked around. I wanted to show her that jewelry store," Joe said. "And," Ryan asked. "We picked out the wedding bands," Ava said. "You know if you two got hitched there, I'm still singing at the wedding in Cabo," Ryan said. "I know you are. I'm looking forward to it," Ava said. "So what do you two have left to put together,' Ryan asked. "Flowers, and the reception stuff," Ava said. "That's it?" Ava nodded. "Well, that and what you guys are wearing," Ava said. "We figured that out already," Joe said. "Oh really?" Joe kissed her. "It looks nice. No worries." "You guys always look good," Ava said. Joe curled up with her. "We'll meet you at my place for dinner," Ryan said. Ava nodded. "You two are seriously too cute."

Ryan left with Rose, and Ava and Joe relaxed by the pool. "Seriously, what are we doing today," Joe asked. "Flowers, cake and food for the wedding." "Okay. Talked me into it," he said as he scooped her up and dove into the pool with her in his arms. They splashed around, which turned into making out in the pool and having sex in and out of the pool. "Still can't believe you talked me into that," Ava said. Joe kissed her. "Wasn't that hard to talk you into." "You know she'd kill us if she knew," Ava said. He kissed her again. "I could stay here all day with you." "Don't tempt me. We have to get that last stuff finished," Ava said. "I know. Then we can relax." "You're gonna love the dress." "Love the lady in it." Joe kissed her again. "We have to get up." They went inside and got dressed, then headed off to do the last minute things they needed to finish.

By dinner, the cake, flowers and menu was done. Ava found a dress for her mom, and he found something for his mom, then they headed to meet Rose and Ryan.

They walked in and saw Ryan and Rose kissing. Joe wrapped his arms around Ava. "Looks like we rubbed off on you two," Joe joked. "Funny. So how was your day," Ryan asked. "Got the rest of the planning done," Ava said. "That fast," Rose asked. "Invites are on the way out," Joe said. "You two are hilarious. There's a job for you when we finish the music career . . . . Wedding planner," Ryan teased. "What are we doing for dinner smart mouth," Joe asked. "Grilled trout and veggies, and cheesecake for dessert," Ryan said. "Sounds good. What restaurant did you get it from," Joe teased. "Just for that, you aren't getting dessert," Ryan said. Ava gave Rose a hug. "Seriously everything done," Rose asked. "Only thing left is the honeymoon." "Already booked," Joe said. "Do I get to know where," Ava asked. "Let's just say all you'll need is a bikini and something to wear at dinner." "Right. Funny," Ava said. "Wasn't kidding." Ava kissed him. "Think I might need a few other things." Joe kissed her. Ryan opened the wine and poured a glass for Rose and himself. "So what were you two up to today," Joe asked. "Showed Rose around the city. Took her downtown and showed her around." "I bet," Joe teased. Ryan threw a towel at him. "You two are like little kids," Ava said. "I'll go turn the grill on," Joe said. They left Ava and Rose inside alone.

"So," Ava asked. "Damn," Rose said. "That good?" "Seriously, he's unbelievable." "Good or bad?" "Really really good." "Next thing you know, you'll be out here too." "I know why you love it here now." "Seriously, what do you think," Ava asked. "Totally like him. We were like teenagers all day. It was awesome. Then we came back here, started cooking, then we sat outside and talked. He's . . . . wow." The guys came inside a few minutes later. "What are you two grinning about," Ava asked. Joe came up behind Ava and wrapped his arms around her. "What?" "Come outside," Joe said. Ava went outside with him and they walked to the back deck. "What," Ava asked. "He told me what song he wanted to sing." "And?" "You're gonna cry if I tell you," Joe said. "No." "He chose it. It's either Like Me or You Are." "My two favorites." "I picked Like Me." Ava nodded and kissed him. He wrapped his arms around her. "Then I'm singing Love Letters." "Serenaded. Now how many girls can say they got that," Ava asked. Joe kissed her again.

"You didn't tell him I picked them right," Rose asked. "Told him I chose them," Ryan said. They finished making dinner, and flirted back and forth all the way through it. "She's so happy. I'm happy she finally found someone she loves that much," Rose said. "Your turn," Ryan said. "What do you mean?" "Now it's your turn. No more worrying about Ava." "She's like my big sister sometimes." "Believe it or not, he has a way of reminding me what I'm missing even when he doesn't think he does," Ryan said. "What do you mean?" "When I got divorced, I thought life was pretty much over for the longest time. He's my reminder that life is pretty great especially with someone to share it with." "You have a point there," Rose said. "So how long are you staying for?" Ryan wasn't about to let go of her for anything. "Until she makes me leave." "At least she'll have someone to keep her company while we're doing our shows," Ryan said. "Something tells me that a plane ride isn't going to separate them." "He loves her, and he is never going to let go. He's like the white knight on the horse," Ryan said. "And what about you?" "What about me," Ryan asked. "Pretty handsome knight yourself." He smiled. "Well you're pretty beautiful too princess," Ryan said. He kissed her. For the first time in months, he felt whole again.

Ava saw them inside. "We're contagious," she said. Joe led her to the chaise and curled up with her. "He likes her." "Ya think?" "Know what? I have a feeling you won't need to go home to visit her." "Really?" "Bet you." "What are we betting for?" "I win, I get one night of whatever I want. You win, you get one night of whatever you want." "Fair bet. She's a tough cookie," Ava said. "So were you and you're here with me aren't you," he teased. "Funny." Joe kissed her. Ryan and Rose came out a little while later. "Fish is almost done," Joe said. "Everything else is ready," Ryan said. "I bet," Joe teased.

They had dinner, then relaxed outside together. "So when do you guys leave for the next concert," Rose asked. "Two days," Joe said. "Where's the concert this time," Ava asked. "An hour from here. We're coming home Friday night," Joe said. He kissed Ava. "Planned," Ava asked. "Convenient," Joe said. Ava curled up in his lap. "You staying this weekend with me Rose," Ava asked. "I have to go home. I only packed for a few days." "You're coming back though right," Ryan asked. "I have to check in at work, but I can come back on Tuesday." Ryan breathed a sigh of relief. Joe nibbled Ava's ear.

A while later, Joe decided it was time to head home. "We're heading back to the house. You coming Rose," Ava asked. "I'll be back in a little while," Rose replied. Joe and Ava left, leaving Ryan and Rose alone. "You could stay here tonight if you want," Ryan suggested. "My stuff is at the house." "We can grab it," Ryan said. "Why are you so anxious to have me here?" Ryan kissed her. "Just tonight."

Ava and Joe got back to the house and went to bed. "She's gonna end up staying there," Joe said. "Maybe tonight." "I'm telling you, we're contagious." "She doesn't fall for guys like that Joe." "He's gonna win her over. You watch," he said. He wrapped his arms around Ava and snuggled up to her and fell asleep. An hour or two later, Rose sneaked in and grabbed her things, then headed to Ryan's.

She came out to the car. "That's all you brought," Ryan asked. "Didn't think I'd be staying for a week." "Come to the concert," he asked. "I have to go home and get clothes." "After." They got back to his place. He turned on the fireplace and opened another bottle of wine. They talked for hours, which led to kissing, which landed them in the master bedroom. They were curled up on the bed together and Ryan stopped himself. "What?" "I don't want to mess this up," he said. "Mess what up?" "I like you." "I like you too." "I just don't want to rush this." Rose kissed him and slid her sweater off. "You sleep in here tonight," Ryan said. "You're staying in here with me." "I'll sleep in the other room." He went to get up and she pulled him back to her. "What are you scared of?" "I don't want to ruin today," he said. "You aren't." "I just don't want to rush this." They kissed and she slid his shirt off. She pulled her shirt off, then he gave into his gut feeling. He made love to her and from that second on, he was hooked. He curled up in bed with her, and for the first time in months, he fell fast asleep.

The next morning, Ava and Joe got up and went for a run. "Still don't know why you need to do this." "It's good for you. Stop complaining." He kissed her. "Know of a much better exercise idea." "Race you." "For what?" "I win, we go into town for a while and walk around. You win, whatever you want this afternoon." They left and he chased her through it. They got back to the house and she won. "That's totally not fair." "Sore loser?" He grabbed her and carried her up the steps to their bedroom. "So not fair." He leaned her onto the bed and kissed her. "You notice? She stayed at his place last night." "Doesn't mean you won." He kissed her again, peeling her shirt off. "I won and you know it." He peeled her workout gear off, then slid out of his and carried her to the shower. "You did not," Ava teased. In minutes, the room was filled with steam. They made love in the shower, then went back to bed. "We're going out today you know." He kissed her neck. "No sucking up to get your way either." They curled up in bed for a little while, then got dressed and headed out.

Rose woke up the next morning with Ryan's arms still around her. She had to admit, it felt good. "Morning," Ryan said. "Morning." "You sleep okay?" "Better than I thought." Ryan had missed having someone to wake up to. "Breakfast," he asked. Rose nodded. He got up, slipping his jeans on, then went downstairs. Rose got up, pulled on her robe, then went downstairs after freshening up. Ryan handed her coffee as she came into the kitchen. "Thank you," she said. "Welcome beautiful," he replied as he kissed her. "So what are you up to today," Rose asked. "Have to pack tonight, but the day's pretty much free." "I should book a flight home," Rose said. "I wish you didn't have to go." "I'm back before you get back Ryan." "Come to the concert tomorrow night then." "I'll see what I can do." An idea popped into her head. She grabbed her phone.

"Hey Rose. What's up," Rachel asked. "Can you do me a huge favor?" "No I am not dumping whoever it is for you." "Right. Funny. Can you grab some stuff from Ava's house for me and send it?" "Where the hell are you?" "Tennessee." "Cowboy heaven? What are you doing there?" "Ava is getting married." "I thought she was with James," Rachel asked. "Better idea. Pack for a few days, grab some of my stuff and come here." "Seriously?" "We're going to a concert tomorrow night." "Girl, you're crazy." "I'll send you the ticket." "What do you need from the house?"

"What was that all about," Ryan asked. "Not going. My friend Rachel is coming and she's gonna bring some of my stuff for me." "I'll get an extra ticket." Ryan kissed her. "I'm so glad you aren't going," he said. "I have to do a conference call to get updates on work, but I can stay," Rose said. He kissed her again then leaned her into the counter. "Guess I came up with a good idea," Rose said. Ryan picked her up, leaning her onto the counter. "Stay here with me." "I have to go home at some point," Rose said. "Why?" "I have work." "You said you were mobile." "I can call and ask." Ryan kissed her again.

Ava and Joe spent the day shopping and sitting at the park. "Who else are you having in the wedding party," Joe asked. "My friend Rachel or Brad's wife. Either or." "Do you have a bridesmaid dress for her?" "I have one put aside." He called Brad. "She'd love to. I'll take her down to try it on this afternoon," Brad said hanging up. Joe and Ava hung out at the park when a paparazzi person caught them and snapped pictures. They left and headed back to the house.

They came back to the house then sat outside. "See, that's why I said we shouldn't," Ava said. "Since it hit the radio and TV, it's going to be hard doing anything," Joe said. "Good thing we already did then." He kissed her. "Can we stay home tonight," Joe asked. "Depends." "On what?" "Where Rose is." He laughed. "I know exactly where she is," Ryan said. "She's going home." "He'll talk her out of it." "So sure about that." "She wasn't here last night. That tells me I'm right. If she wasn't here last night, that means he fell hard. He's not like me." "Meaning?" "Meaning when I saw you, I told them I was going to marry you." "You did not." Joe nodded. "Fell the minute you said hello." He kissed her again and pulled her on top of him. "Considering who I was there with," Ava said. "I told them. Ryan laughed at me. Fact is, when I see what I want, I do whatever I have to in order to get it." "Oh really." He nodded. "I wanted to be with you the minute we met. When you came in to say good night, I told them I was going to marry you. When Ryan finally stopped laughing, he realized that it was a definite possibility." "What if I'd said no?" "I would have done whatever it took to get you to say yes, even if it took years." "Good answer." Joe kissed her. "I love you baby." "I love you too."

Rose made her conference call to work and got approval to work from Nashville, then Ryan and Rose spent the rest of the day relaxing. "What time does her flight come in," Ryan asked. "Around 9. It's almost too quiet here," Rose said. "It's relaxing. That's what I sort of need after the concerts." "Guess I'm used to the city life." "Trust me. You'll get used to this," Ryan said. "That's what Ava said. Gotta say, I love it here. I know why she didn't want to come back." "So whatever happened with her and James?" "She walked away." "Guess that was good for Joe." "Truthfully, I've never seen Ava this happy. You can see it all over her face that she loves him." "He knew the day they met," Ryan said. "She met you guys before that." "What do you mean?" "Years ago at a concert near her hometown." "That's where I'd seen her before," Ryan said. "She had a crush on Joe way back then." "Guess they're a match made in heaven then." "True." "Kind of like fate introducing us," Ryan said. Rose nodded, then kissed him.

Rose and Ryan picked Rachel up at the airport. "I still can't believe you made me pack this much," Rachel said. "Stop complaining." "Couldn't choose which shoes could you," Ryan teased. The two girls laughed and Rose introduced her to Ryan.

Ava and Joe were about to head to bed when Rose called. "Come for a drink with us." "Us who," Ava asked. "Rachel's here." "Come over here." Ava hung up and Joe wrapped his arms around her. "Rachel is coming over with Ryan and Rose." "Who's Rachel?" "One of our girlfriends. Carrie's coming for the wedding." "I guess he talked Rose out of going home then." "Fine. You won that round." He kissed her. He checked the fridge to make sure there was beer for him and Ryan, then threw a bottle of wine in for the girls.

Rachel Chapman was the spontaneous one. She was around 5 foot 7, and was like the girl next door. She was normally the wild and crazy one, the one that always had to set everyone right, and the one that no guy could possibly crack. She was cool, calm, collected and smart as hell. Her dark raven hair and brown eyes had guys stopping in their tracks. Only one man she wanted, and he was gaga over Ava.

They showed about a half-hour later. Ava introduced Rachel to Joe. "So what's this I hear about you two getting married," Rachel asked. "On the 18th of October," Ava said. "Congratulations." Joe wrapped his arms around Ava. "Don't know how I got so lucky," Joe said. "You know, you're right Rose. She does look different," Rachel said. Joe grabbed everyone a drink and they sat down outside. "And since when did you start drinking beer Ava," Rachel asked. "Felt like it," she replied. "Oh you two are just too cute," Rachel said. They sat around talking for a while, then Rose decided to head back to Ryan's. "See you two later," Rachel said saying goodbye. The minute Rachel got back to the house and had some privacy, she called James. "You won't believe this. Ava's engaged to Joe."

———

The next morning, Ava woke up in Joe's arms. "We're staying in bed today," Joe said. "You have a concert tonight." He kissed her, then pinned her to the bed. "I know. We don't have to be there until 2 and I refuse to let go until then," he said. "Deal," Ava said. He kissed her and wrapped his arms around her. "We do have to eat at some point," Ava joked. "I know. I guess I'll let you have breakfast," Joe teased. Ava couldn't help waking up wanting him and having a smile ear to ear. She really was that happy. He made it too easy. Her phone rang at 10am. She saw the caller and pressed ignore. "Don't tell me," Joe said. "You don't want to know." "Why is he calling?" "He's good friends with Rachel. She probably told him our news," Ava said. "Good. If he knew about Vegas, he wouldn't have bothered to call at all," Joe said. "True. But Ryan and Rose and Brad would be pissed, your mom would be mad, and my parents would blow a gasket." "Also true," Joe said. He kissed her. "You know what I'd do today if we could?" "What," Ava asked. "You and me on a deserted island." "Nice try," Ava said. "You're coming to the concert tonight right?" Ava nodded. "Good. You've gone three whole days without being serenaded. Must be a law against that somewhere." "There probably is." Ava's phone went off again. She looked. "Hi." "We wanted to remind you about your appointment this afternoon at 2:30." "I'll be there. Thanks." "Who was that?" "Doctors appointment." "For what?" "Checkup. Figured if I'm going to be here, I might as well find a doctor." "Want company?" "You'll be at rehearsal." He kissed her. "As long as my wife is healthy, I'm good." Joe kissed her and made love to her before he left for rehearsal. "I'll meet you down there after my appointment." He kissed her again and left. Ava showered, then left for the doctor.

Rose and Rachel left with Ryan for the rehearsal. He showed Rachel around, gave her the passes, then got down to work. "I still can't believe you Rose. The lead singer?" "He's a really good guy," Rose said. "Tell me you didn't fall for him." "A little." "The tough cookie does crumble," Rachel said.

——⟡——

"We did the test." "And?" "We're doing an ultrasound."

——⟡——

Ava got to the rehearsal around 3. Joe kissed her as she came in. "Everything ok?" "Tell you later." "Ava?" "I'm perfect." "That I knew." Joe kissed her again, then she went and sat with the girls. "Where were you," Rose asked. "Doctor." "You alright?" Ava nodded.

Once rehearsal was done, Joe grabbed Ava's hand and led her to the change room where they could have some privacy. "Tell me." "One of the tests came back weird." "Which one?" "The one that checks if I'm pregnant or not." He kissed her. "And?" "Just shy of 4 weeks." "Seriously?" Ava nodded. "They said they don't know 100% yet, but that's the way it looks." He kissed her again. "When will they know for sure?" "Have an appointment in two weeks." Joe kissed her and pulled her close. "Everything's going so perfect." "You sure we're ready for this," Ava asked. "Do you love me?" Ava nodded. "Of course I love you," Ava said. "We're getting married," he said with a smirk. "So why is it so scary to think of having a baby together?" "Just wanted to make sure we were ready for this," Ava said. "The house is too big for just us anyway. Now we can start filling the rooms up." Joe kissed her again, as he curled up with her on the sofa. The guys came in with Rose and Rachel and Brad's wife a little while later. "You two coming for dinner," Brad asked. "We'll be there in a few," Joe said. Ryan headed out with the ladies. "I know that look. What's going on," Brad asked. "Not saying until we're sure." "Seriously? Holy shit. Congrats you two," Brad said as he hugged Joe and Ava. "Shh," Joe said. "Can't hide that one buddy. It's all over your faces," Brad said. "We'll be there in a few," Joe said. Ava turned to face Joe. "I had to tell him." He kissed her as she slid her arms around his neck.

They all had dinner, then the guys went off to do the interviews. Joe talked Ava into coming with him. "So we heard you're engaged. When's the big day," the interviewer asked. "Mid October. We're keeping the actual date and location quiet. We're just having a small ceremony and reception," Joe said. "So who is she?" "She's a romance writer. I met her years ago, then saw her again recently and she had my heart from that minute on." "Does she have anything to do with the new single?" "My inspiration actually." "So Ryan, we heard you had some inspiration of your own tonight."

CHAPTER 8

Once the interview was done, Joe kissed Ava. They finished sound check, then did the meet and greet. Joe came into the change room right after the meet and greet was done. "What you doing sexy lady," he asked kissing her. "Was checking emails," she said. Joe slid the laptop out of her hands and pulled her to her feet. "What are you up to?" He kissed her again. "I love you." "I love you too. What time do you start?" "15 minutes. Just thought I would warn you, James is here." "Where?" "He got front row tickets. If you want to stay side stage, you can." "Can't hide from him forever," Ava said. "Considering, I think you should stay up here with us." "I'll go down and see them. He starts, I come back." He kissed her. "I know you're worried. Don't. I'll be fine," Ava said. He kissed her again, pulling her tight against him. Joe went to get ready and Ava went down with the girls.

"Was wondering when you were coming down here," Rachel teased. "Was sidetracked," Ava joked. "I bet. You two are way too cute," Rachel said. "I'm sitting side stage for the concert. I just wanted to let you two know," Ava said. "Why's that," James asked handing Rachel and Rose a drink. "You guys enjoy the concert." Ava went to walk away. "You can't avoid me forever," James said. "What do you want James?" "We need to talk." "No we don't. There's nothing to say James. Joe and I are getting married. That's all there is to it." "How are you gonna go do that," James asked. "My life, my rules." Ava went to walk off, and he grabbed her arm. The security officer stepped in and separated them. Ava went up to the side stage and kissed Joe before he went on. "You okay?" Ava nodded. "I love you." "Love you more," she said.

James tried to get back stage and couldn't. "I need to talk to Ava Ross," James said. "I'll see if I can find her." The security officer came over to Ava. "No. He's not allowed back here, and he's not one of our guests." He walked back over to him. "Sorry. No can do." James went back and watched the rest of the concert with the girls, then they went back to meet the guys. "He's with me," Rachel said. "He's not on the list. No can do," Security said. Ryan came by. "What are you doing here James," Ryan asked. "I need to talk to Ava." "She left with Joe already." James was finally allowed backstage.

"We could've hung out a while," Ava said. "You know he's best buddies with Ryan. He wouldn't have stopped him from coming backstage," Joe said. "Good point." "Besides, means more us time." Ava curled up with him in the car. "I still can't believe we're having a baby," Joe said. "Maybe." "We are Ava. I wonder what he or she will look like." "Probably have your eyes and your smile," Ava said. "Your nose." They giggled and laughed all the way home.

———

"James, she's gone. She's marrying him," Ryan said. "I know, but she was supposed to marry me." "You can't win her back James. There's no winning her back." "She's not hitched yet." "I'd leave it be James. Just move on," Ryan said. "I can't. I love her." "Probably better to just wish them well and move on. It'll hurt like shit, trust me, but you're better off walking away." "She won't even talk to me." "I heard her half too James. You went nuts." "I love her. Even if it takes forever." "It will James." "Why are you so convinced they're going to stay together," James asked. "Let's just say I know. I've never seen him that happy," Ryan said. "Something's different about her too. I have no idea what, but you're right."

———

Rachel went back to the house with Ryan and Rose, and James went back to his hotel. He paced the room for hours trying to figure out what to do next. Every idea he had, he quashed in minutes. He had to get her alone. The question was how?

Ava and Joe got home and curled up on the sofa together. "What did he want anyway," Joe asked. "No idea. Fact is, he's determined to get me back. I was damn near tempted to tell him," Ava said. "Would have loved to have seen the look on his face." "I take it you two aren't the greatest of friends," Ava asked. "I know a snake when I see one." "Well, point being, he doesn't win. You're stuck with me," Ava teased. "Just what I wanted." "So what are we doing tonight?" Joe curled up with her in his arms. "Being really happy, and staying that way," he said. "Good plan. What about tomorrow," Ava teased.

They headed upstairs and had a long hot bath in the tub, then crawled into bed together. "How do you always know just what I need," Joe asked. Ava slid in behind him in the tub. "What are you doing," he asked. She gave him a back rub. "Okay. Now that's heaven." There wasn't one knot left when she was finished. "That's what you need after being on stage all night." "You don't even know." "No more stress," Ava said. He kissed her. "I still can't believe we might be having a baby." "I'll know in a day or two," she said. "Let's not tell anyone until after." "Good plan." Joe kissed her again. He slid out of the tub, then helped her out, wrapping a towel around her. They slid into bed, cuddling up next to each other.

Ryan and Rose got back to the house and relaxed a while downstairs with Rachel. They put in a movie, had popcorn, and laughed for a while, then they headed to bed. Rachel went to go to bed and called James instead. "Hey." "Stop pacing yet?" "Stop." "James, she's engaged. You can't compete with him." "Something is different about her." "She's happy. Really happy," Rachel said. "How did she up and get engaged to him that fast?" "Maybe they love each other. You told me that she never said the words to you." "Rachel, enough." "I heard her myself." "Where are you staying?" "Ryan's place." "I'll be there in 20," James said hanging up.

"Where are we going," Rachel asked. "Back to my hotel. Let Ryan and Rose have some alone time," James said. "James, seriously you have to stop trying to break them up." "She's my soul mate. I won't stop fighting until I win." "You are being crazy. She's like a totally different person since she came here. She's calm, and relaxed." "Did you find out where the wedding is," James asked. "No. I wasn't asked to be in the wedding party." "Did you get an invite?" "No." "I have to find out where," James said. "James, leave them be. There are other women in the world." "I know I'm acting ridiculous, but I just can't." They pulled into the hotel and went upstairs. "If all I'm going to do is watch you plot against her, I'm going back." "I'm sorry," James said. "You need a distraction." "Such as," he asked. Rachel wrapped her arms around him. "We'll go out dancing or something." He kissed her, peeling the shirt off her back. Within minutes, her clothes were on the floor and so were his. It was rough, intense and both of them were into it. After, he got up, showered, and left.

The next morning, Ava woke up and Joe wasn't in bed. She slid her robe on and went downstairs. She saw him outside with his guitar, paper and a pencil. "What are you up to," she asked as she came outside and kissed him. "Got a song idea in the middle of the night." "What time did you wake up?" "8," he replied. "Let me hear it." He played, and sang to her. "So, what do you think?" He looked at her and she had tears in her eyes. "That bad?" Ava kissed him again. "That good," she said. "Haven't finished it, but I think I got a good part of it." Ava kissed him again. He slid his guitar onto the chair beside him and pulled her into his arms. "What's wrong," he asked. "Nothing." He kissed her. She curled up on the chaise with him. "Bad dream?" Ava nodded. "Baby, I'm not going anywhere." "What time is your flight leaving," Ava asked. "Noon. You coming with me?" Ava nodded. "We'll be home after the concert. We don't even need to pack." "Good," Ava said. "It was that bad?" "Had a dream that he tried to stop the wedding." "You know he can't. We're already married." "I know. It's silly." "Babe, whether you like it or not, you're stuck with me for life," Joe said. "You better hope so." "Nothing he says is ever going to stop me from loving you." Ava curled up with him. "I have a good idea," Joe said. "What's that?" He picked her up, she grabbed his guitar and they headed inside and back up to bed.

They curled up in bed. Her phone rang. "Hi," Ava said. "We got the results back. According to the test results, you're 4 weeks." "Thanks," Ava said. "I'll send you the prescription for the pre-natal vitamins." "Thanks." Ava hung up. "Who was that?" She turned to face him. "Ava?" "That would be the doctor." He looked at her as a grin went ear to ear. "4 weeks." "Baby?" Ava nodded. Joe kissed her. "Holy crap." "That's what I said." He kissed her again and she wrapped her legs around him. "When are we due?" "May." "I have to call my mom." "We said we weren't telling anyone until after." "I can't hide this." "Me either, but we shouldn't." "Brad knows." "The man's psychic. No telling anyone." "You know the secret's going to kill me," Joe said. Ava kissed him. "Can I at least tell Ryan?" "No. He'll tell Rose." "I have to tell someone." "Tell me," Ava said. He kissed her. They made love to, then took their time getting changed and left for the airport.

He worked on the song on the plane. "What is up with you two," Ryan asked. "Nothing," Ava said. "You are so full of it. Spill it," Ryan said. "It's nothing Ryan. Just had a long night." Brad looked over. He smirked. Ava threw popcorn at him. "I was right wasn't I," Brad said. "Shut up Brad," Ava said. He smiled and went back to talking to his wife on instant messenger. "What is he talking about," Ryan asked. "Fine, but it stays between us." "What?" "We're having a baby." "When did you find out," Ryan asked. "This morning." "We're not telling anyone yet," Ava said. "Congratulations," Ryan said hugging them both. "So, we aren't going to be doing any performances in May right," Joe asked. "I'll make sure we're home," the manager said. Joe kissed Ava.

The concert went off without a hitch, then they headed home. Joe finally finished the song. He played it for the guys and Ryan smiled. "What?" "Considering you had writers block for 2 months, something tells me you found some inspiration." "Guess I did," Joe said as Ava curled up beside him. They landed, then headed home.

Ava and Joe headed inside, then had a hot bath, Ava gave Joe a massage, then headed to bed. "You know Ryan's going to tell her," Joe said. "He won't. I just don't want to tell everyone until it's been a few months." "Babe, you don't need to worry." "I also don't want them thinking that it's the reason." "Okay. I get it." "You were great tonight," Ava said. "Just like Ryan said, I had some inspiration," Joe said. They curled up together then made love and fell asleep in each other's arms.

A few weeks later, Ava was getting nervous. There were only 3 days left until the wedding. The tour was finished, and even Joe was getting excited. They flew down a day or two before the wedding and relaxed at the villa. "Wow," Ava said. "Nobody around to stress us out." "Until everyone shows for the wedding." "Did you invite Rachel," Joe asked. "I did, but I told her to meet Rose at the airport. I didn't tell her where it was so she couldn't tell James." "She didn't bring anyone with her right," Joe asked. "Nope." He kissed her. "It's gonna be fine baby." "I know. It's us," Ava said. She curled up in his arms by the pool.

Everyone started showing up the next day. They had the rehearsal, then the dinner. Everyone got along so well, it was almost creepy. They said goodnight to everyone then went to head to bed when Carrie and Rose pulled her aside. "What?" "Remember? He can't see you until the morning of the wedding." "Rose," Ava said. "It's true." Joe pulled her aside. "What?" "Baby, humor them," Joe teased. Ava kissed him, one last long kiss goodnight, then went with the girls. Brad and Ryan took him out for a few drinks to a bar in town.

The next morning, Ava got up, got her hair and makeup done, then had something to eat. "I still can't believe you're getting married today," her mom said. Her mom was teary all morning. Rose and Danielle (Brad's wife) got ready, then they did a few pictures. Her flowers showed then a dozen lavender roses showed up. She read the card:

> *Love you forever*
> *Starting today*
> *Now and forever*
> *I'm here to stay*
> *Love you with all my heart and soul*
> *Starting today and every day.*
>
> *XOXO—Joe*

Ava started crying. Rose read the card and got teary-eyed too. "Seriously, the man is totally made for you," Rose said. Ava put them in water, then got dressed. She came down the steps and her mom cried. "Wow," Danielle said. They had 20 minutes before the ceremony. "Can you take this to him," Ava asked Danielle. She nodded and left to go check on the guys.

"Why am I so nervous," Joe asked. "Forever's pretty scary." "Not with her," Joe said. Danielle came in and handed Joe the note from Ava:

Just wanted to remind you of something. Ever since we met, you took my breath away. Everything you've done, said and been was more than I could ever ask for. You are the best thing that ever happened to me. I can't wait to be your wife. I love you more than you even know. Even if forever seems scary now, I'll always be there. I love you. XOXO—Ava

He wiped a tear away, then slid the note in his pocket. "You okay," Ryan asked. Joe nodded. "Better now," he replied. "Note from her?" He nodded. He had the rings in his pocket, and had added a diamond or two to each, and an inscription. He slid on the bracelet she gave him, then went downstairs.

The wedding started shortly after. It was a tiny wedding, but they wouldn't have had it any other way. He walked along the beach and took his place. A few minutes later, the music started for her to come down the aisle. She walked towards him and he was fighting off tears. She finally made it to him and he held her hands in his. Then Joe and Ava were both tearing up.

The ceremony was short, and sweet. "I remember the day we met again. I couldn't stop smiling all night. I knew the minute you walked into that room that we'd be here one day. I've been waiting forever for this, and I promise you forever," Joe said. "The day we met again, I was almost shocked. There was a spark there that made me feel like you were the only one in the room. That first night we spent all night talking, I fell for you even more. Every day since, I feel like I've been in a fairy tale. They always have a happy ending. I promise I'll love you forever, be yours forever, and never ever let you go." They exchanged rings, then wiped the tears away and were pronounced husband and wife. Joe kissed her. Everyone was in tears. "And a special surprise for Ava." Ryan handed Joe his guitar. They sang 'Waiting all my life'. Ava almost cried. As soon as the song was done, Joe walked over to Ava and kissed her. They walked back down the aisle as husband and wife and went down the beach.

"You and your notes got me going," Ava said. "Then there was your note." "Why were we nervous when we were already married?" "This was with everyone. It's officially official," Joe said. He kissed her and pulled her close. Their photographer took a few shots of them. They sat down on the warm sand, and had a few more pictures. "I'll go get everyone for the pictures," the photographer said. He kissed her again. "I missed you," Joe said. "I missed you too." They got up and went to do the pictures.

Once all the formalities were done, they went back to the villa for the reception. They had dinner, then Joe kissed Ava and went and sang a bit for everyone. He did the song he'd written for her, then the two she loved, then came over and led her into the middle of the floor for their song. "A little surprise for the newlyweds, our friend Darius." He sang 'History in the making'. They danced and kissed. She danced with her dad, he danced with his mom, then Joe grabbed Ava's hand and led her outside. "What," Ava asked. He kissed her, leaning her into the railing of the terrace. "We're going away for two weeks." "Where?" "Paradise Island." "Perfect," Ava said. "No cell phones or laptops permitted." Ava nodded. He kissed her. She slipped a small box out of her purse. "What's this?" "Open it." He opened it and found a thumb disk in it. "What's this," Joe asked. She slid it out of his hand and walked inside. She handed it to Brad. "Okay. Everyone, watch," Brad said. Ava had made a video of pictures of the two of them through the years, then pictures of them together since they met again. The ending said:

Forever in love

Joe kissed her. "Rose helped me with it." "Perfect," he said. "And I made a screensaver for your computer of pictures of us." He kissed her. "I love you baby," Joe said. "I love you too." The guys did a few more songs for everyone, then Joe and Ava went back to their suite.

She slid the headpiece off, then he helped her with her dress and she slid him out of his shirt. "Forever." Ava looked up at him. "Definitely," he said. Joe kissed her and they curled up in bed together. "You like the surprise," he asked. Ava nodded. "He volunteered." "It was perfect." "We're leaving first thing tomorrow. Right after breakfast," Joe said. "So noon," Ava joked. They made love for the first time as husband and wife, or as Joe put it 'First officially official time as husband and wife'.

Ryan sat down by the water with Rose. "It was a beautiful wedding," Rose said. "That it was." "What's with the big smile," Rose asked. "I've never seen him get like that." "Like what?" "All teary-eyed. He loves her. I remember when someone loved me that much." "It'll happen again," Rose said. "Think so?" Rose nodded. He wrapped his arm around her and kissed her. "Do you want to stay here a few days with me?" Rose nodded.

Ava and Joe had breakfast with everyone the next morning. "We have some news to share with everyone," Joe said. Everyone got quiet. "We're having a baby," Joe said. Brad smiled, and everyone came over to say congratulations. Carrie hugged Ava and so did Rose. "Why didn't you tell us," Rose asked. "Wanted to be sure." "Is that why," Carrie asked. Ava shook her head. "We didn't know until a few weeks ago." Once everyone finished breakfast, Ava and Joe left for their honeymoon.

"You knew didn't you," Rose asked as she walked along the beach with Ryan. "She told us on the way home from a concert we did. She made us swear not to tell anyone." "Sounds like her. I never would have pictured her as the mom type," Rose said. "She is. I can tell you that much. She has been taking care of you guys," Ryan commented. "I know, but still, a baby's a totally different story." "Joe's so totally the dad type. The minute she found out, he was so happy he couldn't stop smiling." "Thought that was normal for him," Rose joked. "Since he met Ava, definitely."

Joe and Ava landed at Paradise Island and were whisked off to their suite. "This is beautiful," Ava said. "Just like you," Joe replied. They spent the first day on the beach, then spent the next few enjoying the island. They went on day trips on the boat, swam with the dolphins, and relaxed. There was no stress, no drama, and nobody to aggravate them . . . . or so they thought.

Rose and Ryan headed back to Nashville a few days after Ava and Joe left. "You gonna stay for a few days," Ryan asked. "I have to get home and get back to work." "What if I said I didn't want you to leave?" "I still have a job there," Rose said. "See if they'll transfer you." "Ryan, they don't have an office here. We both knew I'd have to go home." "Doesn't mean I have to like it." He kissed her and they headed upstairs to bed. "You sure I can't talk you into it," he asked. "I don't have a job like Ava where I can work anywhere." "Not even if I asked you to move in with me," Ryan asked. He was tempting fate. "I would love it Ryan, but . . ." He kissed Rose and pulled her into his arms.

The next morning, Rose called the office. "We're expecting you for a meeting tomorrow," her boss said. "I'll be there. Quick question. We don't have an office in Nashville do we?" "No." "Didn't think so." "You been out there all this time?" "My friend got married." "We'll see you at the meeting tomorrow." Rose hung up. "What," Ryan asked. "I have to go back. I have a meeting tomorrow." "Company," he asked. Rose nodded. They spent the day together, watching movies, then had dinner together and headed back.

"James, she married him. They're on their honeymoon," Rachel said. "Doesn't matter. Once she realizes it's not what she wants she'll be back." "She's moving her furniture there." "Why are you telling me all of this," Ryan asked. "Because I want you. You can't see past the nose on your face to realize it can you?" "I care about you Rachel, but I can't get past it." "I want to be with you. If you're going to pine over her for the rest of your damn years, then I'm leaving," Rachel said. "Where did they go?" "No idea." "You weren't even at the wedding?" "I couldn't. I had to work." "She really married him," James asked. Rachel nodded. "I really did lose her didn't I?" Rachel nodded and wrapped her arms around him. "But you still have me," she said. "I don't want you to feel like a second choice." Rachel kissed him. He picked her up and leaned her onto the bed. They had sex, then fell asleep. She got up the next morning and he was gone.

———

"Rose, can you come into my office?" She followed her boss into the office she'd always dreamed would be hers. "I looked into your idea. As long as you can come back for the monthly meeting, you can work from there. Just don't slack off. As long as everything gets done when it's supposed to be, you're good." "Thank you," Rose said. "He must be one heck of a guy." "He is. Never would have thought we'd be a good pair, but he's a really great guy." "So tell me." "Long story. My friend married one of the guys he works with." "What's his name?" "Ryan Lee." "Not the Ryan Lee from that country group?" Rose nodded. "I thought the guys were all married?" "Joe married my friend Ava." "That's who he had on stage with him at that concert? Holy crap." "And they're having a baby," Rose said. "Tell Ava I said congratulations." "I will." Rose left, they had the meeting, then she put her things together and headed back to the house. "What happened," Ryan asked. "Don't need a desk there since I'll be working from Nashville." "Seriously? They authorized it?" Rose nodded. Ryan kissed her. "You going to come make me a happy man?" "I'll try," Rose replied. He kissed her again. Within a few hours, and with 3 suitcases in hand, they left for Nashville.

———

Joe and Ava got back to the house and spent the day going through the wedding gifts. Once they were finally finished, Ava put the thank you list together. "I have to go to the studio tonight," Joe said checking his email. "New CD?" He nodded. "Guess I get the bed to myself," Ava joked. He kissed her and pulled her into his lap. "I'll be home around 2." "So I get writing done." "Always making the best of the situation aren't you?" "Always." He kissed her again. "I'm making dinner. You hungry?" He nodded. She made him her famous mango chicken and they sat out on the patio. "You sure you'll be okay tonight," Joe asked. "I'm pregnant, not paralyzed." "Just worry about you." "I love you for it, but baby and I are going to do some writing tonight, then curl up in bed and wait for you to come home," Ava said. They finished dinner and he headed off to the studio after a long kiss goodbye. "Almost don't want to go." "Faster you get there, the faster you get home." Joe kissed her again, then left.

It was the first night Ava was actually alone in the house. She had a hot bath, then got some writing done. Rose called around 9. "What you up to?" "Writing." "Company?" "Sure," Ava said. A half-hour later, Rose was at the house. "So how's work," Ava asked. "Had a meeting at work this morning. I can work from here." "Meaning?" "He asked me to move in with him." "Of all people," Ava said. "I know. I never would have thought it either. How's married life?" "Perfect." "And baby?" "Just fine. It feels like I'm in a dream," Ava said. "You're living the damn fairytale." "What's up with Rachel? She didn't even say she wasn't coming," Ava said. "She's dating James." "Nice." "She really likes him. What can I say?" "I just hope he treats her right." "He's still whining that you should be with him." "Kind of happy where I am thanks." "You should talk to him. Give him a chance to get it out of his system." "You don't remember what happened last time I did that do you?" "Just talk to him." Ava put in a movie for them to watch, then her phone buzzed with a text:

Miss you. What you up to?

She smiled and replied:

Rose is here. Just watching Notebook. Miss you more.

A few minutes later, his reply came:

Chick flick night. Love you.

Ava: Love you more. When you coming home?

Joe: 2:30. Got 2 songs done. Working on third

Ava: See you soon love.

Joe: Forever. XO

"You two are sickening." "What," Ava said. "You two and your text fest." "They're done at 2:30," Ava said. "You'd know." Ava threw an M&M at Rose. "You and Ryan getting along?" "He's not my normal type. I don't even know why the attraction's there," Rose said. "Because he's a good guy, and you can't help but love him. He's like family to me now," Ava said. "It's all your fault too." "Meaning?" "If you two hadn't rubbed off on us . . ." "Don't let Joe hear you say that." "Why?" "He bet me that we were rubbing off on you and that you wouldn't go home." "I'm going but to get the rest of my stuff from the house." "You're moving?" She nodded. "Guess I can sell the house then," Ava said. "You sure you want to?" Ava nodded. "This is home now." "You seem like a different person here," Rose commented. "No stress or drama to deal with." "Just the million and one female fans who want to do your husband." "Nothing I can't handle Rose." "You can't be at every concert." "Ring trumps fan," Ava said. They both laughed. "That's the only part I'm not sure I can handle with Ryan." "The fans? They aren't a threat Rose. Especially Ryan. He's Mr. Tried and True. He has eyes for one girl and only one." "I hope so," Rose said. They finished watching their movie and Rose headed home. Ava went upstairs to bed and finished a bit of writing, then put it away and curled up under the covers.

Around 3:30, Joe came home then got changed for bed and slid under the covers with her, wrapping his arms around her, then kissed her neck. She rolled over and curled up in his arms. Joe kissed her. "How did it go," Ava asked. "Four songs done. I have to go tomorrow night, but we're going in mid-afternoon, so I should be home around midnight." "Missed you." "I missed you too baby," he said. He kissed her again and they made love.

Ryan got home and slid into bed with Rose. He kissed her shoulder and slid his arm around her. Her fingers linked with his. He had to smile. This is the one thing he missed most. He fell asleep with Rose in his arms. Thoughts ran through his mind. He had what he'd wanted. He said a prayer to say thank you, then was out cold.

CHAPTER 9

Ava woke up the next morning to the sound of Joe's cell phone. "When will we be back? Okay. Book it for us." He hung up and curled back up with Ava. "Where you off to now," Ava asked. "Oprah." "When?" "Leaving in 2 hours. Oh, and you should probably get dressed and figure out what to wear." "Why?" Joe kissed her. "No?" "You and Rose are both coming," Joe said. "She has to work." "Then you're coming. Wanna show off my wife." "That I think I can do," Ava said. He kissed her. "I missed you last night." "Missed you too. So you got more done than you thought," Ava asked. "Six more until we're done." "I thought you were supposed to be at the studio tonight?" "Bumped. We have to get two more written." Ava went to get up and he pulled her back into his arms. "Yes love." "I love you." "I love you too." They got up and started getting ready.

"I have to work Ryan," Rose said. "You could just bring it with you." "Conference call," Rose said. "I'll be back around dinner. We doing dinner tonight?" She nodded. "I'll take you to my favorite restaurant," Ryan suggested. "Sounds good." He kissed her. "I'll call you when we land." "Good luck." "Something tells me she's going to love the Love Letters song," he teased. "Wouldn't be surprised," Rose said. Ryan headed out.

By the time they got to Oprah, they had another song written. "This one's perfect for the second single. We needed a faster one," Brad said. Joe looked over at Ava. "I like it." "Concert like, or just like," Brad asked. "It's a perfect one for the beginning of the concert." "That good?" Ava nodded. "I knew she was on the plane for a reason," Ryan joked. "Rose working," Ava asked. "Conference calls." "Well lucky me, I get three guys all to myself," Ava teased. Joe kissed her.

They got to the show and Ava hung out in the back with the guys. "Which song are we singing?" "Love letters and Waiting all my life," Brad said. "Two," Joe asked. "She'll ask when you tell her about the wedding." "Didn't think there would be that much about it," Joe said. "She'll ask. Especially when Ava's here with us," Ryan said. "They get any of the pictures?" "Two were in People after the interview we did before that last concert,"

Brad said. "Forgot about that one." "We authorized two pictures. That's it," his manager said. "Which two," Joe asked. "The one of the two of you on the beach, and the one where you're kissing in front of the sunset," his manager said. "We had to pick two." "You know," Joe asked as Ava slid her arms around him. Ava nodded. "Our two favorites." She smiled. "Okay then," Joe said.

"Give a big welcome to Ryan, Joe and Brad of Aces." The crowd roared and Ava went and watched from the side. They sang Love Letters. Once the song was done, they went to commercial. Joe walked over to her and kissed her, then grabbed a seat. The producer got a seat for Ava right in front of him. The interview went pretty good until she had Joe centered out. "So I hear congratulations are in order," Oprah said. "Thanks." "Joe just got married. So tell us about her." "We met years ago at a concert, then a while ago, bumped into each other at another one. Fell for her the minute she walked in." "So tell us about this beautiful wedding." "We got married at a villa in Cabo. It was just our friends and some family. We didn't want the big fancy thing. Truthfully, we would have been happy just us on a beach somewhere." "And she's in the audience I hear," Oprah said. The lights looked over towards Ava. "Well come up here." Ava sat down with the guys and Joe's fingers linked with hers. "So what's it like being married to the fan favorite?" "It's like a fairy tale. Has been since the beginning. He is such a sweet man. Think I'm the lucky one," Ava said. "So we heard that you're a writer." "On my 5th book." "Here's her latest 'Whirlwind'. So what's the storyline?" "Basic story of a girl who always chooses the wrong guys and gets caught up in the whirlwind of their lives and leaves hers behind." "Sort of like the two of you," Oprah said. "Not really. We just had this instant click that lit the spark." The interview continued. "Can we talk you guys into one more song," Oprah asked. "You might remember this one. It was their wedding song oddly enough. This is Waiting all my life." Ava sat and listened to the rest of the performance, then the taping was done. "Thank you so much guys. You were great," Oprah said. "Most welcome," Ryan said. "And congrats to you two," she said hugging Joe and Ava.

They finally headed home. "I swear I didn't know she'd pull you up there," Joe said. "Liar." He kissed her. "You did great," Ryan said. "Mr. Prince Charming," Brad teased. "Like Danielle wouldn't say the same about you," Joe teased. "Good point." Brad stopped teasing. "So we're going to the studio to try to get one or two more down tomorrow right," Brad asked. "Which ones?" "Home again, and the other one you were working on," Ryan said. "Dude, we can't record when we haven't finished writing it," Joe replied. "We'll do home again then head home." They all agreed. They got home a little while later and Ryan headed home to see Rose, Brad left to take Danielle and the kids out, and Ava and Joe headed to dinner. "Where are we going," Ava asked. "My favorite place."

They pulled in and headed into his favorite steakhouse. "That was definitely an interesting day," Ava said. "I have a feeling your books might sell out." "All because of you no doubt," Ava joked. He kissed her. They chatted and finished dinner, then headed home. Her phone rang the minute they pulled in. "Hello?" "Ava. I need to talk to you," James said. She hung up. "Who was that?" "James." She put her phone back in her purse as he called back again. They went inside and headed outside to the patio. "You know you can't avoid him forever," Joe said. "He tried to break us up. I'm not in the mood for his crap." "Look at our hands. See those rings? That means he can't break us up. We're forever," Joe said. "Just don't feel like hearing him go on for hours." "Just talk to him. Maybe he's just calling to say congrats." "Always have to be positive don't you?" "That's why you married me beautiful." Joe kissed her and she slid into his lap.

"Married you because you were so handsome," Ava said. "Right. Married me for my looks." "And a few other things." Joe kissed her and picked her up, wrapping her legs around him and carried her upstairs to bed. "Now these other things you're talking about . . . what would they be?" She kissed him and undid his shirt. "Because you have a good heart, you make me laugh, you are talented, and you're my kryptonite." "Really?" Ava nodded. "Now when you're saying talented . . ." Ava pulled her to him and kissed him. "That too," Ava said. He kissed her and peeled the dress off of her. "Plus I love you," Ava said. "Well, when you say it that way," he said as he kissed her again. He made love to her.

"Why did you marry me," Ava asked as they were curled up together. "Because every minute of every hour of every day, all I could think about was you. Plus you're beautiful, and sexy and smart and funny all rolled into one." "Really?" "That plus you're pretty damn amazing in bed." She moved away from him then he pulled her back into his arms and kissed her. "I still can't believe you married a crazy guy like me." "Me either," Ava joked. They laughed. "I swear every one of your fans is eternally jealous." "Only one fan I love." "Good. Who's the competition?" He kissed her again. "I don't know what I'd do without you. Seriously. I feel like a new man," Joe said. "Believe it or not, I got inspired enough to finish 5 chapters while you were at the studio." "Seriously?" "It'll be done faster than I thought." "Who's the dedication to?" "This rock star guy I know. He's pretty sexy." "Anyone I know?" He kissed her.

Ryan got home and the house smelled delicious. "Why do I smell apple pie?" "Was in a baking mood," Rose said. "Weren't you supposed to be working?" "I did." Ryan kissed her, pulling her into his arms. "We ready for dinner?" Rose nodded. They left and made their way down to the restaurant. They had a relaxing dinner, cracking jokes all the way through, then went for a walk. "So how did it go," Rose asked. "Good. They interviewed Ava too. Asking about the wedding and everything." "What's wrong?" "I wish you'd come." "Why?" "We could have had a little vacation while we were there," Ryan said. "Better idea," Rose said. "What's that?" "I was thinking today that when we were at the wedding, it wasn't enough time." "What do you mean?" "Thought we could go away. Just you and me." "Where?" "Anywhere. I have two weeks of vacation time owing. Wherever you want to go." "Beach or no," Ryan asked. "As long as it's us, wherever you want." "I'll book it in the morning then." "I just thought you needed a vacation too. Gives you time to relax, maybe get writing done, plus nobody around," Rose said. He kissed her. They headed back to the house. "You sure they'll give you that time off?" "Vacation is vacation. Besides, how are they going to complain when I'm this far away?"

Rose and Ryan got up the next morning and he booked the vacation. Two weeks on a beach that's quiet, private and 5 stars. "When are we leaving," Rose asked. "Tonight." Ryan kissed her and called the guys. "You're seriously going away for two weeks? Can you disconnect yourself from your phone and the internet that long," Brad joked. "Funny. I cancelled the studio time too, which gives you two time to work on some songs. I'm going to work on some too. We'll see what we have when I get back," Ryan said. "Enjoy," Brad joked. Rose was on the phone with Ava. "Have a good time Rose." "Can you believe I'm actually using my vacation time," Rose asked. "It's a first girl. Give me a shout when you two get back."

"Well, we're studio free for two weeks," Joe said getting off the phone with Brad. "What are we going to do with all that extra time," Ava joked. "You have a doctor's appointment today don't you?" Ava checked the time. "And I have 45 minutes to get there." They got up and washed up, then bolted out the door to the appointment. They got there just in time. "Come on in." They did the ultrasound and both of them were excited. "Baby's just fine. I say nine weeks." Joe thought back. That was that first week they were together. "So we'll see you in a few weeks," the doctor said. They printed out pictures for Ava and Joe, then she went in to see the doctor. "You're due May 8. So we'll make an appointment for once a month for an ultrasound just to see how the baby's doing. The last 2 months, it's bi-weekly. That alright?" "Definitely." Ava left with Joe and they headed home. "I still can't believe this," Ava said. "So counting back, that would have been the first concert." "The one that we were at together that first weekend." Ava nodded. He laughed. "What," Ava asked. "The green room." "How can I possibly forget it." "Could relive that one," Joe teased. "Funny." He kissed her at the light. They got home, then got changed into their swimsuits and went for a swim. They splashed around and laughed the rest of the afternoon.

Around dinner, they curled up on the chaise. "I still can't believe Ryan actually went on a vacation." "Rose has a way of talking people into things." "The man is head over heels. I told you," Joe said. "Fine. You were right." "So that means I win." "It does." "So one

74

whole night of whatever I want." "Gloating doesn't look sexy on you," Ava said. He kissed her and pulled her into his arms. "So what am I in for tonight?" Joe leaned her onto her back on the chaise, untying her bikini. "Seriously." He kissed, nibbled, and teased her into forgetting where they were. "Joe." He undid the bottoms. He kissed her again, then she realized his suit was gone too. "What are you up to?" He kissed her, then made love to her in the sunshine. They went from outside, to inside on the sofa. Her legs were shaking, and he was clinging to her like a death grip. Joe kissed her again and they both practically exploded. "I love you baby." "I love you too." "You know if you weren't already having a baby . . ." "I know. I was thinking the same thing," Ava joked. He kissed her. "So what am I in for the rest of the night," Ava asked. "Hmm." He kissed her again. "Seriously." "Dinner. Curling up by the fire, and being alone, just you and me. No phone and no laptop" He kissed her again and curled up with her. "So It's like we're on our honeymoon again?" He kissed her. Ava got comfy. "Come with me," Joe said. "Where are we going?" They headed upstairs. He picked her up and carried her to bed. "This is what I miss from those two weeks," Ava said. "Having nobody else around but you and me. Nobody bugging us. We could stay in bed all day if we want to. We can do whatever we want, whenever," Joe said. "Once the baby comes, there won't be any more in bed all day," Ava said. "Yeah there will. My mom wants to come and help," Joe said. "Doesn't mean that we can do this." "Yeah it does." "Joe, we can't do this once the baby comes unless we go away and get a babysitter." "Hence why I asked her." "You asked her so we could stay in bed all day and make love?" "Not in those words, but so we could have us time." "You have a point, but how does that work," Ava asked "It will babe. We need us time too." "I know." "It'll be perfect babe." "It will," Ava said. The rest of the night, they were in bed, in each other's arms, and made love all night.

———

"James, you can't just go there," Rachel said. "I'm going. My flight leaves in an hour. Either you're driving me to the airport or not," James said frantically packing a suitcase. "You're acting insane." "Fine." He threw his bag in the car and left. He got on his flight and within an hour or two, he was landing. He got a rental car, then left for his hotel. "Come on Ava. Answer," he said waiting for Ava to pick up her cell phone. "Can't take your call right now. We're a little busy. We'll get back to you when we get a minute." It was her machine. He went to bed and decided on talking to her the next day.

———

The next day, they got up, had a morning skinny dip in the pool, then curled up on the chaise with their morning orange juice. "I know you're killing for a coffee," Joe said. "You don't even know." He took a sip of his coffee then kissed her. "That work?" Ava kissed him. "I take that as a yes." They made love on the chaise outside.

———————

"So what do you think of our little paradise," Ryan asked as he woke up with Rose in his arms. "I still can't believe this is real." Their butler brought them coffee and juice. "I had an idea," Ryan said. "What's that?" "Thought you might want to wear this," he said handing her a box. "What's this?" "Open it." She opened it then looked at him with tears in her eyes. "I didn't think I could feel this way again. You opened my eyes. The thought of losing you kills me. Marry me," Ryan said. "Ryan." "I love you." "Seriously?" He nodded. "We're in paradise Rose. Where better for me to ask you," he said. "I love you too." "Yes," he asked. Rose nodded. He put the ring on her finger and kissed her.

———————

Later on in the day, Joe went off to work on some music with Brad and Ava had the place to herself. She turned her phone on and had 3 new voicemails. She zipped through them then got a call. "Hello?" "Don't hang up. I'm in town. I need to talk to you," James said. "There's nothing else to say James." "There is." "Fine." "Can I come over so we can talk?" "No. I'll meet you." They made plans and Ava hung up. She called Joe. "What's up beautiful wife of mine?" "James is in town." "Shit." "Exactly what I thought. I'm meeting him. Hopefully this is enough to get him to stop the crazy shit." "When are you going?" "Leaving in 20. We're meeting up at Starbucks." "At least you can smell the coffee," Joe said. "Funny." "I'll meet you there at 1." "Love you," Ava said. "Love you too baby."

James showed up and ordered himself a coffee. She came in a few minutes later and ordered an Italian soda. He went to hug her and she sat down. "Not even a hug." "I'm married James. This isn't some romantic rendezvous." "I miss you," he said. "As I repeat myself." "I know. Why did you rush into it Ava?" "Because we wanted to. It was right for us." "I just don't get how you could walk away from what we had so easily." "I had the bruises to prove I was right." "I don't get why you two jumped into a wedding so quick." "I knew him before I saw him that night. I met him years ago." "Why couldn't you be happy with me?" "Because you don't know when to back off. Because I wasn't in love with you. What do you want me to say," Ava asked. "That you loved me back." "You're not going to hear it." "I need you." "So does Joe and . . ." "And what," James asked. "Our baby." "You're pregnant?" Ava nodded. "That why?" "No. We didn't know until the week before the wedding." "Ava," James said. "We have a life together. You need to find someone that makes you happy James. It's not going to be me," Ava said. "I love you." "And I love Joe." Joe walked in a few minutes later. "Hey beautiful," he said walking over and kissing her.

"How's things James," Joe asked. "Would be better if I had what I wanted, but good." "I'm sorry if it felt like I stepped on your toes." "Since you did," James said. "Fell for her the minute we saw each other again." "I hear congrats are in order," James said. "Thanks." Joe wrapped his arm around Ava and she kissed him. "So where was the wedding," James asked. "Cabo. It was like a little piece of paradise," Joe said. "Always wanted to go there," Ava said. James tried to make small talk for a while, looking Ava up and down. Finally, she had to just get away from James. "I have to get going. It was nice seeing you James," Ava said getting up. Ava grabbed her purse. "See you later," James replied. Joe left with Ava.

"Couldn't have been that bad," Joe said. "Wrong," Ava replied. Joe pulled her into his arms and kissed her. "You coming home," she asked. He nodded. "Right behind you beautiful." They headed home, then stepped inside and he pulled her into his arms. "What," she asked. He kissed her. "How did things go at the studio?" "Finished the one I was working on." "Good." "It's named after you." Ava smirked. "It's called My Angel." "Now I want to hear it," Ava said. He kissed her and picked her up, wrapping her legs around him. He walked upstairs to their bedroom and leaned them both onto the bed. Her dress slid off.

Joe loved her. There was no doubt in either of their minds. The feel of her skin against his, the feel of her kiss, the goose bumps that her fingertips caused when she held him. This was more than love to him. It was forever wrapped into one woman. He'd got his inspiration back, the always warming smile, and he felt like the piece of him that was missing was finally filled. There was no going back, no walking away. She was his forever.

They curled up in bed, talking and telling silly stories about when they were little. They talked about hopes and dreams they'd always had, and how some of them had come true. They were so close, there was nothing left that could separate them.

Ava got a call that afternoon from her real estate agent. "We wanted to let you know, we have an offer no the house." "And?" "20 grand over asking." "And when do they want to move in?" "Two weeks." "The inspection was alright," Ava asked. "Perfect. I guess they're big fans of your husband." "If that's why they're putting in the offer," Ava said. "No. They actually fell in love with the house." "I'll be back this week to look it over then," Ava said then hung up. "We're going on a road trip aren't we," Joe joked. "Had an offer on the house." "Plus you're gonna have to call a mover to get the rest of your things," he said. "That too." "When do we leave?"

The next morning, Ava and Joe headed back to her place. They came in and Ava started making calls. She cancelled the phone and internet and cable. "It will be done first thing tomorrow Mrs. Morgan." Ava hung up, then called the mover. "We'll be there in a few hours." "I have the shipping address. I'll leave it on the counter." Most of the house was already packed. All that was left were dishes, furniture and memories. They spent the day packing up box after box. By the time dinner hit, all that was left was her bedroom.

They headed upstairs and relaxed a while on the bed with their takeout dinner. "This is a great house," Joe said. "It was." "Reminds me of the house we had when I was little." "Had too many years in this place. I bought it when I got my first book published," Ava said. "That long ago?" Ava nodded. "How many books did you write in this house?" "5," Ava replied. "You sure you want to sell it?" "Home is where you are. This isn't home anymore," Ava said. "You don't have to give the house up." "There's too many memories here. Besides. I kinda like our house better." "You sure?" Ava nodded. "Okay." "Why?" "Could keep the house here. Sort of like a vacation house." "If we're going on vacation, this is the last place I want to be," Ava said. "Got a point." "I'd rather be phoneless, cableless, and without power on a deserted island with you, then be here," she joked. "Now you're talking." He kissed her and ended up making out like teenagers in the bedroom.

—···········—

"James, did you get a chance to talk to her," Rachel asked. "Yeah. I can't help thinking that there's a hint of a chance." "Would you stop already? She's having a baby with him. She's selling the damn house here," Rachel said. "She can't." "There's a for sale sign James." "Look up the concert dates. When are they doing performances out of town?" "What? You think you're going to swoop in and make her divorce him? Did you forget to take your anti-stupid drugs this morning," Rachel asked. "Look it up." "They have nothing booked until March." "Shit," James said. "Would you stop James? You have someone right in front of you asking you to love them and you're seeing right through them." "You don't understand. I love her. The first time we kissed, I loved her." "And now she's going to spend the rest of her life lip-locked with Joe," Rachel said. "Doesn't mean I don't still love her." Rachel hung up. He was hopeless.

—···········—

Ava and Joe got up the next day and watched the movers pack the furniture and the last of the boxes. "Well babe, it's official." "I know," Ava said. The real estate agent showed up a little while later. "Bidding war. This is the highest of the three." She handed it to Ava and she saw the name on it. "Good price," Joe commented. She pointed out the name. "Why in the hell?"

James sat down at his desk at the office and finished up paperwork, hoping that he'd get a reply to his bid on the house. She had to accept it. It was almost $40,000 over the asking price. Just the thought of someone else being there made him want it all the more. When she came to her senses, she'd move home and come back to the house where she belonged. He got a call back about ten minutes later. "Someone topped your offer. I'm sorry James." "By how much?" "8 grand," the agent said. "Any way you can put in another bid?" "No. The house sold. They're taking possession next week." He couldn't believe this. All the plans, all the hopes. They were gone. She was gone.

———————

Ava and Joe headed home that night. "There isn't that much stuff to unpack," Joe said. "Figured you'd have a lot more." "I'm not a shoe addict Joe." "The Christmas tree will be nice." "Had it for years. We could just get a real one like I always wanted," Ava said. "Good plan. I never had time to set one up and have a big Christmas." "Now we can do it together," Ava said. Joe kissed her. "First Christmas, first baby; first everything this year." She kissed him. "First of many," Ava said. He nodded. Their flight finally landed and they headed home.

"Glad to be home." "Me too. No more drama," Ava said. "I still can't believe he thought he'd win the bidding war on the house." "Then that lady throwing in paying for all the closing costs, thank goodness." "You wouldn't have given him the house anyway," Joe said. "Exactly." Ava turned her phone off and left it on the counter. "Back to phone-free vacation?" Ava nodded. He kissed her and picked her up, putting her on the kitchen counter. "This place is more like home," Ava said. "Especially with you here." He kissed her again and wrapped his arms around her. "So what does my handsome and sexy husband want to do tonight," Ava asked. He smiled at her. "Dinner, then home for dessert." "Why don't I just make something?" "We have to go grocery shopping." "Good point." He kissed her again. He grabbed the phone and ordered from his favorite Chinese restaurant. They curled up together on the sofa and had dinner, then he turned on the fireplace. "No TV, no phones, no internet." "Exactly." "I say we last an hour," Joe teased. She slid into his lap straddling him. "Think so?" "If you're gonna be that way about it," he teased as he kissed her. His kisses trailed down her neck, to her shoulder. He slid the sleeve of her dress off. "You know what we were doing a month ago today," Ava asked. "About the same thing as we're doing right now?" He kissed her again. "The first day of our honeymoon." "Curled up in the hotel, ignoring the sunshine." Joe carried her upstairs, turning the fireplace off. "Reliving it?" He nodded and kissed her. She slid her dress off, and he pulled his jeans and shirt off, then they crawled into bed together. "Better," he said.

"Something tells me we're spending vacation in bed," Ava said Joe kissed her. "You shouldn't be doing any strenuous stuff anyway." "Awe darn. I wanted to run that marathon," Ava teased. "Don't make me make you stay in bed," Joe teased. "How were you planning to do that?" "I have my ways," Joe said as he kissed down her neck, to her chest. He kissed her stomach, then her hip. "Something tells me you'd succeed if you had to." One more move and she'd be a goner. "I'd win in a minute," Joe said. He made that move. She heard his phone ringing. "Baby," Ava said. "Crappy timing whoever it is," he said. He kissed her hip. They called back again. He ignored the phone and continued what he was doing. He slid into her arms and made love to her, taking his time. Both their hearts were racing. They kept going and going for what felt like hours.

They curled up together in bed, both asleep. Joe's phone rang again. He slept through it. Ava got up and grabbed his phone. She went to turn it off and noticed who the caller was. She showered, then went back to bed. He curled up next to her, wrapping his arms around her. "Smell good." "Had a shower." She turned towards him and he kissed her. He pulled her into his arms. "What's wrong," he asked. "I turned your phone off for you." "Who called?" "Tara." She handed it to him and went to get up. "Oh no you don't," Joe said. "Let go." "Tara is an old girlfriend. She probably just heard that we got married." "Right." He turned his phone on and she called again. "Hey T." "You around tonight? Thought we could get together." "Just hanging out with Ava." "Who's Ava?" "My wife." "When the hell did you get hitched." "About a month ago." "Congrats. So did you want to get together?" "That would be a definite no T." "Well, congrats anyway." He hung up. "Just like I told you," Joe said. "Why are your exes still calling?" "She only calls when she's in town. Trust me. She won't be calling again." He had 5 messages. He checked them. Two were Tara, one was his mom seeing how they were, and one was from Ryan. "No bloody way." "What," Ava asked. "They're engaged." "Who?" "Ryan and Rose." Ava started laughing. "I know. Now I was totally right." Ava went to get up and he pulled her back to him. He listened to the last message, but wouldn't look at her. He hung up, sent a message, then turned the phone off. "So where were we?" "Secret messages?" "Just a friend. Said I was going phoneless for a few days." "Fine." Ava went to get up. "Would you stop?" "I'm going to plug my phone in," Ava said. "Babe, it's not important right now." "You chat with your friend. I'll be back up in a few." She went downstairs and plugged her phone in, then noticed voicemail. She checked the missed callers and deleted them. James was the last person she wanted to talk to. She turned her phone off, then plugged it in and her laptop.

She went to go back upstairs and he had his jeans on and was coming downstairs. "What's wrong?" "Coming to get you." "Just plugged stuff in." "Get back to bed." "That an order," Ava asked. He wrapped his arms around her and pulled her to him. He picked her up and carried her up the steps. "No more getting worried that there's someone else alright," he said. "It's just when things seem too good," Ava said. "It means you hold on with both hands Ava. I love you. Nobody else is getting me, except you." "Good." "Besides. Something tells me nobody else could possibly get me going like you do." "Gee," she teased. He kissed her and leaned down onto the bed and into her arms. "I don't want you ever worrying about that." "I can't help it Joe." "I know. Remember something next time you worry. There's a ring on your finger. Look at the inscription. Don't ever forget that I loved you so much I wanted to marry you the minute I met you. I love you," he said. "I love you too." He kissed her and they made love again, then curled up and fell asleep in each other's arms.

Ava woke up a few hours later to the sound of him singing and his guitar. Ava followed the sound of the music and wrapped herself in her terry robe. She sat on the steps listening. It had to be something new. She snuck down a few more steps, then realized he had to be in the TV room. She sat and listened until the creeky step gave her away. "Okay superspy." "Didn't want to interrupt you," Ava said sliding onto the sofa beside him. "Just playing around with something." "I don't know why you don't just sing one on your own," Ava commented "I could, but something tells me the fans would rather hear him." "Baby," Ava said. "Except you." "I love your voice, and I love his," Ava said. "Nice save." "You sing to me all the time. Why wouldn't you let someone else hear it, other than just backup stuff?" "Maybe," he said. "So what are you working on?" "Got an idea when I was sleeping." "And?" "Got the tune, the lyrics are the hard part." Ava took a look at them. She threw a little into them then handed it back to him. He sang through what he had. "Better," Joe said. "Just needed an umph." He threw a little more into it, then wrote out the rest of the music. "What about this part," he asked. An hour later, they had it finished. "You are amazing. You know that," Joe said. He kissed her. "You would have figured it out baby." "Helps that I married the creative genius." Joe pulled her to him and kissed her, then slid the guitar to his back. He slid it off and Ava slid into his lap. "Baby, I really don't know how I ever deserved you," Joe said. "Fate."

CHAPTER 10

The next morning, Ava and Joe woke up on the sofa together. "Babe, we should have gone back to bed," Ava said. "Stiff?" He leaned towards her and kissed her. "Don't tease." She slid her legs around him. "Who's teasing," Ava joked. "Ava, seriously." She kissed him. He felt her undo the button of his jeans. "Don't start." She undid the zipper. "Start what?" She slid his jeans off with her feet. He kissed her and within a few minutes, they were making love again. "You are so in trouble," he said. He kissed her again. They got way too carried away. They went from the sofa, to the stairs to the bed. Finally, they both were past exhausted and completely zapped of energy and still throbbing from head to toe. "No more teasing," Joe said. "That wasn't teasing." He kissed her again. "Babe, I'm just damn happy I married you right now," Joe said with a smirk ear to ear. "Oh really." He nodded. "I love you too." Joe pulled her into his arms. They curled up together and were out cold until almost noon.

Brad called the house around 2. The machine picked up. "Guys, it's Brad. Give me a shout. Was gonna see if you two were up for dinner tonight." Ava picked up. "Hey Brad." "So what are you two up to?" "Just relaxing. Dinner sounds good." "Wanted to pick his brain about a song I was working on." "Joe finished up one last night. You're gonna love it," Ava said. "Can't wait. That mean you two are coming?" "When do you want us?" "5?" "See you then. Do you want us to bring anything ? Wine," Ava asked. "Sparkling cider." "Gotcha. See you at 5." Ava hung up and Joe wrapped his arm around her. He kissed her shoulder.

"We're doing dinner at 5," Ava said. Joe kissed her. "Guess that means we'll have to get out of bed." Ava nodded. He kissed her again. They got up and started getting ready. She slid into the shower, and he slid in with her. "You know we're going to end up being late." He kissed her, leaning her into the wall of the shower. "No more teasing then," Joe said. "Until later." One more round in the shower, then they slid out and started getting ready. Ava slid on her black dress then realized she was showing. She slid on her heels, then did her hair and makeup. They left for dinner, grabbing some groceries and the cider on the way. They came in and Danielle was all smiles. "Finally," Danielle joked. "So much for working out,"

Ava said. "You still look amazing." "Guess I'm going to have to go shopping," Ava said. "I'll go with you." They went to finish with the final touches for dinner and the guys started talking shop.

"Ava helped me with the lyrics. It sounds amazing," Joe said. "We'll talk to Ryan. You can do lead on this one," Brad said. "You sure?" "Dude, you have it nailed. Besides, it sounds great." "You sure?" "It'll sell a million copies." They both laughed. Ava came in and brought Joe a drink. "Thanks baby." "Told you so," Ava teased. He kissed her. "You two can write. Ryan will be impressed," Brad said. They all had dinner, then Brad played what he'd been working on. Ava added some lyrics, and he added some more music. "Damn you're good," Brad said. "Honestly, Joe had it as a lyric in something else he was working on that he scrapped," Ava replied. The ladies chatted a while and the guys kept them entertained, then Ryan called.

"How's things," Ryan asked. "Good. Joe and Ava are here," Brad said. "So how's the writing going?" "We both got one done. Had an idea about one of them." Brad told him the idea. Surprisingly, Ryan loved it. "So, what are you guys doing in November," Ryan asked. "Why?" "We're getting married." "I heard. We'll be there." "Tell him we can do it at our place," Joe said. "He heard," Brad replied. "We'll talk tomorrow," Ryan said. "So soon?" "See you tomorrow," Ryan said. They hung up. "We're gonna head home. I know he'll have a million and one ideas when he gets back," Joe replied.

Ava and Joe headed home. "My superstar," Joe said. "You aren't half bad yourself sexy," Ava replied. "I still can't believe they're coming back already." "He isn't the vacation type I guess." "Longest he went away was a week. Trust me. She must have whipped something on him." Ava smirked. He slid his hand in hers, linking fingers, then kissed her hand. "Thank you for tonight," Joe said. "For what?" "Being you." Ava smiled. "I love you." "I love you too." They got home, then went upstairs and slid into bed. He curled up next to her, as close as he could and they fell asleep.

The next day, Ava woke up to him kissing her shoulder. "Morning," she said. He kissed her neck. A smile came across her face. "Baby," Joe whispered. "Mmm." "We only have 3 hours until they're back." "Ooh. Wouldn't want mom and dad to catch us," Ava joked. He laughed. "Before he starts calling and talking us back into the studio today." "So breakfast?" He pulled her to him. "Dessert first," Joe said. They made love and it was intense, passionate, urgent and amazing. There was just something about him that had her entire body willing to give in at a moment's notice. Every inch of her wanted him. They made their way to the shower. Finally, they cleaned up, then had breakfast. Just as he was finishing his coffee, Ryan called.

"We're getting in at 1. Come by?" "See you then," Joe said. "Bring Ava." "I will. Did you at least try to get a tan?" "Funny," Ryan said then hung up. Joe finished his coffee and Ava was doing dishes. He slid the cup into the sink, wrapping his arms around her. "Don't start," Ava said. He kissed her neck. "Baby," Ava said. "What?" He nibbled her ear. "We have time," Joe teased. "I still have to get dressed." "You look perfect the way you are," Joe said. "I'm in a bathrobe." He kissed her neck again. "I'm going to get dressed." She kissed him. He picked her up, sitting her on the counter. "Yes love," Ava teased. He kissed her again. "We have an hour," Joe said. He kissed her and they did it on the counter. Finally, they managed to get ready and headed to Ryan's place.

They pulled in, grabbing Joe's guitar from the back and headed inside. "So how was the vacation," Ava asked as she hugged Ryan and Rose. Rose showed her the ring. "I heard. Congratulations." Ava hugged her friend. "Now I know what you meant," Rose said. "About what?" "Being swept off my feet." "So what you two talking about," Ryan asked. "Girl stuff," Ava teased. Joe wrapped his arms around Ava. "So I hear you helped the boys with some lyrics. I didn't know you wrote music," Ryan said. "I'm a writer Ryan. I can rhyme." Joe kissed her. "You knew exactly what I was going for with it," Joe said. "Because I am a good eavesdropper." They chatted until Brad got there. The guys went into the TV room to work on some music, and the girls went outside.

"So tell me how he did it," Danielle asked. "He said he thought I should wear it. He handed me the box. I think that's the first time ever that I almost cried when I got a present," Rose said "And just think. It means we're all practically family." "Who would've thought," Rose joked. "Still can't believe it. Six months ago, they were working week after week and then you two came along, and now they love being home," Danielle said. "And we made friends," Ava joked. "I still can't believe you two are getting married," Danielle said. "You sure your place is alright Ava," Rose asked. "It'll be perfect. Either that, or we go to the country club," Ava teased. "Or we could have it here," Danielle said. Joe came outside. "Yes love," Ava said. "You three having fun?" "Always. You guys getting lots of work done," Ava asked. "If you call him talking our ears off about Rose over here, then yes," he joked. "So what are you three up to this afternoon," Joe asked. "Thought we should take Ava shopping for some new clothes," Danielle said. "Gee. Like I didn't know that was coming," Joe teased. "You guys have work to do anyway," Danielle said. Joe kissed Ava. "I'll meet you back here," Joe asked. Ava nodded. He kissed her again. "Love you." "Love you too." He went back inside. "You two are too cute," Danielle said. "I have something to show you two," Ava said. She pulled out the ultrasound picture. "That's why," Danielle said. Danielle smiled and Ava showed it to Rose. "Someday," Rose said. "Better get used to it Rose. Your god daughter or godson is in that picture," Ava said. "You sure?" Ava nodded. Rose hugged Ava. The ladies went back in, then decided to head out to the mall to go shopping. Joe walked Ava outside.

"What," Ava asked. Joe kissed her. "I'll be back in an hour or two." "We'll be here," he said. She kissed him, then the ladies headed off to the mall.

Two hours of shopping later, Ava found a few things, then found a few more for the baby. The little shoes were irresistible. They came back and the guys were singing away. The ladies snuck in and Ava listened at the door. When the song was finished, Joe looked up and saw her. "Sneaky," Joe said. "Do what I can," Ava joked. He grabbed her hand and pulled her to him. "How are things going," Ava asked. "You did good," Ryan said. "Do what I can," Ava replied. "We also decided something," Brad said. "What's that?" "Remember the other night when you were singing with me," Joe said. "Don't." "You're coming the first night we sing it to sing with me." "On stage," Ava asked. Joe nodded. "You are all nuts," Ava replied. "Nope. You're doing it. Just the first night," Ryan said. "Give me some notice before we have to do that." "Saturday," Joe teased. Ava looked at him. "You'll be fine baby." "Trying to torture me or what," Ava asked. They all laughed and Joe wrapped his arms around her. "Nope. Showing off the millions of talents nobody knew you had," Joe teased. "Funny." "So we add in Wanting You and Have Faith," Ryan said. "One run through." Joe and Ava sang through it. Ryan smiled. "What," Ava asked when they finished. "You're doing another one with us, and we're recording it that way," Ryan said. "Ryan," Ava said. "How the heck I didn't know about this, I don't know," Ryan replied. "You're seriously a few short of your box of fruit loops," Ava said. Joe laughed. "You don't even know how good it sounds," Brad said. "Before I get signed up to sing with you guys for the entire concert . . ." Ava got up and went into the kitchen.

"That was you," Rose asked. Rose looked at her friend realizing she had never shown that talent. "Stop. If they keep going, I'll be a permanent member," Ava teased. Joe came up behind her and wrapped his arms around her. "Too late. You're stuck with us," he said. "You guys are seriously nuts if you think I'm doing that every night." "Means I get you with me all the time. Totally works for me," Joe joked. "So you guys done for the day," Rose asked. Joe nodded. "We're heading home," Joe said. "I'll see you guys tomorrow," Ava said. She hugged the girls goodbye, then said goodbye to Ryan and Brad.

They got home and he grabbed the three bags from the trunk. "This is all you got," Joe asked. "The red one is for you." "Babe," he said. They went into the house and he put everything down, then pulled out the shirt in the red bag. It was a baby shirt that says 'Daddy rocks' on it. He smiled. "Where the heck did you find this?" "Now you see why it was too irresistible," Ava said. "You were supposed to get clothes for you." "I did. I got one or two things." He put the shirt down and wrapped his arms around Ava. "What's wrong," he asked pulling her to him. "Don't want to get too much. When would I wear any of it again?" He kissed her. "Could find a way," Joe teased. "I bet you could." He kissed her again and had her backed into the wall. "What is up with you today," Ava asked.

"Addicted." "Figured that much." Joe kissed her. "I love you." "I love you too. And no more volunteering me to make a goof of myself on stage," Ava said. "Gives you a reason to come with us." "Don't need one." He kissed her again. "You sound amazing babe," Joe said. "Right," Ava replied. He pulled his phone out and played it back to her. "See," he said. "That was in the living room. Not a stage." "You'll be fine." He kissed her, then they made dinner. After, they curled up on the sofa and watched an old black and white movie.

<hr/>

"Still can't believe you talked her into singing on stage," Rose teased. "She was amazing," Ryan replied. "I've heard her singing in the car but it never sounded like that." "I had a feeling it was in her," Ryan said. "So now that the girls know," Rose said. "Think you should call your parents. I'll call my parents after," Ryan suggested. She called her parents and told them, and they were determined to fly down and see her and meet Ryan. His parents felt the same way. "Sunday dinner. She should meet everyone," his folks said. "I'll see you Sunday then," Ryan replied. They finished their calls and curled up on the sofa together. "So we're doing Sunday dinner. You want to invite Joe and Ava," Ryan asked. "My only allies at dinner." "My folks aren't that bad baby. They just wants to meet you. Mom was a little stunned to say the least." "She worries about her baby boy." Ryan nodded. "What did you want to do for dinner then," Rose asked. "We're going to have to go grocery shopping. Put it that way." Rose laughed. He kissed her. "I'm gonna make you happy baby," Ryan said. "I know. You already do." "How was shopping?" "Baby frenzy. It was good though. We talked her into a few things. I know she's scared, but she doesn't want anyone knowing," Rose said. "Scared of what?" "Same thing I am. That all of it's too good to be true. That the fairy tale isn't going to have a good ending." "Don't worry about it. We're going to make it to forever." "You get why she's worried though?" "Completely. I've already had one try at forever and it blew up in my face. Now, it's a chance I'm taking because I love you." They curled up together on the sofa and talked all evening.

<hr/>

The next morning, Ava got up and went for a run. Joe was still asleep. She took her time. She watched the trees changing color, the regular people she saw on the street, then headed back to the house. She came inside, had a bottle of water, then did her yoga stretches. She went upstairs after and slid into the shower. She came out a little while later and he was still asleep. She slid onto the bed and wrapped her arm around him, cuddling back up to him. "Was wondering when you were coming back," Joe said yawning. "Went for a run." "Babe." "The doctor said it was fine since I was running before this." "You're still beautiful." "Thank you, and you're pretty sexy yourself, even with bed head." He kissed her. "What we up to today?" "Writing. What you up to," Ava asked. "Distracting my wife."

"Nice job. Let me know how that goes," Ava teased. "I know you have to get chapters in." "Almost finished it actually. Not too much left to go on it." "Good. Then you get a break between." Ava nodded. "Just in time for a few appearances," Joe said. "Meaning?" "Two CD release parties, tribute performance, and the awards." "As long as I'm not singing at them." He laughed and kissed her. "Nope. That one's saved for the concert in November." "Seriously," Ava asked. "Stop freaking out. You'll be fine."

Joe and Ava got up and ran errands for a while, then came home and relaxed. They sat outside by the fire pit and chilled. "Why are you so worried about having the baby?" "I'm not worried. I don't know what to expect. Second, I can't fit into anything. I'm not about to go buy all those pregnancy clothes. None of them are my style." "You'd look beautiful in a potato sack. What are you worried about?" "What happens if we don't work Joe?" "Remember what I told you before. Look at the inscription on the ring when you get worried. We're forever." "But . . ." He kissed her. "I'm never walking away. You're stuck with me for life. Like a permanent growth that you can't amputate." He tried joking their way through it, but she really was worried. What if she had to raise the baby alone? What if he cheated? What if he found someone else? What if he changed his mind? The thoughts ran through her head like a broken looped recording. "Baby. Remember something. I will always, want you, love you, need you, and be there. No matter what. We're going to be together until we're 102 and forget each other's names. We're going to see our great, great grandkids and be together until we're old, wrinkled, piles of ashes. Even after that, we're going to be in heaven together forever. You'll never get rid of me." Joe kissed her. "I'm yours." "I know I'm just being silly," Ava said. "No. You're pregnant. You're allowed to be worried. Just don't ever think that I'm going to walk away, because I never will." Ava nodded. He kissed her and they curled up watching the stars. This is what Ava needed and she had the best husband to share it with.

———————

The next two weeks were crammed with wedding preparations for Rose and Ryan. Rose hadn't realized just how hard it was to put it all together in that short amount of time. "I don't know how you managed to do this Ava," she said as they sat at the table going through everything. "Joe planned most of it. I just did the little stuff." "The caterer, flowers, dresses, invitations and DJ isn't little," Rose said. "We didn't need a DJ. We used the caterer they use on tour and all I had to do was the flowers, dresses and invitations, which Joe and I picked out together." "Still." "Everything will be fine Rose," Ava said. "You two are singing that song at the wedding." "What song?" "Don't play stupid Ava. You're singing it." "It's your wedding. Can't say no can I," Ava asked. "Nope." They went out that afternoon and Rose hunted for the perfect wedding dress. "Are you having the big church wedding," Ava asked. "Already booked the church. It's a little one." "Sounds pretty." Rose finally found one she loved. "Well Princess Rose," Ava teased. They pinned it for alterations and found a maid of honor dress for Ava, then left. "I told you. One store," Ava joked. They laughed. They ordered the flowers then headed home. Joe and Ryan were working on something new. Ava shushed Rose.

"I think back on memories, the good and the bad, I think back to the better days, when love was all we had, then I realize, I'm still that guy . . ." They listened as the guys continued on. By the end of the song, Ava's eyes were tearing. "If I tweak this part . . ." The ladies walked through the hall. "So," Ryan asked. "Two more things off the list," Rose said sniffling. "And why does Ava look like she was crying," Ryan asked. "Hormones," Ava teased. She wiped the tears away and went into the kitchen. "The song is beautiful," Ava said. "So that's why," Ryan said. Joe came into the kitchen and saw Ava with a glass of lemonade. "How did it go," he asked. "Got a dress, and so did Rose." "You like the song?" "It's beautiful," Ava said. "Then stop crying." "I told you. It's just hormones." He wrapped his arms around her and kissed her. "Silly head," he said. They got up and went in and sat with Ryan and Rose.

"So, we decided to have the wedding at the country club," Rose said. "That way, we don't have to do the cleanup," Ryan joked. "Good plan." "So all we need now is the DJ, the cake and the invitations," Rose said. "We'll get Brad's brother to be the DJ, and the cake isn't that hard to do. We'll get the invitations tomorrow," Ryan said. "What's left?" "The honeymoon," Ava teased. "You're actually going away and staying off the phone for a week," Joe joked. "We have to get back into the studio and get some of the new stuff recorded." "Hello ADD. Wedding first," Joe teased. "We ordered the tuxes. My niece said she'd be the flower girl," Ryan said. "Did you call Carrie and Rachel," Ava asked. "They're both coming and so is James. He's coming with Rachel," Rose said. "Great," Ava replied. "Anything else we're missing?" "Bachelor party," Joe teased. "You two have had ten years of bachelor partying," Rose teased. The guys laughed. "And bachelorette party," Ava said. Rose looked at Ava. "Don't even think it." "We'll see," Rose replied. After a little more wedding talk, and a hug goodbye, Ava and Joe headed home.

———

"And I went shopping. I got a few things." "Finally stopped trying for the skinny jeans," Joe teased. "Can still fit into them." "So what did you get?" "Dresses." "Mmm," Joe said. "You're hilarious." "Babe, I told you. You'd look good in anything." "Thanks." "Why are you worried," he asked. "Just miss having the tiny waist." "Babe, you're beautiful. You never have to worry about it." "I'm a woman Joe. I always will," Ava said. They got home and went inside. "You need to stop being worried." "Why?" "Because you will always be the most beautiful woman in the planet to me." Ava wrapped her arms around him. "Babe, you don't need to keep being scared," Joe said. "I love you. I know you love me." "And it's not gonna change," he said then leaned in and kissed her. "So what are we up to the rest of the night," he asked. "Seems I owe you a night of whatever you want." "Thought that debt was paid up," Joe joked. "Was an entire day if I remember correctly." "You have a point." "Owe you half a day still." "So what am I going to do with you," Joe asked. "Good question." Ava kissed him, then went to walk towards the office. Joe pulled her to him and kissed her, leaning her into the door frame.

"Have a better idea baby," he suggested. "What's that?" "Bubble bath and dinner in bed." "Oh really," Ava asked. He kissed her again. "Think I need to do writing." "My night." He grabbed her hand and they walked upstairs. He drew Ava a hot bath, put in the bubbles, then grabbed them a drink. He came back in and Ava was in the tub. "Comfy," he asked as he slid in behind her and handed her a glass of ginger ale in a champagne glass. "Needed the bubble bath," Ava said. "Think we both did," Joe said. They relaxed then he kissed her neck. A smirk came across her face. "We have to go do a performance on Friday," Joe said. "Where?" "L.A." "When are you back," Ava asked. "Sunday morning." "So in other words, you're leaving tomorrow?" He kissed her neck. They relaxed until the water went cool, then Ava stepped out. "Where are you going," Joe asked. "Do some writing." She slid her robe on, then walked downstairs. She logged into her computer and checked through emails. There were a few from James, and a few from her agent. The new book was selling, and she was asked to go on a book tour for a few days.

He walked into her office in nothing but a towel.

Ava replied getting the dates for the short book stint. She replied back that it was the week after Rose's wedding. Ava agreed and asked for the information.

He saw the email. "Planning to run away?" "For a few days." "When?" "After the wedding." "Babe," he said. "Work. I have to go to New York and Chicago, then to L.A." "I don't think you should. What about the baby?" "I'm fine. It's nothing major." "I don't think you should be flying." "It'll be fine." Ava went into her writing. He flipped the top of her laptop down, then slid onto the desk in front of her. "Something I can help you with," Ava asked. He looked at her. "What?" He motioned for her to come closer. "Mmm?" He kissed her, pulling her to him. "I guess writing is out for tonight," she joked. He untied her robe. His arms slid around her waist, pulling her to him. "What are you up to?" "Had an idea." "And what's that?" He grabbed her hand and they walked back upstairs.

Joe slid her onto the bed. "I love you." "I know. I love you too," Ava said. His phone went off. He ignored it. "Get the phone," Ava said. He grabbed it off the counter. "Yep?" "It's Sasha." "Kinda busy." "Was thinking about you." "Gotta go." He hung up. "Who was it,"

Ava asked. "Nobody." He kissed her and leaned her onto the bed. They made love. He pulled her into his arms. His phone went off again. Ava grabbed it. "Is Joe there?" "Can I ask who's calling?" "It's Sasha. I need to talk to him for a quick minute." Ava handed him the phone then got up. She went into the bathroom and had a shower, then went downstairs. She grabbed the leftovers from the fridge, then warmed them up in the microwave and locked herself in the office. She was a full chapter in when he came downstairs. He saw her in the office. He grabbed a beer from the fridge, then walked in. "You okay?" "Sure. How's the treat of the week?" "Ava, stop freaking out." "Right. It's 9pm and some chick is calling you on your cell phone that you won't even acknowledge knowing when I'm in the room. Nice." She went back to her writing. "She's a friend." "Right." Ava went back to her writing. He walked into the TV room, then came back into her office in a little while later. "What?" He put a high school yearbook in front of her. "See this? This is Sasha." He pointed out her picture. "We knew each other in high school. I bumped into her at a concert last year." "Fine," Ava said. "I didn't sleep with her." "Funny how you bring that up like you're guilty or something." Ava grabbed her plate and walked into the kitchen and rinsed the dishes off.

"Ava," Joe said. "What?" "A long time ago. That's all." "Fine." She went to go back in to do more writing and he blocked the way. "Ava." "I'm going to do some writing." "I turned it off." Ava turned the light out, then went to turn on the TV and he grabbed the remote. "What?" "What are you all mad about?" "Nothing." "You know you're a crappy liar," Joe said. "What's there to be mad at? How many girls have called you since we got married?" "That's the point remember? You're my wife." "Yep." Ava grabbed the remote. He grabbed it back from her hand. She looked at him. "Just say what you're gonna say Ava." "What other girls are going to pop up?" "That what you're worried about," Joe asked. Ava got up and went upstairs.

Joe went up the steps following her. "Ava," he said. He walked into the bedroom and she was sitting on the edge of the bed crunched over. "Babe?" "I'm fine." "No you aren't," Joe said. Ava got up, then went into the bathroom. "We're going to the hospital," Joe said. "I'm fine." She splashed cold water on her face, then took a deep breath. She walked back into the bedroom and he was pulling on his jeans and a sweater. "Where are you going?" "Taking you to the hospital." "I'm fine." "No you aren't." Ava sat back down then lay down on the bed. "Babe please." "I'm fine Joe." "Then why are you pale as a ghost?" He grabbed her track suit and went to help her put it on. "Would you stop?" "Babe, we're going." Ava slid it on, and a minute later, heard him on the phone. "I'm taking her. I don't know, but I'll call you when I can." He hung up and walked into the bedroom. A twinge of pain hit her.

A half-hour later, she was at the hospital. Security officers were outside the door, and he was staring out the window. The doctor came in. "You're fine Ava. Your blood pressure is a little high, but not too much of a concern. No stress. Try to take it easy." "Thank you. I have a question. Flying. She allowed," Joe asked. "In a few weeks, yes. Right now, no." "Even a short flight to L.A.?" "She's seeing her doctor next week. After she gets the okay from her, fine. Right now, no." The doctor left and Ava went to get up. "Babe." Joe walked over. "I can get dressed myself," Ava said. She pulled her track suit on, then walked out of the room. She went to walk out the door and he pulled her back to him. "What," he asked. "I told you I was fine." "Why are you all pissed off?" Ava walked out. She got in the car. "We're not leaving the parking lot until you talk to me. "Fine. Then the crowd over there can come flip the damn car," Ava said noticing the sea of reporters. He pulled out and they headed off then pulled into the park by the house. "What," Ava asked. "Why are you so pissed off?" "Who were you on the phone with?" "Ryan. Then Kristina called." "Who's Kristina?" "One of my buddies. She's Blake's fiancée. One of the guys from the crew that tunes the guitars for Brad and I." "And?" "I'm coming home after the show Friday and after the show Saturday." "I don't need a babysitter Joe." "You know how stubborn you are?" "Yep." "I don't want you to be home alone if something happens," he said. "Fine. I'll call Rose." He headed back to the house. They went inside and Ava went in and went back to her computer.

Joe walked upstairs and pulled his jeans and sweater off. He sat down on the edge of the bed. Ava came in a few minutes later. "I know you're worried. You being worried scared me alright," Joe said. She walked into her closet and came out a few minutes later with her satin teddy on. "Let me worry okay? Short of carrying our baby for you, it's the only thing I can do," he said. "You understand why I'm worried?" "Babe, just because I'm on the stage every night with the guys doesn't mean I'm going to sleep with someone else on the road. I love you." "I'm still nervous." "Until I prove there's no reason to be, I know you will." "Every concert you've had since we met, I've been there. What about when we have the baby? I can't be there." Joe kissed her. "If you want to be, you can. Just say the word babe." He kissed her again and wrapped his arms around her. "You and the baby are my priority. You come first." His phone rang again. "Hey Joe. It's Tiff." "Hey." "I was going to see if you wanted to go out tomorrow night for a drink." "We're going on the road for a few days tomorrow. Just spending some time with Ava." "Oh. I'll call you in a few hours." He hung up and turned the phone on silent. "Now where were we," he asked. Ava got into the bed and turned the light off. He slid in with her, snuggling up to her. He felt something. "Babe?" "Kicking." "Why?" "When I lay on my side, the baby kicks until it's comfy." "I love you," Joe said. Ava said nothing.

The next morning, Ava got up and went downstairs. She worked on some writing then headed back upstairs. She stepped into the shower and was rinsing the conditioner out when he slid in with her. "Morning beautiful," he said. "Morning to you too," Ava said. She went to step out and he pulled her back in with him. "What?" He kissed her. "Where'd you go?" "Writing." Joe kissed her again and leaned her against the wall of the shower. They made love in the shower, then he carried her to bed and they continued.

The house line rang. "We're leaving in an hour. Do you have your stuff packed," Ryan asked. "Is Rose coming here," Joe asked. "She's popping by after she finishes her work up for the day." "I'll get my stuff together. See you in an hour," Joe said hanging up. Ava went to get up and he pulled her back to him. "You have to pack." "You know I don't want to go," he said. "Go. I'll be fine." "I can get Danielle to come over." "I'm just going to do my writing Joe." He kissed her neck again, then her shoulder, then nibbled her ear. "You have to pack." "Already did," he said. His arm slid around her waist. "What has got into you today?" "Changed the batteries," he joked. Ava had always said he was the Energizer Bunny. They made love again, then he pulled her close. "I'm gonna miss you." Ava slid out of bed. She pulled her robe on then he got up and slid his arms back around her. "If I can, I'll come home Saturday." Ava nodded. "Stop being upset," he said. "Everything is going to change." "And I'm still gonna be in the same spot. Still wrapping my arms around you every night. I don't want anyone else." "Good." She turned towards him and kissed him. "I love you babe." "I love you too." He kissed her again, then went and washed up and got changed.

Ava slid on one of the dresses she bought and drove Joe over to meet the guys. "I'll call you as soon as we get there," Joe said. Ava nodded. He kissed her again. "Remember what I said." Ava nodded. "Love you." "Love you too." Joe left with the guys and Ava went home. She got writing done the rest of the day, then had a quick dinner, a hot bath with a steamy book, then slid into bed. She slept with his pillow in her arms. It still smelled like his cologne. At 3am, she woke up with a shooting pain. She got up and had a glass of water, trying to let the pain pass. After she laid back down, she finally felt better. Then she was up again at 7am.

Ava went into the doctor on her own. "Wanted to check to make sure it wasn't anything." The doctor did the ultrasound again. "Think I know what it was," the doctor said. "Which was?" "There was a cyst on your ovary. It burst. You're fine." "That's what it was?" "I'm checking the other side just in case." She finished the ultrasound, and found another one on the other side. "At least you know what it was." "How's baby," Ava asked. She did the ultrasound, then flipped it into 2-D. "Baby is just fine." She printed it out for Ava then ran a few more tests. She waited in the office. "Everything's fine. All the tests are normal. You haven't gained a heck of a lot of weight with the baby." "I was still going for a run." "Brisk walk." "So I'm okay to fly?" "You can. Where are you headed to?" "I have to go on a book thing for a few days. Three flights." "If you need anything, call me and tell me. I'll come in on a Saturday if you need me to." "Thank you," Ava said. "No worrying." Ava nodded. She headed home and slid into a hot bath.

CHAPTER 11

Ava slid out of the tub and had dinner. Rose and Danielle showed up around six. "So how's mom?" "Good." "Get dressed," Rose said. "Why?" "Go put on one of the sexy dresses. We're going out," Danielle said. "I'm not really in a going out mood." "Tough," Rose said. Ava went upstairs, pulling on one of the sexy dresses she'd bought, slid on her not so high heels, then put on some makeup and did her hair. She came downstairs. "Where are we going," Ava asked. "You better after the hospital?" "The doctor said I was fine. Why," Ava asked. They left. "Where are we going? Seriously." They pulled into the airport a half-hour later. "You're telling me where we're going or I'm not moving from this car," Ava said. "A Concert."

"She's not answering her phone," Joe said. "Stop freaking out Joe. She's probably in the tub." "She'd still answer the phone." He called again, then heard a ringing in the hallway. He finished his beer, then went to go down the hall and saw Ava. "What the?" "Hi," she said. He wrapped his arms around her and kissed her. "You aren't supposed . . ." She kissed him, then slid the picture into his pocket. "Joe . . . what's going on," Ryan asked. Rose slid in behind Ryan and wrapped her arms around him. "What the hell are you two . . ." "Hey beautiful," Brad said to Danielle. "We thought you guys needed a surprise," Danielle said. Joe kissed Ava again. He grabbed her hand and they walked down the hall. "You weren't supposed to be flying." "Look in your pocket," Ava said. He pulled out the picture. "This . . ." He looked at Ava. "I went to my appointment today. I'm fine." "What about the other day?" "We'll talk about it later. It wasn't the baby." He kissed her again then snuck into the change room.

"I was trying to call you," Joe said. "We left at six." He kissed her again. "This one of the new dresses," he asked. Ava nodded. "We definitely needed new dresses." "So you like?" She turned around and he noticed that it was very backless. He kissed her neck, then slid his hands around her waist. "So you like it," Ava asked. He slid his hands up her legs, sliding the skirt part of the dress up her legs. "Joe," Ava said. "What?" "Think I might have missed you." He kissed her and within minutes they were going at it.

Rose and Danielle hung out with the guys. "How the heck did you get a flight out here," Brad asked. "An old friend lent us his plane." "I'm glad you two thought of it," Ryan said. Ryan and Rose were curled up together on the sofa. "What time is the meet and greet," Danielle asked. "Done already. We did it at 5." "Anything else before you go on," Rose asked. "Other than tearing Ava and Joe apart, nope." They all joked around.

After, Joe and Ava curled up on the sofa. "You liked your surprise," she asked. "You have no idea. Plus, this means we can try out the new song." "Great," Ava said. Enthusiastic wasn't her strong suit that night. "You'll do fine." "Still don't know how you talked me into it in the first place," Ava said. "Because you love me." "For now." He kissed her again and held her close. The baby was kicking away.

A half-hour later, the guys were on stage. They got a half-hour or so into it, and the girls were side stage. "So I know everyone heard we've been working on some new stuff. We also added a few people to the Aces family. We have two or three new songs. Here's one of our favorites. To sing it with us, is one of our most favorite people . . . . Ava Morgan." Joe came and grabbed her hand, leading her over to where he was on the stage. She sang with the guys and the entire audience cheered. "Thanks everyone. Now here's another new one for you," Joe said. He wouldn't let Ava leave. They sang Love Letter and the other new one Ava had helped them with, then Joe went to change guitars. He kissed Ava, then headed back out. "You were great," Rose and Danielle said. "So totally not doing that again." "You were really good," Rose said. "Thanks guys." The ladies watched the rest of the concert, then headed back to the dressing rooms.

The guys came in at the end of the concert. "Holy crap," Ryan said. "I know. I didn't know it would go over that well," Joe said. "What," Ava asked. "They loved you." "Don't you dare ask what I think you are," Ava said. "You have to Ava." "Funny." "No seriously," Ryan said. "Hello? Baby?" "I know. But you have to," Joe said. "Three against one," Brad teased. "Make that five," Rose said. "I love being ganged up on." "You were so good," Rose said hugging her. "Fine." Joe slid onto the sofa behind Ava and wrapped his arms around her. "You know what this means right?" "That I'm stuck with you," Ava joked. He kissed her. "I still can't believe you can sing like that. I've never heard you sing before," Rose said. "Yeah you have." The radio in the car doesn't count," Rose said. Joe kissed Ava's cheek. The manager slipped into the room. "So, we have someone out here that is asking for Ava's autograph." "You know we don't do them after the concert," Joe said. "The press is requesting it. Let's go guys." They headed out and Ava was talked into being part of the photo shoot.

Finally, they all headed back to the hotel. "We can leave tonight if you want to," Joe said. "Stop worrying about me," Ava replied. He kissed her. "I always will. I still can't believe you went to the doctor without me." "I wanted to make sure." "What happened?" "Nothing." "You suck at lying." "Had another stomach pain." "And what was it?" "Burst cyst." "You sure you're alright?" Ava nodded. He kissed her. "We're going home tonight." They went up to grab his bag from his room and Ava saw a note on his door:

See you around 12. XO

Ava walked off. He came after her, but the doors to the elevator had closed. She went to Ryan and Rose's room. "I need to get out of here," Ava said. "You alright," Ryan asked. Rose looked at Ava. "You guys stay," Rose said. "Take the plane back," Ryan said. Rose left with Ava. Within a half-hour, they were in the air.

Ava got home and was sick. Rose grabbed Ava a ginger ale and sat with her. "You okay?" Ava shook her head. She pulled the sheets off the bed, throwing them into the washer, then pulled on the satin sheets she loved. "Ava, sit down," Rose said. "I can't." "You have to. The baby remember." Ava sat down. "What happened?" "Nothing." "You always sucked at lying." "Leave it alone Rose." "You walk into our room ready to shoot knives and you say leave it alone?" Ava got back up and cleaned. She flipped the laundry. "Either you tell me, or I'm calling him," Rose said. "Another one of his girlfriends leaving him notes on his door. Then they call his phone, and they try to get him into bed. I'm sick of it," Ava said. "Ava, chill. He loves you." "So his dick is public property?" "Calm down." "No." Ava finished cleaning then went upstairs. "I'm going to my place to grab some clothes. I'll be back in a half-hour," Rose said. "I'm fine. Go home." "Call me in the morning alright?" Ava nodded and Rose left.

Around 4am, Ava finally fell asleep. Joe came in at 9. He walked upstairs and went into the bedroom, finding her out cold. He slid into the bed beside her, pulling her towards him. Ava woke up. "Baby," he said. She pulled away and got up, pulling her robe on and walking downstairs. "Ava," Joe said. She went into the office and logged into her computer. "Stop this." "What's her name Joe?" "Who?" "Don't play fucking stupid with me." "Ava, you realize fans find out where we are right?" "And find out what room you're in," she asked. She went back onto the computer. "Ava, stop this." "Forget it. I'll just go and leave you to whatever the hell you want to be with tonight." Ava got up and walked back upstairs, then got another shooting pain. "I'm taking you to the hospital." "Get the hell away from me," Ava said. She walked back upstairs, texting Rose. She locked the bedroom door and got dressed. Ava heard the doorbell and came downstairs. Ryan and Rose were at the door. Ava walked past them and went out to the car, getting in and leaving.

"Another cyst. Until we get your blood pressure back down, you'll have to stay Ava." "Fine." "What happened," the doctor asked, more than a little concerned. "Nothing. We got in an argument." "Rose, Ryan and Joe are here," the nurse said peeking her head in. "That's nice," Ava said. She curled up and tried to sleep.

"Is she alright," Joe asked. "She had a burst cyst. Her blood pressure is too high. She's staying until it goes down," the doctor said. "I need to go in there." "If it's going to raise her blood pressure, you're staying out here Joe." "I need to talk to her." Joe walked past the doctor and went into Ava's room. He sat down beside her. "Get out." "Ava, let me explain." "Why? How many others am I going to find out about Joe?" "It was Tiff." "So you and her are what Joe?" "She can try all she wants Ava but we both know that I love you." "So you don't love her. No big deal. Guys sleep with girls they don't love all the time," Ava said. She wouldn't even look at him. "I don't." "Right." He got up from the chair and sat down on the edge of her bed. "Baby." "Don't." "Stop this," he said. "You want her, go get her." Joe saw her wiping tears away. "Ava, I'm not leaving. The only woman I want is sitting in this bed crying and trying to pull a tough girl routine." He heard her sniffling and handed her Kleenex. "Just go." "I'm not moving an inch." Ava winced. He got up and called the doctor.

He paced the waiting room again. "Joe, sit down," Ryan said. "No." Rose came back with coffee for them. "You have to have something. Breakfast looked like hell down there," Rose said. They had their coffee. A little while later, the doctor came back out and Joe was asking a million questions. "She alright?" "Spotting, but she's fine." "I'm going in," he said. "She's asleep." He walked in anyway and sat down beside her. "Baby?" He held her hand in his. "Go home Joe." "Please." "Go do whatever you want Joe. Go have fun." "Ava, stop this. I love you." "Go home." "No," he said. There was no way he was leaving her side.

He spent the entire day at her side. "Is she allowed to go home," Joe asked. "As long as she's not under stress," the doctor said in the hall. Joe went into her room and she was sitting with Rose. "You can stay with us," Rose said. Ryan pulled Joe to the side. "She's coming home with me," Joe said. "What did you do," Ryan asked. "Tiff won't back off. I told her that we were done and she won't stop. She knows Ava and I got married, and she still won't back off." "You need to straighten her out," Ryan said. "No. I need to take my pregnant wife home." Joe walked off. Rose was helping Ava get dressed. Joe walked over and picked her up from the bed, carrying her out the door and to the car. "Put me down Joe." "No problem." He put her into the car then got in and pulled out of the parking lot.

They got back to the house and he carried her inside. Joe walked upstairs to their bedroom, and laid her on the bed. She went to get up and he sat down beside her. "We're going to make it through this." "Go call Tiff. Maybe she'll believe it." "Stop. Tiff and I were done a long time ago. I love you." "Then why is she calling? Why is she following you and leaving you notes?" "I don't know. Fact is that I don't care. If I have to change my cell number, I will." "Why bother? You'll just give it to her again." Ava tried to get up and he stopped her. Joe kissed her. "It's not going to change a damn thing." He kissed her again. "Stop it," Ava said. "Ava. I love you. Get it through your head." "Then tell me why you can't stay away from her. Tell me why she's leaving you notes and why she knew what room you were in." "I talked to her at the meet and greet." "Then?" "Babe, nothing happened." "Then why don't I believe you?" Ava got up and went into the washroom.

Ava showered and for once, Joe wasn't hopping in behind her. She came out and he wasn't upstairs. She slid on a shirt then went downstairs. He was gone. Ava made herself some dinner, then took her laptop upstairs. She tried to get some writing done, then curled up and went to sleep. She woke up in the middle of the night and he still wasn't there. She tossed and turned and tried to fall asleep. She wrote a little more, then finally fell asleep.

The next morning, Ava got up and went downstairs. She grabbed her cell phone and realized it was off. She turned it on and had six new voicemail messages:

Beep: I'm staying with Ryan and Rose tonight. I just want you to be okay. I love you.

Beep: I can't sleep without you. Are you up? Are you okay?

Beep: It's Rose. Call me when you get up. Joe's here and freaking out.

Beep: I love you.

Beep: It's James. I'm in town for a week. Come meet me for dinner one night.

Beep: Baby, please. I'm sorry. I changed the number. It's 615-746-9558. Please baby.

Ava called Joe. "Are you alright?" "My phone was off." "I'm sorry babe." "I just wanted to let you know I was fine." "I'm coming home." Ava hung up. She made herself some breakfast, then went upstairs and had a hot shower. When she came out, Joe was sitting on the edge of the bed. She walked past him and grabbed something from the closet to wear.

"Ava." She walked past him again and grabbed her laptop. "Please babe." "What do you want me to say? That it's okay that you were talking to her?" "I love you. Only you. You need to know that." "You get her out of your system that quickly?" "Ava," he said. She got dressed. "Stop already." "Stop what? Stop being pissed off that you're talking and seeing your ex? Fine. I'm not anymore," Ava said. She walked out of the room with her laptop and went downstairs.

Ava sent the chapters she'd finished to her agent, then checked her email. She got a contract from the management company for the group to sing with them. Ava sent it over to her lawyer friend to take a look at. Joe came downstairs a little while later. "Ava, can we talk about this?" "About what," Ava asked. He walked over and took her hand, leading her over to the sofa. "What?" "Babe, I'll tell you what happened." "So now you admit something happened," Ava asked. "Before the wedding, she came to one of the concerts. "And?" "We were talking backstage. I told her that I couldn't be with her anymore. That I'd met someone. She tried to get me to change my mind." Ava looked at him. "Which means you two did what," Ava asked. She could feel her blood hitting a boiling point. "Ava, you aren't supposed to be under stress." "Either you talk now, or leave and don't come back." "I didn't sleep with her." "Just tell me you didn't do anything else." "Almost, but I told her to leave." "Like that would stop her." "Ava, stop," Joe said. "Then what?" "I told her that we got married. She's been freaking out ever since. She's shown up twice already." "You done?" "I love you." "Good. You can leave now." Ava went to get up and he pulled her to him. "I'm not going," he said. "Then I will." Ava got up and went upstairs. He came up behind her. "You can't just leave me alone can you," Ava asked. "No." Ava walked into the bedroom. "Babe, please." "You were with her before we even got married. What the hell was the damn point?" He kissed her. He had her leaned into the wall of the bedroom in a few minutes. He undid her sweater and had to find a way to make it up to her.

"I'm sorry," Joe said. "Just go." He kissed her again. They went from the wall, to the bed. They made love. Ava tried to get up after and he wouldn't let her go. "Let go," Ava said. "No." "Joe, please." "I can't. I can't let you leave." "And I can't stay married to you if you're going to cheat on me." Ava got up and went into the bathroom and turned on the shower.

The room was steamed up. "Ava." "What?" "Tell me we'll get through this," Joe said. "How the hell do I trust you?" "I swear that nothing happened after we got married." "And I'm supposed to believe that how?" "Because that ring means something to me." "Then she wouldn't still be calling would she?" "I changed the number." "Fine." "Please." There was no reply. Joe heard the water turn off and she stepped out, wrapping a towel around her. "Baby," he said. She walked into the bedroom. Ava got dressed, then went downstairs. "Where are you going?" "Doesn't matter Joe." "Baby, please just listen to me." "I've had enough listening. I've had enough bullshit from you." Ava walked out the door. He grabbed his sweater and went after her. "Ava." "Can't just leave me alone can you?" "Come inside." "Why?" "Babe, stop. You're not supposed to be under stress." "Then don't cause it." She kept walking. He followed her. "Would you stop?" "Not until you talk to me," Joe said. Ava turned and headed back to the house. "You're not supposed to be exercising. The doctor said nothing strenuous." Ava kept walking. She got back to the house a half-hour later. He came in behind her. "I'm sorry." "You think that's going to fix this?" "What do you want me to say," Joe asked. "Nothing." Ava walked upstairs, slid on her track pants and sweatshirt and went to bed. "Tell me what I have to say for you to forgive me." "You were with her the one night I didn't go to the damn concert weren't you," she asked. "Ava." "You just proved you can't be trusted." "We'd just met." "Doesn't matter." "I'm sorry. I swear that nothing else happened. Nothing since then," Joe said. "So why was she leaving you notes Joe?" "Because she's stubborn and won't take no for an answer." "How am I supposed to trust that you aren't going to do this again?" "Because this is killing me. It's like a slow death." "Good." "I love you." "Should have thought of that shouldn't you," Ava said.

She turned out the light. "I'm not going to sleep with you being mad at me and either are you," he said. "Just stop." "We promised we'd never go to bed mad." "And you promised a crapload of shit that you lied about too." "Ava, I love you. The first night we were alone, I knew I wanted to marry you. All of this was before that. I was with her the night you were there with James." "And it kept going from there." "Babe," Joe said. "Don't babe me. You want her, go have fun." "I want you." "I'm not a damn toy to be played with Joe," she said. "I want you and only you. I want to wake up beside you, hold you in my arms, feel you with me every minute of the day. I don't want to wake up without you." "You should've . . ." He kissed her and pulled her into his arms. "No more fighting." "I'm allowed to be pissed off." He kissed her again. "I'm sorry. I swear that it's never happening again. Even if I have to get a restraining order." "If I ever find out . . ." He kissed her again.

"I think I should call and see if she's alright," Rose said. "You know they're probably making up," Ryan joked. "She isn't going to let him off easy. I'll tell you that much." "Good. Honestly, it was when they first met. But still, he shouldn't have had her anywhere near him if he wanted to be with Ava." "Good play," Rose joked. He smiled. "What?" "We're never going to be in those kinds of fights," Ryan said. "What makes you think that?" He kissed Rose. "Because I am totally, 100% head over heels in love with you." "He loves Ava too." "Difference is, cheating never has and never will be for me," Ryan said. "Good to know." He kissed Rose again. "Still, I should call," she said. He pulled Rose into his arms and kissed her, then his hands slid up her sweater. "Or I could call her later."

"Where are you James," Kristy asked. "Nashville." "Why?" "Work. It's not what you're thinking," James said. "It better not be." "I'll be home in a day or two." "Don't go over there alright?" "I'm not. I have to go. The meeting is starting." James' new girlfriend Kristy was going to figure this out . . . he just had to outsmart her.

Ava got up the next morning and went to slide out of bed. She was quiet, and made it out without Joe waking up. She went downstairs and got some writing done, then made herself breakfast. She was two more chapters in when he came downstairs. "Morning," Joe said. "Yep." He walked over, poured himself a coffee, then walked over and sat down with Ava. "How's the writing going?" "Trying to figure out the ending." "How did you sleep?" "Fine." "I know you're still mad," Joe said. "Did you expect any different?" "I have an idea," he said. "What?" "We go away for a week." "You can't just take off Joe." "Yeah I can." "You know these impulse trips are a little crazy," Ava said. "And exactly what we need." He kissed her then got up and called their travel agent.

"To Cabo,' he said. "I can get you on the flight this afternoon at 3." "Sold." He booked it, and kissed Ava. "What?" "Flight leaves at 3," Joe said. "For how long?" "A week."

"What do you mean you're going away," Ryan said in complete shock. "We're going to Cabo. We'll do the recording stuff when I get back," Joe said. "I'm holding you to it." "I know. I'll call you on the way back." "I know why you're going. I hope it works," Ryan said. "You and me both." "I'll let Rose know." "Thanks bud. Can you keep an eye on the house for me," Joe asked. "No probs."

That afternoon, Ava and Joe left. He wouldn't let her bring the laptop or her cell phone. They landed and headed back to the villa where they'd got married. "And why here," Ava asked. "Starting over." "I know you want me to let this go, but it's a little difficult." "Just remember something. I married you. We were here in front of everyone we love. We loved each other so much we got married in Vegas. That's never going to change." "If I'd known . . ." "We still would have. I know you love me," Joe said. "I can't believe that you of all people could do that." "I'm sorry. I am. Just tell me what I have to do to make it up to you." "I don't know." He wrapped his arms around her as she leaned against the railing. "Name it," Joe said. "You know how silly this sounds?" "Anything." "Enough." "I want to make this right," he said. "I know." "Are we ever going to get back to the way we were?" "It takes time." He kissed her neck. "You have to win my trust back." "I don't know how Ava." "Either do I." "You're going to be on tour with us for a while right?" Ava nodded. "Then?" "Just means you don't have the opportunity," Ava said still suspicious. "I don't want anyone else Ava. Doesn't matter who it is." "Just give me time." "Come for a walk with me," he asked. They walked along the beach, then sat down in the cove they came across.

"What did you want to do tonight," Joe asked. "Dinner." "By the fireplace." "Could," Ava replied. "I have an idea." "What's that?" "We spend the night playing truth or dare." "What are we ten," Ava asked. "Funny. Are you scared?" "How about have you ever," Ava joked. "Or twenty questions." "Interesting." Joe grabbed her hand and they headed back. "No more fighting. You have to promise me," he said. "Then don't give me a reason to be in a fight with you." "Promise?" "No more secrets," Ava asked. He nodded. "Fine." "Something I have to do first," Joe said. "What's that?" He stopped and pulled Ava into his arms and kissed her, then headed back to the villa. He walked right into their bedroom. Joe kissed her again, kicking the door closed.

He curled up on the bed with her and they made love. Joe never wanted to go through that again. He'd missed her arms around him and the feeling of having her close. This time, they were more passionate, more loving, more romantic and more sizzling than before. He wanted every inch of her wrapped around him. He was determined to make this work, even if he died trying.

CHAPTER 12

After a week in Cabo, alone, with no stress or drama, Ava had managed to give Joe another chance. They were back to the way things were before, for the most part anyway. They got back to Nashville and Ava went for another doctor's appointment. "Blood pressure went down, stress is down and baby is still sucking its thumb. Whatever you did, keep doing it," the doctor said. "We don't know if it's a girl or boy right," Joe asked. "In a few more weeks." Joe was past excited. They headed home, and curled up on the sofa together. "We should put stuff together for the nursery," Ava said. "Pick out what you want, and it'll be here," Joe said. "Don't feel like shopping?" "Depends." "Fredericks isn't included Joe." He kissed her. "Would you stop," Ava said. They curled up on the sofa together and went through the catalogs Ava had received. They finally came across a crib and nursery set they both loved. The mobile had music notes and guitars and the bedding was black, purple and white. "Plus the sheets," Ava said. They picked out the furniture and bedding, then put the order in online. "Still want to go look at other stuff," Ava said. "We can go if you want, but I have to call security first," Joe said. "For you or protection from you," she teased. He kissed her again. Joe called the store, then they headed out.

Joe and Ava made their way into the cleared store. After gushing over all the baby clothes, getting a car seat, picking out a few baby toys, and finding the cutest baby sized version of a guitar, they left. The press was surrounding the store. They finally got in the car and left. "I still can't believe you got the baby pig," Joe said. Ava turned it on and it made oinking noises. "Fine. It's cute," he said. They laughed the rest of the way to the house, then headed inside. Ava's phone rang. "What's up Rose?" "I'm staying at your place." "What are you talking about?" "Ryan's locked himself in the studio. I'm coming over." She hung up, then within about 15 minutes, Rose was at the house.

"What do you mean he locked himself in the studio," Joe said. "He's been in there for 2 hours. A friend of his came to help him with something, and he hasn't come out," Rose said in between sniffles. "What friend," Joe asked. "Cassidy." Joe looked at Ava. "What," Ava said seeing the look in his eye. Joe grabbed her hand and led her upstairs to the bedroom. "What's wrong?" He kissed her. Joe barely let her up for air. Finally, he took a breath. "Who is she Joe?" He closed the bedroom door. "Don't even think you're getting away with not telling me," Ava said. "I have to go over there." "Either you say it, or don't come back here," Ava said. "Baby, you can't tell Rose this." "Speak." "He was 'friendly' with her for the past while." "Is she why he got the divorce?" "No. She was because of it," Joe said. "In other words, she's his sex buddy." "Don't say anything to Rose." Ava went to walk off. He pulled her back to him and kissed her. "She friends with Tiff," Ava asked. He kissed her again, leaning her into the bedroom wall. She pushed him away, then walked downstairs.

"Tea," Ava asked Rose. "Stronger." Ava walked over and handed her a glass of Jack. "Why won't he let me in," Rose asked as Joe came in. "I'll go see if I can get the workaholics out." He walked over to kiss Ava and she turned her cheek. His hand slid across her cheek and pulled her face to his. "I love you. I'll be back." He left and headed off to stop the speeding train known as Cassidy.

"I guess you two made up" Rose said. "Sort of. It's still not 100%." Rose saw the bags from the baby store. "What did you two do? Buy one of everything?" Ava pulled things out and showed them all to Rose. "Did you pick out the furniture," she asked. "Ordered." "Bedding?" Ava showed her the picture. "You two are so cute." "For now anyway." "Ava, after what he's gone through trying to talk you into taking him back, he isn't going to do that again." "Tours are funny things Rose."

"Ryan." Joe knocked on the door to his studio. "Buddy, it's me." Ryan opened the door. "Well hello there stranger," Cassidy said as she slid her bra back on. "You want to lose her Ryan?" "What are you talking about," Ryan asked. "She's at my house with Ava. She's already mad at me Ryan. You start this crap, I am not sticking up for you," Joe said more worried for himself than Ryan. "Was for old times' sake," Cassidy said. "Old times are old for a reason. You need to go Cassidy," Joe said. "This isn't your studio smart ass," she said sarcastically to Joe. "Cass, go," Ryan said. "You're welcome," she said storming out. "Where is she," Ryan asked. "Commiserating with Ava." "She know?" "Buddy, you mess this up, and you're screwing with my wife." Joe walked past Ryan and went to walk out. "Tell her to come home." "Not if this is what you're doing in front of her face." Joe walked out and headed back to his place.

"He wouldn't mess around on me," Rose said still reeling. "I'm just saying, if anything happens, I want you to come to me," Ava said. "Ava, what aren't you telling me?" "I'm just saying Rose, if it happens, then you come to me. No telling him off or starting fights." "Same goes for you, although I'm not sure why we're having this discussion," Rose said. "They're on stage half the damn year Rose. That's why." "Why what," Joe asked as he walked in and wrapped his arms around Ava. "Nothing," Ava said. "Finally got him to take a break," Joe said. "Good," Rose replied. Rose left and headed home. "You going to tell me what you were talking about," Joe asked. "Nothing. Just making sure she's seeing things the way she should when it comes to you two." "Meaning what?" "Meaning that there comes a point where she's probably going to have to fight off groupies." "Ava." "I didn't tell her. Don't think I'm going to forget that easy either." "He knows better," Joe said. "Than you? I'm sure he tries to." "Baby, don't go getting all pissed off again," Joe said. "Never said I stopped." Ava got up and went upstairs, drawing herself a hot bath, then slid into the tub. She put her iPod in, then leaned back. He came in a little while later. He pulled her earphones out. "What," Ava asked. Joe kissed her. He grabbed her hand and helped her out of the tub and pulled her into his arms. "This doesn't . . ." He kissed her again, then walked her backwards to their bed. Ava slid across the bed, then got up. "Ava," he said. She grabbed a towel, wrapping herself with it, then walked downstairs.

―――――✶―――――

Rose came home and walked straight into Ryan's studio. "So. You finally decided to come out." "Meaning?" "You didn't answer your phone, and you ignored me," Rose said. "I was working on music." "Who is she?" "Who?" "Cassidy." Ryan's heart leaped into his throat. "She's a friend." "What kind of friend?" "Where did all of this come from? We were fine this morning," Ryan said. "No answer. Nice." Rose walked off and went up the stairs.

"Ava, what's wrong?" "I warned her." "About?" "What do you think? Her falling into the same problem we have right now." "Ava, I told you. I called it off with her months ago." "She best friends with Cassidy," Ava asked. "Not funny." "I know." Ava went to turn her laptop on. "Babe, there are no more secrets between us. She's gone. Cassidy walked out on Ryan. I told her not to come back." "Great for him." Ava turned the laptop on and logged in. "You're not hiding behind the computer tonight. We're finishing this, and we're finishing it now," Joe said. "The fact that no matter what you guys make it look like, you cheat and so does he. Next thing you're going to tell me is Brad does." "No. He was married before we started." "Two out of three then." "Ava, enough. You're upset. I get that. You care about her enough to tell her and warn her. I understand why. Fact is, things changed. Tiff and I are done. Cassidy and Ryan are done. I want you and only you. He wants to be with Rose more than anything," Joe said. "And if he ever told her the truth, she'd do exactly what I wanted to." "You aren't walking out. Over my dead body," Joe said. "You even breathe on her again." "Ava, stop. I love you. I am never ever jeopardizing us again. Never." "We'll see." "Can't just trust me can you," he asked. "I really don't know." Joe kissed her.

Within minutes, Joe had her on the sofa. "Babe," he said. "I'm never losing you. You know that." "I can't go through this again," Ava said. He kissed her. "You'll never have to." He made love to her on the sofa, then curled up with her and spooned the rest of the afternoon.

———

"Rose." Ryan saw her packing a bag. "Where are you going?" "The only thing I can think of, is that you and her were up to something. Prove me wrong Ryan," Rose said. "We were writing." "That's what you want to call it." She packed her lingerie. "Rose, she's an old girlfriend." "And?" "I told her I was marrying you." "And that changed things how?" "Rose," Ryan begged. She grabbed her jeans, sweaters and shirts and put them in the suitcase. Ryan went to grab her arm and she walked into the bathroom and grabbed her toiletry bag. "Where are you going?" "Anywhere but here." She went to grab her shoes from the closet and Ryan pulled her to him. "Let go." He pulled her back onto the bed. "Ryan." He turned her towards him and kissed her. "Enough," she said breaking the kiss. "You're not going." "And why the hell wouldn't I?" "Nothing happened." "You lock yourself in a room with an ex-girlfriend, ignore my calls and my pages in the room, then pretend like you didn't do a damn thing wrong when I can tell by the smell of her perfume on your damn chest . . ." Ryan kissed her again and peeled her shirt off. The first thing she smelled was Cassidy's perfume. She pulled away from him, grabbed her shirt, then grabbed her bags and walked out. She left and headed straight to Ava's.

———

Rose knocked and Ava came to the door in a towel. "What are you doing back here?" "Guestroom, then I'm moving back," Rose said. Joe wrapped his arms around Ava. "Upstairs. Turn right, third door," Joe said. "Let go Joe," Ava said. "No," he said. "She needs me." "So do I." He grabbed her arm and walked her back into the office. He kissed her again. "Just tell me that you aren't going to let her leave," Joe said. "I'll go with her and make sure . . ." He kissed her. Whether he liked it or not, Joe was pleading Ryan's case. "We can't let her leave," he said. "Yeah I can, if that's what she wants," Ava said. He kissed her again and had her pinned to the wall. "We aren't letting her go back." "Why not?" "Because Ryan loves her. You didn't see him before he met her. He was miserable as shit." "It's better that she is now," Ava asked. "You and I aren't. That's what matters to me right now." He kissed her again. "I love you," Joe said. "I know. God only knows why, but

I . . ." He kissed her again. Ava finally managed to slip out of his arms and went upstairs to check on Rose, after pulling on her satin robe.

Rose was curled up on the bed crying when Ava came in. "What happened," she asked. "He smelled like her." Ava wrapped her arms around Rose. Joe looked in and saw them, then brought tea into Rose. "You'll be alright. We'll figure something out," Ava said. "I'll just move back," Rose said. "No," Joe replied. "I can't stay here." "And running off isn't going to fix it for either of you," he said. "I need to get out of here." "Just stay tonight. We'll figure out what to do in the morning," Ava said. "Maybe you should talk to him," Joe said trying to fix what Cassidy had caused. Ava gave him the cut it out sign. He motioned for her to come.

"What," Ava asked sliding the door closed. "He loves her." "And? That stopped . . ." He covered her mouth. He walked into the bedroom with Ava, closing the door behind them. "Stop taking your anger about me out on him," Joe said. "He did the same thing Joe." "And he loves her." "Your point is?" "Ava, we all make mistakes." "He's engaged. Those kind of mistakes are for when he's single Joe. You should know that." "I do. That's why I changed my number. All of that stuff stops. Let them figure this out themselves," Joe said. "She wants to go back, I'm not letting her go alone." "You aren't going," Joe said. "Says who?" "Says the father of that baby you're carrying." "I can't let her do this alone. You don't know her like I do," Ava said. "She shouldn't be going and you know it." "I'm not stopping her either." Ava went to walk out and he pulled her to him. "I love you. Remember that." "I love you too, but she's my best friend," Ava said. "And he's one of my best friends." Joe kissed her, leaning her back against the door. Within minutes, he had her in bed with him, making love.

Rose got up the next morning and came downstairs to find Ava making breakfast. "What are you doing up so early," Rose asked. "You have to eat. We'll go and talk and figure this out together. We need a proper meal first," Ava said. They had breakfast, then Joe slipped in the kitchen with them. He slid into the chair beside Ava, pulling her close and kissing her. "How are you today Rose," he asked. "A little calmer. I'm still mad as hell, but at least I can think straight. Thanks for letting me stay last night." "You're always welcome," Joe said. "We're going shopping this afternoon." Rose smirked. "As long as you two are happy and having fun, it's good with me." He kissed Ava's neck. "Retail therapy never hurt anyone did it," Ava joked. "Why don't we go out for dinner tonight? I'll find somewhere nice and quiet, and we can meet up there around 5," Joe said. "You going to the studio," Ava asked. Joe nodded. "Sounds good to me," Rose replied then headed upstairs to shower.

Joe pulled Ava into his lap. "What," she asked. He kissed her, leaning her back into the edge of the table. "Please. For me," he asked. "I'm not going to talk her into staying, and I'm not going to talk her into leaving either." He kissed her again. She heard a zipper. "What are you up to," Ava asked. "Nothing," he replied. Ava heard the shower start. They had sex at the table. It was spontaneous, quick, hot and mind tingling. "I love you. Remember that," he said. "As long as you remember what you'll lose." Joe kissed her again. "I already know, and I don't like it." Ava got up and went to head upstairs. Joe followed her. "No you aren't," Ava said. He followed. The two of them showered, then got dressed. Rose was walking out of her room when she saw them kissing at the bedroom door. "I love you," Joe said. Ava kissed him. "See you at 5." Ava nodded. He kissed her again, leaning her into the door frame, then headed out. "You two are almost too sweet," Rose said. "You ready to go," Ava asked. Rose nodded and they headed out.

They shopped, talked, shopped and talked all day. "I don't know what the point of me marrying him is if he's going to do that," Rose said. "Rose, remember something. A ring changes things." "Did it for you and Joe?" "Nobody is perfect. Nothing is. You make the best of the perfect moments, and the happy memories." "What did he do," Rose asked. "Doesn't matter. Fact is, if you want to run off and pretend this didn't happen, it won't work. You'll hear the music, you'll see him, and I'm telling you one thing; if he's half as stubborn as Joe, you have one hell of a fight on your hands." "He knows what he wants. That's all," Rose said. "And he knows what to hold on to. Let's go find something unbelievably sexy for dinner . . . . for both of us," Ava suggested. They shopped a while longer, then Joe called.

"Hey there beautiful," he said. "Hey yourself. How's things going?" "He's miserable as shit. He's coming to dinner. Don't tell her," Joe asked. "It's ok." "I love you." "I know. That's why you keep me around." "I'll see you in a half-hour," Joe said. "Where are we going?" "The seafood place." "Oh really?" "Either there or the fancy place you love." Ava smirked. "I'll make the reservation," Joe said. They hung up. The ladies got changed at the house then left.

"I've been trying all day to call her," Ryan said. "She'll come around," Joe replied. "I can't believe I did that." "If she takes you back . . ." "I know. Why won't she just answer?" "Just drink your beer," Joe said. The guys were paying attention to the TV when Ava and Rose came in. Rose headed straight for the table, and Ava came over to them. She slid her arms around Joe. "Sorry. I'm married," he joked. "I know," Ava replied. Joe turned to face her. "Hey beautiful." "Hey yourself," Ava said. She kissed Joe then gave Ryan a hug. "So how was the studio," she asked. "It was alright," Ryan said still miserable. "How was shopping," Joe asked. "You tell me," Ava replied. Joe looked her up and down and was almost drooling. "You two are seriously going shopping more often," he said. Ava smirked.

"Your table's ready," the hostess said. "We'll meet you over there," Ava said to Ryan. Joe looked at him and winked.

Ryan looked and saw Rose at the table in a sexy red dress. Her hair and nails were done, and she looked stunning. "Rose, I'm . . ." "Sit," she said. Ryan sat down beside her. "I'm sorry. I'm really sorry," he said. "I know. You have reason to be." "I love you." "Ryan, not now." "Just tell me what I have to do to get you to come home." "I'm not coming back until after the wedding." "Baby," he said. "My decision. That way, I can get my work done, you get yours and you remember that in a heartbeat, I can be somewhere else." "I just want to be with you." "Then you can wait." "Rose." "Yes or no," she asked. "Can I come to your place and visit?" "Yes, but then you go home." "I just want you in my arms. I miss waking up with you." "After the wedding," Rose said. "You're killing me." "Yes or no Ryan?" He pulled her towards him and kissed her. "That a yes," she asked. Ryan nodded.

Ava and Joe were across the room. "Okay, seriously, what did you do," Joe asked. "Nothing. We had girl time." "Liar." "We just talked it out. She needed cooling off time. We talked and laughed all day." "And you got her to give him a chance?" "With a few conditions that I think would be a good thing." "Such as miss fix it?" "She's renting a place until the wedding," Ava said. "Why?" "She wants to have her own space." "Ava." "It also means, he has to do right by her or he can't see her." "Hard to freaking get or what," Joe asked. Ava nodded. "As long as it gets him to stop pouting," he said then leaned in and kissed Ava. They all had a quick dinner together, then Joe put Ava's shopping bags in his car, and they left Ryan and Rose alone.

Joe and Ava chatted the entire way home. "Still can't believe you pulled that off," Joe said. "You have to admit, it worked pretty well." "Understatement." Joe couldn't stop staring. "What?" "Nothing," he said with a smirk ear to ear. They pulled into the driveway and headed inside. He grabbed the bags from the trunk. "You know I'm getting a fashion show of this stuff," Joe said. "I'm sure you will at some point," Ava teased. She slid her heels off and headed upstairs. He followed her, dropping the bags on the floor of the bedroom. Ava untied the wrap dress and Joe caught a glimpse of the black lace lingerie. "Now that's what I'm talking about," Joe said with a sexy smirk. "What?" His arms slid around her. The baby kicked, hard enough that he felt it. He kissed Ava's neck. "You know how sexy you are?" "Suck up," she teased. His arms slid up her torso to her breasts. Not a minute later, her phone rang. "You are not answering that," Joe said. Ava went to grab it and he pulled her back. "What if it's Rose?" He kissed her and had her pinned to the bed a minute later.

"I can't get a hold of Ava," Rose said. "Just stay at the house with me tonight." "No." Ryan turned Rose towards him and kissed her, leaning her up against the car. "Please?" "I'm going back to their place. End of discussion." Ryan kissed her again and pulled Rose close. He'd missed this. The smell of her perfume, the feel of her lips on his. He kissed her again, sliding his hands to cup her face. "I love you. Please." "I'm going back to their place." He kissed her again, sliding the phone out of her hand and into his pocket. He got Rose into the car, then they headed back to his house.

"Just drop me off," Rose said. "No." He walked into the house, holding her hand and pulling her in behind him. "I'm not staying with you tonight," Rose said. He kissed her again, leaning her into the closed front door of the house. He picked her up, slipping her heels off and pulling her legs around him. He carried her up the steps to the bedroom. Before she could say a word, he had her leaned onto the bed. He was sliding the skirt of her dress up her legs when her phone buzzed in his pocket. Rose grabbed it and he slid it out of her hand. They made love on the bed for the first time in days. After, he was about to close his eyes, when Rose got up. "Where are you going," he asked. "I told you." She slid her dress on, grabbed her phone, then left.

Rose walked in a half-hour later, took her things upstairs, and went to bed. She couldn't help the little smirk that she had, knowing that she had the upper hand. Her phone buzzed a text message:

Miss you. XO

She smiled, then replied:

I bet.

Ryan: Come warm me back up.

Rose: Going to bed.

Ryan: I miss you. Please.

Rose: Sweet dreams.

Rose turned her phone on silent and went to sleep.

The next morning, Ava curled up in bed with Joe. "Can we stay in bed today," he asked. Ava shook her head. Joe kissed her. "We're not staying in bed," she said. He pulled her close. "I have a doctor's appointment," Ava said. "I know." "We have to be there at 1. I'm not staying in bed all morning." "The doctor's coming here. The press is going nuts." "Over what?" "Guess some paparazzi got pictures of you and Rose yesterday." "So?" "So we didn't tell the press that Ryan was engaged. Plus, nothing was said about you being pregnant." "Doesn't mean we can't go to the doctor," Ava said. "You sure you want to weed through the press?" "Think I can handle it," Ava said. She slid out of bed heading for the shower, and he slid in behind her. "Seriously," Ava joked. He kissed her neck. "The appointment is in 2 hours. Enough." He kissed her. They finally finished in the shower, then went downstairs to have breakfast.

Ava came in and saw Rose sitting on the patio with a coffee. "I thought they made up," Joe asked. "They did. She's getting the condo today." "And she's here why," he asked. "Tough cookie." He kissed Ava. "I have to leave," Ava said. "No we don't." Ava called the doctor. "I'll see you in an hour. Joe asked me to come to the house." "I'll be at the appointment. No need to come all the way out here," Ava said. "I'll see you at the office then." Ava hung up. Joe kissed her, pulling her to him. "What," Ava asked. He kissed her again. Ava went outside to check on Rose. "And how are you," Ava asked. "Good. I'm heading out in a few hours. I have to get the keys around 3," Rose said "You want to come with us," Ava asked. "Where?" "Doctor's appointment." "You two go. I want another baby picture while you're there," Rose said in a much better mood. Ava hugged her. "Lock up when you go." Rose nodded. She replied to another text from Ryan.

"Well, baby is perfect. Kicking up a storm and definitely growing," the doctor said. "Good." "Do we want to know," the ultrasound tech asked. "Yes," Joe said. "No," Ava said. "I promise I won't tell her," Joe said. "Funny." "You don't want to know," Joe asked. "You don't want a surprise?" "We want to know," Joe said. "Thinking that a lot of pink sounds right." "A girl," Joe asked. The doctor nodded. He kissed Ava. They printed off a few pictures. "I don't want anything showing," Ava said. "Gotcha," the doctor joked. They headed back to the house and when they arrived, Tiff was sitting on the front step. Ava got out of the car, walked past her and went inside, locking the door behind her.

"What the hell are you doing here," Joe asked. "I missed you." "Go home Tiff." "Why? Wifey mad?" "Get out of here." "I need to talk to you." "Go." "Joe, we need to talk." "Why? Because you feel like messing up my marriage even more?" "No. Because I love you." "I'm married. We're having a baby Tiff." "You were mine first," she said. He went to walk off and go into the house and Ava had the deadbolt on.

Ava went upstairs and threw enough clothes for a few days into a bag. She threw in a few extra sweaters, grabbed her toiletries and sat them at the front door. It was only a matter of time. He'd walk in and see it, and know he'd lost. All she heard was him telling Tiff off. "Why are you trying to mess with this?" "We've been together for years." "When I was touring Tiff. When I was home, we were done. You know it and so do I." "I need you." "You never had me. The woman inside that house is the woman I promised to be with forever. I put a ring on her finger and promised forever. It was what it was Tiff. It's done." "One last time." "No. Go home Tiff." He grabbed the spare key and walked inside and saw Ava sitting on the steps.

"Baby," Joe said. She looked at him. "Talk to me." She had the baby pictures in her hand. "Ava. Talk to me." "Why was she here?" "To see if I'd cave." "I can't do this. I can't sit here and pretend that her being here . . ." Joe kissed her and pulled her into his arms. "I love you. That's what I told her. I promised you forever. I promised that I'd be here no matter what, and that nobody will ever separate us." "You believe that?" He kissed her again. "Every word." He carried her up the steps to bed then kissed her again. He kissed her like it was the first, the last and every second in between. He made love to her like he did the night he married her the first time. They had a long bath together, relaxed outside, curled up by the fire, and he did everything in his power to get her mind off what had happened, including putting her things back when she fell asleep.

—w~~c~&*@@*~&~w~—

Rose settled into the furnished condo. She had her things put away, and had the satin sheets on the bed in the first two hours. She leaned back in the Jacuzzi tub and sipped her champagne she'd bought on the way there. She turned her phone on and saw message after message from Ryan. She called him back. "What's up," Rose asked. "Where are you?" "The condo." "I still don't know why you had to go there." "I'm doing this for me Ryan." "Baby, come over." "I'm in the Jacuzzi tub." "Rose." "Bubbles and champagne." "Directions?" "Nope." "I miss you." "I know. Just relaxing. Lit all the candles." "Address?" A smirk came across her face. "Rose, enough. I get the hint," Ryan said. She sent him the address along with a picture of her in the tub. He almost whimpered. "See you soon," she said. Rose hung up before Ryan could say another word.

Ryan was at the condo in less than a half-hour. He went up the elevator, then was at her door in minutes. Rose answered the door in a towel. "Hey," she said. He walked in and pulled her to him, kissing her and pinned her to the wall. "You tease me anymore, and you're so getting it," Ryan said. She slid out of his arms and went back into the tub, throwing the towel at him as she stepped in. He walked into the bathroom and saw her surrounded by bubbles. In minutes he was sliding in behind her. "So how was your day,"

Rose asked. "Would have been better waking up with you." "I told you." "I know. I had an idea though." "What's that?" "Vegas," Ryan said. "You're waiting whether you like it or not." "Why? Why should we wait?" "Because. You'd have been pissed if Ava and Joe did it. We're not going to Vegas." "I love you," Ryan said. "I know. That's why we're waiting." They relaxed in the tub and had some champagne, then Rose stepped out, blew out a few of the candles, and slid on her robe. She went into the TV room and slid in a DVD. He blew the rest of the candles out and wrapped himself in a towel, leaning on top of her on the sofa. "What do you want," Rose teased. He kissed her. "Nope." "Rose." He kissed her again and went for the belt of her robe. "Ryan." He kissed her again and slid the belt right off. "What is up with you," Rose asked. "You started it." Rose laughed. He kissed her again, then slid his arms around her. "Fine. I admit I was teasing," Rose said. He kissed her again and made love to her on the sofa.

Ava got up a few hours later, noticing all her things back where they'd been. Joe was out cold with his arms tight around her and his leg wrapped around her. The baby started kicking again. Ava went to get up and he rubbed her back. "Thought you were sleeping," Ava said. "And I felt the kick." After a while, the pain in her back went away. "Better," he asked. Ava nodded. He kissed her shoulder. "We should have dinner," Ava said. He grabbed the phone and called to get takeout Chinese. "I was thinking more like going and taking dinner to Rose's new place," Ava said. "Something tells me that Ryan has her talked out of it." "I'm not betting anymore." "I bet you a back massage." "Fine. I bet you a back massage she stays at that condo until the wedding," Ava said. "And I bet you Ryan has her talked into moving back in a day or two." "And when I win . . ." Joe kissed her. "When you win, I spend the entire day wherever you want." She smirked. "Within reason," she commented. "That leaves a lot." "And we do whatever I want," Ava said. "Ava." She got up, pulled her sweater and leggings on and went downstairs just as the food was showing up. She took it into the kitchen, grabbed her chopsticks, then turned the fireplace on and sat down. He came downstairs in nothing but his jeans, grabbed his food and curled up with her by the fireplace. "Ava." "Yes love." "I'm sorry for that earlier." "I heard what you said." "Outside?" Ava nodded. "Why didn't . . ." She kissed him. "Why didn't you tell me," he asked. "The fact that I never walked out should have been enough of a sign." "You know you drive me nuts right?" Ava nodded. They finished eating, then curled up and watched a movie.

———

Rose got up and went into the bedroom, slipping on a sweater and her shorts. "What are you doing?" "Walking you to your car," Rose said. "Rose." "I meant it." "You realize I couldn't sleep without you." "Guess you'll need a sleeping pill then," Rose said. "One night?" Rose shook her head. "Baby." She slid her sandals on. "You know you're driving me nuts." "I know. Remember it." She cleaned up in the kitchen. He tried distracting her, time and time again, and she still had no intention of letting him stay. "Just tonight." "No. You're going back to the house," Rose said. He kissed her, pinning her to the wall by her front door. "You're still going home." He kissed her again, then made love to her again. "Ryan," Rose said. "Come with me." She shook her head. "Please." "Ryan, go home." "Please come back to the house with me." "I'm staying here." "Nothing I can do to talk you out of it?" Rose shook her head. "I'll miss you." "I'll miss you too." "Rose," he said. She kissed him goodbye. He walked back down to his car, then headed home.

CHAPTER 13

Ava and Joe got up the next morning, went for their morning run past the paparazzi, came home, then relaxed outside by the pool. "I'm calling and finding out who won the bet," Ava said. "You're gonna gloat." Ava nodded. Joe kissed her. He slid the phone from her hand. "What?" "Later," he said. He kissed her and wrapped his arms around her then got up and headed into the pool. "I'm still calling her," Ava said. He pulled her to him and fell into the deep end. They splashed around for a while, then Ava pulled herself up on the edge of the pool. "You know at some point, the pool is going to need more steps," Ava said. He kissed her. "I know."

Ava finally called Rose. "So how goes the condo life," Ava asked. "Good. It's nice and quiet." "And?" "It worked. The man is begging." "And," Ava asked. "He's waiting. This is way too much fun." "You're welcome." "He's probably scared I'm going to do it to get back at him." "Which was the whole reason right?" "Exactly. What you up to tonight," Rose asked. "Babysitting an overgrown kid I know." "He letting you out on good behavior?" "End of the week. I have to do some writing at some point." "Call me. We'll have girls night," Rose said. "I will. Have fun. No playing with matches." Rose laughed and hung up.

Ava hung up and Joe was practically undoing her bikini top. "What is up with you?" "I know you win." "Oh hell yeah I did," Ava said. He kissed her, pulling the top completely off, then went for the bottoms. "Not out here." "Why? Who's going to see?" Joe kissed her again and they made love on the chaise. They headed inside, then curled up together on the sofa. Joe's phone was ringing off the hook when they came inside. "What's up," Joe asked. "Studio." "Now?" "I'm coming to pick you up," Ryan said. "What time are we back?" "Midnight latest." "Dude," Joe said. "She's driving me nuts. I have to do something." "Fine. I'll see you in a couple minutes." Joe was half way up the steps with Ava by the time he hung up. "What are you doing," Ava asked. They got to the bedroom and he leaned her onto the bed. "He's on his way here," Joe joked. They had sex again. It was fast, quick and intense as hell. He had a quick shower, then pulled on his boxers, his jeans and a t-shirt. "I'll call you when I can get him to take a break," Joe said. "Hey." "What?" She looked over at him. He kissed her. "And it's a girl free environment," Joe promised. Ava nodded. He kissed her again as Ava got up. She pulled on her cover-up for her swimsuit, then went downstairs. Ryan showed just as they were coming downstairs. "Hey you two," Ryan said. "Hey yourself bud. What's up," Joe said. "Rose is driving me bananas, but other than that." "Call me okay," Ava said as Joe kissed her. He kissed her again, then left with Ryan.

"Look at you two," Ryan said. "We're good." "I heard that Tiff was over here." "Causing shit as usual. How's things with you and Rose," Joe asked. "She got some condo. I swear, it's like she's turned into a totally different woman." "Only one way to win her back," Joe said. "I know. I was over there last night. It's almost like dating. She made me go home . . . . alone." "Gotta give it to her. She's definitely holding her ground." "It's almost a turn-on," Ryan said. Joe laughed. "I know. Either Rose rubbed off on Ava, or the other way around," Ryan commented. They pulled into the studio and walked in to find Brad playing the piano.

"What's up," Joe asked. "Nothin. How are things with the two party animals," Brad asked. "Funny," Joe said. "I heard that Tiff showed. What happened," Brad asked. He caught Brad up on the whole story. "She was causing shit. I finally coaxed her into leaving," Joe said. "And the paparazzi got a shot of the two of you." "Who?" "You and Tiff." Brad handed him the magazine. There it was on the cover. A shot of Tiff on the verge of kissing him. "She won't see this," Joe said. "Thought there was nothing to worry about," Ryan said. "Keep your mind on your own bullshit Ryan." Joe walked off. "What's going on with you," Brad asked. "Cassidy." "Still? I figured after you and Rose got engaged that it was done." "Until she showed up at the house." "Tell me you didn't do what I think you did," Brad asked. "I'm human. I make a million mistakes." "You know she'll walk away for good. Why would you even chance it?" "It was a mistake. Things are fine now." "You better hope so. She's hanging with Danielle today," Brad said knowing that nothing could break the bond he had with Danielle.

Joe called Ava hoping to catch her before she left the house. "You just left. How could you miss me already," Ava teased. "Are you going out at all today?" "Groceries. Why?" "There's a picture in one of the tabloids." "Of?" "You don't want to know." "Hotel or front porch." "Porch. I called security to make sure it doesn't happen again." "How bad is it?" "It was when she tried to kiss me." "Fine," Ava said. "What?" "You told me the truth. At least you didn't hide it." "Baby, if it's going to get you upset." "I'll order the groceries in." "I love you," Joe said. "I know you do. Can't remember why, but I love you too." "Funny." "When you get home, wake me up alright," Ava asked. "I'll definitely wake you up." "You know what I mean." "And you know exactly what I mean," he teased. Joe breathed a sigh of relief then hung up a few minutes later then headed back into the studio.

Ava called Rose. "What you up to?" "Hanging out with Danielle. Did you want to come over?" "No. Why don't you two come by here? I'm sort of in a non—public mood today," Ava said. "What happened?" "Just not going out today. If you two want to come over, let me know." Ava hung up. She wanted them here, but saying what had happened over the phone, wasn't going to work. She had a hot shower, then went and sat outside and tried to get some writing done. By the time it got close to dinner, Ava was starving. She made something quick, then turned on the gas fireplace and an old romantic movie, and finished up the last of the writing she needed done. She leaned back and watched the end of the movie and watched a little TV. There was something about them at a bar downtown. Ava turned it off then went upstairs, slid on her black satin nightgown, and crawled into bed.

Joe made it home just before midnight. He walked upstairs, washed up, then slid into bed with Ava. She felt his arm wrap around her and the baby kicked. He kissed her neck. "How did it go," Ava asked half-asleep. "We finished at ten. We went to Ryan's for a drink or two." "Oh really?" He kissed her shoulder. "So how was Brass?" "Where?" Ava got up and went downstairs. She grabbed a glass of flat ginger ale. "What are you talking about," Joe asked. Ava turned on the TV to the tabloid show. "We caught Joe Morgan, Ryan Lee, and Brad Martin coming out of Brass. So did you enjoy the show tonight guys? 'Bachelor party'." Joe turned the TV off. Ava walked back up the steps and went back to bed. He sat down on the sofa. He waited a few minutes, then went upstairs. "Babe, we took Ryan instead of throwing him a bachelor party." "After what was in that tabloid, you thought that was a good idea? Wow," Ava said. "Ava, we just went for a drink or two." "And got your picture shot by every paparazzi in town." "Ava, it happened. You have to know that nothing else happened," Joe pleaded. "Fine." Ava went back to sleep. He watched her. He tried to sleep, tossing and turning all night. Around 4am, he gave up. He went downstairs and tried to work on some music. He got half way into a song, then couldn't figure out how to end it. He replayed it over and over, but was stumped. He walked back upstairs and Ava was still asleep. He slid back into bed, wrapping his arm around her and cuddling up next to her. Ava slept through it.

Ava got up at nine, went for a run, intentionally, then came home. She had breakfast, then the delivery showed for the baby furniture. Within about an hour, the furniture was put together. Ava sat down in the beautiful new rocking chair. All of this was really happening. After an hour of crying and smiling, and talking to the baby, Ava took the bedding down and washed it. By the time Joe woke up, the bedroom was completely put together, shy of the paint.

Joe heard rustling in the other bedroom, or at least where they'd thought of making the baby's room. He slid his robe on and walked in. Ava was curled up on the rocking chair. "All this without me," he asked. "The delivery guys put it together." "It's perfect." "I know." Ava went to walk past him. "I'm sorry," he said. "You could have at least warned me. I can get texts remember?" "It was a last minute thing." "I'm sure it was." Ava walked past him, then went and hopped in the shower. She stepped out as he was walking in. "You seriously going to keep avoiding me," Joe asked. "I don't want to have this discussion again. I didn't want to see what I saw. I don't want to have a picture of you and her stuck in my brain, but I do. I kept dreaming last night that she won you back. That you walked away from me. You know what, if you do, then go now." Ava wrapped a towel around herself and walked into the bedroom. "I'm not going anywhere," Joe said. Ava got changed. "Babe." She pulled her hair into a ponytail, put on some makeup and walked out. Within minutes she was out of the driveway.

Ryan knocked on Rose's door. "Hey," Ryan said. "Hey yourself." "What are you up to today?" "Why?" "Thought we could go out for the day. You and me. Wherever you want." "How about Brass," Rose asked. He looked at her. Pissed off was an understatement. "Bachelor party. We were there for an hour." "Then I guess I get a bachelorette party." "If you want one," Ryan said. "Good." "Rose, come with me." "Where?" "We'll go for a drive," Ryan asked. She put on her sunglasses, grabbed her purse and locked the door.

Ava drove until she had to stop. She stopped at the mall and had lunch, shopped a bit, then thought of checking into a hotel. She turned her phone on. "You have eight new messages." Ava went through message after message from Joe. "Where are you? Ava, just call me back." "I'm worried about you. Ava, where are you?" "Baby, I know you're pissed off, but taking off like this. You're scaring me." Ava deleted the messages. Not even a minute later, he called. "What," Ava asked. "Where are you?" "Funny. I didn't need to call you when you decided not to bother coming home until whatever time in the morning," Ava said. "This is ridiculous. Where are you?" "Downtown." "I'm leaving. Meet me at the Union Station hotel." "Why?" "Ava, enough. I 'm on my way." "I didn't say I wanted you here." He hung up. Ava went and checked into the hotel. She got her key and went upstairs.

Joe called a half hour later. "Where are you?" She gave him the room number and he headed upstairs. "What the hell were you thinking," Joe asked. "Giving you time to leave." "Ava, I went out with them. We went to the stupid bar. Nothing else happened." "I hate watching over my shoulder to make sure you aren't doing something wrong. That picture won't get out of my damn head." "And you think walking away is going to fix that?" "I can raise the baby alone Joe." "No. She's our baby. I love you. One night and a stupid picture doesn't change that." "It does if she's who you want Joe." "Is that what you seriously think? Why would I want her Ava? Why?" "Because I know you do." "I want you to look me in the eye and tell me you don't think I love you. Do it." "Fact is, you want that too." "I have that. I have the one woman who can be wild and crazy with me, and make love to me the next in my arms right now. That's who I want Ava. I want my wife." "But . . ." He kissed her. He held her close and kissed her until he knew that the insecurity was gone for the night. "You gonna come home," he asked. "I'll follow you." "Brad took your car back." "He came with you?" Joe nodded. They went downstairs and were surrounded by paparazzi. He checked her out of the room, and they headed home. The only picture the paparazzi got that night was him kissing Ava.

———

"What are we doing here," Rose asked. "I had an idea." "Ryan, don't bring up the quickie marriage thing again." He kissed her. "We have two weeks left. I can't wait that long." "So we move the date up," Rose said. "To now." "You know how crazy this is?" Ryan kissed her. "No." "Rose, come on." "No. Turn the car around Ryan." He pulled into a fancy hotel off the highway and checked them in. "Ryan," Rose said. He grabbed her hand and pulled her into the elevator with him. He had her pinned in the corner kissing her in minutes. They stepped off the elevator and he slipped the key into the main suite of the hotel. "Ryan, really. Let's just go home." "I'm keeping you hostage," he teased. "I bet. With room service and all." He kissed her again, picking her up and carrying her to the bed. Within a few minutes, their clothes were on the floor, and they were making love. After, he pulled her into his arms. "You know you're stuck with me tonight," Ryan said. "No, we're getting changed and I'm going home." "Rose, come on." "I told you." He kissed her neck, then down her shoulder. "I'm still going back to my place, and you're going home," Rose said. "One night." "No." "Why?" "Don't ask me that. You know the answer Ryan." "Please." "The amount of crap that you've caused, and you ask me anyway? Remember something alright? Remember what you did Ryan, and how easy it is for me to walk right out the door and not come back," Rose said. "I know. I'd just rather have you in my arms all night." "Ryan." "At some point, you know you're going to have to forgive me." "And at some point you're going to realize that having me in your life at all is a privilege," Rose said. She slipped out of the bed, hopping into the shower.

Rose called as Ava and Joe were passing the hotel. "What's up?" "Where are you?" "Driving home." "Where?" Ava gave her the GPS location. "Stop at the hotel. I need a ride back." "How did you get out here then," Joe asked. "I'll meet you in the lobby," Rose said. "Why are you whispering," Ava asked. Rose hung up. About ten minutes later, they were pulling up. "You know he's gonna kick my ass if he knows we drove her home," Joe said knowing he had no choice in the matter. "And I'll kick it if you don't," Ava said. When the car stopped Joe kissed Ava. Rose hopped in. They left and headed back towards the driveway. "Tell me you didn't ditch him when he was sleeping," Joe asked already knowing the answer. "He was trying to talk me into eloping." "Can't blame the guy for trying to do something nice," Joe said. "Darling sweetheart love of my life, this has nothing to do with you," Ava teased. "The man loves you. Who wouldn't want to rush and get married," he asked. Joe slid his hand in Ava's. "What are you trying to say," Rose asked. "Ignore him," Ava said. "Did you two? Ava, did you and Joe," Rose asked. "A week or two before." "Are you kidding me," Rose asked. "No. We went to Vegas to check out the location for the video shoot. Ava came with us, and there you go," Joe said smiling. "Are you serious? You got married without me," Rose asked. "Then we got married in Cabo," Ava said. "You little shit." "It was supposed to be a secret," Ava said playfully smacking Joe's arm. "Fact is, he loves you. You want to get hitched then have a party do it. You want the big fancy wedding, then do what you want to do. He loves you. He wants you to be happy," Joe said determined to voice his opinion. "He's waiting. Even if I have to keep him at arm's length until the wedding, we're having the wedding," Rose said. About a half hour later, they pulled in to Rose's condo. They dropped Rose off, then headed home.

"You know he's seriously kicking my butt when he finds out we drove her home," Joe said. They pulled into the driveway and Ava slid into his lap. "Your butt's going to be busy. He can't kick it." "Ava, seriously. He's going to be royally pissed." Ava kissed him. Just as Joe was about to hop out of the car, his phone rang. "What's up," Joe asked. "You drove her home didn't you," Ryan asked. "We were driving back. She asked." "I almost had her talked into it," Ryan said. "She's more stubborn than Ava. She wasn't going to go along with it." "She make it home okay at least?" "Yeah. We just pulled into our place." "Talk to you tomorrow." Ryan hung up. Ava hopped out of the car and went inside. She walked in and checked the voicemail. "Joe, it's Tiff. I'm sorry. I know I said I wouldn't call, but I need you. Something happened. I'm at the hospital." He walked in and heard it from the front door. Ava walked upstairs and drew herself a hot bath, locking the bathroom door. She slid in her iPod and leaned back. Part of her actually wished she could have a drink.

Joe grabbed the key from the hall closet and gave her a little time to calm down, then went in. She was crying. "Ava." "Just go." "I'm not going," Joe said. "She *needs* you." "Stop it." "Just go Joe. She's going to call and bug you until you do. And tell me again how she got the home phone number?" "Ava." "You gave the number to her didn't you?" "No." "Liar." "I'm not leaving," he said. Ava got up, grabbing a towel and wrapped herself with it. The baby gave one hell of a kick. "Go." She pulled on her sweater and her leggings and climbed into the bed. He slid in with her. "Joe." "I'm staying where I belong," he said. The phone rang again. He ignored it. "Joe, it's Tiff. Please call me back. I'm at the hospital. Room 286. Please." Ava picked up the phone. "One sec." She handed it to Joe.

"What," Joe asked. "I had a miscarriage," Tiff said. "Has nothing to do with me." "You're the only person I know to call." "Call your mom." "Please. They won't let me go home alone." "Oh hell no. Don't even think it." "Just for tonight." "No." "Please," she begged. He hung up. No way was he jeopardizing his marriage even more. "What," Ava asked. "I'm not leaving this house." "What did she want," Ava asked. "She needs to have someone take her home and stay with her or she can't leave. I'm not going." "How did she get the house number?" "Ava, please." She got up and went into the guest room, locking the door.

The next morning, Ava got up and Joe was gone and so was his car and cell phone. Ava showered, then left to go for her run, only to be surrounded by paparazzi as soon as she left the street. Ava ran through them, then made her way to Ryan's place. "You ran all the way here," he asked. "They were surrounding me," Ava replied. "I'm taking you home." "Where is he," Ava asked. "We'll call him on the way." They left and he dropped her off at the house. The house was almost quiet except for the humming noise of the refrigerator. Ryan left.

Ryan called Joe the minute he got out of ear shot. "Where are you?" "What do you mean where am I?" "I just took Ava home. The press is all over the front gate." "Damn it." "Where are you?" "I took Tiff home from the hospital." "You didn't. Tell me you didn't," Ryan said. "I slept on the sofa. She was pumped full of drugs before she left. I slept like shit, but I'm on my way home." "Ava's upset," Ryan said warning him. "She told me to go." "Buddy, she is really really upset." Joe hung up.

A half-hour or so later, Joe walked in the door. The house was quiet. Ava was outside on the patio. "Hey beautiful," Joe said. He walked outside and went to kiss her and she turned her face. "Ava." She got up and went and got in the pool. She slid onto the floating chair and put her sunglasses on, closing her eyes. A minute later, she was being splashed with water. He popped up beside her. "You told me to go," Joe said. Ava didn't say a word. He pulled her sunglasses off. "Talk to me." She wiped the tears away, then slid back into the pool. She slipped under the water, then surfaced beside the steps. She got out, wrapped herself in a towel and walked back into the house. He hopped out, grabbing his jeans and shirt, and went inside. "Ava, talk to me." "Did you fuck her," Ava asked. "No." "Don't lie to me." "I slept on the damn sofa. She was pumped full of pain meds when she left. She didn't even know I left this morning." Ava walked upstairs. "Don't follow me." He was 3 steps behind her instead of 2. "I didn't do anything." "I woke up alone. You didn't even leave a note," Ava said. "Babe, you told me to go. I went. That's all that happened." "Then why do I think you are completely full . . . ." He kissed her and knocked her to the bed. "Would you stop," Ava said. "I went over there and got her out of the hospital. That's all. I tried calling you last night. You always have your phone off, and I couldn't exactly go in and wake you up with the door locked." "Never stopped you before." "I don't want to fight with you anymore. She's history Ava. Ancient history." "And when she shows up here?" "She's not going to. She's going home." "I don't believe that for a second." "Only woman I want to be irresistible to is you. Only woman I want in my arms is you. Only woman I want to make love to until the end of time is and always will be you." "I know but . . . ," Ava said. He kissed her and slid his arms around her.

"I don't want to fight with you either," Ava said. "Then don't. I know the singing thing makes you nervous. The fact that for years I could do whatever I wanted makes you worry that I'm going to do something stupid. Think of things this way. When I finish on stage, the only woman I want to see is you. I want to talk to you and feel you in my arms and kiss you until the sun comes back up." "I don't want to worry about it. I hate the feeling that something is going on behind my back." "Then don't worry. Just remember who I come home to every night. Remember who you married in front of everyone." Joe kissed her and for the first time in days, the worry was gone.

Rose got up, ran around and did pre-wedding errands, then stopped at Ryan's house. She recognized the car in the driveway. She walked in and saw him talking to someone in the kitchen. The second he heard the clicking of her heels on the hardwood he turned around. Ryan walked over to Rose pulling her to him and kissed her. "Well hello to you too," Rose said as they finally came up for air. "How was your day?" "Long. They wanted to know what kind of cake we wanted. Couldn't choose," she said. "I bet." Ryan kissed her again, then took her hand and led her into the kitchen. "Mom, you remember Rose." "Nice seeing you again," she said She gave Rose a hug hello. "So are you sure there's nothing I can help with," his mom asked. "All I want is for you to show up. You don't have to do anything," Ryan said. "Let me do something." "You can help me with the food choices. It's narrowed down, but we can't decide," Rose said. "Tie-breaker. Nice," Ryan teased. "Everything else is done and I have a dress put aside for you at the dress shop. You just have to try it on," Rose said. "See I told you she thought of everything," Ryan said wrapping his arm around Rose. "You two are too good to me." "For raising this one, I think you deserve it," Rose said. Ryan kissed Rose's cheek and held her in his arms. "I'll leave you two alone then. We're checking into the Union Station hotel like you said," his mom said. "Good. I'll see you Friday next week," Ryan said. The wedding was coming up that fast. He walked his mom to the door.

Rose sat down at the table and went through the food choices. After nixing the messy stuff, she had it narrowed down to three, and they could only choose two. "Why do you look panicked," Ryan asked. "We need to call them by six." He picked two of the items she'd narrowed down. Rose shot an email to the caterer. "You going to relax at any point," he asked. "One last thing for today, then we can relax." "Which would be what beautiful," Ryan asked. "Cake." "I say chocolate." "It's either chocolate or strawberry shortcake like." "No wonder you had trouble choosing," he teased. "Exactly." "Combo of the two." Rose shot an email to the cake shop. "Top layer strawberry, middle layer chocolate?" He nodded. She sent an email back. "Everything done now?" "Have to pick my dress up tomorrow.

Ava got her dress today. I have to make sure they have the flowers, and that's it until the day of." Ryan sat down beside her. "What?" "We're going out tonight. You and me," he said. "You tried that last night." "I won't bring up the eloping thing again." "Where?" "The lake." "You think so do you?" He leaned forward and kissed her, pulling her into his lap. "I know so," Ryan said. "I'm not staying the night." "I know." "Finally gave up?" "Know when to quit is all." He kissed her again. "About time," Rose said. He stood up and carried her upstairs. In what seemed like minutes, they were on his bed.

They kissed and made out like teenagers. They teased and taunted each other, then snuggled and watched TV. "This is the part I miss," Ryan said. "I know." "Missed me didn't you?" "A little. You do know why I am doing this right," Rose asked. "I know. I'm not going to fight you on it anymore." They watched a movie, then had a nap and headed to dinner.

CHAPTER 14

Rose and Ryan's wedding day finally came. Rose had a massage in the morning with Ava, then they got their hair and nails done. They came back to Ava and Joe's house and Ava went and got changed while Rose had some lunch. Ava went upstairs to pull on her dress and Joe was there. "Thought you were going golfing with the guys," she asked. "Had a better idea." "Which is?" He pulled her into his arms and kissed her. "You realize that Rose is downstairs, and Rachel and Carrie are on their way here." He kissed her again and locked the bedroom door. "Missed me?" He nodded and kissed her again. They had that fast, intense, leg shaking sex that he'd been thinking about all morning. He kissed her as he pulled her to her feet. "I'll see you at the church," he said kissing her goodbye. "Go." He got dressed with Ava helping him with the vest, and with another earth shattering kiss he headed out. Ava pulled on her dress, touching up her lipstick, then came downstairs barefoot. "You look great," Rose said. "Nice try, but thanks. You done lunch," Ava asked. Rose nodded. Just as they were about to head upstairs, Rachel and Carrie showed with Rose's mom. The ladies chatted a bit, then Ava went and helped Rose into her dress. The flowers arrived, including a dozen pale pink roses from Ryan with a note that had Rose all weepy-eyed:

> See you soon. Love you. I can't wait to marry you. Never knew what forever was until I saw it in your eyes. Never knew how forever felt until I felt your hand in mine. Never wanted forever more until I kissed your lips, and now you're mine forever more.

Rose started tearing up and Ava handed her a tissue. Rose had the dress on, then saw herself in Ava's full length mirror. "You okay," Ava asked. "It's really happening isn't it?" Ava nodded. "I'm marrying him." "Now we're almost like family," Ava said. "Always have been." "Who would've thought when we were in that stupid resort, that this would be happening?" Rose laughed. Ava helped her with her shoes and they headed downstairs. Carrie and Rachel were stunned. "You look beautiful," Rachel said. The photographer went through a pile of shots, then they all left and headed to the church in the limo.

"You sure she's going to show," Ryan asked. "Ava told me she got the flowers and the note. Trust me. She couldn't wait to get the dress on." Ryan laughed. "You have the rings," Ryan asked. Brad nodded. "What am I missing?" "She's meeting you at the end of the altar," Brad teased. They laughed. Ryan heard the music starting. He walked his mom down the aisle. Then Danielle and Brad came down, then Joe and Ava. Then Rose came down the aisle with her Dad. Ryan was trying to hold back tears. Rose got to him and wiped his tears away. "You look beautiful," he said. She smiled. "Pretty handsome yourself."

The wedding went off without a hitch. After, they headed over to the country club. The photographer did his pictures, then they had the reception. There were speeches, then dinner, then Rose and Ryan had their first dance. Once it was done, and the dance with his mom and her with her dad was finished, Ryan sang one or two songs with the guys. They sang 'The day before you' and 'The day you kissed me' and Ryan came back over to Rose. He pulled her into his arms and danced with her. The cake was perfect, and he managed to sneak her away from everyone for a quick moment. "What," Rose asked. He kissed her. "I know what you're thinking," Rose said. "What's that?" "Waking up together." "That too. I got you something." He pulled a box from his pocket and handed it to her. She opened it and found a charm bracelet with a diamond heart pendant on it. "This is beautiful." "And, we're going to Hawaii," Ryan said. Rose smiled. "Well, then you can open this," she said handing him a box. "What's this?" "Open." He found a white stick. He looked at it and it said pregnant. He kissed Rose. "When?" "Found out yesterday." He kissed her again. "Did you tell Ava?" She shook her head. Ryan pulled her into his arms and practically spun her in a circle. He kissed her, then they went inside. They danced the rest of the night, then left close to midnight. Rachel caught the bouquet. Rose hadn't noticed and either had Ava, that Rachel had brought James as her date. Carrie had shown up with Jake.

Ava went to leave with Joe and Jake stopped her. "What are you doing here," Ava asked. "I'm here with Carrie." "Nice." "I need to talk to you," he said. "I'm heading home. Jake, you know my husband Joe right," Ava asked as Joe white-knuckled her hand. They knew each other alright. "I'll meet you outside. I'm going to say goodbye to Brad," Joe said. He kissed Ava with one of those goose bump kisses, then headed off. "What's so important," Ava asked. "James needs to talk to you." "I don't really give a crap what he wants." "Five minutes." "No." Ava went to walk off and James was in front of her. "What do you want James," Ava asked trying to calm down the kicking baby in her stomach. "You know why I was so upset when you two got married," James asked. "Mad that I chose him?" "And the fact that he isn't exactly the most faithful." "I can handle my own marriage thanks," Ava said. Ava walked off and found Joe. "Ready," he asked. Ava nodded and he kissed her. They left, walking past Jake and James.

"So what did he want," Joe asked once they were on the road. "To warn me that you're a serial cheater." "And?" "Told them to mind their own business." "You don't believe them right?" "For now," Ava said. They pulled into the driveway of the house. "Ava, you trust me right?" "Until there's a reason not to." He kissed her. "Never ever happening." "I know. You'd be lost without me," Ava teased. They got out of the car and headed inside. They went upstairs, and Ava slid her dress off, revealing the pale pink satin teddy that he didn't know she'd bought. "Full of surprises aren't you?" Ava smirked. "What else are you hiding," he asked. She kissed him. "What?" "I love you." "No more fighting?" "Unless it's tickle fights." He held her in his arms. "I had an idea while we were there," Joe said. "What?" "Me and you on a beach somewhere, just us. Nobody else around." "What are you hinting at?" "Nothin." "Liar." "I found a place in the Caribbean. It's a little island. Only enough space for 20 people. I booked a beach cottage for us for a few days." "Another honeymoon?" He kissed her. "Vacation before the baby comes." "You sure we can?" "The doctor said yes." "Sneaking around behind my back again," Ava joked. "Only for good stuff, I promise." "When are we going?" "Sunday. She's coming to do one last ultrasound before we go just to be sure."

Two days passed and the doctor ensured both of them that the baby was perfect. They left for their trip. Three days of calm, quiet, no phones, internet or TV, and just each other. It was exactly what they needed. Joe even managed to write another song. They headed back after a few days of fun and sun, and everything went back to normal.

———ᴡ•ᴄᴇʏᴏᴏᴋᴇᴅ•ᴡ———

Ava was only a month from her due date. They'd finally gone out for dinner all together, before the guys headed back out on tour. "You sure we can't put it off until after," Joe asked. "You won't want to go after either," Brad said. "There's never a perfect time Joe," Ryan said. "Fine. If I get a call before a show, we're coming back." "I know," Ryan said. "I want to be there." "You're so past excited aren't you," Ryan asked. "Like a kid at Christmas." The baby started kicking again. They chatted through dinner, then everyone headed home. The guys had 48 hours left and they were leaving for the first 3 shows.

"You could come to the shows," Joe said. He was trying to talk Ava into it. "I know you want me there, and I want to be there, but they said no flying." "The first two are 8 hours away." "And you can fly back if you need to." He kissed her. "I don't want to be away that long." "Baby, you'll be fine. We can talk before and after. You can send me a text during if you need to." "If anything happens, you have to call me." "I will. Stop worrying." They slid into bed and he curled up next to her. He rubbed her back, then kissed her neck, her shoulder. "I'm going to miss you too," Ava said. "We've gone to every appointment together." "It's fine. She's fine." They curled up together and a short while later, were out cold.

The guys finally left. Ava, Rose and Danielle had a slumber party the first night. "You okay baby," Joe asked via the umpteenth call that day. Joe was still worried. "I'm fine. I'm here with Rose and Danielle." "I love you." "Love you more. Sing like you're singing to me." "Kiss the baby for me." "I will," Ava said. She had to admit, the phone call caused one big smile. Rose chatted with Ryan, Danielle with Brad. Then the girls watched the end of their movie. They all fell asleep, then Ava went upstairs and curled up in her bed. Joe called as soon as the show was done. "Would you stop worrying?" "Where are you?" "Upstairs in bed. Curled up with your pillow." "Thanks for that earlier," Joe said. "You're welcome. How did it go?" "Everyone wanted our song." "It can wait." The baby started kicking again. "She's awake." Joe sang to her. The baby settled down. "You know you're going to be doing that every night to calm her down." "I plan on it," he joked. "Where you guys going now?" "Heading to Atlanta. I'll be home Sunday." "I slipped something in your bag." "Where?" "Outside pocket." He grabbed it from the bag. It was the baby picture. "What's the other thing attached to it," he asked. "Open the envelope." He opened it and found one of the pictures someone had taken of them together when they had just got married. "You look beautiful." "Thought it would remind you," Ava said. He flipped it over and saw what she wrote:

Love you forever
From the very first day
When I realized forever
Was ours to stay
Love you forever
Until the end of time
Forever
Until the end of time.

"I love you too." "Go get some sleep baby," Ava said. "I still miss you." "I miss you too." "I'm gonna see if we can fly back tomorrow after the concert." "You don't need to Joe." "Yeah I do." They chatted a while longer, then headed to bed.

Ava woke up the next morning and the pain was totally different. The baby wasn't kicking. Ava called Rose. "On my way."

They were at the hospital not even 20 minutes later. "Driving like you're in a race wasn't necessary," Ava said. "Sit in the chair," Rose replied. They took Ava into a private room. Her doctor popped in. "So I see the little one's a little eager to see Mommy." "Just feels totally different," Ava said. The doctor checked her over. "The baby's pressing on your back. Trying to figure out how to make itself more room. Go home. Complete bed rest. No stress. If anything happens, call me and I'll pop over." Ava nodded. They got back to the car. "Don't tell him," Ava said. "I won't as long as you do what the doctor told you," Rose replied.

Joe came back with the guys. "How's my baby," he asked as he leaned down to the sofa to kiss Ava. "We're fine." "I was worried about you two," Joe said. "I knew you would be." "I figured you'd be out shopping for baby stuff by now," he teased. "Back's sore." He curled up with her rubbing her back. For the days that he was there, there was no pain, no aching. The days that he wasn't were bad.

⎯⎯⎯⎯⎯⎯

Finally a week or two later, Ava called Rose. "Come now." Rose was there in minutes. They took off for the hospital. "You're definitely in labor," the doctor said. Rose called Joe. "We're almost back. We'll meet you there." Rose was excited for them, but knowing she'd get to see the baby being born when hers wasn't too far off scared the crap out of her. Two hours passed and security was posted at her door. "I could so go for a slushie right now," Ava joked. "Nice. You laugh through this," Rose asked. "High pain tolerance. James remember?" "Not funny." The doctor came back in. "You're almost there. Another hour," she said after checking Ava again. A half-hour passed. Finally Rose heard Ryan in the hall. "Get him the hell in here," Ava said. Rose went into the hall. "Joe." He ran towards Rose and into the room. "Babe," Joe said "Where have you been?" "Got detained at the stupid airport. You okay?" "No." He slid onto the bed behind Ava and rubbed her back for her. "Better?" Ava nodded. "How did you ever learn that," Ava asked. "Sisters." Ava's fingers linked with his. "We can do this. You are going to be the greatest mom in the world," Joe said. The doctor came back in and Rose went out into the hall with Ryan.

Twenty minutes later, Rose heard the baby crying. "Welcome to Grace Dawn Rose." Rose walked into the room with Ryan. "Seriously," Rose asked. Ava nodded. Joe was crying. Ava was crying. Baby Grace was crying. Ava wouldn't let her go for a second, and Joe wouldn't let go of Ava. Ryan pulled out a camera and took a few pictures. "I still can't believe you made me a Dad," Joe said. "She's perfect." "I can't believe you two. Ava was laughing during labor, you two are like the darn happy team," Rose joked. "She knew Daddy was coming. She just wanted to beat him to bed," Joe joked. He kissed Ava and Ryan snapped another picture or two. Ava handed her to Rose. "Get used to it Godmother." Rose was smiling. Joe kissed Ava. "You're still beautiful. Even after all of that," Joe said. He kissed her again. "You know that's how you two got this one," Ryan teased. They all laughed. Rose slipped the baby into Ryan's arms. He sat down in the chair with her, then started singing amazing grace. Joe chimed in with him. Brad snuck in and joined them. He gave Ava and Joe a hug. Ava got all teary. "If she doesn't turn into a singer or something musical, I think I might be stunned," Brad said. "Oh she will. Going to get her a guitar once she can walk," Joe joked. Ava looked over at Rose who was on the phone with Ava's mom. "She's doing fine. It's a girl. Grace Dawn Rose . . . one minute." She handed the phone to Ava. "Hi mom. I'm fine. Yes he's here. She's absolutely beautiful. I will. He's right here." Ryan handed the baby to Brad. "She is beautiful considering," Brad joked motioning towards Joe. "Not funny," Joe said. He paused his call with Ava's mom to give Brad the finger. "I know. I promised. See you tomorrow." He hung up. "Tomorrow?" "She's coming." Ava leaned her head back against Joe's chest. Joe kissed her again. Brad slid the baby back into Ava's arms. Grace cried for a split second. Everyone headed out leaving Joe, Ava and baby Grace alone. "You know I'm not moving a muscle. They'll have to drag me out," Joe said. "You're not leaving." The nurse came in a few minutes later. "Did you want to try feeding her?"

~~◦◦◦◦◦◦~~

A half-hour or so later, Joe was more in love than ever. The baby was full and back asleep in Ava's arms. The nurse came in and changed the baby, then tucked her into the bassinette beside Ava's bed. "I brought an extra blanket for you two. There are a few things out here. Did you want me to bring them in?" Ava nodded. There were roses, balloons, gifts, and a huge teddy bear which Ava knew had to be from Rose. "Happy," Joe asked. Ava nodded. "How was the concert?" "Pictured you front row with her in your arms," Joe said. He kissed Ava. A half-hour later, they were both out cold.

Joe woke up and Ava was in the chair with Grace. "Morning," he said. Ava smiled. He got up and walked over to her. Grace was just falling back asleep. Ava slowly got up, then slid her into her bassinette. He kissed Ava. "We made a beautiful little girl." "That we definitely did." He wrapped his arms around her, and Ava wrapped her arms around him. "I love you. Did I tell you that today?" "Not for a few hours." He kissed her again. The nurse came in. "How are you doing today?" "Sore, but Grace's little face makes me forget it," Ava said. "She doing okay," the nurse asked. "She ate, burped, then fell asleep." "You sure you don't have any other kids," the nurse joked. "Nope." "We will," Joe teased. Ava looked at Joe. "Either that or we're going to be practicing for a while," he whispered in her ear. Ava slid back into bed and Joe curled up with her. "I'll check on you in a few hours," the nurse said leaving them be. They were both back asleep in a little while.

Around ten, Grace was awake. Ava fed her and Joe walked around with her in the room. Rose and Ryan came by, Brad and Danielle, then Ava's mom and dad showed. They visited for a while, then the doctor came in. "So how are you?" "Tired," Ava said. "Get used to it," her mom joked. Grace woke up and Ava fed her, then handed her off to her mom. Her dad snapped pictures. "So I think we might be able to send you home today if you're up to it," the doctor said. "Perfect," her mom replied. Ava grabbed an outfit from the bag she'd brought with her. "You would," Joe teased. She slid a little lilac sleeper on Grace, wrapped her up in her pink blanket, then they headed home.

Ava stepped inside and took a sleeping Grace to her crib. Joe followed her. He turned on the mobile, the monitor, then slid the sheet over Grace. "She's an angel. You know that right," Joe said. Ava nodded. He wrapped his arms around Ava and kissed her. "I love you." "I love you too." He picked Ava up and carried her into the bedroom. "Still tired," Ava asked. "You're relaxing. I'll go downstairs and take care of your parents and get them settled." "How did I get so lucky," Ava asked. "Truthfully, it was the sexy dress." "I bet." "And the part where you said you'd marry me," Joe teased. He kissed her again then went downstairs.

Her mom had set out the flowers, and was heading for the kitchen. "I'll make us something," Joe said. "Ava sleeping," her mom asked. Joe nodded. They cooked together, while her dad put something together that they'd bought. They ate, then Ava came downstairs. "Well hello beautiful," Joe said as he pulled her into his lap. "She wake up?" Joe shook his head. He handed Ava a glass of orange juice. "You two are too adorable," her mom said. They chatted, Ava had a quick bite to eat then Grace woke up. Joe went upstairs, changed her, then brought her downstairs. She was almost smiling.

A week or two passed. Ava's mom headed home, and the guys had to head back out to the concerts. "Come with us," Joe said. "Who's going to look after Grace?" He kissed her. "Already figured out," Joe said. Rose came with them. "Why are you so determined?" "Because you're singing with us," Joe said. They were at the next show a few hours later. Grace had a routine. It was almost like clockwork. The hair and makeup people did Ava's hair and her makeup, she slid on the backless black dress he loved. Took her over a half-hour to get it on, thanks to Joe. Then the guys finally headed on stage.

After an hour or so, she heard the words. "Do you want to hear the new song?" Joe walked towards her. He took her hand and handed her the microphone. Joe kissed her, then they walked out on the stage. "Please welcome our new favorite member of the band. This is Ava Morgan." Within a few minutes, the song had started. Ava and the guys sang the first song to what sounded like a million cheering fans. "One more?" Joe started the song she'd helped him write on their honeymoon. They sang it together, Ava wiped away tears after, then waved goodbye and went back to Grace. Joe kissed her. Grace woke up and Ava curled up on the sofa with her. Rose came in. "I thought I heard her up," Rose said. "Guess she heard me coming." "You were amazing." "Thanks," Ava said. They played with Grace a while then Ava fed her, and Grace fell back asleep. Rose took her out to the RV.

Joe walked in when the concert was finished. He walked over to Ava, pulling her into his arms, then picked her up. "You were amazing." He kissed her, then walked her towards the sofa. In seconds, he had her on the sofa, kissing her. "She sleeping?" Ava nodded. He inched up Ava's dress. "Remember," Ava said. He kissed her leg. "Don't tease," Ava said. He kissed her hip. "Seriously." Joe kissed her. "I swear you are seriously going to drive me nuts." "Good." He kissed her again. "This was the best night ever." "Why, because I wore the dress?" He kissed her again. "Partly." "Where to next," Ava asked. "Bed." "Funny." "The RV." He kissed her. They got up, grabbed their things, then got in the RV and headed to the next venue.

After two more shows, they headed home. Grace got used to it. A few more months passed and Rose was in labor. Ava was with her all the way through. The guys were in the studio the entire day. Ava called Joe and got voicemail. She left him a message to get Ryan to the hospital. Rose had the baby without him there. "He's gorgeous," Ava said. "Where's Ryan?" "Still in the stupid studio probably," Ava said. She called again. Joe answered. "I just got the message. We're on the way." "No rush. He's fine," Ava said. An hour later, the guys showed. "I bet Jacob and Grace end up dating or something," Rose joked. "Wouldn't be surprised," Ava said. Danielle came in with Grace and handed her off to Ava. "Say hi to Jacob baby," Ava said. Joe came in. "Hey handsome," Ava said. "Hey yourself." Joe gave Rose a hug, then went over and kissed Ava. "You two. The dynamic duo," Ryan said. "I tried to call you." Joe kissed Ava again. "I know. Thank goodness we finally took a break," Joe said. Ryan was curled up with Rose and Jacob. The gang hung out a while, then Ava and Joe took Grace home.

They put Grace down for the night, then Joe carried Ava into their bedroom. "One track mind." He kissed her. "What are you up to," Ava asked. "What did the doctor tell you?" "I know what you're thinking." "She did didn't she," Joe asked. "Yes." "She okayed it?" Ava nodded and kissed him. He peeled her jeans off, then her shirt and she pulled his off, kicking all of it to the floor. "I missed you," Joe said as he kissed her lips, then down her torso. "Joe," Ava said. One warm breath on her had goose bumps popping up. He kissed her thigh, then her hip. "Seriously," Ava said. He looked up at her with that sexy grin. "Don't look at me like that." He kissed her torso, then kissed her lips again. "I missed that look," Joe teased. "What look?" "The look that you give when you want me to ravish you from head to toe." "No idea what you're talking about," Ava joked. He kissed her again and made love to her. This was heaven to him. "I missed this." "Joe," Ava said. He kissed her harder and kept going. There was no way he was stopping now. They both almost exploded. He didn't want to move from that spot. "What," Ava asked. He kissed her again. "Now that's a look I love." "Which would be," Ava asked. "The one of pure love." "That too," Ava teased. He kissed her. They curled up together on the bed. "I missed this," Ava said. "You and me both." A half-hour later, they were both out cold.

Grace woke up a few hours later. Joe got up, gave her a bottle, then rocked her back to sleep. He slid back into bed with Ava, wrapping his arms and a leg around her. He kissed her neck. "She alright?" "Quality time with Daddy," he teased. He kissed her shoulder. Ava linked her fingers with his and he wrapped his arm around her. "I had an idea." "No we're not having another one right now," Ava said. "Better idea." "What's that?" "Stay on tour with us." "Who's going to take care of Grace? Rose has Jacob now," Ava said. "Nanny." "You think so do you?" "Just while we're recording or on stage," Joe suggested. "Baby," Ava said. "We can get someone to help with Jacob too." "She doesn't want to be on tour." "Think about it?" "And the days that we're home, we're home." He nodded. He kissed her neck again. "You had someone in mind didn't you," Ava asked. "Sorta." "You know what I'm going to ask." "She's my cousin." "Nice." "We were best friends when we were younger." "We'll see." "She's popping by tomorrow. Is that alright," Joe asked. "Fine. Only because you're putting me in a good mood." His hand slid down her torso. "Sleep," Ava said. "I will." Before they fell asleep, they made love again.

The next morning, Ava got up, had a shower with Grace, got her dressed, then sat downstairs with Joe. They played with her for a while before his cousin showed. "So you must be Ava," she said as Joe showed her in. "Oh my God. This is baby Grace." "So, Joe tells me you're thinking about ECE?" "I love kids. I can't really have any, but I love having them around me. Besides. Honestly, I'd love to be able to spend more time with you guys." "Where have you been anyway? You were invited to the wedding," Joe asked. "I know. I was in the process of moving back. New York wasn't my style." "Told you so," Joe said. Grace started falling asleep. "I'll take her if you want?" Joe walked upstairs with Emily and showed her Grace's room.

He came downstairs with Emily a little while later, monitor in hand. "I have an idea. We'll go out for dinner. Emily can stay with Grace for a few hours," Joe said. "You sure," Emily asked. He nodded. "I'll call you if there's any problems." "I'll go get changed," Ava said. She walked upstairs, put on some makeup, then slid on the black dress that made him drool, then slid on her heels and came downstairs. "Two hours," Ava said. Joe nodded. "Remember what I said Emily." "I know. Milk in the fridge, and nothing loud." "Just put it in the microwave for 45 seconds." "Have fun," she said. They left. "Are you sure," Ava asked. Joe nodded.

CHAPTER 15

"I think I should call and see if she's okay," Ava said. "Ava, stop freaking out." They pulled into the restaurant, then headed inside. They had a private room, just the two of them. "What's all this for?" Joe kissed her. "Because you're you." He pulled her into his arms. "Distraction?" He smirked. They sat down to dinner. The waitress came over and brought them a drink, then left them alone. "How long have you had this planned," Ava asked. "Since yesterday." "Oh really." He nodded. "What's the real occasion?" "Because I haven't heard the 'I can do this alone' thing in a while. That we're finally passed all the other stuff," Joe said then leaned in to kiss her. They had a relaxing dinner, then Joe asked her to dance. She was in his arms where she belonged. "I missed our date night," Joe said. "Considering you've been on tour." "And I'm going tomorrow. That's why I wanted her to come today. I want you to come do more shows with us." "I know, but . . ." "We have her to help. If you're willing to let her that is," Joe said. He kissed Ava. "If I say maybe?" He kissed her again. He paid for dinner, then they ducked out the back. "Where are you taking me now?" "Thought we could go see Rose and Ryan." "As long as we're back in an hour." Joe laughed, kissed Ava and they left.

"He's fine Rose," Ryan said. "What if he needs something?" "We'll know. Just come and sit and relax." He pulled her into his lap and rubbed Rose's shoulders. "Besides. Ava and Joe are on their way over." Ava and Joe showed a little while later. "How are you," Ava asked. "Tired." They laughed. "Who's looking after Grace," Rose asked. "My cousin," Joe replied. "Talked her into it," Ryan asked. "Plotting against me already?" Joe wrapped his arms around Ava. "That mean that you're doing more shows with us," Ryan asked. "A few. I still want to have time with Grace." "Okay," Ryan said.

They hung out for a while, then Ava and Joe headed home. "When did you two talk about her helping," Ava asked. "When you were practically a walking zombie. Everyone needs help baby. If I can't be there every day, I want someone to help you." "I know, but I don't know how I feel about having her with me at all times," Ava said. "Babe, just relax. You'll see." They pulled into the house and came inside. Grace was playing on the floor with

Emily. Ava's face was red, and so were her eyes. "Hello princess," Ava said. Grace crawled over to Joe. He picked her up in his arms. "Da." "Seriously? That's her first word," he said. "Guess she loves you too Daddy." Ava kissed him. "How was she," Ava asked. "She wasn't too happy that you left, but she was alright." He went to hand her to Ava, and Grace started crying. "I just gave her some water and one of those crackers you had out for her." "And?" "Inhaled it," Emily said. Ava went and grabbed some food for Grace, then handed it to Joe. He fed her at the table, then Grace fell asleep in his arms. He cleaned her up and took Grace upstairs to bed.

"So, if you want to help out every once in a while, it's fine with me. Joe wants me to go with them for a few shows. You up for it," Ava asked. Emily nodded. "We'll see how things go." She hugged Ava. "You won't regret this for a second." Ava hoped she wouldn't. She handed Emily the schedule she had Grace on. "This is sort of a general idea." "Sounds good to me. If you need me to help with anything else," Emily offered. "Thanks." Joe came down a little while later. "So," Joe asked. He slid on the sofa behind Ava. "I'll give you a shout tomorrow," Ava said. Emily hugged Ava and Joe, then headed home. "What?" "Fine. We'll see how it goes," Ava said. He pulled her back into his arms. "See, you know I was doing it for you. I just want you to have help if you need it." Joe kissed her. "So now that Miss Grace is down for the night, what do you feel like doing?" "Could play you what I was working on," Joe said. Ava undid the top knot around the neck of her dress. "Or a better idea," he said as he slid his hands under the sides of the dress. "I'll go throw on something and you can play it for me," Ava said. "I'll have to help you get changed then," Joe teased. Ava got up and started walking for the steps, then he came up behind her. The minute they got past the bedroom door, the dress was off. He kicked his jeans off, pulling her to him.

"What," Ava joked. He turned her to face him and kissed her, then picked her up, leaning her against the door. "I love you." He kissed her again and carried her to bed, pulling her g-string off with his teeth. The man could tease her into a frenzy in seconds. She had the same effect on him. They made love then curled up in bed. "Thank you for all of this tonight," Ava said. "You deserve every second of it." "You sure you want her helping," Ava asked. "Why not? We know her, we trust her, and best part is she's family." "Still." "Baby, there are no worries. There's nothing to freak over," Joe said. "I know. I just don't want Grace getting more attached to her is all." He kissed Ava. "Only person she's attached to that much is us." "Still can't believe she said that tonight," Joe said. "She does when I put her down to bed." "What were you singing to her this time," Ava asked. "Things that matter." Ava smirked. Joe kissed her and held her in his arms, and a half-hour later, they were both out cold.

Rose walked in to check on Jacob and saw Ryan with him in the glider chair. "You know, we're going to have to stick together. I'm going to teach you everything. How to play ball, how to sing. I'm going to be the best dad for you. I wanted you here for so long Jacob. Second to your mom, you're the best thing that ever happened to me. Just remember that I'm going to love you forever okay?" He gurgled. Ryan rocked him to sleep, then tucked him in. Ryan went to step out of the room and Rose wrapped her arms around him. "Eavesdropping again?" She kissed him. "I'll take that as a yes." He kissed her, then they went downstairs and curled up on the sofa watching movies. "You're too much. You know that," Rose said. "We're in the studio tomorrow. You going to be alright here with him?" "I think I'll survive. Ava going in with you guys?" "No. She said she had something she had to do tomorrow," Ryan said. "You'll be back for dinner right?" "Not sure. You saving me dessert," he teased. "If you show up." He turned on an old movie on TV, and kissed Rose. "It's just Brad and Joe and I tomorrow." "It better be," Rose said. "I promised you." "I know." They watched the rest of the movie, then headed to bed.

"You still don't trust me do you," Ryan asked. "I don't have time to worry about you not cheating Ryan. I have Jacob to take care of, and work to get finished." "You know you don't have to," Ryan said. "We're not having this discussion again." "You don't. You know you don't." "I need something to occupy my brain Ryan." "I know, but if it stresses you out, you're better off without it." "Was I better off when you were stressing me out?" "Not the same thing," Rose said. "Yeah it is. I love what I do. I love being with you. I love Jacob, but you have to understand that I can't just sit around all day. I have to do something." "I know baby." Ryan kissed her, pulling her into his arms. They headed upstairs to bed. "I have an idea." "What's that," Rose asked. "Joe's cousin is helping with Grace." "Don't even. Ava's busy as a one armed paper hanger. She has the writing, the music, plus she has Grace. That's why she needed help." "Then you're coming with us this weekend. We're leaving Friday morning," Ryan said. "I can't just take off." "We're bringing him with us." Ryan spent the next half-hour talking her into it.

"James, would you just sit still," Kristy asked. "I have to go." "Why?" "I have something I have to do," James said. He took off and headed for Ava and Joe's place. "Mrs. Morgan. There's a guest here for you," security said. "Who?" "James." "Fine," Ava said. James took off down the street and pulled in to her driveway. He came to the door and Ava had Grace in her arms. "What did you want?" "So this is," James asked. "Our daughter Grace." "I need to talk to you." "I gathered that. Give me five." Ava put Grace down for her nap, then came back downstairs.

"What did you want James?" "I miss you." "I'm still married James." "I love you." "What happened to Rachel," Ava asked. "I can't. I know who I want Ava." "Well, I'm not available anymore. You can't just use her." "I want you." "James, enough." "I tried to get over you." "I know. Try harder." "I just have to do one thing." "I know what it is. Answer is no." Ava got up from the sofa. She walked James to the door and he had her pinned to it, kissing her in a half a second. She pushed him away and pushed him out the door. Ava went back to her desk. She sat back down trying to get back to her writing. A song came into her head and she started writing the lyrics.

———————

Rose headed over to see Ava once Jacob woke up. When she came to the door, Rose saw the look on her face. "What happened," Rose asked. "James was here." "What the heck for?" "He wanted to try to win me back." "He does realize you married the perfect man right?" "Far from perfect, but yeah he knows." "What happened?" "He kissed me." "Shit," Rose said. "I ended up writing an entire song." "Seriously?" Ava nodded. She handed the lyrics to Rose. "Damn." A minute later, Joe sent her a text from the studio:

Miss you. Come. Emm is on her way to look after kids.

Ava replied:

XO. Surprise for you. We're on way.

"What," Rose asked. "Emily's coming to look after the kids. We're going shopping, then to the studio." Ava slid on Joe's favorite jeans on her, her playboy Bunny tank top and her boots. Once Emily showed, they stopped off to get some drinks, and headed to the studio to meet the guys.

Joe looked up from his fidgeting. "What," he said as he looked at the door. He was a little taken aback. "Hey," Joe said. Ava kissed him. "Hey yourself handsome." "So this is the studio," Rose said as Ryan pulled her into his arms. "We needed a female perspective on something," Joe said. "The sexy black jeans," Ava teased. "Nice. Not exactly what we needed the opinion on," Ryan said. Joe grabbed Ava's butt and pulled her to him. "We came up with a song for the CD, but we're not sure how the end should go," Brad said. "So play it," Ava replied. Joe kissed her. They played the part of the song they'd decided on. "Should I let you walk away, or hold on forever. Should I give up or keep us together." "Okay, so if it were a decision you were making, what would you choose?" "Already have that answer," Ava said. "Then . . . I already know the answer. Hold on forever," Brad asked. "That's exactly what I told him," Joe said. They finished up the song. "What's this," Joe asked noticing a paper in Ava's back pocket. "Read it. Something that popped into my head while I was writing." He finished reading it and handed it to Ryan. Joe kissed Ava. "What?" "It's amazing," Joe said. "No idea where it came from either." He kissed her again, pulling her in close. "Get a room," Brad teased. Joe slid the guitar to his back and grabbed Ava's hand leading her out of the room.

"What?" "You know I'm never walking out on you," Joe said. "It wasn't about us." "I know." "Then what's wrong," Ava asked. Joe kissed her again. "What?" "Nothing." "Speak or I'm going home." "Ava, it's nothing." She went to walk off and he pulled her back to him. He kissed her. "Just say it," Ava said. "Kelly." "Who's Kelly?" "An old friend." "What kind of friend?" "Ava." She walked back into the studio and grabbed her purse and keys. "Ava," Joe said coming after her. She walked past him and walked out the door then got in the car and headed home.

"What the hell was that," Ryan asked. "Nothing," Joe said. "You want to hang with us this afternoon," he asked Rose. She kissed him. They spent a few more hours working away then took a dinner break. Joe took off and headed to the house.

He walked in and the house was too quiet. He walked upstairs and Grace was asleep with Jacob. Emily was in the TV room. "Ava come back here?" "She did, then she said she'd be back later." "She call," Joe asked. "No," Emily replied. He called her phone. "You've reached Ava. Can't take your call. Leave me your name and number after the beep." He hung up. He sent her a text:

Where are you baby? Come home.

He got a reply ten minutes later.

No.

Joe: Ava please. We can talk about this.

Ava: Nothing to talk about.

Joe: Please baby. I'm waiting here for you.

Ava: Go back to the studio.

Joe: Come home first.

Then no reply.

He sat down in the TV room with Emily. "What's wrong," she asked. "Nothing." A half-hour later, Ava walked in. "Baby," Joe said. She walked past him and went upstairs. She checked on the kids, then went into the bedroom. "Talk to me," he said. "Why?" "Baby, enough." "No. Enough of the stupid idiot girls hanging off you. Enough of ex's coming out of the damn woodwork. I'm sick of it." Ava put the things she'd bought away. "She was there to meet up with someone in one of the other studios." "Right." "Ava, nothing happened," Joe said. "Right." She walked past him and went downstairs. "Did the kids have a bath," Ava asked. "Just before bed like you said." Ava made herself something to eat. "You eat Emily?" "Yes. Had the leftover mango chicken. It was awesome." "Thanks." Ava went to walk out of the kitchen and Joe blocked the door. "What?" "It was a fluke Ava. Nothing happened. She hugged me. She tried to kiss me and kissed my cheek instead." "And?" "Nothing." "Right," Ava replied. Ava went to try to get past him again. "She slipped me her room key. I put it back in her purse." "She know we got married,' Ava asked. "She must have seen the ring." Ava got past him and went into her office. Joe locked the door behind her. "What?" "Ava, you know I wouldn't." "And how do I know that?" "Because. You know I love you." "Didn't stop you before did it?" "Fine. There were old feelings there. I didn't do anything. Only person I want to be with is you." He grabbed her hands pulling her into his arms. "I love you." She didn't reply. He kissed her. "Only you and Grace." "Then why?" "Ava, why are you so worried?" "Because I am." He kissed her again pulling her as close as he could. He lifted her up, wrapping her legs around him. "You've got me forever." "Until?" "Until nothing." He kissed her again. "No more worrying," Joe said. "Fine." He slid her to her feet. He took her plate and cleaned it off, then grabbed her hand. "Where are we going now," Ava asked. They walked out and headed back to the studio.

They came in and Kelly was hanging with the guys. Ava took one look at her and was about to turn and walk out when Joe linked his fingers with hers and held on tight. "Hey Kelly." "Hey handsome." "Kelly, this is Ava." "Nice to meet you," Ava said. "Ava? As in," Kelly asked. "Yeah," Joe replied. "Oh." Kelly made an excuse and left. "Where's Rose," Ava asked. "She headed home." Ava gave her a quick call. "The kids are asleep together in the crib," Ava said. "Just picked him up." "Call me tomorrow," Ava asked. "You're telling me what's going on Ava." Ava hung up. "Now back to this song," Brad said. The guys got back to work, as Joe kept an eye on Ava.

"You wrote this," Ryan asked. Ava nodded as he read through the lyrics she wrote. He handed it to Brad. "Whoa. Ava?" "I know," she replied. "No, this is amazing." "Thought it would make a good one for you guys," she said. "I'm so working on this tonight," Brad replied. The guys went through a little bit more of the completed stuff, then Brad started playing around with some music to go with her song. Joe added some guitar, then Ryan went at some of the tune.

> Every night I lay awake
> Wondering about what happened yesterday
> Wondering if I lost my chance for good
>
> Wondering if it's worth the fight
> To put an end to my lonely nights
> Wondering if you're wishing it too.
>
> It gets easier
> Forgetting you
> It gets easier
> To get over you.

Ava almost teared up. Brad wrote out the music. The guys kept going.

> I walk down a street of memories
> Thinking I see you there
> When all I find is you've vanished in thin air
>
> I smell that perfume
> You used to wear
> I remember the smell of your hair
>
> Knowing I should go on
> Knowing I should find someone new
> Can't get over you.

The guys finished the song an hour or so later. They played it again all the way through, recording it. Ryan put his touches in, Brad his, and Joe put a bit of his talent into it. They played it back and Ryan was teared up. So was Joe. "Where does all this come from," Brad asked. "My writing." "Seriously?" "Just know what it's like to want to hold on when there's no point," Ava said. "I don't even think I can get through it without crying." Ava smirked. "She's mine guys. I get the super talented writer," Joe said. The guys laughed while he pulled Ava into his arms and kissed her.

The guys finally decided to call it a night. Ryan and Brad headed out with a hug goodbye to Ava. Joe leaned her against the piano. "I love you," he said. He kissed her. She still didn't respond. "What," Joe asked. "James kissed me." "When?" "When I was out. I bumped into him." "And?" "I walked off after slapping him." "He doesn't give up does he," Joe asked. "Just tell me that nothing else happened today." "She was my first girlfriend Ava." "And?" "She still can get my heart racing." Ava looked at him. "But you're the only one I want in my arms." "Joe." "We had lunch." "And?" "She suggested going back to her place," he said. Ava looked at him. "I went for a while. Nothing happened. We talked. She tried to get me . . ." Ava went to try to walk away and he held her against the piano. "She wanted me," Joe said. "And?" "Normal reaction, but I want you." Ava got past him and walked out to the car. He zipped up his guitar and came out behind her, putting the guitar in the backseat.

"Ava." "Just go home," she said. "Not until you get this through your head. I love you. I promised forever. That's never changing." "And I don't share Joe. You want that, then I'll leave you to it." Ava turned away from him. He pulled out and headed back to the house. Ava walked in and went straight upstairs. Emily headed home and Joe said goodbye then headed upstairs. Ava was in the tub. "Baby." He saw her brush tears away. "Don't," Joe said. He walked over to her. He sat down on the edge of the tub. "Can't just leave me alone can you?" Joe kissed her. She grabbed her towel, wrapping it around her and drained the tub. She walked past him, pulling on a shirt and slid into bed. "Talk to me," Joe said. Ava turned her light out. He got changed for bed, then slid in with her, pulling her to him. "Let go." "Never." "Just leave me alone Joe." Ava got up and walked out, going downstairs and grabbed the blanket and pillow from the hall closet. "Ava." She curled up on the sofa and went to sleep. Ava tossed and turned for what felt like hours.

He came downstairs, then sat down beside her on the sofa. "I can't sleep if we're mad," Joe said. "You want her, then go Joe." "I want you." "Then why were you there with her?" "I don't know." "Then figure it out," Ava said. "Ava, I love you. I love you more than I ever thought I could." "It's not enough." "It's more than enough." "Obviously it isn't," Ava said. She was happy the darkness hid the tears. "Baby, I don't want to be with anyone else, ever." "Than enough with the stupid ex's Joe. You don't see me running off with James do you?" "No." "It's because I made a promise. One that I won't ever give up on. You can't do that, then there's no point,' Ava said. "Meaning what?" Ava got up and walked into the kitchen. "No. Don't you dare even think it," Joe said. "Go decide what you want." "I know what I want." "Then do it," Ava said. He pulled her into his arms and kissed her then leaned her onto the counter. "I want us." "I don't know that you do," Ava said. She got down and walked upstairs.

"Where are you going," he asked. "I don't know." "You aren't walking out of this house." "I can't do this. I can't fight off the female population of the world to be with you," Ava said. "Ava, you aren't leaving." "I have to." "Ava." "I can't be here unless you're doing this all the way Joe. I can't wait around for you to walk out." He pulled her to him and kissed her. "Don't go," Joe begged. "Is this what you want?"

"It's what I wanted from the first day we met," he said. "Joe." "More than anything." "What happens when the next old flame sees you?" "I tell her about my beautiful wife and daughter." "Joe." "Friendly and that's all. I swear." A tear fell. "Nothing else, ever again." "I'm not staying if it happens. You know that." "You're never leaving." "Seriously Joe." "If it ever happens again, I'll go." "Promise me." "Anything," he begged. "Promise me that it will never happen again." "It never will. I'd rather die first." "Remember you said it," Ava said. He wrapped his arms around her pulling her close. "Don't go." "It hurt," Ava said. "I never want to hurt you." "It's like that whole thing all over again. You know that." Joe kissed her.

He picked her up, carrying her to the bed then leaned her onto it. He curled up with her, then unbuttoned the shirt. "What are you up to," she asked. He kissed her again, peeling the shirt off. He kissed her neck, her shoulder, then her heart, her breasts, her ribs. "Joe." His kisses trailed lower. She lifted his chin so he could look her in the eyes and he moved back up and kissed her. He made love to her. Every kiss sizzled. Every touch almost burned her skin it was so hot. They took their time and cherished every second. "I missed you," he said. "You know you're . . ." He kissed her again. He fell asleep with her in his arms.

The next morning, he woke up and she wasn't in bed. Grace was gone. The baby bag was gone, and so was her purse, her laptop, her phone and her car. He called. "Where are you?" "The park." "Where," Joe asked. "Grace's favorite." "I'll meet you there." He hung up, showered and got dressed, then left to meet them.

Rose packed a bag for Jacob and one for herself. "We're only going for three days," Ryan said. "I know. I wanted to have something nice to wear at the concert." "I have a suggestion," Ryan teased. He pulled her to him and kissed her. "Silly head." He kissed her again. "You know we're never going to be ready to go." Ryan leaned her onto the bed. "So we're late." He kissed her again, sliding her dress up her legs. "Jacob's going to be up in a minute." He kissed her again. They made love then curled up on the bed together. "I know what I forgot to pack," Rose said. He kissed her again. She went to get up and he pulled her back onto the bed beside him. "Ryan." "Just relax." His phone went off. Rose laughed. He grabbed it. "You ready," Brad asked. "Where's Joe?" "They're meeting us there." "Okay," Ryan said. "We'll be there in 20."

Ava and Joe packed their bags, then packed one for Grace. Emily showed and they headed to the airport. They got there just as the guys were hopping on the plane. Rose came down and got Grace, bringing her onto the plane and sitting her with Jacob. Ava came on with

Joe. "Was wondering when you two were going to show up," Brad joked. "Funny," Joe said as he sat down with the guys and pulled Ava into his arms. "We took little miss princess to the park," Ava said. "Swarmed?" "Nope," Ava replied. The plane headed off. "I have an idea for tonight," Ava said. "What's that," Joe replied. "Remember when you did that tribute concert?" "That song," Brad asked. Ava nodded. "Was one of our favorites," Ryan said. Joe looked at Ava. "What?" He kissed her cheek. "It was an amazing performance," she said. "Just for you tonight then," Ryan said. Ava got up as soon as she could. "Might as well practice it then," Ryan said. They sang it and Joe didn't make it through once without tearing up.

"What are you doing," Rose asked. "Nothing," Ava said. "Ava. I know you remember." "I'm not doing anything." She sat down and got some writing done on the plane." "What happened the other night," Rose asked. "Another ex girlfriend." "Ava." "Don't start." "Are you alright?" "No." The guys worked on the song that Ava had written the words out to. Grace finally fell asleep after Ava fed her, then Ava went and sat back down in the back. Ryan talked Rose into sitting with them. Ava finished her writing that she needed to do for the week. Joe walked over and grabbed her laptop, saving her work, then turned it off. "What?" "Come here," he said. He pulled her to her feet. "What?" "If you're trying to get a reaction, it's working," Joe said. "Good." Ava went to turn and walk away, and he pulled her back. Joe kissed her. "I'm never losing you." "You better hope not," Ava said. She walked off, shrugging him off. She went and sat back down with Rose. "Ava." "Rose, butt out," Ava said. The plane landed a half-hour later. The guys hopped off and Emily got Grace. Rose stepped off with the guys. Joe stopped Ava.

"What?" "Please," Joe said. "I'm not forgetting it." "Ava." She walked past him and hopped on the bus. She got Grace settled, then plugged her laptop back in. "I'm going to go with Ryan and Rose if that's alright," Emily sai. "Sure," Joe said as Emily hopped off. "Will give you and I time to talk alone," Joe said. They got on the other RV alone. "What," Ava asked. "You really think I'd rather be single than be with you?" Ava just looked at him. "If I wanted to be single so badly, I wouldn't have married you." "Fine," Ava said. "Don't fine me. You don't believe me." "How many other girls Joe? Makes it hard to believe you doesn't it?" "There aren't any other women. I want you." "Right now maybe." Joe kissed her, picking her up and carrying her to the bed. "Would you stop?" "Ava, what do you want me to do?" "Mean it." She got up, walking back into her laptop. Joe walked in, picked her up, flipped her over his shoulder and carried her into the bedroom. "Put me down." "We're finishing this, and finishing it now," Joe said. "Meaning what?" "Henry," Joe asked. "Five minutes." "What," Ava asked.

They hopped out. "What," Ava asked. "I don't want to fight with you anymore." "I am not putting up with the ex girlfriends anymore." "Ava, I dated a lot before I met you." "So did I but they don't pop out of the damn woodwork every minute." "I want you to know something." "What?" "I started over when we met. You're the only woman I wanted so badly I could taste it. You're the only one I look forward to seeing every day. I get to the concerts, and I miss you like crazy." "What are you trying to say Joe?" "That's why I wanted you with us. I miss you. I miss having you with me, singing along and making me love my job. It's not the same without you there. I miss you every second of the day." "You know why I can't do this." "And I also know that you love me more than you want me to know. I know that your heart broke when I told you about Tiff," Joe said. "Don't bring her into this again." "She's part of my history. Just like James is part of yours," Joe said. "Difference being, I don't do anything. I don't sleep with old boyfriends." "Is that what it's going to take to get us back to the way it should be?" "No." "Then tell me what to do." "No more exes popping up. If it happens, then tell me. No more walking off with them." "You know I wouldn't ever cheat on you." "If you ever do . . . you know I'll find out." "And my conscience will eat me alive." "Once. Just once Joe." Joe pulled her to him and kissed her. "Never," he said. After making up a little, they got back in the RV and headed to the concert.

CHAPTER 16

"What are you wearing tonight," Joe asked. "The red," Ava replied. Joe's smile gave his thoughts away. "Don't even think it." "Don't think what," he asked sliding in behind her and wrapping his arms around her. "I just finished getting my hair done Joe." He slid the belt of her robe undone. "Joe, quit it." He kissed her neck and slid his shirt off. He walked over and made sure the door was locked. Grace was dead asleep. He walked back over to Ava and turned her towards him. "And where did this come from," he asked noticing the lingerie. "Fredericks." He kissed her and picked her up, leaning her onto the counter. "Grace is going to wake up." Joe kissed her again and went for the buckle of his jeans. "Joe." He kissed her and pulled her close as his jeans hit the floor. They had sex, then he carried her to the oversized chair in the change room. He curled up with her. "Remember what I said," Joe said. Ava nodded. He kissed her. "You have to get ready," Ava said. He hopped up, showered, then pulled on his black jeans and red shirt. Ava slid her robe back on just as Ryan was knocking at the door.

"Hey," Ava said opening the door. "Red," he asked. "Have to," Ava joked. "I bet." Ryan went back down the hall. "I could've changed," Ava said. "Unless you're getting naked, forget it." Joe kissed her. Emily came in. "How's Grace," Emily asked. "She's sleeping. Just like an angel," Joe said. Ava grabbed her dress and slipped it on. Joe couldn't stop staring. "Wow," Emily said. Ava slid on her black heels that had Joe drooling even more. He went to do the meet and greet with the guys while Ava finished getting ready. "If it gets too noisy, her crib's in the RV," Ava said. "If she can sleep through this, she'll be fine." "There's a bottle in the fridge if she needs it." "Ava," Emily said. "What?" "Thank you for trusting me with her." "Like Joe said, you're family," Ava said. She hugged Emily. Ava took Grace into the other room with Rose and Jacob, and Emily followed.

The guys came in after the meet and greet. Joe grabbed Ava's hand and led her into the hall. "What?" He kissed her. "Good luck," Ava said. He wrapped his arms tight around her. His heart was racing. "What's wrong?" "Tiffany was at the meet and greet," Joe said. Ava looked at him. She pried his arms from around her. "Why?" "Fluke." "She still over there?" "She wants to talk to me. I told her you were here with me and I had to go." Ava walked over towards where the meet and greet was and saw her. Joe took off behind Ava. "Tiffany," Ava said. "Hi." "You know who I am right?" "I just needed to talk to him for a second," Tiffany said. "Say what you wanted to say then." "I was going to see if he wanted to come to a party with me tonight," she asked. "Answer's no," Ava said. "He can't answer?" "Tiffany, stop asking. He's married . . . to me. That means him partying with you is out of the question," Ava said. "We're going for a birthday." "Tiff, I'm not going," Joe said. "Why?" "We're leaving right after the concert," he said trying to make an excuse. "Can we go for a coffee before you go?" Ava walked off.

She walked back into the change area and sat down. She fixed her makeup and Joe walked in. "I told her no. That whatever she thought we had is done." "Good." Ava put on her lipstick. "Ava." "What?" "We alright?" "Mmm." She put her makeup away, then went to walk past him. "Baby." "What?" "Just like I promised," Joe said. "Fine." Ava walked past him and went back into the room with the guys. "You're on in two guys," the stage manager said. Joe pulled Ava into his arms. He kissed her. "I love you." "Love you too." He slid in his earpieces and headed for the stage. Ava sat down with Rose and Emily.

"What's up with you two," Ryan asked as he walked to the stage with Joe. "Tiffany's here." "You know she's going to find out," Ryan said. "Tiffany and I were done before we got married Ryan." "Then why is she calling and showing up?" "Cause shit." They said their before concert prayer, then headed for the stage.

"Ava, you're on in 20," the stage manager said. Ava nodded. "What's going on?" "Revenge of the idiot ex week," Ava said. "Ava," Rose said. "His ex is here." "So?" "Long story Rose. Point being, she's a pain in my ass." They chatted a bit, then Ava went towards the stage. "This is one of our favorites. We sang it at a tribute concert a while ago. Sing along if you know the words." He looked over at Ava. The one song that caused tears and goose bumps all at once. Once the song was over, the entire crowd was cheering and screaming. "We brought a friend with us. Anyone want to meet her?" The fans cheered. "Help us get her out here." They started the song and the fans sang along. When the female part came, Ava came out. Joe smiled at her. They sang their two songs. "Think we can talk her into one more song with us," Brad asked. Everyone cheered. "I set out on a narrow way . . . ." Ava sang with them for one last song. "Ava Morgan y'all." Ava waved and headed off stage. She walked back down to the change room, sliding her black jeans and sweater on with her cowboy boots. She came back in and sat down with Rose until the end of the concert.

When the concert finished, Ava headed for the RV. Joe came down and saw her gone. He grabbed his things and carried Grace to the RV. He tucked her in, then saw Ava on the bed on her laptop. "Babe. You were amazing." Ava looked at him as he slid onto the bed beside her. She saved her work. He turned her laptop off and closed it. "Grace?" "Sleeping." "Didn't want to chance waking her up," Ava said. His arms wrapped around her torso. His leg slid around her and she leaned into his arms. "You were really good tonight," Joe said. "If she shows up again," Ava said. "Ring trumps crazy." He tried to make her at least crack a smile. "Sexy red dress trumps crazy girl every time," Joe said. "Funny." "No more worrying. You're pretty much stuck with me." "Can't even trade you in," Ava asked. "Nope. Surgically attached." "Oh darn." He kissed her neck. "Ready," Henry asked. "When you are," Joe replied. They headed off to the next stop. Joe and Ava curled up on the bed.

"Who was that girl," Rose asked. "What girl," Ryan replied. "The one that asked about Joe?" "An old girlfriend of his." "Oh really," Rose said. Ryan nodded. "Why?" "She looked upset." "Joe told her it was done a long time ago. I guess Ava telling her off set her straight." "Seriously," Rose asked. "Ava can take care of herself. Trust me." "That has to be why she was all upset," Rose said. "What?" "When she was sitting with me before she went on with you guys." Ryan called Joe's phone. "What's up?" "Everything okay?" "We're just heading to sleep." "Tiff?" "Done." "My kind of done or yours," Ryan asked. "Mine." Ryan hung up. "What?" "It's all good."

"What was that about," Ava asked. "Nothing. I guess Tiffany got backstage." "Really?" Ava got up. "Babe, nothing happened. I got off the stage and packed up and got on the RV with you." "Would it make me a bad person if I said I wanted her gone," Ava asked. Joe pulled her back to bed. He pinned her down on the bed and kissed her. "Nope. Means I love you too." "I hate feeling like this." "Babe, no more being upset. We're together. That's all that matters," Joe said. He kissed her again and made love to her, then they curled up together and fell asleep.

They pulled into the venue at 10 am. Ava got up and got some writing done while Emily played with Grace. They all had lunch together, the guys did a few interviews, then Joe came back to the RV. Ava was feeding Grace. Grace finished lunch, and Ava cleaned her up. "Mama," Grace said. "Yes beautiful." "Dada kiss." Ava saw Joe come in. "What are my girls up to," he asked. "Grace just finished lunch." "How's the writing going?" "Fine," Ava said. Grace reached for Joe. "Come with me. We're doing sound check," Joe said as he slid Grace out of her arms. Ava grabbed her laptop and followed them. Emily tagged along. The guys did their sound check, then Ava did hers. Ava sat back down as they practiced and went over what songs they were doing and she got some writing done. Grace got up from sitting with Emily and walked two steps towards Ava. She dropped her laptop and watched Grace. "Mama." Ava picked her up. "Joe," Ava said. "I saw it. Baby girl is growing up." She reached for Joe. The guys sat back down on the stage while Grace played with Joe.

Rose came down to the stage. "Ava." She looked over. Rose motioned for her to come with her. "I got her babe," Joe said. Ava walked over and met Rose. "What?" "We're going for a few hours." "Where?" "You need a mani/pedi and a new dress for tonight," Rose said. Ava walked back over and kissed Joe. "What time are you guys getting back?" "2ish." He kissed her again. "Have fun." Emily looked after the kids while Rose and Ava left.

As they were walking out, Rose had a bad feeling. They left for a few hours. After shopping and the all-important mani/pedi, they headed back. Ava looked towards where the guys were and saw someone beside Joe. She put her things in the RV, then walked down towards the stage. Joe jumped up and walked over to her. "Ava, don't freak." "Name." "Amy." "And?" "I dated her. She's friends with the guys too." "And?" "She hung out here with us. That's it," Joe said. "Every town." Ava went to walk off and he grabbed her arm, pulling her back to him. "What Joe?" He kissed her. "Where's Grace?" "Asleep in Ryan's RV with Jacob." He kissed her again. "Don't even think it," Joe said. Ava walked off. He went back down to the guys. "That must have been Ava," Amy said. "That would be her. She had to get some chapters into her agent," Joe said. "So did you want to go for that coffee," Amy asked. "Think I'm going to go chill for a bit. It was nice seeing you," Joe said giving her a hug, then heading for the RV.

Joe walked in and Ava was doing her writing with her iPod on. He slid the earphones out. "What?" "You could have come and said hi." "No reason to. I told you, I didn't want the ex-girlfriend B.S. That means I don't want to meet them either." "Even if it means getting to rub it in that I'm all yours?" "Think you can handle that alone," Ava said. He kissed her. He slid the laptop out of her lap. "Joe." He kissed her again. He grabbed her hand and helped her to her feet. "I made you a promise. I'm sticking to it," Joe said. "Okay." "I mean it babe. No more." He pulled her into his arms and kissed her again. "So how was shopping," he asked. "You'll see later." "I see a Fredericks bag." "Sneaky." He kissed her. "What did you get?" "A dress or two." "And?" "Boots and a pair of comfy heels." "I want a fashion show," Joe asked. "Nope." He kissed her then led her to the bed and curled up with her. "I just didn't want the stress. I would've," Ava said. "It's fine. I know why you didn't." He wrapped his arm around her and they cuddled and relaxed. "We're flying home after the show tomorrow," Joe said. "Good." "Miss our place," Joe asked. Ava nodded. He kissed her.

"I have an idea," Joe said. "What's that?" He got up and made a call. "Get changed." "Why?" "We're going out for dinner." While Ava got changed, Joe went and checked on Grace. "You two have fun. I'll stay here with her," Rose said. Joe came back and Ava was finishing doing her hair wearing nothing but her black satin robe. "Mmm." "Don't even think it," Ava said. He walked towards her. A half-hour later, she was almost ready. He was just doing his shirt up when there was a knock at the door. He answered it and a minute later handed her roses. "What's all this for?" "Happy anniversary," Joe said. Ava handed him a box. "What's this?" Ava smirked. She went into the bedroom and grabbed her new dress. It was black and sexier than the other one. She slid it on as he was opening the gift she bought him. It was a necklace with a seashell. "What's this?" "From the beach outside the villa." He put it on. He looked up and saw her in the dress. His mouth dropped. "Ready," Ava said. She grabbed her purse and went to walk past him. He grabbed her arm and turned her towards him, kissing her. "Happy Anniversary to me," he teased. His hands slid down her back. "Don't even start." Ava slid her heels on and they headed to dinner.

Joe and Ava got to the restaurant and other than being swarmed with people trying to get his autograph, they made it to the private dining room and had their anniversary dinner. "You aren't seriously wearing that on stage," Joe asked. Ava nodded. "Babe." "What?" "You better be prepared then." "For what?" "No sleep," he joked. They finished dinner, then went back to the concert. All the way back, they kissed and flirted. They got back and headed backstage. The guys did their meet and greet, then they came back in and sat down before they hit the stage. Rose came in to give Ryan a lucky kiss. Joe pulled Ava off to the side, while Brad called Danielle. "What," Ava asked. "Babe, you can't wear this," Joe said. She kissed him. "I'm wearing it." "Then you're sitting side stage." "Why? Afraid I might meet some handsome stranger?" "No. Afraid I won't be able to concentrate without you near me," Joe said. He kissed her again and leaned her against the wall. "Guys. We're on in 5," the stage manager said. Joe kissed Ava again. "Wait until you see what's under it," Ava whispered in his ear. "Tease," he replied. Ava nodded. He kissed her again.

When Ava came out onto the stage, there were hoots and hollers and whistles. They sang their songs, then Ava sat at the side of the stage with Rose and watched the concert. At the end, Joe walked right to her and kissed her. They all headed back to the RV's and found a crowd of fans. The guys were asking Ava for her autograph, and the girls were pawing at Joe and Ryan and Brad. They finally made it through the crowd and went into the RV's.

Rose and Ryan left with the kids, and Joe and Ava had a night just the two of them. They went into the bedroom and closed the door. "You were great tonight babe," Ava said. He kissed her. "Even with the sexy distraction watching me." He kissed her again and leaned her onto the bed. Ava kicked the heels off. "Tell me the other one you got isn't so distracting," Joe asked. "You'll see tomorrow." "Seriously." His hand slid up her legs to the black leather g-string. "Tell me you didn't." Ava smirked. Within minutes, he was pulling her dress and the g-string off, and she had his jeans and shirt on the floor. He kissed her from head to toe, then made love to her over and over until they were both exhausted. "I swear woman, you're going to drive me insane," Joe said. "That was the plan," Ava replied as he pulled her into his arms and spooned her.

The next morning, they woke up and Ava went for a run. She outran the security guys that came with her, then they headed back. She hopped on the RV and saw Joe playing with Grace. She came in and kissed them, then had a quick shower and pulled on her tank top and jeans. "Mama," Grace said. "Hey baby girl. You having fun with Daddy?" "Ya." "How was your run," Joe asked. "Good. You two have breakfast?" "Saved you coffee." Ava smirked. She poured herself some, then sat down and finished the last of the chapter she had to finish. "Had an idea for this afternoon," Joe said. "What's that?" "Beach." "Funny. We can't even go to dinner without being surrounded." Joe got up and kissed her. He had a shower, then got changed. Ryan came by. "What's up?" "We have to go do an interview. You two want to come with us," Ryan asked. "Rose coming?" "She went to go visit some friend of hers." Ava realized who it had to be. "She take Jacob?" "Nope. He's with Emily." Joe came out. "Interview bud." "Sorta had plans for us today," Joe said. "Interview. I'm throwing on the blue." Joe pulled on his other shirt. "Tell me you're coming," Joe asked. Ryan headed back to his RV. "Depends," Ava said. "On what?" Ava kissed him. "What?" "Dinner," Ava said. "Unless you're dessert." She kissed him again. Grace grabbed her teddy bear and they went to go meet the guys.

After the interview, they headed back. Rose was still gone. Ava called her while the guys did sound check and she put Grace down for a nap. Emily came and sat with Grace. "Where are you," Ava asked. "Out with a friend." "You're either rubbing it in Jake's face, or you're doing something utterly stupid." "Hey Ava," Jake said. "Hey yourself. How you been," Ava asked. "Good. So how long are you guys in town," Jake asked. "Just tonight. We're flying home after the concert." "You should stay for a day or two," Jake pleaded. "I have to get back. Rose does too." "We'll see you at the concert tonight then," Jake said. "You and who?" He handed the phone back to Rose. "What are you doing," Ava asked. "I'll be back in a half-hour. Just leaving now," Rose said.

Ava went and did the sound check with the guys, then they all had dinner. Ava and Joe headed back to the RV to get changed. "What's up with you tonight," Joe asked. "Nothing," Ava said. "You called Rose, and ever since you've been acting weird." "She was out with Jake." "As in James and Jake?" Ava nodded. "Great." "Not my problem anymore," Ava said. "Good." Joe pulled her into his arms and kissed her. "I want to see this dress." Ava slid out of her jeans and shirt and slid it on. "Ava." "What?" "Damn," Joe said. It hugged every curve, and was perfect. She went to grab a necklace and he slid one around her neck. "Where did this come from?" "Happy Anniversary day two." She smirked. She looked and saw the necklace in the mirror. "It's beautiful," Ava said. He kissed her. She handed him a box from under the bed. "What's this?" She smirked. He opened it and found a new shirt. "Now this is me," Joe said. "Exactly." He slid it on and kissed her. "Babe," he said. He kissed Ava. "And in a few hours, we go home," Ava replied. "Back to our place. Then I get you all to myself." "Meaning?" "My mom's coming into town. She wanted to spend time with Grace," Joe said. "Oh really." "That and I can take you out for a real anniversary night." "And just what might you be thinking in that crazy head of yours," Ava asked. He pulled her close and kissed her again. "One night whatever you want remember?"

The guys headed to the meet and greet. Rose finally showed up with Jake and James. Ava said hi, but nothing else. Joe came in after the meet and greet and saw the guys. Ryan sat and chatted with them and Ava went to walk out with Joe. "Ava," James said. "What?" "Can I talk to you for a second?" "What," Ava asked. "Tell me you thought about what I said." "You don't know what you're talking about." "Ava, I meant it," James said. "I know you did. You're wrong, but I know you meant well." "You always were better off with me." Ava shook her head and went to walk away, when he grabbed her arm. "Let go," Ava said. Joe walked over to them and he dropped her arm. Ava walked away and went into the hall. "What the hell is your problem James," Joe asked. "You know what it is. You aren't going to treat her right. You screw anything and everything that fucking walks." "Remember something smart ass. This wedding ring means one woman forever. That means that Ava and I are together forever. Get the hell over it," Joe said. He walked out and went off to find Ava.

A half-hour later, he still hadn't found her. The guys pulled him back inside and they headed on stage. Rose took off to find Ava. Emily stayed with the kids. Rose looked for the better part of a half-hour, then found Ava. "You're going on in 5 minutes," Rose said. Ava finished her drink, then went backstage. She touched up her makeup, then went on. Joe looked at her trying to figure her out. She barely looked at him. She finished her songs, then went backstage, walking past Rose, Emily and everyone else. She walked out, grabbing a drink and went to the RV. Rose came in 15 minutes later. "What's wrong," Rose asked. "Nothing." Ava poured herself a drink. She slid Grace into her crib and tucked her in. "Ava." She had her drink and slid out of her heels. "I'm fine." "You walked off. You aren't fine," Rose said. "Rose, leave it alone." "Ava." A minute later, Joe came in. "Where the hell did you take off to," Joe asked. "I needed a drink." "Babe, we had drinks there." "I needed a drink. End of discussion," Ava said. Rose left.

"Ava, you're gonna tell me what the hell is going on," Joe asked. "Why?" "We were fine until those two showed up. What the hell is going on Ava?" "He was at the house. He was trying to convince me into leaving you." "You told me." "Exactly. I just don't need his crap anymore." "You're gonna tell me what happened. You two broke up. Ever since then, he's gone nuts. What happened?" "He wouldn't back off. He tried ever since we got together to make me leave and go back to him," Ava said. "Then stop freaking out. Let me take care of his stupid ass." Joe kissed her, then walked off and went to find James.

"What did you say to her," Rose asked. "I want her back," James replied. "I thought you were with Rachel?" "You know I want Ava back. We always were supposed to be together. She's better off with me and she knows it." A minute later, Joe came in. "Find her," James asked. Joe nailed him between the eyes. "Stay away from me, stay away from Ava, and stay the hell out of our lives. You even take one step near her again, and I swear . . ." Joe walked off and went back to Ava. James got up and Jake stopped him from taking off after him. "You've done enough James," Jake said. Ryan came in. "What the hell," Ryan asked. "Joe went to the RV's." "We're going," Ryan said. Jake had his arm around Rose. "You want to stay here with them or are you coming," Ryan asked. She hugged Jake goodbye and walked off with Ryan. "What is going on with you two," Ryan asked. "He's an old boyfriend that I bumped into." "Rose." "We dated at one point. We broke it off. He decided playing the field was more fun." "Lucky for me then," Ryan said pulling her into his arms and kissing her.

"Baby," Joe said. Emily was with the kids. "Where did she go," Joe asked. "She walked off," Emily said. Joe pulled on his sweatshirt then took off after her. He found her on the stage. "What are you doing out here?" "I can't believe him. He's such a damn jackass." "Ava, come back to the RV and we'll head home." He looked at her and saw Ava crying. "Baby, don't," Joe said. She went to get up and Joe pulled her into his arms. He kissed her. "Can we go home," she asked. He nodded and kissed her again. They headed back to the RV, then to the airport.

Within a few hours, they were home. Ava tucked Grace into her crib, then came into the bedroom. Joe closed the door the minute she came in. "What are you up to," Ava asked. He slid his arms around her. "Welcome home baby." He walked her towards their bed. "I missed this," Joe said. He kissed her neck and undid her sweater. "Joe," Ava said. He had the sweater on the floor along with his sweater, their jeans and everything else. She wrapped her legs around him, and he pulled her so close she could almost feel the air coming in and going out of his lungs. He kissed her and made love to her. They were finally home again. Joe kissed her from head to toe, made every inch of skin tingle at his touch. One kiss had him drunk with love. He needed more. They kissed and made love all night. The next morning, Joe got up and checked on Grace. She was playing with Emily. "Just heading back to sleep for a bit. You two alright," Joe asked. Emily nodded. He kissed Grace and headed back upstairs to Ava.

He slid his arm around her waist and pulled himself close. "She up," Ava asked. "Emily's taking care of her. Go back to sleep." He kissed her neck, then curled up with her for another hour or so. Ava woke up to the feel of his hand inching up her torso. Her back arched. His hands slid down her torso, and inched towards her inner thigh. "Guess you're awake," Ava joked. He kissed her neck, then her shoulder. "Joe." Within minutes, he was making love to her again. They finally got up, showered, got dressed and went downstairs. They hung out with Grace for a while, then took her over to Ryan and Rose's place to play with Jacob.

They all relaxed and the guys hung out in the studio with the kids. "Ava, seriously. What happened," Rose asked. "He's an asshole. I swear he knows just what button to push," Ava said. "You and Joe alright?" Ava nodded. "I don't know why I can't get him out of my head." "Because he knows how to push the insecurity buttons," Rose said. "Was I supposed to be with James?" "Stop being ridiculous Ava. You and Joe belong together and you know it." "Then why am I worried?" "Because you're too happy. Because you love Joe so much that you don't know what you'd ever do without him," Rose suggested. "I'm scared I'm going to lose him to someone else. I'm scared that he's going to mess around." "Ava, he loves you. Stop worrying." Joe came outside and slid in behind her in her chaise. "Hey beautiful," Joe said. "Hey yourself." He pulled her into his arms. Ryan came outside and sat down with Rose. "What were you two gabbing about out here," Ryan asked. "Girl stuff." "We had an idea," Joe said. "And what might that be," Ava asked. "Dinner and a movie," Joe said. "Where," Rose asked. "We're going to a drive-in," Joe said. Ava laughed. "Separate cars," Ava asked. Joe kissed Ava's neck. "Did you ask Emily if she can stay with them," Ava asked. "She said she'd be over at 5." "I guess we can go," Ava said. "Can you two look after Grace for an hour," Joe asked. "Sure," Rose said. He got up, grabbing Ava's hand and they left. "Where are we going," Ava asked. "You'll see," he said as they headed off.

"Where are we going," Ava asked again. "You worried?" "No. I'm just wondering why we took off." They pulled into a park. It was quiet, nobody was around and they were near the water. "Where are we?" He got out and opened her door for her. "Seriously Joe. Where are we?" He walked out towards the water. "Joe, tell me." He wandered over towards a tree. She looked. He'd carved their initials into it. "This is where my parents got engaged." "It's beautiful here," Ava said. "So I had an idea." "And what might that be?" She looked and there was a white satin dress hanging from the branch. Behind it was a white shirt and white dress pants. "What are you up to Joe?" "Put it on and follow me alright?"

A few minutes later, Joe took her hand and they walked along the beach. She saw a man in a suit in the gazebo. He walked towards him. "Hey," Joe said. "You two ready?" "More than ever," Joe replied. He'd planned it. They were renewing their wedding vows. "I promise to love you every second of every day for the rest of my life. I promise to be honest, loving, caring, and hold you in my arms every night. I promise to be your best friend, to be faithful and cherish you, to serenade you at least once a day, and to be the best husband and dad there ever was,' Joe said. "And Ava?" "You know, it feels like I've known you my entire life. Every joke, you understand, every story you listen to, every song you sing makes me love you more. I promise to trust you, love you, be faithful, and be with you every night. I promise to make you laugh, smile, cry and love every minute. I promise to be your best friend, to always have you in my heart, to remind Grace of all our happy memories, to be your loving wife forever and ever. I promise to be a pain sometimes just so we can make up, and I promise to never let anyone or anything come between us," Ava said with tears in her eyes. "I now pronounce you husband and wife again." Joe kissed her and she saw cameras flashing. Ava turned and saw paparazzi cameras. They took off across the park, then grabbed their things and headed back to the house, being tailed by paparazzi.

They pulled into the house and he carried her inside and straight to bed. "What is it about this bed," Ava joked. He peeled her out of the dress and kicked his things off and made love to her again. "I could do this every day for the rest of my life." "You're gonna have to," Ava joked. Joe kissed her again and curled them up in the blankets. They finally got up and got dressed and went to leave for dinner when Ava saw messages on the home phone. "Joe, it's Kelly. I need to talk to you when you get a minute." "Joe, it's Steph. You didn't even say goodbye. Call me." "Joe, it's Callie. Was just thinking about what you said . . ." He stopped it and grabbed Ava's hand. "What in the hell?" "Come on. We're going to be late." Ava dropped his hand and went to listen to the last message. "Joe, it's Callie. Was thinking about what you said the other night about keeping it quiet. If it means seeing you, then yes. Call me." Ava walked upstairs, and went for her suitcase when he stopped her. "Let go of me," Ava said. "Ava." She grabbed enough clothes for a few days, then packed a bag for Grace. "You're not going," Joe said. Ava grabbed the bags then grabbed her laptop and cord, her phone charger and her toiletry bag and threw it in her car. "Ava." "Don't you fucking dare," she said. Ava got in, and pulled out. She got to Ryan's and Joe pulled in behind her. Ava walked in, got Grace, put her in the car seat and left. "Ava," Joe said. He took off after her and Ryan was right behind him.

She drove for hours. He followed her the entire way. She stopped for gas and he pulled in behind her. "Ava, stop this," Joe said. "Don't you dare follow me." She filled her tank, paid for it and went to leave when she noticed her keys were gone. "Give me the keys," Ava said. "Get in the car." "Give me my keys." He handed them to Rose. "Rose, keys please," Ava said. "Ava, we're going home and we're talking about this whether you like it or not," Joe said. "Touch me and you're in for it." "Ava, enough," he said. "You think you can pull that shit and I'm not going to leave? I already told you once. That should have been enough," Ava said. She grabbed her keys and went to get in her car. "Ava." "What? It's not what I think," she asked. "No." "Fuck you," Ava said. Joe grabbed the keys. "Get in the car. We're talking about this, and we're doing it now," Joe said. "I'm not moving." He got Grace from the backseat and slid her into the car seat in Ryan's car. He handed the car keys to Rose and got Ava into his car.

"Ava, stop thinking that walking out is going to solve this shit," Joe said. "Then stop with the damn girls calling. Who else has there been Joe? Who? How many," Ava asked. He kissed her. She pushed him away. "I love you." "Why all the phone calls then Joe?" "You really think that little of me?" "Prove me wrong. Prove that you haven't been screwing around. I'm not doing this with you. I'm not staying with you when you can't stay faithful for 5 damn minutes," Ava said. He turned out of the parking lot and headed home. "You think he was right don't you," Joe asked. "Beginning to think so." "Instead of believing him, try this on for size Ava. I love you. I love our daughter. I love everything about us. I thank God for you every minute of every day. I've been with you every concert. Stop just assuming," Joe said. "Which part should I quote? The 'what you said about keeping it quiet' part?" He looked at her. "Ava, I didn't want you getting upset." "Did you or didn't you," Ava asked. "Ava, stop it." "Let me out of the car Joe." "No." He sped up. "Joe, I swear." He pulled over at the park. Ava got out and walked towards the pay phone. "Stop." "You tell me to stop? You promised me. You promised Joe," Ava said. She called Rose. "Come get me." "Where?" She told her where the park was. "There in 5. Just pulling off the highway." "Ava, she's a friend," Joe said. "Bullshit." "I love you. I wouldn't do that," Joe said. "Then you figure out why you're getting calls from how many women that all sound like you're fucking them," Ava said. Rose pulled in and Ava left with her.

Ava got back to the house and Rose took Grace back to their place. Ava walked in, grabbing herself a drink, then sat down on the patio. Joe walked in, grabbed himself a drink and walked outside. "Ava." "Don't even bother. I don't need the excuses anymore," she said. "I didn't do anything." Ava finished her drink. "You have to believe me." She got up to walk past him and he grabbed her hand. "Let go." "No." "Ava, I swear." "I swear? You're full of shit," she said. Ava walked into the house, and he followed her. "Leave me alone." "No." "You want someone else, then be with someone else. I'm leaving. You can see her whenever you want," Ava said. "You're not going." "I'm not staying here when you do nothing but cheat and lie." He pulled her to him and kissed her. Joe leaned her into the wall of the kitchen. She tried fighting him, but he kissed her and fought back. Next thing she knew, they were in bed together. He wanted every inch of her. It wasn't passion, it was more primal need. Joe wasn't making love to her, he was devouring her whole.

Finally, due to nothing but exhaustion, Joe and Ava curled up together in bed. His arms held her tight. The messages ran through her brain. She couldn't stop thinking about what she thought he'd done. She slid out of his arms and went downstairs. She called back every woman that called. "Hello?" "Is this Callie?" "Yeah." "This is Joe's wife." "Hi." "You want to tell me why you were calling my husband?" "We hung out one afternoon. It's not that big of a deal." "And just what did you two do," Ava asked. "We were . . ." "Did you sleep with him?" "No." "You better be telling me the truth." "I really like him. All we did was make out," Callie said. "You better fucking hope so. You call him or even breathe near him again, and you'll have me on your ass like a rabid dog. Got me?" "I didn't know he was married," Callie said. "He is. You want to explain to his daughter what you were trying to do?" "I'm sorry." "Good." Ava hung up. She got changed, locked the doors and walked down to Ryan and Rose's place.

The next morning, Joe woke up and Ava was gone. There was no note. He called Ryan. "She's been here all night." "I'm on my way over." "She's upset," Ryan said. "I'm on my way." Joe hung up, showered, got dressed and headed to Ryan's.

Ava was on the back patio with Rose and the kids. "What happened," Rose asked. "I'm sick of the girls calling. I'm sick of never having one happy moment that stays a good memory." "They're not all bad Ava," Rose said. "I didn't sign up for a marriage where he can have extra-curricular fun." "It's one of those things Ava. You know they're surrounded when they're on tour. Just trust that he won't," Rose said. "That's what you told me." "He has. I know he has," Ava said. Rose looked over and saw Joe.

Rose got up and took the kids inside. "Where . . ." "I don't want to talk to you," Ava said. "We're talking." "Why don't you go call Callie?," Ava asked. "Ava, enough." "You want to tell me what that was?" "Before I met you." "And she took that long to call you? Right. Try a few weeks." "Babe," Joe said. "Don't alright? Just don't." "It was a stupid moment." "Had a lot of those lately." "Come home," Joe said. "No." "Ava, come home and we can talk about this." "Right. Just like we were going to talk last night." "Ava, tell me what you want me to do," Joe asked. "You won't do it." "Ava, tell me." "No other girls. No nothing. No more calls. Nothing. Only women that should be calling are me, my mother, your mom and sisters, Emily, and my girlfriends. No more 'I miss you' bullshit from your fuck of the week." "I never slept with anyone else." "Don't believe it," Ava said. "Will you come home?" "No more of the bullshit." "Ava." She went to walk past him. Joe grabbed her hand. "What?" He pulled her to him. "Please." "I don't know," Ava said. He wrapped his arms around her. He held her face in his hands and kissed her. "I love you." Ava walked away.

CHAPTER 17

The guys were in the studio the next day. They managed to finish one more track. Joe headed home right after. He walked in the door and saw someone sitting on the patio. He walked out and saw Ava curled up with Grace. They were both asleep. He kissed Ava and woke her up then sat down on the edge of the chair. "I'm sorry," Joe said. "I know." "I don't want to lose you," Joe said. Ava carried Grace inside and tucked her into her bed, then came back downstairs. Joe poured them each a drink, handing one to Ava. "I can't do this without you," he said. "Joe, I can't do this. I can't pretend those calls aren't upsetting me." "I know. I swear it's not happening again." "Do I take the risk and trust you?" "Please babe." He sipped his drink. "I mean it. One more woman calling this house . . ." Joe got up and kissed her. "Joe." "No more. None. I promise." He kissed her again and pulled her into his arms. She slid her glass onto the table. He picked her up and carried her to their bed. They made love again, and he devoured her. "I love you," he said. Joe kissed her again as they both were shaking. He leaned onto his back and pulled her to him.

"Don't think I can forget this either," Ava said. "Babe, I swear. I am going to fix this." "You can't fix it. I'm doing this for Grace." "Babe." "I don't know if I can trust you again." "Ava." She broke away from him and showered, then went and checked on Grace. She finally went downstairs and worked on her writing. He came down an hour or so later. Joe walked into the office and pulled Ava away from her desk. "What?" He kneeled down and slid his arms around her waist. "Stop." "Ava, please. Tell me what I have to do." "I don't know. How am I supposed to let you go on tour when I keep thinking that you're with someone else while you're away? It's part of your job." "Then I come home." "You can't every night Joe." "Yeah I can. Either that, or you come with me." "What happens when Grace is in school? I can't just take off." "Ava. Please." "Never ever again. Next time, I'm leaving for good. You know that right?" "I know." "I mean it. I will walk out the door with her and that's it." "Ava, I'm never taking that chance of losing you ever again. Never." "I know." Joe pulled her to her feet and wrapped his arms around her, almost crying on her shoulder. "Babe, I know I've screwed up a million times, and that I don't deserve you." "Joe, enough." He kissed her and sat her on the edge of the counter.

He untied the belt of her satin robe. He slid closer to her, pulling her as close as he could and she wrapped her legs around him. He slid her robe off, then undid his jeans. They did it in the office, then on the sofa downstairs. "How did I get this lucky," he asked. "I honestly don't know." He kissed her and curled up in her arms. "I love you." "I know." "Babe." "What?" "What would you think about another baby?" "Why?" Joe kissed her neck, then her collar bone. "Not now we aren't." "Why?" "Think about it. Now is not a good time." He kissed her again. "I have a book tour to do in a week or two." "For how long?" "A few days." "Where?" "New York, Chicago, then Dallas." "I'm going with you." "You have other things to get done Joe." "And I'm going with you anyway." "Joe, you have a CD to finish." "You come first." He kissed her. "You do," he said. They curled up on the sofa together and relaxed until Grace woke up. He pulled on his jeans and went upstairs. Ava went upstairs and pulled on her jeans and tank top.

She came back downstairs and Joe was playing with Grace. She threw Joe his shirt and went in and grabbed two glasses of lemonade. She handed one to him and Grace tried to grab an ice cube. They played and hung out together the rest of the day, had dinner, then put Grace down to bed.

—————

"Are you sure they're alright," Rose asked. "Rose, stop worrying." "Just tell me that it's not going to happen with us." "I know neither of us is perfect babe. Neither of us. We're going to make mistakes, but we'll get through them. We'll make it through," Ryan said. "I love you." "I love you too baby." They curled up by the fireplace and just watched the fire. "I need to know something." "What," Ryan replied. "Did he cheat on her?" "Rose, it has nothing to do with us." "Just answer me." "We've all made stupid mistakes." "Did he Ryan?" "Once. He's been kicking himself ever since." "Was she right about that Callie girl?" "Yes. You have to know that it was a mistake. We all make them. Fact is we don't make the same mistake twice." "If you ever . . ." "I told you. It's not happening," Ryan said determined to convince her.

Rose and Ryan finally headed to bed. Rose was worried all night about Ava. She'd never seen her this upset. Finally around 2am, she called to see if Ava was alright. "Hey," Ava said. "You okay Ava?" "Getting there." "Did I wake you up?" "No." She heard Joe. "Seriously. Are you two alright?" "We will be. Thank you by the way." "Ava, you need me, you got me." "I know. I love you for it," Ava said. "Just say the word." "I know. You too." They hung up a while later. Rose fell asleep in Ryan's arms, and Ava tossed and turned and finally fell asleep.

———— ·····❦····· ————

The next morning, Ava got up with Grace and was playing outside with her. Joe got up and walked outside to see his two favorite ladies. "What are you two up to," he asked handing Ava a coffee. "Grace decided that she wanted to play outside with her toys." "Get any writing done?" Ava nodded. They all hung out for a while, then Ava went inside and got dressed. When she came back downstairs, Emily was talking to Joe and playing with Grace. "So that's cool?" "Fine with me," Emily said. "What are you planning?" "She's looking after Grace this weekend while we're doing the two concerts," Joe said. "Two?" "Friday and Saturday. We can fly back Saturday after the concert." "Oh really," Ava asked. He nodded and pulled her into his lap. "You sure that's alright," Ava asked. "I'll stay in the guest room." "I guess," Ava said. Joe kissed Ava, then went upstairs to pack. Ava went upstairs behind him. "What are you up to," Ava asked. "We need us time," he said. "We also have a daughter." "Babe, we need to fix this or we aren't going to be any good to her." He kissed Ava. They both packed. Just before Grace headed to bed for her afternoon nap, they headed out. "You sure she's going to be alright," Ava asked. He kissed Ava. "Positive. My mom's coming over tomorrow to stay with them." They pulled into the airport to meet the guys. "Ready?" Joe kissed Ava. "Yep."

They all left for the next concert. They showed up, the guys did an interview or two while Ava did her writing, then they did sound check. As they were finishing up, security came over to Joe. "What's up?" "There's a guy here that said he needs to talk with Ava. Should I let him in?" "Who is it?" "Kevin James." "Check with her," Joe said. Joe went to talk with the guys. "Ava, there's someone here to see you." She followed him.

"What the hell are you doing here," Ava asked. "Heard you were singing with them. The girl of a million talents," Kevin said. "Too bad you passed on them." "Ava, I'm trying to make up for it." "What do you want Kevin?" "Talk." "No," Ava said. "Coffee?" "No." "Ava give me a break." "I don't have to. That's the best part of breaking up. I don't owe you a damn thing," Ava said. "Please." "No." "Can't handle being that close to me?" "I'm married Keith," Ava said. "To who?" Joe came out a few minutes later and slid his arms around Ava. "Joe, this is my stupid ass of an ex Kevin. Kevin, this is Joe." He saw their matching rings. "Are you seriously trying to tell me you two are married," Kevin said. "For a while now," Joe replied. "So, no. I had no problem getting you out of my system. Go home," Ava said. Security walked him out and she walked back with Joe to where her things were.

"You alright," Joe asked. "Fine," Ava said. She went back to her writing. "Babe," he said. "What?" Joe kissed her. "Go finish talking to the guys." He kissed her again. "Go." He went back and finished their discussion with them. Ava finished up her writing, and Joe walked towards her. "Come on." "What?" "Dinner," Joe said. Ava packed up her laptop and followed them. They had dinner, then Brad went to call his wife, and Ryan went off to call Rose. "So what was what's his name doing here," Joe asked. "He heard I was singing with you guys." "Seriously?" "And he thought he could probably get something out of it if he showed. The guy's an idiot," Ava said. "I love you." "Love you too." "So, now that we have a few hours to ourselves," Joe teased. "What are you thinking?" He slid her into his lap and kissed her. She straddled him in his chair. "Come with me." "Where?" Joe kissed her and got up. He grabbed her hand and walked her out by the water. "What are you up to?" He pulled her into his arms and kissed her. His hands slid up the back of her shirt. "Joe." "What?" "What are you up to?" "Just happy that you're in my arms." "Suck up." They played around a while on the sand, then headed back to get changed. Ava slid into the shower and not a minute later, Joe was in behind her.

They showered, then played around, then Ava slid out and started getting ready. The hairdresser and makeup artist came in and did her hair. "What you wearing," Joe asked coming out in his black jeans. "You're fine." "Tell me." Ava shook her head. They finished with her hair and makeup. Ava slid on a jean shirt and leggings and went and sat down until the guys were done the meet and greet. Joe came in after and slid onto the sofa with her, pulling Ava into his arms. "Am I changing?" "Nope," Ava said. "Can I have a hint?" Ava shook her head. He kissed her neck, then her shoulder. "Try all you want. I'm not telling." The opening act finished and the guys headed on stage. He kissed Ava with one long kiss, then ran to catch up with the guys. Ava went in and slid on the black dress—another one that Joe hadn't seen. She touched up her makeup, then warmed up. She called to check on Grace. "She's fine. Auntie came to see her. They're staying in the other guest room," Emily said. "If you need anything, call me." "I will. Have a good show." Ava hung up. A minute later, Kevin called. "What?" "Can't just come and talk to me can you?" "I'm on in ten minutes." "Good. When you're done, come meet me for a drink," Kevin said. "Where?" "I'm at the concert. Third row." Ava hung up. "You ready," the stage manager asked. Ava nodded. He handed her the microphone. "Please welcome Ava Morgan."

They did the songs, then she sang another one with the guys, then headed backstage. Joe grabbed his other guitar and kissed her. She went backstage. "Ava, that guy that was here this morning is at the gate," security said. Ava went and met him. Security surrounded them. "What do you want," Ava asked. "When did you start singing?" "Fluke thing. Why are you here?" "I miss you." "And I'm married to Joe." "Ava, can't we even just have a drink?" "No. Something you forgot Kevin. The 'I'm out. I don't do relationships' thing isn't valid anymore. I'm married." "I made a mistake." "One you don't get a do-over with. I'm done. I have a baby girl at home,' Ava said. "You finally had one." "I don't need your shit Kevin." "What if I told you I still loved you?" "Then I'd tell you to take whatever you took the day you dumped me and get the hell over it." Ava finished her drink and walked backstage. She came back just as the guys were doing the last song on stage.

Ava sat down and went through her emails in the dressing room. She replied to a few, then deleted the junk mail. One stuck out:

Urgent—Message for Ava Morgan

She went through the email:

I know you don't know me, but you need to know. I've been seeing Joe on and off for a while. When you two met, we broke it off, but we got together recently. He said he couldn't see me at all anymore and that it was over. That he'd made a commitment and he was sticking to it. I love him with all I am and I hope you two are happy. I know you make him happy.—Jess

Ava forwarded it to his email. She logged off her computer and put it back in her bag, then threw her leggings and jean shirt back on. They came in and sat down for a few before they started getting ready to go. "You have an email," Ava said handing Joe his phone. She got up, took her things and hopped on the bus with the guys for the airport. Joe came on after her. "Babe," he said. Ava pulled her laptop back out and went back to writing. They got to the plane and hopped on, and Ava sat separately from them. Joe got up and went and sat with her. "Don't," Ava said. "Ava, it was a long time ago." "When did you see her?" "Meet and greet." "And?" "Nothing. I told her not to bother. That I was married and sticking to it." "How many more are going to come out of hiding Joe?" "None." "One. Just one." Joe kissed her. "It was before we were together. I told you that I was not the greatest person before we met." "Fine." He kissed her again. "Come sit with us." He got up and grabbed her hand, walking back over to the guys.

The plane finally landed and they headed to their hotel. Ryan called Rose, Brad called Danielle and Ava went to bed. Joe curled up with her. "I love you," Joe said. She didn't say a word. He fell asleep with Ava in his arms. The next morning, he woke up and she was gone. He looked around. "She went down to the gym," Brad said. "Thanks," Joe said. "What happened now?" "Jess emailed her." "Guess all the skeletons are officially out." "Ha ha not funny," Joe said. He pulled on his shirt and his baseball hat and went downstairs. Ava was just walking out of the gym when he saw her. He walked over to her. "Good workout?" Ava nodded. He kissed her. They headed back upstairs. "We have a few hours before we have to go. Was thinking we could grab something for Grace and Jacob." "Sure," Ava said. She showered, then pulled on her jeans and cowboy boots and they headed out. Ava put her things on the bus and they left.

An hour later, they had a bag for Grace and one for Jacob, and a few things for them. They got back to the hotel, had lunch, then headed to rehearsal and sound check. "Instead of God Bless, sing this one with us," Ryan said. "Of course you'd choose that one," Ava teased. They practiced a bit, then it was decided. That was their new song. The guys did sound check, then Ava did hers, and they headed off to dinner. Joe went off to talk to Ryan. "You two okay," Brad asked as he sat down with Ava. "Tell me he didn't really have that many girlfriends at once before we met." "He was the flirt. He had girlfriends out the wazoo. Difference being, the minute he met you, they didn't exist. I've seen them pop up at meet and greets. Fact being, he loves you. You don't need to worry about the other women around," Brad said. "Brad." "I know what you're gonna say Ava. I'll make a deal with you. I'll keep an eye on him and kick him in the ass if he needs it. You stop worrying," Brad said. He gave Ava a hug. "Thanks." "Have to take care of family right," he said. Ava nodded. The guys came back in. "Everything good," Joe asked. Ava nodded. He curled up with her. "So what time does the meet and greet start," Ryan asked. "We're doing an interview first," Brad said. "Where," Joe asked. "Here. You're doing the interview with us Ava," Brad said. "I am, am I?" Joe kissed her. Ava got up and got her makeup done, then tried to fix her hair. She pulled on the dress she was going to wear that night." "Damn," Joe said. "Thanks. Get dressed." He pulled her into his arms and kissed her, leaning her against the wall. "What time is the interview," Ava asked. "45 minutes," Joe said. He kissed her again, picking her up and wrapping her legs around him. "Joe." He leaned her onto the sofa. "You know you have the worst timing," Ava said. His hand slid up her legs.

They had sex. Hot, sizzling, fast and earth-shattering sex. They cleaned up then went into the interview. The reporter interviewed the guys, then they left and the interview continued with just Joe and Ava. "So tell us how you met." "I'd met her years ago. This time, she came backstage with an old friend of ours. She walked in and it was like time stopped. I couldn't take my eyes off of her," Joe said. "What about you Ava?" "Honestly, we talked and I couldn't stop smiling. It was the call a few days later that got me. He called and invited me to the concert. I got there, and they walked me down to see him." "So it was love at first sight?" "If first sight meant years ago when we'd first met, then yes. Had a crush on him for years," Ava said. "So how did you ask her to marry you?" "We'd celebrated my birthday. I slid it on her hand when we were sleeping. When we got up the next morning, I told her I loved her and that I wanted to be with her forever. She saw the ring, then said yes," Joe said. "So we have some shots of your wedding in Cabo San Lucas." "It was just a small wedding with our friends and some family. Honestly, I couldn't wait to be with her," Joe said. "So now that you've had your beautiful baby girl, what's next for you two?" "The new CD's coming out in a few months, Ava's new book is coming out, which is a great book by the way. I read it. Other than that, whatever the world throws at us. Forever's a long time," Joe said. "Thanks you two." The interview finished and he kissed Ava. "Ava, I have some other questions for you. Is that okay," the interviewer asked. "Sure," Ava said. Joe kissed her again, then headed off to sit with the guys. "So when did you start singing?" "Honestly, it was a fluke thing. The guys were working on a new song, and I helped them out. From that day on, I was singing with them every concert," Ava said. "So tell us about your daughter." "She's adorable. She's growing up way too fast, but all babies do." "Any plans for more kids?" "Not right now. I want to enjoy every second with her." "So we know that Joe is the notorious playboy of the group . . . or is that just rumor?" "He probably was before, but I can tell you that now, he's the best father and an amazing husband." "So you tamed the bad boy?" "I guess I did," Ava said. Joe smirked. "So tell us about the new book."

The interview finally finished, then the guys got ready for the meet and greet. Ava walked past Joe and slid out of her heels. "Babe," Joe said. Ava closed the door. "You were great." Ava sat down and called to check on Grace. "She's fine. How are you two doing," his mom asked. "We're good. We went shopping for some stuff for the kids today." "Why don't you fly home in the morning? Just relax tonight," his mom suggested. "I'll let you know." "She wouldn't let go of your wedding picture today. She said mine over and over." Ava laughed. "I miss her," Ava said. "Enjoy tonight." "Thank you for this." "Give my boy a kiss for me," his mom said. "I will." Ava hung up. "Told you she was fine," Joe said. "Your mom said to give you a kiss." "What's wrong?" "Nothing. Just didn't want the bullshit today." "Babe," he said. "You're fine. Everything went fine. I lied, but fine." Ava got up, slid on her slippers and went to leave. He grabbed her hand, pulling her back towards him. "You didn't." "Yeah I did. You are still the playboy of the group. Always will be," Ava said. "Not anymore." "Fine." "Ava, not anymore. Nobody else. Period." "Fine," Ava said. "We okay?" Ava nodded. He kissed her. Ava headed into the other room and as soon as Joe finished getting changed he came in and sat with Ava and the guys.

The concert went off without a glitch. As soon as Ava got back to the sitting area, her phone went off. "Hello?" "Ava, it's James." She hung up. Ava slid into her jeans and sweater, then got some writing done. When the concert finished, the guys headed backstage, they grabbed their things and headed for the airport. "Rose waiting up," Joe asked. Ryan nodded. "Jacob said Dada and grabbed the picture of me," Ryan said. "He'll be walking soon," Ava said. "Then he'll be chasing Grace," Brad teased. They joked around and Ava fell asleep on the plane. They finally landed, then Joe carried Ava to the car. He threw the bags in the back and they headed home.

Ava woke up half way back to the house. "I'll wake you up when we're home," he said. "Can't." Ava leaned onto his shoulder and he linked his fingers with hers, kissing her hand. They pulled into the driveway and headed inside. They slid upstairs, making sure they didn't wake anyone, then Ava checked on Grace. She was out cold with her teddy bear. Ava came back into their bedroom and slid out of her jeans and into her satin teddy. She washed up, then crawled into bed. Joe unpacked and slid into bed with her. "Welcome home baby," Joe said. "I have to leave tomorrow for New York." "I know," Joe said. He wrapped his arms around Ava, then they both fell asleep.

The next morning, Ava got up with Grace and played with her while she packed. "Mama." "Yes you're coming. You get to hang out with Daddy too." "Mine." Grace held onto their picture from their bedside table. A half-hour later, they were all packed. They had breakfast with Joe's mom and dad, then the three of them headed to the airport.

"I missed you." "I missed you too baby." "How did the concerts go?" "Good. Gotta tell you, singing that song that Ava so loved, not easy without you there." "You can throw in a new one instead." "Good idea." Ryan played with Jacob and spent more time with Rose. They passed on the studio until Joe got back. They tucked Jacob into bed, then Emily looked after him and they had a date night. "Where are we going?" "A movie." They went in and got their tickets, then went to the movies. After, they went out for drinks, then headed home.

Ava and Joe checked in to the hotel, then headed to the first book signing. Joe hung out with Grace. Ava was in her zone. She looked beautiful, and there were almost as many fans as at his concert. When the book signing was done, Ava headed back to the hotel with Joe and Grace. They had dinner, then gave Grace a bath and put her to bed. As Ava was tucking her in, Joe filled the tub for them. Ava came back in and he slid her shirt off, then her skirt. Ava got undressed and slid into the steaming hot tub. Joe slid in a few minutes later, after handing Ava a glass of wine. "Seriously, when do we get to take a break," Ava asked. "Wednesday night." Ava laughed. "We don't have that many concerts left. Once they're done, we're going away," Joe said. "Oh really?" He kissed her neck. "I'd suffice for a descent night of sleep." He kissed her shoulder. "You know you used to be fine after all of this," Joe said. "Just tired." "Babe." "Don't even think it Joe. We aren't." "I'm just saying." "We're not having another one until she's at least 2." "We've been practicing," he joked. "And I am on something until we decide to have one." "Party pooper." "You don't have to be in those dresses Joe. You also don't have to carry the baby for 9 months." "I know. I just think that having another one . . ." "When it's time, then we will," Ava said before he started getting carried away. "I love you." "I know." They had their wine and relaxed.

Ava finished the book signing the next day. They went back to the hotel to pack up and head back when Kevin knocked on the door. "Ava." She went into the hall. "What the hell are you doing here?" "We have to talk." "No we don't." "Ava we're talking or you're not leaving." Joe put Grace in her crib and came out into the living room. "What could you possibly have to say after what you did," Ava asked. Kevin pulled her to him and kissed her. Ava pushed him away. "Get out." "No." Joe walked into the hallway hearing it all and Ava stopped him. "Kevin, if you're trying to start a fight . . . ," Ava said. "I'm not. I know that I screwed up before. I want you back." "It's not gonna happen. Joe and I are married. End of discussion." "No. Not end of discussion." Kevin made a move towards her and Joe clocked him in the face. "Get out," Ava said. She pulled Joe back. Kevin finally left. "Your hand alright," Ava asked. Joe nodded. Ava went and grabbed ice and a towel, wrapping his hand up. A little while later, they checked out and headed home.

CHAPTER 18

Ava and Joe finally got home. They tucked Grace in for her afternoon nap, then curled up in bed having a nap themselves. They got up a few hours later to the sound of Grace giggling away with Emily. "Didn't know you were coming by," Joe said peeking his head into Grace's room. "Thought you two might need some time to chill," Emily said. "Hungry?" "Sure," Emily said. Joe brought Grace downstairs and Emily followed. He put on something for dinner and Ava came down and helped. "So how was the book thing," Emily asked. "Don't ask," Joe answered. Ava grabbed the ice pack from the fridge and handed it to him. "What happened?" "One of her friends is a dick," Joe said. He wrapped his hand up. "You didn't have to hit him," Ava said. "Yeah I did." "You seriously did that? Since when are you a scrapper," Emily asked. "Ha Ha very funny," Joe said. "Somehow I don't think I need to worry about him bugging me anymore," Ava said. "He needed a butt kicking." "Understatement, but still," Ava said. He walked over to Ava. "Nobody messes with my wife," Joe said then kissed her. "So how did the concerts go," Emily asked. "Great." "And?" "Nothing. It was good," Joe said. "So when's the tour done?" "Right before Christmas." "Speaking of . . . ," Ava said. "Everyone's coming here. Danielle's bringing Turkey for dinner, Rose said she's bringing dessert." "Already planned it without me," Ava asked. "It's just us and my parents during the day. I was going to call your folks . . ." "I'll call them tonight," Ava said. "Second Christmas." "Like last year wasn't enough," Ava joked. "Grace's first Christmas." "True," Joe said. He wrapped his arms around Ava then taste tested dinner. "Babe." "I know," Ava said. They had dinner together, then Emily headed home. Ava and Joe gave Grace her bubble bath, then Joe sang her to sleep.

Ava curled up on the sofa downstairs and turned on the TV. "I still can't believe I only get two days to relax," Ava said. "So what do you want to do for your birthday," Joe asked. "Nothing." "We have to do something." "Nope." "Ava, come on." "I want to relax, sleep in, and do nothing." "No dinner?" "Just us." "We have to do something. You know that Rose and Danielle aren't going to let you do nothing," Joe said. "I just want to relax and have a non-stress day." "Beach?" Ava smirked. "What are you thinking," she asked. "Somewhere warm. Grace can make a sand castle." Ava smiled. "Or dinner here, with them, then you and

165

me locked in the bedroom," Joe said. "So like every other weekend after we get home . . ." He kissed her. "Seriously." "Massage for two," Ava said. "Like the way you think." "I know." They curled up together on the sofa and relaxed, then headed to bed.

Ava's birthday came up quickly. "Get her to the restaurant around 6:30," Danielle said. "How do you expect me to pull that off without her knowing," Joe asked. "Tell her you made a reservation for the two of you to have a quiet dinner." "She's here. Gotta go." Joe hung up. "Better," he asked. Ava nodded. "What are you up to?" "Nothing. Made a dinner reservation," he said. "Oh really." He nodded and kissed her. "We have to go pick Grace up," Ava said. "She's staying with Emily." "Oh really?" Joe kissed her. They got changed, then headed home to get ready for dinner.

Ava slid on her black dress that Joe loved, with her heels that made her legs look 20 feet long. She came downstairs and he handed her roses. "Thank you," Ava said. He kissed her. "Happy birthday beautiful." Ava slid them into the vase, then they headed out for dinner. They walked in and Ava knew. "Couldn't stop her," Joe said. They had dinner with Ryan and Rose, Brad and Danielle and Carrie and Rachel. Joe slid Ava's gift into her hand during dessert. "What's this?" "For my wife." "Should I pass it to her," Ava joked. He kissed her. Ava read the totally sappy card, then opened the gift. It was a white gold heart locket with a picture of Grace on one side, and a picture of him on the other. "It's perfect," Ava said. "Thought you'd like it." Ava kissed him. "There's something else in there." Ava looked and saw diamond earrings, and a paper. She pulled it out. It was the info on two tickets to Maui. "What's this," Ava asked. "In January. After the concerts are done." Ava wrapped her arms around him. "You and me. Just a few days," Joe said. "Think we're gonna need it." Rose and Ryan gave her a charm bracelet with a white gold guitar and a diamond heart. "It's beautiful." "Ryan picked it," Rose said. Ava hugged them. Brad and Danielle gave her a gift certificate for the spa, and Carrie and Rachel gave her three of her favorite old movies on DVD. "You guys," Ava said hugging everyone and saying thank you. "So there's one other gift from Grace," Joe said. "Oh really." Joe handed her a box. It was a picture of Grace and Joe in a Swarovski crystal frame. "When did you . . ." "Father-daughter day." They finished dinner then headed home. Ava put the picture beside her lamp. "So birthday girl. What else did you want to do tonight," Joe asked. She curled up in his arms. "Got it already," Ava said. "Which is?" She kissed him. He slid his arms around her and undid the back of her dress. She kicked her heels off.

He kissed her from head to toe. He teased his way down her body, then back up, taking his time to tease every inch of her into goose bumps. He licked, teased, nibbled and kissed his way back up and kissed her. They made love over and over again. When they were about to fall asleep, Ava heard a car pull in their driveway. "What was that," Ava asked. "Nothing." "It sounded like a car pulling in." "Probably just the neighbors." He pulled her into his arms. She heard the sound of keys dropping at their front door. "Joe, that wasn't a neighbor," Ava said. "It's fine." Ava slid on her satin robe and walked downstairs. There was a package with a red ribbon in the mail slot. Ava grabbed it. "What the hell?" Joe came downstairs in his jeans. "Well," he asked. "What's this?" He grabbed the package. "It's for you." "Who would be dropping off . . ." Ava looked at the writing. She opened it and found a set of car keys. She looked at Joe. "I can't surprise you can I," he asked. Ava walked outside and saw the new shiny SUV that Joe had made her look at a million times. "What is this doing here," Ava asked. "Open the envelope." She opened it and found the ownership in her name along with the insurance papers. The license plate:

Joes Baby

Ava smiled and walked over to him. "Oh really," Ava asked. "As in you're my baby." "Uh huh." She kissed him. "Everything else was more than enough," she said. "We're gonna need it." "Says who?" "Says you haven't taken the pill in a week." "And?" "Unless you changed to the shot, we're gonna need a bigger car," Joe said. Ava kissed him again and he walked her over to the door, opening it for her. It was black leather interior, sunroof, power everything, and every button and whistle available, including the tinted windows. "Question," Ava asked. "What's that my beautiful wife?" "Mine or yours?" Joe smirked. "We both have keys." "I guess I could share it," Ava said. He kissed her again. "Deal being, no taking off. There's a GPS in it in case anything happens. Don't make me use it for other things," Joe said. "Guess I'll have to tell my boyfriend he'll be driving." He laughed and pulled her into his arms. He wrapped her legs around him and locked the SUV, carrying Ava inside and right back to bed for another round.

The next morning, Ava and Joe got up and started packing. "So, we'll be back Sunday morning," he said. "Why not Saturday right after," Ava asked. "The guys wanted to stay. Danielle and Rose are coming." "Nice." "Will be. You need girl time with the girls," Joe said. "Oh really?" Joe pulled Ava into his arms. "Really." "Dress shopping it is," Ava teased. "If you come back in anything like those other ones . . ." "Those were the tame dresses Joe," Ava said. Grace came into the bedroom. "Hey baby," Joe said picking Grace up. "Me." "Yes you're coming too baby girl." They finished packing and Joe played with Grace. Ava finished getting everything together, and they headed for the plane in Ava's new SUV. "You sure it'll be safe here," Ava asked. "Trust me," Joe said. He kissed her. They hopped on the plane with Grace and the guys were already on the plane with Rose, Danielle, Jacob and Emily. "About time," Brad said. "Wanted to take it for a scenic drive," Ava said. "Take what," Rose asked. "Ava got the wheels," Ryan said. "You didn't." Rose looked out to the parking and saw the SUV. "Okay, I'm jealous," she said. "We'll go out for a bit when we get back," Ava said. The kids played during the flight while everyone chatted. Ava curled up with Joe and did some writing. "So, I figure we'll hit Macy's first,"

Danielle said. Ava looked at Joe. He looked back with a grin. "You two have a cat that ate the canary look. What's up with you two," Brad asked. "Nothing," Ava replied. "Liar," Brad said. They chatted the rest of the flight. By the time they landed, the kids were asleep. They all headed for the RV's, then to the venue.

The guys did sound check, then Joe pulled Ava off to the side. "What would you like oh sexy one," Ava asked. "Other than you?" "We're going shopping. Any requests," Ava teased. Joe kissed her, picking her up in his arms. "I'll see if I can find it." "If anything happens . . ." Ava kissed him. "I know. I love you too," she said. The ladies headed off shopping and Emily stayed behind with the guys and the kids. "We should get her something," Danielle said. Ava nodded.

After two hours of shopping, Ava had found dresses to top the other ones . . . . and a few things that Joe had requested. They came back and Ava packed the dresses away. "So," Joe asked sneaking up behind her in the RV. "What?" His arms slid around her. "You'll love it," Ava said. "No more teasing." "Trust me." "Ava." "Might forget the words or the music, but you'll like it." Ava handed him a shirt she'd bought for him. "Nice." "You needed something new." "Babe." "It'll fit." "You are in way too good of a mood," Joe said. "Could be better." He picked her up and they ended up in a tickle fight on the bed. That led to making out like teenagers. Just as they were about to take it further, her phone rang. She looked at it, then threw it into her purse. "Who?" Ava kissed him. He grabbed the phone. "Who's this?" "Kevin." "Guess you didn't get the fuck off and leave my wife alone thing did you," Joe asked. "I know she still wants me." Joe hung up, turning her phone off. He kissed her again. "Told you it wasn't important," Ava said. He pulled her into his arms. "Don't let him ruin the mood." "We're changing your cell number. You know that right," Joe said. "Already put in the request." He kissed her. They curled up on the bed together.

"Who would have ever thought," Joe said. "I never would've. I expected to be in that little house forever to be honest," Ava said. "I have to tell you something." "What," Ava asked trying not to get pissed. "Before we met, I wasn't the guy I am now," Joe said. "I figured that." "I was lost. Honestly, I didn't know what was up." "And I met every sleeze in the planet," Ava joked. "Then I met you. Honestly, I feel like a totally different person." "Why?" "Because I feel like things make sense now. That old saying 'no pain no gain'. The BS of every other girl in the damn planet and the crap I went through, makes me value us even more," Joe said. "Just had to find the right one." "That changed my life." "And hopefully the others will stay in the woodwork where they belong," Ava said. He pulled her back into his arms and kissed her. He made love to her, then they had a shower, got changed and headed to dinner. "Do I even get a hint about the dress," Joe asked. Ava shook her head. "One hint." "Pale pink lace." "What?" She walked ahead of him and he chased her to dinner. Ava gave Emily the little present that her and Rose had bought. Emily ran off and put it on.

"What has got into them," Rose asked. "They're back to normal," Brad teased. Grace had dinner with them, then the kids ran off to play. "So what color tonight," Ryan asked. "Black jeans, white shirt," Joe said. "Oh really," Ryan asked. "New shirt," Brad teased. "You can wear yours," Danielle teased. "Planned the outfits?" Ryan wrapped his arm around Rose. "You needed something new," Rose teased. "I have something new alright," Ryan joked. For once, the guys didn't feel like doing the meet and greet. The guys got ready and Ava hung with the girls. Rose put Jacob and Rose down after they fell asleep on the sofa with them. Joe pulled Ava into the hall. "What?," Ava asked. He kissed her. "Nice shirt sexy man." "This hot and sexy lady I know bought it for me," Joe said. "Missing something." "What?" She slid a box out of her pocket. "Ava." "Open it." It was a white gold bracelet with a small cross on it. "It's beautiful." Ava slid it on his wrist. It fit perfectly. "Matches," Ava said. Joe kissed her again. "Ava, we need you for hair and makeup." Ava nodded. Joe kissed her again and the guys headed off to the meet and greet.

After, Ava hung out with the girls until the guys went on. She went back and slid on the black and white dress she'd picked out that hugged her curves. She slid on the pale pink lace lingerie underneath. She knew Joe was going to love this. The minute she headed on stage, his eyes were stuck to her. Ryan was singing 'Make her love me'. Ava came in and sang part of it with him. They did her songs, then Ava headed off. Joe smirked. At the end, Ryan talked her into one more song. Joe slid his hand in hers and brought her back on stage. They sang one last song, then they were done. Joe pulled her into his arms and kissed her. They went back and hung out for a while. "You were amazing baby," Danielle said hugging Brad. "Must have been the new lucky shirts," Rose teased. Joe was on the sofa with Ava in his arms. "Pink lace," Joe whispered. Ava nodded. "So what's the plan," Brad asked. "Hang out until the mobs are gone, then on to the next one," Ryan said. "The kids are asleep in yours," Rose said. Ava nodded. "Guess we'll have to be quiet," Joe whispered. Ava elbowed him.

They all finally left and headed to the next venue. Ava and Joe quietly slipped past the kids and washed up, then slid into bed. He had Ava's dress half off before they even made it to bed. She came into the bedroom and he looked over. "Damn." "I warned you," Ava said. Within minutes, he had her pulled back onto the bed. "You know how sexy you look?" "Think that's why I bought it," Ava said. He kissed her, then down her torso, sliding the lace underwear off on his way down. "Babe," he said. "Mmm." "I think I might just keep you." "Personal sex slave. Sounds interesting," Ava teased. Joe kissed her and she slid his belt off. He kicked his jeans off. "What am I gonna do with you," Ava asked. "Keep me. Surgically attach us." "Think we already are," Ava teased. He made love to her again, then they curled up and fell asleep.

"I had an idea," Brad said curled up in bed with Danielle. "What's that?" "A baby." "Good idea." She handed him mail that she pulled from her bag. "What's this?" He noticed an envelope with her writing on it. "Open it." He opened it and saw a pregnancy test. "Baby," Brad asked. Danielle nodded. "Seriously?" "Hence why we were shopping."

"So now that I finally get you all to myself for the night," Ryan said. "Other than sleeping in," Rose said. "Have a better idea," Ryan said pulling Rose into his arms and kissing her. "I'm glad you're here babe." "Me too. I missed you," Rose said. "I love the touring and the concerts and the fans, but honestly, I wish I was with you more." "Soon enough," Rose said. "We should make the best of this." "Such as?" "Next time we do a concert and come home, I slide into bed with you and wake you up." "Hmm. That could work," Rose joked. He made love to Rose. "I don't know how I got so blessed." "One of those unexplainable things." "And just think, if it hadn't been for Joe and Ava, we wouldn't have met," Ryan said. "You know he bet her that I wouldn't go home after we first met." "And she must have lost that bed miserably." Rose kissed him. "I missed having you to curl up with." "Sleep better together." He nodded. They curled up and fell asleep together.

The next day, Ava and Joe took the kids for a run, then brought Jacob over to Rose and Ryan. "I see they got some fresh air," Rose said. "Needed a run," Ava said. Jacob was hand in hand with Grace. "I'll take them for a bit," Rose said. Ava and Joe teased each other, playing tag all the way back to the RV. "Where they find all the energy, I don't know," Rose said. Ryan wrapped his arms around Rose. "So we have a few hours before we have to be back. What do you want to do today," he asked. "What time," Rose asked. "1," he replied. They took the kids to the park for a while, then to the beach.

"Would you stop," Ava said. He tackled her onto the bed. "Never." "What am I gonna do with you?" "I have a few ideas," Joe said tickling Ava. There was a knock at the door. "Joe, it's Andrew." He kissed Ava and they got up. "What's up bud?" "Visitor." "Who," Joe asked. "Jane Martin." He hopped off the RV and Ava was right behind him. "Joe." "One of my high school friends. I promise." He kissed her and linked his fingers with hers. "What the hell are you doing here stranger," Joe asked. "Came to see if you're still being a snob," she said. "Ava, this is Jane. Jane, this is Ava." "Congrats. I heard you two got hitched. Thanks for the invite snob," Jane teased. "Last minute thing in Cabo. How are you?" "Good. Adam and I got married." "And you call me a snob," Joe said. "You were on tour smart ass," Jane replied. "You coming tonight?" "I guess." "Funny." "He bought us tickets." "Did you want to come by for a drink before," Joe asked. "Sure. I'll pop by. I'm just heading off to pick him up. Thought I'd poke my head in and say hi." Joe hugged her goodbye. "See you tonight." Andrew put her name down on the list and Jane headed off. Joe and Ava headed back to the RV.

"Snob," Ava asked. "Long story." He walked Ava backwards towards the bed. "Now where were we," Joe asked. His arms slid around her and he tackled her to the bed. "We should go out and do something with your time off." "We are." He kissed her as they laughed and joked around. "Seriously." "What were you thinking? Matching tattoos," Joe joked. Ava looked at him. "You are nuts." "Tattoo on my butt that says property of Ava?" "No." "A little one that only we know about." "Such as," Ava asked. "Two rings linked." "With Forever underneath it." "Would kill an hour," Joe teased. He kissed her but he had other ideas. They made love, then showered, then they got the tattoos.

They headed back just as Rose and Ryan were coming back. "Where did you two disappear to," Ryan asked. "Got a new tattoo," Joe said. Rose smirked. "What? You two have a secret language I don't know about," Rose asked. "Nope," Ava joked. Joe picked Ava up, flinging her over his shoulder and carried her back to the RV. Brad and Danielle had spent the day baby shopping. Nobody else knew. Ryan and Rose put the kids down for their afternoon nap with Emily and hung out for a while.

"You have to do the interviews at 1," Ava said. "And it's only 12:15." Joe leaned her onto the bed. "You're hilarious." "Determined," Joe said kissing her. They had sex, then changed.

The guys met up for the interview while Ava, Rose and Danielle watched. "You know you're glowing," Ava said to Danielle. "In a good mood." "So either you two took full advantage of your alone time, or . . ." "Or what," Danielle asked. "Are you," Ava asked. "What?" Ava looked. "You are!" "Shh," Danielle said. "Congratulations." Ava hugged her. "How far?" "Two months next week," Danielle said. "Holy crap." "I know. We were just talking about it yesterday. I put the pregnancy test in an envelope and handed it to him." "So where did you two disappear to today," Ava asked. "Baby shopping."

The ladies sat around chatting. Joe waved Ava to come closer. She checked her makeup and came over to them. "This is my wife, Ava," Joe said. "You've brought a new dynamic to the concerts. Where did you come up with the songs," the interviewer asked. "We wrote them together," Ava said. "You and the guys?" "Pretty good team," Ava said as Joe slid his arm around her shoulders. "We also have some news for you. The single for Love Letter is #1." "Seriously," Ryan asked. "And the single has sold a million copies as of today." "It's a great song," Brad said. "That it is," Joe said. "So you going to tell us the story behind it?" Joe looked at Ava. "Honestly, one night I was thinking about what I would write if I was to write her a love letter. I got stuck at one part, and she came downstairs. She sang it with me, then added the last piece. It was perfect. It was all about how much I love her." "Easily relatable for everyone. So when are you doing the video for it?" "Soon," Joe said. They asked a few more questions, then finished up. Ava went to head back to the girls. "Babe," Joe said. "I know." He picked her up, spinning her around and kissed her.

Joe put her down and they headed back to the RV. "What?" "What were you guys giggling about," Joe asked. "Danielle's pregnant." "Seriously?" "Brad just found out. I guessed." Joe kissed her. He walked her backwards towards the bed. "I still can't believe we did it," he said still in shock over the single. "I knew people liked it, but that much." Joe held her close. "You know what that means don't you?" "What's that," Ava asked. "You're stuck with us for life." "I guess I am." He kissed her again and they curled up together. "Something is so right with us," Joe said. "I know. Don't know what I'd do without you." "Get used to it. I'm not going anywhere Ava." "Good." Joe kissed her again. Ryan came by with the kids. Grace walked over to Joe. "Dada up." He picked her up kissing her and snuggling her close as Grace giggled. "We're celebrating tonight," Ryan said. "Oh really," Ava replied. "We're all going to dinner. Don't ask me how we're supposed to get back through this insane crowd," Rose said. "Better idea," Ava said. She checked something on her laptop, then made a call. "What are you doing," Joe asked. "They're delivering." "Seriously?" Ava nodded. "They'll be here around 5." Joe wrapped his arm around her. "See, this is why I love her," Joe said. "But I thought . . . ," Ava teased. He kissed Ava. "Funny." Brad came in with Danielle. "So what's the pow wow for," Brad asked. "Celebrating." "Oh really," Danielle said. Ava looked at Danielle. "Good thing I ordered it for six people," Ava said. "Or six and a half," Brad said. "What are you talking about," Ryan asked. "Danielle." "What about her," Ryan asked. "We're having a baby." Joe and Ryan hugged Brad and congratulated them both. "Tell me Ms. Smarty pants didn't figure it out first," Joe said. "Of course. I knew when Ava was," Brad said. They all joked around a bit, then Ryan and Rose left, and Danielle and Brad went for a walk.

"Finally," Joe said. "What," Ava asked. He picked her up and carried her back to bed, kissing her. "Aww. Mr. Neglected," Ava teased. He kissed her again and his hands slid up her shirt. Ava saw Grace sneaking up at the end of the bed. "You're supposed to be napping missy," Ava joked. She slid Grace onto the bed with them. "I know what will put her to sleep," Joe said. "What's that?" He grabbed his acoustic guitar. He sang 'Now and

Forever' to Ava. By the end of the song, Grace was asleep in Ava's arms. He kissed Ava, then took Grace to her bed and slid her in for her nap. He came back into the bedroom and curled back up with Ava, kissing her. "Babe," he said. "Yes love." Joe kissed her again. "Who knew that all that insomnia would lead to this," Joe joked. "I wouldn't exactly call it insomnia." They laughed and kissed. "We should write more together," Joe said. "Good idea. Smart and sexy too," Ava said. "And all yours." "Best part." "You think so do you," he said brushing her hair over her shoulder. Ava nodded. "Always has been." He kissed her again and they made love.

"I still can't believe Ava figured it out," Rose said. "I still can't believe Brad's finally gonna be a dad," Ryan said. "Danielle is beaming." "I know. It's about darned time for those two," Ryan said. They went and got Jacob and went for a walk by the water and let Jacob play with the sand. "You know we're raising a beach bum right," Ryan said. Rose nodded. "And something tells me someday he's going to marry Grace." "You think so do you?" Rose nodded. They relaxed on the beach a while, then headed back and put Jacob down for a nap.

Dinner showed right on time. They all had a nice relaxing dinner while the kids napped, then did a quick sound check and the guys went to get ready for the meet and greet. "Well," Joe asked. "I say go shirtless," Ava teased. He kissed her and pulled her into his arms. "Fine. If you insist. Blue jeans," Ava said. "What are you up to," Joe asked. "Red dress." "Ava." "Not telling." "You're killing me with these dresses." "I know. And you love it," Ava replied. He kissed her and had her pinned to the wall of the RV. "You're going to make me late you know," Joe said. "I'm not the one with the problem." He kissed her and they had sex again, then he washed up and headed to the meet and greet. When they finished, Ava was still in her blue jeans. "At some point, you're going to have to let me see it before you walk out," Joe said. "Nope," Ava teased. He kissed her again. They finished doing her hair, touched his up, then the guys went out. Ava grabbed her red shirt and her blue jeans, slid on her cowboy boots and walked out when she had to. Joe smirked.

Ava sang her two songs, then Ryan headed off stage. "Thought we'd pull a little surprise on Ava tonight. See, she always pulls surprises on us. It's our turn." "Meaning what," Ava asked. Joe came out with his acoustic guitar and sang 'Now and Forever'. "Guys, if you have a girl, now is a good time to wrap your arms around her," Ava joked. He sang and Ava got a little teary-eyed. She sang one last song with the guys, then headed back. He looked over at her when he switched guitars. Ava blew him a kiss.

CHAPTER 19

Finally, they all headed home after the concert. Grace and Jacob were dead asleep with Emily at their sides, and Brad and Danielle were curled up in their seats together, Ryan and Rose were snuggling and Ava and Joe were curled up together. "I saw the tears Ava," Joe said. "It's one of my favorite songs." "I got you and you know it," Joe teased. "Fine. You already had me, but fine." He kissed her.

"So when are you due," Rose asked. "July," Danielle replied. "You know you're getting a baby shower," Ava said. "Thanks. There's so much to do before the baby comes," Danielle said. "Now it's really like a family," Ryan said. "That it is," Brad said wrapping his arm around Danielle. Ryan and Rose chatted with Brad and Danielle most of the way back. Ava and Joe fell asleep curled up together.

They finally landed. Grace and Jacob were still asleep. They were snuggled up side by side. Ava slid Grace out of the crib and tucked her into her car seat. Joe grabbed their things, throwing them into the SUV, and Ava gently belted Grace in. Everyone was heading home within a half-hour.

Ava took Grace in and tucked her into her crib with her teddy bear, then slid out and went and helped Joe with the bags. She threw laundry in, then headed upstairs. Joe pulled her to him the minute she walked into the bedroom. "What?" "So much for a red dress." "Felt like the cowboy boots tonight," Ava said. "That top should be illegal." "Oh really?" He kissed her. "I have to see the other ones," Joe said. "Not until I walk on the stage." "Intentional teasing." Ava nodded. "Totally not fair." "I know." Ava kissed him then went in to wash up for bed. She washed her makeup off, and when she looked up, he was behind her. "What?" "Totally get the Fast Cars song now," he joked. "Only time I really put any on is when we're on stage." "Still sexy without it." "You're pretty sexy with bed head yourself," Ava said. He slid his shirt off. "Ava." "Yes baby." "Promise me something.' "What?" "That no matter what happens, we'll always be this much in love." "Probably more," Ava said. "Good." "Worried that you're too happy?" Joe kissed her. He picked her up and carried

174

her to bed, pulling the shirt off and sliding the jeans off the minute they fell into bed. "It's good being home," Joe said. "No disruptions?" He nodded. They made love. They curled up together and were out cold in minutes.

Ava woke up 4 or 5 hours later and was playing with Grace downstairs when Joe noticed she wasn't in bed. The smell of the coffee gave her location away. He slid his track pants on and walked downstairs. "Dada. Look." Grace had drawn him a picture and Ava had posted it on the fridge. "It's beautiful baby," Joe said. "Daddy work." "Looks just like me." He picked Grace up and kissed her. "Num," Grace said. He grabbed Ava's breakfast and made it, then fed her while Ava made her and Joe some breakfast. She brought it over to him with his super mug of coffee. "Thank you beautiful." "Welcome sexy." Joe kissed her. Grace giggled. "What are you giggling for," Joe asked. He tickled Grace. They played around all day outside. Ava got a little writing done and sent the finished chapters in. "So what do you think of this as a cover," Ava asked. She showed Joe. "Where did we take that," he asked. "We didn't. It was one of their suggestions." "I like," Joe said. It was a picture of his hand with Grace's. He kissed Ava, then went back to playing with Grace.

Ava watched Joe with Grace. He really was a new man. He was playing music every day, spending quality time with Grace, being a pretty great husband, and was in a great group with a great bunch of guys. Ava couldn't help thinking that it just seemed a little too good to be true. When it seemed that way, it normally was.

The next morning, Ava woke up and Joe was gone. Grace was in bed. Ava went downstairs and looked around to find a note—nothing. She put on the coffee. She poured herself a cup, then gave Grace her breakfast. They played for a while. Ava went and looked. The new SUV was there, but his car was gone. She checked her phone for a message, but there wasn't one. She called Joe's phone and it went straight to voicemail. "Where did you take off to? Call me."

After a full afternoon of playing with Grace and writing, Ava fed Grace, gave her a bath, and tucked her in. She did some more writing, then slid into a hot bath. There was still no call, and still no message. Ava leaned back and tried to relax. She had a glass or two of red wine. When she finished the second glass she heard a noise. It was his car alarm. Ava leaned back. He walked in, noticing the open bottle of wine. Joe poured himself a glass, then walked upstairs. He saw her in the tub, then walked over and filled her glass back up. "Hey beautiful," Joe said as he leaned down to kiss her. She turned her cheek. "What's wrong?" "Where were you?" "Studio." He leaned down and kissed her again. "Didn't return any messages either." "I left my phone here." "No note," Ava asked. "I thought I told you yesterday." Ava shook her head. "Baby, I'm sorry." He slid his shirt off, then wrapped his arms around Ava. "What are you doing," Ava asked. A minute later, his jeans hit the floor, then his boxers and he slid into the tub with her. "What are you doing?" He kissed her. She saw a lipstick mark on his neck. He kissed down her neck, to her shoulder. "Stop." He pulled her into his lap. He kissed her again. "Joe, stop." "What?" "Might want to wash the lipstick off." Ava got out of the tub, wrapped herself in a towel, and walked off with her wine. She walked outside and sat on the chaise by the pool. He came out a few minutes later, with a towel wrapped around him. "Ava," he said. "What?" "I thought we were past this." She took another sip of her wine. "Ava, seriously. I was at the studio with the guys. Ryan invited my mom down." "So where did the lipstick come from?" He sat down on the edge of the chaise. "Stop being an idiot. I have what I want, and I'm never letting it go." He kissed her and slid into her arms. "You can't get rid of me that easily you know."

The next morning, Ryan got up and Rose and Ava were on the phone. "I'll be over in a half-hour. Is she looking after the kids," Emily asked. "Rose," Ryan said. "Ryan's up. I'll call you when I'm on my way . . . . okay, then call me when you're on your way," Rose said hanging up. "What's wrong," Ryan asked. "Going out with Ava for a bit. Girl day." "We're going back into the studio today. We won't be back until late," Ryan said. "I'll miss you," Rose said curling back up with him in bed. "You two have fun on your girl day. I'll be back around midnight," Ryan said. Rose wrapped her arms and legs around him. "Not sleeping in anymore," Rose said. She laughed as he leaned in to kiss her.

Joe woke up as soon as he felt Ava slide out of bed. "Where you taking off to," he asked. "Out with Rose." "Baby," he said. "What?" "I had a better idea." "I'm sure you did," Ava said. He got up and chased her into the bathroom. He had her pinned to the wall in a heartbeat. "Would you stop? I have to get ready," Ava said. He kissed her, picking her up and sliding her legs around his waist. "She can wait," Joe said. They went from the wall, to the shower, to the counter, then he carried her back to their bed. "What time are you coming home," Ava asked. "What time you want me home?" "Seriously Joe." "Probably midnight unless we can get this stupid song done." "The magic touch will be there to help if you need it," Ava joked. He kissed her. "Now that's what I wanted to hear." "Take your phone this time," Ava suggested. He nodded and kissed her. "I seriously have to get ready." Not even a minute later, Grace was awake. Joe kissed Ava again, then got up to take care of Grace while Ava got dressed.

Ava slid on her leggings, tank top, her boots and her rings and went to leave. "Missing something," Joe said. "What," Ava asked. He grabbed his leather shirt from the closet and threw it to her. "Your lucky shirt?" He kissed her. "Mama," Grace said. "Hey baby girl." "Me go." "I'll take her over," Ava said. Ava picked her up. "You don't want to hang out with Daddy?" "Me go Daddy." "Okay baby," Ava said. Grace reached for Joe. "Hug," Grace said. Joe slid Grace out of Ava's arms and wrapped his arm around Ava. He kissed her. "I'll call you." He nodded. "Don't forget your phone this time alright," Ava said. He kissed her again this time harder. Grace giggled in his arm. "Daddy loves mommy you know." "Me lub Daddy," Grace said. He kissed Grace's cheek. "See you in a few," Ava said. He nodded. Ava left to pick up Rose.

"What's wrong Ava? I thought you two were happy as hell," Rose asked. "I just keep thinking that something's gonna happen and I'm gonna lose him." "Would you stop? You couldn't get rid of him if you tried," Rose said. "Like every other time I've thought something was going to happen and the relationship blew up in my face?" "You're married. It's different." "Weren't you the one that always said, 'Fine. Leave then," Ava asked. "Yeah. You screwed that up by introducing me to Ryan." "Seriously. I'm scared." "You have Grace. You have Joe for the rest of your life. He isn't going anywhere," Rose said. "Then why am I worried that something huge is going to happen?"

They shopped until they couldn't walk anymore. Ava dropped Rose off, then called Joe. "Good timing," he said. "Why's that?" "Just come over here," Joe said. Ava grabbed dinner and brought it over to the guys. "Now what's this I hear about you needing assistance," Ava asked as she saw Joe alone in the studio. He slid the take-out from her hands and kissed her, leaning her against Brad's piano. "So where did everyone else take off to," Ava asked. "Dinner." Joe kissed her again. They had a picnic on the floor of the studio, then tried to figure out the part of the song the guys were stuck on. Ava wrote something down. "That's it," Joe said. He played through it with Ava's extra words and it was perfect. "See, I knew," Joe said. He kissed her again. "Nope. It was all the lucky shirt's fault," Ava replied. He kissed Ava. "Babe, what are you all upset about?" "Nothing." "You promised you'd never lie to me," Joe said. "I just have this feeling like something bad is going to happen." "Babe, only thing that is ever separating us is death. Even then, I'd still be taunting and teasing you every minute of the day." "I know, it's just when things seem like they're going too well . . ." "They always backfire. I know. Stop worrying." He kissed her again. When Ryan and Brad came back in, he was serenading Ava with another song. "I guess shopping went well," Ryan joked. "And we finished the song off for you," Ava said. "You figured out an ending," Ryan asked. Joe nodded. He played through the end. "It's awesome." "So now we can finish it and go home early," Brad asked. "What about the other one," Ryan asked. "Tomorrow," Brad said. "Fine. We finish recording it, then we can head out," Ryan said. Ava kissed Joe and went back into the booth with the producer. They got the song in one take and Ryan and Brad headed home.

Joe got Ava back into the studio. "What?" "Ryan wants to put our songs on the CD," Joe said. "The two we wrote that I sing with you guys?" Joe nodded. "I guess." "Which means another tour." "It's fine." "Babe, if you don't want to," Joe said. She kissed him. "It's fine." He kissed her again as the producer turned the lights off. Joe had her leaned back into the piano. "What?" "You know how much it took for me to not pounce on you this morning,"

Joe asked. "Good thing I left quickly." "Grace is staying with Ryan and Rose tonight." "Oh really." He kissed her again. "I know exactly what you're thinking." "Can't help it," Joe said. "Sweet talker." He kissed her again. Finally, they headed home in the SUV.

They walked in and Ava took the things she'd bought upstairs. "I get a fashion show tonight." "Funny." "I'm not joking. No more taunting me when you walk out." "It's to surprise you." "No more surprises unless you want to get tackled on the stage." He kissed her and leaned her onto the bed. "I see the red bag," Joe said. "And?" He reached in and found a black and pink lace bra, matching g-string and a pink lace teddy. "Babe." "Can't handle surprises can you?" He kissed her and slid her boots off. "Never," he said. He grabbed another bag. "Would you stop? Just let it be a surprise." "Nope." He kissed her again. He pulled out a pink dress. "Where's the rest of this?" Ava smirked. "Oh hell no," Joe said. Ava nodded. "No. You walk on stage in this . . . ." Ava went to get up and he leaned her back onto the bed. "What else did you buy?" "Look in the blue one." He reached in and found a men's dress shirt. It was white with a silver design. "Now this, you can wear," Joe joked. "Funny. It's for you." "It's perfect." "I know." He kissed her again. "So you either bought white, or silver," Joe said. Ava grabbed the last bag sliding the dress out of it. It was white and silver to match his shirt. "Okay, you are so totally styling us from now on," Joe teased. He kissed her. "What," Ava asked. "I wouldn't give this up for anything. You know that?" Ava nodded and kissed him. "Seriously. You don't have to ever worry about anything. Never." "Babe, it's a girl thing," Ava said. "Then stop it. I will never ever leave you. Ever." He kissed her again and made love to her. Ava fell asleep in his arms. A few hours later, he was awake. A million things were running through his brain.

Joe went downstairs and tried working out, working on music, writing. He couldn't fall back asleep. Ava rolled over part way through the night and noticed him gone. She went downstairs and saw him in his studio. "What are you up to in here?" "Couldn't sleep." Joe kissed her. "What are you working on?" "Fidgeting with something I had in my head." He sat with his jeans on, bare feet, and played for her. "Babe," Ava said. He looked over at her. "I know why you're stuck." He kissed her. "Low on inspiration?" She laughed. "You were reading," Ava said. "A little." "Sneak." "I wanted to see it." "How much did you read?" "Chapter six." "Want me to tell you what happens next?" "Nope." "What do you think happens?" "He wins her over and they have a beautiful baby girl, and they're happy forever." "Not quite." "Babe, I know I've made a million mistakes, but I don't want to ever lose you." "Now you're worried," Ava asked. "I'm just saying. No matter what stupid crap I do, don't walk away." "What did you do?" "Nothing." "Joe, tell me." "Before you got there . . ." "Joe, just say it." "Tiffany showed up." "That why you can't sleep?" "Ava, nothing happened. Fact is, I knew you'd be gone if anything did. Last time was enough. I'm not doing it again." "Then why are you sitting down here instead of curling up in bed with me?" "She kissed me." "And?" "I told her she had to go." "And?" "Then you called and said you were on your way." "Stop worrying then," Ava said. He kissed her and pulled her into his lap. "I love you." "No secrets," Ava said. "Babe, I don't want to screw this up." "I'll talk to her then." "Babe, not necessary." "Yeah it is. Woman to woman." Ava got up and put in the code to block the number and called Tiffany.

"Hello?" "Tiffany, this is Ava." "Hi." "I have a favor to ask." "What's that?" "Stay away from Joe. That means no phone calls, no showing up where he is, nothing. I'm sick of the stress you're causing. We're married. That means he's my husband, he's the father to my daughter. That also means that you don't need to be anywhere near him. Go to a concert, but if you even try to make one move, you aren't going to like what happens. You understand?" "I'm in love with him," Tiffany said. "And Joe's in love with me. He sleeps beside me, kisses me every morning and a million times every day. Enough is enough." "I can't help loving him." "No but you can be a real woman and stop being a home wrecker." "I'm sorry." "Good. We have an understanding?" "Yeah," Tiffany said. "Goodnight." Ava hung up.

Joe pulled Ava into his arms. "You coming back to bed," she asked. He shook his head and leaned her onto the floor, wrapping his arms around her. "Have I told you I love you today," Joe asked. "Not yet." He kissed her as she slid her leg around his. "I love every inch of you. I love your heart, your soul, your mind, your kiss, everything," Joe said. "I love you too." They made love again, then they curled up together in the TV room on the sofa with the quilt his mom had made them. "I think we should have another baby," Joe said. "Oh really? Sick of practicing?" He kissed her again. "Never. I could practice a million times a day if you'd let me," Joe said. They both laughed. "After Christmas." "Yeah," Joe asked. Ava nodded. He smiled and kissed her again. "Sleep," Ava said. They curled up and a half-hour later, they were both asleep.

The next morning, Ava woke up and Joe was still asleep with his arms around her. She slid closer to him and he woke up. "Go back to sleep," Ava said. "I have to go back to the studio." "We will," Ava said. He kissed her. She curled back up with him and they were asleep in minutes. Around 11, Ryan called the house. "What are you two up to," Ryan asked. "He's sleeping." "I bet." "What time did you need him there?" "You're coming too Ava. We need to get those two songs down," Ryan said. "Fine. Bring Rose and the kids. We'll meet you in an hour." Ryan hung up and Joe rolled over and pinned Ava to the sofa. "We have to be there . . ." He kissed her and untied her robe. "Babe," Ava said. He peeled his jeans off. "We have to be there," Ava said. He kissed her again and they made love on the sofa, then he carried her upstairs into the shower. He washed her back and she washed his, then they finished their shower and got changed. Ava slid on leggings and a tank top. "Tease," he joked. "Consider yourself lucky I'm not going for the over the knee boots," Ava joked. He walked over and handed her the flat ballet slipper type shoes from her closet.

"Oh really," Ava asked. She kissed him and slid them on. He wrapped his arms around her, kissing her again, then walked her back towards the bed. "We have to be at the studio in 20 minutes," Ava said. "Party pooper." "Nope. Means I get to tease you every minute of the day," Ava joked. He kissed her again. "Up." He smiled, then pulled her to her feet and they left.

They walked in and the kids were playing, Ryan was talking to Brad and Emily was hitting on the producer. Joe kissed Ava. "Go," she said. He went in to go over the plan for the day with Ryan and Brad. "So," Rose asked. Ava smiled. Grace ran over to her. "Mama, look." She handed Ava a picture she'd drawn. "This is beautiful baby," Ava said hugging Grace. "Sing Daddy." Ava nodded. Joe came back in. "What's up," Ava asked. "You're up." "Now," Ava asked. He nodded. "Mama sing?" Ava nodded. Grace wrapped her arms around Ava's neck and kissed her then reached for Joe. "And how's the princess today," Joe asked. "Love Daddy." "I love you too baby girl." Grace kissed him. "Miss Daddy." "Missed you too. What are you and Jacob doing?" "Color." "Draw me a picture of Mommy and I." "Kay," Grace said. He kissed her and put her down to play. He came back into the studio. "Ready," Ava asked. "One last thing." He kissed Ava. "Now I'm ready." They worked on the two songs and an hour or two later, they were done. Brad and Ryan took Rose and Danielle and Jacob to lunch and Ava, Grace and Joe had lunch just them. Joe and Ava curled up together after while Grace fell asleep on the sofa. He leaned against the edge of the sofa with Ava in his arms. "You should play them what you were working on," Ava said. "I don't want to be here until midnight." "Good point." "I want to have dinner with my two favorite ladies," Joe said. "You just had lunch with them." "I know. Dinner, just you and me and candlelight while Grace sleeps." "How are you going to pull that off?" Joe kissed her. "I have my ways you know." They were kissing away when Rose, Brad and Ryan came back in. "Told ya," Brad joked. "What," Joe asked. "The two of you haven't changed since the day you got married." "You expected us to," Joe asked. Brad laughed. They got up, the guys did a little more work and they all headed home.

Grace was out cold in the backseat as Joe and Ava headed back to the house. They pulled into the driveway and headed inside. Joe tucked Grace into her crib and Ava checked the ever flashing voicemail. "Joe, it's Carla. I have the clothes put aside for this week. Can you give me a shout to go through the choices." "Ava, it's Rachel. Call me." "Ava, it's Carrie. You aren't gonna believe this. Rachel and James are engaged. Call me." The phone rang. "Ava?" "Yes." "It's Gwen. Joe's mom. We need you two to come to the hospital," she said. "We'll leave in 2 minutes." Emily was just walking in. "Stay here with Grace. We need to go to the hospital." Ava ran upstairs. "What?" "Car. Now." He ran down the steps behind her. They took off for the hospital. "Babe." "What?" "Where are we going," Joe asked. "Hospital. Your mom called." They pulled in and he ran in while Ava parked the car.

"Mom. He alright," Joe asked. "He had a heart attack. They said they caught it early. He's okay. I just . . ." He pulled his mom into his arms and hugged her. "It's okay. I'm here." She cried. She saw Ava walking down the hall. "Go in and see him," his mom said wiping her nose. Joe let go just long enough for Ava to take his place with his mom. "Is he alright," Ava asked. His mom nodded. "I got him here as fast as I could." "Thank you." "Why don't you go in? I'll grab some coffee for the two of you," Ava suggested. Ava went and grabbed coffee while his mom went in. Joe came out just as Ava was coming down the hall with the coffee. "How's he doing?" "Better. Thank you babe." "You're welcome." He opened the coffee and put his mom's down on the table beside him. "You should be in there," Ava said. "He said he wanted to talk to you." Ava kissed Joe, then went in and saw his dad.

"Thank you," he said. "For what," Ava asked sitting down beside him. "For taking care of him. For making him into a good man. For giving me a grand-daughter. He's a good man Ava. I know he isn't perfect, but he's a good man." "I know," Ava said. "He loves you something mean." "I love him too." "Just take care of him for me. Make sure he's always happy and knows someone's there for him." "He knows he has me no matter what." "He needs us. We're not going to be around forever. I love my son, but he's been a mama's boy forever," his dad said. "That I do know." "Just take care of him." "I promise I will. Now onto less serious moments, what did you do to get you in here?" "Horseback riding. I started getting chest pains. I took something, then they rushed me here," his dad said. "Didn't I tell you before that you weren't allowed to scare anyone anymore?" "Had to keep everyone on their toes." "Well cut it out." "I'll try." "You have to be alright to get to the concert near here," Ava said. "Why?" "I want you to hear him." "Alright then." He hugged Ava. She went into the hall with Joe and his mom went back in to sit with his dad. "The man is a mush ball," Joe said. "He definitely is." "Imagine that being us someday." "Think I know how you'll end up with a heart attack," Ava joked. "One more of those dresses and it will happen sooner than later." They joked around until his mom came out. "He's asleep." "We'll take you home," Joe said. "I want to stay with him." The nurse came by. "Can my mom stay tonight with my dad?" "Aren't you," the nurse asked. "Yes. Answer the question." "We're not supposed to, but I can set up a cot by his bed." "I'll bring some clothes over for you in the morning," Ava said. She hugged Joe and Ava, then went back in and sat with him. Joe and Ava headed home.

They walked in the door and Joe noticed Emily asleep on the sofa. He picked Ava up and carried her upstairs to bed. "What is up with you," Ava asked. He kissed her and leaned her onto their bed. "You know my parents absolutely love you." "Love them too." "My dad told me something. Been thinking about it ever since." "What's that?" "He said I have done a million crazy things in my life. But marrying you was the best thing I ever did." "Oh really," Ava said. "He's right. I'm not the same crazy guy I used to be." "Nope, now you're a great Dad, and play with a great group of guys, and are a pretty good husband."

"Pretty good?" Ava rethought the comment. He kissed her as they both laughed. "Pretty great," Ava said. "Better," he replied. He made love to her and they curled up together, falling asleep.

The next morning Ryan got up to the sound of the phone ringing. "Hey," Ryan said. "Are we going in today," Joe asked. "No." "Good. I have to go down to the hospital." "What happened," Ryan asked. "My dad had a heart attack. He's fine. We're going down to take them home." "Give him a hug for us." "Will do."

Ava and Joe headed to the hospital with Grace. "How you feeling Dad," Joe asked as they walked in. "Better. I'm going home today." "You're going home with a new diet. No more bacon and fatty stuff," his mom said. "I'm not eating rabbit food." "It's not that bad Dad," Joe said. "For a skinny kid. I need man food." Joe laughed. Grace reached for Ava. "You remember Grandpa right," Ava asked. Grace nodded. "Do you want to say hi?" She reached over and hugged him. "Well, you're okay to head home," the nurse said. "Good." The nurse handed Joe's mom the bill. Joe slid it out of her hand and paid it on the spot.

They got back from the hospital and Joe and Ava curled up together on the sofa. "We have to leave tomorrow," Ava said. "I know. My mom has the number to call us if she needs to." "Are we bringing princess Grace?" "Up to you," Joe said. "Is Rose coming?" Joe shook his head. Ava called to check and see if Grace could say with her. "No prob. I'll see you when you guys get back on Monday." They spent the day together at the park, then the zoo, then headed home and fed and bathed Grace then tucked her into bed.

Joe and Ava sat down and had dinner just the two of them. "Babe," he said. "Mmm." "I love you." "I love you too," Ava said. They had dinner, then curled up and watched a movie, then headed upstairs to pack. "You aren't putting the pink thing in there are you," Joe asked. Ava slid it in the suitcase. "Ava." She put the dresses she'd bought, plus the heels and the lingerie she'd snuck past him. She threw in her leggings and boots and tank tops, then threw in a sweater or two and the rest of her toiletries. "Which shirts," Joe asked. "White and silver, black and grey, and the black one." "And I'm putting this one in just in case you decide to put on the pink dress," Joe said. "Oh really?" He nodded. "So if I throw this in," Ava asked as he noticed the black and pink lace bra. "You won't need the dress because you won't make it on stage." She slid it in the suitcase. "Ava." She smirked at him then went to walk out of the bedroom. He pulled her back into his arms. "What?" He kissed her. "Just a hint of it and you're all hot aren't you," Ava teased. "For you? Name a day I'm not." He kissed her again and leaned her onto the bed. "You know you're crazy." "That's why you married me," Joe joked. "Nope. That wasn't the reason." "Oh really?

What was it then?" Ava looked at him with the smile that always was contagious. "Ava?" "The concert tickets." He tickled her. "Liar." "Fine. It wasn't the tickets. It was the sex." "Getting warmer," he teased as he slid her jeans off. "Nope. Was definitely the sex." He kissed her and had her pinned to the bed. "Ava." "Honestly, it was everything. It was you, the way we are when we're together, the way that you're there for my friends even when you think you shouldn't, the way you snuggle up with me when you're asleep . . . and the tickets." He kissed her and made love to her through the giggles, the kisses, the laughing and the teasing.

The next morning, everybody got up, grabbed their things and headed for the airport. Ava dropped Grace off. "Mama," Grace said. She ran over to Ava. "No go." "I have to baby." "No." Rose packed Jacob up and came to the airport with them. By the time they got there, Jacob and Grace were both asleep. Ava and Joe kissed Grace and left. "I'll call you tonight," Ava said. Rose nodded and hugged Ava. Joe gave her a hug too. "Thank you," Joe said. "No problem. We'll keep an eye on the house for you too." "Thanks. If you need anything, call Ava's cell." "I will." Ava and Joe hopped on the plane and Ryan said his long goodbye to Rose. "Call me when you land," Rose said. Ryan nodded. He pulled Rose into his arms and kissed her. "I'm gonna miss you." "I'll miss you too. I'll see you on Monday," Ryan said. He kissed her again.

CHAPTER 20

They got to the venue, went through interviews and sound check, then had a dinner break. "Ava," Ryan said. "Yep." ""You know you turned this crazy ass into a home body," Ryan said. "I know." "She did not. I just found what I wanted," Joe said. "And turned into a home body instead of the party man," Brad joked. "Funny." "What are you guys getting at," Ava asked. "After the concert we're going out. A bar or something." "Okay then," Joe said. "Ava?" "Hey. I had Grace. I love her, but we need a night out," Ava said. Joe wrapped his arms around her. "See, this is why I married you." "I thought it was because you couldn't stand to see her with anyone else," Brad said. "That too." Ava laughed. They joked around through dinner. Ava got her hair and makeup done for the show, then came back to get changed. She walked into the trailer and Joe had already left. She slid on the pink dress, then the heels and headed for the stage. She heard someone calling her. She turned around and James was at the gate. "What the hell are you doing here?" "I had to see you," James said. "You're engaged." "Please." "No. Go back to Rachel." "Ava." "What," Ava asked. Security let him through. He walked towards her and kissed her. Ava pushed him away. "Don't even start that." She went to walk away and he pulled her back into another kiss. Ava finally pushed him away and headed for the stage. She touched up her lipstick, then headed on.

She got through her two songs, then sang one with the guys and headed back. When the concert was done, Ava had a drink in hand and was in the backstage seating. Joe came in and walked towards her. "What did I say about the pink dress," he joked. "That it was your favorite." Joe leaned down and kissed her. "Something's wrong." "Nothing." "Ava." "James." "Where?" "When I was heading to the stage." "And?" "I'm just glad we're out of here." "Babe." "He kissed me." "I'm kicking his ass," Joe said. They headed back outside and James was there again. Joe walked towards him and Ava tried to hold him off. "I can handle him," Ava said. "No. Go get in the trailer." "Joe, don't." He walked past her. "I told you once," Joe said. "I need her," James said. "She doesn't want you. If she did she wouldn't have married me. Get the hell out of here before I call the cops on your ass." "I can't go through with the wedding," James said. "Well you aren't marrying my wife." "She was mine first," James said. "Fucking little damn kid. Get the hell out of here before you're in shit," Joe said. "Meaning what?" Joe clocked him, knocking him flat on his ass. Security took James out of the gated area and walked him out the front gates. Joe walked back to the trailer. "You know you're insane," Ava said. "He came after you." Ava wrapped his hand with ice. "I can handle him. I told you that," Ava said. "He doesn't get to do that to you. Not now, not ever." He kissed Ava. "You are seriously insane." "Protecting what's ours." He kissed Ava again and pulled her into his lap. "Now about this dress," Joe said changing the topic "What about it?" He kissed her again, undoing the back of the dress. "Sexy on, better off." "Oh really," Ava said. He felt the lace underneath it. "You didn't." His hands slid up her legs and felt the lace. "Ava." "What?" "Tease." "No. This would be teasing," Ava said sliding the dress off and showing him the lace lingerie. Joe chased her into the bedroom.

He had her pinned to the bed in no time. Bad hand or not, she was his. All his. Joe peeled his shirt off, then kicked his jeans off. "Babe," he said. "What?" "Nobody is ever putting their hands on you." "I know. Stop worrying and getting yourself hurt." "I don't care if I get hurt. I don't want anyone hurting you." "I'm fine," Ava said. "I know what he did before. I know the kind of guy he is and what he's like when he doesn't get his way." "So do I. That's why I took kickboxing." "Ava." "I know. I love that you want to defend me," Ava said. "Nobody ever." Ava kissed him and he wrapped his arms around her. "Enough with the playing around. Take care of your hand," Ava said. "I know what will cure it." "So do I. A cold shower." "Funny," Joe said. Ava went to get up and he pulled her back to him with his good arm. "What do you want," Ava asked. He kissed her again. "I'm sorry. I had to. The guy's got on my last nerve." "I know. Just cut out the hand hurting okay?" "If you promise to not go near him," Joe said. "I won't." Joe kissed her. "Can you stop molesting me long enough to let the ice do its thing?" He shook his head and kissed her. He made love to her, then they curled up in bed. "You know you're crazy," Ava said. "Always." He pulled his jeans on. "Where are you going?" "Two minutes." "No. Don't you dare do what I think you are." He left to go make sure they were ready to head out. Ava pulled on leggings, flip flops and her sweater. She walked up behind him sliding his shirt on. "You ready Joe," Ryan asked. "We ready to head out," Joe asked. Brad nodded. They headed back to the RV's then pulled out, heading to the next concert. "What did you think I was doing," Joe asked. "You don't want to know." Joe kissed Ava and carried her back to bed.

Ava gave Rose a quick call to check on Grace. "She's fine. She's curled up with Jacob." "Thank you," Ava said. "What are godmothers for? How did the concert go?" "James showed." "He's engaged," Rose said. "I know. Didn't stop him from kissing me." "Ava." "I walked off. Joe clocked him." "Are you kidding me?" Rose was laughing. "No. My protector," Ava teased. "I bet. How's his hand?" "Fine now. I made him ice it." "He loves you. I never thought I'd see it." "I know. I'll call you tomorrow. I have to get some sleep while I can," Ava said. "Love you." "Love you too." Ava hung up. "Grace is fine," Ava said. "I told you so," Joe said. "I just feel like I'm missing everything." "Babe, you aren't." "I miss her." "So do I. Do you want to get them out there for the next concert," Joe asked. Ava smiled. He kissed her. "That's the smile I love." He called their manager and arranged for Rose to fly out with Grace and Jacob. "We'll surprise Ryan," Joe said. "We're going out tomorrow night." "Emily." "Already done. Now can you stop worrying and come here." "For?" "Need your help with the words." They worked on a song for an hour or two, got most of it done, then curled up and fell asleep.

They pulled in the next morning to the next venue. Joe and Ava went shopping for a while, then had lunch and headed back. They did a few interviews, then Ava snuck Rose and Jacob onto Ryan's RV. Grace wouldn't let go of Ava for a second. Brad came and hung out with Ava, Grace and Joe. "I can't wait until we have our little munchkin," Brad said. "You realize they're all going to be best friends." "Oh hell yeah. They're all practically family as it is," Brad said. "We are like family." "Road family," Brad said. Joe wrapped his arms around Ava. Grace fell asleep in Brad's arms. "See, you're already a natural," Joe said. Brad slid Grace into her crib, tucking her in. They all headed out and Emily went in and sat with her. Within a few minutes, Ava saw Ryan's arms fly around Rose and Jacob. "What are you two doing here," Ryan asked. "Ava missed Grace. She thought Jacob might be missing you." Ryan kissed Rose. He looked over. "What," Ava asked. "Girl, you read my mind." "I know." Ava went with Joe and sat on the stage working on the song with Brad. They had a good portion of it done when Ryan and Rose came up with Jacob. "What you workin' on," Ryan asked. "Got an idea last night and ran with it. We have most of it, but we need the Ryan touch," Joe said. They all worked through the song. By the end of it, Brad had it written down. They played through it two or three times. The other guys in the group added their touches. Brad loaded it into his laptop and played it back. "Damn," Joe said. "It's definitely going to get the crowd going," Brad said. "And it's another one Ava's going to have to sing with us," Ryan joked. "Keep adding to my work," Ava teased. "Longer for him to stare at you in those dresses," Ryan teased. "See I knew you noticed," Ava joked. "So where are we going tonight for our night out," Ava asked. "Wherever you want," Ryan said. Ava asked around. She got names of a few places and looked them up, then picked one. Their manager called and arranged for VIP etc. "Finally." Ava laughed. "What," Joe asked. "Knew it." He kissed her. They all relaxed the rest of the afternoon. The kids played, then they had dinner and the kids went to bed. Ava got ready with Joe, Ryan and Brad got ready, and Rose relaxed. The guys did the meet and greet while Rose helped Ava pick out what to wear.

Joe walked in after the meet and greet and saw Ava in the white and silver dress. "Babe." She smirked. "Do not mess the hair," Ava said. He walked towards her and kissed her, pulling her into his arms. "See, I told you," Rose said laughing. "Well?" "You don't wanna know," Joe said. He kissed her again. Ava went to slide her heels on and he walked her backwards towards the bed. "I'm going to check on Ryan," Rose teased. "Thanks. You got me into this," Ava said. Ava heard her leave. "What," Ava asked. He kissed her and leaned her onto the bed. "See I knew I should've made it a surprise," she said. Joe kissed her again and wrapped his arms around her. "Nope." "You have to go on." "In 20." "Don't even think it," Ava said. He kissed her as his hand slid up her leg. "Joe," Ava said. "What?" "Now?" He saw the white lace g-string and the decision was made. It was fast, intense and hot. He got up, washing up, kissing Ava again, then took off and headed on stage. Ava fixed up her makeup, slid on her flip flops, then grabbed her heels and headed backstage. She watched the concert from the side. Ava walked on and Joe had a silly grin. After her two songs, Ryan opted to try out the new one on the crowd. "So we have a new song to try out on you. Let us know what you think," Ryan said. They got through the song and the crowd loved it. "So in the past years we've been together, we've had a lot of changes. We gained Ava, the hair has definitely changed. I can remember back in the day where the three of us were playing just for fun. What was your favorite song back then Joe?" "Faithfully." He sang a bit of it while the girls screamed. "What about you," Brad asked Ryan. He sang a little of Old time rock and roll by Bob Segar. "What about you Brad?" "This was my favorite," he said as he started playing Ava's favorite song. He sang a bit of it and Ava joined in, then the guys did. It was 'The day before you.' Ava finished, then headed off to stand with Rose. Joe came over in between changes and kissed her. They finished the concert, and Joe grabbed his acoustic guitar, bringing it back to the RV. Grace and Jacob were asleep in Ryan's RV. Everyone came and hung out with Joe and Ava.

The guys played a few songs, worked on a bit, then once things were clear, everyone headed back to their own RV's. Ava slid Grace out of the crib with Jacob and tucked her into her bed in the RV with her and Joe. They headed off to the next and final stop for that week. They pulled in a few hours later, then they headed off to a hotel for the night. Ava slid Grace into the crib, then curled up in the bed with Joe. "Babe," he said. "What?" He nuzzled her ear. "Of course," Ava joked. "What?" His arm slid around her. "Aren't even tired are you," Ava asked. He nibbled her ear, then her neck. "Can't sleep," Ava asked. He nibbled her shoulder. "Joe." He pulled her closer to him. "Trying to be quiet so we don't wake her up," she asked. Joe nodded. He slid the leggings off. "What has got you in this mood?" "Stupid thought," he replied. "What?" "What I wanted to do when you walked on the stage." "I don't want to know." "Bent over the piano." It got him even more turned on. "Oh really," Ava commented. In minutes they were going at it again. He had her pinned and it was hotter than ever. He felt like he could go on forever. He turned her to face him and kissed her, then she wrapped her legs tight around him and they came together. "Babe," he said. "I know." He curled up in her arms with his head on her chest and fell asleep to the sound of her heart beat.

They got up around 12, checked out and headed to the venue. They did interviews while Ava and Rose played with the kids. "So you and Joe are okay," Rose asked. "He's crazy, but we're good." "See, I told you." "I know. It's better," Ava said. "No more exes from outer space?" "None that I've heard about." "So where are we headed tonight," Rose asked. "It's called North." "Country?" "A little of everything. You'll like it." Joe walked over to Grace after the interview. "Dada. Hug." He picked her up and wrapped his arms around her and kissed her. "How's Grace?" "Me good. Miss Daddy." "I missed you too baby." Joe kissed Ava. "Hi Mama." "Hi baby girl." "I big." "I know." Grace yawned. "Know what time it is," he asked Grace. "Sing." He carried Grace to the RV and Jacob came along. Ryan and Joe sang the kids to sleep. They came out a little while later. "Tell me it wasn't God Bless," Ava teased. Joe kissed Ava. "My wife the mind-reader." Ava laughed. They relaxed a bit while Emily sat with the kids and fell asleep with them. "I'm so glad you got her here," Ryan said. "Had to do something for your birthday," Joe said. "You better not do what I think you are tonight," Ryan said. "Why?" "Joe." "Ava can," Joe said. "I'm not getting on his bad side." "See, she knows," Ryan joked. Rose handed Ryan his birthday present. "Babe." "Open it." He opened it and found a gold chain with a cross. "It's beautiful." Ryan kissed her. "We'll leave you two alone," Joe said. He grabbed Ava's hand and they headed to the RV.

"I already called for a cake," Ava said. "One step ahead of me aren't you," Joe joked. "And, we got him a new shirt and a new watch." "Seriously?" "Shopping." Joe laughed. Ava handed him the card to sign. He wrote a note in it, then slid it in the envelope. He kissed her. "See, this is why you married me," Ava said. "One of the reasons." He kissed her again.

Ava and Joe came back out a few minutes later and Joe handed Ryan a birthday gift. "When the heck did you find time for this," Ryan asked. "I have connections, and a personal shopper." Ryan opened it and found a shirt that he loved. In the sleeve, he found the box with the watch. He opened it. "Buddy," Ryan said looking at Joe. "From me and Ava and Grace." "Look at the inscription," Ava said. It read:

Family forever.

He hugged Joe and Ava. "You two are too much." "We had to," Ava said. Brad came over a few minutes later with Danielle. "How was the flight," Rose asked. "Good," Danielle said. She handed Ryan his gift and said hi. "Seriously. You guys are spoiling me," Ryan said. He opened the box and found an old CD he had been trying to find for months. "Where did you find it," he asked. "A used CD store. It was a total fluke," Danielle said. He opened it to put it in the CD player and saw a note inside it. It was a gift certificate for a massage and a note:

For the godfather.

There was a sonogram picture of their baby. He wrapped his arms around Danielle and Brad. "So it's yes?" Brad nodded. "Guys, this is the best birthday." "Not yet," Joe teased. "What the hell else did you plan?" "Nothin," Joe teased. He looked over behind Ryan. Ryan's Mom and Dad were walking over. "What," Ryan asked. He heard his Dad laughing. Ryan hopped up. "What are you two doing here," he asked hugging them. "Spending your birthday with you." He hugged them, then hugged Ava, knowing full well her and Rose had planned it with Brad and Joe. "We'll leave you guys to catch up," Joe said. He headed off with Ava, and Brad headed back to his RV with Danielle.

Joe curled up on the bed with Ava. "So fill me in on the other surprises," Joe said. "Black and pink dress." "No." Ava nodded. "Woman." "What?" "You can't do that," Joe said. "Oh yes I can." Ava backed up and headed towards the door. Joe took off after her. They ran towards the stage. "Don't even think it," Joe said as Ava hopped on the stage. "Think you can outrun me," Joe asked. Ava nodded. They played tag for at least 15 minutes before he caught her and had her pinned to the piano. "You are not wearing it," Joe said. "Yeah I am." "You can't." "Why?" "Don't ask that question," Joe said. She slid out of his arms and took off. Joe grabbed her and pulled her back into his arms. "I'm wearing it." "Unless you want to seriously not make it out tonight," he said. "Meaning?" "You wear it, you won't make it on stage and either will I," Joe said. "Promises promises," Ava teased. He kissed her and pinned her to the edge of the piano. "What?" He smirked. "No." He lifted her up on the edge of the piano. "Don't even think it Joe," Ava said. His hand slid onto her ass, pulling her towards him. "Why," Joe asked. He kissed her again. "Everyone will see." He kissed her and slid his hands up her skirt. "Stop it." He kissed her with a breath taking and intense kiss and in seconds they were at it on the piano. It was fast, dangerous, and they were liable to get caught in seconds. After, he slid her off the piano and leaned her against it. "You're crazy," Ava said. "That's why you love me." "One of the million reasons," Ava said. He grabbed her hand. "Where are we going," Ava asked. He kissed her. They headed back to the RV.

"I can't believe you," Ava said. He kissed her and walked her backwards into the bed. They went at it again. They curled up on the bed. "What has got into you," Ava asked. "Pulling surprises on you." "See, after everyone else was gone, just us on the stage would have made sense," Ava joked. "Don't put ideas in my already dirty mind," Joe joked. He pulled her close. They had a quick cat nap, then showered and headed to dinner. Ryan, Jacob and Rose had dinner with Ryan's Mom and Dad. Danielle and Brad had dinner with Ava, Joe and Grace. "Where Jacob," Grace asked. "He's having dinner with his Daddy. It's his birthday." "Cake." "Yep." "Where mine," Grace asked. Ava smirked. "Chocoholic. You'll get some cake," Joe said. "Kay." Grace played with her dolls. Ryan came back with Rose and Jacob. "They staying for the concert," Brad asked. "Front row. Thanks you guys."

"You needed family on your birthday," Joe said. "More than you know." He sat down while Jacob and Grace were playing. Ava got up. "Where are you off to," Ryan asked. "Be back in a minute." Ava went off and grabbed his birthday cake (one of two he was getting). They sang happy birthday and Ryan blew out the candles. "I knew you were gonna do that," Ryan said. "Not a birthday without a cake." He cut the cake and the kids made a huge mess, but devoured it. They all had a piece, then the guys went to get changed. "Ava," Joe said. She looked up. Joe motioned for her to follow him. "I got the kids," Rose said. Emily helped Rose clean them up. "What?" "You aren't wearing it." "You never know." He leaned her into the side of the RV. "Unless you're trying to get yourself in trouble, don't," Joe said. "So, the really low back black one instead?" He almost whimpered. "Ava." "I'll do the coin toss," Ava teased. He kissed her hard, intense and almost had her legs shaking with one kiss. "Need help," Ava asked. He nodded.

He showered with Ava after he devoured her on the bed. He slid on his black shirt and black jeans. "Very sexy," Ava said. She handed him her favorite cologne. "Oh really," he asked. Ava nodded. Joe kissed her. "Go." He went and fixed his hair, then took off for the meet and greet. "I want to see it before we go on," Joe said. "Oh you will babe." He kissed her again then he took off and hair and makeup came in to get Ava ready. They finished a half-hour later and Ava slid on the black dress with the almost non-existent back. She slid his leather shirt on with it and her heels. She headed in. Grace ran to her. "Hey princess," Ava said. "Daddy say be good girl." "You or me," Ava joked. "Dunno." Ava kissed her. Grace yawned. She put her to bed in the crib in the RV. She sang her to sleep, then headed off to sit with Rose. She walked in and Joe was sitting there. He looked over and saw her in the black dress with his leather shirt. "Nice," he said. "Thought you'd like it." Joe kissed her. "Grace is out cold." "Nice to know you listened to her," Joe teased. He kissed Ava again then the guys headed on stage. "Somehow I remember that dress looking a little different," Rose said. "It will be," Ava replied. After a few songs, Ava slid the jacket off and grabbed the birthday cake.

"So ladies, I know you know what today is. It's Ryan's birthday, which means he gets his way with the tunes tonight. Just one we're doing without his consent," Joe said. Ava came out with the cake and everyone started singing happy birthday. Ryan glared at Joe then they all started laughing. He blew out the candles and the stagehand took it backstage. "Now that we got that out of the way . . ." "So how old are you now Ryan," Joe teased. "Old enough to know good music," Ryan replied. "Such as," Joe teased. They sang a few old ones, then sang the new one, then the two with Ava. Ryan hugged her. Ava headed off. Joe watched her. He had one of those 'You're so gonna get it' looks. Ava walked over and stood by Rose. "He's so kicking your butt tonight," Rose said. "Not exactly what that look means Rose." "And the fact that he can't stop staring over here?" "Means I love this dress," Ava replied. "When does the other one come in," Rose asked. "One in Navy, and one in pink, then in white with the silver on it." "Well, can't say that being married and a mom hasn't changed you," Rose teased. "No, just means you wore off on me." The guys finished a half-hour later, and Joe walked directly towards Ava.

"What," Ava asked. "What do you mean what? Trying to torture me," Joe teased. "When I am, you'll know," Ava said. She walked back towards the sitting area, and he slid his arm around her, walking her towards the change room. They walked in and he locked the door behind them. "What," Ava asked. "I warned you." "True." Joe walked towards her, and she backed up until her bare back touched the concrete wall. "Seriously. No more of the dresses. You're killing me," Joe said. "You didn't look tortured," Ava teased. He went to kiss her and she slid away from him. "Ava." "We have somewhere to go tonight. Don't start this," Ava said. "You're changing." Ava shook her head. She unlocked the door and slid out, then they headed off to the bar. "I have to grab something. One sec," Joe said. He went into the RV, grabbing his leather shirt and handing it to Ava. "Don't need it," she teased. "Yeah you do." She intentionally didn't sit with him. "The dress looks amazing on you," Danielle said. "Thanks," Ava replied. "Don't encourage her," Joe said. "Considering that she carried Grace and she still looks that good, she should show it off," Danielle said. "Girls gotta stick together," Ava joked. "I swear, if you three turn into the three musketeers of torture dressing," Brad teased. "All of you would love it," Rose said. "Seriously, stop encouraging it.," Joe said. "They only get better Joe," Ava teased. They pulled into the bar. Ryan and Rose hopped out, then Brad and Danielle. Joe begged Ava to put the shirt on. She hopped out and he slid it over her shoulders. Ava ordered drinks and they headed to the VIP area. "Babe," Joe said. "Relax. We're in the bar. We're having fun."

After a drink or two, Ava and Rose headed for the dance floor. Ava made sure to stay just far enough away that Joe would be tempted to get up and find her. They danced and joked around, then a group of guys came over to dance with them. "Don't trust her," Ryan teased. "Not funny," Joe said. "They're having fun. Relax," Brad said. The guys had another drink while Joe watched Ava like a hawk. "So, what's up at Christmas? We doing the big party thing again," Brad asked. "We could. Her folks are flying in and mine are coming over. We could do a big dinner thing," Joe said. "I'll talk to Rose. Would you quit worrying? Either go over there and dance with her, or chill out," Ryan said.

Ava was dancing and fending off the guys surrounding them when she felt arms wrap around her. Joe kissed her neck. "What's wrong? Dress too much for you," Ava teased. "Wait until I get you home," he whispered. Ava turned to face him and danced with Joe. Ryan slid over behind Rose, and Brad behind Danielle. They danced for a while, then headed back for another drink. Joe pulled Ava into the hallway. "What?" Joe kissed her, pinning her to the wall. Ava slid her hand into his. "You know this is torture," Joe said. Ava nodded, then walked back out to the dance floor with him as they danced close and like nobody else was there. Finally after another song or two, they headed back to the table. They had a drink and celebrated for another hour or two, then headed back to the RV's. Ava still sat across the other side of the limo from Joe. They got back and within a half-hour, they were packed up and heading for the last concert.

Ava slid her heels off, and Joe walked up behind her. "What?" "Promise me," Joe said. "Promise what?" "Promise me that you aren't going to torture me." "You like the dress?" He turned her to face him and he kissed her, leaning her against the wall of the hallway. Emily was asleep with the kids. He grabbed her hand and pulled her into the bedroom, closing the door, then pinning her to it. "I take that as a yes," Ava asked. He slid the dress off as he noticed the black lace g-string she slid on under it. "Tomorrow, jeans. Promise me," Joe said. "Didn't bring any." "Liar." "None that I'm wearing on stage," Ava said. "Then we go shopping when we get there," Joe said. He had her pinned to the bed in minutes. His shirt and jeans hit the floor at lightning speed.

That night was unbelievable. Joe and Ava were almost like they were possessed. He devoured every inch of her. They made love and practically exploded with fiery passion. He fell asleep, exhausted, holding her as tight as he could, and not wanting her to move one inch.

The next morning, the RV's pulled in and the guys went and did interviews. Ava showered and bathed the kids. Rose came and picked Jacob up, and Ava got changed and went and watched the interviews. As soon as they were done, Joe pulled Ava into his arms. "Dada," Grace said. "Hey baby girl." "Up." He picked Grace up and she hugged him and kissed his cheek. One of the photographers snapped a shot of her with Joe and Ava. "You know I want a copy of that one," Joe said. "I'll leave it in the RV for you." "Ready," Joe asked. "What," Ava asked. He took her hand, went to the RV and grabbed her purse and their phones, then they headed to the mall. "Babe, we can't just take off," Ava said. "I told Ryan and Brad." They left in the security SUV and pulled in to the mall, then headed to his favorite store for jeans shopping. They closed the store and blocked the windows, while Joe decided on a shopping spree. They got two pairs each, and a shirt for him. "One store I need to take a look at," Ava teased. "If you're thinking of that dress place . . ." Ava slid out with Grace in hand and he wrapped his arm around her. "One."

Ava tortured him with little dresses, then found one he loved . . . . from the front. She bought it. "Wait a sec." "What," Ava asked. "Ava." She smirked. They headed back, grabbing some lunch on the way and a coffee for the guys. They pulled back in, then put Grace down for her nap with Jacob. "So he talked you into jeans did he," Ryan joked. "Sort of," Ava replied. "What do you mean sort of? You promised." "You never know what I could come out in." Ava teased him. "You realize next weekend, I'm packing for you," Joe said. Ava kissed him. "So what are you guys up to," Ava asked as Brad and Danielle and Rose came and sat down. "Just relaxing." Ava went back to grab her laptop and do some writing, but Joe was right behind her.

"What can I do for you," Ava asked. "You can't do the dress tonight." "Why?" "Don't make me remind you of the other day. The piano." "After the concert, could be interesting," Ava teased. "Ava, seriously." "The classy one then." "Which one?" Ava slid the black and navy dress from the bag. It was sexy, but nothing like the one she'd worn the night before. "Or you can do the red top with the new jeans." "Determined?" Joe kissed her. "All those stupid guys lusting after my wife is driving me nuts." "Except you're one of them," Ava teased. "I get to. I also get to sleep with you every night and . . ." "And what?" "I don't wanna share," Joe said. He kissed her wrapping his arms around her. "All yours and you know it." "Did you know that you got a letter asking if you wanted to be in playboy," Joe said. "Really? They tell you that in the interview?" "Ava." "I never would and you know it," she said. "Promise me." "Only one who would get to see pictures like that at all is you." "Oh really," Joe said. Ava kissed him. They curled up on the bed and relaxed and snuggled a while. Snuggling turned into a nap.

Ryan knocked an hour or so later. Ava got up. "What's up?" "We have to go do sound check." Ava nodded. She walked over, sliding her jeans off, and her top, then slid on top of Joe. She slid his belt off, then silently undid his jeans. A second later, she was flat on her back. He had his shirt peeled off and his jeans were inching towards the floor. "Since you're up, sound check," Ava teased. "He can wait ten minutes." He kissed Ava, taking what was left of her breath and they had quick, fast, intense sex. Joe kissed her again. "So I should wear the dress tonight then," Ava teased. She pulled her jeans on with his shirt. "Where are you going," he asked. "Sound check." She slid her flip flops on and took off with him chasing after her. "Told you I'd get him here," Ava joked. Joe picked her up, flipping her over his shoulder and walked on stage. "Tease." "And you love it," Ava said. Joe kissed her. Ava hopped off the stage, then grabbed her laptop and did some writing while they were going through their sound check.

Ava finished her sound check in no time, then got a little more writing done. "I don't know how you get it done with all this noise," Joe said. "Inspiration is closer this way." He kissed her. She emailed the chapters off to her agent. "Seriously, no dress," Joe asked. "Naked it is," Ava teased. "Ava." "Thought you liked the dresses?" "My sister's coming tonight," Joe said. "Should have told me that. Fine. Jeans and a top." He kissed her. "I haven't met this sister have I," Ava asked. He kissed Ava again. "I take that as a no." "She's never around. I invited her, but she was working."

They head dinner, then got ready. Ava pulled on the jeans and a sexy black top to match Joe and the guys, and her black heel boots. He kissed Ava. "Better?" "Still sexy." He kissed Ava again. "Go do the meet and greet." He kissed her and headed off Ava played with Grace a bit, then Rose tucked her into the crib with Jacob. A woman came walking towards Ava. "You're Ava right?" She nodded. "I'm Caroline. I'm Joe's sister." She hugged Ava. "Nice to finally meet you," Ava said. "I'm sorry I couldn't make it sooner than this. Work is insane." "So what do you do?" "I work at a fashion house in London," she said. "Wow." "I know. It's a dream job and a half. So where's Grace," Caroline asked. "We just put her to bed." Ava pulled out a few pictures and showed her while the guys finished up the meet and greet. When Joe came in after, he hugged her. "About damn time sis." "All you guys are hitched now. There's nobody for me to play with," Caroline teased. "So how long you here for?" "Two days. I have to pick a few things up," she said. "You staying for the concert?" "The boyfriend is front row already," Caroline said. "Good." They all chatted a while, then Joe pulled Ava into the hallway.

"What's wrong," Ava asked. Joe kissed her, pinning her to the wall. "And just why couldn't I have worn the dress," Ava asked. He picked her up wrapping her legs around him, then carried her into the change room. "Because that wouldn't have looked that good," Joe said. He kissed her again, nibbling her ear, then her neck. "You're nervous." "No." "Babe, you're allowed," Ava said. "I'm not nervous." She slid her hands in his back pockets. "You're always amazing. That's why I love you." "What if tonight sucks?" Ava kissed him. "It won't." Ryan came in to change shirts. "Jasmine left this for you," Ryan said. "Who's Jasmine," Ava asked. "One of the fans." "Try she's practically a stalker," Ryan said. "Not helping." It was a picture frame with her meet and greet picture of the two of them in it." "Awe," Ava said. "Ryan, seriously." He tossed the picture and kept the frame. There was another knock at the door. There stood the blond haired, blue eyed chick that every boy dreams of. "Joe, I need you for a second," she said. Joe kissed Ava. "You're going on in ten," Ava said. He kissed her again and left. "Ryan." "You don't wanna know," he said. "Speak." "Can't. Swore on the guy bible." Ava walked out to the RV. Rose took off after her. "What's wrong," Rose asked. "Help me find the other black dress."

"Had to make a scene didn't you," Joe said. She kissed him. "I told you before." "I had to," Jessica said. "She's here. We can't." In seconds she was on her knees. He heard Ava pass by where they were, but they were out of eyesight.

"He's going to kill you," Rose said. "Good thing I'm wearing boots then," Ava said. She sat down and saw Joe run by ten minutes later.

"What did you do," Ryan asked. "Nothing. I told her not to come here," Joe said. "Ava's gonna find out," Ryan said. "No she won't. Besides. It's done."

The guys did a few songs, then Ava came out in another black dress. He looked over at her and she wouldn't make eye contact. They got through the songs, then Ava walked off. He looked for her backstage and all he saw was Rose.

Ava packed her things up, packed up Grace's things, then got one of the security guys to take her to the airport. Grace and Jacob got tucked into the crib and Ava slid on her leggings and sweater and did some writing. "Everything okay," Emily asked. "It's fine. Go back to sleep." Ava grabbed herself a drink . . . . a large one.

"Where did Ava go," Joe asked. "Airport," Rose said. He went out and her things were gone, and so were Jacob and Grace. Joe packed his stuff and security took his bag to the SUV. "She's on the plane," security said. Joe went back inside. "Rose." "What's up?" "Was she alright," Joe asked. "No idea. She didn't say a word. Just that she'd meet us at the airport and she was taking Jacob and Grace with her." "When did she leave," he asked. "When she walked off the stage."

CHAPTER 21

Joe left before everyone else did. He hopped on the plane and saw Ava with a large drink. "I was wondering where you took off to." She glared at him. "What?" She went back to her writing. "If there's something you want to say," Joe said. "You're not sitting with me." "We have a 3 hour flight." "I don't give a shit where you sit, but you aren't sitting here." "What's wrong," Joe asked. He went to sit with her and Ava got up. "Ava." She went and sat over by the kids. Not ten minutes later, everyone showed up. The flight took off a few minutes later. He slid Ava's laptop out of her hands and pulled her to her feet, walking them towards the back of the plane where they could have some privacy. "What's wrong," Joe asked. Ava slapped him and went and sat back down. He sat beside her the rest of the flight, but not a word was said. When they finally landed, Ava put Grace in her car seat, threw the bags in the SUV and left.

"She's pissed," Ryan said. "You're so freaking smart old man," Joe said. "We'll drop you off. Kids in the back," Ryan teased. Ava pulled into the house, tucked Grace into bed, then drew herself a hot bath. She leaned back and tried to relax. She knew what she saw. She saw his boots and her knees in front of them. It didn't take a brain surgeon to figure it out.

Joe walked in 45 minutes later. He walked upstairs and saw candles flickering in the bathroom. He walked in and Ava was wrapping a towel around herself. "Babe." She walked past him and went into the bedroom. She slid on her t-shirt and boxers and went to bed. "Ava. Talk to me." She turned the light off. He walked over and turned it back on. "No going to bed mad," Joe said. She got up, grabbed her laptop from her bag and went downstairs. He followed her. "Ava." She plugged it in and opened the last webpage she'd looked at—It was real estate in Nashville.

"Ava, talk to me." She looked at a few other houses. He slammed it shut. "We're talking." "Why?" "Why are you looking at real estate?" "Thought I would move." "Why?" "Give you your bachelor pad back," Ava said. "Ava." "Don't you dare tell me that I didn't see what I know I did Joe. "Ava, it's not . . . ." "It's not what I think right? Well I'm not waiting around for the truth part of that." "Where are you going?" "Anywhere but here." "You're not walking out," Joe said. "And why not? You doing whatever you want with whoever you want isn't already doing that?" Ava walked up the steps and locked the guest room door. She slid into bed and was asleep in minutes.

Wouldn't you know that was the only door he hadn't got the key to? He slid into bed, spending the entire night tossing and turning. He got up once or twice, trying to figure out how to get in to that room, then went back to sleep.

Ava got up at 9, fed Grace and got her dressed, then took Grace and went out. She needed breathing space . . . . badly.

Joe woke up and didn't hear Grace. Didn't hear anything. No noise at all. He looked and Ava wasn't in the spare room, or the office, and Grace wasn't there. He looked outside and the SUV was gone. He called Ava's phone and it went to voicemail. "Ava, call me. Please. Babe, just come home so we can talk this out." He hung up and showered, got dressed, cleaned up a bit, then had coffee and tried to work on a song to distract himself. When it got to six o'clock and Ava wasn't back, he started getting worried. He called Rose. "She dropped Grace off at 5." "Where did Ava go?" "No idea, but she wasn't happy. What happened," Rose asked. "Nothing." Joe hung up. She wasn't with Rose, Danielle or Emily, and she sure as hell wasn't home.

It hit 10pm and he was worried. He called her phone again for the 5th time. "Ava, where are you? Babe, just come home so we can talk. I'm sorry. Baby please." He poured himself a drink. As he was finishing his second glass, Ava walked in. She walked up the steps, then locked their bedroom door. Rose called the house. "She just walked in. Thanks Rose," Joe said. "Whatever you did, fix it." "I know." "You know I can kick your ass," Rose replied. "I know that too Rose." He hung up and walked upstairs. Joe unlocked the bedroom door and walked inside. Ava looked over and saw him. "What?" "You took off. You tell me," Joe said. Ava just looked at him. Her eyes were a crystal blue that almost glowed. It was the one way he knew she'd been crying. "I'm too tired for this." "Where were you?" "Franklin." "Don't tell me." "Yeah. I was looking at a few." "Ava." "I told you once Joe." "Babe." "Don't pull the nothing happened bullshit either. I know what that looks like, and I'm damn sure it happened," Ava said. "She tried and I pushed her away." "Right. Why go outside with her at all? Even worse, trying to stay out of sight so nobody would see you unless you had something to hide?" "Ava, please stop." "Why don't you? You want to be single so bad, then go be fucking single." Ava went to walk past him and he grabbed her. He wrapped his arms around her and no matter how hard she fought, he wouldn't let her go.

"Let go of me." "No. Ava I stopped her before she even got close to." "I don't believe you." "Baby, I wouldn't do that to us." "Bullshit," Ava said. She managed to break free of him, but he caught her hand, pulling her back to him. "You don't want to be married to me, then let me go." Ava walked off and went downstairs. She sat down on the sofa and turned on the TV. He sat in the bedroom as his eyes welled up. Ava sat downstairs on the sofa and cried until she fell asleep. Around 1am, he walked downstairs and carried her up to bed. He laid her on their bed and wrapped his arms around her. This is what he wanted. He didn't want the stupid single bullshit. He wanted her.

The next morning, Ava woke up in bed with Joe's arms around her. She went to get up and he pulled her back to him. "Let go of me." "No." "What the hell do you want from me? I can't play the stupid game anymore Joe. Either you want to be married or you want to play. Pick one." "I did. See that ring on your finger? That was my decision," Joe said. "Then stick the fuck to it." Ava got away from him and walked downstairs. She made coffee, then sat down outside on the chaise to drink it. He came out a little while later. "Stop assuming," Joe said. "You let her . . ." "No I didn't. I said that I was married. That any of the stupid ass shit I did when I was single, wasn't happening anymore. That I loved you. That she was a good person, but I married the woman I love. She was upset. I told her that someday she'd understand it. That I wasn't being fair to you," Joe said. "Ever listen to your own damn words?" Ava got up and went back inside. He walked in a few minutes later and saw her coffee cup on the counter. He heard the shower running.

Ava had to wash the feeling away. Somehow, she had to. She had to wash away the pain, the anger, the feeling of being lied to. She had to get her strength back again. She heard the bathroom door. Joe sat on the counter. The minute the water stopped, he tossed Ava a towel. "What," Ava asked. "Feel better?" "No." Ava walked into the bedroom. "You know walking away from me isn't going to change this." "I'm not fighting with you over something you can't change. I know what you did Joe." "And I'm telling you that nothing happened." Ava slid on the black and pink lace bra and the g-string that matched, then slid on her jeans. "Where are you going," Joe asked. "To pick Grace up." "I don't want to fight in front of her," Joe said. "Then stop causing fights." Ava grabbed a shirt and pulled it on. "Ava, just hear me out." "Why? So you can keep lying?" Ava went to walk out of the bedroom and he grabbed her arm, pulling her back to him. "What? What do you want from me Joe?" He kissed her. "I want you to know that I didn't. That I love you." "Prove it." "Ava, stop with the hard-ass act. I know you better than that." "I'm hurt. What do you want from me?" "I want you to think about this. I told you that I'd never do anything again," Joe said. "And I was stupid and believed you once. Doesn't mean . . ." He kissed her, pulling her tight to him. "It doesn't mean I believe it," Ava said breaking away from him. "Ava, you know I'm telling you the truth." "Then you explain how I saw what I saw," Ava said. "She tried. I pulled her up and told her what I told you." "What happens next time?" "There's not gonna be one." "Maybe we shouldn't have rushed into the wedding," Ava said. "Don't say that." "We should've taken more time." "Ava, don't say it." "Maybe we just need some time apart." He pulled her back to him. "No. I don't want to be away from you. I love you," Joe said. "Maybe it's a good idea." He kissed her again and held her close, kissing her and devouring her lips.

He had her on the bed in less than 5 minutes. He was inching her shirt back off. "Joe, stop." "You're not leaving." "We need to," Ava said. "No. You aren't going," Joe said pinning her to the bed. "Stop." "I'm not losing you. I can't." "For a day or two." "No." "We have to do something," Ava said. "Ava, we figure this out together. That's all there is to it." "I can't." "Babe, we got into this together. We're fixing it together." "Do you know what it feels like?" "Babe, I swear on Grace that nothing happened. Please." Joe kissed her again. "Please don't go," he said as he wrapped his arms tight around her. "I can't just sit here." "Babe, please." "We'll go get Grace." He kissed Ava. "I love you. Just believe in me alright," Joe said. "I'll try." "Good." They kissed a while longer, then went and picked Grace up.

Ava put her in the SUV while Ryan pulled Joe aside. "I told you," Ryan said. "We didn't do anything Ryan. I wouldn't be that stupid." "You better hope you didn't. If you did, you screwed yourself for life," Ryan said. "I know." He hugged Ryan goodbye and left with Grace and Ava. "What was that," Ava asked. "Nothing. Just a kick in the butt," Joe said. "Where are we headed?" "Anywhere you want." "Horseback riding." "Babe." "She can ride with me," Ava said. "Seriously?" Ava nodded. "If it makes you smile once today, then we'll go."

The rest of the afternoon they went for a ride, had lunch, went to the park, then headed home around dinner. They fed Grace dinner and Joe gave her a bath and tucked her in with a song while Ava did her writing. He came downstairs, poured them each a drink, then took one into Ava and sat down on the sofa by her desk. "Thank you." "What are you doing Monday next week," Joe asked. "Grace's doctor's appointment first thing. Other than that nothing." "Can we move it to Thursday morning?" "Why," Ava asked. "Just an idea." Ava called and checked and had it moved to Wednesday morning. "Why am I moving the appointment," Ava asked. "We're going away for a few days." "Where?" "Not sure yet. I think we need to," Joe said. "You are supposed to be in the studio next week." "I'll tell him we're going away for a day or two," Joe said. "Okay." He motioned for her to come closer. "What," Ava asked rolling her chair towards him. He pulled her from the chair and on top of him. "What are you up to," Joe asked. Ava leaned on top of him. He slid her shirt off. "Joe." He kissed her. She straddled him on the sofa. He sat up, then leaned her backwards, kissing her stomach, her breasts, then her shoulder and her neck. "I still have writing to do," Ava said. He kissed her and undid her jeans. Not a second later, his phone went off. He slid it out of his pocket and put it on the desk.

She peeled his shirt off, then he kicked his jeans and boxers off. It was intense, animal instinct and passion. Ava's body craved him. He always knew just what to do, what to say, how to kiss her and where. He knew her body better than anything. Both of them were hot and sweaty. Finally, they came like a bang. "I love you," Joe said. He kissed her neck again. "Joe," Ava said. "Babe, I'm sorry if I made you think that anything happened. I'm trying to do right by you." "I know. I just keep thinking that things are working too well for nothing to happen." "Babe, only woman I want is you. I want to be with you every second of every day. Don't ever think that some chick like that could tempt me." "But . . ." He kissed her again. "Bed?" Ava nodded. He slid his jeans on, she slid his shirt on, then they grabbed the clothes from the floor and went upstairs. As Ava was turning the lights off, the doorbell rang. She went and answered it. "Is Joe home?" "Babe, door." He walked down the steps and saw her. "Kyra, what are you doing here?" "I got in a fight with him." "What kind of fight?" The second she got into the light Joe saw the bruise. He sat with her calming her down and Ava went and got dressed. She came downstairs in her leggings, boots and black sweater. "Where are you going," Joe asked. "Emily's on her way over." "Where are you going?" "To the police," Ava said. "I can't," Kyra said. "Yeah you can. We'll be there with you," Ava replied. Emily showed a few minutes later and Ava scooted Kyra into the SUV. "Babe," Joe said. "I'll go. I'll call you." He kissed Ava. "Thank you," Joe said.

After an hour at the police station, Kyra came out in tears. "We'll send someone to pick him up tonight. I'll call you when we leave," the officer said. Kyra wrapped her arms around Ava. "I don't even know why I stayed with him. Joe's gonna say I told you so forever," Kyra said. "No he won't." Joe called Ava. "We're on our way back." "I love you," he said. "Love you too." Ava hung up. They hopped in the SUV and were back at the house in 20 minutes. Ava walked her upstairs and drew her a hot bath. "Just relax a while. I'll make you some tea," Ava said. She came downstairs and Joe pulled her into his arms. "She okay?" "She will be. Save the I told you so's for her okay?" He nodded. "Call your sister," Ava said. "Babe, it's almost 11." "Call or I will Joe."

Ava made tea while Joe told his sister what was happening. "She's staying here with us tonight. I would offer the house to her this weekend, but it's not a good idea," Joe said. "We'll come get her tomorrow. Thank Ava for me," Caroline said. "I will." Ava took Kyra some tea, then gave her some warm pajamas and tucked her into the bed. "If you need anything, just ask. You're safe here," Ava said. "But . . ." "He can't get past the front gates. I'll let them know to be on the watch." "Thank you Ava." "That's what family's for." Kyra hugged her and finally stopped crying. "Sleep. It'll be better in the morning."

Ava came into the bedroom and Joe was laying on the bed in his boxers. "You are amazing," Joe said. "About time you noticed." "Babe." "What?" "How did you know," Joe asked. "Been there. Lived through it and thanks to a few good friends I made it through," Ava said. "Who?" "Doesn't matter. It's history." He wrapped his arms around her and pulled her into his arms. "Anyone ever lays a finger on you again." "It was a long time ago." "Babe, I mean it. Anyone," Joe said. They curled up on the bed and fell asleep.

The next morning, Ava got up with Grace. Kyra woke up a little while later. Joe was still asleep. "How we feeling today," Ava asked. "Best sleep I've had in a while." "So, Joe and I are leaving tomorrow for the weekend. I'm gonna call a friend of mine that does security. If you need anything, you call him," Ava said. "You don't need to." Ava called her friend. "No problem Ava. Anything you want." "Here's Dane's number. Even if you just get scared, call him. He's a pretty good listener too," Ava said. "They called and told me he's in custody." "Kyra, I know what you're going through. Having him in jail is a good step, but it doesn't fix it," Ava said. She wrapped her arms around Ava. "Thank you for all of this." "If you need to talk, call my cell." "Okay," Kyra replied. They had a quiet breakfast. Kyra played for a while with Grace while Ava went to get dressed.

She slipped back into the bedroom and Joe woke up. "Where you going?" "Shower." "Be in there in a minute." Ava slid out of her clothes, throwing them into the laundry hamper and turned on the hot water. By the time he came in, the room was filled with steam. Joe pulled Ava into his arms and kissed her. He picked her up, wrapping her legs around him and leaned her into the wall. "Your niece is downstairs," Ava said. He kissed Ava again. "Good." They did it in the shower, then on the bathroom counter. Ava did her hair and Joe shaved and got ready for the day. "We have to leave in 4 hours," Ava said. "I know." "Rose isn't coming this weekend," Ava said. "We're leaving from the concert Sunday and going." "Where?" "Bring a bikini or two. Maybe a dress or two." "Joe." "Not telling," Joe said. He kissed her with a colgate kiss. Ava slid her leggings on with the tank top that was almost too low for him to not pounce on her. Ava slid her over the knee boots on, then did her makeup. "Babe," Joe said. "What?" "Tell me you aren't wearing them on stage. Promise me." "No." "Then the piano is gonna be the least of your worries," Joe teased. "I know." He kissed her. Ava finished getting ready, then packed. "One night. Jeans," Joe said. Ava threw in 2 or 3 pair and a few sexy tops that Joe glared at her over. She threw in the bikinis, and a few other dresses, plus heels etc. She took her bag downstairs and put it in the SUV, then came in and packed Grace's things. "So I couldn't change anything," Joe asked. Ava nodded. He kissed her. Ava finished packing for Grace and took her toiletry bag downstairs, then went to check on Kyra and Grace.

"Mama, look." Grace ran over to Ava with a picture. "Well aren't we the artist this morning," Ava said. "She wanted to color," Kyra said. "It's fine. I have an idea." "What's that?"

"Gimme a minute." Ava went upstairs. "What would you think of bringing her to the show tonight," Ava asked. "Already got her tickets. My sister's coming and meeting us there," Joe said. Ava went downstairs. "We have a pit stop to make before the airport." "What?" "We're bringing you with us to the concert tonight," Ava said. "I can't," Kyra said. "You can play with Grace all day. Just a change of scenery." "I don't have any other clothes." "I have an extra suitcase. We'll go to your place with you and throw some things together." "You sure?" "Yes," Joe said coming downstairs and grabbing a coffee. She hugged Ava. "Thank your uncle. His idea," Ava said. She went and hugged Joe while Ava got Grace into her car seat. They headed to Kyra's place and packed her things, then headed for the airport.

The flight landed a few hours later and they headed to the venue. They did sound check, an interview or two, then Joe's sister showed up. "Kyra," Caroline said. She turned around from playing with Grace. "What are you doing here," Kyra asked. "Joe called me." "Mom, I don't need to hear a lecture." She pulled Kyra into her arms. "Are you okay?" Kyra nodded and started crying. "You're coming home with me. You need family." "Mom." "We're staying for the concert and having a girl day tomorrow, then we're heading back," Caroline said. "Hug," Grace said walking towards Kyra. Kyra picked her up and hugged her. "Mama," Grace said pointing at Ava. "How's things over here," Ava asked. "Thank you for taking care of her last night," Caroline said. Grace slid into Ava's arms. "She knows who to count on now," Ava said. The ladies relaxed and then went to the hotel and changed for the night.

Emily looked after Grace while Ava and Joe got ready. "Not the white one," Joe begged. Ava nodded. "Babe," he said. Ava slid it on and put on her silver sparkle heels. Joe walked towards her and Ava slipped past him and went towards hair and makeup. "Ava." She slid her heels off and ran to hair and makeup with Joe trailing her. She sat down just as he was getting to the door. "You aren't," Joe said. Ava nodded. "Don't blame me when you get no sleep," he teased. They started on Ava's hair. He kissed Ava. "Don't you have a meet and greet to go to," Ava asked. He kissed her again, with a blood rushing kiss. He left and they finished Ava's hair and makeup. By the time he was finished the meet and greet, Ava was done getting her hair and makeup done. She slid her heels on, then went and relaxed in the sitting area. Joe came in and kissed Ava. "Well," Joe asked. "It's all good," Ryan said. "Oh really." Joe wrapped his arm around Ava. "I'm wearing it," Ava said. He kissed her neck. "You two are hilarious," Brad said. "Just thought the jeans would be better," Joe said. "Buddy, she's hot. And I can say that because I am married to my beautiful pregnant wife," Brad said. "Keep your eyes on your own prize," Joe teased. Brad called Danielle to check on her. "You two better." Ryan asked. "Never better," Joe said. Ava got up and grabbed herself a drink. Rose called Ryan.

"Babe," Joe said. "I'm fine." Ava drank her drink. He grabbed her glass and took a swig. "Liar." He grabbed her hand and pulled her into the change room. "What," Ava asked. "What's wrong?" "Nothing." "Ava, something's wrong," Joe said. "It's nothing." "Stop." Ava went to walk out and he pulled her back. "Tell me." "Just brings back all the memories. I'm worried about Kyra," Ava said. "We're talking tonight." "No." "Even if it takes an entire bottle," Joe said. He kissed Ava and they walked out. She walked him to the stage, then watched the show from the side. She looked out into the crowd and saw Kyra and her mom, then behind her, Ava saw him. She went back and grabbed another shot, then went and did her songs. She came back in after and slid her heels off, then walked to the RV. She sat with Grace and Emily until the show was done.

Joe was about to head back to the RV when he saw his sister and Kyra with a man. "Hey," Joe said. "Good concert. You guys were great," he said. "Thanks." "Where's Ava," Joe asked. "In the RV with Grace." "Haven't seen her in years," the man said. "I'll get her." Joe hopped in the RV. "You okay," Joe asked. Emily was asleep. "Fine." "There's some guy out there that says he knows you." Ava pulled on Joe's shirt and her heels, then came out. "Holy shit Ava. Long time," the man said. "Yep." Ava's hand tightened on Joe. "No hug," he asked. "No." Ava walked over towards Ryan's trailer. The guy followed her. "Ava." "Get the hell away from me," Ava said. "It's been a long time." "Not long enough." He grabbed her arm. Ava turned to face him. "Let go of me," Ava said. "You tell him?" "Tell him what? That a long time ago I dated a Neanderthal? No." "Don't push me." "Get your fucking hands off me." "Or what?" Ryan saw what was happening and tried to distract him. "Hey Ava. You did great girl," Ryan said. "Thanks Ryan," Ava said as Ryan hugged her to get her out of the man's grip. "I have that thing you needed," Ryan said. Ava got in the trailer with Ryan. He texted Joe. Ava stepped out and the guy grabbed Ava dragging her away from the guys.

"What do you want Owen?" "Same thing I always did." "I'm married now." "Who the hell was that stupid to marry you," he asked. Joe tapped him on the shoulder and nailed him in the face. Security was behind him. He grabbed Ava's hand and they headed to the SUV. "Grace?" "In the SUV." They took off for the hotel. "You okay," Joe asked. Ava stared out the window. "Babe." She shook her head. They got to the hotel and security walked them in and up to the suite. Emily took Grace to the bedroom and tucked her into the bed, then fell asleep in the bed beside her. Joe walked into the bedroom with Ava. She slid out of the dress and went into the shower. Joe poured them a drink and left the bottle beside the glasses.

Ava came out a little while later. She wrapped herself in the towel and Joe saw the bruises. "Looks like I'm wearing what you wanted after all," Ava said. He pulled her into hisarms. He carried her to bed, then curled up beside her. He handed her a drink. "Tell me." "It was years ago." "Babe, you have to tell me," Joe said.

She told him about meeting Owen at a bar one night. How he went from possessive to controlling, then things got physical, sexual then emotionally abusive. How with one look or one word, she was scared for her life for months. How it was because of Rose, Rachel and Carrie that she got away. "What did he do to you," Joe asked. She told him about the rape, the assaults, the torture tactics. "Babe, I'm not letting him near you again," Joe said. "He knows where I am." "And so do I." He filled Ava's glass and his own. "I didn't think it would still scare me," Ava said. Joe kissed her. "He never will again." "Joe, you can't promise that." "Yeah I can." He slid the glass out of her hand and kissed her. He called security and notified them of the situation. "We'll get a cop over here in the morning." Joe hung up and curled up with Ava. She had nightmares and was white knuckling Joe when they woke up.

He kissed her the minute her eyes opened. "You were either watching me sleep or you didn't sleep." "You flinched," Joe said. "Did I keep you awake?" "No. Just remember something. It doesn't matter that you aren't perfect. Either am I. I love you the way you are. Just don't shut me out." Ava nodded. They got up, got dressed, then got Grace breakfast. They headed back, got their stuff together and headed for the next venue. Ryan didn't say a word. They pulled in and Ava was surrounded by security. They did sound check and an interview or two, but he wouldn't let Ava out of his sight. She played with Grace, rocked and sang her to sleep for her nap, then Joe finished up.

"Come on," he said. "I'll take care of Grace," Rose said. "Joe, seriously." He kissed her. They went for a walk, then sat down on the beach. "You need to relax." "Where are we going," Ava asked. He kissed her again. They hopped in the SUV and 15 minutes later, pulled in to a spa. "What are you up to," Ava asked. They walked in and headed to the massage area. He'd booked a hot stone massage for two. Joe kissed her. They had their massages, then headed back. Grace got up and they played on the beach with her, then they had dinner. Joe started getting ready. Ava grabbed the sexy black dress and slid his jacket on top. She put the boots on, then headed in to get hair and makeup done. Joe sat with her. "Go do the meet and greet," Ava said. "Are you alright?" Ava nodded. Security came in and sat with her. He kissed her, then went off with the guys.

As soon as she was done, Ava was on the phone with Rose. "You sure? You were freaked for weeks last time," Rose said. "It's fine." "Liar." "I told him. We got the restraining order re-activated," Rose asked. "When are you back?" "Next week after the concerts." "Where are you going?" "He won't tell me. We're going on vacation for a few days between shows," Ava said. "I can look after Grace." "We're bringing her," Ava said. "Take care of you. You need me, call me." "I will. Love you." "Love you too." Ava hung up and the guys came back in. Joe slid onto the sofa behind her. "Rose said to call her," Ava told Ryan. "How you doing," he asked. "I'm better. Thanks for the save," Ava said. "Family does for family." "Still, thanks," Ava said. He kissed Ava's cheek and went and called Rose.

"You look beautiful," Joe said. "Just because I'm putting the shirt over it," Ava said. "No. Because you are," he said pulling Ava into his arms. "You know you don't have to baby me." "I'm taking care of my wife. That alright?" "Depends." "On what?" "You gonna be mad if I slide the shirt off," Ava asked. He kissed her. "Brad, tell her the shirt looks good with it," Joe said. "I like the dress." "Thanks," Joe said throwing a pillow at him. "I'll see. It's hot up there," Ava said. Joe kissed Ava. "Hotter when you walk out in another one of those dresses." He kissed her again as Ryan came back in. "You going to tell me where we're going," Ava asked. Joe shook his head. "Taking off for a few days," Ryan asked. "Thought we might," Joe replied. "We can look after the house for you if you want." "Cool." Ava and Joe relaxed a while before they headed for the stage. "If you start getting freaked out, just say something," Joe said. Ava nodded. He kissed her again with a spine tingling kiss, then headed on stage.

By the time Ava headed on stage, she was a little more relaxed. She sang a few songs with the guys, then headed off. She stood side stage until the concert was finished. They headed off and Joe walked towards her, kissing her and leaning her into the wall. "Had to didn't you," Joe joked. Ava nodded as she slid the shirt back on. He picked her up, wrapped her legs around him and walked to the dressing room. "Where are we going?" He kissed her with another unbelievable kiss and locked the door behind them.

CHAPTER 22

The next night, right after the concert, they headed for the airport. Joe handed in their tickets. "Do I get to know where you're kidnapping me to?" "Flight 807 to Scottsdale." He took her hand and led her towards the plane. Grace was asleep in Ava's arms. Within a few hours, they were there. It was quiet, relaxing and private. There was nothing to distract them from their time together.

After a few days of relaxing, playing with Grace and de-stressing, they headed home. "Was I right," Joe teased. "For once," Ava replied. They pulled in and put Grace down for her nap. "What time do we have to be there tomorrow," Ava asked. "Leaving at 11." "Good." "Why?" "No reason," Ava said. They unpacked and spent the day doing normal household stuff. They spent the night in. They played with Grace a while, tiring her out and Joe tucked her in with a song. When he came downstairs, Ava was on the patio in her robe. He handed her a drink and they curled up together. "Feeling better," he asked. Ava nodded. "Good. You know seeing you like that scared the crap out of me." "Scared me too." "I have to ask you something you aren't gonna like," Joe asked. "What?" "Anything else I need to know? Anything you haven't told me?" "Nothing that important. I just didn't want all the past brought up." "I know babe, but if it means you being safe." "I know. I promise there's nothing." "Good." He kissed her temple and snuggled with her. "The pool looks good." "Turned the temperature up a bit. It's not as cool as it was." "Oh really." "What are you thinking in that beautiful head," Joe asked. Ava got up, dropped the robe and dove in, wearing a barely there string bikini. He looked and watched as he undid his shirt. "Coming," Ava asked as she swam to the side. A few minutes later he was in the water and they were splashing around.

Finally after a round of pool tag, he had her pinned to the wall of the pool. "Had to wear it," Joe joked. "You said it was your favorite." "Consider yourself lucky that I didn't peel it off you when we were at the hotel." "Thought you did," Ava teased. He kissed her and her heart almost skipped a beat. "You always get me don't you?" "Teasing? Always." He untied the bottoms. "What are you doing?" He kissed her again and threw them on the pavement.

Ava slipped away and went for her robe. He grabbed it and pulled her back into his arms and onto the chaise. "What are you up to," Ava asked. He kissed her again and slid the top off. "You realize we have neighbors." He kissed her again and pulled her legs around him. "I love you." "Love you too baby." "Trust me?" "What?" "Yes or no?" "What are you up to?" They made love outside under the stars, and somehow she forgot about neighbors, about anything but what they were doing. He picked her up and carried her inside to the sofa, turning the fireplace on and they made love again. "You are addictive as hell, do you know that," he asked. "Ditto to you." "You know you forgot to pack something when we left." "I know." "Babe," he said. "If it happens, it does." They curled up together, and fell asleep on the sofa.

The next morning, they got up and Ava started packing again. He got Grace ready when Rose showed up. "Hey stranger," Joe said as he answered. "Hey yourself. Where's Ava?" "Packing. Can you talk her out of the little dresses?" "I highly doubt it, but I'll see what I can do." "Rose," Grace said. "Hey beautiful." Rose gave her kisses and Grace snuggled back up to Joe.

"So the dresses got worse did they," Rose joked as she came in. "No. It's the pink one and the two black ones." "Tease." "And he loves every second of it." "Why don't I look after Grace this weekend?" "You sure?" Rose nodded. "What is with your super huge grin," Ava asked. "Jacob's getting a baby brother or sister." "Seriously?" Rose nodded. Ava hugged her. "I can't believe you two. What did Ryan say?" "He's past happy." "I'm glad you are too." Rose hugged Ava. Ava kept packing, then threw lingerie into the bag with her things. "So really, how are you," Rose asked. "Better. I think his idea of the vacation was good." "It was great actually," Joe said as he walked in and kissed Ava. "So does Miss Grace want to come spend the weekend with Jacob?" Grace nodded. "Let's go pack a few toys." Rose went into the bedroom with Grace while Ava and Joe finished packing.

They headed to the airport, then hopped on the plane with the guys and they were off. "So how was the vacation," Brad asked. "Was perfect. Just like you said," Joe replied. "So you knew," Ava asked. "He asked. That's where Danielle and I went on our honeymoon." "It was definitely relaxing," Ava said. "Good. You two needed some down time together." Ava's phone went off as soon as they were about to close the doors. "Ava." "Cat?" "Finally. You know how hard it is to track your famous ass down?" "How are you?" "Good. You guys flying into Michigan today?" "Yeah why?" "I'll see you there." "Come to the security gate. We can hang out a bit," Ava said. "What time?" "2ish?" "See you there. Love ya." "Love you too." Ava hung up. "Details," Joe teased. "It was my friend Cat. She's coming to say hi." "I don't think . . ." "She wasn't at the wedding. She's been travelling everywhere." "Now this should be interesting," Ryan joked. "Meaning? Seems to me the last friend of mine you met, you married Ryan." "Point taken," he teased. "So tell me about Cat," Joe asked. "Too many stories to tell. We've been best friends for years. We email back and forth, but it's been a long time." "So that's who you're chatting to," Joe asked. "Funny." He kissed her. "I want details," Ryan joked. "We've definitely had a few adventures." "Such as?" "Not bringing those skeletons out," Ava joked.

They chatted the rest of the flight, then Ava did some writing while the guys worked on a new song or two. They finally landed and headed for the venue. They pulled in and Ava was thanking her lucky stars she brought a coat. "Seriously? It's freezing." "That's why I packed your leather jacket," Ava said. "Smart ass," Joe teased as he kissed her. They pulled in and unloaded, then went inside. Ava left a pass with security for Cat. They did sound check and the guys were just about to head to interviews when Cat showed.

"Ava." She turned and got up, running for Cat. "Oh my god. It's been forever." They hugged. "You look amazing," Cat said. "His fault," Ava joked. "You look great Cat." "That's all me baby," she joked. "So what you been up to?" "Nothing exciting. Same crap different day. Nothing like Miss Superstar over here." "You wouldn't believe me if I told you." "I saw in the paper that you two got married. I could have sworn the last time we talked you were dating that Kevin guy," Cat said. "Who is officially history. We met by fluke." "It's always a fluke Ava." "I went to a concert with a friend who knew them, and ended up talking to Joe all night. Been inseparable ever since." "See, you probably wore the boobie shirt," Cat joked. Ava smirked. "See, I know you better than you think Ava." "It wasn't that." "Right." Joe walked over towards them after the first interview. He kissed Ava. "This must be Cat." "And you must be Joe. Heard so much about you," Cat said. "Ava told me the two of you have too many skeletons. You telling me that she has a naughty side?" "You mean the queen of flirtation? Oh hell yes." "Then you're telling us at dinner." "Would love to." Ava shot her a look. Joe wrapped his arms around Ava. "So how did the interview go," she asked. "Good. They asked the question you thought they would." "Told you." "Told them we were working on it." "Shit disturber." Joe kissed her. "Have to go back for another one in ten. I'm just gonna call and see how Grace is." "She's fine. She's sleeping." "Instant messaging?" Ava nodded. He kissed her again, then headed back.

"Girl, you are happy as hell aren't you," Cat asked. "There are good and bad days." "He is so totally your type." "Always had a crush on him." "Tell me about it." The two ladies chatted for an hour or two, then headed to dinner.

"I know you have juicy stories," Joe teased. "You mean the one where she had guys fighting over her and left with someone else completely, or when she had 4 guys competing for her attention?" "Oh really," Ava said. "Take it back. That was me." "Just like I said." "She was always a flirt, and always the one that got attention from the sleazebags." "Exactly," Ava said. "There has to be a good story or two," Ryan teased. "Well, there was the time that we went to a peeler bar and she disappeared with one of the dancers." "Like you didn't," Ava teased. "And just what were you doing," Joe asked with his arms wrapped around her. "Dumping him," Ava said. "Ooh," Brad said. "I'm sorry guys. You know better. I refuse to share." "Always did," Cat said. "Don't even." "What? We all make mistakes." "Cat," Ava said. "Speak," Joe said. "The one where she was on and off with a guy for years and ended up having the poor guy begging for her." "Just meant I played the right card," Ava said. "Was wondering when I'd find out about that side of you," Joe teased. "No more stories," Ava said. "Not even the one about poor old what's his name where you had him practically scared to come back into the bar?" "That was deserved and you know it." "Very true." They all chatted a while longer, then Ava went to get her hair and makeup done. "Tell me you're wearing jeans," Joe begged. "Okay . . . . I'm wearing jeans." "Ava." "I'm wearing the white and silver." "Babe." "The one that matches your shirt." "You know what's gonna happen." Ava nodded. He kissed her and went to go get changed.

The guys headed into the meet and greet while Ava and Cat talked. "So what happened with that chick," Cat asked. "She finally screwed off. Seriously, I didn't know if I was going to be able to put up with her being all over him." "Ava, the guy loves you. It's written all over him. Stop being worried." "You try being married to someone who's loved by millions of people Cat. There are women that are damn near obsessed." "And he put a ring on your finger and promised to love you forever." "And what happens when he finds out that I'm not perfect, and that I'm never gonna be?" "He wraps his arms around you and loves you even more." "But." "But nothing. Stop being worried about the what if's," Cat said. "I love him, but I'm still scared." "I get it. Stop being worried. He loves you. Nothing's ever gonna change that." Ava hugged Cat. "You better get out there," Ava said. "Love you." "Love you too. See you after." They hugged then Cat took off.

Cat Jameson has been best friends with Ava forever. Ever since they were teenagers and meeting because of a common friend or two, they'd always been close. Cat stood around five foot nine and had curves that guys lusted over. She had dark hair, green eyes, and had a contagious laugh that everyone loved. She'd seen her share of heartbreak, but her and Ava were always there for each other. Ava would walk through quicksand for her and vice versa. Cat had her share of secrets, but Ava knew all. Cat had finally found a job she loved and had everything going right, that was until one of their skeletons came back to haunt them.

Cat sat with a friend and watched the concert, totally surprised at how great it was . . . more importantly, how great Ava did. After, Cat's friend left and she went back to hang out with Ava and the guys. "You were great," Cat said. "Thanks," Joe replied. "Dang, I didn't know you could sing like that Ava," Cat replied. "Thanks. So what are you doing for the next few days?" Joe smirked. "Why do you ask?" "Thought you could come hang with us for a while." "You know I have to work Monday." "You'll be back for work," Ava said. "Then, I'm all yours." "Good." They packed up, then headed to the airport.

The next two days the girls hung out, shopped, then were back for sound check, interviews and concerts. When Cat headed home Sunday, Joe knew something was up. "So, that was the famous Cat." "I wish she was closer." "Babe, you never know what could happen." "That I do know." "So why do I get the feeling something is up with her?" "Something's always up," Ava teased. "I mean it." "It's nothing. Just something that happened years ago." "No secrets." "An old friend of ours that she wished she hadn't seen." "And?" "The guy went a little nuts on her. He's a control freak." "What did you tell her?" "That when she thinks she can't handle it, to call in for reinforcements." "Not if it means you getting hurt," Joe said. "I love you for worrying, but it's not that. The guy's scared of me." "Oh really," Joe teased. Ava nodded. "And just why would that be?" "Kickboxing." "Ooh, I'm scared of you," Joe teased as he tickled her and leaned her back onto the bed.

"I missed you," Joe said. "I was right beside you." He kissed her and slid his arms around her, pulling her close. "That kind of missing me," Ava teased. He smirked and kissed her again. "Missed you too then," Ava said. She slid her legs around him. "You know I never stop learning interesting things about you." "You know parts of me that nobody else knows." "I know. That's the best part about loving you." He kissed Ava and one thing led to another. They made love and this time, things seemed different. She'd missed that feeling of just letting herself go. There were no more secrets now. There was nothing to hide, nothing to be scared of. It was intense and passionate. He wouldn't let go of her, even after. "I really missed you." Ava smiled and kissed him. "Never lost me," Ava said.

The next morning, they picked Grace up and spent the day playing in the park with her. She was running a bit, trying to chase Joe. The more Ava watched them, the more she knew that the spur of the moment decision she'd made so long ago was the best one she ever made. This was what she'd always wanted. There never really was a reason to be scared. Grace came running for her and before they knew it, Grace had tackled Ava and Joe had tackled Grace. They were all playing around in the grass like little kids. "Daddy, hug." He pulled Grace into his arms. She wrapped her arms so tight around him. "I love Daddy." "Love you too baby girl." "I love mommy." "Me too." Ava smiled as Grace reached for her and turned it into a group hug. "Mama, teddy." "You left teddy at home baby." "Me know." "We should get back anyway," Joe said. "Hot date," Ava teased. He gave her that look and that smile that let her know just what he was thinking. "Could say that," he teased. They packed up and headed home. The entire way home, her hand was in his. He had a silly smirk ear to ear. "What," Ava asked. "Nothin," he said as they stopped at the light. He leaned over and kissed Ava. "Pay attention to the road." "Can't. Sexy woman beside me." "Funny." They finally got home and had dinner, then gave Grace a bubble bath and tucked her into bed. Ava came downstairs after and he was working on another song.

"What are you up to?" "Had an idea." "Oh really?" Ava slid onto the sofa beside him. "A few actually, but the song idea is working." "I bet. About as well as all those other ideas in your head right now are." He laughed and kissed her. "Grace asleep?" "As soon as her head touched the blanket." He played a bit of the song he was working on. "Sounds good." "It's about you." "Aww." He laughed. "What do you think of this part?" They ended up spending an hour or two working on it. "You know this isn't gonna be another one of those songs." "Party pooper." "I can't be out there with you all the way through the concert." "You could." "I love you for wanting me there, but honestly, I love watching you guys out there. I always did." Joe kissed her. "I know. That's how I found you in the first place." "Exactly," Ava replied as he kissed her again. He wrote a little more, then he put the guitar away.

"Babe," he said. "Yes my handsome husband." "Like that. I have an idea for tonight." "And what would that be?" Joe kissed her. "Thought we could stay in bed." "Oh really." He nodded and rubbed noses with her. "And just what would we be doing in bed?" "Making a baby." "Gee, unlike every other night." He kissed her again and slid his arms around her torso, kissing her again and scooping her into his lap. "What?" "We want another baby right?" Ava nodded. "This time I want him to look like you." "A boy?" Ava nodded. "We can handle two right," Ava said. "Babe, we can do whatever we have to." "But still." "What are you worried about? I thought that was my job." He kissed her again. She slid her legs around him. "We make pretty awesome babies," Ava said. "Very true." "If we have another one, nothing's going to change." "Promise me." "Babe, Emily's helping us. It's only going to change when Grace starts school." "Good point." "Then we figure it out together." "I want to be at the concerts with us." "So do I. Stop worrying. We'll figure it out when it happens." "But . . ." Ava kissed him. "Stop worrying." He kissed her and leaned her onto the sofa. "So what if we do have another one?" "Then Grace will have someone to play with." "I want to be home more." "Tell Ryan that." "Babe, do you always have the right answer?" She kissed him. "Nope." He kissed her again and they snuggled, made out, snuggled, then made out until they both decided to head to bed.

Joe carried Ava up the stairs and leaned her onto their bed. "What," Ava asked. "I wanna do this every day for the rest of my life." "Good thing we got married then." He kissed her again and peeled her out of her sweater. A few minutes later, her jeans were off and she was peeling his shirt off. He kissed every inch of her. Then . . . . her phone went off. "You even think it," Joe said. She went to grab it and he pulled a move he hadn't since they first met. She looked and saw that it was Cat. "Don't do it, or I'm . . ." Ava texted back that she'd call in a few. She put the phone down and Joe continued his taunting. "Baby," Ava said. She heard his zipper. When she heard his jeans hit the floor, she looked at him. He was working his way up her torso. It was ridiculous, but he still made her nervous. He kissed her and made love to her, this time determined to take their time. Every inch of her was humming in minutes.

He curled up with her after. "I love you," he said. "Nah. You're just addicted." "That too," he said. Ava snuggled up closer when her phone rang again. Ava grabbed it. "You alright?" "No." "Where are you?" "Airport." "What time?" "Three hours." "I'll come get you." "Love you." "I know. Text me the flight number." Ava hung up. "Cat?" Ava nodded. "She's flying here. Something's wrong. Can we book her a room at that hotel?" He kissed her. "I'll book it." "Thank you baby." "You realize this means we have three hours." "Two and a half." "Ooh." He kissed her again. "Don't you start," Ava said. "Better idea." "What's that sexy husband of mine?" "Was thinking." Her fingers linked with his, and his hands slid down her torso. He pulled her in close. "You know I'm not gonna sleep until you get back." "I know. I'll come back as soon as I get her checked in." He kissed her and leaned her back onto the bed. "What," Ava asked. He kissed her again. Ava slid her legs around him. "You know I should get up and get changed." "You have another two and a half-hours." "Don't you start." He kissed her again and was teasing her again.

Finally, Ava slid out of bed, under protest from Joe, and showered, then got changed and headed off to pick Cat up from the airport. Joe called her half way there. "Yes baby." "I checked her flight. It's landing in ten minutes." "Thank you baby." "Come home quick okay?" "I will." "Got a present for you when you get here." "Did I just get a sneak peek?" "Just come home okay?" "I will babe. Love you." "Love you more." Ava hung up and pulled in to the parking lot, then went in and met Cat. They headed for the SUV and were snapped by paparazzi. They headed out and Ava checked her into the hotel. "You gonna tell me what happened?" "He came back. He busted in to the house, then threatened me." "Did you call the cops?" "They aren't gonna stop him." "Just trust that someone might know how to do their job alright?" "I can't stay there." "I know. We'll find you a place out here." "Ava, I can't run away, but I can't stay there either." "Get some sleep Cat. We'll figure it out." "Ava, I'm seriously scared." Ava was sending a text. "What are you doing?" "Texting one of my buddies that does security. He'll be here tomorrow." "Are you kidding me?" "Go for a swim in the tub, then try to relax. No dirty movies either." Cat hugged Ava. "I'll pop by tomorrow and we'll figure this out after a good night of sleep." "Thank you." "You don't even have to say it." Ava headed out and Cat slid into the Jacuzzi tub.

Ava got home and heard Joe on the phone. She walked into the TV room and saw him in his boxers on the phone. She slid onto the arm of the sofa. "I have to go. I'm glad you're okay. Call me tomorrow." He hung up. "Kyra?" He nodded. "How's Cat?" Ava slid onto the sofa and his head was in her lap. "She's okay. That guy is a dick." "What happened?" "He scared the shit out of her. He busted into the house and was threatening her. She left and packed as much as she could. I told her we'd see if we could help her find a place near here." "Okay miss fix-it. I'll call the real estate agent tomorrow." He got up and kissed Ava, then picked her up and carried her back upstairs to bed. "Missed me?" Joe kissed her again and leaned her onto the bed. "Couldn't sleep." "Kyra alright?" "She moved back in with my sister." "Good." He slid her leggings off, and Ava peeled her sweater off, then her shirt. He undid her bra, then curled back up in bed with her. "Now where were we," he teased. Ava's g-string hit the floor. "Sleep." "Nope." "Joe." He kissed her shoulder and pulled her close. "Better idea," he said. "What's that?" He rubbed her shoulders. "Your shoulders are all tense." "Thank you," Ava said. He kissed her shoulder, then her neck and gave her a much needed back massage. "Babe," he said. "What," Ava asked. "I have to go into the studio for a bit tomorrow." "So that's why." "Funny, no." He kissed Ava and pulled her into his arms. "I promise I'll be home before Grace heads to bed." "Right," Ava teased. "I'm not leaving until 1." "I guess I can't really complain. A week ago, we were relaxing in the pool." Joe kissed her. "See, I knew you'd understand." "I'll bring down dinner," Ava said. "Sounds good." He kissed her. "Was thinking." "Don't even. We have to get some sleep." "Well now that you mention it," he teased. "Sleep." He kissed her and curled up with her and a little while later, they were asleep.

Ava got up the next morning with Grace, had her coffee while Grace played and colored, then gave her some breakfast and made some for her and Joe. The smell of the coffee woke him up. He slid downstairs and wrapped his arms around her as she cooked at the stove. "About time you woke up." He kissed Ava. "Bed was lonely." "I bet. Grace drew you a picture." He kissed Ava again, then went over and saw Grace. "See Daddy." She held up another Grace masterpiece. It was a picture of Joe with his guitar singing to Ava. "This is great baby girl." She hugged Joe and jumped into his lap. Ava brought breakfast over and she ate with Joe while Grace ran around with her toys.

Emily popped over later in the morning to take Grace for a run outside. The minute the door was closed, Joe kissed Ava and leaned her into the door. "You know you have to leave in a little while?" "We need to have a shower." Ava smirked. "You need to." He walked her backwards towards the steps. Ava ran up the steps with Joe chasing her. He tackled her onto the bed. He peeled her shirt and jeans off, then kissed her. She had his jeans undone in minutes. They had sex then hopped into the shower and finished. "You know, I think at some point we're supposed to not be doing this," Ava said. "Never." He kissed her again. They showered, then hopped out. Joe shaved and did his hair, while Ava got changed and pulled on her jeans and sweater. He walked into the bedroom and pulled on his boxers and his jeans, then wrapped his arms around Ava. "What?" "Nothing," he said. He kissed her and pulled her close. "I love you too." "So sixish?" Ava nodded. "I know. It's gonna be a long afternoon." He kissed her. "If you need anything, just tell me." "I will." He pulled her close and picked her up, wrapping her legs around him and leaned her onto the bed. "You have to leave." He kissed her again, pulling her to close she could feel his heart pounding. Ava's phone rang. He grabbed it and saw it was her doctor.

"Hey Ava. Just wanted to remind you of your appointment at 1." "I'll see you in a little while." Ava hung up. "Oh really?" He kissed her. "Stop." "You never know," Joe said. "Would you cut it out?" "If not, it means we practice more." "Would you just go already?" Joe kissed her again, then pulled her to her feet. He got dressed while Ava finished getting ready, then Emily came back with Grace. "I'll stay with her. You go," Emily said. They both headed off after another long kiss. "Call me and let me know." "I'll see you at six." "Gonna keep me in suspense aren't you?" Ava nodded. Joe kissed her again and they both headed off.

CHAPTER 23

"We might as well do a test while you're here." "It's gonna be negative anyway." "Just to be on the safe side." Within ten minutes, Ava had her answer. "Guess you were right," the doctor said. "I didn't think I would be," Ava said. "Are you two trying?" Ava nodded. "We'll see what happens. When the time's right, it'll click," Ava said. "You're perfectly healthy. Matter of fact, you're healthier than I was at 22." "It's his fault." "I'll call you when I get the blood tests back." "Okay," Ava said. She headed home, picking Cat up on the way. When they pulled in, the real estate agent was just showing up.

"Good timing," Cat said. "Have a couple places to show you if you want to go take a look," she said. "You two talked this morning I guess," Ava asked. Cat nodded. "Go. I have writing to get done." Cat hugged Ava and left with the agent. Ava walked inside to a quiet house. Emily was watching a movie and Grace was sleeping. "Any calls?" "No, but something showed up. I put it in your office." "Thanks." Ava headed into her office and saw a vase of sterling roses and white lilies. She read the card:

> To my everything. Love you forever. Joe

She smiled. Ava got a little writing done, then went upstairs and slid on the pink dress. She made Grace and Emily some dinner, then headed off to meet Joe.

Ava walked in as they were working on one of the new songs. Ryan looked over and saw her, then Joe looked up. They took a dinner break and Brad and Ryan headed off to dinner with Rose and Danielle. Ava sat down as Joe walked in to sit with her. "Tease," Joe said. "Always." "So what did the doctor say?" "You get to keep practicing." "Sounds good to me," he replied. Ava handed him his favorite Chinese food, and they laughed and snuggled while they ate. "So how's the music going?" "It's going. We're stuck on another one," Joe said. Ava went and grabbed the lyrics and took a look. "This what you were working on?" He nodded as he inhaled his noodles. Ava read through it, then wrote a line in. She had two more written when he finished dinner. She handed it to him. "Babe, it's awesome."

He kissed her. "I knew you'd work your magic." He kissed her again. Ava got up to clean up dinner, and he wrapped his arms around her. "Something you needed?" He kissed her neck, then her shoulder. "Joe, they're gonna be back soon." He kissed her again and walked her into the studio. "What are you up to?" Joe kissed her and leaned her against the piano. "One-track mind." "Like you wearing the dress didn't warrant it." He kissed her again. They did it against the piano, then Ava tried to slip away. "Where you going?" "To put Grace to bed." He kissed her again. She slid the bottom of her dress back down and slid her heels back on. "Damn." "Would you?" Joe kissed her and leaned her back into the piano. Ryan came in and knocked on the window. "Interrupting anything?" "No. Got some more lyrics for that song we were stuck on," Joe said. "Bet I know where you found the inspiration," Ryan teased. Ava kissed Joe then left the guys to it. She headed home and walked in to find Grace bawling her eyes out.

"Baby," Ava said. Grace ran towards her. "What happened?" "I was going to give her a bath and she screamed." "Baby." "Mommy bubbles." Ava rolled her eyes. "It's fine. She wanted the lavender bubbles." Ava took her upstairs, gave her a bath, then dried her off and tucked her into bed. "Where Daddy?" "He'll be home soon baby." "Song." Ava rocked her in the chair and sang to her until Grace was asleep. She slid her under the covers and quietly snuck downstairs. "I think she misses you," Emily said. "Probably. You can head home if you want." "Your friend Cat came by. She said she'd be back around 7:30." Not a minute later, Cat was at the door.

"So how did the house hunting go," Ava asked. "Good. I found one I actually liked," Cat replied. "Where?" "Ten minutes away." "And?" "I put an offer in. I'll find out tomorrow." "That's great," Ava said. They sat down and Cat showed her the pictures. "It's perfect for you," Ava said. "I know. Plus, if we go out one night, it's not that far between the two places." "As long as you love it." "It was a hint," Cat said. "I know." The ladies had a coffee and chatted outside by the pool. Joe came in a half-hour or so later and saw them outside. He poured himself a coffee, then went and sat outside with them. "So how did house hunting go," Joe asked as he slid onto the chaise behind Ava. "Put an offer in on a place." "That's great. She's a great agent," Joe said. "Definitely," Cat replied. "And, you have a date tomorrow night," Joe said. "With who?" "An old friend of mine we bumped into on the way home," Joe said wrapping his arms around Ava. Ava looked at him. "Scott," Joe said. "Seriously," Ava asked. He nodded. "Tell me about this Scott person," Cat joked.

After giving Cat all the details she asked for, Cat headed to her hotel and Joe and Ava had some alone time. "So, how was your evening," Joe asked. "Okay. Walked in to Grace screaming her head off." "Why?" "She wanted the lavender bubbles. I think she misses us Joe." "Or she's getting to that time." "Don't even say it." "Ava," Joe replied. "She's getting cranky. She needs us here." "Babe, we are." "We're taking her with us this weekend." "No concerts this weekend. It's thanksgiving." "Good point. We're doing dinner then." "With?" "Ryan and Brad and Danielle and Rose and Jacob, plus Cat and Scott." "Mom," Joe asked. Ava nodded. He kissed her. "You know you don't have to do all this." "You're gonna be glued to the football games Joe." He laughed. Ava slid into her teddy, then washed up and got ready for bed. He slid up behind her in the bathroom. "Babe." "Yes?" "What did the doctor say," Joe asked. "She did blood tests, but the other test was negative." "So, that means maybe?" "Would you cut it out?" He kissed Ava. "Fine. Until after thanksgiving." They headed to bed. Joe curled up with her. "I love you." "I love you too smart ass."

The next day was filled with turkey, family, friends and football. Joe tried teaching Grace and Jacob all the rules, but they were more into the toys that Grace had. Dinner went perfectly with a little help from Rose. Ava knew exactly what she was thankful for. No way was she telling Joe; not yet anyway.

The next morning, Ava got up, got some writing done, then they took Grace to the zoo for the day. They headed home, had dinner and curled back up in bed. The next morning, Ava woke up with a call from her doctor. Joe had taken Grace outside to play. "Ava." "Don't say it." "I had a feeling." "How long?" "Two or three weeks." "Thanks." "See you in a few." Ava showered, then went downstairs. "Hey beautiful," Joe said playing with Grace. "Hey yourself," Ava said. "Mama, come." "What are you making?" "Castle." Ava played with her a bit, then went inside to grab some breakfast. She came outside with orange juice and an omelet for Joe. He looked over at her. "What," Ava asked. "No coffee?" "Didn't feel like it this morning." He smirked. "What?" "Did the doctor call?" "Yep. I was right." "Unh huh." Ava kissed him, then finished her breakfast. "You can't lie to me," Joe said. "I'm not." He kissed her again. Grace came over and jumped into Joe's arms. "Mama, fly?" "Not today baby." "Jacob?" "That we can do," Joe said. Grace curled up in Joe's arms, then kissed Ava and ran off to play with her sandcastle. Joe motioned for Ava to come closer. "What?" He pulled her into his arms and kissed her. "Ava." "What?" "Are you?" "No." He kissed her and held her in his arms. "Did you want to do dinner with Ryan and Rose tonight?" "Sure. We could invite Cat and Scott." "We could," Joe said then leaned in and kissed her. "Why do I get the feeling you're up to something?" He smirked and kissed her again, then he got up. He took Grace inside and got her cleaned up and dressed, and Ava headed inside, doing the last of the dishes, then went upstairs and pulled on her jeans and tank top.

A little while later, Jacob and Grace were playing and Joe dragged Ava for a day out just the two of them. "Is this what you were up to," she asked. He kissed her. "At least tell me where we're going." They pulled in to a fancy hotel and spa. "What's all this for?" Joe kissed her again and they hopped out. They went inside and had a day of pampering, then got changed, and headed off to meet Ryan and Rose for dinner. Before they stopped at the restaurant, he made a stop. "What are we stopping here for," Ava asked. "Nothin." "Liar,"

Ava said. He pulled her towards him. "What?" "I love you." "I love you too." "Trust me?" Ava nodded. He hopped out and opened her door. "Babe." He took her hand and locked the SUV. "Joe, seriously." He knocked on a glass door. It was too dark to see anything at that point. The door opened. "Don't we have to be at dinner?" He pulled her into his arms and kissed her. "Not until 8." "You said . . ." "I know. I had to stop here." "For what," Ava asked. The room lit up. It was a small jewelry store that he loved that had personally designed rings and jewelry. "That piece you wanted," the man said laying out a tray. Ava looked over and saw a ring that literally left her stunned. "I appreciate the help," Joe said. He took it from the tray and slid it on Ava's finger. "Perfect." "Holy . . ." "Had a feeling you'd love it," he teased. "Sneaky." It was a platinum eternity band. He slid it on beside her wedding band and engagement ring. "If you need anything else let me know," the salesman said. "I will. Thank you." Joe shook his hand and they headed out the door.

"What has got into you," Ava asked. He kissed her. "Can't just do something nice?" "You know you don't have to buy me jewelry." He slid his hand in his pocket and pulled out a box. "Yeah I did." It was a small band to go with his wedding band. "Joe," Ava said. He kissed her. "I saw it and I liked it." "Why?" He kissed her again. "Because I know," Joe said. "Know what?" He kissed her, smirked and they hopped in the car and headed to the restaurant to meet Ryan and Rose.

"Was wondering when you two were showing up," Ryan said as they came inside. Ava looked over at Rose. "Would you quit giving them a hard time," Rose said. Ava gave her a hug, then said hi to Ryan. "We had a stop to make," Joe said. "I bet," Ryan joked. "What can I get you," the waitress asked. "Ice water," Ava said. Joe looked over at her. "Same," he replied. He smirked. "What," Ava said. He shook his head with a silly grin on his face. They chatted over dinner, then they headed home. "I'll drop Grace off in the morning," Ryan said. Ava hugged Ryan and Rose goodbye and they headed home. "What is the smirk for," Ava asked. He locked the doors of the SUV and pulled her to him. "I know Ava. When you pass up wine at your favorite restaurant, I know." "Would you stop?" Joe shook his head. "Ava, I'm right. You know I am." "She said that it was negative." "And if you wait another week or two it won't." He kissed her. "You're convinced you're right aren't you?" He nodded. Ava smirked. "Seriously," Joe asked. Ava nodded. "You were seriously going to not tell me?" "Until I knew 100%." He kissed her again and pulled her tight to him. "Ava." "Home." Joe kissed her and Ava slid back into the passenger seat. They headed straight to the house.

They pulled in and headed inside. The minute Ava slid her heels off, he had her pinned to the wall. Joe kissed her. It was intense, passionate and mind-numbing. He picked her up wrapping her legs around him, then walked up the steps and leaned her onto the bed. He undid her dress, sliding it off. "Joe," Ava said. "Baby," he replied. His phone buzzed in his pocket. He kissed her again and peeled his shirt off. It went off again. "Answer it." He pulled it out and threw it on the side table, then kicked his jeans off and kissed Ava. When it went off a third time, Ava grabbed it. He peeled her lace underwear off, as she answered it. "Hey. It's Ryan." "I know. What's up," Ava asked. "We'll meet you in Texas." "Why?" "Long story. You two are flying out just the two of you. We'll meet you at 1," Ryan said. "We can wait." "No. You two go." "What are you up to," Ava asked. "See you tomorrow." Ryan hung up and Joe kissed her hip. "We're . . ." "I know," Joe said. He kissed his way up her torso. "Joe." He kissed her. The kiss was enough of a distraction to completely make her lose her train of thought.

They made love. It was intense and passionate. Every inch of her was kissed, licked, nibbled, until literally she couldn't stand it anymore. "Joe." He kissed her again as they both exploded. He held her in his arms. "They decide on the later flight,' he asked. Ava nodded. Her legs were still shaking. "Know what that means?" "We can catch up on the sleep we're missing tonight," Ava teased. He kissed her again. "I still can't believe we're having another one," Joe said. "The doctor said 60% chance." He kissed Ava. "You're full of it and you know it." "Just don't get ahead of yourself. I don't want to tell anyone until I'm sure." "Babe." "Please Joe." "Why?" "Because I don't want to until I'm at least 2 months." He kissed Ava. "That would be Christmas." Ava smirked. "Fine." He kissed her again and they were asleep in minutes.

The next morning, Joe and Ava got up and packed, took their time getting to the airport then left. They relaxed on the plane, getting a cat nap in before they landed. They got to the venue and everything was getting set up. They joked around while the crew was finishing up, and went for a walk. "You sure you won't let me tell the guys," Joe asked. "No." He kissed her. ""Not going to change the answer either." He kissed her again and they headed back towards the RV. "Joe, there's someone here for you," security said. He walked to the gate with security. "Hey." "What the hell are you doing here?" "You told me to come by." "Nice damn timing," Joe said as he walked in with the man. Ava looked. "Babe, this is my buddy Craig from high school." Ava looked. The guy looked familiar. "Nice to meet you," Ava said. Joe wrapped his arm around Ava. "So what have you been up to," Craig asked. "We got married, had a baby, touring. The same old shit," Joe joked. They guys joked around. "I have to get some writing done. You two hang out," Ava said. "You sure," Joe asked. Ava nodded. She kissed him, then headed off, grabbed her laptop and found a quiet area.

An hour or two passed when her phone went off. "Where'd you disappear to," Joe asked. "Where we were walking earlier." "Be there in a minute." Ava hung up and went back to her writing. A little while later, Joe walked over and sat down with her. "So how's your buddy?" "Good. He got married. I still can't believe half my old friends are married now." "You started a trend," Ava joked. He kissed her. "Right. How's the writing going?" "Okay.

Just needed some quiet time." Joe wrapped his arm around her and pulled her into his lap. "Still not gonna let me read it are you?" "The edits are almost done." He nuzzled her ear. "Now why did you really come out here?" She turned to face him and he kissed her. She wrapped her legs around him. "You know we have time before the guys get here." Ava went to laugh and he kissed her again. Her phone went off a minute later. "Hi Rose." "We just landed. We'll be there in 20." "See you in a few." Ava hung up. "Already?" Ava nodded. "What if I don't want to go back," Joe asked. "Then you don't get to see the white and silver." He kissed her again, then leaned her onto the grass. "Joe." "What?" She smirked. He kissed her again. After making out a while, they finally headed back.

Sound check went fine, Grace was hilarious as usual being the entertainer before falling asleep in Ava's arms. She tucked Grace in, then kissed Joe for luck, then went and got changed. "What is up with you two," Rose asked. "What?" "The two of you have been giggles since we got here," Rose said. "It's nothing," Ava said as they touched up her makeup and finished up her hair. "You are such a bad liar." "Fine. It's something that we're not sharing." "Don't you dare tell me you're pregnant." "Maybe." "Holy shit," Rose said. "I know." Rose hugged her. "We're not sure yet alright?" Rose nodded. "I mean it." Ava headed on a little while later. She finished her songs, then headed off and walked directly into Jake.

"What are you doing here?" "Coming to talk to you," Jake said. "You aren't supposed to be back here," Ava said. He grabbed Ava's hand and led her down the hall to a quiet corner. "Let go." "You know he's freaking out." "Jake, I'm married. I have been for a while, and that isn't changing anytime soon." "He still loves you." "Point being what? My situation hasn't changed." "Ava, please." "What would the point be? You said it yourself at the beginning Jake. Fun in the sun and that's all," Ava said. She walked off and sat with Rose until the guys were finished.

As soon as they were done, Joe walked in and grabbed Ava's hand. "What?" He locked the door of the dressing room and leaned her up against the door. He had that look in his eye. The one that warned her she was about to be devoured whole. He kissed her and her toes curled in her heels. She felt his hands slide from her back to her backside. "Joe." He kissed her again. "Stop," Ava said. Her heart was racing so fast her chest hurt. He picked her up and sat her on the counter. "What's that look for," Ava asked. He kissed her again and slid her g-string off. "Joe," Ava said. Within a minute or so, they were going at it. It was unbelievable. Once he came, he slid her off the counter and sat down on the sofa and curled up with her. "You are seriously crazy," Ava said. "I love you." "I love you too," Ava replied. "Babe, I gotta say, you are so not wearing this on stage again." "You say that about every dress." "Unless you want a piano incident . . ." They laughed. "You know we have to get up." "We're going out," Joe said. "We are, are we?" He nodded. "Where?" "Go West."

"Gee, maybe I need shorter heels." "Jeans." Ava shook her head. He kissed her neck. They got changed, and Ava slid on the jeans and a sexy top that Joe was totally against her wearing anywhere than on stage. They headed off making sure that the kids were alright, then left for a night out.

Joe and Ava were dancing most of the night together, then came back over to everyone else, had a drink and a quick chat, then headed to the hotel. They walked in and checked on Emily and the kids, who were dead asleep, then they headed into their bedroom and changed for bed. Joe snuck up behind her after she washed the makeup off, and kissed her neck. "What?" "I don't even know why you need to wear it." "Don't start quoting the songs," Ava teased. "You're beautiful without it." "Thank you baby." Ava kissed him with a colgate kiss, then he pulled her into his arms and hugged her. "What's going on in that head of yours?" "Just thinking." "What are you worrying about," Ava asked. "Us." "Why?" "Two." Ava laughed then kissed him. "Was wondering when it was gonna hit you," Ava said. He carried her to bed and snuggled up with her.

They did two more concerts then headed home. Ava was asleep curled up with Joe, and Rose, Ryan and Brad were wide awake. Emily was asleep by the kids. When the plane finally landed, everyone headed home. Ava tucked Grace into bed, then changed, and slid into bed with Joe. His arms wrapped around her and he kissed her neck. "She still asleep?" Ava nodded. "I love you." "Love you too," Ava replied. A little while later they were fast asleep.

The next morning, Joe woke up and Ava wasn't in bed. Grace was still asleep. He came downstairs and saw Ava asleep on the sofa. He picked her up and carried her back upstairs. She woke up with his arms around her. The second she moved, he nuzzled her neck. "Morning." "How did I get back upstairs?" "Carried you. Everything alright?" Ava nodded. "Liar." "Just thinking too much." "And you said I worried," Joe said. He kissed her neck. They got up once Grace woke up, and sat outside with her. The doctor called around lunch. "Just reminding you of your appointment at 1," the receptionist said. "Thanks. See you in a few hours." Ava hung up. "Where you going?" "Shower and get dressed." "Oh really." Ava went to go inside. "Mama, me come." Ava walked over and snuggled Grace. "You can come baby," Ava said. Joe took Grace into her room and got her cleaned up and dressed, while Ava had a shower and pulled on her jean skirt and tank top. "Ooh," Joe said. "Don't even," Ava replied. She did her hair while he finished his shower. She was finishing her makeup when he stepped out. He wrapped the towel around him and walked towards Ava. "Don't start," Ava said. He slid his arms around her torso. "You don't need the makeup." "It's mascara. Relax." She put it down and he turned her towards him. Joe kissed her and held her in his arms. Ava saw her watch out of the corner of her eye. "I have 45 minutes," Ava said. He kissed her, then went in and got changed and they headed off.

Ava went into the doctor's office. "We're running the test again," Ava said. The doctor re-did the test. "Three weeks. Um." "Um what," Ava asked. "It's probably nothing." "What?" "You're spotting." The doctor came out and went for the ultrasound machine. Joe saw the look on her face. He got up with Grace and went in. "What's wrong?" The doctor did an ultrasound. She looked at Ava. "Next time." "I'm sorry Ava." "Sorry about what?" "I'll give you a call to check up on you next week." Ava got up and they headed home. Joe called Rose to look after Grace for a little while.

They walked into the house. Ava went into the kitchen and made herself some tea, then went outside. "Babe," Joe said. "What?" He slid onto the chaise behind her and wrapped his arms around her. "This is why I didn't want to tell anyone." "You'd rather have me not be here to help you through this?" "No. I just didn't want anyone else knowing." He kissed her cheek. "You alright," he asked. Ava shook her head. "Come inside. We'll curl up by the fire and watch a movie." Ava nodded. They went inside and curled up and watched a movie. Joe picked Grace up before dinner while Ava was having a nap. He came home and Ava was in the tub. He went upstairs with Grace and she ran into the bedroom, then into the bathroom. "Mama." "Hey baby girl," Ava said. "My bubbles." "Sharing," Ava said. "Okay." Grace kissed her, then went into her bedroom and played.

Joe leaned down and kissed Ava. "Drink?" Ava shook her head. He kissed her again and slid his shirt off. "Don't think it." He kissed her again and kicked his jeans off. He slid into the tub with her. He added more hot water, then she leaned into his arms. "You feeling better after the nap?" "A little. I'm just glad we didn't tell anyone." "I know." They relaxed a while, then got up and he went and put dinner together. Ava came downstairs and they had dinner, then gave Grace a bath and tucked her into bed. Ava sat at the top of the stairs and listened to him sing to her. As soon as he came out he saw her and sat down with her. "Nothing to worry about now right?" He nodded. "Just means we still get to practice some more." "Always making the best of a bad situation," Ava joked. He kissed her. "I love you. Whether we have another one or not." "I love you too." Joe got up and they went downstairs, curling up by the fire and talked.

———

"Something's wrong with Ava," Rose said. "Rose, stop worrying." "I know something's wrong." She called Ava's phone and it went to voicemail. Rose called the house, same thing. "Would you stop worrying?" "No." "What's going on," Ryan asked. "Nothing." "Rose, whatever it is." Her phone rang. "Finally. You alright," Rose asked. "I'm fine. We're just having a chill day." "Then why do I get the feeling something is wrong?" "I'm not." "You?" "Yeah. Tomorrow okay?" "First thing." Rose hung up. "Feel better," Ryan asked. "At least I know she's alright."

CHAPTER 24

After a week or so, Ava finally felt better. The concerts went well, and Ava had a weird feeling. She called Cat. "Hey girl," Cat said. "Hey yourself. Where are you?" "Vegas with Scott." "Oh really," Ava asked. "We won $5,000." "Good one. Everything else alright?" "Yeah. You feeling better?" "Yep. Give me a call later alright?" "I will."

Ava spent the day playing around with the kids, while the guys worked on some music. Ava put Grace down for a nap and Emily stayed with her while Ava took off to the mall. After an hour or so, Ava wasn't feeling that good. She went to head home and had to pull over. She pulled into the doctor's office and they took her straight to the hospital.

"Joe," Emily said a little frantic. "Emily?" "You have to go to the hospital." He dropped the phone and took off without a word to the guys. He pulled in and saw Ava's SUV. Security saw him and walked him to Ava's room. "Babe. You okay," he asked. Ava shook her head and he saw the tears streaming. The doctor came in a few minutes later. "What's going on," Joe asked. "She'll be fine. We're going to do a procedure, then everything will be alright." "What are you talking about," Joe asked. They wheeled Ava out. A half-hour later of him pacing the halls, and seriously wishing they served something stronger than coffee in the cafeteria, they brought Ava back. He sat down beside her and held her hand. "Babe, you okay," Joe asked. Ava nodded. "Just sore." "What the hell happened?" "She thought I had lost the baby. I thought I had. I went out today and was fine, and doubled over in the SUV on my way home." "She lost the baby this afternoon. We just did a procedure to stop the bleeding." He looked at Ava. She was crying. "When can she go home," Joe asked. "We'll check her out in a few hours, then she can probably come home tonight." The doctor left and Joe kissed Ava. "Babe, why didn't you call me?" "I didn't have time. I went straight to the doctor and she brought me here." He slid onto the bed beside her and slid her into his arms. The doctor finally let her head home later on that afternoon. He got Brad to drive her SUV home and he drove back to the house and carried her to bed.

Ava woke up the next morning, still sore. Joe made her breakfast and brought it up to her in bed, sliding back in with her. "You feeling any better," Joe asked. "Just glad I'm home." "Babe, you gotta quit scaring the crap out of me like that." "I was just as scared Joe." "I don't know what I'd do if you weren't here." "Probably have a lineup of women begging to take my place," she tried to joke. "Nobody ever could." "Sucking up gets you everything." Joe kissed her and wrapped his arm around her shoulders. "We should get packed." "We aren't going," Joe said. "We have to." "No. Not after this." "Joe, we can't just not go. At least one of us should go." He kissed her. "Not without you." "I'll be fine in a day or two." "Ava, no." "I'm not stopping my life. We need to do this. We have Grace. It's not like I can just stay in bed for a week." Joe kissed her again. "Until the doctor says it's okay." "Fine. Call her." "Stubborn as hell as usual." "That's why you love me." Ava had her breakfast, feeding at least half to him, then got up and took the dishes downstairs. "Babe." "I can handle doing dishes." "She said off your feet." "She also said no sex. You following that rule?" He kissed her neck. "Please, just let me take care of you?" "Joe, I can handle this." He picked her up and carried her back up the stairs to bed and leaned her onto the bed. He kissed her. "Can we at least go get Grace?" "If you stay in bed, I'll get her." "Can't even be in the car?" "You want Rose knowing?" Ava agreed. She showered while he went to get Grace.

"Ava okay?" "Yeah. Just getting a million things done. She's in cleaning mode again." "Tell her to call me." Joe gave Rose a hug, then brought Grace home. "Mama necklace," Grace said. "She'll love it baby." They stopped at the store for some flowers and a few groceries then came home. They went inside and Ava was sitting on the sofa. "Mama." "Hi baby. How was the sleepover?" "You." Grace handed her the necklace. "And it matches the outfit. Where'd you and Daddy go?" She ran into the kitchen, then came back in and handed Ava a dozen roses. "Well. You two were shopping." Grace nodded. She hugged Ava, then sat with her and played with her dolls. Joe came in and saw her. "What did I tell you," Joe said. "No TV." He walked over and kissed her. "Babe." "I'm fine." He slid onto the sofa behind her. "Mama, movie." "Pick one." Grace grabbed their wedding video and Joe got up and put it in the DVD player.

Grace watched it over and over. Joe and Ava smirked and were silly. "Mama pretty." "Thanks baby girl," Ava said. "Uncle Ryan." "Yep." She tried to sing along with the music. They had a quiet day, then had dinner with Grace and Joe gave her a bath and tucked her in. Ava came upstairs with the suitcase. He caught her as she was walking up the steps. "Stubborn." "You got it." She slid it onto the bed. "We're not going." "Yeah we are." Ava's phone went off.

"How we feeling," the doctor asked. "A little sore, but better." "Bleeding stop?" "Yep," Ava said. "You can go this weekend, but if you are in pain, you aren't going on." "Promise," Ava said. "Let the man take care of you." "I'm sure he'll love to hear that," Ava said.

"Call me when you get back. You're coming in next week." "Okay." "Don't push yourself either." "Gotcha." The doctor hung up and Ava smirked.

"Fine. We'll go, but I mean it. One twinge," Joe said. Ava slid her arms around his neck and kissed him. "Seriously Ava." She kissed him again and he slid his arms around her. "I worry about you," Joe said. "I know. I love you too." "No dresses." Ava laughed. She slid her arms down and he pulled her close. "I mean it." She kissed him, then went and started packing. She threw in one black dress, her leggings and tops, then her dressy leggings. "Better," Joe said. They finished packing, then got ready for bed. "So what else did she say," Joe asked. "To let you take care of me." "You gonna listen to her?" Ava kissed him. "That a yes?" Ava nodded. Joe picked her up and carried her to bed, then got changed and slid in beside her. "Just don't tell the guys alright?" "Em knows. She was the one that called me remember?" "Shit." He called Emily. "I won't. She doesn't want anyone knowing, that's fine," Emily said. "Thanks." "You got it." He hung up and slid his arm back around Ava.

The next morning, they got up and got changed, then packed up a bag for Grace and headed for the airport. Three concerts in a row. The guys showed with Emily a half-hour after Joe and Ava. They worked on a song or two on the plane, then finally landed. They got to the venue and got settled in and Joe sat with Ava in the RV. "Babe." "Stop worrying." "You know I'm going to." Ava kissed him. "I'm just going to relax with Grace and do some writing. Go." Joe kissed her. "You sure?" Ava nodded. He kissed her again then kissed Grace and went off to do the interviews. Ava took Grace with her and watched. "Mama, why Daddy TV?" "Because people want to talk to him." "Sing?" "He will." "Me first." Grace tried to sing a little, then giggled as Ava tickled her. "Me sing Daddy." "Yes you do baby girl." "Mama sing." Grace climbed into Ava's lap. "What you up to?" Grace wrapped her arms around Ava and yawned. "Tired?" "No." Within a half-hour, Grace was asleep in Ava's arms. She got up and took her to the RV for a nap with Emily, then went back and watched the rest of the interviews. In between, Joe walked up to her and sat with her.

"How's the most beautiful wife in the world," Joe asked. "Don't know. You should ask her." Joe kissed her. "I'm fine. Grace was being adorable," Ava said. "Singing again?" Ava nodded. "She still can't figure out why they're interviewing you guys." "I'm sure she'll figure it out soon enough," Joe said. "She wants to sing with you." "Just like her Mama." They laughed and he kissed her. "Seriously. How are you feeling?" "Fine." "You sure," Joe asked. "Better now." "Suck up." He kissed her. "You two lovebirds think you can tear yourselves away for another round of interviews," Brad teased. "Ha ha," Joe replied. He kissed Ava and left with the guys.

Once the interviews were done, he headed back to the RV. Ava was curled up on the bed with her laptop and Joe slid onto the bed beside her. "How's the writing?" "Good. How'd the interviews go?" "Long. Same stuff over and over." "So what time are you starting sound check?" "An hour. The guys were hungry." "And what about you?" He leaned her towards him and kissed her. She closed the laptop and leaned into his arms. "Missed you," Joe said. "Silly head." He kissed her again. "Besides, thought you and Grace might be hungry." "She ate." "Then?" They got up to head off to have lunch after making sure Emily was with Grace.

"You two are like surgically attached today. What's up," Brad asked. "Nothing," Joe said. "Liar." "Just looking after my lady Brad." "I know. Something's up and I know it," Brad said. "Radar?" Brad nodded. "It's nothing Brad. Just been swamped the past few days with errands,' Ava said. "Right. Get a personal assistant. Truth please," Brad joked. "What you want the truth about," Ryan asked. "Something is up with those two," Brad said. "Nah. They're just being extra mushy," Ryan joked. "Thank you," Ava said. "And keeping secrets," Ryan said. "Enough." "Then spill," Ryan said. Joe linked his fingers with hers hinting that it was up to her. "We're keeping it quiet. Doesn't go past us." "What," Ryan asked. "We were pregnant, but we lost it," Ava said. "You alright," Ryan asked. Ava nodded. "Why the hell didn't you . . . . wait. That's why you took off like a bat out of hell," Brad said. Joe nodded. "What the hell are you doing out here then? Woman, you should be at home," Ryan said. "I'm fine." "Pain in the ass and a half to make her stay home. Trust me," Joe joked. Ava elbowed him. "You sure you okay," Ryan asked. Ava nodded. "Not one more word about it." The guys agreed.

They did sound check with Ava, then went back to the RV's and chilled for a while. They all watched some TV on the big screen, then relaxed and got changed. They had dinner, then the guys headed off to the meet and greet while Ava got changed. She slid on a sexy top with her leggings and high-heeled boots. She finished with hair and makeup, then sang Grace a lullaby and tucked her into bed. "Sing Mama?" Ava nodded. "Love you." "Love you too baby. Sweet dreams." Grace was asleep a little while later. Ava headed back in and Joe walked right towards her. "You look amazing." "Thank you. Pretty sexy yourself," Ava said. Joe kissed her. "How'd it go?" He kissed her. "Spill," Ava said. "It's nothing." "Joe, no secrets." "Janelle." "Who?" "An old friend." "Nice." "She left. Totally platonic," Joe said. "Um hmm." He kissed Ava again. "How you feeling?" "Fine." "How fine," Joe asked. "I'm fine." He kissed her again, then headed on with the guys. Ava came on and did her songs, then headed off and sat side stage and watched. He noticed a girl begging for Joe's attention. Ava looked. Joe looked over at her. Ava looked at him. They came off for a quick intermission. "That's her?" He kissed Ava and they went back on. Ava went and sat back in the dressing room and relaxed.

Joe came in when the concert was done. "Hey beautiful," he said. "Hey yourself." Joe sat down with her and the guys followed. "So." "Good show," Ava said. "Ava, quit the tough girl routine." "And I thought Joe was bad," Ryan said. "How you doing," Brad asked. "I'm fine. Just tired." "You sure," Ryan asked. Ava nodded. "We're out of here in a half-hour," the manager said. The guys packed up and Ava went and hopped into the RV. Emily went and hopped in the RV with Ryan and Brad. Joe came in, put his things down, then sat down with Ava. "What?" "Was worried about you," Joe said. "Would you cut it out?" He kissed her. "I'll work on it." They left ten minutes later.

The next two concerts went off without a hitch. The doctor called as they were boarding the plane to head back. "How are you feeling?" "Good," Ava replied. "No more pain?" "Nope." "You're coming in tomorrow at 10am." "See you then." Ava hung up.

They headed home once they landed. Ava tucked Grace into bed, then walked into the bedroom and got changed. "Babe," Joe said. "What?" "What time did the doctor say?" "Ten." "Good." "And why's that?" He slid his arms around her. "What you sucking up for," Ava asked. "Ryan wants to go in and record the song at 1." "You don't have to come with me," Ava said. "Yeah I do." "Joe." He kissed her neck. "I'm coming." Ava rinsed her makeup off. She turned towards him. "I can go by myself," she said. He kissed her and picked her up, then carried her to bed. "I'm going." He laid her on the bed and curled up with her.

The next morning, they got up, got Grace dressed and washed, then headed to the doctor. "Much better," the doctor said. "Like I said." "So I have a question," Joe said. "Answer is yes," the doctor replied. "How did you know?" "Guys always ask." Joe and Ava left and headed home, stopping at the park for Grace. Once she got tired out, they took her home, gave her lunch, then Joe put her down for a nap. Ava went and tried to get some writing done.

Joe slipped into her office once Grace was asleep. "Ava." She turned to face him. "Yes love." "Come with me." She followed him up the steps. He'd lit candles in the bathroom, and drawn them a hot bath. "What's all this for?" Joe pulled her into his arms and kissed her. "Us." "Figured that." "Us time." "Oh." Ava smirked. She got undressed and slipped into the tub. He followed. "Good idea," Ava said. His arms slid around her. "Babe." "Mmm." "You know I was afraid I lost you," Joe said. "I know." "Never ever losing you again." "Why are you so worried?" He kissed her neck. "Joe, what's wrong?" She turned to face him and his eyes were tearing. "You're never going to lose me," Ava said. He kissed her. Her heart was racing. They kissed and cuddled until the water got cool, then slipped out and went to bed. "No more worrying. I'm fine," Ava said. He kissed her again and she wrapped her legs around him. He made love to her and it felt like it had been forever. Her body was shaking after and so was his. Joe kissed her again. Ava heard Grace crying. "I'll get her," Ava said. She kissed him and got up, grabbing his shirt and sliding it on.

"What's wrong baby? Bad dream?" Grace nodded. Ava flipped her pillow. "No more bad dreams." "Dream Daddy go bye bye." "He's here." "Okay," Grace said. "Try to go back to sleep." A minute or two later, Grace was out cold. Ava slipped out of her room and came back to bed with Joe. "You are so hot in that shirt," he teased. "Why gee," Ava replied. He kissed her and leaned her onto the bed.

Grace came walking in just as Ava was making dinner. "Mama, Daddy TV." They walked in and saw the last interview the guys had done.

"So when does the new CD come out?" "We're working on it now. We're aiming for around Valentine's Day or earlier." "Any surprises?" "A few. There's a song I know all the fans are loving that we've made sure was on the CD," Ryan had said. "Does that mean that Joe's wife recorded with you?" "A few tracks. I gotta say, she's definitely a good inspiration for us," Brad said. "So Joe, we heard that your little girl is starting to try to sing. Think she'll turn out like her Dad?" "Honestly, I hope she's whatever she wants to be. She has two pretty creative parents to look up to," Joe said. "Any plans for another baby?" "At some point." "So when does the tour wrap up?"

Ava went into the kitchen. Joe followed her. "Babe." "It's fine," Ava said. "You sure?" Ava nodded. He turned her to face him. He kissed her and wrapped his arms around her. "It'll happen when we're ready." "I know. Still get to practice." Joe kissed her again. "Very true." "Daddy singing." They went back in. "They've hit number one with Love Letter. Now, they're adding Ava Morgan to their group. What's next? The new CD. We got a release date and it's just in time for Valentine's Day next year. Get ready everyone. They're gonna sell like hot cakes." Joe wrapped his arms around Ava. "All thanks to my wife," Joe said. He kissed her then called Ryan.

Ava gave Grace her lunch, then Grace demanded to see the wedding video again. Ava put it in and finished up the last of the edits for her new book. Joe slid onto the sofa behind her. "Finished," he whispered as Ava saved her work. "Now." Ava logged into her email and send the final work to her agent. "That mean I can actually read it," Joe asked. "When it's in book form." "Babe." "We have other things to do." He kissed her cheek. Grace was asleep watching the video again. Joe took Grace to bed and put her down for a nap.

Joe's phone went off. "So when are you and the guys heading back in," Scott asked. "Tomorrow. We are flying back out Friday." "Alright. Moving on Saturday anyway." "Where," Joe asked. "In with Cat." "Ava's friend?" "Yep." "Buddy, why? I love that condo," Joe asked. "We got a little carried away in Vegas." "Seriously?" "We are gonna try to see if we can pull it off before we try to erase it." "You two got hitched," Joe asked. "It wasn't planned." "We're so doing dinner." "Joe, try to keep it to yourself." "Okay," Joe said. "Nobody else. If it works, we do a real wedding." "Nice," Joe joked. "See you tomorrow."

After dinner and putting Grace to bed after her bubble bath, Ava and Joe curled up in bed. "I still can't believe they got hitched," Joe said. "Why did you have to go tell her about Vegas," Ava said. "Babe, we've been together for almost two years. I think the guys will forgive us." "And if the press gets a hold of it . . ." He kissed Ava. "Wouldn't have changed it for the world. It was what we wanted. Just you and me," Joe said. "Still." He kissed her again and slid on top of her. "That's probably when Grace was conceived." "You are seriously being ridiculous." "And I'm right," Joe said kissing and nibbling her neck and her shoulder. "Always did have a way with words." He kissed her and wrapped his arms around her. "Nobody is ever gonna take that day away from us." "I think I still have the pictures," Ava teased. He kissed her. "Seriously?" Ava nodded. She slid out of bed and grabbed them from her desk, then brought them upstairs. She had two 8 x 10 and 2 wallet size. He put one into his wallet on the counter, and slipped the 8 x 10's in the drawer. He slid back into bed with Ava and pulled her to him. "Remember what happened that night?" "Hmm." He kissed her and slid her teddy off. "Think it's coming back to me," Ava teased. He leaned her onto the bed and made love to her. "Love you more than I did back then," Joe said. "Oh really." He kissed her. "More than you know babe." He kissed her again and curled up with her. "So what are we up to tomorrow?" "Ryan messaged me. We're going to the studio." "Scott doing the next song?" Joe nodded. "Have fun." "You're coming," Joe said. "Do distract Cat?" Joe shook his head. "Another one?" He nodded. "You guys seriously need to quit adding me." "Nah. More fun watching you in the dresses on stage instead of on the sideline," Joe teased. "Oh really Mr. I don't want you wearing the dresses." He kissed her. "Dresses are for me. Everyone else can wish." He kissed her again. "You should get some rest then." "True." They fell asleep still curled up together.

The next morning Ava got up and Joe wasn't in bed. She heard music from the back patio. She checked on Grace, and realized she was probably outside with him. She turned on the coffee, made a cup for each of them, then went outside and handed him one. "Thanks babe." He kissed her. Grace was playing with her toys. "Tell me you got sleep." "Got up with Grace at 7." Ava shook her head laughing. "Got an idea for another one. Started working on it last night." "Joe." "I was up for an hour, then curled back up in bed with my sexy wife." "Really." He nodded and kissed Ava. "What's the song about?" "It's called secret," Joe said. "Don't you dare tell me you're writing a song about that." He kissed her again. Ava took a gulp of her coffee. "You know they're gonna kill you." "Nope. They'll think it's about Cat and Scott," Joe joked. "Sneaky." He kissed her. Ava got up and went over to see what Grace was up to.

Emily showed just as they were getting ready. "Give me a shout on the way back," Emily said. "If you need anything, call Rose," Ava said. "I will. Have a good one." Joe and Ava pulled out and headed to the studio. They walked in and saw Cat and Scott. "Hey lovebirds," Joe said. Cat shot him a look. "Oh give him a break. Congrats." Ava hugged Scott and Cat. "So where's this song you were working on," Scott asked. The guys went off and Joe played a bit of it for him.

They got straight down to work. When Ava's part came, she had it down in two or three takes. "Damn girl," Scott said. "Thank you," Ava said. Joe kissed her. "Babe. Need your touch on this one." He handed her the lyrics for the song and played a bit of the music for her. "Okay." Ava went into the booth while they were finishing up the tracks. When they stopped for a break, Ava handed the lyrics to Joe. He read through them. "Babe." "Don't even. I know what you're doing." He kissed her. "It's good," Joe said. He played the rest of the song as he heard it in his head and finished the tail end of the song. He went in and recorded it to play it back to the guys.

"Damn." "Where did you come up with this one Joe," Ryan asked. "Scott and Cat." "Right," Brad teased. "What are you getting at Brad," Joe asked. "Nothin." He threw a little piano and bass into it, Ryan put his touches on it and they recorded it. They played it back and it was definitely going to be the first release. Once they finished for the day, Ava and Joe headed to dinner, Ryan and Brad headed home, and Cat sat with Scott at the studio.

CHAPTER 25

Joe and Ava got home and Grace ran to the door. "Mama, come." She dragged Ava to the TV room and saw one of the videos the guys had done on TV. "Daddy." "Yep." "Who that?" "That's Uncle Brad." "Who lady?" "No idea." "Mama prettier." "Thank you baby girl." She hugged Ava's leg. "You have a point Grace. Mama is definitely prettier," Joe said. He kissed Ava's cheek. "Okay, seriously. I'm starving," Ava said. "Mama, made cookie." "Well that's a start," Ava said. Joe kissed her. "I'll go grab something." He headed off and Ava sat down with Grace. "So everything was okay," Ava asked Emily. "She turned on one of the concert DVD's. She was dancing around until she finally conked out." "Oh really. Well then," Ava said. A little while later, Joe walked in to Grace dancing around again. He put dinner in the kitchen, then walked over and danced with her. Ava grabbed her camera and snapped a few pictures. When the song was done, they had dinner, then gave Grace a bath and tucked her into bed.

He came into the bedroom and Ava was putting on her lotion. "What ya doin," he asked. "Nothing. She asleep?" "Had to sing two songs. She kept trying to sing along." "She's going to be your backup singer in no time," Ava joked. Joe kissed her. "Now wouldn't that be hilarious." He got changed for bed and washed up and curled up in bed with Ava. "Ever noticed that when we're home, we go to bed early, but when we're not, we're night owls," Joe asked. "Blame it on Grace. She tires me out just watching her." "Good point." She curled up next to him. "Babe." "Mmm." "What would we do if it was just you, me and Grace," Joe asked. "Enjoy every minute just like we would if there was another baby. Why?" "Just thinking," Joe said. "She said I was fine." "I know, I just worry." "Then stop worrying. You're stuck with me." "Good." Joe kissed her. "So now that we have us time . . ." He kissed her again and Ava's arms wrapped around him. He made love to her, like it was the first time. They took their time and cherished every second. He didn't want to let go of her. They cuddled, kissed and made love for hours. Finally they tried to get some sleep. At 3am, Grace woke up crying. "I'll get her," Joe said.

"What's wrong baby girl?" "Dream you went bye bye." "I'm right here." "You lost." "Baby, I'm here." "You went away." "I'm right here. I'm not going anywhere." She wrapped her arms around him crying. He flipped her pillow over. "I'm never going to be gone baby." "Yes." "Only at work. I always come home." "Daddy." He sang to her a bit until she calmed down and tucked her back into her bed. He sat by her until she was asleep, then slipped out and hopped back into bed with Ava. His arms pulled her close and he nuzzled her neck. "She okay?" "The dream where I disappeared." Ava kissed him, then went back to sleep. He snuggled close and they were out cold.

The next morning, Ava got up and went for a run with Grace while Joe slept. She got back, then gave Grace her breakfast and made coffee. She heard Joe coming down the stairs as soon as the smell of the coffee made its way to him. She poured him a cup and handed it to him as soon as he came in the kitchen. "Morning babe." "Morning handsome." Grace giggled. "And morning to you too giggles." "Hi Daddy." Grace finished her French toast and Joe made omelets for him and Ava. "Thank you baby," Ava said. He kissed her. "Daddy love Mama?" "A lot," Joe said. "Mama love Daddy lot." "I know," Joe said. "Mama loves me." "So does Daddy," Ava said. "Me sing Daddy." "Whenever you want baby," Joe said. "Uncle Ryan." "I'll ask him," Joe joked. Grace giggled. They all finished breakfast, then Joe played with Grace while Ava got showered. He came upstairs just as she was stepping in the shower.

He slid in behind her. "Who's looking after Grace?" "Em." He kissed her and pulled her close. "When did . . ." Joe kissed Ava again, leaning her into the wall of the shower. "Two minutes after you headed upstairs." He kissed her again then picked her up, and she wrapped her legs around him. They did it again in the shower. Her legs were shaking. She could barely stand. "You drive me nuts," Ava said. "Totally planned." He kissed her again. "So why is Emily here?" "We're going shopping." "Oh really." Joe kissed her. They finished their shower, then got dressed and the four of them headed to the mall. Ava went to her favorite dress store. "Need something dressier." "For what?" "Awards," Joe said. "Seriously," Ava asked. Joe nodded. They headed to the other stores and finally came across the dress. It was black satin, low back, just above the knee and sexy and classy all at the same time. "Now that's what I'm talking about," Joe joked. "Thank you." Ava kissed him then tried on another one. It was red hot red. It was sexy, it was backless, and was perfect for the stage. Joe took one look at it and stood up. "Well?" "Um," Joe said. Ava smirked. She went in and got dressed, then came out and got more than just the two. "Ava, you trying to kill me with the red one?" Ava nodded. He kissed her shoulder. "Mama pretty." "Thank you baby," Ava said grabbing the bag and carrying Grace. "You're gonna need something to wear too," Ava said. Joe kissed her and they headed to the men's store that he loved. There was a small crowd following them. Security came and walked them to the next store. They went through a few shirts, then found a few. He tried some on, literally getting Ava turned on. If she smirked when he came out, he kissed her and put the shirt in the buy pile. They got a few things, then Ava headed to the lingerie store. He wandered around while Ava bought a few things, then they headed back to the SUV.

They got home, put Grace down for her nap, and sat outside. "I still can't believe you got the red one." "You didn't see it all," Ava said. "Meaning?" "Got a few more tops at Victoria's Secret and Fredericks." "Tease." Ava nodded. "What am I gonna do with you," Joe asked. "Hmm." He leaned towards her and kissed her. "Is Emily still here?" Joe nodded. "She's in the guestroom." He kissed her again, undoing the back of her shirt. "What you doing back there," Ava asked. He kissed her neck. "Thought we could go for a swim." Ava got up and went inside. She came out a few minutes later in a string bikini and dove into the water. He noticed she'd left his swimsuit on the table. He dove into the pool. He came up behind her, pulling her into his arms. "Now what were you saying," Ava asked. He leaned her into the wall of the pool. "So where exactly were you gonna wear the red dress," Joe asked. "Friday night." She could feel his heart start racing. "I don't think so." "Babe, I'm a girl. I'm not supposed to be one of the guys," Ava teased. "If the guys at the concert aren't already drooling, they will when they see you in that." He kissed her again, and their animal instincts took over. He had the bikini top on the deck and was going for the bottoms when Emily came out. "Grace is calling for you," Emily said. "Be up in a minute," Joe replied. Emily went back inside. "Saved by Grace,' Ava teased. He kissed her again. "Meet you upstairs." Ava nodded. He hopped out and went in to see to Grace.

Ava slid her bikini top back on, did a length or two, then wrapped the towel around her and headed inside. She went upstairs and slid her sundress on. A half-hour or so later, he came into the bedroom. Ava was on the phone with Rose. "I think we're just chilling tonight." "But you're back off again tomorrow. We are in need of a girl's night," Rose said. "I know. We have next weekend off. I promise." "I'm holding you to it." Joe kissed Ava's neck and slid his hands up the skirt of the dress. "I have to go. I'll call you before we go," Ava said. Ava hung up and he kissed her. "Grace asleep?" He nodded. "The Daddy disappeared dream again?" "I don't know why," Joe said. "Me either. I think we should bring her this weekend." "Babe, she'll get better sleep at home," Joe said. "I know, but considering." "What if I said I wanted you to myself," Joe asked. "We have Grace." "Ava." "I know what you're getting at." "Good." He peeled her g-string off. "We need practice time," he whispered as he leaned into her and pulled her legs around him. They made love again. It was quick, but still intense. "So just what did you have planned for later?" "Dinner, a little wine." "Oh really." "You and me curled up by the fireplace with just a blanket," Joe teased. He nibbled her ear. "Should I wear the red dress?" "Don't need it." "So what should I wear?" "The satin robe." "Hmm." "Don't," Joe said. "The white lace lingerie under it." "Baby." "Or just the g-string." "Tease," Joe joked. Ava slid out of bed. She pulled her sundress back on and went downstairs.

Ava checked to make sure the edits were done on the book, then cleaned up a bit. Joe came downstairs. "Someday woman," Joe teased. "I know." Joe kissed her. They both cleaned up, then Grace was awake. He took her outside and played while Ava put something together for dinner. An hour later, the kitchen smelled like her famous fried chicken and corn on the cob. Just as they were walking in, Ava pulled fresh biscuits from the oven. "Dang," Joe said. "Sit. Dinner's in a little bit." "Hungry?" Ava shot him a look and a smirk. "Mama chickie?" "Just like you like it," Ava said. Grace hugged her leg. A half-hour later, they had dinner, then played with Grace a while longer. "Mama bubbles." "Okay." "Daddy come." "You got it baby girl," Joe said. Ava took Grace upstairs and Joe ran the bath for her. Grace jumped into the tub of bubbles. She was giggling away and splashing around. Ava washed her hair and cleaned her up, while Joe distracted her with the bath toys, then Joe scooped Grace up and wrapped a towel around her and tucked her into bed. "Daddy?" "Yes baby." "Stay forever right?" He nodded. "Promise?" "Yep." "Daddy sing." "Which one?" "Mama song." He played and sang a bit until Grace was asleep. He kissed her, then came downstairs. Ava was curled up by the fire with the warm blanket from their bed.

Joe sat down beside her and Ava handed him a beer. "And what's the special occasion?" "Wanted one," Ava joked. He laughed. "She asleep?" "Listening to your song." Joe kissed her cheek. "I think I know why she's having the nightmares," Ava said. "It's nothing. Everyone has nightmares." "She's having them because when you're performing, we're not with her." "She can't stay up Ava." "You know what I mean." "Being away from home you mean," Joe asked. Ava nodded. "You have a point." "I know once she grows up she'll understand, but I don't want her having the nightmares." He kissed Ava. "I know one way to eliminate them," Joe teased. "A little brother won't fix them." "Psychic." "You know it," Ava teased. "Babe, its either we bring her or one of us stays home." "She wants you." "We're taking a break before Christmas," Joe said. "Until?" "End of February." "Then what?" "Then most of march and we're off until the end of August." "Good." He kissed her. "Why?" "That way I don't have to share," Ava said. "Only once in a while for the odd one off thing." "And we can bring her." He kissed Ava. "I know you're worried about her. She's gonna be fine," Joe said. "Just being over-protective." He kissed her again.

Ava slid into his lap, wrapping her legs around him. "You are an amazing mom and an amazing wife. She's never gonna worry about anything baby." "So back to that idea of what to do tonight," Ava said changing the topic. He kissed Ava and pulled her close. "Practice time?" Ava giggled. "That's where she gets it from." Ava kissed him. Within minutes, he was pulling the sundress off. "You put it on," Joe asked. He noticed the white lace g-string and bra that had him so turned on, that clothes were hurting. He kissed her again and Ava tried to slip out of his arms. He pulled her back to him and peeled his shirt off. Ava's phone rang. "Don't you even think it." He kissed her again and reached to undo her bra. Within a few minutes, they were wrapped up in the blanket on the floor, just like he'd said earlier and were making love by the fireplace.

———

"Why the hell isn't she answering," Rose said. "Just leave a message and tell them to come here," Ryan said. "I can't leave a message like that on her voicemail." The doctor came in. "You pulled a muscle, but other than that, you're fine." "I told her," Ryan said. "I want you off your feet for a day or two," the doctor replied. "We're doing a concert tomorrow," Ryan said. "Then, I'll give you something. As soon as you can, you're back home in bed. No RV beds either." "You got it." "I mean it. Firm bed. I'll give you something to get you through." "There's only two shows. We're back early Sunday morning." "You're in here Sunday afternoon." "Okay." "She's still not answering," Rose said. "We're going home," Ryan replied. "Fine." They left and headed home. Rose walked Ryan back upstairs and put him to bed. "I'll grab the heating pad." She came upstairs a few minutes later with the heating pad, ice water and the muscle relaxers the doctor had given him. She turned the heating pad on and slid it under his back and he pulled her to him. "What," Rose asked. "Stop fussing." "You scared me." "Baby, we're fine. I'm fine. I've done this before." He kissed her. "Come to bed." Rose slipped into her satin pajamas and slid into bed beside him. "You sure you're okay," Rose asked. "Yes." She kissed him. "No more over-doing it okay?" He nodded. They curled up and went to bed early. Emily fell asleep by Jacob.

———

After round two by the fire, they curled up and snuggled, leaning against the sofa. "Babe, if you want to stay this weekend, just tell me." "And leave you out there without adult supervision," Ava teased. "Funny." Joe kissed her. "Seriously." "It's fine. I don't think we should bring her. We're back Saturday after the concert anyway right?" Joe nodded. "48 hours won't be that bad." He kissed her. "Know what that means," Joe asked. "Don't you even start." "You and me, the plane." "I said don't say it," Ava joked. He kissed her again and she slid her arms around him. "Oh I'm gonna say it, and remind you tomorrow when we're on the plane." "The guys are on with us." "So?" Ava got up and slid her sundress back on and walked upstairs. He turned off the fireplace and followed her with the blanket. Ava checked her phone and saw 5 calls from Rose. She checked voicemail and heard what happened. "Ryan was in the hospital. Something about his back," Ava said. "We'll find out tomorrow," Joe said. "Call." "He's probably sleeping. It's happened before. They gave him a muscle relaxer shot and sent him home." Joe slid her phone out of her hand. "You should . . ." He kissed her and picked her up, carrying her to the bed pinning her onto the bed. "I get you all to myself for the weekend." "No plane." "Yes plane," Joe joked as he leaned in and kissed her. The dress hit the floor and so did the blanket and his clothes. Her legs wrapped around him. "You're mine. All mine this weekend," Joe said. "Better not wear me out." They made love again, then curled up and went to sleep. Finally, a night with no nightmares.

They got up the next morning and everyone headed to the plane. Rose stayed home with Grace. "How's the back," Joe asked as he was holding onto Grace. "Better. Thanks." "That's what you get." "Bite me." They hopped on the plane and Joe gave Grace a hug and kiss. "Daddy no go." "Baby, Mama and I will be home tomorrow night." "No." "I promise baby. You can call me whenever you want." "No. Daddy no going." "I love you baby girl." "No go." "Remember when I went out the other day and came home?" "Um hmm." "We're coming home tomorrow. You can call us whenever you want to." "Sing to sleep?" "Promise." "I love you Daddy." "I love you too baby." He handed her to Rose and Ava hugged and kissed her goodbye and they hopped on the plane.

The flight wasn't long. Joe kept hinting all the way there. "You two are hilarious," Brad said. "Why's that," Joe asked. "I know what Mr. playboy over here is thinking, and you trying to talk him out of it is hilarious," Brad said. "One-track mind." "Always has had one," Joe said. "Remember back in the beginning with that chick that showed to one of the concerts? The one that you almost drooled over," Brad said. "The one who showed up to how many concerts that year," Joe joked. "Who was in a black playboy hat," Ava teased. "What," Joe asked "So forgetful," Ava teased. "Don't you dare tell me . . ." "Front row. You stared," Ava said. "I know. Couldn't help it. Are you trying to tell me . . . . ," Joe asked. "Smart ass," Ava replied. Brad and Ryan both started laughing. "Like either of you remembered," Joe said. "Knew you looked familiar,' Ryan teased. "Liar," Joe said. Ava laughed. They finally landed and headed to the car to head to the venue.

They pulled in through a mass amount of fans and went inside. Ava put her things in the RV and turned to find herself face to face with Joe. "If that was you all those times, where's the hat?" Ava pulled it out of the shelf in the RV. She slid it on and smirked. He kissed her, knocking the hat off and leaning her onto their bed. A minute later, there was a knock at the door. Ava managed to get up, then answered it. "Joe around?" "Sure," Ava said. A woman stepped on the RV. Ava stepped off. She went and sat down with her laptop and tried to brainstorm ideas for a new story.

"What the hell are you doing here," Joe asked. "Emily told me. It's been forever." He hugged her. "So how have you been," Kendra asked. "Married." "I heard. That must have been Ava." "That was my beautiful, intelligent, sexy as hell wife." "Lucky lady." "Come on. I'll introduce you two." He headed towards Ava with Kendra in tow. "Babe, this is an old friend from grade school. Kendra, this is my wife Ava. Ava, this is Kendra." "Nice to meet you," Ava said. "How's the writing," Joe asked. "Brainstorming." "Take a writing break," he said. "Can't." "Yeah you can." Joe grabbed Ava's hand. They walked over towards Ryan and Brad. "That can't be Kendra," Brad said. "Hey stranger," she said hugging Brad. "Be back in a few minutes," Ava said. "She's fine babe," Joe said. "Just want to check on her." He kissed Ava. "She's fine." "I know." Ava went and called to check on Grace.

Joe went back to the RV after hanging with Kendra and the guys and Ava was on the bed. "Hey beautiful," Joe said. "Hey." "What are you doing in here all by yourself?" "Thinking." "About?" "I miss her," Ava said. "Baby." "I miss her falling asleep on my chest. I miss seeing you rock her to sleep and you two having the father daughter talks that you thought I couldn't hear." "She's growing up." "And we're missing it." "Baby, we aren't. We have two weeks left until we're done for the year." "I know." Joe kissed her. They curled up together and talked, then headed to sound check.

———

Kendra was watching sound check. She sat there remembering how bad she'd wanted Joe to herself. How the second she saw him, all the feelings came rushing back. What she would do for one kiss. Her phone went off. "Hey James." "How's things," he asked "Fine. Just visiting some friends." "Oh really?" "What do you want?" "Nothing. Was gonna see if you wanted to get together," James asked. "I'm three hours away." "I'll meet you." "I'll call you when I'm done here." Kendra hung up. James was seriously getting on her last nerve. She'd met James because of Joe. One fluke night at a damn concert and now he'd popped back into her life.

———

They finished sound check and Joe kissed Ava. "Babe." "If you want to go hang out with her . . ." "I want you to come with me," Joe said. "Joe, I know that look." "We're friends." "And I know the look of someone who's so hot for you she can barely prevent herself from jumping you at a moment's notice." "Oh really." "Had that look yesterday," Ava teased. He smirked and kissed her. "And what about today?" Ava smirked and kissed him. "Oh really? Well, maybe I should leave her with the guys and disappear with you for a few hours to the hotel." "You'd never make it back here in time." He had this silly look like she was literally turning him on just with one touch. "You're choice." She kissed him then headed back towards the RV. He caught up to her, grabbing her hand and walked over towards Kendra.

"So, you coming to the concert," Joe asked. "Of course. Like I'd give up the chance to watch you in action." "Funny. Seriously though, who's coming with you tonight?" "Just me." Joe looked at Ava and she shook her head. "We're doing dinner around six if you want to join us," Joe said. "Thanks. I'd love to." "We're just gonna head back to the hotel and freshen up. We'll see you back here around six?" She hung out with Brad and Ryan a while then went and got changed.

The car pulled off to take Ava and Joe to the hotel. "I swear, if you even thought of doing what I think you were . . ." Joe kissed Ava. "You said no. The answer's no." "Thank you." "Babe, I'm not about to get on your bad side. I know what can happen," Joe joked. Ava smiled. "Not easy to forget that." "Good. You better not." Ava curled up with him until they pulled into the hotel. They went up the elevator to their room, then the minute the door closed, he chased her to bed.

He had her pinned to the bed when her phone rang. "Crappy timing whoever it is." He slid the phone from her pocket. "What's up Rose?" "Hey Joe. Just wanted to let you know that Grace finally fell asleep. I put on the concert DVD like Ava said." "At least we know what to do next time right," Joe teased. "And I checked on the house. There was a package at the door for Ava." "Does it say who from?" He undid Ava's shirt. "It's from Owen." "I'll get it on the way home," James said. "Don't freak out alright?" "I won't." "Joe, the man's a nut. I already called the cops." "Thanks. Talk to you soon." Joe hung up and kissed Ava. "What?" "Nothing." "Joe, what," Ava asked. "Not letting that asshole ruin the mood." "Either you tell me . . ." He kissed her and wrapped his arms tight around her, rolling them onto the bed. "Tell me." He shook his head. She pinned him to the bed. "Tell me or I'm showering alone," Ava said. "Ava." "Now." "There was a package at the house from Owen." "How the hell?" "They left it on the porch. Rose called the cops." "Damn him." "Babe." "I can't get rid of him can I?" Ava got up and walked out to the balcony.

There was a warm breeze of salty air that she hoped would calm her. She took a few deep breaths and leaned against the railing. "Babe, he can't get to either of us." "I know. It just pisses me off that he won't go away." "He's being dealt with." "I know." Joe wrapped his arms around her. "We're together. That's what matters." She closed her eyes and slid her arms around his. "We have us. Always will." "I love you," Ava said. "I love you too beautiful." He kissed her neck. "Do me a favor?" "What's that?" Ava turned towards him and kissed him. He picked her up, wrapping her legs around him and carried her back into the room. He undressed her, while she undressed him then made love on the bed. He kissed her from head to toe, she had him literally begging. They kept going and going until both of them were tired. His phone went off as they were falling asleep. "Hey Ryan," Ava said. "You two are hilarious. Dinner in 45 minutes," he said. "We'll be back." "I bet." "Enough. See you in a few." Ava hung up then went to get up. "How are you not tired?" "45 minutes until dinner," Ava said. "Shit." Ava got up and turned on the hot shower. She slipped into it and had just put the conditioner in when he slid in behind her. "Power nap?" He kissed her shoulder. "Funny." "Can't blame a guy for trying," Joe said. "True." She rinsed out the conditioner and leaned over to shave her legs while he showered. "Babe, seriously cruising," Joe joked. She giggled. She finished and stood up, rinsing the shampoo from his hair and putting conditioner on it. "Nice." Her body pressed against his and his arm slid around her and down to her backside. "Down boy," Ava teased. He kissed her. She turned the water off and stepped out, then handed him a towel. "Which one you wearing?" "Red." "No." Ava nodded. She slid her leggings and tank top on, then her sandals, towel-drying her hair while he shaved. She handed him his black jeans and red and black shirt and he pulled her closer. "You're gonna make us late," Ava said. He kissed her. She freshened up, then he finished getting changed and they headed back.

CHAPTER 26

They came in through the crowd, then headed to dinner with the guys. "So where'd you two disappear to," Brad asked. "Quiet time. I had a pounding headache," Ava teased. "I bet." Brad laughed. "Not funny." "I'm surprised you two don't have like 20 kids by now," Ryan said. Joe held Ava's hand a little tighter. They had dinner, then Joe went and got changed for the show. Joe kissed Ava with a long kiss goodbye then headed to the meet and greet. Ava slid into the red dress, got her hair and makeup done, then relaxed until they were finished. Joe came in and came up behind her, kissing her neck. "Hey handsome," she said. "Hey beautiful." He sat down with her and she laid her legs across his lap. "You seriously are gonna kill me with that dress," Joe said. "I know." "Aww. They're so cute," Brad joked. "Careful or you're getting a heel to the head," Joe joked. The guys laughed. Ryan called Rose and talked to her from the change room and Danielle called to see how Brad was. "So, where were we," Joe asked. "I'm wearing the dress." "Hotel." "And," Ava asked. "Piano." "Tease." "Nope." "Balcony." "Better." "Joe." His arm slid around her. "You have to go on." He kissed her. "I know," he replied. "Don't start." Joe kissed her again. "Guys you're on in 10 minutes." Ava giggled. "Smart ass." "Hello? The clock's right there," Ava said. He kissed her then got up. She stood up. "Damn," Joe said. "Would you stop?" He kissed her and she walked them down to the stage. "Good luck baby," Ava said. He kissed her.

The guys hopped on stage, then after a few songs, Ava came on with them. Joe was watching her like a hawk. "So Ava, think you can put up with us for a while longer," Ryan asked. "Why you asking?" The manager came out with a plaque. "As of this morning, the single has sold a million copies," the manager said. The crowd roared. "So, Ava? Think you can put up with us," Brad asked. "As much as family can," Ava replied. The crowd roared again. They sang a few more songs, then Ava headed off. She sat at the side stage, and watched them. Joe kept looking over and smiling. When they finished, he put his guitar with the others and wrapped his arms around her and kissed her. "You know we're going out to celebrate," Ryan said. "You got it," Joe said. The guys changed and they all headed out to a club in town.

They each had a drink or two, celebrated and danced for a few hours, then headed back to the hotel to get some shut-eye. They walked into the hotel and Ava saw the message sign on the phone. She went and checked them. "Ava, it's Rose. The cop was here. I know Joe told you. You wouldn't have wanted to see it. They called to tell me he's in custody. They denied bail. He pleaded guilty. He's not coming back. Love you. Call me." Ava put the phone down. "Babe," Joe said. She turned towards him and kissed him. "Ooh. Good news." He kissed her and picked her up, carrying her to bed. "Good mood?" Ava nodded. "You know, you were amazing tonight," Ava said. "So were you babe." "So where you want to hang it?" Ava smirked. "Ooh. The smirk is back," Joe said. She smiled and he kissed her. She undid his shirt. "Oh really." Ava nodded. He kissed her, wrapping his arms around her. "I love you." "I love you too babe."

She slid his shirt off, and he had her dress off in minutes. "You had to wear the red lace," Joe teased. Ava nodded. He kissed her again and she peeled his jeans off. "You know someday." "Someday what," Ava asked. "Someday, we're gonna be alone. Just you and me on that stage." "And then what," Ava teased. He kissed her. "I'll get you back for the dresses." "Threat or promise?" Joe kissed her and made love to her. It was intensely passionate and she wanted him so bad she could taste it. He drove her wild and he knew it. He knew exactly how to turn her on, and she knew the same about him. Every inch of him craved her touch. The second he felt her nails on his back, he was putty in her hands. They were almost possessed. After, he leaned back onto the pillow and tried to catch his breath. He held Ava in his arms as her head rested on his shoulder. "Holy crap." "Tell me about it," Joe said. He kissed her. His phone rang. Ava went to get it and he pulled her back to him. "Whoever it is can screw off." Ava laughed and grabbed the phone. He answered it.

"Joe, it's Kendra." "Hey." "You guys were awesome." "Thanks. You headed home," Joe asked. "Was gonna pop by for a drink." "Where?" "I know where you guys always stay." "I'll see if Brad's up." "Okay." Kendra hung up. Ava straddled Joe. "No way," Ava said. "I know." "We have to get up in like 7 hours." "I know. One drink." "She's not coming in here," Ava said. Joe nodded. She called over to Brad's room while Joe kissed her stomach. "You still up?" "Sorta," Brad said. "Kendra's coming for a drink. Need assistance," Ava replied. "Nice. I bet you do. I'll be over in a minute." Ava hung up and pinned Joe to the bed. "One drink," Ava said. He pulled her to him and kissed her. "We may not get any sleep," Ava said. The smirk came out again and he kissed her. Ava got up and slid on her leggings and Joe's shirt. "Nice. Dropping her a hint," Joe joked. Ava nodded. He wrapped his arms around her. "Only one thing missing." "What?" He picked her up and carried her to the sofa. "Oh yes. The latest accessory. My husband," Ava teased. He kissed her as they laughed.

Brad came in a few minutes later and saw Joe and Ava. "Nice. Third wheel has arrived," Brad joked. "His fault," Ava teased. Ten minutes later, Kendra was at the door. Brad let her in. "Babe, drink," Ava asked. "You already know." Ava laughed. "Brad?" "You have that fruit thing," he asked. Ava nodded. "Kendra?" "Beer?" Ava handed Brad and Joe their drink, then grabbed hers and Kendra's. "Thank you beautiful," Joe said as he kissed Ava. They snuggled on the sofa. "You really were great tonight. Congrats on the single Ava," Kendra said. "Thanks." "Who would've thought," Joe joked. "I have no idea where that talent came from, but remind me to thank your mom and dad at Christmas," Brad said. "I will." "I read a few of your books Ava. They're great," Kendra said. "Thank you." "Still want a sneak peek of the one you just finished," Joe said. "Never know what Santa could bring you," Ava joked. "Or I sneak onto your computer again." Ava smacked his shoulder and he kissed her. "So what else has been going on with you guys? I heard Ryan got hitched to Ava's buddy. Why am I not in the loop anymore," Kendra asked. "You're fault you were dating that James guy." "He was your friend Brad," Kendra replied. "Ryan's thank you very much," Brad replied. "James who," Ava asked. "James Perry." "Nice," Ava said. Joe's arm wrapped around her knees pulling her almost into his lap.

After two drinks, Kendra was determined to hang out. "We gotta get some sleep Kendra. We have an early flight tomorrow," Joe said. "I'm gonna head to bed," Ava said. "Be there in a few minutes," Joe replied. Ava kissed him. "I'll walk you down," Joe said. Kendra hugged Brad goodbye and Joe slid on his sweatshirt and walked her to the elevator.

"I missed you guys," she said. "You made your decision Kendra. You wanted to be with him." "What if I changed my mind," she asked. "Then I hope you find what you want. I know I found exactly what I wanted," Joe said. "You really love her don't you?" Joe nodded. "More than ever." "I have to confess something." "Kendra, I'm not stupid," Joe said. "I know. I missed you." "Friendship's all you get Kendra. Nothing else." "Come on." "No. I mean it. I love her. I'm not jeopardizing it," Joe said. "She wouldn't . . ." "Yeah she would. I love her." "One last kiss goodbye?" "No." He gave her a hug and she left. Joe walked back down the hall to the room and walked in, turning the lights off and walked into the bedroom. He kicked his jeans off, and his sweatshirt, and slid into bed with Ava. His arm wrapped around her and she linked her fingers with his. He snuggled up with her and they were asleep a few minutes later.

The next morning, they all showered, got changed, then headed to the next venue. They shared one RV this time. The guys worked on some music while Ava tried to do a little writing. When they pulled into the venue, Joe slid the laptop out of her lap and kissed her. "Hey," Joe said. "Hey yourself handsome." "You doing okay?" Ava nodded. He took her hand and they headed into the venue. The crew finished setting up while the guys did some interviews; they even managed to pull Ava into one.

"So congrats guys on the new single." "More like congrats to Ava," Brad said. "I heard that the famous Ava helped in writing that song." "Actually, it was her. We wrote it together," Joe said. "Oh really?" "I was working on it one night, and Ava came in and saved it from the trashcan," Joe said. "Wow." "Definitely lucky to have her with us," Ryan said. "She's like part of the gang?" "More like part of the family," Brad said. "So how's married life Joe?" "Amazing. I'm the luckiest guy in the world." "So any plans for more kids?" "We're hoping," Ava said. "Oh really? What about you Ryan?" "Our son is a handful, but we'll see what happens." "And Brad, I hear you're gonna be a daddy." "That I am. After watching these two, I think I might make a pretty good dad." "Of course you will buddy," Joe said. "So tell us about the new song you're working on." "It'll be on the new CD. The release date is the week before Christmas instead of Valentine's." "Oh really. Nice." "Something for our fans as a gift from us," Ryan said.

The interviews finally finished and they went to the hotel for a power nap. Joe and Ava curled up together. "So miss snuggles." "What," Ava asked. "I know you heard it last night." "And I knew she was up to something. Who calls at that time of night?" He kissed her. "You know her so well." Joe slid his arms around her. "Thought you were tired." He kissed her and undid the buttons on her shirt. "Sleep." He kissed her again and peeled the leggings off. "Joe." The leggings hit the floor. He kissed her hip and her g-string hit the floor. "Joe." He moved up her torso and pulled his shirt off. "Sleep." He shook his head. He kissed her and kicked his jeans off. "You're not tired?" "Nope." They got up and he ran them a hot bath in the Jacuzzi tub. "Definitely not tired," Joe said. They slid into the tub and he grabbed them each a drink. "This is what I needed." "I know," Joe said. He slid in behind her. "This is what we both needed. No more stress." He put his drink down and rubbed her shoulders. "You do realize that this doesn't mean you're getting any," Ava teased. "I know. I also know that you're not getting much sleep." "We're flying home tonight," Ava said. "Exactly. The plane awaits." "Don't even." "You get on the plane in a dress, you're asking for it," Joe teased. "Funny." He wrapped his arms around her and kissed her neck. He nibbled her ear.

Ava got up and wrapped a towel around her, then headed for bed. "Where you goin?" "A nap." He got up, grabbing a towel and wrapping it around him and following her. Ava laid down and he slid onto the bed beside her. She curled up in his arms. "And if you're good tonight, you might get a back massage," Ava said. "Ooh." "Exactly." He leaned towards her and kissed her. "And if I'm not?" Ava looked at him. The slight smile crossed her lips. "Even better." "No. If you're not good, then you're sitting alone on the plane." "After," he teased. "No." He kissed her. "Guess I'll have to be good, at least until we get home." Joe laughed and kissed her again. She snuggled back up with him and they had a nap. An hour later, Ryan walked in to wake them up. "Black or blue," Ryan asked. "Blue," Ava said. "Get up." "We are," Joe said.

A little while later, Joe and Ava headed to the venue with the guys for dinner. "So what you shocking him with tonight," Brad teased. "Navy blue dress." "Thought you didn't get it," Joe said. She smiled. "How's your back doing Ryan?" "Better. It always takes a day or two." "You know she only took you because she loves you," Ava said. "I know. God bless her, she's a worry wart." "She just takes care of the people she loves." "I know. Love her for it," Ryan said. They chatted during dinner, then the guys went off to call their wives, and Joe and Ava went and got changed.

"Babe." "I'm wearing it," Ava said. "Can't." "Why?" She turned to face him. She knew just the reason why. "Wearing it." He locked the door to the RV. "I'm wearing the dress," Ava said. He kissed her. He had her leaned over the counter in minutes. "Holy shit," Ava said as they went at it and her legs were shaking in seconds. "Babe, you are so in for it." They finished just as fast as they started. "Babe." "We have to go." He kissed her again. Ryan came and knocked. "Let's go," Ryan said. He kissed Ava again and pulled her close. "You can't," Joe said. "I'm wearing it." They cleaned up a bit, then headed inside. Ava went and finished getting her hair and makeup done. She stood side stage when the concert started, went out and did her thing, then watched the rest. Once the concert was finished, they headed straight to the airport. "I need sleep," Brad said. "You and me both," Ryan replied. Joe wrapped his arm around Ava. She shook her head. She got up and went and sat away from the guys. Joe got up and sat with her, turning out the light for them.

"What," Joe asked. Ava shook her head. He kissed her, then pulled her into his lap. He kissed her again and it turned into a mind-numbing, body tingling make out session. "I want you so bad," he whispered. "I know," she replied. He heard Ryan snoring (or faking it). Ava got up and sat across from Joe. He got up and headed towards the washroom. Ava shook her head. He motioned for her to come. That smirk crossed her face again. She slid her heels off, and walked towards him. He locked the door and had her on the counter in seconds. "What is up with you today," Ava asked. "You wearing the dress that rocks every single curve has nothing to do with it," he said. He kissed her again and a minute or two later, they were having sex. They tried to be quiet, knowing that the guys probably knew exactly what they were doing. They both came so hard, they were shaking. "Holy shit," Joe said. She kissed him and he tried to regain his strength. Ava slid off the counter and he pulled her into his arms. "You know this dress is never leaving the house again," Joe said. "Yeah it is." Ava slid out and sat down. Joe came out a few minutes later and sat down beside her, raising the armrest between them so they could cuddle.

A half-hour later, they were asleep when the pilot announced they were landing. Ava woke Brad and Ryan up and they landed. They grabbed their bags, then headed home. They walked in and Emily was asleep on the sofa. Ava walked upstairs with Joe one step behind her, dropped her bags in the bedroom and went in to look in on Grace. She was asleep in her crib. Ava smiled, then went into the bedroom. Joe was unpacking. Ava slid her arms around him. "Hey beautiful," he said. "She's out like a light." "Babe, I was thinking," Joe said. "About what," Ava asked as she kissed his neck. "Remember the other day when you were thinking we're away from her too much," Joe said. "Yep." "If you don't want to be on tour with us . . ." She sat down in front of him. "I never said I didn't." "I know, but you're worried." "We're missing things, but we're also spending time with her. I just don't want to miss the big things," Ava said. "Okay. But if you change your mind." Ava stood up and kissed him. "I love being with you on tour." "And it wouldn't be the same without you there." "Then stop worrying," Ava said. He kissed her and pulled her close.

They curled up in bed together and snuggled, then kissing led to more. Ava slid her leg around him. "Thought you were tired," Joe said. Ava kissed him and slid her arms around him. "Oh I get the hint." "Good." He kissed her and pinned her to the bed. He made love to her and ravished her. They finally fell asleep still entangled, and completely exhausted.

"How's your back," Rose asked. Ryan pulled her to him and picked her up, carrying her to the sofa. "That good," he joked. He leaned her onto the soft leather and unbuttoned her sweater. "Missed you." "I missed you too," Rose said. He kissed her and made love to her. "You really can't take off anymore." "Why's that," Ryan asked. "Missed you way too much." "Oh really," he asked as they curled up together. "You don't even know." "What did you do?" "Was thinking about you last night." "What kind of thinking?" She gave him that look that always had him turned on. "You didn't." Rose nodded. "I missed you." He grabbed her hand and walked her upstairs then curled up with her. "Show me." "Not the same." "Rose." She linked her hand with his and repeated what she'd done the night before, which led to round two.

The next morning, Ava got up with Grace. "Mama home." "Daddy's home too baby." Grace wrapped her arms around Ava and wouldn't let go. "Missed Mama." "I missed you too baby." "Where Daddy?" "He's sleeping." "Pictures Mama." "Show me," Ava said as Grace slid out of her arms and walked her into the kitchen. There were pictures everywhere. "This Daddy." "With his red guitar." "And Rose paint finger." Ava looked and saw the silver sparkles on Grace's little fingers. "Did you have fun?" "Ya." "Good. Did you have fun with Jacob?" "My boyfriend." "Oh really," Ava said. Joe came downstairs a few minutes later and Grace ran to him. "Daddy." He picked her up in his arms and kissed her. She wrapped her arms around Joe and Ava went and grabbed her camera and snapped a few pictures. "Missed Daddy." "I missed you too baby." "Love Daddy." "Love you too princess." He walked over to Ava and kissed her good morning. "Thought you'd still be sleeping." "Couldn't. My teddy bear wasn't in bed." Ava giggled. She made breakfast for them and Emily, then Emily headed home and Joe and Ava spent the day with Grace.

Rose got up with Ryan, and Jacob came into the room and jumped onto the bed. "Daddy." "Hey buddy. What are you doing out of bed," Ryan asked. "Awake time." He wrapped his arms around Ryan. "I missed you Jacob." "Missed Daddy." "I got you something." Ryan got up and grabbed the teddy bear he'd bought Jacob. "Teddy." "Thought you'd like him." "Hi Teddy." Jacob hopped off the bed and ran into his room. Rose wrapped her arm around Ryan. "I had an idea," Rose said. "What's the idea from that beautiful brain?" "Had an idea about Christmas." "We're doing the big all the family thing." "What if we had a few friends over for dinner," Rose asked. "Such as?" "Rachel and Carrie were going to come." "And Rachel's going to bring James." "No. They broke it off." "Good. The guy was trouble." "True. We could invite a few of your old friends, Ava and Joe, Brad and Danielle, Cat and Scott . . ." "Already planning it aren't you?" "Miss my friends," Rose said. "If it puts a smile on your face, you got it." "So when are the concerts done?" "Two weeks. Break until March." "Good. Jacob really missed you." "You did too," Ryan said with a smirk ear to ear. "True." "You know what this means right?" "Christmas decorations, Christmas shopping and caterers?" "Presents, decorating and mistletoe." "We should just put a pile of it over the bed." "That's what got us Jacob in the first place," Rose teased. "I know. Was thinking we should have another one." "Or did you just want to practice?" Ryan kissed her. Jacob came running in. "Daddy, come play." Ryan slid out of bed, then headed into Jacob's room with him.

After a long morning at the park, Ava and Joe brought Grace home for her afternoon nap and some lunch. After she finished her lunch, Grace was asleep in Joe's arms. He carried her up the stairs to her bed, then came downstairs and curled up with Ava. The minute he sat down, her phone rang. "Hey Kay." "They loved the book. It's out the same day as the new CD," her agent said. "Seriously?" "And you have two interviews lined up." "With?" "One with Glamour, one with Cosmo, and the other is a TV one." "Who?" "Oprah." "Seriously?" "If you're up for it." "Just let me know when," Ava said. "Thursday." "This Thursday?" "Yep." "Holy shit," Ava said. "Right. I'll meet you and Joe at the airport." Kay hung up. "What?" "We're going to Chicago on Thursday." "We are, are we?" "Oprah's calling." "Then we need to find you something to wear," Joe said. "When Grace gets up." "That means we get Mom and Dad time." "Laundry, then practicing." Joe laughed. He kissed her and they got up and started on laundry. They chilled after doing some laundry, and cleaned up, then curled up on the sofa and watched a movie for a while.

They got 20 minutes into the movie, and Joe kissed her. "What happened to relaxing and watching a movie?" He kissed her neck. "Practicing," Ava teased. His hands slid under her butt. Just as he was about to undo his belt, Grace woke up. They both laughed. "Something tells me she doesn't want a little brother or sister yet," Ava teased. He kissed Ava, then got up and went and got Grace. She almost jumped into his arms. "Hey Gracie. How did you sleep?" "Miss Daddy." "I bet you did." He changed her and brought her downstairs. "Hi Mama." "Hi princess." "What doing?" "We were just going to watch a movie." "Shrek." "Okay." Joe slid it in the DVD player and slid onto the sofa behind Ava. Grace grabbed her favorite teddy bear and curled up with Ava. "See, this is what Sunday's are supposed to be like," Ava said. "Aren't you supposed to go to the doctor?" Ava checked her phone. "Tomorrow at 10:30." He smirked. "Don't even think it." He kissed Ava's neck. "Mama, hug." Ava snuggled Grace. "Grace, what would you think about a little brother or sister," Joe asked. "Okay." Ava giggled. "See what I mean," Ava said. "You want a little sister?" "Yeah." "What about a brother," Joe asked. "Okay Daddy." "She'd say yes to almost anything you ask," Ava said. "Mama, hungry." "Okay baby." Ava went to get up and Joe kissed her. Joe got up and went and made them dinner. Grace went in and helped him while Ava flipped the laundry.

Rose called just as Ava went to sit back down. "So, how did it go," Rose asked. "Good. And I have news." "What's the news?" "Oprah on Thursday." "Seriously," Rose asked. "Joe and Grace are coming with me." "Holy bananas." "I know." "Ryan. She's going on Oprah," Rose said. "Thanks for announcing it," Ava replied. "It's big news." "True. We're gonna need shopping time," Ava said. "Not without me," Joe said from the kitchen. "I heard that. I guess the blue dress worked," Rose asked. "Understatement." "Ooh." "I know. Anyway, we have to find something Oprah worthy." "You know she's going to ask you to sing," Rose said. "Yes you and Ryan and Jacob can come." "Ava." "She won't ask if we're not all there," Ava said. "She will," Joe replied. "Then Brad and Danielle are coming too." "I'll call them." "Sounds good to me," Ava said. "So they accepted the changes?" "And the book's coming out the same day as the CD." "That's next week." "Shit." "I know." "We're totally going shopping," Rose said. "I just hope there aren't any more book tours." "Not now." They finished their call, then Ava and Joe had dinner with Grace, gave her a bath and tucked her in. Joe sang to her a bit while Ava watched, and Grace was asleep in no time.

Joe came into the bedroom while Ava was going through her closet trying to figure out what to wear. "What are you doing," he asked as he slid his arms around her. "Trying to figure out something I can wear." "Babe, we'll get something tomorrow," Joe said. "I have to have something in here." "You could do the black dress." "Funny." "True. More for my benefit," Joe joked. She finally gave up. "We'll find something after the doctor tomorrow." He kissed her. She walked him towards the bed and he pulled her into his lap, straddling him. "When are the awards," Ava asked. "Tuesday next week." "Crap." "I know. At least you have a dress for it." "You wearing the black?" "The one that matches your dress." Ava smiled. "Just think. We could have something else to celebrate," Joe said. "Determined aren't you?" He nodded. He kissed Ava. "And where did we find this sexy teddy?" "Wouldn't you love to know," Ava said. He kissed her. "Babe." "Don't even. We need sleep." He leaned her onto the bed. "We are going to actually get sleep right," Ava teased. He smiled and kissed her again. They made love, then curled up in bed together. "You know, I'll never get enough of this," Joe said. "What?" "You. I love falling asleep with you in my arms." "Me too. Especially when you hold me all night." "Never gonna let you go Ava." "I know. I love you." "Love you too." They finally fell asleep.

The next morning, Joe and Ava headed in to the doctor with Grace. "So, how we feeling," the doctor asked. "Good," Ava replied. "Good. I'm going to do the tests, then you can head out. You're probably fine." "I know. Just routine." She did the tests, then came in to see Ava. "You're fine. I'll give you a shout if anything comes back on any of the tests." "Thanks." They headed out and took Grace to the mall. After a few stores, they finally found something to wear. "It's perfect," Joe said. "You sure?" Joe nodded and kissed Ava. "Mama pretty," Grace said. "Thank you baby." They got the dress, then went and found something for Grace. "Pretty like Mama." "Yeah you are," Joe said.

After dinner and tucking Grace into bed, Ava and Joe curled up together. "Disappointed," Ava asked. "No. I didn't expect it to happen immediately." "We just lost a baby." "I know. Are you okay," Joe asked. "I guess I sort of wished it too." He kissed Ava. "It will. When it's time, it will."

A few days later, they were on Oprah. A million and one questions later, she talked Ava into singing with the guys. "This is their newest song." They sang Love Letter, then Our Secret. After, they headed home and got packed for the last few shows.

The awards were a huge success. The guys won every award they were nominated for. It was gonna be their year. Once the awards and the after-parties were over, they got back to work. The next week or two flew by in a flurry of interviews, concerts, Christmas shopping and decorating. The CD and book came out to rave reviews, then finally they were all home for a while.

CHAPTER 27

Christmas neared. They had a tree covered in decorations, and were finishing up their wrapping for Grace when Ava started feeling sick. "You okay," Joe asked. "Just light headed." Ava grabbed some orange juice and sat back down with him, trying to get more wrapping done. "So, we have all the shopping for Grace done, right?" Ava nodded. "Babe, you're all flushed," Joe said. "I'm fine." She put the last of the presents for Grace under the tree. "Any shopping left for you to finish," Ava asked. "A little." He smirked. "I have to get something for Ryan and Brad." "Already done," Ava said. "One or two things left." "Do you want me to go with you?" "You can't. You could look after Grace tomorrow," Ava said. "Sounds good. Daddy daughter day." Ava smiled. They turned the fireplace off and headed upstairs to bed.

The next morning, Ava left with Cat to do the last of her shopping. Ava had to stop twice at the ladies room. "You alright," Cat asked. Ava nodded. "Ava." "What?" "Are you," Cat asked. "You and Joe are determined." "If you're feeling like this." "Stop." They finished the last few things, with Cat literally jaw-dropped, then they headed home. "Stop and get a test," Cat said. "No." "Stop and I'll get it for you." Ava stopped and Cat ran in, coming out ten minutes later. "Do it at my place."

"Hey beautiful," Joe said as he met Ava at the door. "Hey yourself." "Hi Mama." "Hey baby girl," Ava said as Grace hugged her leg. "Where was you," Joe asked. "Helping Santa." "Oh." Grace ran back in to play with her toys. "So where'd you really take off to," Joe asked as he slid his arms around Ava. "Fredericks, Victoria's Secret, and a few other places." "Tease." Ava nodded. He kissed her. "Missed you," he said. "Good." He kissed her again and led her into the kitchen. "We made you dinner." "Very nice," Ava said as he slid his arms around her. "What is with the silly grin," Joe asked. Part of her wanted to tell him, but the other part thought it would make the best present ever. "Nothing. Just had a good day with Cat." They sat down and had dinner while Grace colored. After dinner, they gave Grace a bath, then Ava and Joe tucked her into bed. "Mama?" "Yes baby." "Sister."

"Did you ask Santa?" "Daddy lettered." "I'll e-mail him," Ava said. "Okay." Grace kissed her and was asleep a few minutes later.

"Oh nice Joe," Ava said. "What? You asked her." "I swear at some point your determination is going to drive me nuts." "Oh it is, is it," Joe asked. He slid his arms around her. "Yeah it is." He kissed Ava and walked her backwards towards the bed. "Babe." "What?" "Bubble bath." "Ooh. Good idea," Joe said. He kissed her and peeled her shirt off. She undid his belt. "I get a hint to what you bought," Joe asked. "On Christmas morning just like Grace." "Party pooper." "I have to surprise you somehow." "I know how you can," he said. Joe kissed her and peeled her jeans off as she undid the zipper of his. He picked her up, wrapping her legs around him and leaned her onto the bed. "Where were you really," Joe asked. "The mall." "No security?" Ava shook her head. "Nice." "I finished my shopping." "Good. Means more time here," Joe said. Ava laughed. "Haven't had daddy and daughter time in a while." "I know. She just kept asking all day when Mama was coming home." He slid her tank top off and saw the white lace bra. "I knew," Joe said. "Liar." He kissed her and slid her g-string off. They were going at it in minutes. It was almost like he was her drug and she was his. The two of them together were like fire and gasoline. The sex was intense and amazing. He had her body shivering with pleasure and his heart pounding so hard she thought it would pound out of his chest.

They curled up together on the bed. "Bubble bath?" "Can't move," Joe said. Ava giggled. He pulled her close. "You know you've had that grin ever since you came home." "Your fault." "Right. I know the one now is because of me. What was the one for when you came home?" "Nothing." "Full of secrets aren't you?" "Nope." "You know I have my ways of getting the secrets out of you," Joe said. Ava kissed him. She got up and drew them a hot bath. He slid in behind her. "And just think. No concerts this weekend," Ava said. "What are we gonna do with all this extra time." His hands slid under the water. "I can think of a few things." "Christmas party it is," Ava said. "Nice." "What were you thinking," Ava asked. "Giving Grace something from her Christmas list." "You never know. We could find that doll she was desperate for." "Funny," Joe said. He kissed her and wrapped his arms around her. After relaxing a while, they slid out of the tub and went to bed.

Half way through the night, Ava sneaked downstairs. She couldn't wait to tell him. She slid the baby socks into a little gift bag and walked upstairs. She slid it in the side table drawer and his phone rang. He got up. "Hello?" "Joe, it's Kendra." "Why are you calling at this time of night?" "I need your help." "With?" "Can you pick me up at the airport," she asked. "I'm half asleep." "Joe, please." "Tell me or I'm not going anywhere." "James. End of discussion." "There's a hotel near the airport. I'll call and get you a room and come by in the morning." "Joe." "Kendra, she'll kill me," Joe said. "Please." "I'll call you back." He hung up.

"What did she want," Ava asked. "She's at the airport. Something's wrong. I have to go pick her up." "No you don't." "Something's wrong." "I'll go," Ava said. "Babe, I have to go." "Fine." Ava rolled over. "Don't get mad." "She's waiting." "Babe, tell me you aren't mad," Joe said. "If anything happens, so help me." He turned Ava towards him. "Babe," he said. "Don't suck up Joe. She calls you at 3am . . ." He kissed her. They had sex. Quick, fast, erotic as hell sex. "I'll be home in a half-hour." "If you . . ." "I'm not going to." "Joe, I mean it." "I mean it too. I'm never going to," Joe said. He kissed her again, then got up and pulled his jeans and shirt on, heading for the airport.

He pulled into the airport and she hopped in, throwing her bag in the back. "You gonna tell me," Joe asked. She peeled her sunglasses off and he saw the black eye. "What the hell?" "He saw me with someone else and pushed me. I fell into the damn counter." He drove her to the hospital. They walked in and security surrounded them. "Well, you bruised the bone, but other than one heck of a bruise, you're alright." "Kendra," Joe said. She went to get up and flinched. The doctor checked her out and saw the bruise on her arm and back. "Was this him?" "I got attacked. This is the only place I knew I'd be safe," Kendra said. "Who did it?" "I don't know. I think he was friends with James." "What makes you think that?" "The voice was familiar." "Meaning?" "I don't know." The doctor checked her out and spent hours running tests. "Sprained wrist, bruised ribs." The police came in and talked to her and Joe went to call Ava.

"How did I know," Ava asked. "I'm at the hospital with her." "Why?" "Trust me. You don't want to know." "Whatever," Ava said. "I'll be home in a little while. I'm going to check her into her hotel." "Do what you want." "Babe, I'll be home in an hour. I promise." "Fine." "And I'm bringing Starbucks." "Getting warmer," Ava teased. "I love you." "Better. I love you too." He went back in and walked Kendra outside through a crowd of press and took her to her hotel. "I'll get security to keep an eye on you." "Thanks." "No prob. Just no more 3am calls ok?" Kendra nodded and kissed his cheek.

Joe walked into the house and smelled cinnamon rolls. He walked into the kitchen and saw them on the stove. Ava wasn't there. He heard her upstairs. He walked upstairs, putting the coffee on the bedroom counter and slid into the bathroom behind her. He walked in and saw her in nothing but a towel. He peeled his shirt off, then wrapped his arms around her, going for the towel. "Don't." "You alright," Joe asked. "Not feeling well." "Babe." "Rose is looking after Grace." "Ava." She walked back into the bedroom and laid down. He put the coffee beside the bed and slid into bed with her. "You're like an ice cube," Joe said. "I know." He wrapped his arms around her, trying to warm her up.

An hour or so later, the nausea finally passed. Joe was asleep with her in his arms. When she moved, he woke up. "You okay," he asked yawning. "Better." "Babe, just relax." "Sleep. I'm going to grab some juice," Ava said. He kissed her. "Go back to sleep." "Not until you come back to bed," Joe said. Ava went downstairs, gulped some ginger ale, then went upstairs with another glass of ginger ale. He pulled her back into bed. "If I didn't know better, I'd think you were pregnant again." "What do you mean," Ava said. "You were like this when you were pregnant with Grace." "No I wasn't." "For a month or so you were." An idea popped into her head. She messaged her doctor and asked for a refill on what she'd given her when she was pregnant last time. "What are you doing?" "Nothing," Ava said. The doctor messaged her back that she'd get it delivered that afternoon. Ava curled back up with him and had another cat nap.

They woke up just after lunch and picked Grace up. "Hi Daddy." "Hey princess. You having fun with Jacob?" "Yeah. Home now?" He nodded. Grace ran into his arms. "Mama better?" "Yep." He brought Grace home after a quick chat with Ryan and Rose. Grace came running inside and saw Ava in her office. "Hi Mama." "Hey baby." "Mama better?" Ava nodded. Grace jumped into her lap. She wrapped her arms around Ava. "Babe," Joe said. "Thank you." He went into the kitchen and saw an old medicine bottle on the counter. He looked at it and thought it was familiar. He put it out of his mind and made lunch for him and Ava and Grace. After lunch, Grace went down for her nap.

"So, I have to ask you something." "What," Ava asked. "That bottle on the counter." "Yeah." "Why does the name of it look familiar?" "No idea. They gave it to me when I had that flu bug," "That must be it." They curled up together on the sofa. He saw a gift bag hanging from his guitar. "What's that," Joe asked. "What's what?" "On the guitar." "No idea," Ava said. "Early gift?" Ava shrugged. He got up and grabbed it. There was a small note inside:

The next hint: Where are you most creative?

"A treasure hunt?" Ava laughed. "Nice." He got up and went outside. He saw another note:

Where we lay our head every night.

He went into the TV room and kissed Ava, then grabbed her hand and walked upstairs. He saw a bag on the bed. He reached inside and saw an envelope:

What's the one thing you want more than anything?

He looked at Ava. He opened the envelope and saw baby socks, a pacifier, a baby bottle and one of Grace's toys from when she was a little baby. He looked at Ava. "Babe." "What,"

Ava asked. "Are you telling me what I think you are?" "Nope." Ava went to walk out of the bedroom. He grabbed her hand and pulled her back to him. "Are we?" "I think so." "Babe." "I took a test. It's not 100% unless the doctor says so." He pulled her into his arms and kissed her. "We're pregnant." "No telling anyone," Ava said. "That's what the grin was for. I was right." Ava nodded. He kissed her again, then almost knocked her off her feet and onto the bed.

Rose and Ryan curled up on the sofa after Jacob went to bed. "I bet you anything." "Would you stop? You're almost as bad as Joe." "The last time I saw her look like that was when she was." "Ryan, she isn't. Trust me." "If you say so." "I wouldn't say it to Ava if I were you," Rose said. "Okay." They watched a bit of TV and Rose started wondering if maybe he was right.

The next morning, Ava went into the doctor to get checked out. "If my test and your test say positive, you actually going to believe me," the doctor asked. "Well?" "I'll send the prescription for the prenatal vitamins." "We don't know how far right?" "According to this, probably the first month." "I'm not getting my hopes up," Ava said. "Ava, last time was bad, but it will be fine. We'll keep a close eye on you. No stressing about anything." Ava nodded. "I mean it. None. If you want this baby then you aren't going to get all huffy. Remove stress." "Okay." Ava hugged her and left. She got home and Joe was working on some music. "Hey beautiful." "What you two doing in here," Ava asked. "Picasso over here is drawing a picture." Ava walked over and kissed Grace. "So." Ava kissed him, then went into the kitchen and made lunch. "Woman, tell me." "No." "Ava." "Nobody gets to know until I'm sure it's going to work." "We are, aren't we?" Ava nodded. He kissed her, pinning her against the counter. "Babe." "Nobody," Ava said. "Come on." "No." "Mama, what going on?" "Nothing baby. Grilled cheese for lunch?" "Okay." Grace hugged her leg. "Where you go?" "Just went to the doctor." "For why?" "It was the Mama doctor." "Okay." Grace hugged her leg. "I love Mama." "I love you too baby." Ava picked her up and put her on the counter to help her make the grilled cheese. "Yummy." Joe wrapped his arms around Ava's waist. "Don't you have music to make," Ava teased. He kissed her neck. "I love you." "I know." He kissed her again. "I love you too," Ava said.

Ava finished wrapping the rest of the Christmas presents while Joe gave Grace her bath and put her to bed. There was only a week left, and Joe was worse than a little kid. He was itching to open a present. He came downstairs and slid onto the sofa with her. "So," Joe said. "You aren't opening anything." "Why?" "Stop. If Grace can't, you can't." "Nice. You seriously going to tempt me for an entire week?" Ava nodded. Rose called just as Joe was attempting to coax Ava into coming to bed.

"Hey." "So your parents and Joe's confirmed they're coming. Cat and Scott, Rachel and Carrie and your friend Andrew," Roses said. "Haven't seen him in years," Ava said. "I know. So you still bringing the cookies?" "Half are done. Just have a few left," Ava replied. "You still bringing the egg nog," Rose asked. "Yep." "Ava, why do I get the feeling that there's something you aren't telling me?" "You know everything there is to know," Ava said. "Right." "Other than what your Christmas gift is." "Emily said she would look after the kids," Rose said. "We're bringing Grace for a little while." "She can curl up with Jacob." "Okay." "Find something to wear yet," Ava asked. "I'm going tomorrow." "The awards are tomorrow." "Shit." "I know." "Tomorrow morning first thing." "See you at 9 then." They chatted for a few minutes, then Ava headed upstairs with Joe.

"You know it's going to take all the strength I have not to tell anyone," Joe said. "You spill the beans you're in shit." "I know. Still though." "We can tell them after I know nothing's going to happen." "Babe, you can't worry." "I'm going to," Ava said. She got changed for bed and he slid his arms around her. "Would you still get mad if I said it after we won all the awards we were nominated for," Joe asked. "Yes." "Even if I said I love you a million times on stage?" Ava nodded. She brushed her teeth and washed up before bed. "What if I just told . . ." "Nobody. Ryan would tell Rose, Brad would tell Danielle." "What about Cat? She is your best friend," Joe said. "No." "I still can't believe it." "I know baby. I know you're excited but after what happened . . . ." He kissed her. "No more worrying." "I'm just saying," Ava replied. "I know. I won't. I promise." "When we tell everyone, I'll let you do it. Sound good?" He kissed her. Joe took her hand and led her into the bedroom. "Come lay down." "Don't start with that again." "I'm not." Ava laid down and curled up in his arms. "I still can't believe it." "You were definitely determined." "Doesn't mean we can't still practice," Joe teased. Ava laughed and he kissed her.

The next day, Ava got up early with Rose and headed to the store. They got a dress for the party, and a pair of heels. "You know you're glowing," Rose said. "I'm just happy." "Liar." "You're hilarious." "Are you," Rose asked. "No." "You sure?" "Positive." "So what time are you coming by at Christmas," Rose asked. "Your crew is coming to our place for dinner. It's already put together." "You aren't seriously cooking for that many people," Rose asked. Ava nodded. "Okay. I'll bring the dessert." "Danielle's bringing salad and veggies." "Anything else?" "Nope. Joe said he was helping," Ava said. Rose giggled. "Don't even. He can cook. He's not just a sexy guitar player you know." Rose laughed again. "What?" Joe slid his arms around Ava's waist. "You know I'm married right?" "Damn right I do," Joe said. "Hi Mama," Grace said. "Hey baby girl." "Grace wanted to do shopping," Joe said. "I bet she did." He kissed Ava. "So what are you gonna wear tonight," Ava asked

Rose. "The royal blue one. I'll save the red one for Saturday," Rose said. "So I'll meet you at my place to do hair?" "At 3." Ava hugged her and left with Joe and Grace. "Couldn't wait for me to come home could you," Ava asked. He shook his head and kissed her again. A crowd formed. They headed to the SUV. "Babe." "What?" He slid Grace into her car seat. He closed the door and kissed Ava. "I love you too." She slid into the SUV and they headed home.

They pulled in, had lunch with Grace, then put her down for a nap. The minute he stepped out of her bedroom, he was face to face with Ava. "Hey beautiful wife of mine." "Hey yourself." He kissed her. "What you doing?" "Nothing," Ava said. "Come with me then." She smirked. He slid his hand in hers and they walked into their bedroom. "Something I forgot to tell you this morning." "What's that?" He pulled her into his arms and kissed her. "I love you." "I love you too." "She really did miss you." "I know who else did," Ava said. "Fine. I admit that I missed you." "Oh really." "I rolled over and there was nobody there." "And just what were you rolling over for?" He unbuttoned her jeans. "Something." "Really," Ava said. He kissed her again. "What you doing?" "Do-over." Ava smiled. He undid his jeans and they crawled into bed, kicking their jeans to the floor. He peeled the tank top off of her and kissed her. "Better," Joe said. He wrapped his arms around her. "Babe." "Yes love." "You know we're singing tonight right?" Ava nodded. "They want us to sing Love Letter." "On national TV?" He nodded. "You didn't tell me that," Ava said. "I know." "Shit." "Sound check is done." "When?" "While you were shopping." "Sneaky. Why didn't you just tell me," Ava asked. "Stress." Ava shook her head and laughed.

She kissed him, which led to more kissing and the rest of their clothes on the floor. They made love while Grace slept. They showered and made love in the shower, then finally started getting ready for the awards. They showed to do her hair and Rose's around 3:30. Joe sat downstairs with Jacob and Ryan and played a little music. Grace went in to sit with Ava. "Pretty Mama." "Thanks baby." They finished hair and makeup, then the hair and makeup team headed to see Danielle. Joe came upstairs as Ava was sliding the dress on. "Wow." "Zip," Ava asked. He kissed her neck while he zipped her dress up. "You know the zipper should go down," Joe said. "Stop." He kissed her again. "Mama pretty right Daddy." "Very," Joe said. He went in and shaved while Ava got the kids settled. He came downstairs a half-hour later looking 'sexy as hell' as Ava put it. Emily showed and they kissed the kids goodbye and headed to the show.

CHAPTER 28

They walked down the red carpet, answered what seemed like a million and one questions, then headed inside. They chatted with a few of the guys' friends then sat down. The first award came up. "Best Video goes to Aces for Love Letters." Joe hugged Ava and kissed her. She walked up to the stage with the guys. "Firstly, I have to thank my beautiful wife Ava for being part of this with us. The song wouldn't be here without her . . . ." The guys did their thing, Ava said a little something, and they headed off. The minute they were backstage, Joe picked her up and kissed her. "Holy shit." "You know we have three more," Ryan said. They went back to their seats. Joe's fingers were locked together with Ava's, and his arm was around her. After a few more awards, they got ready for the performance. "No getting nervous," Joe said. Ava nodded. "I love you." "Love you too." They headed on, did their song, dedicating it to Grace and Jacob, then headed back to their seats.

By the end of the night, they'd won for every award they were nominated for again. They went home with one for each of them. "I still can't believe this," Ava said. "Believe it. We did it baby." Joe kissed Ava. They headed to the after party, went through another barrage of press, then relaxed. "Babe," Joe said. She looked. He nodded and grabbed two sodas with lime. "You have to have a drink to celebrate," Ryan said. "Headache," Ava said. "Joe." "Fine." He had one or two with the guys. She danced with Joe, Rose with Ryan and Danielle with Brad. Finally, after the guys had one too many, they headed home. They snuck past Emily, and Joe and Ava went to bed. Ryan and Rose got home and were asleep on the sofa, and Danielle and Brad got home and curled up in bed.

Ava woke up and the award was the first thing she saw. Joe wrapped his arms around her and kissed her neck. "Morning beautiful." "Morning to you too my sexy husband." "Ooh," Joe said. He kissed her. "You were great last night." "So were you." "I was just going to have soda with you," Joe said. "Babe, you're allowed to celebrate with them." "I know I just didn't want you to feel . . ." Ava kissed him. "I love you for not making it weird. It's fine." "How's baby this morning?" "Fine." He kissed her. She wrapped her arms around him. "Emily took the kids to the park," Joe said. Ava nodded. He kissed her again and one led to two. He made love to her, then they curled back up in bed together. "You know I have to go do another book reading," Ava said. "Where?" "Vegas, L.A. and New York." "After new year's though right?" Ava nodded. "Good. Road trip." Ava smiled. "You're always there to support me and the guys. I'm always going to do that for you too," Joe said. "Thank you." "Babe, we wouldn't have got those awards without your help." "Had nothing to do with the fact that you three are blessed with that talent right," Ava asked. "The right song is what makes us good." "Then we're a good team." He nodded and kissed her. "Always will be," Joe said. She leaned her head on his shoulder and they curled up together.

Saturday came. Rose was spinning with things to do, while Ava and Joe spent some time with their parents and family. Grace played with her grandparents and cousins, and they talked all afternoon. Joe and Ava took them to their hotels, then went home to get changed. Grace was asleep in the SUV. They pulled in and put her down for a nap, then went to get ready. Ava slid on the black lace lingerie that Joe loved. "I wouldn't if I were you," Joe said. "Why's that?" He looked at her and she laughed. "We're going," Ava said. "We can be fashionably late," Joe teased. Ava shook her head. He wrapped his arms around her in her satin robe and walked her backwards towards their bed. "We're not . . . ." He kissed her and leaned her onto the bed. He kissed and teased until she gave in. Her body was humming. "We don't really have to go do we," he asked. "You want your mom asking what we were doing," Ava asked. He smirked. "Don't you even answer that." They got up and finished getting ready. Ava slid into the black velvet dress he'd picked out and they got Grace changed, then headed to dinner.

After a few hours with family and laughs, jokes and stories, Ava and Joe headed home with Grace. They tucked her into bed, then curled up in bed. "You know how tempted I was to tell them," Joe said. "Thank you." "We have to say something." "No." "Ava." "Not one word." "At Christmas dinner?" Ava shook her head. He kissed her. They snuggled together. "Babe." "Yes love." "Can we tell Grace," Joe asked. "No." He kissed her again and slid his arms around her. "You are such a party pooper." Ava smiled. "You still love me anyway," Ava said. "Very very true."

Christmas finally came. Grace woke up Christmas morning and saw everything Santa had left her. She ripped into every present for her, and was excited. She played with all of her toys while Ava and Joe opened their presents to each other. Grace fell asleep around 11am. She was immersed in her toys. Ava carried her to bed and tucked her in. "Just think. In 7 more months, there's going to be a baby in that crib," Joe said. "Good thing we got her the bed then," Ava said. He kissed her. "This has been the best Christmas," Joe said. "Oh really?" He nodded. "Got the best gift ever." "The guitar?" "Funny." He kissed Ava. "No telling the world at dinner either," she said. He kissed her and took her hand. They closed Grace's door and he talked Ava into going back to bed. "Everyone's going to be here at 4."

"I know." "I have to . . ." "Turkey's in. Everything's fine." Everything was set for everyone to come. He curled up with Ava. "Thank you." "For what?" "All of this," Ava said. "Babe, you haven't seen anything yet." "Meaning?" "I got you one other present." "Oh really?" "Giving it to you at dinner." "You've done more than enough. I just wanted Grace to have a fairytale Christmas." "I know. You deserve a little something too." "Already got what I wanted," Ava said. She kissed him. "You're the best present anyone ever gave me, but still." "You're peaking my interest." "Good." He kissed her again and she slid her leg around his.

———

Jacob was asleep amongst the wrapping paper and presents by 10am. Ryan and Rose watched him and couldn't help smiling. It was the exact reaction they wanted. They opened their presents to each other. A little sparkle, a little satin and lace, and a few gadgets and they were happy. "You know, I never understood what people meant about kids making Christmas special, but now I get it," Ryan said. "He looks so happy," Rose said. "I know. Santa was definitely good to him." "Don't think I could ask for anything more to make this day better." "Oh really." "Babe, you outdid yourself. How did you know about the watch," Ryan asked. "A little bird in a black SUV told me." "Seriously?" "Was shopping with Joe and Ava and he pointed it out." "I love it. Do you like the necklace?" She nodded. "It's beautiful." "What are we gonna do now?" We can't wake him up," Ryan said. Rose got up and motioned for her to follow him. "What?" She slid her hand in his and walked up the steps. "You know you read my mind," Ryan teased. "We were up late. We need more sleep." They slid back into bed then fell asleep curled up together.

———

After another two rounds, Ava and Joe finally started trying to get dressed. She slid on her red dress that almost delayed them more, and did her hair. "You know you could just not do the makeup." "Good point," Ava said. She put on a little mascara and some lip gloss. "Mmm." "We have a half-hour before everyone's coming." Joe kissed her and leaned her into the bathroom door. "I love you." "I love you too. Thank you for all of this today." "Thank you for being willing to put up with my crazy family." He kissed her then he heard Grace wake up. One last kiss, and he went in and got Grace. She hopped out of his arms and ran to the bathroom, then came out a few minutes later. "What you doin?" "Potty," Grace said. He looked over at Grace. "Surprise," Ava said. He laughed. He brought her into her room and helped her pick out a party dress. Joe got her all changed, then headed downstairs where Ava was checking to make sure everything was done. The food was ready and staying warm in the oven, the bar was set up and everything was together, and just in time.

Rose and Ryan showed with Emily and Jacob, then Ava's parents pulled in. An hour later, everyone was there. They were oohing and aahing over Danielle and her pregnant tummy, and playing with the kids. They all had a drink, while Ava started putting dinner out. "Babe," Joe said. She looked over at Joe. "Yes love." He motioned for her to come. "2 minutes," Ava said. He shook his head. He slid his hand in hers and led her to the steps.

"First, Merry Christmas to everyone. Secondly, I'm glad all of you could be here. We've had a really long year, and we're glad Ryan finally decided to let us take a little time off," Joe said. Ryan laughed. "This year has been an amazing roller coaster ride. We've had a few additions to the family with Brad and Danielle's new baby to be, and I think Grace found her first boyfriend," Joe said. Everyone laughed. "I'm just happy we could all be here together and celebrate Christmas the way it should be . . . . with family." Everyone said cheers and they went back to talking. Ava put dinner out and Joe called everyone to eat.

Ava finally sat down beside Joe and he laughed. "What?" "Can you sit for 5 minutes," he asked. "Think I might be able to." "Good." He handed her an envelope. "What's this?" Everything got a little quiet. Ryan smirked. Rose looked at him. "What do you know," Rose said. He motioned for her to be quiet. Ava opened it and found two envelopes. She opened the first one and saw pictures of Grace and Joe. They were beautiful. There was a black and white shot, and a color one. Then there were two of just him. She looked at him. "I know," he said. She opened up the other envelope and found two tickets to Cabo. "Oh really." Joe nodded. "Back to the scene of the crime." Ava wrapped her arms around him and kissed him. "Thank you baby," Ava said. "It's for me and you and Grace. Just us on the beach." Everyone looked. "We're going back to where we got married," Joe said. Everyone clapped and then went back to talking. "Scene of the crime?" "Where I stole you away forever," Joe said. Ava kissed him. Rose snuggled up to Ryan. "See, guys know just what to do to make their women happy," Ryan said. "That you do," Rose replied. Ryan leaned over and kissed Rose.

After a few more hours, and a few family presents, everyone started heading home. Only people left were Ava and Joe, Ryan and Rose, Danielle and Brad and Emily. "There was something else in the envelope," Joe said. "No there wasn't," Ava said. Joe nodded. He slid his hand in his pocket. Ryan looked. Rose smiled. Danielle and Brad were snuggled up together. "How could you possibly . . . ." He pulled out a platinum eternity band. "Baby," Ava said. He kissed her. "You know what this means right?" "Don't mind being stuck with you forever," Ava said. "Good." Joe kissed Ava. "I gotta ask something," Ryan said. "What's that," Joe replied. "Why didn't Ava have champagne?" Rose elbowed him. "I was too busy running around to have bubbles go to my head." "Okay. I'll buy that," Ryan said. Joe had his arms around hers and slid his hand to her stomach. Rose noticed. "Ava." "What,"

Ava asked. She looked at her. Ava shook her head. "You sure?" Ava nodded. "What," Ryan asked. "Nothing." "Liar," Ryan said. Joe kissed her and went in and made coffee.

Ava walked into the kitchen behind him as Ryan and Rose sat down with Danielle and Brad. "I swear." "Didn't even realize it," Joe said. "Stop." He kissed her and leaned her against the counter. "You drive me nuts." "And you love me," Joe said. "No idea why." Joe kissed her again. "Did you want some," he asked. "Funny." "One cup." "Better make the Starbucks then." He kissed her. They went back in and sat down with the rest of the group. They chatted a while, then Ava got up and got the coffee. She carried everything in and they had coffee. "So, I'm gonna ask, even though I probably shouldn't. The last time you decided no coffee and no wine or anything ended up with the adorable Miss Grace. Anything you want to tell us," Brad asked as Danielle elbowed him. "You just stuck on that tonight aren't you," Ava asked. "She's having coffee Brad. Leave her be," Danielle said. Joe looked at Ava. "Thank you Danielle." "We're trying," Ava said. "I think Grace might love having a little sister to play with," Danielle said. "That's why you're having the baby," Joe teased. "Funny." They talked a while later, then Brad and Danielle headed home. Finally Ryan slid Jacob out of the bed with Grace and they headed home.

Ava finished the last of the dishes. "Babe." "They're done," Ava said. Joe slid his arms around her waist. "You almost gave it away you know." "I know." "We're not telling anyone," Ava said. "I know. I just wish we could." "You know why Joe." "Yeah. I do. I also know that the longer we wait, the more they're going to ask. I mean last time you started showing after 2 months." "New year's," Ava said. Joe kissed her. "You can't wait that long can you?" "Depends." "On?" Joe turned her towards him and kissed her with a mind blowing, knees buckling and toe curling kiss. He picked her up, sliding her heels off and wrapping her legs around him, then carried her to the sofa. There wasn't a word between them the rest of the night . . . . that is unless they spoke body language.

The next morning, Ava woke up sick. Joe took care of Grace while Ava tried to calm her stomach. "What Mama doing?" "She's laying down baby," Joe said. "Can we go play with Mama?" He picked Grace up and slid onto the bed with Ava. Grace jumped over to Ava and snuggled her. "Mama sick?" "No." "Okay." After an hour or so, they got up. Joe fed Grace some breakfast, and Ava made breakfast for her and Joe. Grace ran off to play with her toys, and Joe and Ava relaxed. "You feeling any better," Joe asked. Ava nodded. "The only part you hate. I know." "Just dizzy." He got up and grabbed a Gatorade from the fridge and handed it to her. "Thanks." He kissed her. "So what we up to today?" "You already know the answer." "Not without security," Joe said. "Joe, I don't need security." "Yeah you do. Especially now." "Joe." "I mean it. I'm not letting anything happen to you." "You're sweet, but I'm not going to be gone that long." "Then we're going with you." "Then we'll definitely need security," Ava said. "Babe, please just let me take care of you. We don't need to go anyway." "Yeah I do." "For what?" "Bathing suit for Cabo." He kissed her. "Then I'm going. I'll call and tell security." Ava kissed him. She went upstairs and hopped into the shower. As she was stepping in she heard the front door open and close and Joe was chatting with someone.

Ava slid into the shower and within a few minutes, he was in there with her. "Emily?" He nodded. He kissed her. He grabbed her loofah and washed her back. "You know how beautiful you are?" "Not so bad yourself handsome." He kissed her. "You sure you're up for trying on bikinis," Joe asked. "Stop." "Just saying." "Then we wait until after the baby. Your choice." Ava stepped out and went into the bedroom. She slid on her leggings and a top with her boots, put her hair up, then put on some makeup. She was about to walk out of the bedroom when he pulled her back towards him. "I'm just saying," Joe said. "I know. If you're coming, then get dressed." He kissed her. "We're going together." "Then you really should put something else on other than the towel. Could cause a really big crowd," Ava teased. He kissed her again and slid his hand down her torso, then to her butt. "Don't you start that again." He pulled her towards him and picked her up. "Put me down." He shook his head. He went back into the bathroom and sat her on the counter. "We have to go." He kissed her. He shaved, then kissed her. She wiped the shaving cream off his nose. He kissed her again, then he got dressed.

Joe and Ava headed to the mall with security, went to the stores Ava wanted to check out and one of his favorites, then headed home. They came inside and relaxed with Grace, watching a movie until she fell asleep. Ava tucked her into bed, then came downstairs. "Where did Emily go," Ava asked. "Home. She has a date tonight." "I'm glad. She needs to get out more." "Promise me you'll stay home tomorrow with me," Joe said. "Okay." "And I get to pamper you tomorrow." "Joe." "Nope. Not one finger." "Fine." "And no phones." "All the rules," Ava joked. "You don't stick to them you're in trouble." Ava smirked. "And that isn't getting you out of it either." "What isn't," Ava asked as she slid into his lap. "You start it . . ." Ava kissed him. "You are starting something woman.," Joe said. Ava nodded and got up. He pulled her back to his lap. "I told you." "Yep." Ava got up and went into the kitchen, grabbed herself a vitamin water and he slid up behind her. "What are you doing?" "Grabbing a drink." "I see that." She turned and faced him. "What you doin?" He kissed her and pinned her to the fridge. "Come back to the sofa," he said. He turned around and grabbed her hands, leading her back to the sofa. She leaned into his lap. "What movie are we watching," Ava asked. He kissed her. "So no movie?" He laughed and leaned her onto the sofa pillow.

"Babe." "Mmm." "You love me?" Ava nodded. "So if I told them before New year's eve . . . ." "What did you do?" "Nothing." "Liar," Ava said. "Ryan called when we were at the mall." "And?" "I told him we were shopping for a bikini." "Joe." "He asked why we didn't go earlier and I told him you were sick this morning." "Great." "Babe, it's not that big of a deal." Her phone rang two minutes later. "Ava." "Hi Rose." "Sick all morning?" "Fine. Come over." Ava hung up and called Brad and Danielle over. She called her mom and dad and told them, then Joe's parents. "All your damn fault," Ava said. He kissed her. "Don't you dare start sucking up now." Joe kissed her again. Everyone showed up ten minutes later.

"So what's going on," Danielle asked. Ava looked at Joe. "Go ahead," Ava said. "Remember the other night when you asked why Ava wasn't drinking, and then you asked if she was pregnant?" "You are, aren't you," Rose asked. "Almost 2 months." "Why didn't you tell anyone," Danielle said. "We had our reasons. Just decided we're trying to keep it quiet. Nobody else knowing." "Seriously guys," Ava said. "Okay," they said. They all agreed. Rose wrapped her arms around Ava and hugged her and Danielle hugged her. Everyone headed home after and Ava went into the kitchen. She poured her vitamin water into an ice cold glass and sat outside. Joe came out a few minutes later and wrapped them in a blanket. "I am so kicking your butt," Ava said. "You love it though." "Stop trying to be cute. I'm mad." "I'm sorry," Joe said. "Let's just hope they keep it quiet." "When we get back on stage, the fans will notice." "Not if I wear something different." "Babe, you can't hide it forever." "I can try. I don't want the press all over us," Ava said. "I know, but it's something we should be celebrating." "And what happens if . . ." "Don't even think it." "I'm being realistic Joe." "You're not allowed to be stressed out." "I'm going to be." "Babe. Please." "I was fine when nobody else knew. If something happened, we could just deal with it just us." "I know. The baby's going to be fine. I promise," Joe said. "You don't know that Joe." "You that worried?" Ava nodded.

Joe pulled her into his arms. "I'm going to take care of us." "I know." "Babe, please stop worrying." "We already lost a baby." "And we have Grace," Joe said. "I know." "So whatever happens, we figure it out together. You have Rose to help if you need it." "I just wanted a little while of it just being our thing." "I know babe." They curled up outside for a while, then headed in and curled up on the sofa and watched a movie. Grace finally woke up and they had dinner, then played with Grace a while before they gave her a bath and put her down for the night. They headed to bed and curled up together. "You feeling any better?" "I just was trying to make things easier," Ava said. "Stop worrying." "I was thinking." "Oh damn." "Funny. I think we should get a real nanny." "Babe, Emily's fine with it." "I know, but it's not fair to ask her to put our kids first." "Ava, this is what she wants. She wanted to be their nanny." "I know, but she has a man in her life now." "And he knows that she's a nanny and the kids come first." "You sure it's not going to cause a problem," Ava asked. "She's family." "I know. That's why it will never be a problem. Besides, Grace loves her. If she left . . ." "I know," Ava said. "Stop trying to take the world on Ava. We're all supposed to work together. You can't do it alone." "I know." He kissed her to distract her from everything that was running through her mind.

"Now that Grace is asleep . . ." "What?" "You going to let me read it," Joe asked. He was itching to read the new book that she'd been hiding for months. "Maybe." "Tease." "If you want to. I put a copy on the shelf in the office," Ava said. "About darned time woman." "You've been busy too smart ass." "I know. Now we get a few weeks for just us." "You know what's going to happen when word gets out right," Ava said. "Other than the fans probably sending us baby stuff like last time?" "The press is going to be all over us." "And?" "Not funny," Ava said. "And you're going to be as beautiful as you always are and I'm going to love you even more than yesterday." "Suck up." Joe laughed and kissed her. "Just know how to get you in a good mood." "And how's that," Ava asked. He slid on top of her and she wrapped her legs around him. He pulled her close and kissed her, then moved down to her neck, and her shoulder. She felt the shirt slide up her back and he peeled it off, followed by his own. Just as he was going for the button of her jeans, Grace was crying. "Don't move," Joe said getting up.

"Baby, what's wrong," Joe asked. "Monster." "Where?" She pointed at the window. Joe looked and saw someone running across the front lawn. He went into the bedroom, grabbed the cordless and called the security gate. Within a few minutes, they had the person in custody. He tucked Grace back in and sat with her until she was asleep. Joe came back into the bedroom and Ava was curled up on the bed, in lingerie, asleep. He slid his jeans off, turned the light off, then curled up in bed beside her. He wrapped his arm around her and kissed her neck. "She okay?" "Yes babe," Joe said. "What was wrong?" "Nothing." A minute later the security officer was calling.

"It's been handled. She won't be on the premises again." "Who was it?" "Jada James." "Seriously? Didn't I tell you to keep an eye," Joe asked. "I know. She got passed the gate." "Next time." "I know." Joe hung up. "What was all that," Ava asked. "Nothing." She turned to face him. "Tell me." "Grace saw someone at her window. When I went in, they took off," Joe said. "And who was it?" "Nobody." "Joe, just say it," Ava said. "An old girlfriend." "She was trying to get in the house," Ava asked. "It's handled." He slid his arm around her. Ava got up and slid on her leggings and his shirt, then went downstairs. She slid on her flip flops and walked down to the gate.

"Mrs. Morgan," the security man said. "She still here?" "Yes." Ava walked into the room they had her in. "Any reason in particular you think it's alright to scare a little girl," Ava asked. "I wanted to see Joe." "You want to see him, you went about it the wrong way. Get a ticket for a concert like everyone else." "Who do you think you are," Jada said. "His wife." "Stupid move. You know he's a player." "And we've been married well over a year.

Almost two actually," she said. "He knows me." "What's your point? We both know a lot of people." "I want to talk to him." "Not happening. Instead you get me. You even think of showing up at our house again, I will get you in major shit. Got me," Ava asked. Ava turned to walk out and Joe was talking to the security guys with Grace in his arms. She went to walk past him and Joe grabbed her hand. "Where you going?" "Home." She slid Grace out of his arms and started walking home. "Babe." She kept walking. She went inside and tucked Grace back into her bed. Within a few minutes, Grace was out cold.

Ava walked back into the bedroom and he was sitting on the bed. "Don't even," Ava said. "Babe, no taking off. You don't know how risky that was." "Why?" "Babe, just don't." "Joe, after kickboxing for years, and putting up with your fans for 2 years, I think I can handle her." "I know you're tough, but she's not exactly totally all there." "If she comes back here, she'll see I meant what I said." "You realize that you risked the baby? They said no stress," Joe said. "Fine." "No more stupid shit. I don't care if you're trying to defend Grace or not." "Fine." "I mean it." "I know. So I have to ask, who the hell is she," Ava asked. "An old girlfriend." "There's more to it and you know it." "She's nuts. It was a long time ago. Not a good time." "I bet." Ava walked back downstairs and grabbed herself a drink, then curled up on the sofa with her laptop. He came downstairs and slid the laptop off her lap. "Come back to bed." "No." "Ava, I know you're mad." "Understatement." "Babe." "Don't Joe." "Come to bed." "Then tell me the rest of the story." "The I wanna be a rockstar phase. I was stupid, self-destructive and not thinking with the right brain." "Like now," Ava asked. She got up. "Babe." "Don't. Joe, if it means moving away from here to get some peace and quiet for Grace, then I'll do it, with or without you." "Stop it," Joe said. "I'm not going to sit here while your legion of ex's decide to stalk you." "Babe, you're losing it." "No. First it's ex's calling, then showing up at the concerts. Now they're trying to break into our house." "And that's why we live where we do. It's better security," Joe said. "Then how did she get this close?" Ava walked upstairs, checked on Grace and went and slid into a hot shower.

She came out and he was sitting on the counter. "Babe." She slid a towel around her. "I know why you're mad." "I'm not fighting with you about it," Ava said. "Good." She went to walk into the bedroom and he slid in front of her. "What?" "You don't seriously want to move." "I want her safe." "She is." "Promise me," Ava said. Joe kissed her. "She's safe. Baby is going to be fine, and so are we." "All of this is getting to be too much." "Baby, we're fine. Everything's fine." "No it isn't." "Babe, we're going to be fine. Just keeps us on our toes," Joe said. "I don't want to worry that Grace isn't safe." "Then we upgrade the security system." "Joe." "First thing tomorrow. I promise." "I'm sick of worrying," Ava said. "Then don't." He slid his arms around her. "Babe, no more stressing out. I know you're upset. I'm pissed that she got this far." "I just want to relax." "Then we leave right after New Year's." "What about the recording?" "We're more important," Joe said. "Joe."

"We both need a break for a while." "That scared the shit out of me." Joe wrapped his arms around her and held her close. "I know babe. It scared me too." He held her then kissed her shoulder. Then her neck, smelling the sweet scent of her lavender body wash. "No more worrying. I'm here," Joe said. She nodded and they curled up in bed. "I'm gonna keep you and Grace safe, and you are stuck with me for life remember?" "Never forget it," Ava said. "I love you babe." "I love you too." Ava kissed him and they tried to get some sleep.

CHAPTER 29

The next morning, Ava woke up and Joe wasn't there. Grace was gone, and so was his car. She got up, had a hot shower, then had breakfast and relaxed. She got a few chapters into the new book and noticed the time. She called his cell and there was no answer. She took a deep breath, then decided to go shopping. After a few hours at the mall, she headed home. Still no sign of either of them. Ava had dinner, then curled up with her laptop and got some writing done. She fell asleep on the sofa waiting for them to come home.

Around 3am, Ava heard the front door. She got up and headed to the door to ask where he'd been. "Hey beautiful." "Where the hell," Ava asked. "Studio." "Where's Grace?" "With Rose." "You didn't even leave a note." "You knew I was in the studio today and tomorrow." "I was up at 8 Joe." "I'm sorry." "Good." Ava walked upstairs and slid into her pajamas and went to bed. He came upstairs, got undressed and slid into bed with her. "So what did you do today?" "You mean other than wonder where the hell you were," Ava asked. "Babe, I told you." "No you didn't. There was no note, no nothing." "You were worried." "You think," Ava asked. "I'm sorry." "Good." He slid his arms around her. "I thought you needed a day to relax." "Too bad I didn't." "Did you get any writing done?" "Yep." "Babe." "It's fine. Next time, leave me a note," Ava said. "I will. I have to go back tomorrow." "Okay." He kissed her neck. "I missed you." "If I'd known you were there, I would've popped by." "We got a few more songs together." "Good." "Finished one I wrote for you." "Oh really," Ava asked. "About us." "Suck up." Joe kissed her neck again. "I missed you." She slid her hand down his arm and linked her fingers with his. "One more week and we're out of here." "We need a vacation." "I know. You know what the best part is," Joe asked. "What?" "You and me on a beach, no phones, no stress and no studio." "What are we doing for New Year's Eve?" "You me and the fireplace." "No party?" "Nope." "Dinner?" "Dessert," Joe teased. "Funny. I meant dinner with the guys." "Just you, me and Grace." "Sounds cozy." "We need us time." Ava turned to face him.

"We do, do we?" Joe nodded. "Miss me?" "Hell yes." He kissed her and his hand slid up her leg. She slid her leg around him. He held her close and kissed her. "I want you so bad,"

Joe said. He kissed her again, holding her face in his hands. He made love to her and things seemed so different. He was different; almost like he was possessed. After, they were both out of breath and their hearts were racing. "Damn." "Who needs to work out after that," Joe asked. He kissed her. He curled up with her and they were asleep a few minutes later.

The next morning, Joe woke up and Ava wasn't there. He went downstairs and she was on the back deck on the phone. He grabbed himself a cup of coffee and went outside. "Hey sexy," Joe said. She hung up. "Morning." "What you doing up so early?" "Couldn't sleep," Ava said. "Babe." "Relax a while. I'm going to get changed." "Where you going?" "Out." Ava walked past him and went inside, then headed upstairs for a shower. He came upstairs a few minutes later and saw her throwing on her leggings, her boots and a sexy top. "Ava." "Yes." "What's going on in that head of yours," Joe asked. "Just have some things I need to do if we're going after New Year's." "Babe." "What?" He slid his coffee onto the counter behind her. "What's wrong?" "Nothing." He slid his arms around her. Joe kissed her. "That's better." "You're hilarious," Ava said. "I didn't get my morning kiss." "Don't you have to go into the studio?" "For 10am." "Then you should probably get dressed." He kissed her again. "Better idea." His hands slid up the back of her shirt as his kisses trailed to her neck. "You have to be there in 45 minutes," Ava said. He kissed her again. "Shower. I'll drive you over," Ava said. He kissed her and peeled her shirt off. "Joe." He picked her up and sat her on the bathroom counter. "I just had a shower," Ava said. "I know." He undressed her and pulled her into the shower with him.

They made love in the shower, then hopped out and started getting ready. Ava slid her things back on, fixed her hair, then sprayed on some perfume. "You know that's my favorite," Joe said. "I know. That's why I have it." Joe kissed her neck and they left. Ava picked Grace up, then dropped Joe off. "You coming by," he asked. "Dinner." He kissed her. Grace giggled from the back seat. "Have fun with Mama baby girl." "Bye bye Daddy." He kissed Grace's head, then went into the studio with the guys. "Where Daddy go?" "Work baby." "Okay." "Did you have fun with Jacob?" "We played." "I bet you did," Ava said. Ava talked with Grace all the way to the store. They got a few more of the last-minute things they needed, then grabbed some groceries and headed home. Ava pulled in and saw someone on the front step. She took Grace in the side door, then went to the front. "Can I help you?" The woman turned around. "Cat," Ava asked. "Hey." "What are you doing here?" "Figured you'd be home." "How long have you been here?" "Ten minutes." "Where's the car," Ava asked. "He's at the studio with the guys." "What's wrong?" Cat stood up and wrapped her arms around Ava. She brought her inside.

"What's wrong," Ava asked. "I'm sorry." "For what?" "I was at the studio with them yesterday." "And?" "I walked in on something," Cat said. "Who?" Cat looked at her. "What happened?" "He was talking to some woman, then they kissed. He saw me and walked out," Cat said. Ava walked upstairs, grabbed her bag and packed. "What are you doing?" She threw a week's worth of clothes in the bag, then packed one for Grace. She called the travel agent. "I need to change the date on two of the three tickets," Ava said. "To when?" "Now." "There's a flight that leaves at 3." "Perfect," Ava said. She hung up. "Where are you going," Cat asked. "He knows you're going to tell me." "Ava, where are you going," Cat asked. "Vacation." Ava dropped Cat off at the studio, then left.

Ava pulled into the airport, checked their bags, then left with Grace.

Cat walked into the studio. She kissed Scott and sat down with him. "How's my baby," he asked. She looked at him. "What?" "I saw what happened yesterday," Cat said. "You mean Joe?" She nodded. "Tell me you didn't say anything to Ava." "I'm her best friend Scott." "Shit. Joe, you might want to hear this." He came into the room. "What's up?" "I saw you yesterday," Cat said. "She's a friend." "I'm not blind Joe." "What did you do?" "Nothing." "You talked to Ava." She nodded. "You're gonna pull this, she deserves to know," Cat said. "Fuck." He called her phone and it went straight to voicemail. He called the house and there was no answer. He called Emily. "I don't see her SUV there." "Emily, go check and see if the suitcase is there." "It's not," Cat said. "Where did she go?" "No idea." Joe called the travel agent. "She changed the date for the tickets. The flight just left."

Ava got to the villa and put Grace down for a nap. She sat down on the balcony and put her feet up and turned her computer on. She logged into email and saw one from Joe:

Babe:

I'm on my way. I swear it's not what you think.

She deleted the message. She saw one from the band manager. It was a listing of the new tour dates. They'd knocked it down to three every two weeks. There was another one from her book agent. The book was selling really well. They wanted to book some more readings. Ava emailed them back and said to book one day a week. She logged off and tried to relax. She slid her bikini on, then sat outside and enjoyed the warm weather. An hour or so later, she had dinner with Grace and curled up in bed. She read to her for a little while, then tucked Grace into bed, turned off the light and went to sleep.

Two hours passed and Ava heard the door. She heard Joe's bags hit the floor. He walked into the bedroom and saw her asleep on the bed. She heard him kicking his things off and he slid into bed with her. Joe pulled her into his arms and curled up with her. He kissed her neck. She shrugged him off. "Babe." "Don't," Ava said. She got up, sliding her satin robe on and went out to the balcony. "Ava." "Don't even bother making an excuse Joe."

"It isn't what you think." "Heard it a million times." "Baby, you have to believe me." "No I don't," Ava said. She sat down on the chaise. "Please." "No. You act like your damn near possessed last night, then I find this out. I can add one and one Joe. A plus B doesn't equal F." "Ava." "No. Nothing you could possibly say could change this." "Come inside." "No." "Ava, it isn't what it looked like," Joe said. "Then you damn well tell me what it was? You were kissing someone else. Cat saw it, and you took off with whoever it was. Tell me how that wasn't what she said." "Babe." "Don't you dare," Ava said. "First, she kissed me." "And that makes a difference why?" "I walked her out and told her not to come back." "Funny how your exes pop up whenever you're alone isn't it?" Ava refused to let him see her cry. "Ava, come on." She got up and went inside then went and made tea. "Would you stop?" "Why don't you? Nothing you can say is changing this," Ava said. "I love you." "And every other woman who walks past you." Joe pulled her to him. "Let go." He kissed her, holding her face in his hands. "I love you. I'm not going to intentionally hurt you." "So you accidentally kissed her? Nice try." He pulled her back into his arms and kissed her again. "Stop," Ava said. "Don't you dare . . ." He kissed her again and leaned her up against the kitchen counter.

"This ends now," Joe said. "Good. Go home then." "I mean the fighting." "So do I," Ava said. "Ava, I didn't do anything." "Other than kiss her you mean." "She kissed me. I walked her outside and made her leave." "Who was she?" "Kelly." "As in your ex-girlfriend?" He nodded. "The same Kelly I told to stay the hell away from you?" "I told her to leave." "How'd she get into the studio Joe? Security is there." "I don't know." "Dumb move," Ava said. "Babe, I swear." "Don't." "I swear I didn't." "Move," Ava said. "No." "Move." "Not until you believe me." "Move." She pushed him away and went for the bathroom. She came out a few minutes later and went back to bed. She was shivering when he came back into the room. He sat down on the bed beside her and heard her teeth chattering. "Babe." "Just leave me alone," Ava said. "You're shaking." "Go." He slid into the bed with her and pulled her close. "Joe, just go." "Not until you stop shaking." He curled up with her and held her until the shaking stopped and she was asleep.

The next morning, he woke up to Grace jumping onto the bed. "Hi Daddy." "Hey baby girl. Where's Mama?" "She outside." "Oh. Let's go find her then." "Okay." He pulled his jeans on and picked Grace up, tickling her in his arms. They went outside and Ava was doing yoga on the beach. He grabbed himself some coffee, then when Ava was finished, they went down to the beach.

"Hi Mama," Grace said as they walked onto the beach. "Hey princess." "Daddy's up," Grace said. "I see that." Joe went to kiss Ava and she turned her cheek. This wasn't exactly how he'd planned the week to go. They played with Grace as she ran around on the beach, then went in the water for a bit, then came in and had lunch. After lunch, Grace went down for a nap and Ava went and sat outside on the balcony with her laptop. "Babe." She ignored him. He slid the laptop out of her hands and put it on the table. "What," Ava asked. "We gonna be like this all week?" "Why? Backup planned?" "That's not fair Ava." "You expected me to be nice," Ava asked. "Ava, please." "Please nothing. You did what you did." "Babe. Enough." "No." He kissed her again, pulling her into his arms. "I didn't do anything. I asked her to back off and stop the stupid crap." "Then what? You two kissed in front of Cat, then you walked her out. What happened then," Ava asked. "Nothing." "Then why . . ." He kissed her. "Cat left. She passed me coming in the door." "Joe." "I swear Ava. Nothing else happened." "You ever . . ." He kissed her and wrapped his arms tight around her. He had her on the sand in minutes. "I love you. You know I'd never be with someone else. Not after what happened," Joe said. "If you even think it." He kissed her again. "Never." "Fine." "Good." He helped her to her feet and led her inside. They walked in and within a few minutes there was a knock at the door. "Message for you sir," the man said. "Thanks." Joe opened the note. He looked at Ava. "What?" "Something happened to my sister," Joe said. "Kyra?" "She's with her," Joe said. He grabbed the phone and called.

"What's going on?" "He busted into the house." "Who," Joe asked. "Don't ask. You already know," Kyra said. "She alright?" "Concussion." "Kyra." "I know. I called your friend to come help." "You want me to come," Joe asked. "It's fine. I'll take her home." "I'll get two tickets to you." "For what?" "You're moving closer," Joe said. "Joe, I don't need this." "You're coming." "Fine." "We'll find you a place nearby." "Joe," Kyra said. "I know. I'll meet you." They talked and Ava made lunch. "Babe." "Go take care of them," Ava said. "No. I'm getting Ryan to pick them up." "Where are they going to stay?" "We'll find them somewhere." "Go." "No. We're finishing our vacation," Joe said. "She needs you." "And I need you. We're staying." He kissed Ava and grabbed half of her sandwich. They sat outside on the patio. "I'm sorry I got you all upset last night." "Let's not discuss it again," Ava said. "Okay babe." They finished lunch, then relaxed on the balcony.

"I had an idea for tonight." "I bet you did." "We can go to dinner." "What about Grace," Ava asked. "We can bring her." "Where?" "Don't worry about it." "Joe, seriously." He kissed her. "We can go downstairs. They're setting up dinner for us." "Oh really." "I asked them last night," Joe said.

They got changed, played with Grace a bit, then headed down for dinner. They talked and went for a walk along the beach, then tucked Grace into bed. The rest of the night, they were curled up together. Somehow things worked themselves out. They always had.

After a week of relaxing, they headed back. Grace was asleep the entire plane ride. They pulled back into the house and Joe put Grace down in bed. Ava unpacked. She saw the answering machine flashing and wasn't even going to chance it. Joe went and pressed play downstairs and Ava heard the messages. "Joe, it's Kelly. I'm sorry about that the other day. I didn't mean to get you in trouble. Give me a call." He laughed and pressed delete. "Ava, it's John. Call me." He pressed delete hoping she wouldn't hear it. "Joe, it's Kyra. We're here. Call me at the hotel. We're in suite 2017." "Bud, where the hell did you disappear to? Call me." Ava heard him pick up the phone.

"Where the hell did you take off to," Ryan asked. "Long story." "She found out about Kelly?" "Cat told her." "I told you," Ryan said. "It's fine. We're home." "How was New Year's Eve?" "Quiet. Just like we wanted." "We're in the studio in the morning." "I'll see you there." "She gonna put a hidden camera on you," Ryan teased. "Funny." "Maybe she needs to." "Don't make me pull out your skeletons." "See you in the morning. Tell Ava to call Rose." "Yep." Joe hung up and walked into the laundry room behind Ava. "What you doing?" "Laundry," Ava replied. "Ava, come to bed." "Not tired." "Even better," Joe said. "Nope. Going to do some writing." "No you aren't." Ava nodded. She turned the washer on, then went and grabbed the phone. "Ava." "I have to call and see what John wanted." She dialed and he was chasing her for the phone.

"Hey stranger." "Hey yourself," Ava said. "How was the vacay?" "Good. Relaxing. How's things?" "Better if you were here," John said. "Funny." "I mean it." "What did you want?" "You." "Seriously." "Was going to see if you wanted to join me for New Year's," John said. "Was away for New Year's." "Ava, tell me you didn't let him talk you into staying," John said. "I have to go." He heard Joe kissing Ava then heard the phone click.

"Joe." "No phones. We're still on vacation until the morning." "Which means," Ava asked. He kissed her and pinned her to the counter. "Joe." He smirked. "I'm tired." "Liar," Joe said. She smirked. He kissed her hard. He picked her up with her legs wrapped around him and walked upstairs. Her phone went off a minute later. "Joe." He shook his head. "Vacation." He walked into their bedroom and leaned her onto the bed. The house phone rang. Ava grabbed it when he went for the bedroom door. "Ava, it's Kyra." "We just got back," Ava said. "Can you come over?" "What's wrong?" "Nightmares. Plus I'm kinda worried about Mom," Kyra said. "We'll be there as soon as we can." "Thanks." Ava hung up. He kissed her. "We have to go to the hotel." "Not right now we don't," Joe said. He peeled her leggings off. "Joe, seriously." He kissed her again and kicked his jeans off. "We should call Emily." He kissed Ava.

One move and he had her full attention. He kissed her and made love to her. "Better," Joe said. He was still just as crazy as the last night they'd spent in this bed, but this time, it had her entire body humming and throbbing. "Joe." He kissed her hard, so hard that he almost wiped out the only breath she had. Her heart was pounding in her chest when they both almost exploded. "Now what were you saying," Joe said catching his breath. "Don't remember."

He kissed Ava. "You know how amazing you are?" Ava laughed. "After that?" He laughed. "Remember something from now on." "What's that?" "Remember that nobody will ever get me in bed with them other than you. We're together forever." "Don't test it," Ava said. He kissed her. She slid her arms around his neck. "Never." The house phone rang again. "Call Emily. I'm going to have a quick shower so we can go." He answered the phone.

"Joe," Kelly said. "What the hell are you trying to pull?" "I'm sorry. I just wanted to apologize so you two wouldn't be fighting." "You did enough. I told you to never come there." "I wanted to see you." "What do you want," Joe asked. "You." He hung up. Ava walked out a minute later in a towel. "Company," he asked. "No. Go see Kelly. While you're at it, see if she'll let you stay." "Ava." "I heard it Joe." "Babe." She pulled her jeans on and her shirt and walked out.

"What's wrong," Ava asked as Kyra answered the door. "I don't get why we had to move. I mean having the bodyguard there should be enough." "Just go along with him," Ava said. "Where is he?" "Don't know. About the nightmares." "Ava, are you two okay?" "No. Thanks for asking. The only thing I can tell you is that the nightmares go away after a while. You have to take control of them," Ava said determined to change the topic. "What happened?" "Nothing." Ava started getting light headed and sat down. "You alright?" "I'll be fine." "I'm sorry I caused all this stress," Kyra said. "It's not you. This I can handle." "What's going on Ava?" "Nothing. Nothing you can do anything about anyway. Just try to be calm. Try yoga. Helps when you're stressed," Ava said. "Okay." "Joe will take you house hunting tomorrow." "Ava." "I'm going to head home." Ava left a few minutes later. She pulled out as Joe was pulling in. "Babe." She kept driving. She went home and relieved Emily. "You two okay," Emily asked. "Just perfect." Emily headed out and Ava went upstairs and sat in the tub. She locked the bedroom door and the bathroom door. She even parked in the garage so he wouldn't know she was there.

Ava relaxed a while, then once the water cooled for the third time, she slid out of the tub, into her pajamas and into bed. Ava took his pillow downstairs and threw a blanket onto the sofa with it. She walked back upstairs and slid into the bed, turning the lights off. She tossed and turned. She looked at the clock. 3am and she hadn't heard a door or his car pull in. Ava rolled over and tried to go back to sleep.

She woke up at 8 and went downstairs. The blanket and pillow were still on the sofa. Ava walked upstairs and got Grace and brought her down for breakfast. "Where Daddy?" "Studio." "Can we go see Daddy?" "If you want to." Ava made breakfast, then they got dressed and went down to the studio. Ava walked in and Grace ran into see Joe. "What are you doing here," Joe asked. "Mama brought me." He looked over and saw Ava on her cell.

He looked at Ryan. "Grace, do you want to try singing with me," Ryan asked. "Okay." He distracted Grace while Joe went and tried to talk to Ava.

Ava saw him coming in and walked outside. "Ava." "What?" "Don't do this." "She wanted to see you." "Babe." "Don't you dare," Ava said. "I told her never to come to the studio. That we were done. That's what she meant." "She wants you. Better run just in case she changes her mind." Joe grabbed Ava's hand, pulling her back to him. "Let go." He kissed her and pinned her to the wall. "Stop." Ava tried to fight him. "Ava, stop it." "Get away from me." "Not until you make it stick. Kelly and I are done. She came here to tell me she's moving." "Oh goodie," Ava said. "Stop it." "She give you her forwarding address so you could pop in?" "Woman, you are driving me nuts." Joe kissed her again. "I love you. I always will. Stop being so damn pissed off. I did the right thing." "Sure." "Ava." She walked away and went back into the studio and saw Grace singing with Ryan and Brad. Ryan looked over and saw Ava. "Stay here with Brad for a minute okay," Ryan said. "Kay," Grace replied.

Ryan walked over to Ava. "You okay?" "No." "Ava, the man attracts the crazies." "Fine," Ava said. "Nothing happened with them. He told her that her showing up was stupid. That he wished her the best and she tried to kiss him. He walked her out, then walked back in. Nothing else happened. I'd know if it did." "Then why is she calling our house," Ava asked. "Because she's panicking about moving on with someone else." "We've been married 2 years." "I know. She's been hoping that he'd be with her all that time. Trust me. Crazy is an understatement with that one." "Ryan." "I know. I told you I'd keep an eye on him. I'd tell you." Ava hugged him. "All things considered, you shouldn't be stressing," Ryan teased. "Shut it." He laughed and kissed her cheek. Ava walked back into the studio and Joe was walking towards her. "Grace, come on baby girl," Ava said. "Can I stay with Daddy?" Ava looked over at Ryan. "Good with me." Ava handed Ryan the baby bag. He hugged her. "Have fun with Daddy." Joe walked up to her. "What?" He slid his hand into hers, linking fingers. She looked him in the eye and was still past mad. She left and spent the afternoon trying to relax while Joe and the guys hung out with Grace.

Ava got a manicure and pedicure, a massage, then got some take out and went home. She relaxed in a hot bath, got some writing done, then curled up in bed. Joe came in at ten, tucked Grace into bed then came into their bedroom, closed the doors and sat down on the bed. "I know you aren't sleeping." "Couldn't," Ava said. "Babe, I swear nothing happened." "Fine." "I wouldn't do that and you know it." "I know." "Thank you for today." "She wanted to be with you. I wasn't about to say no." "She was adorable," Joe said. "I bet." "Am I allowed to sleep with you?" "Your pillow's here." "That mean you forgive me?" "For now." "Ryan told me what he said to you," Joe said. "And if he doesn't stick to it, he has two women to deal with." "I know. I promise you nothing is going to happen." "Good."

Ava turned to face him. "I don't want to doubt you," she said. Her eyes were filling with tears. "And I don't want you getting all mad over nothing." "Here's the deal from now on. I don't give out my cell and you don't give out yours. The home number is for friends and family only." "Works for me." "Even if we have to change the number." "Okay. You gonna tell me who John is," Joe asked, "An old boyfriend I bumped into at the mall." "And?" "I told him how happy we were." "Oh really." "He misses me, but he knows that I'm off limits." "Babe," Joe said. "What?" "I was a little jealous." "Figured." "You don't know what was running through my head." "Lived it." "I hate that feeling." "Difference being, I'd never cheat. Secondly, we're pregnant. Who's going to want a pregnant woman," Ava said. "Me." "Other than you?" "I love you. I don't want to fight with you anymore." "Me either." He leaned down beside her and kissed her. "I missed you." "I missed this too." He kissed her again and slid his arms around her feeling the satin teddy. "Come lay down." He kissed her and kicked his things off, then curled up under the covers with her.

"New?" Ava nodded. "I like." "Had a feeling you would." He kissed her and slid his arms around her. "I have to go back in tomorrow," Joe said. "Okay." "Come with me." "No more volunteering me for songs." "Deal. Just eye candy." He kissed her and she wrapped her leg around his. "You smell good," Joe said. "Lavender bubbles." He kissed her neck, then her shoulder. "You know how I love that smell on you." Ava nodded. He kissed her again and they made love. It was gentle, loving, romantic and erotic. After, he held her close and she fell asleep in his arms.

Around 8am, Grace ran into their bedroom. "Mama." "What's up baby?" "There's a door knock." "Okay." Grace ran into her room and Ava pulled her satin robe on and went downstairs. "Who is it?" "Ava, it's Ryan." She opened the door. "What's up?" "Woke the lovebirds up did I," he teased. "Funny." "Wanted to talk to you for a minute." Ava headed for the kitchen and Ryan followed staring at her in the robe. "Coffee?" "I'll drink yours," he joked. "So what's up?" "Remember when I told you I'd keep an eye on him?" Ava nodded. "I don't want you worrying." "I won't." "You know how many girls flock to him," Ryan said. "And I know a few who think you're pretty great too." "Thanks. Ava, there's always going to be a fan who has a thing for him." "And if he does anything he shouldn't, he'll be in shit," Ava said. "There's only two women I know that he needs to watch out for." "Other than Kelly?" "She isn't a problem anymore." "Get to the point." "I'll tell you if they're around. Just put a little trust in him okay?" Ava nodded. "He loves you something fierce." "Good. He better." "No. I mean the other night when you freaked on him, he was really upset," Ryan said. "And?" "He stayed with us." "Good." "I'm not going to play private eye for you, but I will give you a heads up. Sound fair?" Ava nodded. "And if you even think of being a playboy, I will kick your butt all the way to Mexico," Ava said. "I know. You know you're like family to us." "I know." He hugged Ava, finished his coffee and headed home.

CHAPTER 30

Ava went back upstairs to bed and curled back up with Joe. "Who was it?" "Ryan." "There is no damn way it's 11am," Joe said. "Nope." "Good. More bed time." "Go back to sleep," Ava said. His arms slid around her and he undid her robe. "Grace is awake." He got up and slid his robe on, then turned Grace's favorite movie on that always knocked her back out. Joe gave her some breakfast, then slid back into bed with Ava. "Something tells me the Cheerios are going to be gone in a minute or two and she'll be out cold," Joe joked. "How would you know that?" "She was already yawning." Ava laughed. "Plus, Emily's on her way over. She promised she'd take Grace to the park this morning." "How convenient," Ava teased. "See what happens when you plan something?" He kissed her neck. Within a few seconds, her robe hit the floor. Ava heard the door open. "Hi Emm," Joe said. "Go back to sleep lazy butt." He laughed. "Hey Gracie. Ready for the park," Emily asked. She left with Grace and Joe kissed Ava's shoulder. "So where were we?"

Ava turned towards him. He kissed her and she slid into his arms. "Much better," he said. Joe kissed her again and his hands slid down her side. "Gotta love the lavender bubbles." "Still soft?" He kissed her. Joe's phone went off two minutes later. He ignored it. He made love to Ava while his phone went off two and three times. He kissed every inch of her until her body was trembling, then teased her into orgasm over and over again. His hormones took over for what felt like hours. Finally, Ava managed to get out of bed and had a hot shower, with him by her side. "Don't know how I'm supposed to resist you all day," Joe said. "Could just stay here and hang with Grace." He kissed her and pinned her to the shower wall. "Not in a million." She finished her shower, then slid out and let him wash up. She slid the towel around her and dried off, then went to head into the bedroom when he pulled her into his arms. "What?" "Did I tell you I love you today?" Ava shook her head. "I love you too." They got dressed and Grace came home with Emily.

She came running up the steps and into the bedroom. "Mama, people pictures." "Where?" "At the park." "That's why we're back. It was paparazzi," Emily said. "Thanks Emily," Joe replied. "Not sure why they'd be following us, but I thought she was safer with you two." Joe went and talked to Emily and Ava sat with Grace. "Why was they taking pictures Mama?" "Because you're so beautiful." "Really?" Ava nodded. She had a feeling she knew why. They grabbed some lunch for Grace and brought it with them, heading into the studio.

Ryan saw Ava the minute she walked in with Grace. "Well hello lovely ladies." Ryan kissed Ava's cheek and Grace ran over to hug him. "Playing Daddy today?" "Think we might," Ryan said. "Me play," Grace asked. "In a little bit," Joe said. "Okay." She hugged Ryan and kissed his cheek, then ran in to say hi to Brad. "So how's things," Ryan asked. Joe kissed Ava. He went in and got set up. "I guess that's an answer," Ryan said. "Better." "The man's all smiles today." "I know," Ava said. "I hate you two fighting." Ryan gave her a hug and went in with the guys.

They joked around and got some music down, then Grace came running in and jumped into Ava's arms. "Mama, me sing like Daddy?" "If you want to when you grow up." "Mama, is Uncle Ryan uncle?" "Sort of." "I like him," Grace said. "Me too." Ava finally calmed her down and Grace colored, then watched a movie on the DVD player. Around 2, she was asleep. Ryan and Brad went and grabbed lunch with Scott, and Joe motioned for Ava to come into the studio. She stepped in. "What's up?" "Grace sleeping?" Ava nodded. "What we doing for lunch," Joe asked. "What did you have in mind?" "Dessert." "Other than that?" "Whatever you want," Joe said. "Stay with Grace. I'll run across the street." He kissed her. "I love you." "Love you too." He kissed her neck. "They'll be back in an hour. Food." Joe kissed her and Ava left to grab something. She came back ten minutes later and he was on the phone. "She just walked in actually . . . . I will Ma." He hung up and kissed Ava. "My mom said hi." "How's she doing?" "Good." Ava handed him his lunch and curled up on the other sofa with him. "This is awesome," Joe said. "The sandwich place you never wanted to go into." "Nice." He kissed her. "So what we doing tonight?" "Sleeping." "Better idea." "What's that?" "Date night." "Seriously?" He nodded. "You can pull on that black dress and the heels." "Your favorite." A smile came across his face. She could read that dirty mind anywhere. "And just what else did you have planned," Ava asked. "A few things." He kissed Ava's neck. "I bet I know what they are." "You're probably right too." They relaxed after lunch. Her phone rang just as the guys were coming back in. Ava grabbed it.

"Hi Ava. Just making sure you remembered your appointment at 4." "I did. I'll see you soon." Joe looked over at her. "Doctor appointment." "Seriously?" "I can do this alone," Ava said. "I wanted to go." She kissed him. "I'll be back in an hour." "Pictures." Ava laughed. "I mean it," Joe said. Ava nodded and kissed him. "I'll take care of sleeping bear." Ava kissed Grace then headed to the doctor.

"So how we feeling?" "Good." "Did you lower the stress?" "Tried." The doctor laughed. "Considering, that isn't bad." She checked Ava over, then did the ultrasound. "Just perfect." "You sure?" "You're at the end of the first trimester. You're fine." She printed out 4 copies of the picture and handed them to Ava. "How did you know," Ava asked. "Had a feeling. Wouldn't be surprised if he posted them online." "We haven't told anyone." "Think you're safe to tell the world Ava. You're starting to show already." "Great." The doctor laughed. Ava booked her next appointment then headed back to the studio.

She walked in and they were recording one of Joe's songs. Grace was sitting with Scott. Joe saw her and looked over smiling. Ava had a smile ear to ear. "Hi Mama." "Hey baby." She was dancing in Scott's lap. Once they finished the take, Joe hopped up and went to check on Ava. "Well?" Ava handed him an envelope with the pictures. "Totally alright," Joe asked. Ava nodded. He picked her up spinning her in circles. He kissed her. "Definitely a date night." He kissed her again. "What," Ryan asked. He opened the envelope and showed the guys. Ryan hugged Ava and Brad hugged Joe. "So, this means what I think it means," Joe asked. "No." "Why?" "Emily had paparazzi following her at the park. No way are we telling the world." He kissed Ava. "Guys, back to work. We'll be done by 7," Scott said. Joe kissed Ava again, kissed Grace then went back in and got another take or two, then finished another song.

Finally, they headed home. Ava made Grace some dinner, then Joe tucked her in. Emily came by to keep an ear out for her, and Ava went and got changed. She slid the dress on with the heels, did her hair and put some makeup on. She stepped out of the bathroom to him in his dress pants and no shirt. "Wow." "What time is the reservation," Joe asked. "8" "We have a half-hour." "I know." He kissed Ava. He slid his shirt on, pulled on his boots and they left.

They walked into the restaurant and went back to the private dining room. A few people looked just as they were being seated. "You look beautiful," Joe said. "Pretty sexy yourself." He smirked and kissed her. "I still can't believe it." "What?" "The picture." Ava smiled. "Which one," Ava asked. "Gotta say, it almost topped the one at Christmas." "Right." They had dinner and talked and flirted their way through it. They finished up, then headed out. "Can we get your autograph," a fan asked. Ava nodded. She signed one and so did Joe. They headed to the SUV and he pulled out. "Where are we off to now husband of mine?" "Dancing." "Oh really?" He nodded. They pulled up to the club and headed inside. Within a few minutes, he had her on the dance floor in his arms. They danced for an hour or two before anyone even noticed. They made their way up to the VIP lounge and had a drink, then headed home. The minute they were leaving, they were surrounded by paparazzi. They let them take a few shots, then they hopped in the SUV and headed off. "You realize home is the other way," Ava said. He nodded and smiled. "Where we going?" "You'll see."

Joe and Ava pulled into the park a little while later. "And what are we doing here?" He hopped out, then opened her door for her. "Come on." They walked through the park, then down by the water. "What are you up to?" They stopped at an old tree. Ava was looking out onto the water and he laughed. "What?" "It's still here." "What is?" He showed her. He'd carved their names into the tree when he first met her. "Don't tell the press," Ava joked. He pulled Ava into his arms. "This is where I first realized how bad I had it for you," Joe said. "Oh really." "And where I was the minute I knew I wanted to marry you." "Maybe we should transplant this into our yard," Ava teased. "Funny. Seriously Ava." "Right here?" Joe nodded. "I was sitting against the tree. Ryan kept laughing at me. He said there was no way I could fall for someone I barely knew. That there'd been tons of other girls. Why not them." "And what did you say?" "There was something about you. That I wanted to see you again." "So who's idea was it to get me to the concert," Ava asked. "His. He said if you said no, I should let it go." "Good thing I showed then." Joe nodded and kissed Ava, leaning her against the tree. "Really good thing you did." "What would you have done if I hadn't," Ava asked. "Hunted you down until you gave in." He smiled and kissed her. "Darn. Should've played hard to get." He laughed. "Admit it. You wanted me too." "Thought you were a sweetheart," Ava said. "That's it?" Ava smiled. "At the beginning. Think it was the kiss and being pinned to the wall within 2 minutes of walking in that did it." They kissed for a while, then went back to the SUV after stopping to make sure they had a picture of the tree.

They went back towards the SUV and the paparazzi were snapping pictures. "Seriously guys, come on," Joe said. Ava hopped in and they headed home. They pulled into the driveway and headed inside. Emily headed home and Joe and Ava headed to bed. Ava slid out of the dress and pulled her silk chemise on. She washed the makeup off as he watched her from the door. "What?" "You're more beautiful without it." Ava kissed him. He picked her up and carried her to bed and curled up with her. "Still remember the first night I talked you into staying," Joe said. "Didn't take much." "Took all the will power I had not to pounce on you the minute I saw you again." "If my memory serves me right, you did." Joe kissed her again. "Who would've thought I'd still be here?" "You know the funny thing, I don't think this place really felt like home until you were here." "Oh really." "You in my shirt at the kitchen table." "And you stealing my coffee as usual," Ava joked. He kissed her. "Now we have Grace and another baby on the way. I finally did something right," Joe said. "You did a long time ago." "What's that?" "You married the right girl." He snuggled with her. Within an hour or so, they were both asleep.

The next morning, Ava woke up to Joe nuzzling her neck. "Morning," Ava said. "Morning yourself." He kissed down her neck to her shoulder and Ava turned to face him. Joe kissed her and slid his arms around her. He slid one hand down her torso and pulled her leg around him. "What about Grace?" "She had breakfast. She's out with Emily." He kissed her again. Within a few minutes, they were going at it again. "Joe." He kissed her. He nibbled her shoulder as his body shook. Ava was trying to catch her breath when she came. "Good morning to you too," Ava teased. He kissed her. "You have to go in today," Ava asked. "We do." "We?" He kissed her again. "I'm coming with you am I?" He nodded. "Definitely." "And Grace?" "Rose is coming with Jacob too. They can run around together." "Thought of everything," Ava said. "Almost." "Meaning?" "Meaning we have to leave at 4." "For what?" "Talk show. For the CD." "So you won't be home for dinner?" "We won't. We have to fly to New York." "What about Grace?" "She's staying with Rose." "And just how long did you know about this?" "You mean did I book us a suite at the hotel you love," Joe asked. Ava smirked. "It's booked." He kissed her again. "We should pack then." "And you should figure out what to wear." "What?" "Love letters." Ava shook her head. "The red dress," Ava said. "You wouldn't." Ava nodded and kissed him. She slipped away from him and showered, then slid on her satin robe and packed. He slid up behind her as she packed and undid her robe. "Would you stop?" "Nope," Joe said. He slid his arms around her and pulled her back towards the bathroom.

Once they finally got changed and packed, they headed to the studio. Grace played with Jacob, then Ava and Joe headed to the airport with the guys. They had a quick flight, then started getting set up at the show. They all joked around and got changed in the dressing room, while Joe tried to talk her out of the dress. Finally, they were ready to go. They did the song, then had an interview after. They asked a million of the usual questions, then asked Ava something. "So, we heard a few rumors that you have some news to share." "What rumors would those be," Ava asked. Joe slid his arm around her. "I'll just get to it. Are you and Joe having another baby?" "If it happens, it happens." "So are you pregnant?" "Not that I know of," Ava replied. "Can't always believe the rumor mills. We have a few questions from some fans. First thing they wanted to know was how you and Joe met." "We actually met years ago when I was at one of their concerts. We met the second time when I showed up to a concert with an old friend of mine. Joe and I spent most of the night talking and have been pretty much inseparable since." "She's the best part of my life," Joe said. "Next fan question. When is Ava's new book out." "It's out now actually. It came out the same day as the new CD," Ava said. "We heard it's a definite page turner. How do you come up with the ideas?" "Sometimes its seeing people together. Like when you walk through the park and see a couple and wonder what their relationship is all about. Sort of like that." "So you don't base it on anything in your lives?" "What we do is our thing. I don't put it in the books," Ava said. After another ten minutes, they were finished, did one more song and headed to the hotel.

They all had dinner together then the guys headed to bed. Ava and Joe went and relaxed in their suite. They walked in and he kissed her, walking her backwards towards the bedroom.

"Hold on," Ava said. "What?" "This is . . ." It was the hotel they were at the first time they were alone, and the hotel that the guys were staying in the night she met them for the first time. "Was wondering when you'd notice," Joe said. Ava kissed him. She walked into the bedroom and saw candles, satin sheets and rose petals on the bed. "What have you done," Ava teased. "I had a feeling." "And what would that feeling be?" "That we could re-do that night." "Which one? If you're talking about the night we were here last time, I thought it went perfectly," Ava joked. He kissed her. "It did." Ava smiled. "Wanted it to be a good memory," Joe said. "It always has been." Joe kissed her again and leaned her onto the bed. Within a minute or two, he was peeling her dress off. "You know how much I love this dress," Ava said. He looked and saw the black and red lace g-string and bra. "Baby," Joe said. She slid onto the bed and he peeled his shirt off, then Ava undid his jeans. He kicked them off and kissed her. "You know you could've just told the truth," Joe said. "About?" "Ava." "No. It's our business." "You know that's probably why the paparazzi was following us." "I don't want to tell the world yet," Ava said. He kissed her. They made love more than just once on the king sized bed. He blew the candles out, then they curled up together. "What time are we heading back," Ava sked. "7." "AM?" He nodded then kissed her. "I am so sleeping on the plane." "Nope," Joe said. "Why?" He smirked. "Don't you dare start that again." He laughed and kissed her. They curled up and were asleep in minutes.

The next morning at 6am, Ryan called to wake Joe and Ava up. "Hey." "We're up," Ava said. "No sleep?" "Funny." "See you downstairs in a half-hour." Ava rolled over and Joe wasn't in bed. She went in and had a quick shower, then put her things together. Joe's bag was gone. She called Ryan and met him and Brad downstairs. "Where's Joe," Ava asked. "What do you mean where's Joe? He was with you last night." Ava called his phone and got no reply. "There's a note for you Mrs. Morgan." Ava grabbed the note:

Meet you at home. Have a surprise for you. XOXOXO

Ava shook her head. "I know you two knew about this." Brad smirked. They headed home. Joe met her at the airport. "Where did you disappear to?" He kissed her and pulled Ava into his arms. "Tired?" Ava nodded. "When did you take off?" "Two." "Why didn't you . . ." Joe kissed her again. Ryan laughed. "You two both knew?" Ryan nodded. "Butthead," Ava said. Ryan laughed. "He swore me to secrecy," Brad said. They all hopped in the car. Joe dropped Brad and Ryan at home, then took Ava back to the house. "Where's Grace?" "At home," Joe said. They pulled in and headed inside. Grace ran straight to Ava. "Hi Mama." "Hey baby girl." "I sawed you TV." "Oh you did?" "Yeah." "PVR'd it for her," Emily said. Ava laughed. Ava picked Grace up. "Daddy." "We are baby." "We are what?" He took Ava's hand and led her upstairs. He led her into Grace's room and showed Ava the new bed he'd picked out for her. "Too cute." "Big girl bed," Grace said. "I see that." "One more surprise," Joe said. Grace hopped out of Ava's arms and jumped on her bed.

He opened the guest room door. It used to be one of the two guest rooms in the house. Now, it was the perfect nursery. It was painted pale lilac, with a white crib and lilac accessories. It was absolutely perfect. Ava wrapped her arms around him. "So you love it," Joe asked. Ava nodded and wiped a tear away. "What?" "Nothing. It's just like I wanted." "I know." He kissed her. "You told me when we were doing Grace's room remember?" Ava nodded. "And Rose went a little crazy at the clothing store. Ava went into the closet. There were dresses and pants, tops and sweaters and sleepers galore. There were chenille blankets in the closet. Ava smiled. "Now we can relax." Ava nodded. "Mama, I gots Teddy," Grace said running into the room "Very cute teddy." "Sister?" "Not sure." "Me ask?" "I don't know if baby can hear you." "I love you," Grace said kissing Ava's stomach. Ava hugged her. She picked her up. "Baby, you have to promise Mama something." "Okay." "No telling people about baby okay?" "Why?" "We aren't yet." "Okay Mama." She kissed Ava and hopped down, then ran downstairs and played with Emily.

"You know we're gonna have to tell people," Joe said. "When did you plan to?" "Tonight." "And just how did you plan on doing that?" "We have a concert." "Where?" "Downtown." "I'm wearing the backless black one." "No," Joe said. Ava nodded. "No way." "Why?" "Ava." "I'm wearing it. Not telling what with." Joe kissed her and leaned her against the door frame. "You can't taunt me." "Yes I can." She slipped out of his arms and headed downstairs. "So what time you two headed down for sound check," Emily asked. "We have to leave at 2," Joe said. "Then I'm going to catch some actual sleep," Ava teased. "Thought so," Joe teased. She headed to the bedroom with Joe one step behind her.

She slid out of her jeans and crawled into bed. Joe peeled his sweater off. "Where you going?" "To bed with this hot woman I know," Joe teased. "Tired?" "Grace woke me up at 5." "Serves you right," Ava said. He laughed. "You like your surprise?" Ava nodded. She yawned and turned the light off. He pulled the shutters closed and slid into bed with her. Joe wrapped his arms around her and kissed her shoulder. Ava linked her fingers with his and was asleep in minutes.

At noon, they both woke up, got changed and headed to the concert. They did sound check, then had dinner, did interviews and had the meet and greet. Then the guys headed into the dressing room. "I have an idea," Joe said. "No," Ava said. "Ava." "Here of all places?" He nodded. "We played our first real concert here." "I don't know." "Ava, why not?" "I don't feel like having cameras stalking us." "They are anyway," Joe said. "I'm announcing it." Joe kissed her. "And no jokes either," Ava said. Ryan laughed. "So no rabbit jokes," Brad teased. Ava smacked his arm. Joe wrapped an arm around her. "Whatever you want to do." "I still can't believe you two kept it a secret this long," Ryan said. "You know why." Brad nodded. He hugged Ava and the guys headed out. Joe gave her one heck of a kiss.

The guys did a few songs, then Ryan introduced Ava. "Now folks, be nice. This is her first night in our favorite hangout." The crowd roared. "Thanks for the warm welcome everyone. You having fun tonight?" They roared again. Ava sang a song with Ryan, then looked at Joe. "So, I have to admit. I'm kinda loving it here. It's almost like home." They roared. Ava sang another song with them then headed back to the dressing room. The concert finished and Joe headed backstage. "Chicken," Joe teased. "Better idea." "What?" "We have another interview right?" He nodded.

They headed into the interview and went through a million questions. "So Ava, I have to ask if the rumors are true." "What rumors?" Joe and Ava both laughed. "We heard that you two might be expecting. Are the rumors true?" Joe kissed her cheek. "They are. We're due in July." "Congrats you two." "Thanks," Joe said with a grin ear to ear. They finished the interview and headed back to the dressing room. "Nice." "You said you wanted to tell the world," Ava joked. He wrapped his arms around Ava. "You know we're going to be surrounded." "That's what security's for," Ava said. He kissed her and slid his hand down her back. "Don't even." Joe kissed her. They headed outside, and as predicted were surrounded by the press. They hopped in the SUV and took off for home.

The next morning, it was all over the news. It was on the website, the internet and every channel. Ava woke up to Joe talking to his cousins and her relatives. He hadn't left her side. Ava finally got up and he hung up after the millionth phone call. "Everyone know now," Ava asked. "You won't believe. We have 3 interviews today just us." "You and me?" He nodded. "Great." Ava kissed him and he leaned into her, pinning her to their bed. "What time is the first one?" "Noon." "We have to get up." He kissed her. "Nope," he said. "Joe." He kissed her and slid his arms around her. His hands slid down to her backside. "Don't you . . ." He kissed her and she slid her legs tight around him. They made love, devouring every inch of each other, then showered and went off for the interviews. Ava had on a pale pink dress that had Joe drooling. "Babe." "I'm wearing it," Ava said. They walked in, got ready for the interview, then sat down.

They asked a million questions about how they met, and about the wedding and Grace. "So what's next?" "We're having another baby. We're due in July." "Do we know if it's a boy or girl?" "Don't really want to know," Ava said. "Sort of hoping for a boy," Joe said. "But as long as the baby's healthy, we're good." "How's Grace taking it?" "She can't wait. She keeps asking the baby if it's a boy or girl." "How do you two make it work? I mean you're recording, touring, writing, and you two look like you're still as happy as you were when you first met." "We are. Every day I am thankful for her. She's the best part of me," Joe said. "But how do you two make it all work?" "I write while we're travelling, or when we have some quiet time. Believe it or not, it's just like a normal marriage during the week,"

Ava said. "Oh really?" "He's an amazing dad. He plays with Grace, has father and daughter time, and still manages to cook a mean fried chicken once in a while." "So how do you two keep it alive?" "Honestly, we make whatever time we have special. We have date nights, and I sweep her off her feet all over again," Joe said. After the interview was finished, as well as the two after that, they headed home.

Joe and Ava headed inside and she saw the candles. "Where's . . ." "She's with Rose." "What are you up to?" "Romancing the most beautiful woman in the world." He walked her upstairs and carried her to bed. "Kinda glad we did it your way," Joe said. "A lot better than telling the fans first." He kissed her. He slid her out of the pink dress and took her hand. "Where are we . . . ." She saw the tub filled with hot water and lavender bubbles that she could smell from the door. "I see." He kissed her and she shed the rest of her clothes and slid into the tub. He kicked his things off and slid in with her. "You don't know how good this feels." "Yeah I do," he said kissing her neck. "What's all this for?" "The most beautiful mom on the planet." "Nice." Joe's arms slid around her. "I still can't believe we told everyone. You know we could've kept it quiet like you wanted," Joe said. "If it means the paparazzi quits stalking us, then I'll do it." "Still, you know the interview's going to be played a million times." "And I still might keep you around." He kissed her cheek. "Oh really," Joe joked. Ava nodded. "Pretty good at warming up my cold toes." "And warming up a few other things," Joe said. Ava turned towards him. "Think so?" "Tempt me." Ava slid to the other side of the tub. "Where you going?" "Nowhere." He grabbed her feet and pulled her towards him.

"What," Ava asked. "I love you." "I love you too." "I have an idea." "What?" "We rent a place away from everything for a while." "Like what?" "Have a few ideas," Joe said. "What about the guys?" "Close enough that I can still meet them at the studio, but away from all the city stuff." "No mall." He kissed her. "What do you think?" "For a month or two," Ava asked. He nodded. "Okay." "I want us to have a normal life with Grace for a while. Just us and the plain simple stuff like we had when we were little." "I like it." "Good." He kissed her again and slid his hands down her back, pulling her in close.

Not long after, he had her curled up in bed with him, making love to her. "You know how right all of this is?" Ava nodded. "I never thought I'd ever meet a girl like you. Must have done something really right." "You called. That's all you needed to do," Ava teased. "Oh really?" "When we talked that first night, I couldn't stop thinking about you." "And after?" "Craved you," Joe said. "I wanted you the minute I saw you." It was more intense, more passionate. The two of them were insatiable. They kissed, made love, snuggled, made love, then finally fell asleep curled up together.

"Ryan." "Hey beautiful." He handed Rose a dozen roses. "What are these for?" "For putting up with me," Ryan said. "Think I'd do it anyway. Kind of used to having you around." "Oh really." He kissed her. "I have some news." "What?" "Come sit." He walked into the TV room and pulled Rose into his arms. "I was at the doctor," Rose said. "Right." "Um." "Rose." "I was late. I asked her to check." "Are you telling me what I think you are?" Rose nodded. "Babe." "I'm only a month," Rose said. "Holy shit." "I know. I had to tell you." "This is amazing." Ryan kissed her and held her close. "Silly question." "What?" "Do we want another baby," Rose asked. He kissed her. "Do you?" "I do, but Jacob's so little." "He was a blessing Rose. This one is too." "I know, but Jacob's a lot of work." "Why are you worried? He loves you. You're an amazing mom." "And when you're gone . . ." "We'll figure it out. Joe and Ava are having another baby. Just means we change the schedule a bit." "You sure?" He kissed her. "I know," Ryan said. They kissed and were making out like teenagers when Jacob came running in. "Hi Daddy." "Hey little man." Jacob ran back out and ran into the kitchen with Grace. Ryan and Rose got up and went into the kitchen.

"Where's Mama," Grace asked. "On a date with your Dad." "I see Daddy." "He's coming first thing to get you." "Call Daddy." She got up and went for the phone. "Why don't you two hop into bed," Rose said. "Sing?" "If you're good." Grace ran up the stairs and climbed into the bed. Jacob curled up in his bed and Ryan sang them to sleep. He came out of the bedroom and saw Rose on the bed. She was reading Ava's latest book. He slid his shirt off and kicked off his jeans and slid into bed with her.

He kissed her shoulder, then her neck. She finally put the book down when he reached towards her and pulled her face to meet his. Ryan kissed her. "They asleep?" He nodded as she melted into his arms. "I missed you today," Rose said. "Me too. The interviews went on forever." "Did you get any more of the song done?" "My part's done. It's just Joe and Brad left." "She announced it," Rose said. "I know." "It's all over the internet." "And when people get wind of us . . ." "We're not telling anyone until necessary right?" "I'd keep it a permanent secret if we could," Ryan joked. "I have to tell Ava." "I know. Family's different." Ryan kissed her. "I love you," Rose said. "I love you too babe." They curled up together, kissing and making love until they were both asleep.

CHAPTER 31

The next morning, Ava woke up to Joe's phone ringing—again. Ava grabbed it as Joe pulled her back to him. "Hey Brad," Ava said. "He up?" "No." "Can you wake him up?" "Not likely." "I'm on my way over," he said. "What's wrong?" "Danielle and I got in a fight." "Brad." "I'll be there in ten." He hung up and Joe pulled Ava back under the covers and kissed her. "Brad's on his way here." Joe kissed her again. "Babe." They did it and he was just about to explode when Brad rang the doorbell. He came hard. Ava kissed him as he pinned her to the bed. "Baby, Brad's here," Ava said. "Don't move." "I have . . . ." He kissed her again. "Not one step." He kissed her, got up, pulling his jeans on, then headed downstairs as he pulled his shirt on.

"What's up," Joe asked. "Where's Ava?" "Sleeping." "You two never stop do you?" "What's wrong?" "She's scared and she's freaking on me." "About what?" "That I'm never gonna be home. That we're away too much. That she will practically be doing this alone." "Brad, Ava thought the same thing. It didn't turn out that way. It's your first baby," Joe said. "I know, she's just losing it." "I thought the same thing. We came up with a good idea." "What?" "We cut back on the concerts. Max two a week. The rest of the week we're home with them," Joe said. "Think it'll calm her down?" "Maybe. Take her out Brad. Remind her why you love her. Gees. I shouldn't have to tell you that," Joe joked. "I know. I'm just freaked. She got mad and told me to leave." "Flowers," Joe said. They laughed and Brad calmed down a bit. Brad headed home and Joe walked back upstairs. Ava was asleep in bed.

He kicked his jeans off and threw his shirt in the hamper, then crawled back into bed with Ava. "Hey." "Hey yourself." He kissed her. "Brad alright," Ava asked. "Yeah. Danielle was pulling an Ava." "Meaning what?" "Remember when you started worrying you'd have to do all of this alone?" Ava nodded. "She's starting into panic mode," Joe said. "You know we have reasons for it." "And you also know that even if I have to talk the guys into one concert a week, I'm going to be here." "I know. I think I know what Danielle needs," Ava said. "What?" "Spa day." "Good plan." Ava went to roll over to grab her phone and he pulled her back towards him. "Later," Joe said. "Why?" He kissed her. "Other plans." He slid his arms around her and curled back up with her.

Ava called Rose around 11. "What's up," Rose asked. "Get changed. The guys are looking after the kids." "Why?" "We're having a spa day." "I'm up for that," Rose said. "See you in 20." Ava hung up then called Danielle.

"Hi Ava." "Hey mama. How are you?" "Sore." "Perfect timing then." "For what," Danielle asked. Brad gets to practice being a Dad and we are having a spa day." "Ava." "It's already booked. I'll be there in a half-hour." "Thank you," Danielle said.

Ava hung up as Joe wrapped his arms around her. "What time you three coming home," Joe asked. "Dinner." "We'll go out." "Grace." "Emily," Ava said. He kissed her. "Fine." He held her close. "You know how beautiful you are?" "Think you told me this morning a few times," Ava teased. "I love you." "Love you more." Joe kissed her and walked Ava to the SUV. "Babe." "What?" He kissed her again and tried pulling her into his lap. "Nice try," Ava teased. They headed off to pick up Rose. They showed up and Grace came running out the front door. "Mama." "Hey princess. What you doing?" "Tag. I win." Ava put her down. "Guess what Grace?" "What?" "We're hanging out just us today," Joe said. "Where Mama going?" "She'll be home in a little while." "Yay." Joe kissed Ava goodbye and she left with Rose. They picked up Danielle and a half-hour later were at the spa.

The guys played with the kids all afternoon while Ava, Rose and Danielle got massages and mani-pedi's. "I have to tell you two something," Rose said. Ava looked at her. "You aren't," Ava asked. Rose nodded. "We're all pregnant together?" Ava started laughing. "Danielle, you know no matter what you have us on your side. You need help, you have us," Ava said. "But I want the baby to know Brad," Danielle said. "Trust me. The three of them are like Mr. Mom's already," Rose said. "I know. I've seen Ryan and Joe." "Exactly. They'll rub off on him. Trust me," Ava said. "I guess I'm just freaking out." "Danielle, you only have a month left. You're allowed," Rose said. Danielle hugged Ava. "So what we up to now," Rose asked. Cat came in and sat with them. They laughed and joked around for a while, got facials, then got changed and headed to dinner.

The ladies walked in and saw the guys. Joe walked over to Ava. "Hey." "Hey yourself," Joe said. He kissed her. Ryan and Rose snuggled, and Danielle kissed Brad. Brad looked over at Ava and smiled. They talked and chatted through dinner. "So how were the kids," Ava asked. "Grace is so totally going to be a rock star," Brad said. "Singing again?" He nodded and they laughed. "Don't tell me she was singing Britney again," Ava said. "It was hilarious," Ryan said. "Wait until Jacob starts singing Madonna," Danielle teased. "Nice." "You know he will." "Not if I can help it," Ryan joked. They joked around and finished dinner, then Joe and Ava headed home while Brad and Ryan hung out with Rose and Danielle.

The minute they walked in, Joe picked Ava up and carried her upstairs to bed. "You had to wear the dress didn't you," Joe asked. Ava smiled. "Woman, you are so asking for it." They were kissing on their bed when Ava heard Grace. She managed to slip away from Joe and went in to check on her. "Mama." "I'm right here baby." "Bad dream." "It's alright baby." Ava kicked her heels off. "Mama, no more leave okay?" "Just you and me tomorrow," Ava said. "Kay." Ava flipped her pillow and within a few minutes, Grace was back asleep.

Ava came back into the bedroom and Joe was laying down on the bed. "You know she's getting all upset again." "I know. She went down for her nap and woke up crying. She had a dream I left her," Joe said. "So did you find anywhere for that home away from home?" He smiled. He grabbed the pictures he'd printed off of the little house. "It still has everything we need, but it's away from everything," Joe said. "How far away from everything?" "A half-hour drive to the doctor, 45 minutes to the mall." "And what about the studio," Ava asked. "An hour." "Okay." "We took her and Jacob to take a look at it." "And?" "Hot tub." "And?" "Sunroom so you can do your writing," Joe said. "And?" "Nice quiet room for Grace." "You fell in love with it didn't you," Ava asked. "Not as hard as I fell for you." She smiled. "It's really quiet." "Too quiet?" He shook his head. "Just enough for us." "Did you make an offer?" He nodded. "I low-balled and they accepted," Joe said. "Meaning?" "Meaning it's ours." "Joe." "The inspector took a look before I even went. It's perfect. All it needs is some paint." "And a crapload of cleaner," Ava said. "Nope. The woman that owns it is a housekeeper. It's spotless." "We seriously doing this?" "If you're up for it." "When?" "We put stuff together and we're there," Joe said. "You aren't thinking what I think you are?" He kissed her. "You know how crazy you are?" "That's why you love me." He kissed her again and she slid her legs around him. "I can't wait for you to see it." Joe kissed her again. "You know how much I love you?" "Let me guess," Ava teased. He kissed her again and they made love.

The next morning, Emily looked after Grace for an hour or two while Joe took Ava to the house. It had a wrap-around porch. "I always wanted one of these," Ava said. "And a porch swing." Joe wrapped his arms around her. It had an amazing view. They headed inside and Ava saw the hardwood floors, the old country home feel. He took her on the grand tour. "And this is our room," Joe said. They walked in. Ava saw the private balcony, the wrap around windows, the old claw foot tub and the closet the same size as her one at home. "So?" "You did good," Ava said. He kissed her and pulled her into his arms. "Just for when we need alone time. When we want to get away from everything." "It's perfect. Sort of reminds me of my place," Ava said. "That's why I knew you'd love it." He kissed her again and backed her up towards the old bed. "Joe." "What?" He picked her up as she wrapped her legs around him. They made love on the bed, then after a world of complaining from him, they headed home. "Party pooper," Joe said. "Grace will freak." "Fine." He kissed Ava and they pulled away.

They headed back to the house and went through a cloud of reporters again. "What is up with them?" "Babe, they want to see you," Joe said. "Too bad." They pulled in and headed inside. "Hey Emm." "So?" "It's beautiful." "Thought so." "You know this means we have to pick out paint colors," Ava said. "Oh goodie," Joe said with fake enthusiasm." "Mama, I pick." Joe smirked. "Okay then. We'll go together." "Babe," Joe said. "Don't you even . . ." He kissed her. "I have to go do an interview with the guys this afternoon," Joe said. "Nice." "I'll meet you back here for an early dinner." "Party pooper," Ava said mocking him. He laughed and kissed her.

Ava spent the afternoon with Grace picking out paint colors for the house. Everywhere she went, the press was all over her. Ava headed towards her favorite furniture place when she saw Joe's car. She looked over and saw him talking to someone. Ava slid into the furniture store, watching him. She saw the woman wrap her arms around him and kiss him. He got in the car and pulled away. She sent Ryan a text:

What time's the interview done?

He replied: We're heading there in a half-hour. I'll let you know.

Ava tried to distract herself. She got a few pieces, asked for immediate delivery and gave her the address. She managed to slip away from the press and crossed the street. She had to know.

"Can I help you?" "Yeah you can." "Ava," Tiffany said. "Nice seeing you again Tiff." "What you doing down here?" "Shopping. You still sleeping with him?" "Ava." "Don't BS me. Yes or no?" "It's . . ." Ava walked off, tucked Grace into her car seat, then headed home. She put her things into a bag, packed up Grace's things including the portable crib, then left. She sent him a text:

I saw you. PS. How's Tiff?

Ava drove until her rumbling stomach stopped her. She realized how close she was to the new place. She grabbed groceries and headed there. She tucked Grace into her crib, then started cleaning. The furniture showed, as well as the TV and the electronics that Ava had bought. She started a fire in the fireplace, had something to eat, and wrote as long as she could.

Joe looked at his phone and saw the message. She couldn't have. All he was doing was talking to Tiffany. Her mom had passed away. She needed a friend. The fact that he almost slept with her was a stupid thing to do, but he hadn't done anything. He walked back into the house and saw Ava's things gone as well as a good portion of Grace's. He called Ryan. Within a half-hour, Ryan was there. "What the hell did you do now?" "Tiff's mom died. I went over to talk to her and Ava saw her try to kiss me. She sent me this." He showed him the text. "You know you're in shit." "I didn't do anything. I swear on the baby I didn't." "Where'd she go?" "No fucking idea." "She go to the house?" "No. She refused to step foot in there with Grace until we had it the way we wanted it." "Hotel?" "Called the only one she would go to. She's not." "Did you call her cell?" "For the past hour." "She wants off the radar." "Ryan." "We're going to the other house." "She's not there." "I bet you anything she is," Ryan said.

Ava made some dinner for her and Grace. They curled up by the fire and played. Ava was determined to make everything normal. There was no way that Grace was going to be effected. Ava gave her dinner, then a bath in the tub, then tucked her in with a song. "Where Daddy?" "Doesn't matter." "Why?" Ava kissed Grace's cheek. She got up and slid out of the bedroom. She walked downstairs and Joe was there with Ryan. "Ava." She shook her head. "Out," Ava said. "Babe." "Now." "Ava, stop this." "Out." Ryan walked towards her. "You too. Out." "Ava don't do this." "Get out," Ava said. Ryan grabbed her hand and led her into the solarium. "Her mom died. He went to talk to her. That's all." "And you were there? Screw you." "He didn't Ava. I swear it." "I don't want him here," Ava said. "Fine. I'll bring him over tomorrow. You two can talk this out." "No more damn talking." A single tear slid down her cheek. "Ava." "Just go," she said. He walked back over to Joe. "No. I'm not leaving." Ava's lip started to quiver. She went outside and sat on the back porch on the swing. "I'm not walking out of here. Not like this," Joe said. "Joe, trust me. I'll bring you over tomorrow." "No." He walked outside and saw Ava. "Babe." "Leave me alone." "Don't do this. I didn't do anything with her," Joe said. "And you promising me you'd stay away from her meant nothing. Get out Joe." "Babe." "Now." "Her mom died." "Go." "Ava, please." "No," Ava said. He sat down beside her. "Leave me alone." She went to get up and started cramping. "Babe." "Get away from me," Ava said. She walked back into the house and went and sat down on the sofa. "Ava, come on." "No. You come on. You promised me," Ava said. "And I told you it was because her mom died." "Then go console her." Ava walked upstairs and started cleaning in the bedroom. She remade the bed, cleaned the floor, then another kick of pain. She tried to ignore it. Then another one that had her crumbling to the floor.

"What was that," Joe asked. Joe looked at Ryan. He hopped up and ran upstairs. Ava was curled up on the floor. "Babe." "Screw the hell off," Ava said. Joe picked her up, ran down the stairs and put her in the SUV and took off. Ryan stayed with Grace. The entire way to the hospital, Ava was in tears. When they pulled in, the security officers whisked her into the hospital and Joe followed.

The doctor checked her over, ran test after test, then came into the room. "How you feeling?" Ava shook her head still curled up in the fetal position. "Ava, you can't keep stressing out. If we hadn't stopped it, you would've lost the baby," the doctor said. "Is she okay," Joe asked. "She will be. No stress. I don't care if it's yoga or taking off to a deserted island until this baby is born. No more stress." Ava nodded. "Can she come home?" "I'm keeping her here until the morning. Just to be on the safe side." "Then I'm staying," Joe said. The doctor nodded and left the room. Ava turned away from him. "Babe, please." She went to sleep. He sat in the chair and watched her. "I didn't Ava. I swear I didn't. Please just hear me." "Where's Grace," Ava asked. "Ryan's with her." "She's going to be upset if one of us isn't there." "Ava, I'm not leaving you here." "Just go," Ava said. "No." He sat down on the edge of her bed. "I didn't sleep with her. Nothing." "I saw her kiss you." "Ava." "You promised me." "She . . ." "I don't care what she wanted Joe." "Babe, please." "You made me a promise. You broke it. No more chances." "I'm not hearing this," Joe said. "Yeah you are." "No. I'm not losing you." "You can see her whenever you want to." "No." "Just go." "Ava, stop this." "Just go." "No. I didn't do anything. I swear I didn't." "You were there. It's enough," Ava said. "Ava. We're married. You can't walk away." "Then we're taking a break." "No." He wrapped his arm around Ava and turned her towards him. He saw the tears streaming and her eyes welling up. "You don't want me to go any more than I want to go," Joe said. "I'm not going to spend the rest of my life worried that you are going to screw around with someone else. I want my old boring life back." "Ava." "I'm not doing it anymore." "Ava, stop it." "Do you know what it felt like Joe?" "Ava, it wasn't what you thought it was. You have to give me the benefit of the doubt," Joe said. "I did. Saw Tiffany." "Then she told you." "Didn't have to." "Ava, stop. I didn't. I left and went to the interview." "And?" "Then I came home and you were gone."

They talked the rest of the night, slept, then the doctor came in. She woke Ava up. "I have to redo the tests." Ava nodded. Joe yawned. He went and sat back in the chair. The doctor did the tests and sent Ava home. "No more stress." Ava nodded. They left and he took Ava back to the new place. They came inside and Ryan was asleep on the sofa and Grace was playing with her toys. Joe went to kiss Ava and she turned away. "Hi Daddy." "Hey baby girl." She ran over and hugged him. Ryan woke up a few minutes later. "Ava alright?" "She will be," Joe said. Ava walked over and handed Ryan a coffee. "Thanks Ava. How you feeling?" "Better." "See what happens when you go on a cleaning rampage?" She smirked and walked upstairs. She finished cleaning up the bedroom and Joe walked in. "Babe." "What?" "I'm taking Ryan home. Do you want me to get anything?" "No. Go home." "Ava." "I'm fine," Ava said. "I'm grabbing some clothes and I'll be back in an hour or so." "Yep." He slid up behind her and wrapped his arms around her. "I'm glad you're alright."

"Go." He turned her towards him and kissed her, leaning her up against the wall of the bedroom. One kiss led to what seemed like a million more. She finally broke the kiss. "I love you." "Go get Ryan home," Ava said. "I'm bringing dinner back and we're talking." "Whatever." He kissed her again, wiping away whatever breath she had left and her heart almost pounded clear out of her chest. "I'll be back in an hour and a half." Ava nodded. And he went downstairs.

Ava saw him pull out and she went downstairs. "What you up to baby girl?" "Coloring." "What you making a picture of?" "Uncle Ryan sleeping." Ava laughed. She grabbed herself a drink, then looked over and saw Grace yawning. She made her a grilled cheese, had lunch, then took Grace to bed for her nap. She came back downstairs and cleaned everything. When Joe came back, she was asleep on the sofa. He put his things away, then went downstairs and picked Ava up and carried her to the bed and curled up with her. "You're back are you," Ava asked. "Didn't want to wake you up." "Where's Grace?" "In bed." Ava went to pull away from him and he slid her back, kissing her neck. "Joe." "Just relax." "I'm still mad." "I know." "I want to trust you but how the hell do I do that," Ava asked. "Believe me when I tell you that I wouldn't and didn't." "How do I know that?" "Because there is only one woman, that I've ever loved who I want to be with every time I'm near her. I'm laying beside her." "Joe." "I mean it." "Would you stop?" "Ava, I don't want to be with her. I want you." Ava got up and washed her face. His arms wrapped around her. "I love you. I'm never jeopardizing that." "Fine," Ava said. She walked away and went downstairs and started making dinner. He sat down at the counter. "What?" "I like the furniture." "Good." "We going to talk about this?" Ava went back to cooking. She put dinner together and set the table. Joe got Grace and brought her downstairs. She wouldn't let go of Joe. He played with her until dinner was ready, watching Ava out of the corner of his eye.

They had dinner and Grace nibbled away. "Ava," Joe said. She shook her head. "Daddy, I like here." "Me too baby." "We staying here?" "For a while." "Good. No monsters here. Mama checked." He smirked. Ava finished her dinner, then got up and did the dishes. Joe cleaned Grace up, then helped as Grace took off to play with her toys. "You know you're going to have to talk to me at some point," Joe said. "Not starting this in front of Grace. I'm attempting to lower my stress not raise it again." She finished doing the dishes and sat down on the sofa beside Grace. "Mama, we watch Mama and Daddy movie?" Joe grabbed it from his bag and slipped it in the DVD player. Ava grabbed her laptop and did some writing. Two or three paragraphs in, he slid it out of her lap, saved her work and typed something:

I don't want to fight anymore. Please. I love you.

She deleted it and wrote something:

Are you still in contact with her? How would you know about the death if you weren't still talking to her? You told me no contact.

He replied: She called the manager. He told me. Please.

She deleted what he wrote and shut her laptop off. She got up and made tea. "Daddy." "Yes baby." "Mama was pretty." "She still is." "You sing to Mama like me at bed?" "I should," Joe said. "Think Mama needs bed song." Ava starting tearing up again. She made her tea and went outside to the porch swing. She sipped her tea and tried to get rid of the tears before Grace saw them. She relaxed and by the time she was done her tea, the tears were gone. Her eyes weren't puffy, and she went inside. She saw Joe taking Grace to bed. She went back to the sofa and went back to her writing.

Ava heard Joe singing to Grace. It was the song he had sung to her all that time ago when he was trying to sweet talk her into one thing or another. When he finished, she heard him slip out of Grace's room and head back downstairs. She saved the one sentence she'd managed to write and tried to keep going. "She asleep?" He nodded then kissed Ava. It was one of those trying to convince you to feel something kisses where her heart skipped and raced and pounded out of her chest and the tingles shot down to the tips of her toes type of kiss. The kind where a man can almost get anything he could ever want. He sat down on the sofa beside her. Ava looked at him. He rubbed her feet. "Stop." "Ava I don't want to fight anymore." "I meant stop my foot hurt," Ava said. He noticed the bruise on her toe. "Cleaning again?" "Stubbed it on the bed." "We going to talk and finish this?" "You promised me Joe." "I went to offer condolences. She tried to kiss me and I walked away." "But." "You saw her put her arms around me. Doesn't mean she kissed me." "Never again. Promise me." "I wouldn't have gone in the first . . . ." "Promise." He nodded. "I'm trying. You know I am," Ava said. "I know. I'm sorry Ava. I am." "I know. We've been fine for so long, then this." "Ava, no more worrying. Remember something. No matter where I am, no matter who I am out with, I always have and always will be thinking about you and loving you every second of every hour of every day." "Joe." "I'm not finished. At some point, something is going to happen again. I'll be out with the guys, or out with a concert promoter and rumors will fly. Remember that I love you. I'm never going to wander into someone else's bed. I want you and only you." Ava went to get up and he pulled her into his lap.

"Joe, stop it." He kissed her. It was another of those kisses. Even her toes curled this time. He had her flat on her back on the sofa in minutes. They made love. They christened the house. First the sofa, then the floor of the living room. They curled up with a chenille throw that Ava had bought. "You did good baby," Joe said. Ava laughed. "With the house." "We still have to paint." "I know, but everything else looks great." Ava went to get up and he pulled her back into his lap. "Where are you going?" "Was going to get up and get a drink." He shook his head and kissed her. "I'm still mad," Ava said. "Ava, I didn't sleep with her." "Fine. But if I even think for a second . . . ." He kissed her. "If I even think for one second you are screwing around, that's it." He kissed her again, pulling her legs around him. "Only one woman who gets me whenever she wants." Ava went to get up and he pulled her back on top of him "What?" He kissed her. "Joe." "I missed you." "I bet." Ava got up and grabbed his shirt, slipping it on, then walked upstairs.

CHAPTER 32

Danielle woke up at 4am with pain. Her nails dug into Brad's arm. He was awake in seconds. "Baby," Brad said. "Ow." He got up and tried to help her to her feet. "Ow." It stopped long enough for her to pull on her one piece dress that Ava had demanded was the most comfortable thing ever. She slid her flats on with it and then doubled over. A minute or so later, she brushed her teeth and put some makeup on. Two more contractions later, Brad had the bag in the car, and was helping Danielle to the car. He called the doctor, Ryan and Joe on the way to the hospital. They pulled in and the doctor took Danielle straight to labor and delivery. "How long," the doctor asked. "Six hours. Now they're every two minutes," Danielle said. The doctor checked her out. "You're definitely in labor. You're 8 already." A half-hour later, Ryan and Rose showed up. "Where's Ava," Danielle asked. "Long story." "I'm here," Ava said running in.

A half-hour later, Danielle was holding a beautiful baby boy. His name was Christopher Andrew. "Congratulations Dad," Ava said hugging Brad. "Thank you for being here. I was a damn mess," Brad said. "And you will be for about another 18 years," Joe joked. Ava went to leave and Rose pulled her aside. "You okay?" "Getting there." "I went to the house yesterday and you were gone," Rose said. "We bought a place away from the city." "You are still going to stay at the house though right?" Ava nodded. "You two alright?" "Been better," Ava said. Ryan came towards them. "He with Grace," Ryan asked. Ava nodded. "He'll be by tomorrow," Ava said. "Need to talk to you for a minute," Ryan said.

He pulled Ava aside. "He didn't," Ryan said. "Ryan, enough." "Her mom did pass away. I told her to stay away from him and she said she didn't expect him to show up. Nothing happened." "Fine." "Ava, just have a little faith alright?" She nodded. He hugged her and Ava left. She took the long route back to the house. She grabbed some Starbucks coffee and a few other things, then pulled in. She went inside, then walked upstairs and slid into bed with Joe.

Joe wrapped his arms around her the minute he felt her slide into bed. "Danielle okay?" "Christopher Andrew." "Holy crap." "I know." "We're going over tomorrow," Joe said. "I know. I told Brad and Danielle you'd be by." He nuzzled her neck. "Joe." He kissed her neck, then her ear. Ava turned towards him. "Well?" "Well what," Ava asked. He kissed her. Ava curled up with him and fell asleep. He fell asleep thinking that finally the fight was over.

The next morning, he woke up and Ava was gone. He went downstairs and heard Ava outside with Grace. He pulled his sweater on and went outside. "What are you two up to," Joe asked. "Mama's showing me garden." He walked over and wrapped his arm around Ava. "Morning beautiful." "Morning sleepy head." Ava went for a walk with Grace. A half-hour or so later, and they were back. "How was your walk," Joe asked as Grace jumped into his lap. "I saw birdies." "Wow." Ava went in and made Grace some breakfast "Thanks Mama," Grace said. "Welcome baby." Ava went into the TV room and grabbed her laptop. Joe walked over and pulled it away from her. "I have to do writing." He shook his head. "Joe." He grabbed her hand. They walked over to the table and he brought her an omelet. "Nice," Ava said. He kissed her. Grace giggled. Joe kissed Grace and grabbed his breakfast. The second Ava saw him with the coffee, she stared. "Noticed a few things in the fridge," Joe said. Ava smirked. "Knew you couldn't live without it." "Mama, we going to see Jacob?" "Nope. We're hanging out at home." "Can we go see Jacob?" "I can take you over if you want," Joe said. "Okay." Grace played with her food as usual and managed to actually eat most of it. After breakfast, he kissed Ava, took Grace up to her room to get changed, then headed off to drop her off to see Jacob, go see Danielle and Brad, then come home for more make-up time.

Joe walked back into the house and it was quiet. Ava was in the solarium doing her writing. "Hey," Joe said. "Hey yourself." "She fell asleep with Jacob. I'll go get her later," Joe said. "Okay." "What you up to?" "Writing." "Wanna come for a drive?" "Sure." "Let's go then." He slid her laptop out of her hands and Ava got up. She slid off the massive cozy writing sweater, then slid on her sunglasses and they headed out. "Where are we going," Ava asked. "For a drive." "No kidding. Where are we going?" They pulled into the park. "Trying again?" "No." "Then what are we doing here?" He hopped out and came around the car to get her. A man started walking towards them. "Hey Andy." "Hey. Just got everything set up like you asked. "Thanks." "What are you up to?" The makeup people from the concert came over and touched her makeup up. "You look great," they said. "What is he up to?" "Thought you needed some good pictures of the two of you." He walked over and grabbed Ava's hand. They walked over to the tree and he kissed her. "What are you up to," Ava asked. "Romancing my wife." She smirked. They curled up under the tree, while she leaned into his arms. The photographer snapped a few as the breeze blew through her hair.

A few hours later, the photographer had snapped hundreds of pictures. "I'll send them over," he said. "Thanks," Joe said as he walked back towards the SUV with Ava. The paparazzi came out of the woodwork and started snapping pictures. "Is it true that you caught him with another woman," one asked. "Ava. Is it true that it's not his baby?" They got in the SUV and pulled out, heading home. "So." "No freaking," Joe said. "Where the hell do they get that crap from?" "Now it's not mine?" "Somehow I don't think that's possible." "Good point," Joe said. He kissed her. They picked Grace up, then headed home. She was still asleep in the back seat when they pulled in. Joe took her inside, tucked her into bed, then came downstairs. Ava was curling up on the sofa. "What you up to?" "Just relaxing." He slid onto the sofa behind her. Joe wrapped his arms around her and he felt a thump in her stomach. "Tell me that wasn't." Ava nodded. He rubbed his hand over her stomach and felt another one. He sang to the baby a bit and the kicking stopped. He kissed Ava. They curled up together again, and Ava had a quick nap.

He sat in the solarium and got some writing done himself, then Ava came in when she woke up. "What you doing?" "Writing. How was your nap?" "Good." "Babe," Joe asked. "Mmm?" "I have to go back to town." "You're the one that said you wanted to stay out here for a few months." "I know. We have an interview tomorrow." "Have fun." "We as in you and me and the guys." "No." "Yep." "Joe, I have book stuff to do," Ava said. "We have to." Her phone went off. "Hi Ava. It's Karen. We booked the dates for the readings." "When?" "Wednesday night." "Where?" "In Nashville. Then one in Memphis and one in Dallas." "I'm home on the weekend though right?" "Yes. You're back Friday night." "Good." "See you in Nashville," her agent said. Ava hung up. "What?" "Have three readings." "Where?" "Nashville, Memphis and Dallas." "Road trip." "No," Ava said. "Why not? You aren't thinking you're going without me." "Joe, the one in Nashville we can drive to. The other two, I can do alone." "No." "Why?" "Babe." "Just means catching all that extra sleep," Ava said. "After what the doctor said, no way in hell." "I'll be fine." "No." "Joe, stop it. I'm going." Ava walked out and went into the kitchen and tried to come up with something for dinner. "We're getting Chinese," Joe said. "Stop starting another fight." "You aren't going alone Ava. You just got out of the hospital." "And?" "No."

Ava walked upstairs and went through the closet trying to figure out what to wear. "You're not going without me," Joe said. She put a few things into a bag. "Ava." "I have to go. Like it or don't." He walked up behind her and turned her towards him. "Why?" "Why what?" "Why are you so determined for me not to go," Joe asked. "Because I don't want Grace to have to be shuttled around everywhere." "Real reason." "I'm going. End of discussion." "No it isn't," Joe said. "Yeah it is." "Ava." "You take off to the studio and go on tour and go to interviews alone. I'm doing this." "So you're doing it to make me miss you?" "No. This is part of my job. Let me do it," Ava said. She walked downstairs and he tried to grab her hand. She walked outside and sat on the edge of the porch. Joe sat inside and stared at her. She called Rose.

"Hey Rose." "Hey. You okay," Rose asked. "I have to go do some book readings and he's freaking out." "Ever think it might have something to do with the fact that he's scared you're going to do something to get back at him?" "I'm not the one who can't be trusted." "Ava, you have to either let it go, or stop with the BS," Rose said. "Rose." "I mean it. If you're doing it to get back at him and to upset him, it's working. Just let him come with you." "No." "Fine. Then let him meet you in Dallas. The two close to home aren't that bad." "Why should I," Ava said. "Because you love him. If you didn't, you would've left by now." "Fine." "Stop torturing him." "Rose." "I know you're still mad. Just let go of it." Joe came outside. "Go and talk to him Ava. No more causing shit," Rose said. "Fine. I'll talk to you later." Ava hung up. "Come inside," Joe requested. "For what?" He reached for her hand.

They went inside and he sat Ava on the sofa. "I know you have to go. What's the big deal? I can't be there to support you?" "Joe, it's three hours of sitting in a stupid book store. You don't want to do that, and it's boring for Grace. I'd rather that she have time with you at home." "Fine. Nashville and Memphis you're coming home after right," Joe asked. Ava nodded. "We're coming to Dallas. We can stay overnight, then come home the next morning." "If that's what you want." "Babe." "One night is going to kill you that much," Ava asked. He kissed her and leaned her onto the sofa. "Yeah it will." He kissed her again and started trying to slide her tank top off when Grace woke up. "Joe." He kissed her again. "Daddy," Grace said. He heard Grace coming down the steps one at a time. He got up. "Hey princess," Joe said. "I thirsty." He went into the kitchen and grabbed Grace a sippy cup of milk and took her back upstairs. He tucked her back in and came back downstairs. He walked back over to the sofa and Ava was on the phone.

He kissed her and slid his hands under the back of her shirt. She hung up the phone and Joe put it on the table. "She back asleep?" He kissed Ava again. He went for the zipper of her jeans. "Joe." He kissed down her torso, then peeled them off. "What if . . ." He kissed her again and a few minutes later was having sex with her on the sofa. After, Ava got up and pulled on a shirt, then went upstairs. She came back down in leggings and his favorite shirt. He went upstairs and had a quick shower, then came back down. Grace woke up as he was walking past her bedroom door. "Daddy." "Yes baby girl." "Where going?" "Getting dinner. Road trip," he asked. "Okay." He slid her out of bed, threw on her leggings and her favorite shirt and took her with him to get dinner.

When they came back, Ava had a fire going in the fireplace and had the table set. "Hi Mama." "Hey baby." "I gots a cookie," Grace said. "Looks yummy." "Daddy got one for you too." Joe kissed Ava. They set up for dinner, then sat down and ate. Grace nibbled away at hers while Ava and Joe finished everything else. Ava cleaned up while Joe went and turned on Cinderella for Grace for the millionth time. "Babe." "What?" "I love you." "And you're going to miss me when I'm in Dallas." "Friday night you're home right," Joe asked. "Not if I stay overnight." "Babe." "Just you and Grace." "And what if I wanted to take you out Friday night?" "Then you'd be waiting until Saturday," Ava said. "Ava." "I'll be home most likely. Depends on how tired I am." "I don't want you to go." "I know. You also know I'm still going." "You're going to call me when you land right?" Ava nodded. She kissed him then went to go in and sit with Grace. He pulled her back into his arms and kissed her, leaning her into the counter in the kitchen.

Grace fell asleep watching the movie for the millionth time. Joe carried her upstairs and put her in bed then saw Ava heading to their bedroom. He walked in and saw Ava packing her things. "You're leaving Friday?" Ava nodded. She went through the closet and found two dresses for the other two readings. "Think you should go for the pink one," Joe said. "Too tight." "Black one." Ava pulled it out and put it aside for the first reading. She pulled out the red one next, and packed another one. "If you start feeling sick again, you need to call me," Joe said. "You aren't going to be able to do anything Joe. I'll be fine." "Still gonna worry." "I know you will." Ava zipped the suitcase up. "So what time do you have to be there tomorrow?" "Noon." "I'll drop Grace at Ryan's," Joe said. "Joe." "I want to be there with you." "Fine," Ava said giving in. He kissed her "About time you gave in." He laughed. Ava got changed for bed then grabbed her book and crawled into bed. "What you doing?" "Reading?" He kissed her. "Don't need the book," Joe said. "You might like it." "Oh really?" She handed it to him, pointing out a section in the book. He read it realizing that it was a little steamy. Three lines in he slid closer to Ava. "How do you read this," Joe asked. She smirked. "Babe." "Mmm." He slid his arm around Ava, then marked the page and put the book on the side table. "I have an idea." "What's that," Ava asked. "We could sing when you go to your signing." "Always trying to figure out how to get it so you come with me aren't you?" "Can't hurt to try," Joe said. "Nice one, but no." "You and I could sing the love letters song." "And all your fans would show." "They probably will anyway," Joe said. "I know." He kissed her neck. "You know it's supposed to be about the book." "I know babe. Still, I'm going to be there." "And I'll be back Friday night from Dallas. I promise." "Good." He kissed her and pulled her close. "What?" "What you wearing tomorrow," Joe asked. "The black one I bought." "Better idea. "And what would that be?" "The black top with the leggings," Joe said desperately trying to talk her out of the sexy black dress. "Now there's an idea." He kissed her and they curled up together. A half-hour later, they were both asleep.

The next morning they got up, Ava went for her run with Grace, then they got ready and headed to do the interview. Grace came with them. After an hour and a half of questions, the interviewer came down to the important stuff. "So we wanted to say congrats to Ava and Joe. When are you due?" "Late in July," Ava said. "Is your daughter looking forward to it?" "She is. She keeps asking the baby if it wants some cookies. Someday the baby's going to say yes," Joe joked. "So you hoping for a boy or a girl?" "I know Joe is hoping for a boy, but honestly, I just want a happy and healthy baby," Ava said. "So Brad, what's it like being a new dad?" "It's amazing, tiring, and pure love all wrapped into one." "Did any of the guys give you any advice that worked?" "Ava gave me the best advice actually. No matter what happens, it's going to be nothing but a memory when the baby grows up. Love him every day more than the day before," Brad said smirking at Ava. "Sounds like good advice." "It was the same advice Brad gave me when Joe and I got married," Ava said. Brad laughed.

They finished up the interview then headed home. Ava picked Grace up and took her back to the house. They pulled in and Ava saw Cat on her doorstep. Joe took Grace inside. "What's up?" "I need to talk to you." "What's wrong Cat?" She took Ava's hand and they headed out into the back. "What's wrong?" "It's not gonna work." "What isn't?" "Scott and I are fighting like cats and dogs." "What about?" "He wants to have a baby," Cat said. "And?" "He's gonna be gone in months. What's the point?" "What are you doing Friday?" "Working." "You're working from home right?" Cat nodded. "Good. Pack. Our flight leaves at ten," Ava said. "Where?" "Dallas. We're staying Friday night." "Ava." "You need a girl night too." "Okay." "I'll come get you." Cat hugged her. "Just hear the man out. Stop overdoing the stubbornness," Ava said. "Nice. Especially coming from the queen of stubborn." Ava headed back inside and Cat left.

"She okay," Joe asked. Ava nodded and came inside. "I'm staying in Dallas Friday night." "Why?" "Cat's coming with me. We're gonna have a girls night." "We have a concert Saturday night," Joe said. "I'll be home around lunchtime." He kissed Ava. "Mama," Grace said. "Yes baby." "Why for Cat here?" "She just came to say hi." "Bye bye Cat." Grace ran to the window waving goodbye. Joe and Ava had to laugh. She was way too cute for words. A minute later Cat called. "Tell me she wasn't saying what I think she was," Cat asked. "Bye bye kitty Cat," Grace said at the window. Ava and Cat both started laughing. Joe was laughing even harder.

After dinner, Ava finished putting together what she was going to wear for the next few days and Joe watched her. "What?" "Nothing. You know that you're beautiful in everything you have." "And I don't want to look like a whale." "Ava. You don't. You never could," Joe said. "Nice try." "You're beautiful. A baby bump isn't a bad thing. Think of it like an accessory." Ava laughed and threw a pillow at him. "Don't start that." Ava threw another one. Before they knew it, it was an all-out pillow fight. They ended up curled up together on the bed in a tickle fight. They laughed and giggled for what felt like hours, then finally cooled down. "Seriously. Why are you so worried?" "Because the little dresses aren't possible. I loved the black one." "Babe." "Don't say I can wear it anyway," Ava said. "So wear the longer one." "The tight one?" "You are beautiful in that dress." "And less to show off," Ava said. He laughed and kissed her. "You know that everyone wants to see you. Why does it matter?" "Because." "Ava. You look beautiful in that dress. You put on those boots you love and it's perfect," Joe said. Ava thought about it. "You have a point." "I know. That's why you married me." Ava laughed and kissed him. "Stop worrying about what you look like." "I love you." "I know." He kissed her again. Ava curled up on the bed with him and he slid his arms around her. "Just think. Saturday night, you're on stage. No hiding it," Joe said. "Then I have to go shopping." He laughed again. "We'll go after the reading." Ava kissed him. "Just one more reason why." "What's another one?" "Practicing." He kissed her again and slid her out of her jeans.

The next morning was a whirlwind. They got ready, Grace went to Rose and Ryan's, and Joe and Ava left for the reading. He sat with her agent and the publishing house rep and talked. Ava read from the book that Joe hadn't even got to read yet. He watched her and watched the fans as they were into every word. "She's amazing when she's dealing with a crowd," her agent said. "Know that first hand," Joe replied. He watched Ava talk to the fans, sign autographs and do pictures. Once it was finally over, they went to leave when a fan or two saw him. They ducked out the back and took off to the mall.

Ava went to a few stores, completely surrounded and blocked off to everyone else by security. After a few stores, Joe was starting to laugh. "I don't know why you're so worried," Joe said. "Meaning what?" "Babe, you look amazing. So what if the baby is showing." "Nice." "Ava, stop. The last two looked beautiful." "Joe." "Babe, you looked sexy." Ava looked at him. He slid his arms around her and kissed her. "You sure," Ava asked. "You wanted the short dresses. They look amazing. Stop worrying." He grabbed them and went to the cash and paid for them. Ava slid back into the other dress, then they headed to another store, got a few things, headed to his favorite stores, got a few items there, then headed home. Only one store he wanted her to go into.

"So are we going for stiletto's," Ava asked. "No." Joe started laughing. "I need heels but not ones that are going to kill my feet." "No problem," the salesman said. After a half-hour, Ava had found a few pairs and so had Joe. They headed towards Ryan's to pick Grace up, then went to the house. "Thought we were . . . ," Ava said. He kissed Ava. He tucked Grace into bed and grabbed Ava's hand, leading her into the bedroom. "What?" "Why are you so worried? You weren't so worried last time," Joe said. "Because this time I'm on stage in front of all those people." "And they all know we're having a baby." "And I don't want to look like a . . . ." "Don't even say it. You're beautiful. You were beautiful when you were pregnant with Grace too," Joe said. "Guess the public eye thing was bothering you."

"Just makes things completely different," Ava said. "Babe, no matter what just remember that Ryan and Brad and I all think you're beautiful pregnant or not." "Joe." "I mean it. No worrying allowed." Ava sat down in his lap and he wrapped his arms around her. "You're still sexy, and beautiful, and tempting as hell. Get used to it." Ava smirked. "Better," Ava said. He kissed her. "What are we doing back here anyway," Ava asked. "Closer to take Grace to Ryan and Rose's." "You aren't seriously coming with me tomorrow." He nodded.

"I watched you with that crowd today. I've never seen people that enthralled." "Liar. That's what your fans are like," Ava said. "Not like that babe." "All I did was read part of the book." "I know. You're amazing." "Thank you." "Never saw you in your element like that." "Like it," Ava asked sliding her arms around his neck. He nodded. "Really?" "You don't wanna know." Ava kissed him and he leaned her back onto the bed. He slid the zipper of her dress down. Within a minute or two, her dress was on the floor with his jeans and shirt and everything else. "You are so sexy," Joe said. He kissed her again. They made love, then curled up under the covers. "So when are we supposed to start the tour again," Ava asked. "Two weeks." "Seriously?" "Stop worrying." "I have to book the ultrasounds," Ava said. "Babe, no stressing." "I need the dates." "Ava, the doctor said she'd come to us if necessary." "When did you talk to her?" "While you were signing books." "Busy were you." Joe nodded. "Checking out the sexy lady signing books," Joe said. He kissed her. "Mama." He let go. Ava got up after a few more kisses, slid her robe on and went and checked on Grace.

"What's wrong baby?" "We going home?" "We are home." "Other home." "Not tonight." "Movie?" Ava laughed. She slid Grace out of bed and went downstairs. Grace picked a movie from the shelves and Ava slid it in and curled up on the sofa with her. A little while later, Grace was asleep in her arms. Ava gently took her back upstairs to bed and tucked her in. She went back into the bedroom and Joe was asleep. Ava walked over, kissed him, covered him up and slid into the shower. She came out a little while later in her towel and he was staring right at her. "What?" "Not allowed to stare at my wife," Joe asked. "Depends." He motioned for her to come closer. She walked towards him. "What?" "Tease." Ava walked closer and he pulled her into bed. "What?" He kissed her neck. "Smell good." "Lavender soap." He started serenading her with their wedding song. Ava slid her arms around him. He kissed her and snuggled her back under the covers. After more kissing and more snuggling and making love again, they got up, cleaned up and got dressed . . . and just in time. "Mama. I hungry."

Ava got Grace something to eat, then they curled up together. Grace had her bath, they finished watching the movie, then Grace went to bed. Joe ran out to get something. Ava sang her to sleep. She slid out of the bedroom and smelled her favorite dinner of all time. She walked downstairs and he had the table set with candles and sparkling cider.

Joe walked over to Ava and she wrapped her arms around him. "Hey beautiful." "Hey yourself handsome." He kissed her. "Come eat." Ava nodded and kissed him. They sat down and had dinner, then he handed Ava her fortune cookie. "What?" "Nothing." He watched her open it. A bracelet slipped out. "What?" He smirked. "So this is what you were up to." Joe kissed her. He slid it on her wrist. "Perfect." "Joe." "No it won't." It was just a little loose. Ava kissed him. "So you can always wear it." "Thought of everything." He kissed her and did the dishes. She slid her arms around him. "What you doing?" "Nothin," Ava teased. She undid his belt. "Don't start." She slid his shirt off. "Didn't want it to get wet," Ava joked. "Um hm." Ava walked back into the TV room.

CHAPTER 33

Joe came in and saw Ava curled up on the sofa. He looked at the TV and saw her watching the wedding DVD. "What are you watching," he asked sliding onto the sofa and rubbing her feet. "Still remember how nervous I was." "Why? We were already . . ." "I know. Think I was as nervous as Cat was." "Why?" "Didn't know what to expect," Ava said. "And?" "Other than the road bumps, it was worth it." "Oh really," Joe said. "Unless I'd made you wait to get married." "I couldn't wait to marry you." "I gathered that. Would it have been different if we'd waited?" "I would've chased you anywhere." "Good to know," Ava joked. "Caught you before you could play hard to get." Ava smirked. "And you loved every second." "True." "You telling me you would've been able to hold back," Joe said. Ava looked at him. "Liar." "I could've really made you chase me," Ava said. "How?" "Not coming back here with you." "No, that would've been totally wrong." "And if I hadn't?" "I still would've followed you anywhere." "If we'd waited though." "I would've been drooling on you 24/7 until I got you down the aisle," Joe said. Ava laughed. He slid in behind her on the sofa and wrapped his arms around her. "I knew the minute you walked in that room that I was going to marry you." "Even though I was there with . . ." "Even though you had crappy taste in boyfriends at the time." "Still remember the look on Rose's face when you came to the house." "So do I." "If I'd known then that you could sing like that . . ." "What," Ava said. "Would've pulled you on stage with us that night and never let stupid take you home." Ava laughed. He kissed her. "Look at that." "I know. I couldn't help it. You were beautiful in that dress," Joe said. "Looked pretty sexy yourself." "Why thank you." He kissed her shoulder. "We should get some sleep," Ava said. "What time do we have to leave?" "8:30." He hopped up and picked her up, carrying her up the steps to their bedroom.

The next morning, they got up and got ready to go. Joe drank his Starbucks coffee on the way while Ava did her makeup. "You look beautiful without it." "Sweet, but if they're taking pictures, I need it." Ava turned around and saw Grace singing along with the radio. "You singing?" Grace nodded. "Like Daddy," Grace said. Joe laughed. They sang and were silly most of the way there. He pulled in and got Grace while Ava headed inside. This time, they'd set up a stage. Ava headed on stage. She read a little bit of the book, then someone asked if she'd sing. She looked at Joe. He grabbed his guitar and came up with her. Grace sat in Ava's arms. "It's a family affair today," Ava said. The crowd squealed. They sang a song together, then one that nobody had heard yet. Joe kissed Ava, and took Grace, then she started signing the books. He watched, but this time she kept looking over at him.

After, they headed back to the house. Grace had some dinner, then Joe tucked her in. Ava made dinner for her and Joe. He came downstairs and heard her humming the song. "It was perfect just the way you did it," Joe said. "Did you write it down?" He kissed her. "Of course." He wrapped his arms around her. "What?" "I don't want you to go without me." "I'll be home Saturday morning," Ava said. "I know. Won't be the same." "Think you can handle one night alone." He kissed her. It was a passionate, makes your knees buckle kiss. Ava slid her arms around him. "Saturday night." "Piano. I'm warning you," Joe teased. He kissed her again, leaning her against the counter. He could smell dinner. "You didn't." Ava nodded. He took the mango chicken from the oven and slid it onto the plates. Ava handed him the veggies and he put them out. "You know how addictive this is," Joe asked as he inhaled the mango chicken. Ava nodded. He helped her with the dishes, then demanded she go to bed. Ava headed upstairs and he followed a few minutes later.

He walked in and stared at her. "What?" "You're not wearing the little dress without me," Joe said. Ava laughed and kissed him. She slid the black dress into her bag and put everything together for her trip. "I don't want you to go without me," Joe said. "The first show is in Houston. I'll meet you there," Ava said. "Better idea. You, me and the plane alone on the way to Dallas," Joe said. "Or Cat and I meet you in Houston," Ava repeated. "Then I'll meet you at the airport in Dallas," Joe said. "Cat's coming." She slid her arms around him. "You know everything is going to be fine," Ava said. "And you're calling me to make sure," Joe replied. "Cat's with me. Anything happens." "No. Anything happens, you pick up the phone and tell me." "Stop worrying." "Why do I get the feeling like there's a reason I should," Joe asked. "The worst that's gonna happen is Cat has a drink or two and we get giggly." "Ava." "Fine. We get giggly minus the alcohol." He kissed her with a toe curling kiss and picked her up, carrying her to the bed. He laid her down and curled up with her. "I know why you're worried. You don't need to be." "But . . ." "Joe, trust me okay." He nodded. "Just want to take care of my wife." "I know," Ava said. They curled up together, then fell asleep on the bed.

The next morning, he woke up to Ava packing the last of her things. "I'm driving you," Joe said. "Emily's here with Grace," Ava replied. He pulled his shirt on and freshened up, then took everything to the SUV." "Mama," Grace said. "Yes baby." "Where going?" "Dallas." "See horses?" Ava nodded. "I'll see you tomorrow," Ava said. "No." Grace started screaming her head off and wouldn't let go of Ava. "Grace." "I no want you go." "I have to go to work." "No." "Grace, I promise I'll be home tomorrow." "No." She picked Grace up and held her. "I want come." "What about Elmo," Ava asked. Grace turned and saw Sesame Street on the TV. She nuzzled Ava. After a kiss goodbye and some strategic distraction, Ava and Joe headed to the airport. "Don't you start crying," Joe said. "What are you two going to do tonight," Ava asked. "Was thinking we could do some painting, and some singing, and maybe a little father/daughter stuff." "I have an idea." "What's that?" "Invite Jacob for a sleepover. You and Ryan can work on some music, and they'll distract each other," Ava said. "Good idea." "Plus Rose can have the night off to hang with Danielle." He slid his hand in hers. "Don't worry about me." "Just don't do something stupid okay," Ava said. "Like fly to Dallas?" Ava laughed. "Like calling old girlfriends." "Don't remember any." "Good." "Though I do remember one." "Who's that?" "This girl I met at a concert. Talked her into moving in with me and everything," Joe joked. "That's the only number you should remember." They pulled into the airport a little while later. He walked her in, they checked her bags and he gave her a long kiss goodbye. Cat, and half the paparazzi in town caught it. "Call me when you land," Joe said. Ava nodded. "I love you." "I love you more." He kissed her again and Ava and Cat headed to security.

Within a few hours, Ava and Cat were landing, rushing through getting bags and headed to the hotel. Ava called Joe while she was getting changed. "Babe." "What," Ava asked. "You're the sexiest woman in the entire planet. Don't forget that." "I love you too." Cat watched her and was a little envious. Scott dropped her off with a quick goodbye kiss and was in the studio the rest of the day. She got the answering machine when she called.

They left for the reading, and walked through a cloud of fans. Ava read from the book, answered questions, then people started requesting that she sing. "No backup. I'm sorry guys." She signed the books and did a million pictures, then she headed back to the hotel with Cat. "So, what you want to do first?" "I can't believe he won't answer," Cat said. Ava grabbed Cat's phone. "Stop waiting Cat. Just tell him that we're here and we'll see him tomorrow." "I don't get it," Cat said. "Just like when Joe's in the studio. He's concentrating on work. Just text him and let it go."

After a long text to Scott, they finally left. They got a few things for Joe, Scott, Grace and the new baby, then went for dinner. They managed to get through the appetizer before someone asked for Ava's autograph. They finished dinner, then headed back to the hotel. Cat finally got a message back:

Sorry babe. Was in the middle of something. How's the trip? Miss you already.

"See." "He's full of shit," Cat said. "Call him." Ava went and showered, while Cat called and talked to Scott. When Ava stepped out, they were in a fight on the phone. "Why didn't you just answer?" "Cat, I was working. What am I supposed to do? Say 'Guys, wifey's on the phone. Wait a minute." "Stop being a smart ass." "What's the real reason you're all mad," Scott asked, "Shut up." "Cat, talk to me." "You don't have the time to talk to me, so why the hell . . ." Ava grabbed the phone out of her hand. "Hey Scott." "Hey Ava. How you feeling," Scott asked a little relieved to be talking to the calmer of the two. "Good." "She is freaking out." "I know. She's just upset that you didn't do what Joe did," Ava said. "Don't tell me you two were making out at the airport?" "Kiss goodbye." "I had to get to work." "I know. Remember something. She loves you. Stop treating her like one of your girlfriends that you used to have at the studio." "This coming from . . ." "As I said," Ava replied. "I get it." "Romance the woman dumb ass." "Thanks." Ava handed the phone back to Cat and it went from tense to mushy.

Ava curled up on the sofa and turned on the TV. "Today we spotted Joe Morgan and his wife at the airport getting rather mushy. 'It's good to see that a couple like them can stay together through all the craziness.' 'And a source tells me they're having another baby.' 'Congratulations to the two of them'." Ava smirked. Her phone went off a minute or so later. "Hey," Ava said. "Hey yourself. How's girls night," Joe asked. "She's talking to Scott. They've been fighting all day." "I miss you." "I miss you too. How's Grace?" "She's playing with Jacob." "So you decided on the sleepover?" "Figured I should get used to taking care of two." "You have a point." "Still." "I know. I saw the thing on TV," Ava said. "Still can't believe the things they think are newsworthy." "You looked sexy." "Oh really? And what kind of mood are we in," Joe teased. "No mood. Curled up in my PJ's." "My favorite ones?" "Mmm." "We're staying tomorrow," Joe said. "Why's that?" "Piano." Ava giggled. "Don't think it isn't happening," Joe teased. "Oh I know you well enough to know you're serious Joe." "Hence why we're staying." "As long as I can make it on stage." He laughed. "After." "I love you." "I know. I love you too crazy husband of mine." They chatted a while longer, then Cat came in. "Talk to you tomorrow okay," Ava said. "Sweet dreams." "Give Grace a kiss for me." "I will," Joe said. They finally hung up. "So." "Thank you," Cat said. "Everything all good?" "Yeah. I guess I'm just freaking a bit." "Cat." "I found out before we left. I didn't tell him," Cat said. Ava hugged her. "Congrats Mama." They spent the rest of the night joking and being silly, then finally fell asleep.

Ava got up the next morning with a wake-up call from Joe, showered, then got changed. Cat pulled her jeans and tank top on, they packed up and headed for breakfast, then to the airport. They showed up and Joe was sitting outside the plane. "Well hello handsome. Know where I can find my sexy husband," Ava asked. He walked towards her and kissed her, picking her up in his arms. "I missed you something fierce," Joe said. He kissed her again. Cat went to walk onto the plane and saw Scott. She walked up the steps and he kissed her. Finally, she had the reaction she wanted. Ava and Joe got on the plane and put Ava's stuff with theirs. "Mama," Grace said. "Hi baby girl." Grace jumped into her arms.

"Got something for you," Ava said. She handed Grace a stuffed horse. "Horsie." Grace hopped out of her lap and went and played with Emily.

They showed up to the venue, did sound check, a few interviews, then relaxed for a while. Ava put Grace down for a nap and curled up with Joe. Scott and Cat took off and went shopping and some tourist stuff and Ryan and Brad called home to check on their wives.

"So." "Tell me you aren't wearing the black dress," Joe said. "Only one I packed." "Tease." "No, that would be the black lace lingerie for underneath," Ava whispered. He kissed her. One kiss led to another, then he grabbed her hand. "Where are you going?" He looked at her with a smirk ear to ear. "Joe." They headed backstage. Everyone was gone for dinner. He picked her up and slid her onto the piano. "Determined," Ava asked. He kissed her and slid her skirt up her legs. "Joe." He kissed her again and within minutes they were doing it. "I told you," he whispered. Ava laughed. They kept going until they came so hard they thought the floor was shaking. She slid off the piano and into his arms. "Think I missed you," Joe said. "Missed you too." Ava kissed him and zipped his jeans back up. "Babe." "Mmm." He smirked. "Don't even." He kissed her and they went and showered and started getting ready.

They had dinner, then Ava finished getting ready. Joe walked up behind her. "What?" "You're coming." "To what?" "The meet and greet." "I'm not . . ." He grabbed her hand and led her to the meet and greet. She walked in. They did the meet and greet and then chilled until they had to head on. Joe kissed Ava for luck and Scott and Cat sat side stage and watched. Ava went on as planned, then when she was done, she sat with Emily and Grace. Joe came out after the show and kissed her. "You were great baby," Joe said. "Had some inspiration." He kissed her cheek. They packed up and headed to the hotel. Emily was asleep the minute her head hit the pillow, and Grace out cold.

Ava and Joe curled up on the bed. "I love this dress," Joe said. "You were watching my butt again weren't you?" His hand slid down her back, undoing the zipper of her dress. "What you doing?" "Nothin." He slid her dress off. Ava turned towards him. "You had to do the really sheer lace didn't you?" Ava nodded. He kissed her and peeled her out of it. She slid his shirt off, and went for his jeans. "I missed you." "I know." He kicked his jeans off and was making love to her in minutes. It was like they were like they were on their honeymoon again. They finally fell asleep around 1am.

Around ten the next morning, they showered, had breakfast and packed up and headed back to the plane. Grace played with Ryan and Brad, while Joe and Ava relaxed. They landed, and headed back to the house, dropping Ryan and Brad off. "Mama, we go home," Grace asked. "Yep." They pulled in and Ava saw Cat's car. "What's she doing here," Joe asked.

"No idea." Joe parked, then kissed Ava. "I'll be inside in a few." Joe nodded. He kissed her again, then got Grace and headed inside.

"Cat?" Ava saw her sitting in the car. She knocked on the window and Cat got out. "What are you doing here?" "Can I crash for a few days?"

Joe took Cat's things to the other guestroom and came back downstairs. Cat was playing with Grace, coloring. He went into the kitchen and Ava was making Grace lunch. He slid his arms around her. "Hey handsome." "What you up to beautiful," Joe asked. "Giving Grace lunch. She's already yawning." "Think we need one too." "Oh we do?" He kissed her neck. "Think I might be able to arrange that." Ava gave Grace her lunch, then Cat started crying. "Bathtub is calling," Ava said. "Think something stronger." "No." "Ava." "No." Cat headed upstairs and slid into the hot bath like Ava suggested. "What happened?" "Long story." Grace fell asleep half way through her grilled cheese.

Ava took her to bed and tucked her in. As Ava was coming out of Grace's bedroom, Cat was coming out of the bathroom. "Better?" Cat shook her head. "What happened?" "He turned back into his normal stupid ass self as soon as we got back last night." "We'll find you a new place," Ava said. "Never sold my old one." "What?" "He moved his shit in. I told him he had 48 hours to get it out." "Cat." "I don't care. It's my house." "If you're sure this is what you want." Cat nodded. "You aren't drinking." "One drink." "9 months." "Shit." "Exactly. Go for a run. You can borrow my iPod." Cat did just that. Ava went into her bedroom and slid onto the bed beside Joe.

"World isn't coming to an end without you," Joe teased. Ava shook her head. "She alright?" "No. Scott's lost her." "Ava." "I already talked to him once Joe. He can't figure it out, then he needs a virtual reality smack." "Come here." She slid her arms around him and wrapped her leg around his. "I love you. Always will." "I know. I love you too. Don't know what I'd do without you." "Be pretty lonely," Joe teased. "Nah. Would've found another pretty boy." "Nice." "Pretty. Not handsome and romantic and sexy and amazing." He kissed her. "Good comeback." They curled up in bed, making out and snuggling. "So we going back tomorrow," Ava asked. "Missing it?" "A little." "No more book stuff?" "Not for a while. If it takes off, then I can sit back and watch everyone love it. I won't have to do anymore." Her phone went off a minute later.

"Hey," her agent said. "What's up?" "Wanted to let you know the big news." "Which would be," Ava asked. "Sold out." "The book?" "Either you and Joe singing at that event caused a major buying spree, or they loved it." "Couldn't have anything to do with the fact that you put it under Ava Morgan," Ava joked. "Had to take the chance Ava." "Right." "We're putting out a second edition. Sorta helped that Oprah had it on her favorite things." "Smart mouth."

"Just threw the check in the account. Emailed you the copy," her agent said. "Thanks." "That's what agents are for." Ava hung up and slid her phone onto the table.

"What was that?" "Nothing." "Tell me." "Better idea," Ava said. "What's that?" "We're going to dinner." "Oh really?" "And I'm wearing the red backless one." "Babe." "What?" "You have to tell me what that was about," Joe said. She kissed him and wrapped her arms around him. "Let's just say the world loved it." "The book?" "Second edition." "What?" Ava nodded. "Babe." "Either it was your fans, or they actually loved it," Ava said. "You finally going to let me read it?" Ava nodded. He kissed her and pulled her in close to him. Her leg slid over his. After more kissing and cuddling, Grace was awake. She came into the bedroom and Ava saw her head peek over the edge. "Good nap?" Grace nodded. She helped Grace onto the bed. "What doing Mama?" "Just talking to Daddy." "Why for?" "Kinda like him." "Me too." Joe laughed. "Think I kind of like you two too," he teased. "Grace, can you ask Auntie Cat to help you pick out a party dress?" "Okay." Grace hopped off the bed and ran into Cat's room.

Ava and Joe got up and he went to hop into the shower. "One minute." Ava went and talked to Cat. "What's going on?" "We're going to celebrate." "What?" "Second edition. First one sold out." "Holy shit," Cat said. "Exactly." "I'll find her something." "Get changed." "I'm coming?" Ava nodded. She went back into the bedroom and slid into the shower with Joe. "There you are," Joe said. He kissed her and slid her under the water. They finished their shower, then Joe got changed. Ava did her hair, her makeup, then slid on the red lace g-string and the red dress. Joe watched her. "You look like a cat eyeing its prey," Ava said. "Don't tempt me." He walked towards her. "What?" "Missing something." He grabbed her necklace with the diamond pendant out of her jewelry box and slid it around her neck. "Then I should wear the bracelet." He kissed her. "Think you need a little something. He went to grab one of his necklaces, and saw a box. "What's this?" "Don't know." Ava went to walk out of the bedroom and he pulled her back into his arms. "Ava." "Open it." He opened it and saw the necklace he'd been staring at for months. "When did you," Joe asked. "When we were away. I saw it and figured why not." "Babe." "You deserve it." "You know how crazy you are?" "That's why you married me." "One of the million reasons." He kissed her and they headed downstairs. Grace was in her black sparkly dress with her shiny shoes and Cat was in a black dress.

They headed to dinner, being asked for autographs through it from a few fans, then headed home. Grace was asleep in the SUV. They pulled in and Cat hopped out with Grace. "Thanks Cat," Joe said. "Thanks Cat what," Ava asked. They pulled off. "Hello? Where are we going?" "Our own celebration," Joe said. "The park?" He leaned over and kissed her at the security gate. "Where are we going?" "You'll see." "Joe." "We're going to go have an Ava and Joe night." "Dancing?" "No." They drove until all Ava could see was dark sky. Then she started seeing familiar lights. "We aren't?" He laughed. They pulled in to a parking spot, parked and headed into the bar. She saw Ryan, Brad, Danielle, Rose, and a few of their friends, including Joe's brother Derek. "What are you guys doing here," Ava asked. "Like we weren't going to celebrate with you." "So it was either Joe or Cat," Ava said. "Joe told me and Brad via text. This is a big day girl," Ryan said. He hugged Ava. "Thank you guys." "Ava." She turned and saw Scott with his arm around a blonde. "Hi Scott." "What you guys doing here," he asked. "Celebrating." "Let me buy you guys a drink." Ava looked at Joe. He kissed her and went and pulled Scott to the side.

After Joe talked Scott into growing up a bit, they celebrated a while and headed to the car. They went through another cloud of paparazzi then pulled out and headed back to the house.

They came inside and Emily was on the sofa. "Hey Emm." "Hey. Cat went out for a coffee with Scott. She said she'd be back in a half-hour." "Thanks. You need a ride back?" "No. I'll head back over to Ryan and Rose's with Jacob." She left a few minutes later. Ava slid her shoes off and went into the kitchen, grabbing herself some vitamin water. "What you doing," Joe asked. "Getting a drink." He grabbed another one, then carried Ava upstairs. "What?" He slid his arms around her and pulled her close. "I am the luckiest man there ever was." "I love you too." "I mean it. The music is going so well, your writing is unbelievable, Grace is perfect, and baby coming is doing fine. What more could we ask for," Joe asked. Ava smirked. "What?" "Nothing." "Babe." "Only thing we need now is to have some time just the three of us. Before we know it, the touring starts again . . ." He kissed her. "Stop being silly." "Can't," Ava said. "Why?" "I miss the house." "Tomorrow it is." He kissed her again and slid one strap off her shoulder. She slid his shirt off, then went for the belt. "Babe." "Mmm." "Your phone." Ava looked over. "That would be yours," Ava said. He slid it out of his pocket.

"Hello?" "Joe, it's Jodi." Just the look on his face had Ava sliding the dress back on. She opened her drink and went and washed her makeup off. "Why exactly are you calling me?" "Miss you." "Funny. Didn't miss me 3 years ago," Joe said. "Joe, we broke up." "And I'm married." "Your point? We dated for years. Never seemed the one-woman type of guy." "I am. Been that way for a while. Just took the right woman." "Care to take a wrong woman out for a drink?" "No." "I'll come over tomorrow." "No you won't Jodi." "Why? Might make her uncomfortable to know all the shit we did in that house?" "Don't bother." "Remember that time . . ." He hung up. He walked into the bathroom and Ava was putting her lotion on. "Babe." Ava shook her head. She got up, put the lotion away and went and got into bed. He changed and slid into bed with her, wrapping his arm around her.

CHAPTER 34

The next morning, he got up and Ava wasn't in bed. Her phone was gone, and so was her purse. He slid his robe on and went downstairs. The SUV was gone. Grace's baby bag was gone. He had his coffee then tried calling Ava. "What?" "Where are you?" "Mall." "Ava." "I'll be home in an hour or so." "Babe." "Not now." Ava hung up. His stomach was officially in a knot.

"What's up with you two," Cat asked. "Nothing." "How was the party?" "Fine. How's things with Scott?" "Joe must have talked to him. We talked, but I still don't know." "You have to do what you think is right." "Something's up." "No." "Mama, look," Grace said. She saw a giant teddy bear in the window of the toy store. "Do you want to go in?" Grace nodded. They headed in, went through the teddy bear section, and got her a teddy. Ava got one for Cat too. "Did you tell him about the baby yet," Ava asked. "I can't. I don't want that to be the reason." "Grace, Auntie Cat needs a hug." Grace reached over to Cat and wrapped her arms around her and kissed her cheek. They got a few things, then headed towards the SUV.

Out of the corner of her eye, Ava saw James. She slid Grace into the car seat and turned to hop in when James was in front of her. "Hi," he said. "What do you want James?" "I need to talk to you." "I'm on my way home." "Ava." "No." James grabbed her hand. "Let go." "Ava, I need to talk to you." "And I'm on my way home. What the hell are you doing here anyway? I thought you were getting married or something," Ava asked. "We didn't." "Go figure." "I need you." "That's nice." "Ava." "I'm not letting you back into my life James. That was over a long time ago,' Ava said. "And if I said I wanted you?" Ava broke away from him and got in the SUV. She pulled out before he could get to her and headed for the highway. "What was that?" "Ex history," Ava said. "Mama, where Daddy?" "We're on our way home." "Okay." Grace played with the teddy bear in the back seat the rest of the way home.

A little while later, Ava pulled back in and saw Joe sitting on the front step. She went to get Grace and Cat got her. "Go," Cat said. Ava leaned against the car. "Babe." "What?" "Okay. You're pissed off." "You think?" "Where did you go?" "Shopping." "Ava." "I needed to get out of the house," she said. "Stop." "Who is she," Ava asked. "I dated her before we met. It was the only semi-long term thing I'd had." "And the reason she was calling was?" "She wanted to go for a coffee." "How was it?" "Don't know. I had one at home and hoped you'd come sit with me," Joe said. "Right." Ava went to walk away and he grabbed her hand. "Ava." "I told you. Don't make me say it again." She broke away and went upstairs. "Ava." "What?" "Stop this." "I'm going back to the house. Don't bother coming." She went to grab her things and he stopped her. "Ava, we're not having this fight." "Yeah we are," Ava said. She threw a few sweaters into a bag with some of her things. "I love you." "Yep." She went to walk out and he slid the bag off her shoulder. "Stop it." "Ava, you aren't walking out." He pulled her into his arms. "What?" "I love you." "And you smell like perfume," Ava said. She pushed him away and walked into Grace's room. She grabbed some of her things and walked downstairs.

"Mama." "What baby?" "Can we play in the pool?" "We're going to the house." "I want to play in the pool." "We will when we get there." "Mama," Grace said. "Grace, stop. We're going to the house. You can play in the pool all afternoon if you want to." Joe walked down the steps. "Come on Grace. We'll go get in the car and watch Lilo and Stitch," Cat said. She took her to the SUV. "Ava." "What?" "Stop. Think about this," Joe said. "I am." "No you aren't." "You told me no more calls. You promised me. Then you get a call from her at that time of night?" "She got divorced. She cheated on me with him. I told you there would never be anyone else." "Whatever." He pulled her back to him and kissed her. He slid the bag off her shoulder without breaking the kiss. Finally after 20 minutes, he let her up for air. "That seem like a man who doesn't want you," Joe asked. "No. Feels like one who gets tempted too much." Ava grabbed the bag and walked out.

Ava cried all the way to the house. Grace watched her movie and fell asleep. Cat didn't say anything. They pulled in and Ava took Grace and tucked her into her bed, leaving her sippy cup of water by her bed. She walked into the bedroom and slid on her sweater and leggings, and walked downstairs. "I made chicken soup," Cat said. Ava nodded and they took a mug of soup to the porch. "You two okay?" Ava shook her head. "You want to talk about it?" Ava started crying again. "Ava." "Why the hell do I not know everything yet? I mean I say to change his number and his ex gets it. I say no more ex's, and she calls." "And?" "I don't know," Ava said. "Ava, he loves you," Cat replied. "And I can't compete with them. I can't compete with the little twigs with big boobs and six pack abs. I can't compete with the girls that can practically do acrobatics in bed. Look at me. I'm pregnant. I have to buy clothes that are bigger than usual just to cover my stomach." "And you're pregnant with his baby. He loves you. The two of you are married. He put a ring on your finger and gave you a dream wedding. He does things right Ava," Cat said. "And? I still get to compete with the entire female population of the planet." Ava got up and ran for the washroom. "You alright?" She heard her being sick. She came out a little while later. "You alright?" Ava shook her head. She was clutching her stomach.

Cat sat her on the sofa and wrapped her up in the chenille blanket. "I don't know what's wrong with me." "Pregnant?" "Funny ass," Cat said. "Just chill. I'll grab the ginger ale and crackers." Grace got up a little while later and Cat and Ava played with her. Around dinner time, Ava heard Joe's car pull into the driveway. "Daddy." Grace ran for the door and ran outside straight for him. "Hey baby. What you doing?" "Playing with Cat. Mama sick." Joe picked Grace up and walked right towards Ava. "Grace, come on. Let's go play in the pool for a while before dinner," Cat said. She took her outside so Ava and Joe could talk.

"You okay?" "What are you doing here," Ava asked. "Answer me." "I'm fine." "What's wrong?" "My stomach was upset." "We're talking." "Joe, I don't want to talk anymore." "Then you're listening." "Joe." "Listen. I dated her before we met. I couldn't handle being with her. She was never going to be the right woman for me. We broke up six months before I saw you again." "Then why," Ava asked. "She found out we got married. Said that I was never the one-woman type man. I told her straight out that it took the right woman and she wasn't it." "Did you?" "She showed up at the gate. We talked outside and that's all." "Was she with you when you had the house," Ava asked. "Ava." "Yes or no?" "Yes." Ava got up and was sick again. She went into the kitchen and grabbed herself a glass of ginger ale. "Are you alright?" "Leave me alone," Ava said. "No." Ava was holding her stomach. "Come lay down." "Don't tell me what . . ." He picked her up and carried her to the sofa. He sat down beside her. "I didn't do anything. I called you and texted you a million times." "You don't get why I was upset." "Yeah I do. Ever think maybe instead of worrying about your competition, she was worried that being with you would make me forget her?" "Nice to know it didn't." He kissed her. "Yeah it did." Joe kissed her again with a sweeping her off her feet and into the air type of kiss. "I love you. I told you that a million times. I don't know what else I have to say or do." "I can't handle the calls Joe. I told you that." "And you think walking off was going to change it?" "No. I'm sick of competing with every other woman in the damn planet." "Guess what? You won. There isn't a competition."

They talked a while longer, then he made her dinner. Grace came in with Cat. "Good timing. Dinner will be ready in a few," Joe said. Grace hugged Joe's leg. He put dinner on the plates, then picked her up. "Hi baby girl." "Mama sick." "I noticed. How was the pool?" "Fun." "Good. You hungry?" Grace nodded. He sat her down and gave her dinner, then took Ava's dinner and ginger ale to her on the sofa. Cat sat with her.

"You feeling any better?" "I guess." "You needed to talk to him," Cat said. "You called him didn't you?" "No. Still, you needed to talk to him." "You tell Scott where we were going," Ava asked. "Don't bring him into this. If I pulled something like this, he would let me leave." "Not true." Joe came in. Grace hopped on the sofa with Ava. "Hi Mama." "Hey princess." "Better," Grace asked. "Getting there." Grace hugged her. Joe kissed Ava, then cleaned up. Cat went and helped him. "Why don't you pick out a movie baby," Ava said. "Okay." Grace hopped off the sofa and went through her movies. She came back and giggled. "Which one?" She handed Ava the wedding video. "Again?" Grace nodded. "Okay. Go slide it in." Grace put it in the DVD player and Ava turned it on. She got up and went into the kitchen. Cat went in and sat with Grace.

"You're supposed to be laying down." "I need to say this and you need to hear it." "What?" "I love you, but I'm not going to compete with your past. I need to know that the ex's will stop popping up," Ava said. "You know that we both have a past. Fact is, we're together. We're married. I want to be with you for the rest of my life. If I didn't, then I wouldn't have married you." "I know, but still." "But still nothing. It doesn't matter who it is. We married each other. That means no ex's are going to separate us," Ava said. "Joe." "I mean it. I dated a lot Ava. Fact is, nobody was right until I met you. I love you." "Then why?" "Because people always try to mess up things that they know are indestructible." "Joe." "Get used to it. You're going to see me every morning for the rest of your life," he said. Joe kissed her and pulled her into his arms. "Stop." "Never." He kissed her again. Ava heard Grace giggling at the entry way. Joe turned around and saw Grace. "Like on the movie Daddy." He laughed. "Love Mama more now than I did then." "Love me," Grace asked. "You too." He picked Grace up and hugged her. "You ready for bath time," he asked. "Okay." He tickled her and kissed Ava. Ava went and sat down with Cat. She was sniffling. "What?" "I wanted that," Cat said. "What?" "The wedding like this. I always did." "Cat, if this is what you want, then tell him." "I don't know if I want him," Cat said. Ava laughed.

They finished watching the end of the video and Joe was just putting Grace to bed. Cat heard him. "He do that every night," Cat asked. Ava nodded. "Wow." "She loves it. It helps him get her to sleep." "I bet." A few minutes later, Joe snuck downstairs. "She asleep," Ava asked. He nodded. He grabbed a beer from the fridge and curled up behind her on the sofa. "What we talking about?" "Nothing," Ava said. "Why is it that you and Ryan and Brad are such good guys and he's such an ass," Cat asked. "He's been around the block a few times. He does crazy shit that he never really thinks through. Just remember something. He does love you," Joe said. "When you two got married, why did you do all this," Cat asked. "Because I wanted to have family with us. Ryan wanted to sing at the wedding, and I wanted the white dress," Ava said. "I wanted the guys with us and my family there to celebrate with us," Joe said. "I mean, we're married, but why don't I get to have the hoopla," Cat asked. "Ask him for it," Joe said. "What are you talking about?" "Tell him," Joe said. "Seriously," Cat asked. He nodded. She got up and grabbed her phone, then went outside and called Scott.

"And as for you," Joe said. He turned Ava towards him. "What?" "You going to stop the crap, or am I going to have to surgically attach us," Joe asked. "Funny." Ava went to get up and he pulled her back into his arms. He kissed her literally making her heart race in her chest. She finally managed to get up and he followed her to the bedroom. "Joe." "What?" "You aren't . . ." He kissed her and picked her up, carrying her to their bedroom.

A few minutes later, they were making out on the bed. "Stop." "What?" "You know this doesn't mean I'm not still mad," Ava said. "Ava." "You really expect me to not be?" "No. I expect you to be reasonable. Nothing happened." "And the reason why you smelled like her perfume," she asked. "Ava." "None of this changes it. Your old girlfriends keep popping up and trying to sneak into your life." "You telling me James hasn't hunted you down," Joe asked. "Fact is, he doesn't get more than 5 feet before I tell him off and walk away." "Ava." "No. It's not fair. Why do your ex-girlfriends think that you're free game," Ava asked. "I love you. Only you. I don't want someone else. I'm sick of people trying to get between us too, but there's nothing we can do except deal with it." "Joe." "Hear me out. We know we love each other. Our fans know. Who cares what everyone else does," Joe asked. "When it means you getting calls or being propositioned?" "Who says I'd agree to it?" She looked at him. She knew what was right. It hurt her as much as it did him. Ava felt a thump in her stomach. "What was that?" "Baby telling you to stop being a butthead," Ava said. He laughed. "How about baby saying to stop fighting?" "Nope." He kissed Ava. "I love you. Nobody's going to ever change it." "If . . ." Joe kissed her again, taking her breath away.

Joe slid her leggings off, then Ava went for the belt of his jeans. His phone went off. He threw it on the bed. He went for her sweater, kicking his jeans off. His phone rang again. "Get the phone," Ava said. "No." He kissed her and had her naked in his arms in minutes. He made love to her until her legs shook, and his body was humming in passion. He curled up with her after and his phone went off a third time. Ava grabbed it and saw the caller. "Answer it," Ava said. She got up, pulled her sweater and leggings back on and walked downstairs.

"What?" "I need to talk to you," Jodi said. "You did enough." "She upset?" "What do you want?" "I need your help with something," Jodi said. "No." "Joe, come on." "Let me make myself more clear. Hell no." "Joe." He hung up. He blocked the number and set it to go to voicemail when she calls. He pulled his jeans back on and went downstairs.

He saw Ava outside with Cat. He grabbed his sweater from the closet and went outside. "Ava." "What?" "Come inside." "No." Cat went to get up. "You don't have to go in. Sit," Ava said. Cat looked at Joe. "I'm going to make some tea," Cat said. She went inside. "So what did she want?" "Don't know. Told her not to call and hung up." "Right." "Why are you doubting me?" "Because I don't know what to think anymore." "Listen to what's in your heart." "I can't." "Why?" "Because the smell of her perfume is clouding it," Ava said. She got up and went for a walk. Joe followed her.

"Babe." "Don't." He grabbed her hand. "Stop it," Joe said. "Did you kiss her?" "What?" "Yes or no?" "Of course not." "She lived there with you didn't she," Ava asked. "A long time ago." "Joe." "You can't walk away," he said. "Breathing space." "No. I love you. I know you're upset Ava, but come on." "She calls Joe. I don't want the calls from every ex you've ever had." "Then we change the numbers again." "Fine." "Good. You letting me take you back to the house," Joe asked. "I'll be back in a little while." "No." "Joe, I need time to clear my head." "Then do it there." "Stubborn aren't you," Ava asked. "Just like you are." He grabbed her hand and pulled her close. "No more history. Just us." Ava looked at him. "I promise you," he said. He pulled her to him and kissed her and they headed back. "No more freaking out. We talk it out." "And if she calls again, I'm kicking her ass pregnant or not," Ava said. He wrapped his arm around her and they went back inside.

They relaxed a while with Cat, then Joe hinted that they should go to bed. "I'll be up in a minute." Joe kissed Ava and headed upstairs. Ava talked to Cat. "It's over Ava." "You sure," she asked. Cat nodded. Ava hugged her and they chatted on their way upstairs. "Get some sleep," Ava said. Cat nodded.

Ava walked in and got changed for bed. As she was washing her face, Joe walked in and slid his arms around her. "What?" "You still mad?" "As long as your phone doesn't ring like that again." "Good thing it's turned off. What's going on with Cat?" "What do you mean?" "She's not really walking away from him is she?" Ava nodded. "Come to bed." "Why?" "Need my teddy bear." Ava laughed. They slid into the bed and curled up together. "I love you." "Love you too." They were asleep a little while later.

The next morning, Ava woke up to the sound of Cat in the hallway. "Ava," Cat said. She got up and went straight for Cat. "What's wrong?" "Hospital." Ava went and pulled her leggings and sweater on with her Uggs and left, purse and phone in hand and went straight for the hospital. She called Joe once Cat was seen. "Where the hell," Joe asked. "Cat's at the hospital." "What happened?" "Not sure yet. I'll call you when I can." "I'm coming down there." "It's fine. My doctor's in with her." "Your O.B.?" "I have to go." Ava hung up and went to sit with Cat.

Scott showed a while later with Joe and Grace. Cat refused to see him or even let him in the room. Ava walked down the hall to Joe. "Babe. How's she doing?" "She wants him gone." "What happened?" Ava looked at him. "Is she alright?" Ava shook her head. "She?" Ava nodded. He wrapped his arms around her. "Where's Grace?" "Asleep beside Scott." "She can't deal with him." "She has to talk to him." "He's being served papers." "Seriously?" Ava nodded. He kissed her. "You alright?" She nodded. "Do you want something to eat?" "I'm fine." "No you aren't." Joe handed her something to eat. "I'll take him home. Want me to take Grace?" "She can come sit with me in there." "What time they letting her out?" "Going to try to get her out of here after lunch," Ava said. "I'll be back. I love you," Joe said. "I love you too." He kissed her and Ava went over to Grace. She picked her up and carried her into the hospital room. "Ava, please get her to talk to me," Scott begged. "She will when she feels up to it. Go home." "I'm staying at my brother's place." Ava nodded.

After lunch, Joe came back and they took Cat back to her place. "If you need anything, call me okay," Ava said. "Thanks. Think you're buddy can come by and do security," Cat asked. "I'll call him," Joe said. "Thank you." Ava hugged her and she headed home with Joe. He pulled into head towards the house.

"Joe." "I'll get the stuff from the other house," he said. They pulled in and Ava wouldn't get out of the car. "Come on." She stepped out and they headed inside. He put Grace down for her nap, and Ava went and sat outside. He grabbed them each a vitamin water from the fridge and went outside. "Babe." "What?" "What's wrong?" "I can't." "Can't what?" She went to walk past him and he pulled her into his lap. "Ava." "Just tell me you overhauled the house after she left," Ava said. "Ava." "Just tell me." "I changed a lot of stuff, but I didn't overhaul it." Ava went to get up. "I know what's going on in that head of yours," Joe said. "You mean picturing the two of you on every surface in that house." He kissed Ava. "And the better memories of us in that house washed the memories of her out." "Joe." "Stop. It's our house. Not hers." "You know we're renovating." "Figured," Joe said kissing her. "Grace's in her bed. Come inside." "Joe." He picked her up and carried her inside. They curled up together on the sofa. "You know this is the first thing I bought when she left," Joe said. "I like it." He smirked. "And I bought a new bed." "I bet you did." He kissed Ava. The rest of the day, she relaxed with him and he told her everything else he hadn't told her. Best part was, the calls stopped.

A few weeks later, Joe got the brilliant idea of inviting his brother to dinner. "We could invite Cat over," Joe said. "What are you up to," Ava asked. "Just saying," Joe replied. "Fine. Call her," Ava replied. The day of the dinner came. Cat showed and played with Grace while Ava and Joe got changed.

Joe walked in and saw Ava sliding into her black dress. "Look beautiful, Joe said. "Thank you." Ava went to put her hair up and he grabbed the clip from her hand. "Joe." "Looks better down." Ava turned to put her makeup on and he slid his arms around her. "What?" "You don't need it." "I'm putting it on." He kissed her neck. "He's going to be here in a half-hour," Ava said. "And?" "Don't start." The baby kicked when his hand crossed her stomach. "See," Joe teased. "Don't even think it." He kissed her cheek. "I know she'll like him," Joe said. "And what about him," Ava asked. "Don't worry." Ava put on her makeup and he slid her necklace on for her. She turned and kissed him and he had her half way to the bed when the doorbell rang. "Told you," Ava said. He kissed her again.

"Cat, can you grab the door," Joe asked. He kissed Ava. "No you don't." She slipped away from him and walked towards the steps. He had his arms wrapped around her by the time they got to the bottom of the steps. "Hey Will," Ava said giving him a hug. "Hey Mama. How's baby," Will asked. Grace had her arms locked around his neck. "Good. How's work?" "Busy as hell." "So you met Cat?" "Nice to see a beautiful lady when I come by," Will said. Joe grabbed the steaks and gave a man hug to his brother. "Come on in. Can I grab you a drink or anything," Joe asked. "What you two having?" "Iced Tea," Ava said. "Good for me." They sat down while Grace drew pictures for everyone.

By the time they got through dinner, Cat had a little crush on Will, and Grace was asleep in Ava's arms. Ava got up to do the dishes and Joe kissed her. Instead, she took Grace and tucked her into bed. She came downstairs and Will was outside with Cat. "So," Joe said. He leaned her up against the counter and had both hands in the bubbles. "Told you so," Joe said. "Oh really?" He kissed her. She slid her arms around him. "Remember what happened last time you thought of something like this," Ava asked. "That was supposed to be just so she could meet some people to hang with," Joe teased. "Okay. Whatever you say." He kissed her again. "I'm going outside." "No you aren't. I told them I was making coffee. Spy on them from in here." "What makes you think . . . ." "I know you." She kissed him. "Fine. Then I'm going to clean up Grace's stuff," Ava said. "Spy from the other room. Good plan." Ava laughed and went in to clean up a bit in the TV room.

Cat and Will snuck inside, grabbed a cup of coffee and came and sat down. Joe and Ava were curled up on the sofa. "So when are you two back out on tour," Will asked. "Two weeks." "I can look after Grace for you once in a while on a weekend if you want," Cat said. "Thanks. Kinda hoping to bring her with us, but may take you up on it," Ava said. "Hold you to it. You know how much I love her," Cat said. "Do you have any kids of your own Cat," Will asked. "No. Always wanted them though." Cat looked over at Ava. They sat around and chatted a while, then Cat headed home. Will walked her out. "It was really good meeting you." "You too. Didn't know Joe had a handsome brother," Cat said. "Thanks. If I'd known how beautiful you were, I would have demanded dinner together before this." He got to her car. "So, about Friday," Cat said. Will leaned in and kissed her.

Ava went to close the front door and saw Cat and Will. Joe walked over to her. "About time." "What?" He closed the door and slid his hand into Ava's. "What?" "I knew. Just like I knew you'd marry me in a heartbeat." "Oh so sure of yourself." He kissed Ava. "You're going to bed." She looked at him. In one swoop he carried her up to their bed. "What are you up to?" "Nothing. Making sure my prediction is right." "And what would that be?" He leaned her onto the bed and curled up with her, kissing her. "So?" "That Cat's not going to be calling with bad news after their date." "Sure that's what you were going to say." "Well, that and something else," he said as he leaned in and gave her one of his breathtaking kisses. It seemed to go on for what felt like hours. He slid her out of the dress, she slid his jeans and shirt off. He peeled the lace g-string off of her and nibbled her leg and her hip. "Joe." He kissed her again and they made love. "I will never get sick of this," Joe said. His hand slid around her and the baby kicked. He nibbled Ava's ear, then her neck. "I love you." "I love you too babe." He wanted every inch of her, and had it more than once that night. He curled up with her, one hand on her stomach, and watched her. "What?" "Nothing." "You're watching me again," Ava said. "Was thinking back to the first time we were here together." "And?" "If I'd known I was going to be this in love with you, I would've married you that day." "Aww." "Sometimes I want to pinch myself. First you and me and Grace are a family and now we're having another baby, the music is going great and there's no more stress." "For now. If you say could this get any better I'm going to sleep," Ava teased. "It couldn't." She went to roll over.

"If you could ask for anything what would it be," Joe asked. "Honestly, to have the baby here already and be a size 5." "Ava." "To have the baby here, and have more time to enjoy it," Ava said. "You don't have to come tour with us." "Yeah I do." "Babe." "Not after last time." He kissed her. "If I could wish for something, it would be for Grace and the baby to have a happy and healthy life without all the drama I've had," Ava said. "Really?" "I have you, my writing, the house with you. I sort of want things that can't be guaranteed," Ava said. "Only one thing I never knew I wanted." "What?" He kissed her. "Didn't know I wanted you until I met you," Ava said. "I knew. The first time I met you." "Oh really." "It's like we were the only two people in the room, other than Ryan and Brad," Joe said. "I remember it." "You and your corny jokes." "Had to. You looked a little nervous. Besides. How could I resist the beautiful woman I saw," Joe said. "Nice try." "Fine. It was the shirt." "Better." He kissed her as they laughed. After more silliness, they finally fell asleep.

CHAPTER 35

Ava woke up to her cell phone ringing at 7am. "Hello?" "Ava, it's Cat." "Hey." "You up," Cat asked. "No." Cat heard Joe kissing her. "He called." "Who?" "Will." "And?" "He's coming to take me to breakfast." "Good," Ava said. "What should I wear?" "Whatever you do, no low cut boob tops." "The purple or the black?" "The dark purple." "The lilac one it is." "Be careful." "I'll call you and let you know." Cat hung up and ran around to get ready. A half-hour later, Will was at her door.

Joe and Ava got up with Grace, after Joe pleading with her to stay in bed. "Come on. I'll make your coffee," Ava said. They went downstairs with her and Grace ran off to go play with her toys. "Daddy, go Uncle Ryan?" "Miss Jacob," Joe asked picking her up. She nodded. "Do you want to go hang out with him today?" "Okay." Ava grabbed the phone and called over to Rose. "Hey girlie." "Hey yourself. How did things go last night," Rose asked. "They're out on a date." "Now?" Ava laughed. "He must have liked her." "Eintstein's prediction," Ava said. Rose laughed. "Ryan said the same thing." "Miss Grace wanted to know if Jacob could play?" "Have to head in for a doctor's appointment in a few, but after that, sure." "Thanks." "Hey, you know payback's coming. Babysitting duties," Rose said. "I know. Seriously, I have to get some actual writing done." "Nothing like a little inspiration." Ava laughed. "Should be back around ten," Rose said. "Thanks." "I'll nab her on the way." "Love ya." "You too." Ava hung up. "Jacob," Grace asked. Ava nodded. "Yay!!!" Grace hopped out of Joe's arms and ran off to play. "Writing,' Joe asked. "Yes. Actual writing." "Then I'm gonna get some work done on that song." Ava kissed him. "Or not." "You're going to work on it for a while, while I get writing done." "See how long we can last," Joe teased. Ava laughed again. She handed him his coffee and made breakfast for them. She gave Grace her favorite cereal, and made egg white omelets for her and Joe.

Once Grace headed off with Rose, Ava went into the office to try to do some writing. She clicked into her emails and saw 5 from James. They were all filled with 'I need you,' 'I want you back', and a million words she never wanted to hear from him. Then she saw one from Carrie:

I lost the baby. James and I were pregnant, and we lost it. He's in love with you. I don't know why I even thought he could love me. I'm sorry Ava. I wish I'd listened when you told me not to bother. When are you guys coming back to visit? Miss you.

Ava looked at it and thought she must be seeing things. After that long, he's still like that? She leaned back in her chair and deleted the message. She called Carrie, making sure to block the number. "Hey," Ava said. "Ava?" "How are you?" "Okay I guess. We broke up," Carrie said. "Carrie." "I know." "There are good guys out there. One who's going to love you the way you deserve." "Where? Nashville?" Ava laughed. "Need a serious scenery change," Carrie said. "You're welcome to come for a visit. There's a few hotels nearby." "I might. We are in need of girls night." "Sounds good." "What's new with you?" "Nothing much." "How's the sexy husband we all dream of?," Carrie joked. "Fine. He's still sexy." "Lucky ass woman." "Very true." Joe leaned over and kissed her. "I heard a rumor." "About?" "Are you pregnant again?" "Almost 5 months." "Dang." "Miss Mama. You had a shitload of practice babysitting us when we were partying," Carrie said. "I know." "I have to get back to work. I'll call you and let you know when." "Sounds good. Give Rose a hug for me." Carrie hung up. "So who's the sexy man," Joe asked. "Like you have to ask." He kissed her, then started trying to work away at his song.

After an hour or two, Ava needed a break. She got up and grabbed a vitamin water. She brought him one, then tried to get back to her writing. "Stuck?" "Sort of." He played a bit of the song and Ava listened. Something about the way he was writing gave her a little help. "I got it," Ava said. She went back to writing and didn't stop until lunch. "How many chapters did you finish?" "5." "You had to send them how many?" "3." "Ahead of yourself?" Ava nodded. "Good. Now you can relax for a while." "What were you thinking," Ava asked. "Baby shower for Danielle." "Already planned." "Seriously?" Ava nodded. "What about Rose?" "She doesn't want to tell anyone until later Joe." "Before we go on tour would be a good time." "Shit." "I know." Ava shot Rose a text about Danielle's shower. "What," Joe asked. "Had an idea." "You and your crazy ideas." "We can do Danielle's and Rose's at the same time." Joe laughed. "Never would've thought of it." She sent an email to some of Rose's friends, then called the restaurant to make sure the head count was alright.

Finally, he had Ava to himself. "We're going shopping." "For what?" "I need shirts for the tour," Joe said. "Joe." "You get dresses, I get shirts." "And pants." "Need a few pairs of jeans." "Good thing you're taking me," Ava teased. "Why's that beautiful?" "I get to tell you your butt looks good in public." Joe laughed. Ava went upstairs and pulled on her leggings and a top and they headed off to the mall. It was a pretty quiet day, and they manage to make it through most of the mall without security detail. He got a few shirts and jeans, Ava got a pair or two, then grabbed some shoes, and some baby gifts and headed home. They walked in and started getting dinner together. "So when's the first date," Ava asked. "Next weekend." "Good thing the shower's Sunday." "Still think you need to get some other dresses or something," Joe said. "We can figure that out." "I know. Just don't pull the 'I look like a whale in that' thing again." "The last month or two, I'm not flying." "I know. We can take the RV." "Great." "All the dates are near here." "Oh." "I want to be close to home," Joe said. "We have to be." "I know. If you get closer to and you want to take a break, just tell me." Ava nodded.

Just as Ava was getting ready to put dinner on, Grace came running into the house. "Hi Mama." "Hey baby girl." Rose walked in. "So, how's mama?" "Good. How are you doing," Rose asked. "Good. Thinking that whales probably won't look good on stage, but . . ." "Would you stop," Joe said walking up behind Ava and kissing her neck. "The last two months I'm staying here." "If that's what you want to do," Joe said. Ava nodded. "Babe, you're beautiful. Stop worrying." "Listen to this one . . . So how was their date," Ava asked. "They played, made dolls out of play doh, painted, ran around until they both passed out, then played with his hot wheels." "Awe." They both laughed. "So what time do we have to be there for the party," Rose asked. "The restaurant said ten." "Okay. Did you get her anything?" Ava nodded. "We got it this afternoon." "And?" "Blankets, sleepers, bibs. Joe picked out the 'Daddy loves me' shirt." "Cute," Rose said. "There's still tons on the list." "Thanks." Ava handed it to her. "Was going to grab something for you to give her," Ava said. "I love those stores." "I know. Figured on that one." "So what are you two up to tonight," Rose asked. "Trying to talk her into giving up the crazy talk," Joe said. Rose laughed. "Been trying that for years." "Something tells me I have alternative powers," Joe teased. "True," Rose replied laughing. Ava walked her out and hugged her goodbye. She walked back in and went back into the kitchen. Joe finished cooking the dinner, and Grace ran into the kitchen. "Daddy, I made present." "What's that?" "Picture." Ava took over with dinner while Grace brought him in to show off her artistic skills. "Daddy, Uncle Ryan, Uncle Brad and Mama." "In her red dress." "Pretty," Grace said. "Always." Ava looked at him as he winked. "Coming to dinner," Ava asked. Grace nodded and ran for the kitchen.

After dinner, and while Grace chatted their ear off, they relaxed while she played. When Grace finally started yawning, Ava took her upstairs for a bath. "Mama, do I share with baby?" "Why?" "I like Daddy sing." "Something tells me you'll each have your own song baby girl." "Good. Like my song." "I bet you do." "And bubbles." Ava rinsed her hair and Grace hopped out of the tub and into her arms. "And Mama hugs." "Those are my favorite," Ava said. She dried her off and slid her pajamas on. Grace ran downstairs to Joe, then he brought her back up, guitar in one hand and Grace in the other. He kissed Ava, then went to tuck Grace in. Ava kissed Grace good night, and went into the master bedroom. She slid out of her clothes, and into the shower. It hit her all of a sudden that maybe Grace might not be ready for a little brother or sister. Then she thought about it. She was ready.

She was willing to share the toys and the table, just not special time. They had to have done something right with Grace. She went to turn the water off and Joe slid in with her. "Hey." "Hey yourself," Joe said. He kissed her and wrapped his arms around her. "She asleep?" "Barely managed to stay awake." "Good." "Babe." "What?" "She said her prayers tonight." "And?" "Thanked him for the baby," Joe said. "Oh really." He nodded. "We did something really right." "That's exactly what I was thinking," Ava said. He kissed Ava again as the room filled with steam. "You know how beautiful you are?" "Thank you." "Stop worrying about what people are going to say. We're having a baby. It's a celebration," Joe said. "I know." "No more worrying." Ava nodded. He kissed her.

That night, Joe curled up in bed after they made love, and wrapped his arms around Ava. "You know, this is what I always wanted." "What?" "A family of my own. Having everyone I love around me, enjoying every second of every day of my life," Joe said. "Remember a time when all I wanted was a good man," Ava said. "And?" "Must have found him." "Oh? Why's that?" "Because I wake up in the morning beside you, and I see Grace and I can't imagine wanting to be anywhere else." "Me either. Wonder what we're going to be like in 50 years," Joe said. "Old." They both laughed. "And still together." He kissed Ava. She nodded. "Might still let you snuggle up to me in bed." "You better," Joe said. Finally, they were both asleep.

The next morning, Joe got woken up by his cell screaming again. "Hello?" "Hey. It's Brad." "Hey." "We were asked to do a show on Saturday night. That cool?" "Where?" "The old bar. What you think?" "What did Ryan say?" "He said to ask the old married guy," Brad said. "Nice." "Well?" "I'll talk to Ava when she gets up." "Just us," Brad said. "Oh. Well, sounds good to me." "Cool. I'll tell them yes then." Brad hung up and Joe slid his arm back around Ava. "What did Brad want?" "We have a show Saturday night." "Where?" "Downtown." "Just you three?" Joe nodded. "Good." "Why?" "Then I can be part of the crowd and hit on you from a distance like all the other girls." Joe laughed. He kissed Ava's neck. "Something tells me you'd be the only one taking me home." "Especially since you'd be driving," Ava said. He kissed her shoulder. "You know she's going to be awake any minute." "Yep." His hand slid down her torso, then to her hip. "Joe." "What?" "Sleep." He kissed her. One kiss turned into ten, which turned into mind-blowing quick sex before Grace was awake. After, he kissed Ava. "What?" "Good morning to you too." They both laughed. A minute or two later, Grace came in. "Mama." "Yes baby girl." "I went potty." Joe looked over at her. "By yourself," he asked. She nodded. Ava got up, sliding her robe on and Grace walked into the bathroom. "Baby." "Yes Mama." She gave her a huge hug and a kiss. "I'm a big girl." "Yes you are." "We watch cartoons?" Ava nodded and flushed, then walked her downstairs. Joe followed a little while later. "I am so proud of you baby girl." "Big girl Daddy." "Big girl. You know you're always Daddy's baby girl though right," Joe said. Grace nodded and hugged him. Ava put the coffee on for him and made Grace's breakfast. "Mama, can I play with Cat?" "She's working." "Please?" Ava called her and handed the phone to Grace.

Joe slid his arms around Ava's waist as she poured the orange juice. "What?" "I love you." "Love you too." "Good." "Why," Ava asked. "You're stuck with me for life." "Awe Darn," Ava said. He laughed and kissed her. "Mama, Cat and Uncle Will are coming." Grace went to grab the phone and Cat had already hung up. "You sure she said Uncle Will?" Grace nodded. Joe looked at Grace. He started laughing. He took Grace in to watch cartoons while Ava got ready. They showered, then Ava was just pulling her sweater on when they showed. She headed downstairs and saw Cat and Will, hand in hand. "Hey you two," Ava said. "Hey yourself," Cat said. Ava hugged them both and kissed Will's cheek. Grace ran towards Cat. "Hi." "Hey munchkin. How are you?" "I missed you." "I missed you too." Grace dragged her into the TV room. Joe walked down the steps pulling his shirt on. "Nice of you to get dressed," Will teased. "Nice of you to not be in a suit on a workday," Joe teased. "Long story." "I bet and one that we need a coffee to talk about." Joe and Will headed outside, coffees in hand.

The girls chatted a while as Grace drew pictures for everyone. "I like him," Cat said. "Please don't tell Joe. He's beginning to think he's a matchmaker," Ava joked. They laughed and were silly until the guys came in. "Hi Uncle Will." "Hey Grace. How's the princess of the world this morning?" "Good. You need hug." She wrapped her arms around him and hugged him. "Well, that just fixed everything," Will said. She kissed his cheek. "Cat, you have competition," Will joked. "How do I compete with Princess Grace?" "I love you too Auntie Cat." They hung out and talked a while, then Cat offered to take Grace for the afternoon. "Can I wear my dress Mama?" "No." "Can I wear my . . . ." Ava got her dressed and she ran downstairs in leggings and her pink top. "I ready." Ava handed Cat a bag with a few things in it, and Cat and Will headed off with Grace. Ava went and started cleaning up the kitchen. "What you doing," Joe asked. "Cleaning up." He put the dishes in the washer and kissed Ava. "What?" "Told you so." "Don't you have somewhere you have to be?" He nodded. "Good." He slid his hand in hers and handed her purse to her. "What?" "We're going out." "Where?" "So you can see the bar."

They pulled in a little while later. "So?" "Nice." He grabbed her hand and they headed inside. The guys were set up on the stage and checking the guitars when they came inside. "Hey Joe," Callon said. "Hey." "So what time are we supposed to be here tonight?" "8." Joe slid his hand in Ava's. "What?" "Remember something okay?" "What's that?" "There's only one woman that I'm going to be singing to." "Do I know her," Ava teased. He pulled her close and kissed her. "I love you. No more worrying." Ava nodded and he kissed her again. "No stress permitted." "Okay." They headed outside. "Now where are we going," Ava asked. "To visit a friend of mine." They hopped back in the car and headed off. They pulled into a little shop and he talked her into coming inside. "Hey," the shop owner said coming over towards Joe. "Hey." "This must be Ava. I've heard so much about you." Ava tried to make nice, but she had no idea who the woman was. "So were you able to find it?" She nodded. She pulled a dress out of the closet and handed it to Joe. He handed it to Ava. "Try it on," Joe said. "Joe." "Go." Ava went and slid the dress on. "Babe." "What," Ava asked. She stepped out and his mouth dropped. "Perfect." "All I have to say, is thank goodness for friends." "It's perfect," Ava said. "Glad you like it. I have one or two more if you wanted to try them." Joe nodded. Every dress she came out in was more beautiful than the other one. "Silly question, but these don't look like maternity clothes," Ava said. "Joe told me you were having trouble finding something your style that fit." "You made this?" "I designed everything in here," the woman said. Ava hugged her. "So you like?" Ava nodded. After a few more thank you's and talking to her about a few more dresses, they headed home. "Better," Joe asked. Ava kissed him outside the store. Seconds later she saw flashes. They hopped back into the SUV and headed home.

"I still can't believe they followed us," Ava said. "You surprised about the dresses?" "Where did you meet her," Ava asked. "I went in at Christmas. I was going to get you something, but they didn't have what I was thinking of." "So you asked her to make something?" "Picked out a few things and asked her to make them in your size," Joe said. They stopped at the light and Ava kissed him. They pulled back into the house and headed inside. He wrapped his arms around her. "And." "And what?" "Jasmine is coming to do your hair and your makeup," Joe said. "You are just full of surprises aren't you?" "I have to go do sound check at 4." "Are we going there together?" "Wouldn't have it any other way." "Good." Ava went upstairs and hung the dresses up. "So which one you wearing," Joe asked. Ava pointed out the dark blue one. "Nice." "I still can't believe that they fit, and cover baby." "That's what you said you wanted." "I know, but these are beautiful." "You're the one that makes them look good," Joe said. Ava kissed him. He picked her up and carried her to bed. "We're having a nap." "Oh really?" He kissed her again and slid her leggings off. They made love then curled up for a nap.

Around 4, Ava got up with him and walked him to the door. "I'll be back. I promise I'm bringing dinner," Joe said. "You are, are you." He kissed her, leaning her against the front door. "I'll see you at six." Ava nodded. He finally headed off and Ava went upstairs and slid into the tub. Once the tub cooled, she hopped out and started getting dressed. Jasmine showed and started on her hair. By the time Joe got home, Ava looked like a supermodel. She came downstairs in her heels and his mouth dropped to the floor. "Wow." "You like," Ava asked. He grabbed her hand and pulled her into his arms. He kissed her and pulled her in close. The baby started kicking. "You look beautiful." "Thank you." "I'm lucky if I remember the words or the music tonight," Joe said. Ava laughed. A minute later, Cat was there with Grace. "Hi Mama." "Hey there princess." "Wow." "Thanks," Ava said. Cat smirked. "So what are you two up to tonight," Ava asked. "Being your bodyguards," Will teased. Ava laughed. Joe kissed her cheek. "Don't you think you should get dressed," Ava asked. Joe nodded. "I have to go home and get changed," Cat said. "I'll call you when we're leaving," Ava said. Cat nodded and she left with Will. Emily showed up just as Joe was stepping out of the shower. "Mama, where going?" "Daddy has to work tonight." "No." "We're coming right home after." "Mama." Grace started crying. Ava slid the heels off. "I made your favorite for dinner." "No." "Grace, stop being silly." "Mama stay." "I'll make a deal with you. When we get home, I'll come in and give you a kiss." She went from crying to sniffling. "And you get to play with Jacob tomorrow and come with Mama." "Okay." Ava wiped her tears away, then took her in and got her some dinner. After dinner, Ava drew her a bath with her bubbles, and slid her into her jammies. Joe and Ava kissed and hugged her, then headed off to pick Cat and Will up and go to a quick dinner.

They showed at the bar after dinner and Joe was whisked off to start putting things together. Cat sat down at the bar with Ava and had a drink. "You look amazing," Cat said. "Thanks." "What's wrong?" "Nothing," Ava said. "Ava." "Just was thinking." "About?" "If I let him do the tour without me." "Ava." "I know." "He's not going to," Cat said. "I know. I'm just saying, it's not the easiest thing in the world." "You're going until you can't." "I know." Will headed over to them. "Joe needs to talk to you," Will said. Ava got up and went towards the backstage area.

"Hey," Joe said. "Hey yourself." He pulled her into his arms and kissed her. "What did you want?" "You." "What else is new," Ava teased. He kissed her again. "Don't you have some music to play or something?" He nodded. "They put a chair by the stage," Joe said. "For?" "The most beautiful woman in the entire room." "I'll let her know." He kissed her again. "You know you don't need the kiss for luck," Ava said. "I know. Got the whole package instead." She gave him another kiss, then went out and sat down. Cat handed her a ginger ale, and the show started. After the first few songs, he was staring right at Ava. They did a few more, then finished up. The last song, Joe dedicated it to Ava. "This one is especially for my beautiful wife. I love you." She blew him a kiss. They sang her favorite song, then finished and headed backstage. Ava spotted someone she swore she knew. She tried to brush it off, but something told her not to. Joe came out a few minutes later and walked right over to her and kissed her. "You did good baby," Ava said. "Thank you." He kissed her again. Ava spotted the woman again. She walked towards Joe. "Joe." "Kim?" She hugged Joe. "What are you doing here?" "Heard you were in town. Like I was going to miss it," she said. Ava slid her hand in his. "Kim, this is Ava. Babe, this is Kim." "Nice to meet you. I'm going to grab a drink," Ava said. He kissed her then she walked off.

"What are you really doing here," Joe asked. "Thought we could talk." "My wife is here." "Ten minutes." "Kim." "I'll meet you in the back." Ava was watching him. "Ava," Joe said.

Cat walked over to her. "Hey." "What's wrong," Ava asked "You look like you're going to pull out the boxing gloves," Cat said. She was still watching Joe. Then he disappeared. "I'm going home," Ava said. "Why?" "Now." Ava walked towards the door. "Ava." "Ryan, can you take me home," Ava asked. "Sure." They left a few minutes later.

Ava walked into the house, slid out of the dress and pulled on her pajamas. She went in and kissed Grace goodnight, then washed the makeup off and went to bed.

"Where'd Ava go," Joe asked. "She left with Ryan," Cat said. "When?" "A half-hour ago. Where the hell were you?" "Talking to a friend." "Might want to rub the lipstick off your neck," Will said. "Stop." "Joe, I would leave her alone tonight." "Why?" "Because she looked pissed off when she left." "Cat, nothing happened." "And that's why she's touching up her lipstick. Nice." "Cat." She went to walk off and Will tried to grab her hand. "Don't." "What's wrong," Will asked. "Ask your brother." She walked towards the door. "What the hell did you do?" "Nothing. I went to talk to Kim," Joe said. "As in the Kim?" "Will, don't start." "The girl you were with for years? You think she isn't going to be able to tell," Will said. "Nothing . . ." "Don't pull the line on me. I have to calm Cat down before she goes over there to tell Ava." "Will, I talked to her." "Right. The bed Bunny. Sure you did." He walked off and headed home with Cat. Joe hopped in the SUV and took off towards the house.

He walked in and everything was quiet. He walked upstairs and Ava was in bed. He got undressed and slid into bed beside her. He went to wrap his arms around her and she pushed him away. "Ava." "No." He kissed her shoulder. "Leave me alone Joe." He leaned back over. "Ava." She got up and grabbed her pillow and walked downstairs. He didn't want another fight with her. He went downstairs and saw her on the sofa. "Babe." "Go back to bed." "Come with me." "No." "You're pregnant," Joe said. "Then you're sleeping down here." "Stop over-reacting." "I'm not." "Ava, you're not supposed to be stressing." "Then don't cause it." She walked past him and went upstairs. She curled back up in the bed and went back to sleep.

The next morning, Ava got up and Joe was in bed with her. She went in and Grace was just waking up. "Hi Mama." "Hey baby girl." She got Grace dressed, then scooted her downstairs. Grace went and played with her toys. Ava got changed and threw her makeup into her bag, then walked downstairs. "Where going," Grace asked. "We're going to the house." "Pool?" Ava nodded. She gave Grace her breakfast, then they went to leave when Joe was walking down the stairs. "Where are you going," he asked. "Out." Ava closed the door. She was putting Grace into her car seat when he came outside. "Ava." "What?" "We need to talk." "I'm going to the house." "Grace." "I need my quiet time." "I know you're upset." She went to walk off and he grabbed her hand. "Leave me alone." "No." "Why don't you go hang out with Kim then," Ava said. She broke away from him and got in the

SUV. She pulled out a few minutes later and headed towards the house. Cat was about to pull in and saw Ava. She followed her.

A half-hour later, Ava pulled in and went to head inside with Grace. "Ava." "Auntie Cat," Grace said. "Hey Gracie." Grace wrapped her arms around Cat's neck as Cat picked her up in her arms. "Mama said pool day." "Sounds like fun." "Come?" "Sure." She put Grace down and she ran inside. Grace went up to her room and grabbed her bathing suit. "What's going on," Cat asked. "Meaning what?" "Ava." "I need quiet time." "You two fighting?" "What happened with her after I left," Ava asked. "I wanted to make sure you were alright." "Tell me." "Ava." "That's why I walked out." She went upstairs and pulled her bikini on then took Grace out to the pool. Cat grabbed vitamin water for them from the fridge and followed her outside. Ava got in the pool with Grace and played a while. Her phone went off. Cat saw the caller and answered it. "Where is she," Joe asked. "In the pool with Grace." "I need to talk to her." "She's pissed." "Cat, please just get her." "Ava." She shook her head. "She's not getting out of the pool." "Give her the phone," Joe asked. Cat walked towards her. "No." "Ava." "No." She grabbed the phone and pressed end, then handed it back to Cat.

Grace went down for a nap after lunch and Ava sat down outside with Cat. "You have to talk to him." "No I don't." "What about the baby shower?" "It doesn't start until 2." "You said you were picking Rose and Danielle up." "Rose is picking her up." Ava went and got changed. Just as she was finishing getting ready, Grace was up. She slid her dress on and her shoes and they left. They pulled into the shower a half-hour later. Grace ran off to play with Jacob. "Hey," one of the girls said. "Hey. Are they here yet," Ava asked. "No." Ava called Rose. "Hey. We're just pulling in." Ava hung up and the ladies all hid. Rose walked in with Danielle a few minutes later. "Surprise!" Rose saw the signs. One said 'Congrats Rose' and the other said 'Congrats Danielle'. "Are you kidding me," Danielle said. Danielle cried and hugged Ava, and then Rose started. They chatted a while, had lunch, then opened the gifts. Just as they were finishing, the guys showed. Grace ran over to Joe. "Hey princess." "Hi Daddy." He walked towards Ava. She got up and went and grabbed herself a drink. "Ava." She walked past him. "Hey Ryan," Ava said giving him a hug. "Blew her away didn't you," Ryan said. Ava nodded. She gave Brad a hug. The ladies started disappearing and Grace ran over to Ava. "Mama, we go home?" "Yep." She went to walk out and Joe stopped her. "I'll take Grace," Cat said.

"You have to talk to me." "No I don't actually. Freedom of speech," Ava said. She went to walk away and he grabbed her hand. "Ava." "Why don't you go see what Kim's doing tonight?" "Ava, stop it." "No." She walked off and left with Cat. "Joe," Brad said. "What?" "Where'd Ava go?" Joe went and ordered a drink. "No you aren't." "What," Joe asked. "Go get your woman." "I'm not playing the stupid game." "What happened?" "Kim was there last night." "And?" "We sat down and had a drink," Joe said. "What is with you?" "Nothing." "You don't want Ava now?" "Hell yeah I do." "Then fight for her," Brad said. "No." "Why not?" "Because she isn't supposed to be stressing about anything." "You need to go get your woman," Brad said. Joe drank his drink then grabbed a bottle of water and left.

CHAPTER 36

Ava gave Grace her dinner, then tucked her into bed. She came downstairs and Cat was making virgin margaritas. "Cat." "Aren't even willing to talk to him," Cat asked. "What for?" Ava sat down and started working on some writing. "Call him." "No." "You're going on tour with him in a week." "And your point is what?" "You have to make up at some point." "No we don't." Ava went back to her writing. "I'm going to head home. Stop being so damn stubborn." "I'm not backing down," Ava said.

A week passed. Ava went home and grabbed her things and called Rose. "I think you two need to talk," Rose said. "I'll see you in a few. You still looking after Grace?" "Yes. See you." Ava pulled in and dropped a snoring Grace off, then went to the airport. They packed up the plane and Ava sat at the opposite end from Joe. "Okay, this is just plain weird. What are you two fighting about," Brad asked. "Brad, enough," Joe said. Ava went back to her writing with her iPod on. An hour in, Joe walked over to her and slid her earphones out. "What?" "Talk to me," Joe said. She put her earphones back in. He pulled her computer off her lap. "What?" "Ava, we need to talk." "No we don't," Ava said. "We're talking or we aren't stepping off the plane." "Too bad for you then," Ava said. The flight landed and the guys hopped off, leaving Ava and Joe on the plane. "Ava, please." "Don't you dare think that I'm giving in. I'm done," Ava said. She walked past him, with her purse, iPod and laptop in hand and got on the bus with the guys. A half-hour later, they pulled into the venue. Ryan, Joe and Brad headed off to go do sound check and Ava sat down in the stands. She went up and did her bit, then walked out to the bus. Joe stepped on behind her and locked the door. "What?" "Why are you being so damn stubborn," Joe asked. "How is Kim?" She grabbed her dress and her heels and went to get off the bus. "You're not going anywhere," Joe said. "Yeah I am." He took the dresses out of her hands. "Ava, stop. Enough is enough." "I know," she replied. She grabbed the dresses and walked off. She got security to take her to the hotel.

She showered, got her hair and makeup done, called to check on Grace, then went back to the venue. Joe was just finishing the meet and greet when he saw her. Ava went into the waiting area and relaxed, sliding her heels off. Ryan knew there was tension, but this was crazy. "Go. I have to call Rose, and Brad's calling to check on Danielle," Ryan said. Joe walked into the room and saw Ava. "We need to talk before we go on." "Why bother," Ava asked. "Ava." "No. You go have fun with whoever you find tonight." "Ava." "I'm done. I hope you and Kim had a blast." "Stop it." She went to walk out and he grabbed her hand. "You don't get to walk away," Joe said. "And why's that?" "Because I love you. Stop this." "I thought you did. Guess I was wrong." Ava walked out. She sat in the change room until they went on. They touched up her makeup, she did her songs, then left and went to the hotel. She slid right into the tub, then crawled into bed. Around 2, Joe came into the room. "Ava." "Go back to your own room," she said. "We're talking." "No we aren't." He turned the light on.

"You have to stop." "No I don't. I told you and you did it again. I'm done. You want to be single, then fucking be single," Ava said. She got up and grabbed her pillow and slept on the sofa. The next morning, she got up, showered, packed and left before he even got up. She was having breakfast with the guys when he came downstairs. "Ava, sit," Ryan said. "Ryan." "I'll sit on you if you don't." "Why," Ava asked. "You two are talking if I have to make you stay here." "Ryan, just let her go," Joe said. "I'm not going to listen to you whine another night." "Ryan." "No. You two are acting ridiculous." "Why? Because he can't seem to stay away from every woman that crosses his path," Ava asked. "Because he loves you. He's not going to mess around on you." "You'll believe anything won't you?" Ava got up and walked off. "Joe, go after her." "Why?" "Get up." "She doesn't want me around. I'm not making her want me," Joe said. "Yes you are." Ryan dragged him off and Brad paid the bill. "Go." Ava paid for her room and walked out the door waiting for the car back to the airport. "Ava." "Leave me alone." "We can't keep doing this," Joe said. "You made your choice." "No I didn't. If I had my choice we'd be curled up in bed with Ryan bugging us to get up and on the plane." "Guess you aren't getting your wish." The car pulled up and Ava got in, after throwing her bag in the back. He threw his in and got in the car with her. "You can't just leave me alone," Ava asked. "No. We're not getting on the plane if we're still fighting." "Then you're walking." "Ava." "No. You start this crap. You always start it. What the hell would you do if I did what you've done," Ava asked. "You wouldn't." "What if I did?" "Ava." "Fine. You watch how pissed off you get." They pulled into the airport and Ava went to get out. He pulled her back in and kissed her.

Ava got out of the car, slamming the door, then went and got on the plane. He got the bags loaded and got on with her. "Don't even breathe on me." "Ava." "Don't you fucking dare," Ava said. "I know you're pissed off." "You think so?" "Ava, stop it. I love you. I don't want to fight with you anymore." "Oh fucking well." He kissed her again. She pushed him away. "Enough." "Ava, I want my wife back," Joe said. "Maybe you should check with Kim or whoever else you're having fun with." Ava sat down and pulled out her laptop and iPod. He grabbed them away from her. "We're talking this out." "Why bother? You're just going to do it again." "Ava." "What?" "I am sick of fighting with you," Joe said. "Then don't." "What do you want me to say?" "Nothing. There's nothing you can say that's going to fix this." "We're ending this fight now." "And just how the hell do you think that's happening?" He kissed her and pulled her to him. It was the mind-numbing, heart pounding kiss that always made her give in before. She broke it and walked off the plane. Ryan and Brad were just pulling up. "You two talk?" "I'm not getting on the plane unless you two are on it," Ava said. "Ava," Ryan said. "No. He doesn't get to play the damn field while we're married. That's what he wants, then we won't be anymore." "You don't mean that," Ryan said. "Hell yes I do." He pulled Ava into his arms. Within minutes she was crying.

"Ava, you have to stop this," Ryan said. "He's the one that keeps walking off." "He loves you." "And that's why Kim, Tiffany, and whatever else . . ." "Ava. Stop it." "I can't. I'm going to be raising two kids alone." "No you aren't," Ryan said. "Ryan, you don't understand. I'm done with this crap. I'm done with his million and one ex-girlfriends." "Ava." "What?" "He loves you. That's never going to change." "I'm not dealing with his ex's." "I promised you months ago that nobody's getting in his pants but you," Ryan said. "And?" "Ava. He hasn't done anything." "I'm done worrying. I can't do it anymore." "Then stop getting all upset over nothing." "You saw him with Kim. Don't fucking tell me that was nothing," Ava said. She started crying again. He wrapped his arms around her. "Come get on the plane. We have to go," Ryan said. They got on and Ava sat with Ryan. Joe sat and watched her. The plane took off and Ava slept the entire flight.

They landed an hour or two later and got off the plane. They checked into the hotel, then went to sound check. They finished early. Ava did her part, then went to head to the hotel. "Ava, you have to talk to him," Brad said. "Why?" "Do it for me," Ryan said. "I love you like a brother Ryan, but I can't." "Please? I'll stay here if you want me to." "Fine." Joe walked towards her.

"Babe." "What?" "I wasn't with her." "The lipstick was enough," Ava said. "Ava, do you trust me?" "No." "Come on." "No. You want the truth? No. You and your exes have proven that I can't." "Ava, stop thinking that I'm automatically messing around," Joe said. "Give me one instance that you didn't." "Never stop do you?" "Nope." "Ava, I wasn't with Kim." "No. You just come home with lipstick on." "Would you stop. Ava, nothing happened." "Whatever." "Ava, I love you. All I did all night was look at you." "Until Kim walked in and you two disappeared together," Ava said. "That's why you're mad." "That and Tiffany, and every other damn woman you disappeared with." "Ava, I want you to hear this. I love you. If I have to say it every ten minutes for the next fifty years I will," Joe said. "Right. That's why you walk off with her, and whoever else. I'm done. It's finished." "No it isn't." "Yeah it is." Ava walked off and went back to the hotel. She called Cat on the way and begged her to come. "Just come home after the concert tonight," Cat said. Ava hung up and called the manager. "I can get you home tonight if you need to." "I need to minus the guys." "I'll get it together for you." Ava hung up and went to the hotel. She showered, then went to step out and Joe was right in front of her. "Move." "No." "Joe." "Ava, I'm not fighting with you anymore. I miss you," Joe said. "Should've thought of that before." She walked out, then got dressed. She slid the black backless dress on and grabbed her heels, then went to head out. "Ava." "What?" "Come here?" "No." Ava went to walk out and he grabbed her hand. "Let go." "No." "Joe, stop." "I'm sick of fighting with you." "I'm not playing this stupid game with you anymore." "Meaning what?" "Meaning I'm done." Ava grabbed her purse and her shoes and headed back to the venue to get her hair and makeup done.

She got to the venue, had something to eat and got her hair done. They started on her makeup when Joe walked in. "Can you give us a minute," Joe asked. Jasmine left them alone. "What?" "Don't you even think of walking out," Joe said. "Or what?" "Ava. We're not done." "Hope you have a good night tonight." "Ava." "Don't. Don't think that you kissing my ass is going to change all of this," Ava said. "I need you." "For what?" "I need you. I need us." "Joe, maybe you need to think about what you actually do need. You want to have your cake, and eat it too. I'm not going to sit around and wait for you to grow the hell up. I have two kids to raise. Either you're going to be there or you aren't. Either you're going to fuck everything that walks, or you're going to be faithful and married. Make your decision." "I did." "Maybe you need to think more about it then," Ava said. She walked out. Jasmine finished her makeup and the guys went and did the meet and greet. Ava confirmed the flight details and checked on Grace. "She's fine," Rose said. "I'll be over tomorrow morning." "I thought you were flying home with them tomorrow afternoon." "Tonight." "You alright?" "No." "I'll meet you at the house," Rose said.

The guys went to head on stage. Joe stopped and walked into where Ava was. He grabbed her hand and pulled her to her feet. "What?" He held her face in his hand and kissed her. She pushed him away and he walked out onto the stage with the guys. Ava called to make sure they grabbed her bag from the hotel. "It's loaded. We'll see you in an hour." A little while later, she was on the stage, did her songs, then went to head off. He hopped off to grab his guitar and pulled her into his arms and kissed her. "I love you," Joe said. She walked off, kicked her heels off, grabbed her laptop, iPod and purse and her phone, then went and hopped in the car to the airport. "I'm surprised you aren't waiting for the guys," the driver said. "I don't want them knowing." "They're going to know." "After I've left." They got to the plane and Ava left before the concert was even finished.

The guys headed off the stage and Joe walked into the sitting area and Ava was gone. "Anyone seen Ava," Joe asked. "She said she was leaving." "What do you mean leaving?" "She got in a car." Joe called the manager. "She's on a plane home now." Joe hung up. "I need a flight back." "Four hours." "Damn it." He hung up. Brad heard all the commotion "What?" "Ava's on the plane home." "What did you do?" "Nothing." "Joe." "We talked." "And?" "She told me to decide if I wanted to be faithful and married, or single." "Damn." "Brad, not now." "You need to get on a plane home." "I know." Ryan called the manager back. "Commercial flight. What time's the next one out?" "An hour." "First class left?" "Empty." "He's on it." "Fine." Joe went back to the hotel and packed then took off for the airport. He rushed through security and was on a plane home. Ava landed and headed home. She walked in and Rose was curled up on the sofa.

"I'm home." "What the hell happened," Rose asked. "If he wants to be single, then I can be." "Ava." "What?" "You can't be fucking serious." "I am. I'm sick of him getting to be the guy who has it all. I'm not going to sit around and wait for him to get someone else pregnant." "Ava!" "I'm done. That's the end of it." "Do you know what you're saying," Rose said. "Yep." Ava walked upstairs. "You need to get your brain cleaned out." "Why? What the hell do I have to sit around here for?" "She's sleeping in her bedroom," Rose said. "I'm not going to stay in a marriage where he's going to bang everything with two damn legs." "Ava, stop this." "No." "You are seriously freaking out," Rose said. "And I have a reason to." "You're seriously going nuts." "No. I'm regaining my single girl brain." "What has got into you?" "Seeing him with Kim, Tiffany, and every other chick he's 'not done anything' with." "You need to calm down." "No. I need a locksmith," Ava said. "Ava, stop it." "I'm sick of it." "You aren't divorcing him." "No. I'm taking a break." "Your touring with them." "Which means when he plays, so can I," Ava said. "You need to get off whatever you're on." Ava went upstairs and slid on her satin teddy and crawled into bed. "We'll talk in the morning." Rose went and curled up in the guest room and was asleep a few minutes later.

Two hours later, Joe walked in and went straight to their bedroom. He saw Ava asleep in the bed. He leaned onto the bed and wrapped his arms around her. "Let go." "Never," Joe said. "Joe, stop." "Why did you take off?" "Because I've had enough." "Ava, I want you. I want the only woman I loved from the minute I saw her. Just stop the silent treatment." "No. You walked off with someone else . . . . this after telling me for the millionth time that you wouldn't. I don't believe you anymore." "Ava, please." "How the hell did you get back here so fast anyway," Ava asked. "I took the first flight back." "Did you ever think . . ." He kissed her and pulled her to him. "Stop it." "Ava, I want this over." "Fine. We're done," Ava said. She got up and went and put her things into a bag. "Ava." He grabbed the bag out of her hand. "What?" "I want the fight over, not us." "Tough." She grabbed the bag and started grabbing her things from the closet." He grabbed her bag and pulled her into his arms and kissed her. He pinned her into the bedroom wall. "You're not leaving," Joe said. "And why the hell wouldn't I?" He picked her up and kissed her, and within a few minutes, they were having sex. He carried her back to the bed and pinned her to it. He tried to get her to curl up with him and she got up, pulled her jeans and sweater on, then walked out.

The next morning, Rose got up and went in to check on Ava. Joe was sitting on the floor by the bed. "What the hell?" "She walked out," Joe said. "Where did she go?" "I have no fucking idea. If I did, I'd be there." Rose grabbed her phone and called Ava. "Where are you?" "The house." "Woman." "Don't start." Rose hung up." "Where is she?" "We need to talk," Rose said. After a half-hour of talking, Joe knew what he had to do. He kissed Grace and headed to the house.

Since Ava hadn't slept all night, she'd finished 5 or 6 chapters of the book. She curled up on the sofa and was asleep when Joe slipped in. He wrapped her up in the blanket and sat down beside her. Ava woke up an hour or two later and saw him. "What are you doing here?" "Being with my wife." "Joe." "I know you're pissed off. I know why. I know that I'm an idiot. Fact is, I love you. I don't want to be without you," Joe said. "You always say it. Then Kim . . ." "I know. I talked to her. That's all I did. She's the one that gave me the idea about the dresses," he said. "Joe." "I love you. I married you because I love you." "Then when is all of the other crap going to stop?" "Now." "Joe, don't just tell me that because you think I want to hear it." "I'm not." "Joe, I've heard it." "I know. I can't do this without you." "What?" "Be here. I don't want to be without you, I don't want us to be apart and raise our babies." "Joe, I can't. Not if I'm worrying and seeing this crap 24-7." "And what if you don't?" "I know it'll be happening behind my back." "Ava, I don't want to be with anyone else." "And?" Joe kissed her. "I love you." "Joe, I don't know if I trust you." "I only want you." "I'm not doing this if you aren't serious," Ava said. "I sat on the floor of the bedroom all night. I need you." "Joe." "We're staying together. I love you." "Joe, I can't." "Can't what?" "I can't just forget all of it." "Ava." "I can't forget it," Ava said with tears streaming down her face. "I love you." "It's not enough," Ava said. She went to get up and he got up and was face to face with her. "I can't." He grabbed her arm and pulled her to him. He kissed her and they ended up back on the sofa in a few minutes. "Joe." "What?" "Just stop." "Ava, stop this." "I can't." "I'm not letting you go." "Every time things go right, some woman gets between us and they go wrong." "There isn't going to be anyone screwing us up again." "Joe." "I'm not leaving," he said. "What about Grace?" "She told me to bring Mama home." "Liar." "I'm sorry," Joe said. He kissed her again.

An hour or two later, Ava headed to her doctor's appointment with Joe. "Baby's doing just fine. You're blood pressure is down from the other day, so it's good." "Two weeks," Joe asked. The doctor nodded. They left and headed home. They still weren't back to normal, but at least they were trying. They got back to the house and Ava went upstairs.

"So," Rose asked. She was sitting in the TV room with the kids. "Getting there." "Joe." "I know." "Are you two talking at least," she asked. "Sort of. We went to the doctor on the way home." "And?" "Perfect." Ava came back downstairs a few minutes later. "Ava." "Hey Rose." "You okay?" "Fine." Ava walked back out the door. He walked out after her. "Where are you going," Joe asked. "Out." "Ava." "I'm going back to get the SUV. Either get in or not," Ava said. "Two minutes." He went in and told Rose where they were going and he headed back with Ava.

"I know you're mad." "Joe, enough." He slid his hand over and tried to hold her hand and she wouldn't let him. "Ava." A half-hour or so later, they pulled in. Ava hopped out and went inside. He followed her. "We're not leaving until we finish this." "Joe, leave it alone," Ava said. "No. Why are you so worried," he asked. "Because you proved I have a reason to." "Babe." "Don't babe me Joe. You know damn well that I'm right." "Ava, she's a friend." "Have a lot of those don't you?" "Seriously?" "Yes seriously. Every time I turn around you're surrounded." "And I have my ring on and tell everyone about you." "Right." "Ava." "Joe, I don't see how you talking about me is supposed to make things better," Ava said. "Because I love your crazy ass." "And?" "What do you want me to do?" She looked at him. "Tell me what I have to do Ava." "No more women." "Ava." "None. You walk off with someone for anything other than a pre-booked interview, that's it." "If you're there," he asked. "Joe." "You know that sometimes I have to talk to people." "Fine. Talk. One stupid idiot move and I'm not coming back." "You can't actually mean that." "You think it's easy? You don't even know how much it hurt," she said. "Ava." "No. You think you felt it when I wanted nothing to do with you? What do you think it's like trying to explain to Grace why you aren't tucking her in? I'm scared as hell," Ava said. "Ava." "Joe, you don't understand. I never wanted to do any of this alone, but I will if I have to." "You won't." "I will." She went to walk off and he pulled her into his arms. "I'm not losing you. If that's what it's going to take," he said. "You always say that." "I'm not losing us. This is more important to me." "If you . . ." Joe kissed her.

He picked her up in his arms and carried her to their bedroom. By the time they hit the bed his shirt was on the floor and so was her dress. He kicked his jeans off and peeled the rest of her things off and made love to her. He kissed every inch of her. They kept going and going until they were both exhausted. "Ava." "What?" "Tell me we aren't going to fight anymore," Joe said. "Up to you." "I love you." "I know." "Babe. I don't want to fight with you anymore." "Good." "I just want us back." He held her in his arms. The baby was kicking again. "See, baby agrees," Joe said. He kissed Ava. His phone went off. "Hi Rose." "You two alright?" "We'll be back in a few," Joe said. "I guess that's a yes." "Grace sleeping?" "Yep." "Thank you Rose." "Yep. You two are back to normal." He hung up. Joe kissed Ava again, then they showered and headed back. He pulled in and Ava was behind him. He walked in and Rose came over to them. "They just landed. I'm heading home."

"I'll bring Jacob over after dinner," Ava said. "Ooh." "Go." Rose left after a quick hug to Ava and Joe.

———————

Ryan walked in and Rose jumped into his arms. "Hey beautiful." "Hey yourself." She kissed him. "Where's Jacob?" "With Ava and Joe." "They're . . ." Rose nodded. "How the hell did you pull that off," Ryan asked. "Girl thing. I know her better than anyone." "Little Miss Fix-it." He kissed her. "I missed you," Rose said. "I bet." He carried her up the steps and right into their bedroom. "You told me to fix it," Rose teased. Ryan kissed her and leaned her onto their bed. "I missed you." "Oh really?" "You don't know how bad it was," Ryan said. "Saw it." "We're never fighting like that." "Definitely not." He kissed her and curled up in the bed with her. "How's baby?" "Perfect." "Good." "How did things go?" "Other than refereeing the two of them, it went good," Rose said. "Where are the next ones?" "Atlanta, and Baton Rouge. You coming with me," Ryan asked. "Thinking about it." He kissed her again. "I missed this." "Me too." They were curled up in the bed, in a quiet house just the two of them. They made love then had a nap before Jacob came back. Around 7, Joe dropped Jacob off. "And," Ryan asked. "It's good." "It better be." Jacob hugged Ryan. "I missed Daddy." "Missed you too," Ryan said. Joe headed home and Ryan and Rose played with Jacob before taking him to bed.

———————

Joe came back in and Grace ran over to give Joe his picture. "It's great baby," Joe said. He picked her up. "Where's Mama?" "In office." He peeked his head in. "You okay?" "Yeah. Just trying to figure some things out." "Such as?" "Book readings," Ava said. "You don't think you might be a little over-worked?" "One a week." "Oh." "On a Sunday." She was trying to put the readings together with tour dates. Joe kissed her cheek. "Say night to Mama." "I love you Mama," Grace said. "Goodnight baby." Ava kissed her and Joe took Grace to bed.

Ava came upstairs a while later and slid into the tub. Joe came in after tucking Grace in. "Hey." "Hey yourself." "She's a lot smarter than she looks," Joe said. "I know." "She asked if you were mad at me." "And?" "I told her that you weren't. Then she asked if you were moving." "And?" "I told her that we weren't going anywhere," Joe said. "She knows I was upset. Plus the million and one questions before putting her to bed." "From now on, we talk things out. No more walking out." "You know . . ." Joe kissed her. "No more fighting." She looked at him. "What?" "Nothing." He kissed her again. "Company?" Ava nodded. He got undressed and slid in with her. "I missed this," Joe said. "Your own fault." He kissed her neck. He felt the baby kicking. "Think this one's a boy or a girl," he asked. "Doesn't matter." "Ava." "Probably a girl." "Never know." "No I am not finding out." "Can't talk you into it," Joe asked. "No." He rubbed her shoulders. "Not going to work." He nibbled her ear. "Joe." "Fine. Can't talk you into it?" "Nope." "Fine." He flipped the radio on. "We just got some breaking news. The Aces have been nominated for 5 awards at the Country Awards . . . ." He kissed her shoulder. "Call Ryan and Brad." "We found out this morning." "And?" "Our song is one of them," Joe said. "Oh really?" He nodded. "When?" "May." "Great." "You're still going to be beautiful." "Better start dress hunting now," Ava said. "You know who can help." "It's an awards ceremony." "I meant me," Joe said. Ava laughed. She turned the water on to warm the tub back up. "What we up to tomorrow?" "Nothing. Laundry and cleaning. Why?" "I have to go into the studio." "Oh really?" "It's just us." Ava was quiet. "Ava." "What?" "You okay?" She nodded. She got up and wrapped herself in a towel, then got ready for bed. "Ava." "What?" "Come back in here," Joe said. She walked into the bedroom and slid her pajamas on.

He hopped out and drained the tub, walking into their bedroom in his towel. "Ava." "What?" "What's wrong?" "Nothing." She put her lotion on. "Ava." "What?" He sat down beside her. "It's just Me, Brad and Ryan." "Fine." "Then why do I get the feeling that you're thinking something else?" "Paranoia?" He leaned her into the pillows. "You sure," he asked. "Joe, I'm fine." He kissed her. "I love you." "I know." He leaned onto the bed linking her legs with his. "You going to come down and have dinner with me?" "Maybe." "Ava." "Depends on Grace." "Nice." "If she wants to come down, then we will." "Guess I'll have to ask her in the morning," Joe said. He kissed Ava again. One thing led to another and they were making out on the bed, in the bed and then made love. "You know what," Joe said. "What?" "I couldn't want anyone else." "Oh really?" "You're too damn addictive." Ava laughed. "You are." "How?" "I miss the feel of your lips on mine." "Mmm." "The feel of your skin next to mine." "Mmm." "The way you feel in my arms." "Should remember that," Ava said. "I missed you." "Sometimes we just need a reality check." "I know. Just not apart anymore alright?" "We'll try." He kissed her again. "Going to be kind of nice tonight." "Why?" "Think I might actually get sleep." "I couldn't sleep either," Ava said. "The going to bed mad thing doesn't work." "I know." Ava curled up with him and they were both asleep a little while later.

CHAPTER 37

Ava got up the next morning with Joe's arms around her. She kissed him and got up. She got changed and heard Grace in her room. She peeked her head in. "Hi Mama." "Hey baby." "Where's Daddy?" "Sleeping." "Can I wake him up?" "No." Grace jumped into Ava's arms. They went downstairs and had breakfast and Ava turned the coffee on. Grace ran to play with her toys and watch her program and Ava went upstairs and put his coffee on the side table. "Hey." "Hey yourself." "Where's Grace," Joe asked. "Watching Dora." He pulled her to him and kissed her. He pulled her into bed. "Joe." He had her shirt half off when she stopped him. "She's downstairs." "And?" He kissed her again. "Get up." "I'm up." He kissed her, and Ava managed to get up and head back downstairs. He got up, pulled his track pants on and walked downstairs. "Hi Daddy," Grace said. "Hey baby girl." She ran over to him and he picked her up. "I made you a bracelet." "Oh really?" Grace handed it to him. "Well thank you baby." She kissed his cheek and hugged him. "So what time you heading in," Ava asked. "1." "Where going," Grace asked. "I have to go to the studio with Ryan and Brad." "Can I come?" Ava smirked. "Mama's going to bring you down for dinner." "I can't stay with you?" "For a little while," Joe said. "Okay." Ava smirked. Grace totally had him wrapped around her little finger. Ava handed him his breakfast and Grace ran off to make Ryan and Brad a bracelet.

Ava laughed. "What?" "Has Daddy wrapped around her finger," Ava teased. "A little." "I'll come down with her around six." "Five." "Why?" "They're going for dinner at 5." "Meaning?" He leaned her into the kitchen counter. One kiss and she was melting in his arms. "Getting my hint," Joe asked. "Nope. Need a bigger hint." She laughed. He kissed her again and picked her up, putting her on the counter and pulling her legs around him. "Oh. That's what you meant," Ava teased. "Funny." His phone went off. "Yep." "Pick you up at 12:30." "I'll meet you there," Joe said. "Guess you two are back to normal." He hung up. "What?" "They're trying to get me to go in early. "Guess you should go then." Joe kissed her. She slid off the counter. "I'm not going until after 12." "Why's that?" "Nap time." Ava laughed. She went into the TV room with Joe and Grace was curled up with her blanket. Ava walked over to her and she looked up at Ava. "Come up on the sofa with me." Grace climbed up and curled up with Ava. An hour later, Grace was asleep. Ava took her upstairs and tucked her into bed. She stepped out of her bedroom and Joe kissed her. "What?" He took Ava's hand and led her back into their bedroom.

"What?" He kissed her and wrapped his arms around her. "She's going to be up in an hour." "We're two weeks behind." "On what," Ava asked. He kissed her. "You know you're hilarious." "I know. That's why you love me." "I have things to do Joe. We have to put stuff together for this weekend, figure out what we're doing with Grace . . ." He kissed her again. "It can wait," he said. He curled up on the bed with her and kissed her. "I missed the us time." "When we have two there's going to be even less," Ava said. "All the more reason." "I have a question." "What?" "We can't keep Emily here. We have to do something," Ava said. "Emm is great with her." "It's not fair to her Joe." "What you thinking?" "A real nanny." "Babe, you and I both know family is a better idea." "Like who?" "Just until the end of the tour," Joe said. "Then there's another one and another one. We need to figure this out." "Babe, we will." "Emily has her own life. She can't just pick up and run every time we ask." "She offered. She wanted to." "Joe." "Fine. We can split it." "Better." "Cat." "Seriously?" "Will loves Grace." "True." "Then," Joe asked. "You're asking." He kissed her. "Now that we settled that . . ." "One track mind?" "Always." They curled up together. Her phone went off. Ava grabbed it.

"Hello?" "Hey." "What," Ava said. "Don't hang up." "And why wouldn't I?" "Ava, just talk to me." "No." She hung up. "Who was that," Joe asked. "James." "He's still calling?" "Guess I'm irresistible to him too."

Joe grabbed her phone and called him back. "Finally," James said. "Try again." "Joe, I just need to talk to her." "No, you don't." "Come on." "She said don't call and she meant it." "And if you hadn't stolen her away from me, I'd be the one married to her." "Think she has more sense than that," Joe said. "I know she still wants me." "Something tells me that you are off your meds." "Joe." "Leave us alone." "I'm coming over." James hung up.

Joe looked at Ava. "What?" "He's coming here." "Why?" "To see you." "What the hell for," Ava asked. "Good question." "He's not getting past the gate." "Do you still care about him?" "Hell no." "No feelings at all?" "Joe." "I need to hear it," Joe said. "Of course I don't have feelings for him." "If you hadn't met me?" "I wouldn't have married him." "Good answer." He smirked and kissed her. "You know you're being silly." "If you can," Joe teased. "Nice." "Ava, I'm just saying, if he makes one move, I am kicking his ass to next century." "Good. Can I videotape that," Ava teased. He laughed and kissed her.

A half-hour later, James showed up. Joe walked downstairs with Ava right behind him. Joe opened the door determined to keep his cool. "What do you want?" "Ava." "Other than my wife," Joe said. "I need to talk to her. Is that a damn crime?" "Yes." "Joe, chill the hell out." "No. You are on private property." "Five minutes." "What's so important," Ava asked. "Alone." "Hell no." Joe wrapped his arms around Ava. "I can't do it." "What," Ava asked. "I can't just move on." "Joe and I are married." "And I know that he's not worthy of you," James said. "Either are you," Joe said. She linked her fingers with Joe's. "Ava, I miss you." "I told you last time. You lost the chance to be with me. I'm not going to be with someone who can't stick to one woman at a time," Ava said. Her nails dug into Joe's fingers. "And you think he can." "I've had enough of this. James, get the hell off my property," Joe said. "You aren't going to be faithful to her. We all know it. You're the worst at monogamy." "Meaning?" "Meaning Jodi. You screwed that one up. What makes you think Ava's not going to come to her damn senses," James asked. Joe inched towards him. "The two of you are acting like children. Enough. James, get the hell out of here and leave us be. Someday down the road if you end up being right, you can say I told you so, but I'm still never going to take you back. Joe, inside." "Ava," James said. "James, now." "I just want us back." "Two words James. They start with F O," Joe said. Ava walked back inside and went and sat down on the sofa. "I know she still loves me," James said. "Maybe you need to up your meds. She said she didn't," Joe said. "And you know damn well she does." "Why the hell do you feel the need to be such a damn prick," Joe asked. "Because I love her. I'd walk through broken glass for her." "And so would I. Difference being, she married me," Joe said. James finally left and Joe came inside. "Who won the contest," Ava asked. "What contest?" "Whose dick is bigger?" "Ava." She walked off and went into her office and got some more writing done.

Grace got up a little while later and Joe headed to the studio. They got a few more songs started by the time Ava showed up with dinner. She was just going to drop it off when Rose showed with Jacob. "What you doing here," Ava asked. "Thought I'd come meet Ryan and Brad for dinner." "Ready babe," Ryan asked. Rose nodded. Jacob was hugging Grace. "Okay lovebirds. In the car," Ryan said. "You sure," Ava asked. Rose nodded. "We'll be back in an hour or so." Grace ran off with Jacob which left Ava and Joe alone.

"Still mad," Joe asked. "I don't understand why the hell you need to fight with him." "Trying to prevent him from coming back," Joe said. "Like that's going to work." "Ava." "What?" "When's the last time you saw him?" "At the mall with Cat," Ava replied. "When?" "Jodi." "Seriously?" "I didn't talk to him. There's the difference." "Ava." "What?" "Is that why you were so mad," Joe asked. "What?" "Why you said all those things about being faithful?" "I didn't let him get away with it and I'm not letting you. It was in the damn vows Joe," Ava said. "Ava, I love you. Remember that." "If you ever even think of . . ." He kissed her. "Never going to happen." "It better not." He leaned her onto the loveseat. "Thought you were hungry," Ava said. He kissed her again. "I am." She straddled him on the sofa. "What time are you guys back tonight," Ava asked. "If I can get Ryan to stop being a perfectionist, around ten." "Oh." "Why?" "Was going to let Grace stay up until you got home, but she'll be out cold by ten." "Real reason," Joe asked. He kissed her and had her pinned onto the sofa. "Guess I'll be having the bubble bath all alone." "Tease." Ava got up and grabbed something to eat.

They relaxed a while and curled up together until the guys got back. Grace ran over to hug Joe. "Let's let Daddy finish work," Ava said. "No. I stay." "Baby, Daddy has work to do," Joe said. "No." "I want stay too," Jacob said. "Grace, let's go. We'll go watch Shrek with Jacob," Ava said. "No." Ava picked her up and she reached for Joe. "I'll come in and give you snuggles when I get home." "No." "One song," Joe said. Grace hugged him and kissed his cheek. "Sucker," Ava teased. "For a pretty girl, definitely." He kissed Ava, then he grabbed his guitar. They sang something for Jacob and Grace and then kissed them goodnight and headed in to finish up. Ava left with Rose, Grace and Jacob.

Ava pulled back into the driveway and Grace was asleep in the backseat. She carried her in, slid her into her pajamas and tucked her into the bed. She managed to slip out of the bedroom before her phone went off again. "Hello?" "Ava," James said. "Like you didn't already do enough." "I miss you." "Enough." "No." "It's been two years. Enough is enough," Ava said. "Ava, I tried to move on." "With my damn friends. Just lose my number." She hung up. A minute or two later, Cat called. "Hey." "How's Will," Ava asked. "Really good." "Oh really." Cat laughed. "I'm at his place." "Why?" "He said he wanted to make me dinner. How hilarious is that?" "It's called he's a good man." "How are you two?" "Fine I guess." "You're so full of it." "It's fine. James showed up and was causing crap." "Change your cell number." "Tomorrow morning. So really, how are things going with you and Will." "I really like him. He's a good man." "About darned time." "He asked me to move in." "And?" "Told him that I didn't want to rush it." "Good." "But I have some of my stuff here. I mean, I'm here all the time." Ava smirked. "I know what you're thinking." "That Joe was right for once," Cat teased. Ava's call waiting went off. "Call you in a bit." "Okay."

"Ava." "Will, what's up?" "I need your help with something." "What?" "Don't tell Joe." "Seriously. What's up?" "I'm going to the jewelry store tomorrow." "For?" "Ava." "You are not doing what I think you are." "Fine. Joe's damn spontaneous shit is hereditary," Will said. "Will, you two just met." "And you two met and got hitched two months later. What's your point?" "Guess I'm going shopping with you then," Ava said. "Have it narrowed down to two. I just need your opinion." "Holy shit." "I know." "Just take your time alright? Long engagement." "You two didn't." "Don't remind me. I wish we had." "Why?" "Long story. Give me a call tomorrow when you're ready to go." "We're coming on the weekend to the show Saturday. Do you want us to look after Grace Friday night," Will asked. "I'll talk to him. Thank you for the offer." "Anytime. She's the most adorable little munchkin in the planet." They chatted for a few minutes, then hung up. Ava sent a text back to Cat that she'd talk to her the next day, then hopped into the tub.

After an hour or so, Ava slid out, slid into her satin pajamas and slid into bed. She woke up at 2 and Joe wasn't in bed. She went back to sleep. The next morning, she woke up and his side of the bed was still empty. Ava got Grace up, then got dressed and gave Grace her breakfast. She left with Will. "Thank you for the help with this." "No problem." She wasn't going to let this bother her. They found a ring and Ava headed home. She gave Grace her lunch, then put her down for her nap. When she came out of her bedroom, she heard Joe at the door. She walked down the steps, then went into the kitchen and made herself some lunch. "Hey." She shot him a look. "Fine. I deserve that," Joe said. She went into her office and locked the door then put her iPod on and got some writing done. An hour or two later, she came out and he was on the sofa. "You talking to me yet," Joe asked. "Why? Thinking that disappearing might be a good idea?" "Ava." "Don't you dare even think it." Ava walked upstairs and Grace woke up. Grace walked downstairs and curled up with Joe. Ava walked in and told Joe she was going out. "Where?" "Doesn't matter." She walked out and pulled out within a minute or two. She drove, then pulled over at the park. She sat down by the tree that he'd had so much pride in carving their initials into. Within a few minutes, she felt sick. She hopped back in the car and left for the other house. She pulled in, headed inside and made herself dinner, then curled up by the fireplace and read for a while. She walked upstairs and read in the tub, then curled up in bed. She was out cold in no time.

The next morning, Ava got up, made herself breakfast, then curled up on the sofa. She heard the door. She didn't even bother looking. "Ava. Where in the hell," Joe said. "Don't you dare start with me." "You took off." "Sort of like you do." "You know Grace was freaked out." "Good." "Fine. You're pissed at me." "Damn right I am." "I was at Ryan's." "Fingers broken," Ava asked. "Ava." "Well?" "No." "No excuse." "You can't just take off." "And either can you." She went to walk away and he grabbed her hand. "Let go." "No." She pulled her hand back and walked outside. "Ava." "What?" "I shouldn't have stayed without letting you know." "And?" "I'm sorry you were worried." "I wasn't. I just assumed." "Why would you assume something else?" "History." She walked back inside and grabbed her purse. "Ava." "Don't." "Babe." "Don't think that you can just kiss my butt and all is fixed. It's never going to be." Ava walked out and left. She walked around at the mall, then headed home.

Ava packed for the concert, then went to bed. Joe walked in around ten. He sat down beside her. "I'm sorry." She didn't reply. "Ava, I know you're awake." "So?" "I'm sorry." "Good." "If it makes you feel better, we finished the two songs." "It doesn't, but thanks." "Babe." "What?" "I missed you." "Don't even think it." "After last night I know what you meant." "Meaning?" "Had a nightmare you and James were together." "Nice hallucination." "I'm sorry I didn't come back." "It takes two damn minutes Joe." "I know. I should've." He leaned onto the bed beside her. "What?" "I missed my wife." "Remember it. Next time you pull stupid ass shit, I'll be gone." "Ava." "It's a damn promise. Don't even think of trying me." "Would you stop?" "No." He wrapped his arms around her. "You'd miss me," Joe said. "Point?" "I love you." "Joe, you know you drive me nuts." He kissed her. "Forgive me," he asked. "And what would you do if I said no?" He kissed her again with a kiss that would turn a glacier into a pond.

Within a few minutes, they were making out and his clothes were hitting the floor. He curled up in bed with her, holding her in his arms. "Mama," Grace said. "Yes baby." "I had bad dream." Ava got up and carried Grace back to her bed. "What was the dream?" "That you and Daddy left me behind and moved away." "Grace. You know we'd miss you too much to ever do that." "Promise?" "Definitely." "Mama." "What?" "Are you and Daddy going to work?" "We're all going tomorrow." "Me too?" "Yes." "Oh." "And Jacob," Ava said. "Yay!" "Just get some sleep." "Okay." Ava flipped her pillow, kissed her goodnight and came back to bed. "See, she needs you," Joe said. "So do you." "Very true." "No more disappearing okay?" "That goes double for you," Ava said. "I have to go to the doctor tomorrow." "I know. We're leaving after the appointment." "You staying with Grace," Ava asked. "No. She's coming with us." "It's just a checkup." "We're all going together." "Surgically attached," Ava asked. He nodded and kissed her. The baby kicked. "I saw that." He kissed Ava again. They curled up together and finally got some sleep.

The next morning, Ava got up. Joe woke up as she was stepping out of the shower. "Party pooper." Ava slid her leggings and shirt on, then went in to get Grace. She walked in and Grace was trying to dress herself. Ava helped her, then Joe came in. "Hi Daddy," Grace said. "Hey princess." He kissed Ava. Grace hopped into his arms. They had breakfast, then headed to the doctor. "Well, baby is doing good. Your blood pressure is a little high." Ava looked at Joe. "Grace, do you want to hear the baby," the doctor asked. She nodded. She put the monitor on and Grace got to hear the baby. "Mama, what's the thump?" "That's the baby." Grace was so excited Joe started laughing. "So, if we were to ask if it were a boy or a girl," Joe said. "I know." "And you're not telling either of us," Ava said. "Ava." "No. It's going to be a surprise." "Babe." "No telling either of us," Ava said. "Gotcha." They left the doctors and headed for the airport.

A few hours later, they were at the venue. Grace was playing with Jacob while Ava and the guys did sound check. Rose was playing with the kids. "So how's Danielle and Chris," Ava asked. "Perfect. Seriously, the only time I actually get sleep is when we're away," Brad said. "So she liked the shower?" "Definitely. Think it was a better idea to do it after we had him." "She said it was a jinx if it was too far ahead." "And Rose was stunned," Ryan said. "Still can't believe you had her thinking it was all just Danielle's party." "I had to," Ava said. "I know." Brad got a call a few minutes later and walked off talking to Danielle. "So how you two doing," Ryan asked. "Fine," Joe said. "Joe, you piss her off again?" "You're fault." "Told you to call," Ryan said. "Before or after the 5 or 6 shots?" They laughed. Ava walked off. She went and grabbed her laptop and sat down and got some writing done.

"Joe." "What," Ryan asked. "You two at it again?" "She was pissed that I didn't call." "And why the hell you were talking to Jodi anyway I have no damn idea," Ryan said. "It's over." "Tell your dick that." "Ryan." "If you love her, don't talk to Jodi. Trust me," Ryan said. "Then don't cause shit." "I promised her something. If you fuck it up, she won't even trust me." "I'm not going to." "Joe." "It's done," Joe said. "You know if Ava finds out you're a dead man."

Ava relaxed a while with her iPod and got some writing done while the kids were napping. Joe walked in a half-hour or so later and handed her roses. "What are these for?" "For being an amazing wife." He kissed her and leaned onto the bed. "How's the writing?" "It's going." "I had an idea." "What would the idea be," Ava asked. "We go out after the show tonight." "Grace." "Rose said she'd look after her." Ava looked at him. "Why do you have a guilty look on your face," Ava asked. "I don't." "Yeah you do." "Ava, I want a night out with my wife." "Where?" "A nightclub." "We're back before 2." Joe nodded. "Fine." "Good. I feel like showing you off." They relaxed a while, then had dinner and started getting ready for the show. The guys went off to do the meet and greet and Ava got changed, with help from Rose and the kids.

Joe's phone went off. "What's up?" "It's me. I'm here. Are we still meeting up later," Jodi asked. "Plans." "I'm going to Z Bar." "Okay." "See you there." He hung up and walked out towards where Ava was with Rose. "Hey." "Hey yourself," Ava said. Joe kissed her. "How was the meet and greet?" "Good. You look great babe." "Thank you." He kissed her then grabbed his red shirt to go with her dress.

The concert went off without a hitch, then Ava switched shoes and they left. They pulled into the bar, went in, had a drink, then danced. Ava saw someone watching them. She looked the next time she spotted the woman. She looked at Joe. "What?" Ava went to walk out and he pulled her back into his arms. "Let go." "No." "Have fun with Jodi," Ava said. She walked out and got the driver to take her back to the hotel. She called Rose. "The kids are here with us. What's wrong?" "I'm staying at the hotel, but in another room." "Why?" "Don't ask." "Call me when you get in the room," Rose said.

Ava walked in and slid into her leggings and her shirt. Rose walked in a few minutes later. "What the hell do you mean Jodi was there?" "Just like I said," Ava said. "He can't be that stupid." A minute later, Ryan was at the door. "Who's looking after the kids," Rose asked. "Brad." Ava laughed. "What's going on," Ryan asked. "Nice to know you're full of shit too." "Ava." "Jodi was at the club. I'm going home," Ava said. "You can't." "Hell if I can't." "Ava." "I'm not going on stage with him." "You can't just leave," Ryan said. "Why not?" "At least let me talk to him." "Too late." "Ava." "No. I'm done." "You're not thinking straight." "Just go Ryan." "Ava." "Go." "I'll be up in a few baby," Ryan said as he kissed her. "I'm going to kick his ass myself." "Good," Ava replied.

Ryan left and went down to the bar. He saw Joe, then he saw Jodi. "What the hell are you doing?" "Having a damn night out," Joe said. "How much you have to drink?" "A few." "Get in the damn car." "Why?" "Because you're about to lose your wife. That's why," Ryan said. "What are you talking about?" "Walk." They left and Ryan talked to him all the way back to the hotel. Ryan sobered him up a bit before he went upstairs. He walked into the room and Ava's things were gone, so were Grace's. He sat down on the sofa. "I know where she is," Ryan said. "I didn't do anything." "Dumb ass. You think you can hang out with Jodi and she's not going to find out?" "We were hanging out. Friends." "Then maybe you should've told Ava straight out." "Where is she?" "Another room," Ryan said.

Ava fell asleep. A half-hour later, she woke up with the sound of someone at the door. She went and answered it. "What the hell do you want," Ava asked. "You deserve an explanation." "You still talking to her," Ava asked. "We're friends. Platonic friends," Joe said. "Right. And I'm the queen of fucking England." "Ava, I mean it. Platonic friends." "Turn your ass around and go back to your room." "No." Ava went to slam the door and he walked in.

"Ava, we were talking and having a drink." "Couldn't have told me that she was there," Ava asked. "What would the point have been?" "The fact that you probably arranged to meet her there? The fact that as of right now, we're done." "Ava." "I told you. You said it wouldn't happen and I told you if it did, we were done. As of now, we're done." She walked over to the door and opened it. He pushed it shut. He pinned her to the wall and kissed her. She pushed him away. "Ava." "Get the hell out Joe." "You aren't serious." "Yeah I am. Get out." "No." "Is that where you were the other night? Were you out with her?" "Me, Brad, Ryan and her." Ava went into the bedroom, packed her bag, grabbed her purse, phone and laptop and went to walk out. "You're not leaving." She slapped him so hard his face was red and walked out. She got half way to the elevator when he stopped her. "Move," Ava said. "No." "Move or you're getting it worse." He grabbed her bag and her hand and led her to his room.

They walked in and he locked the door. "What?" "I was talking to her. That's all." "Right." "Ava." "I'm not having this discussion with you again." "We are until we figure this out. Nobody's walking out of this room until we do." "I'm not putting up with this," Ava said.

"Ava, nothing happened. Ryan knows it. He drove." "You promised me." "And I didn't do anything. I didn't even hug her goodbye." "Right. And I can walk on water." "Ava, you can't just trust me?" "No. Not after everything you've done." "I didn't do anything. I swear to you I didn't." "You know you need a serious ass kicking. Maybe I should call Will to do it." "You want it in blood," Joe asked. "I don't trust you." "I haven't cheated." "No. You take off with the guys and an old girlfriend instead. How's that supposed to be better?" "We were talking about you. How I totally changed after you and I met." "Sure." "Ava, I did. I want you. That's all I want." "And still you seem to get pulled away by every damn ex you ever had," Ava said. "Ava, I love you." He pulled her into his arms and kissed her, cupping her face in his hands. "I love you." He repeated it until he had her backed into the king sized bed. "Stop," Ava said. "Ava." "Just stop." She walked off. "Come back in here." "No." "Ava." "No. Not after this." She took her bag and her purse and walked out.

Half way down the hall, she stopped in tears. He came up behind her. "Just come back in and talk." "What's the point?" "I love you." "Nothing's going to change," Ava said. "Ava." "Let go." "No." He kissed her and walked her back towards his room. "I'm not going back." Ava walked towards the elevator and stepped in. Joe had the door blocked. "Ava." "No." He got on the elevator, grabbed her hand and led her back to the room. "Let go." "Ava, we're staying in here until this is settled." He locked the door and put on the do not disturb sign. "What's the point of trying to settle it? It's just going to happen all over again." "Ava, what do you want me to say?" "That you aren't going to be an idiot anymore." "Babe." "Don't suck up to me. You have to know that I'm not just over-reacting because I'm pregnant." "You're not supposed to be under any stress." "Nice try." "Ava." "What?" "Tell me what you want me to do." "I don't know." "I'll tell you if I go out with . . ." "Joe." "Won't go out alone." "You think that's supposed to make me feel better? It's like confining you to my side. I can't trust you Joe." "Baby, you can." "Name once that my gut feeling was wrong." "When you had second thoughts about getting married in the first place," Joe said. He cupped her face in his hands and kissed her. "I love you." "This isn't going to fix this." "Ava, I don't want to fight with you." "I don't want to fight with you either, but I can't keep feeling like all of this is going to be ripped away. Like when we have the baby, it'll get worse. I'd rather just do this alone period," Ava said. "Ava, you don't know what you're talking about." "Yeah I do. It's either alone, or with you. Make a decision," she said. Ava walked out, then went to Ryan and Rose's room and fell asleep on the sofa.

The next morning, they got up and Grace walked over and jumped onto the sofa with Ava. "Where Daddy?" "I don't know baby." She grabbed Ava's phone and handed it to her. Ava dialed and handed the phone to Grace. She freshened up, then they headed to the plane. Ava walked on and saw Joe. He looked horrible. Grace ran over to him and hopped into his lap. He wrapped his arms tight around her. Ava sat down at the back, turned on her iPod and closed her eyes. Just as they were about to land, Joe walked over to Ava and grabbed her hand. They went into the bathroom. "What?" He kissed her and slid her dress up. "Stop." "Ava." He kissed her again and had her on the countertop in minutes. They had sex. Fast, intense, urgent sex. It wasn't pretty, or romantic. After, he pulled her into his arms. "I'm sorry. Just tell me what you want me to do to fix us." "Tell me the truth." He kissed her again and pulled her close as the baby started kicking again. "I am not living without you." "Joe, we can't keep fighting like this." "I'm not losing you." "What are we supposed to do then? Pretend this didn't happen," Ava asked. "Keep going until this looks like a bump in the road." "Joe." "It is. I promise you. From now on it'll be like cruise control." "You know how . . ." He kissed her again and held her in his arms. "Did you sleep," Ava asked. He shook his head. "Nap." He nodded. They went and sat back down and Grace curled up in Joe's lap.

They finally landed and headed to the hotel for a quick nap. Grace played with Rose and Jacob and Joe and Ava caught up on their missed sleep. At 1, Will and Cat came up. "Hey," Joe said. "Why do you look like you just woke up," Cat asked. "Ava's still sleeping." "Nice." Joe hugged his brother and kissed Cat's cheek. "I am not still asleep," Ava said. She came in yawning with her flawless makeup and her hair done. "You look fantastic," Will said. "Thank you Will." Ava hugged Cat. "So where's snuggles," Cat asked. "With Rose. I was exhausted." "I bet." "Long story. We have to head to sound check. You want to join us," Joe asked. They agreed and they all headed to the venue together.

After an hour of sound check and an interview or two, they all relaxed by the RV. The kids played and drew pictures, while everyone else tried to relax and have a nap before the show. Ava left with Cat and Rose for an hour or two and the kids stayed with the guys. "Where are we going," Cat asked. "Shopping," Ava said. "For?" "Joe's birthday gift," Rose said. "Woman, his birthday's tomorrow," Rose said. "I know," Ava replied. "You at least have an idea?" "I'm just going to pick it up," Ava said. "So the mall is just for fun?" "Yep." They got to the mall and walked around, got a few things, and Ava picked up a gift or 4 for Joe. She wrapped the gifts, then they headed back. Just as they were pulling in, the dinner was arriving. They ate with the guys and then Joe and Ava headed off to get changed.

Joe slid into the shower behind Ava. "You're up to something." "Why would I have to be up to something?" "Because I know better," Joe said. "Not up to anything." She rinsed her conditioner out. "Babe." "What?" "If you're planning something for my birthday." "I'm not. You hate parties." "Ava." "You said it." "Don't," Joe said. She kissed him, then stepped out and started getting ready. He slid a towel around his waist, turned the shower off and came up behind her. "I know you're up to something," Joe said. "Now you want a party don't you?" "You and me on a beach having a you and me party," Joe said. "Interesting plan, but you have a concert to do." He nuzzled her neck. "I have to get ready," Ava said. His arms slid around her, untying the satin robe. "Joe." "What?" "Get dressed." He turned her towards him and kissed her. She slid her arms around his neck. "We have to get ready," Ava said. "I know." He kissed her again. "We're going to be late." "They can wait," Joe said. Just as he was about to walk her towards the bed, Cat knocked at the door. "Get dressed," Ava said. "Black?" Ava nodded. She went and let Cat in. "Hey." "Hey yourself. I can't decide what to wear." "The white one," Ava said. "Seriously?" Ava nodded. Cat went back down to her room and Ava went into the bedroom. "You're wearing the red aren't you," Joe asked. Ava smirked. "Damn." Ava grabbed her lingerie and started getting ready. "Babe." "What," Ava asked. She slid the dress on. "Damn." "Forgot I had this one didn't you?" He nodded. She walked over to him and slid her arms around him. "Now who's delaying who," Joe teased. Her hands slid down to his butt. "Oh really." Ava nodded. Within minutes, he had her pinned to the bed and was making love to her.

Finally, they headed back to the venue. He went to the meet and greet and Ava went into hair and makeup. Joe came in after and slid his arms around Ava. "Don't mess the hair." He slid his hands on either side of her neck and kissed Ava. "What?" "Nothing." "You so suck at keeping secrets," Ava said. "Need you to do something." "And what would that be?" "Bring Will with you on stage," Joe said. "He's not doing what I think he is." Joe nodded. "Cat's front row right?" He nodded again. "Holy shit." "And good ring choice," Joe said. "He asked. I had to help him." He kissed Ava. "How long?" "15." They finished with the last piece of Ava's hair, then she got up.

"Wow," Cat said when Ava came in. "Thank you." Ava grabbed her hand and led her into the hair and makeup room. "What?" "Nothing." They touched up Cat's hair and makeup while Ava helped Will plan things out with the guys. Cat came in a little while later, then headed down to watch the concert with Will. The guys went on after one heck of a good luck kiss from Ava to Joe. "What's going on," Ryan asked. "Just helping Will." Grace came running in. "Hey baby girl." "Hi Mama." "So I have a question," Ava asked. "What?" "Do you like Auntie Cat?" Grace nodded. "And Uncle Will?" "He cool." "What if Auntie Cat and Uncle Will got married?" "I want help." "I'll let her know," Will teased. "Seriously," Rose asked. "With a little help from Me and Joe." Rose laughed. "Ava. 15 minutes." She nodded. "Mama, luck." Grace kissed Ava. "Thank you baby girl." Ava sent a text to Will.

Ava came out to do her songs. Two in, Ava put the plan into action. "You know what the best part of being here with you all is? It's hearing the stories and your memories with the songs. Tonight, we're making a wish come true. Everyone, give a warm welcome to our good friend Will." Cat looked and saw him come out with a rose. "I have to tell you, if it weren't for Ava, and Joe, Ryan and Brad, this would never have happened. I met the love of my life. I owe it to Ava. Now, I'm following Joe's footsteps." Security walked Cat onto the stage. "Cat, I love you. Make me the second happiest man in the planet and marry me."

Her mouth dropped. Cat nodded. "And there you have it. Another memory." Joe and Ava sang love letter as Will and Cat went backstage.

"Holy shit." "What?" "How did you . . ." "Sneaky." He kissed her, picking her up in his arms. "Seriously though, I love you. I don't want to live without you." "We can take our time right?" He nodded. "I just wanted to give you the ring. I don't want to waste any more time with people who aren't right for me. I know you're my dream girl." "You sure you want this so soon?" He nodded. "Then I will." He kissed her. Ava came backstage after finishing their last song and Cat hugged her. "Grace wanted to ask if she could be your flower girl." "Wouldn't be a wedding without her." "I'll let her know. Congrats." "Now we really are family." Ava laughed. Cat and Will watched the rest of the show, then when it was done, they went back to the hotel.

Ava got champagne for everyone and she had ginger ale. They talked, laughed, talked some more, then Ava excused herself and headed to their room. She went in, washed up and slid into the bed. Just as she was falling asleep, she heard Joe come in. He kicked his things off and slid into bed beside her. "You sleeping," he asked. "Not yet." "Good." "Why?" He kissed her neck, then his arms slid around her. "Joe." "Ava," he teased. He kissed her shoulder. "You are in a mood tonight aren't you?" "Always." Ava leaned over towards him. "Thank you for helping him with the ring," Joe said. "I had to. Besides. Gave me time to hang out with him." "The two of them are hilarious." "You did good Mr. Matchmaker." "Did even better when I married you," Joe said. "This is true." "You realize that I asked you three years ago today?" "Yep." "Still remember the look on your face," Joe said. "The look of shock?" He laughed. "I was so nervous. It's the biggest decision I ever made." "Even when you started with the guys," Ava asked. "This was bigger. I was up half the night trying to figure out how to word it." "Think you did pretty good." "I was so scared you were going to say no." "You know that word never came into my head," Ava said. "You know how different life would have been?" Ava nodded. "How different it would've been if I hadn't come to the concert that night," Ava said. "Think I would've put the concert on hold and driven to your place to bring you there myself." "Joe." "Seriously."

He was having one of those moments. One of those 'what would have happened if' moments. "I knew one thing for sure," Joe said. "What's that?" "When you walked in with stupid head, I knew I was definitely attracted. I wanted to kiss you the minute we met." "Oh really." He kissed Ava with a mind buzzing, breathtaking passionate kiss that had her legs quivering in seconds. "I love you." He kissed her again and made love to her. Every inch of her wanted him like she did that first night. Like she did on their honeymoon, the night they secretly married in Vegas.

After, they curled up together, the feel of his lips on her skin still making her body hum with happiness. "Joe." "Yes babe." "Happy birthday." "Thank you love of my life." He kissed her neck. "Get some sleep old man," Ava said. "Why?" "You have a birthday to celebrate tomorrow." "I love you." "I love you too." Finally, they fell asleep, curled up together.

The next morning, Ava got up and started calling around. She had the entire party booked in a half-hour. She went and got Grace from Rose and Ryan's room, then came back just as he was getting up. "Daddy," Grace said. He came out of the bedroom, jeans on and Grace ran and jumped into his arms. "Happy bert day." "Thanks baby girl." She handed him a little bag. "What's this?" Grace giggled. He sat down on the sofa and opened the card that Grace had made. "I love you too baby girl." "Open." He opened it and found a necklace. "Wow. It's great baby." She hopped off his lap, kissed him, then ran off to play with her toys. "Morning birthday boy," Ava said. He pulled Ava into his lap and kissed her. "Good morning to you too." "You like?" He nodded. "You want to open another one?" "Ava." "Had to," she replied. He opened it and saw the leather bracelet he'd been looking at. It had 'Ava and Joe Forever' burned into it. "Babe." "What?" "How did you know?" "Ryan told me." He kissed her. "There's more than that you know." He saw another box in the bottom of the bag. "What's this?" "Something." He opened it and saw a diamond band. "Ava." "Matches the one you bought me." "Where in the?" "Found out where you got mine." He slid it on and it fit perfectly. "Plus, it will remind you of something," Ava said. "What's that?" "You're stuck with me and Grace and this baby forever." "That's a really good thing. Don't think I'd ever let you go anyway."

CHAPTER 38

They finally got home and Joe walked in and put Grace down for a nap. Ava went upstairs and started unpacking, then put his other presents on the bed. "What is all of this?" "Nothin," Ava said. "You spoil me." "Someone has to." He opened the shirt, the jeans, the belt with the fancy buckle, then saw one peeking out from under the bed with a huge silver bow on it. "Ava." "What?" "What's this?" "Open it." "What did you do?" He pulled the box out. It was a familiar shape. He opened it and saw the guitar he'd been staring at for years. "Ava." "It's from me, Ryan, Brad, Rose, Cat, Will, Grace, Danielle, Jacob and baby Chris." He kissed her. "Babe." He tried it out quietly in their bedroom. "Ryan said it was about time you got a new one," Ava said. "Only been staring at it for 5 years." "Why didn't you just get it?" "Got something more important first." "Which was?" He laid the guitar back down in the case and pulled Ava to her feet. "I got the woman of my dreams to marry me." "Sweet talker." He kissed her again. "So." "What?" "Get changed." "For what?" "Dinner." "Ava." "Don't tell me. Tell Ryan," Ava said. "Better idea. Sort of had other plans." "I bet." He kissed her. "I know what you were thinking. He made me promise Joe." "Well, we can un-promise." He leaned her onto the bed and they curled up together. "Would rather be doing this tonight." "You can after." "Promises promises," Joe said. Ava laughed. "Where are we going?" "He said to come over there." "Then we have time." "For what?" "Proper thank you." They laughed. The worry he'd had for weeks was gone. The gifts weren't important. He wanted Ava back. That's all he wanted.

After they finally managed to get changed, and Grace woke up, they headed to Ryan's. He walked in to a room filled with his friends, family, and a pile of people he forgot he knew. "Ava." "Party. Check," Ava teased. He kissed her. "That's how you two ended up with two in the first place," Will said. "I still can't believe you guys. What happened to no parties," Joe asked. "Was necessary this year." Joe kissed Ava's cheek. He went around and talked to everyone while Ava helped Rose in the kitchen. The kids were playing at the table. "Couldn't have done it without you," Ava said. "I know. That's because I'm super woman." "True." "So everything is done?" Rose nodded. "His mom gave the caterer his favorite recipe. It's not half bad." Just as Ava was pouring herself a ginger ale, he slipped into the kitchen behind her. Rose took Grace and Jacob to the other room to have their dinner. "Hey." "Hey yourself birthday boy." He kissed her. "What?" "How the heck did you pull this off without me knowing?" "Rose and Cat." "Babe." "Mmm." He cupped her face in his hands and kissed her. "Having fun," Ava asked. as he let her up for air. He nodded. He kissed her again. "What's wrong?" "Nothin." "Joe." Ava turned and saw Kim.

"What," Rose asked. "Nothing." "Ava." "It's nothing. Go enjoy the party." "Fine." Joe grabbed her hand and pulled her into the hall. "What?" He linked fingers with her. "Hey baby boy," his mom said. "Hi Ma. How you doing?" "Great. How are you two?" "Good." He wasn't about to let go of Ava. Not after what had happened previously. They chatted with his family a bit. Everyone had dinner, then cake, then started heading home. The end of the night, it was Will and Cat, Joe, Ava and Grace, Ryan and Rose, Danielle and Brad and baby Chris. "Surprised," Brad asked. "Now I really need some sleep." "Getting old buddy," Ryan teased. "Funny ass." He threw a pillow at Ryan. "You seriously starting this?" Ryan threw it back at him. "I appreciate all of this guys." "It's all Ava. She knew you wanted a party," Cat said. "I left the guest list up to these guys," Ava said. He kissed Ava. "See, that's how you two got the second one in the first place." "Jealous much," Joe teased. "Nope." Will laughed. Ava started the yawning. "We're going to head home guys." They headed for the door and Ava carried Grace to the car and put her in her car seat. Ryan came out behind her. "Thank you for the help with this," Ava said. "I didn't invite her," Ryan said. "Doesn't matter." "You alright?" Ava nodded. He hugged her. "I promised you. Not backing out on it." He kissed her cheek and went inside. Ava and Joe finally headed home. Joe took Grace and tucked her in while Ava washed up for bed.

She came into the bedroom and slid her satin teddy on. "Babe," Joe said. He walked in and saw her. "What?" "Wow." "Last part of your present." "Happy birthday to me." He wrapped his arms around her. "You have fun," Ava asked. He nodded. "Even better now that we're home." "And why would that be?" "Because I can do this . . ." He kissed her with one of those intense, passionate, take your breath away kisses that seemed to last forever. Before she knew it, they were curled up on the bed together, clothes in a pile on the floor beside the bed. They made love and curled up together under all the blankets. "Babe." "Mm." "Are we okay?" Ava nodded. "I didn't know she was going to be there," Joe said. "Stop worrying. We're fine." "I missed you in my arms." She had to admit that she'd missed him too. "You in the studio this week," Ava asked. He nodded. "Two or three more songs and we're done. Then you get me all to yourself." "I have a doctor's appointment." "Whatever day it is, I'll tell them I'm not coming in." "Joe." "I'm coming with you." "It's a check-up." "Still. Gives me a day with you before we go back out this weekend." "Finishing the CD comes first." "Nope." He kissed her. "You and Grace and baby come first," Joe said. "Heels dug in on this one?" He nodded. "You are the most important person in the world to me Ava." Why was it that the simplest of phrases had her completely at ease?

The next day, Ava woke up and Joe wasn't in bed. His phone was gone. She slid her sweater on with her leggings, then walked downstairs. He was on the sofa playing a song for Grace. Ava went into the kitchen and made him coffee, then brought Grace her breakfast and him a large mug of coffee. "Hey beautiful," Joe said. Ava kissed him. "Daddy play song for me." "I know." "Sparkly." Ava smirked. Ava went to go back into the kitchen and he pulled her onto the sofa with him. "Daddy silly," Grace said. He kissed Ava. "Mm. Coffee." He laughed. They all joked around a while, then Ava went to get ready for her appointment. Grace ran upstairs behind her. "Mama." "Yes baby." "When baby coming?" "In the summer." "Oh." Joe came upstairs and slid his arms around Ava. "Daddy, you love Mama," Grace asked. "Definitely." "How much?" "A cagillion." "How much that?" "Enough to wrap around you a million times," Joe said. "Oh." Ava went to hop into the shower and Grace ran off to play with her toys.

Just as she was about to step out, Joe stepped in. "Hey." "Hey yourself." "What you doing?" He kissed her and within a few minutes, her back was against the shower wall. "Didn't give you a proper good morning kiss." He kissed her again. "Well good morning to you too," Ava said as he let her up for air. She went to try and step out and he blocked her. "What?" "I told the guys that we were going away for the day." "We are, are we?" He nodded. He kissed her again and Ava stepped out. She started getting ready. He stepped out, wrapped himself in a towel and came up behind Ava. "I have an idea for somewhere to go," Joe said. "And where's that?" He kissed her shoulder. "Joe." "Grace can hang with my parents." "Think she might want to be with you." "We're going just you and me." "Where?" He turned her towards him. "Remember what I said before?" She knew that look. "I was being sarcastic about the tattoo." He kissed her. "Seriously? That's what you want to do on your day off?" He kissed her again. "You're nuts." "It'll take an hour. Then we're going to the house." Ava laughed. "I was dead serious," Joe teased. "I know." He kissed her and hugged her. They got changed, took Grace to his mom, then left.

An few hours later, they'd got a clean bill of health from the doctor and he had the tattoo done. Her initials were in it, though not noticeable unless you knew the design. They headed off to the other house. About half way, he stopped and they grabbed some groceries, then pulled into the house. "You know what we were doing three years ago today," Joe asked. "Think I remember." "Funny." "You really thought I'd forget?" He kissed her. "The day that you surprised me at 6am with a ring." "Gotta admit something." "What?" "I seriously thought you'd say no," Joe said. They headed inside and Ava saw roses on the counter. "Where'd these come from?" "No idea." Ava grabbed the card:

I love you. Forever—Joe

Ava looked at him. "What?" She kissed him. "Thought you'd like them." He put the groceries away then curled up on the sofa with Ava. "So what else did you want to do today?" "Just wanted some us time." "What's going on?" "Why?" "Because you never get like this unless something's wrong," Ava said. "Just was thinking last night." "About?" "How worried I was at the beginning. I never thought we'd be here." "It's hard work. We know that." "I seriously thought I was going to lose you." "We almost lost each other." "I don't want to lose you." "No more worrying." "I tried to get her to leave last night," Joe said. "It's fine." "Babe." "We were side by side. I know you were trying." "I didn't want you getting all upset." "Joe, I know that I worry over stupid things sometimes. I love that you don't want me getting upset." "Ava." She put a finger to his lips. "I'm going to be upset once in a while." "I know, but if I can stop it . . ." "As long as I don't hear or see anything going on, we're fine." "I promised you." "I know. Stop worrying okay?" He nodded. "I love you. Always will." He kissed her which led to more kissing. They ended up upstairs in bed in a half-hour or so.

Just as they were curling up together, the phone went off. "No phones," he said. Ava grabbed it from his hand. "I saw you look." Ava looked and saw Kim's name come up on his phone. "Answer it." "Ava, I'm not talking to her," Joe said. Ava answered. "Is Joe around?" "He's here. What can I do for you?" "I just need to talk to him." "You do realize that he's happily married right?" "Not what I hear," Kim said. Ava handed him the phone and got up. "What did you say to piss my wife off now?" "We need to talk." "No we don't." "Joe, I'm serious." "So am I. Stop causing shit. I'm not coming back to you." "Oh really. What if I told her what we did the other night," Kim asked. "Since we didn't do anything." "Oh really?" "Stop the calls or I'm changing my damn number to one you don't know." "I'll meet you at the park at midnight." "I don't think so." "That short of a leash? Good move on her part." He hung up. He walked downstairs and saw Ava on the sofa with her laptop. "What," Ava asked. "Ava." "Have a nice chat?" "No." "Figured I'd give you some privacy." "Babe, I told her to screw off." "The woman is trouble. You know that right?" "That's why I told her to screw off." "Maybe she needs more of a reminder that you're supposedly happily married." "Meaning?" "She knows the button to push on me," Ava said. "You aren't doing anything. No stress, especially because of her." "Then make her go away." "That I can do." He kissed her. He slid the laptop out of her lap and grabbed her hand leading her back upstairs. "Now back to where we were." He kissed her as they curled back up together on the bed. He did a pretty good job of distracting her, but the words still rang through Ava's head.

Later on that day after a nap, and some alone time, they went and picked Grace up then headed home for dinner. Ava made one of his favorites and Grace (as per usual) made a mess. He cleaned Grace up when she was done, then relaxed and finished dinner with Ava. They curled up together on the sofa and watched a movie with Grace, then Ava took Grace upstairs and gave her a bath. She slid on her pajamas and Grace ran downstairs to Joe. "Ready for bed?" Grace nodded and hugged him. He walked upstairs, put Grace into her bed and went to grab his guitar. He saw Ava running the tub in their bathroom. He kissed her, then went to get Grace to sleep.

Ava relaxed in the tub, trying to forget the stress from the day. The baby started kicking again. She rubbed her stomach trying to calm the baby. She leaned her head back and a little while later, the baby calmed down. After two songs, Grace finally fell asleep. He snuck out of her bedroom and went in to sit with Ava. "Hey beautiful." "Hey." "You okay?" Ava nodded. "Company?" Ava nodded. He slid in with her and wrapped his arms around her. He kissed her cheek, then her neck. "Took two songs to knock her out." "Think she does it intentionally." "Probably." "What you up to in here?" "Just thinking," Ava said. "About?" "Nothing." "Ava." "Something she said on the phone." "Which would be?" "That you aren't happy." "Why the hell would she think that?" "She told me you said it." "Baby." "I know. Buttons." "I wouldn't trade today for anything. You know that?" Ava nodded and leaned her head onto his shoulder. "You're so calm." "I know. I guess I'm getting numb to her crap," Ava said. "You know she's only trying to cause shit." Ava nodded. "You coming with me to the studio tomorrow?" Ava shook her head. "You have work to get done. Not going to happen with Grace and I there." "Ava." "Nope." "Party pooper." He kissed her cheek.

They curled up in bed after the bath, and talked. They talked through everything. Every fight they'd had, every funny story, every joke. "No matter what anyone ever says, I wouldn't give up one second with you for anything." "I know I'm a pain sometimes," Ava said. "Ava, you have a reason for everything that's ever happened. You don't freak out for nothing. I love you for standing by me no matter what." "Just realize that sometimes I won't. Doesn't mean I don't love you." "I know baby. And just remember something alright? The fans and the fame and the music doesn't mean a damn thing to me without you." "Joe." "I mean it. The best concert I ever had was when you were there the first time." "Oh really." He kissed her. "The night I kissed you for the first time." "That definitely was a good night." He kissed her again and made love to her. Finally, it felt right. Everything was out in the open, and he had Ava beside him. It was more intense and more explosive than ever. She literally was his kryptonite.

<hr />

Cat woke up in the middle of the night with a nightmare. Her phone went off. "Cat." "Scott?" "I need to see you." "Why? You didn't give a shit then." "I'm coming over." "No you aren't." "I'm on my way." He hung up. Cat got up and pulled her leggings and sweater on and went to the door just as he was about to knock. "What do you want?" "My wife back." "We aren't." "Cat." "Don't you dare think you're going to fight for me now." He kissed her. She pushed him away just as Will came into the TV room. "What the hell?" "Will, this is Scott." "I know. What are you doing here?" "Trying to get my ex-wife to damn well talk to me." "What?" "I want her back." "We're engaged," Cat said trying to rub salt into his wound. He pulled Cat towards him and tried to kiss her again and Will walked back into the bedroom. He grabbed his things, got dressed and walked out the door. "Scott, we're over. Get it through your head." She went into her bedroom and saw Will's things gone. She called him and got no answer. She turned to go back into the living room and Scott kissed her, pinning her to the bedroom wall. "I want you back." "No. Scott, we're over." "Then why are you so turned on?" He picked her up and had her pinned to the bed when she finally managed to stop him. "Scott, enough." She got up, grabbed her keys, phone, overnight bag and purse. "Where are you going?" "To get my man back." She got Scott out, then went straight to Will's place. His car wasn't there. There was only one other place she could think of.

Around midnight, Ava's phone went off. "It's Will." "Hey." "Crash in the guest room?" "I guess." Ava went downstairs and let him in. "What's going on?" "Fight with Cat. Scott showed up. I caught them kissing." "You know it's just a last ditch effort to win her back." "I'm not playing second fiddle to him." "Okay." "I'm not fighting for her either. What's the point anyway? She wants me then it's her choice." "Rationalizing?" "Why can't it just be simple?" "Your brother didn't have it easy either." "You two are happy. You love each other. You got married because you couldn't stand being apart." "We're not perfect either." "Why can't she be more like you?" "Meaning?" Joe came in before Ava answered. "Because Ava's my wife. That's why. What's wrong with Cat?" Ava told him. "He's fighting for his woman." "Joe." "That's what he told me to do. You should be fighting for Cat if you love her." "She would rather be with him, then fine." "Now what were you saying about my wife." "I just wish that everyone could find a girl like Ava." "Meaning?" "Sit," Ava said. "You trying to say something," Joe asked. "Stop it." "She loves you Will. I know she does." "Then why is she with him?" "Asked myself the same thing about this one." "Ava." "And I figured out the answer. Joe loves me. We can figure almost anything out. You have to figure this out with her." "She's probably . . ." He saw lights pull into the driveway. "She's pulling in the driveway." "I don't want to talk to her." "Either you talk or I'm locking you two in that room together."

Cat came to the door. "I can't find Will." Ava opened it and saw Will. "So this is where you went." "Meaning?" "Meaning I've been everywhere." "I bet." "I kicked him out." "You two talk. I'm taking cranky to bed." Ava grabbed Joe's hand and walked upstairs. "Ava." "Let them talk." "He was hitting on you." Ava closed their bedroom door. "You didn't even stop him." Ava kissed him. "Stop with the jealous thing. He's upset. We are friends. That's it." "I'm just saying." Ava kissed him again. She got back into bed and Joe curled up with her.

"You want to be with him, then go." "Would I be here if I did?" "I don't know. Would you?" "Will." "What?" "I want to be with you. I wouldn't have said yes if I didn't." "You still love him don't you?" "There are feelings, but love, no." "Now you're lying." "No I'm not." "You know how flushed you were when you two were caught?" "I pushed him away." "You want him, then just go and get the hell away from me." "Will." He walked upstairs and went to bed. Cat left. She cried the entire way home.

———

Ava woke up at 5am with the baby kicking up a storm. She came downstairs and saw Will on the sofa. "Can't sleep?" He shook his head. "What happened?" "Told her that I know what love looks like. That I know she loves him. Then I told her to leave me alone." "Will." "Ava, if I could find what you and Joe have, I'd be happy. It doesn't exist." "We fight. We scream and yell, walk out. You name it, we've done it. We're far from perfect," Ava said. "If you weren't married to my brother . . ." "What?" "If you weren't, I'd be with you in a heartbeat." "Will, you're just in the grass is greener mode. I'm stubborn. I'm a fighter. That's the difference." Ava saw the glass and the bottle of alcohol on the table. "Ava." "What?" "She doesn't want me," Will said. "Why would you ever think that?" "She wants the bad boy. She doesn't want the good guy." "Will." "Then why the hell would she want him?" "She doesn't." "Only one guy for her. If he'd stop feeling sorry for himself and get off my sofa, he'd be in her arms," Ava said. "She doesn't." "Will." "Ava, she wants to be with him." "Then why did she say yes to marrying you?" "Sex." "Will, that's not enough of a reason." "She didn't want to lose me." "You aren't going to lose her. I know you love her." "Then why am I tempted?" "To do what?" He kissed Ava. She managed to get him away from her before Joe came downstairs.

"What you two gabbing about," Joe asked. "Nothing." "Ava, come back to bed." "I'll be up in a minute," she said. He walked back upstairs. "You're only doing that because you're upset." He kissed her again and her toes tingled. She pushed him away again. "You're going to bed." "Fine." Ava put the glass in the dishwasher and the bottle back in the cupboard. She walked upstairs and Will followed her, then went to the spare room. Ava curled back up in bed with Joe. "Everything okay," Joe asked. Ava nodded. She kissed him. They made love, then fell asleep curled up together, a mess of arms and legs.

Ava woke up around 9. Grace came running into their bedroom. "Hi Mama." "Morning baby." "Hi Daddy." "Hey baby girl. You sleep well?" Grace nodded. "What doing?" "Mama and Daddy snuggles." "Oh." Joe kissed Ava's shoulder. "Why don't you play for a bit in your room? I'll come downstairs with you in a little bit," Joe said. "Okay." She ran off to play in her room. Ava went to get up and he pulled her back into the bed. "What?" He kissed her with a seriously intense kiss that literally had her knees shaking. When they finally came up for air, he hopped out of bed, showered, and threw his jeans on then took Grace downstairs for her breakfast. Ava took her time getting up, showered, then came downstairs in her leggings and a shirt. "Morning," Ava said sneaking up behind him. "Come here for a sec," Joe said. She walked over to him. "What?" He wrapped his arms around her. "I love you." "I know. I love you too." He kissed her again and handed her breakfast. Ava smirked. "What?" "Nothing." "Same thing right?" Ava giggled. He smiled and sat down with her and had breakfast. They were just finishing when Will came downstairs. "Morning," Joe said. "Morning." Will took a gulp of the coffee, then poured more. "What time do you have to be there," Ava asked. "11." "Hi Uncle Will." "Hey Grace. How are you this morning?" "Drawed you picture." She handed Will the picture then took off. Joe had both arms wrapped around Ava. "I'm sorry about interrupting your night last night," Will said. "You need to call her," Ava said. "Hell no." "We'll figure something out." "Can you watch Grace for a few," Joe asked. "Why?" "Need to talk to Ava." Will nodded and Grace dragged him off to play with her.

"What was so important?" He took Ava's hand and led her upstairs to their room, closing the door behind them. "What happened last night," Joe asked. "With?" "Something's up." "Meaning?" "Did he try something last night," Joe asked. "He was drinking. Saying a bunch of crap he didn't mean." "Ava." "No." "You came back upstairs and something was definitely different." "Just heard something from him I didn't think was possible," Ava said. "Which was?" "It's almost like he wishes he was you." "Right. My brother? Mr. Lawyer?" Ava nodded. "Ava, just tell me he didn't try something." "He didn't." "Nothing?" Ava shook her head. "Besides. You were the one that started it last night," Ava said. Joe smirked. "And I have another idea." "You have to be there in an hour," Ava said. He kissed her. "Come drive me over." "So I have to come back and get you?" He nodded. "You, me and the piano," Joe joked. They both laughed. He kissed her. "Thank you." "For what?" "Helping him," Joe said. Ava kissed him. They headed off and after a half-hour kiss goodbye, Joe went into the studio. Ava came back home and Grace was asleep.

She cleaned up a bit, then Will came into the kitchen. "Ava." "Yep." "We need to talk," Will said. "Sure." "Look at me." She turned and looked at him. "I meant what I said last night." "You were drinking. You were acting ridiculous," Ava said. "Ava." "What?" "There's only one other woman I want." "I'm married to your brother." He kissed her again. Ava pushed him away. "Will, stop." "No." "Go and call her," Ava said. "Why? So she can reject me again?" "Will, stop acting like an idiot. She loves you. You love her or you wouldn't have asked her to marry you." Ava turned to grab the phone. "If I love her so much, why do I want you?" "Because you're upset and I was the first one there." Ava called Cat. "He's not going to talk to me," Cat said. "He's right here." "I love him Ava." "Tell Will that." Ava handed him the phone. He covered the receiver and kissed her again. Ava pushed him away and went into her office.

She got into her writing. Heavily into it. It took on a life of its own. Grace came downstairs at 12:30. "Mama." "Well good morning." "I grumble." Ava picked her up and took her into the kitchen and made her some lunch. She gave her a grilled cheese, gave one to Will, then sat down and had one with Grace. "Mama, Will stay?" "He's going home." "No." "You want him to stay?" She nodded. "Go tell him then," Ava said as Grace finished her sandwich and hopped from her chair. Ava cleaned up, then Grace talked Will into turning a movie on for her. He came into Ava's office. "And?" "We talked." "And?" "I still want you," Will said. "Will." "She apologized." "She loves you. I don't know why you can't understand that." "Ava, she admitted there were still feelings there with him." "And?" "She loves me. Doesn't change things." "Will, go over there. Kiss her. Remind your brain who you love." "I know." "Will." "We're getting together for dinner." "Good." "I think you and Joe should come." "I think we should stay home and you two go figure this out together." "Come on." "You started a relationship without us at your side." "Now, it's harder." "No it isn't. The only reason you did that last night is because you were upset. Go and talk to her." "What if we don't figure this out?" "Then keep trying until you do."

After the movie finished, Grace went down for a nap and Will laid down. Cat called. "Hey," Ava said. "I have to figure out how to fix this." "Cat, do you love Will?" "Yeah." "Do you still love Scott or are you through," Ava asked. "I love Will." "Then do what you have to." "Meaning?" "Meaning tell him that you want to be with him. That Scott is a royal pain in the ass and you want to be with him." "Ava." "He started a damn fight with Joe last night. He's upset. I know he loves you." "What do I do," Cat asked. "What you know you should."

CHAPTER 39

Ava showed up around 7 at the studio. "Where's Grace?" "With Emily." "Oh really?" Joe kissed her. Ryan and Brad came in a few minutes later. "Hey Ava." "Hey yourselves." Ava hugged them. "How's the music going?" "Got two of the three done." "Back in a sec," Joe said. He walked her out to the hallway. "What?" He kissed her. "I missed you." "How's it really going?" "Stuck on the last damn song. Ryan keeps changing his mind on the way the words should go." "Half-written?" Joe nodded. "You look amazing," Joe said. "Missed me that much?" He nodded. "More." "Will went to work things out with Cat." "Something is up with him," Joe said. "Why?" "He was looking at you like you were his dessert." "Sort of like you do you mean?" "I'm allowed. I married you." Joe kissed her. They went back in. "How's the last one going," Ava asked. "Haven't finished the dang words," Ryan said. Ava grabbed the notepad. "Play the part you have down." He played it for her. Ava wrote a few lines down then handed the paper back to him. They played it through with Ava's words thrown in. "Perfect." They played it through, recorded the vocals, then played it back. "Damn you are good," Brad said. "Heard every darn song you guys have ever done. I know the style Ryan." "Joe, you have a brilliant wife," Ryan said. "I know." Ava curled up in his arms. "So everything done?" "One more to go for the CD." "Which would be?" "Need your help on it," Joe said. "Why?" "Girl part." "Trying to include me again?" He nodded and kissed her neck. "The fans love you and you know it," Ryan said. "They won't in a month or two." "We're releasing it in September," Brad said. "Nice." "Gives you a few months," Ryan said. "So we all set for the video shoot tomorrow," Brad asked. "Still can't believe you want to do it that early," Ryan said. "Easier." "Brad." "I'm already going to be up." Joe laughed. "Fine." "Starbucks morning tomorrow?" They laughed.

Ryan and Brad headed home and Ava curled up with Joe on the sofa in the studio. "Where," Ava asked. "Downtown Nashville." "Dreamer?" He nodded. "You're coming with me." "Why?" "You're in it." "Like this?" He nodded. "Joe." "Babe, it's a slow one," Joe said. "You kill me." "Powers of persuasion." They laughed. "Come on beautiful. I'll take you to dinner," Joe said. They got up and headed out. He grabbed Chinese and they went to the park. They talked, laughed, kissed, then talked and kissed some more. Finally, they headed home. They pulled in and Ava saw Will's car. "Thought they were at dinner," Joe asked. "So did I." Joe parked and they headed inside.

Will was sitting in Ava's office with a glass of Irish whiskey. "Um, hello. What are you doing in here," Ava asked. "Reading." He looked at Ava. "Who said you could read it?" "Wanted to see what you were doing." "And how did dinner go," Joe asked. "She said she loves me and that she wants to be with me." "And?" "Told her I wouldn't play second fiddle to him. That if she wanted me, he was gone." "Will." "I'm not going to wait for the idiot to try it again." "Then do something about it," Ava said. "I did. I told her to move in with me." "And?" "She said she'd call me." He took another gulp of his drink. "Will, enough." Ava took the bottle and put it away, then locked the cupboard. He kept reading. Ava went and checked on Grace while Joe went in and talked to him.

"What's with you and the damn ultimatums anyway?" "I don't want to have to go through the stupid ex trying to break us up crap you two have gone through. I'm telling you right now, you mess up, there's a waiting list to take your place," Will said. "Never happen." "Okay. Whatever you want to believe little brother." "Will, seriously," Joe said. "Cat loves me. Fact is, I didn't think I had to fight to win her love." "You don't think I had to fight with every ounce of energy to win Ava's heart? Did you forget she was dating James," Joe said. "You lucked the hell out." "No. I loved her down to the core of my soul. No point in marrying someone you wouldn't die for." "Joe." "Hey. Fine. I'm the younger brother. Fact is, I'm the one married to her. It's a constant fight. The fight of my damn life. I am never losing Ava. No matter what it takes. If you don't feel that way about Cat, then you shouldn't be getting hitched." "I'm hurt." "I know. You have to know that you love her that much. Do you," Joe asked. "I love her." "Enough to walk through lava?" "Nice dramatic touch." "Well?" "Enough to win her back." "Go move her in if that's what you want to do. Just know you can't outrun her past. All you can do is love her." "Joe, you're woman is one hell of a writer." "Why's that?" "You should see this stuff she wrote." Will went into the kitchen and threw his glass in the dishwasher. Joe went through the six chapters she'd written.

Will came upstairs. "You two have a nice chat," Ava asked. He kissed her, then walked off, grabbed his bag and left. Ava changed into her nightgown and slid into bed, checking her email via blackberry. Joe messaged her from the office:

Come downstairs.

Ava got a smirk on her face and walked downstairs. "Yes love." "Wow." "Wow what?" "The chapters." "You two are such snoops." "Where did you get the idea?" "Drunk rantings of your brother," Ava said. "You gonna tell me what he said?" "He was drunk." "Ava." "That he wanted what we have." "Really." Ava nodded. "What else?" "Meaning?" "He made a move on you. I know he did," Joe said. "Joe, he was drunk." "He did." "I stopped him before he did and made him talk to Cat." Joe stood up and leaned Ava onto the desk. "Babe." "What?" He kissed her and slid her nightgown up her legs. "What are you up to," Ava asked. She heard his belt drop. "Nothing." He kissed her again and they did it on the desk, then they went upstairs and curled up in bed. "Got you that hot and bothered," Ava asked. "As long as you weren't using my brother as an example in the story babe." She just curled up with him. How was she supposed to forget the kiss that Will had laid on her?

They were asleep a little while later. Ava tossed and turned then finally fell asleep. Joe snuggled up next to her. By 6am, the baby was kicking up a storm. They got up and Emily showed as Ava was about to hop into the shower. "Thanks Em," Joe said. "How's things going," she asked. "Good. Video shoot today." "I bet." "Shh." He went upstairs and hopped into the shower with Ava. A half-hour later and after another round mid-shower, they hopped out and got ready. "And just what did you decide I was wearing," Ava teased. "Leggings and the boots." Ava smirked. "And the dark blue," Joe said. "Your favorite." He nodded. Ava finished getting changed. He kissed her. "What?" "Nothing," Joe said. He finished getting ready, throwing on his black jeans with his dark blue shirt. They left a few minutes later. They showed up and went into makeup and hair, then they handed Ava the dress they'd picked out. "Just because," Ava asked. He nodded. She slid the dark blue dress on and they spent the rest of the morning shooting the video. By ten they were done.

Ava and Joe headed home and Grace came running out the door towards them. "Hey baby girl." "Hi Daddy." She wrapped her arms around Joe's neck and kissed his cheek. "What you up to?" "Coloring." "Oh." Ava walked in and Emily was getting juice for Grace. "How was she," Ava asked. "She's going to be a singer when she grows up." "Another band to play with," Joe teased. Emily headed home. "Ava. There's a note on your desk for you," Emily said as she was heading out. Ava went in and saw Will's handwriting.

Ava,

I'm sorry. What a stupid thing to do. Think you were right. Still, damn. Fireworks. Cat's moving in like you thought she would. Trying to turn the anger off with her. Still want you. Hope the shoot went well. I know you were beautiful.

XO

Will

Ava threw the note into the shredder. "Who was the note from," Joe asked. "Will. Just saying he was sorry for being a pain in the butt." Joe kissed her. "Grace wants to go to the movies." "I bet," Ava said. "What do you think?" "As in the movie room or as in the actual movies?" Joe smirked. "Nice." "Either that or we go rent her some movies." "Good plan. Have fun," Ava joked. "Weaseling out of it?" "Writing." He kissed her again and left with Grace.

Ava tried to wrap her head around what had happened with Will and couldn't figure it out. She got more into her writing and Joe came back in with Grace. "Movie marathon," Ava asked. "Understatement. Plus I got a few for us." "And when would we be watching them all," Ava asked. Joe kissed her. "Think we might find time." "Mama, come." "Give me two minutes. See if Daddy will make you popcorn." "Nice," Joe said. He kissed Ava, then went in and got movie snacks together. Just as she was about to get up, her phone went off.

"Hello?" "It's me," Will said. "How's things with Cat?" "She's heading over now." "Good." "Ava." "I don't want to hear it," Ava said. "I was drunk. We know that. Still, I didn't expect that." "Maybe you shouldn't have then." "I don't regret it. That's the stupid part," Will said. "You should." "You know how many times you two have been in fights over his ex's that try to get in his pants? Come on." "Revenge never cured anything," Ava said. "Ava." "I mean it." "So do I." "Out of mind." "Can't. I was turned on in seconds," Will said. "I have to get going." "I want to see you." "Not gonna happen." "You know I can find ways." Ava hung up. This was absolutely and totally insane. "Babe," Joe said. She almost jumped in her chair. "Hey." "You okay?" Ava nodded. She turned her monitor off and got up. Joe slid his arms around her. "Scare you?" "Stupid phone call." He kissed her. "Come on before Grace drags you in there." He wrapped his arm around Ava and they went in and sat down to watch the marathon of movies Grace wanted.

After a few hours, they had dinner, then gave Grace her bath before bed. "Mama?" "Yes baby." "Where Will?" "With Auntie Cat." "Why?" "He's home." "Coming back," Grace asked. "We'll see." "Mama?" "Yes." "I love you." "I love you too baby." Grace kissed her. Joe took a picture of them. Grace giggled. "Okay Mr. Photographer," Ava said. He kissed Ava, then sang Grace to sleep. Ava went into the bedroom and got changed for bed. He came out and she was rubbing lotion on her legs. She heard the door close. "She asleep," Ava asked. He nodded. "Something's up with Will." "Why do you say that?" "He wants to come this weekend," Joe said. "They were just there for your birthday." "I know." "You didn't say yes did you?" "Why not? They can look after Grace and I can take you out on the town." "Or just have some quiet time." "Even better idea." He kissed Ava.

Every time Joe looked at Ava he fell more in love. He'd done a million things wrong, but she still loved him. He was so far from perfect. Deep down he almost felt like he didn't deserve her. There was no way he was ever letting her go. Nothing was ever going to come between them. Every time she'd have that smirk, or be worried that she didn't look right, or was showing too much, he just looked at her and told her that she was even more beautiful. It's all he could do. There was something in her soul he loved. It wasn't just the little dresses, and the heels. It was her heart. Her loving, caring, hold on for dear life heart that made him fall so hard. What he'd ever do if someone tried to get between them . . . .

He curled up with her in bed, kissing her neck. "Hey beautiful," Joe said. "Hey yourself handsome." "I have to ask you something." "What?" "What you doing for the rest of your life," Joe asked. "Married this hot, sexy guy. Think I might hang around a while." "Really?" Ava nodded. "Lucky guy." "I know." "Think you could stay around forever," he asked. "Think I just might." He kissed her shoulder. "What?" "I love you." "I love you too." "Ava." "Mm?" "What would you think about getting away for a few days?" "Like where?" "Beach somewhere." "You, me and Grace," Ava asked. "You and me." "Joe." "Well?" "Can't fly until after the baby." "Yeah we can." "The tour." "Monday and Tuesday." "This Monday?" He nodded and nibbled her ear, then kissed it. "Joe." "I'll book it," he said. Ava turned towards him. "You're serious?" He nodded. "Sure. Why do I get the feeling you're worried about something though," Ava asked. "Just never want to lose you again." "You won't." "Babe, I've learned. Hold on to what you want. I'm holding on forever." "I'm not going anywhere." Joe kissed her. "What are you worried about," Ava asked. "Just had a stupid dream last night that I couldn't shake. Been thinking about it all day." "What happened?" "Had a nightmare you found someone else." "Joe, you know I'd never walk away from us." "I don't want you to. No matter what stupid crap happens, we're sticking together." "Joe." "I just want to make sure we have us figured out. That's all." "Stop worrying." "I know it's stupid." "Remember something." "What's that?" "When you start worrying, look at the ring on your hand. That's what you told me. Remember what we said in front of all of our friends. Remember the look I had when you asked me to marry you. You'll stop worrying." He kissed her and they snuggled and talked until they both fell asleep.

That weekend, they headed off to the concert with Will and Cat. They landed for the first venue, then went to the hotel to settle in. Will was in the hall talking to Joe when Cat came in to hang out with Ava. "What are they gabbing about now," Ava asked. "He asked Will to take care of you when he was on tour." "I can take care of myself. Geesh." "Plus you have me, Rose and Danielle," Cat said. "Exactly." "He's worried about you. It's actually kind of cute." Ava walked out into the hall. "Hey babe," Joe said. "Get your butts in here." Joe wrapped his arms around her and kissed her. "Was just talking to Will." "I know." Will went into the room with Cat. "Just want to make sure someone's around to help you if I can't be there." "Joe." "If." "I can take care of Grace all by myself," Ava said. "I know. Still. If anything ever happened to you, I'd never forgive myself." Ava kissed him and they went into the room. Grace was asleep in her room and Cat and Will were watching TV when they came in. "So, what time do we have to be over there," Will asked. "We have to be there in an hour or so. You two can chill until tonight," Joe said. "We'll go hang in our room for a bit." Will left with Cat still staring at Ava.

"Why are you so worried about me?" "Babe." "Joe, you know I don't need your brother babysitting me." "If I'm not there . . ." "If you're not there and I need someone, then I'll call you." "You said you didn't want to tour when you got into the last two months." "Doesn't mean I'm not coming with you. It means not walking out on stage." "Babe, the doctor said no flying." "I will until I can't." "Stubborn as usual." He kissed her. "So what exactly did you have planned to do until we have to leave," Ava asked. "We have an interview." "Who?" "You and me." "Since when?" He kissed her again. Ava heard a knock at the door. Hair and makeup came in. "So much for a nap," Ava joked. They laughed. Ava got changed and they came in for the interview.

"So now that you two are on baby number two, what's changed?" "Honestly, sleeping in doesn't exist. Other than that, it's unbelievable. Grace definitely keeps us going. Thank goodness we have the energy for it." "So how do you two keep the magic going?" "It's putting time in for us, quiet time away from all the press and being a normal family when we're home." "We take a break when we need one, and still have a date night. It's like I'm still trying to win her heart." "We heard recently that you two had separated." "It was all work. We finished up the new CD and Ava was away with Grace. I have to tell you, I missed them like crazy when I was here." "So there was no separation?" "Not for a second." "So Ava, I've had lots of fans ask this . . . . how did you meet Joe?" "The first time, was lucking out winning a meet and greet with the guys." "Couldn't take my eyes off her then either." "Forgive me for asking, but why did you two wait so long?" "Oddly enough, a friend brought me as a guest to a concert 3 years ago. I walked in and that was it. We talked right up until they were about to hit the stage." "Something tells me that was the night I almost tripped over my feet." "It was one of those things. He asked me a day or two later to come to the concert. The minute I walked in I was head over heels." "First kiss fever." "So how long did you date before you two got married?" "A month or two?" "Still can't believe he talked me into doing something so silly." "You wished you'd waited?" "Not for a second. Wouldn't change it for the world." "Think I might have won her over after the first kiss." "Definitely." "So, we heard you're now a writing duo." "I wouldn't call it a duo." "She's an amazing writer. Comes in handy when I have writer's block but have a tune stuck in my head." "So are you still going to tour after you have baby two?" "After a while." "I'll get her back on stage with me. I know she'd miss it." "We'd all miss it."

After a little while longer, the interview was finally done. They did some pictures, then Joe and Ava took Grace and headed to sound check. They walked in and Will was talking to the guys. "Hey." "Where's Cat?" "Shopping." "Nice." "I can take her while you're doing sound check," Will said. "No, it's fine." Ava walked off. She sat and colored with Grace while the guys got ready. "Ava," Will said. "What?" "I need to talk to you." "No." Joe called her up for sound check. Once they were done, the guys rehearsed a bit, then they headed back to the hotel to relax a while before dinner. Joe took Grace upstairs and left Will to talk to Ava.

"What?" "We need to talk." "No we don't. Secondly, I don't need a babysitter. Go and be with Cat." "Ava. I think I might be . . . ." Ava walked away. There was no way she wanted to hear it. "Ava." He hopped into the elevator with her. "I think I might be falling for you." "Then stop it and go be with Cat. I'm married and you know it. Secondly, I'm married to your brother. Enough is enough." He went to try to kiss her and Ava got off the elevator. She got down to the room and slammed the door in Will's face.

"Hey beautiful." "Hey yourself. What's Grace up to," Ava asked. "Coloring. Emily's here." "Oh really." He nodded. He had a look on his face that Ava hadn't seen in months. "What is going on in that crazy head of yours?" He kissed Ava and picked her up, carrying her to bed. "What are you up to?" "We're having a nap." "And who said I was tired," Ava teased. "Babe." They curled up together in bed and they actually fell asleep minutes later. Ava woke up with Grace jumping onto the bed. "Hi Mama." "Hey baby girl. What you up to?" "Was playing with Daddy." "Where's Daddy?" Ava heard the shower running. "Going." "Well, Mama has to get ready too." "Okay. I play with Emily." Grace jumped into Ava's arms and kissed her, then ran into the TV room to play with Emily. Ava got up, walked into the bathroom and went to hop into the shower. "Hey. Was wondering when you were going to wake up," Joe teased. She slid in with Joe and in seconds was leaned into the wall. He kissed her. "Couldn't sleep without you." "You did for an hour," Joe said. "What?" "Grace woke me up. She wanted to watch a movie." "You should have woken me up." "Nope. You looked like an angel." He kissed her again then slid her under the hot water. She showered and he washed her back. "Babe." "Mm." "Why were you so pissed when I asked Will to help?" "You don't need to find me a babysitter," Ava said. "Ava." They finished their shower, then stepped out. Ava dried off and started getting ready.

"You gonna answer me?" They hopped into the car to head to the venue and have dinner. "Joe, not now." "Ava." "Not now." They got there and had dinner, then Ava went to get changed. He followed her locking the RV door. "I know something is going on." "Meaning?" "He's now avoiding you like the plague," Joe said. "Good." "Ava." "He was drunk." "And?" "It doesn't matter." "What did he do Ava?" "He kissed me." Ava could see his blood start to boil." She stopped him and made him sit down. "Why the hell didn't you tell me?" "Because he was completely drunk. People do stupid shit when they're drunk." "He kissed you. My brother kissed my damn wife. That's not just stupid. That's . . . ." Ava kissed Joe. "Ava." "What?" "When?" "What do you mean when?" "As in the other night when he showed up?" "I went downstairs. Grabbed a drink and saw him sitting in the TV room." "How many times did he try?" "Meaning what?" "Meaning how many times?" "Joe." "Is that when you came upstairs and we . . ." "Joe, stop." He pushed Ava aside and got up. He stormed out and went to find Will. Ava stopped him. "Stop it." "Ava." "Look at me. I love you. I always have and I always will. Nobody else," Ava said. "I'm not going to sit here and let him get away with that." "Then do it for the baby. You promised no stress." He took Ava's hand and they went back into the RV.

The minute the door closed, he snapped. "Why the hell didn't you tell me before this?" "Because. He was drunk Joe. You do stupid things when you're intoxicated too." "I would never . . ." "Remember something. You have a ring on your hand. It means forever. Remember the speech? Nobody can divide it. We have Grace, and this baby. We are a family. People are allowed to be idiots sometimes." "But making a move on my wife is like suicide." "Joe." "How the hell can he . . ." Ava kissed him. "I love you. I want you. That's all there is to it." "But . . ." "But nothing. I'm your wife. We're having a baby. That's it." He kissed her, and his ego must have taken over. They went at it in the RV, then went and had dinner. The minute Will and Cat showed, Ava had Joe's hand in hers and he was white-knuckling it.

The guys went to do the meet and greet and Will and Cat grabbed their seats. Before they hit the stage, Ava kissed Joe. "I love you." "I know baby. I love you too." "Aww." Ryan and Brad in duo were making fun of them. Joe kissed her again, then headed onstage. Ava came out to do her songs. Before she headed backstage, Joe got the spotlight. "I gotta say guys, I am one lucky man." "That you are," Brad said. They sang one of her favorite ballads, then Ava went back to the dressing room. Joe came in and she was curled up on the sofa. He kissed her to wake her up. "Hey." "Hey yourself. How was the rest of the show?" "Good. We're flying to the next venue tonight." "We?" "You, me, Grace and Emm." "Joe, you're over-doing it." "Unless he wants a broken jaw, we're going," Joe said. "What's going on," Ryan asked. "Will made a move on Ava." "He what," Brad asked. "What an idiot," Ryan said. "Guys, really," Ava said. "I want to go early," Joe said. "We'll all go then." "We can send them home tomorrow," Brad said. "Guys," Ava said trying to calm them down. "Hey. We're a team. All for one and that stuff," Brad said. "Thanks." Joe kissed Ava and they headed back to the hotel, packed and headed off. Will and Cat were coming back when they saw the car pull out. Within seconds, Ava's phone was ringing. "Hey Cat." "Where you off to?" "We got roped into an early interview in the morning. Get some sleep," Ava said. "You flying out tonight?" "I'll see you when we get back." "What aren't you telling me," Cat asked. "Nothing. I'll see you Sunday." There was no point in getting Cat upset and letting the guys in on what had happened.

They finally got to their hotel and Ava and Joe tucked Grace into bed, then fell asleep. Joe's arms were wrapped around Ava for dear life. He had nightmares over and over again that he lost her, that Will married her, that Grace called him Daddy. Every time, he'd wake up with Ava in his arms and calm himself down. Finally around 11, they woke up. Grace was playing with Emily, and Ava was drying off from her shower when he woke up. "Hey handsome." "When did you get up," Joe asked. "Half-hour ago. You looked like you needed the extra sleep." He pulled her to him and kissed her. "Joe." "You know what I'm gonna say," Joe said. "And I also know, that none of the bad things would ever happen." She kissed him, then got up to finish getting ready. He hopped into the shower as she was doing her hair. "Ava." "Yep." "Thought of something this morning," Joe said. "What's that?" "When were you thinking of taking a break from the travelling?" "Middle of next month. She said it's not a good idea in the last 6 weeks." "What if we paused the tour," Joe said. "Joe, stop worrying." "I just don't want to be a 5-hour flight away." "All the venues are within an hour." "Still." He hopped out of the shower and wrapped a towel around him. Ava sat on the counter. "Stop worrying okay," Ava said. "But . . ." "I have the doctor on speed dial. I have Rose and Danielle, Emily and Cat. I'll be fine." "I don't want to go without you." "I'll see if I can get two more weeks out of her." "I just don't want to be that far away," Joe said. Ava kissed him. "Stop worrying. You will." "You think so?" Ava nodded. "I love you." "I love you too. No more worrying." He nodded. Grace knocked at the door. "Daddy." "Hey Grace." He went over and let her in. "Can I watch a movie?" "Which one?" "Cinderella." He nodded. "Have fun baby," Ava said. Grace ran off to watch a movie with Emily and Joe locked the bathroom door.

"What are you up to," Ava asked. "Nothing." "Just wanted alone time?" He kissed Ava. "Just wanted you." "Oh really," Ava asked. He kissed her again. "Grace is in the next room." He leaned towards her and she slid her legs around him. "Just tell me one thing." "What," Ava said. "That what happened the other night wasn't because of him." "It was because I love you. Period." He kissed her. "Good answer." They did it on the bathroom counter, then with the 'cat that ate the canary' grins, they finished getting dressed. "We going home tonight," Ava asked. He shook his head. "Where?" "My grandma's." Ava smirked. "I promised her," Joe said. He kissed Ava again and they went in and saw Grace asleep on the sofa. "We have to go to sound check. Did you want to stay here with her," Joe asked Emily. "I have to make a call or two. Is that ok?" Ava nodded. "Then I'll stay."

CHAPTER 40

Ava headed to sound check with the guys. "You know you're gonna have to tell us what's going on at some point," Brad said. "Trust me. Not worth repeating," Ava said. Ryan looked at Ava. They pulled up, went through a crowd, then went in to start the sound check. Ryan pulled Ava to the side. "What's going on with him? He's wound up tighter than a damn clock." "It's nothing," Ava said. "It's not nothing. He is freaked out over something. Just tell me." "Ryan." "I'm gonna ask him myself if you don't tell me." "Fine. Someone made a move on me and he lost it." "Who?" "Doesn't matter." "Ava. Tell me," Ryan said. "Will." Ryan looked at her. "He came to the house when he got into a fight with Cat. We told him he could stay. I went downstairs to grab a drink and he kissed me." "I'll kick his butt myself," Ryan said. "Don't bother. It's done." "Ava." "I know." "Why didn't you just tell me," Ryan asked. "It's between Joe and Will. Leave it alone. Let him cool off." "I thought it was something else." "I know." They headed in to start sound check and Joe was already playing around with the guitars. They sang a song or two to get warmed up, then went through the song list for the night. Just as they were finishing up, Will and Cat showed.

Ava and Joe went to leave and head back to the hotel when Ava saw Cat. "Hey." "Hey yourself. What is going on with you two," Cat asked. "We had an interview first thing." "You going to see grams," Will asked. "Tomorrow." "Was going to go over with Cat if you two wanted to join us." "We have to get back to Grace. Plus we have two more interviews this afternoon," Joe said. "We'll see you for dinner then." They both went their separate ways. "Still want to kick his butt," Ava asked. "Better idea." "What?" Ava made a call and they headed back to the hotel. "What did you get me into," Joe asked. "We're having a massage."

After their long massage, they headed back to the room and played with Grace a bit before dinner. Joe went and made a call. "What time are we heading down for dinner," Ava asked. "It's on its way up." Ava smirked. They played until dinner, then ate and started getting ready. Grace gave Joe a kiss for luck and they left. They got back, ran into hair and makeup, then Joe left for the meet and greet. Ava slid on the red dress just to throw him. She was about to get up when Will came in. "Ava, I need to talk to you." "You shouldn't be in

370

here." She walked past him. "I'm sorry." "He knows." "What do you mean he knows?" "He knows what happened." "Ava." "I'm not gonna lie to him." "Did you tell him about the note?" "No." "Thank god." "What do you want?" "I was going to take her somewhere warm and get away for a while. Was going to see if I could talk her into a wedding on the beach. I needed your help convincing her." "If you need it, then ask. Go before Joe comes in." He took off and just as Ava was sliding her heels on, Joe came in. "Hey." "You had to didn't you," Joe asked. "The dress? Definitely." "You do realize my aunt and my cousins are in the audience." "Didn't know. Thanks for letting me know." Joe kissed her. "Did I just see Will leave?" "He is taking Cat somewhere warm and talking her into getting married on the beach." "He is, is he?" "Thought it was a good idea," Ava said. "All the better to keep his hands to himself with." Joe laughed. "You look beautiful baby." "I knew you loved this one." He left to go on and Ava finished getting ready.

"You know, we've been a family on our own for so long now. When one of us gets to go home, it's a special night. Joe always has family with him, but we're happy to say there's even more family here with us tonight. Welcome guys," Brad said. Ava sang with them for a few songs, then headed off. She went and relaxed in the dressing room until the guys were done. She slid her flats on until the guys came back. Ava could hear Joe in the hallway. "She's in here," he said. They walked in hugging and kissing Ryan and Brad, then hugged Ava. "I'm so glad you could make it down," Ava said. "Not only is she beautiful, she can sing too," his aunt said. "Don't know where she gets all that talent from," Joe teased. "Been taking care of our Joe," his cousin asked. "Someone has to," Ava joked. They all sat and chatted until Will came in with Cat. "Joe." "Why is he here," Joe whispered to Ava." "Family." "I'm just going to go get changed. I'll be out in a minute or two. Joe, I need your help with the zipper," Ava said. Ava got him out of the room before he did something stupid. "Stop freaking out," Ava said. "He . . ." "I know. Remember what I told you." "Ava, I don't want him in there." "He's your brother. Either forgive and forget or let it go." "How am I supposed to do that?" "I did," Ava said. "Babe." "Do it for the baby then." He kissed Ava, undid the zipper on her dress and she slid into her leggings and a shirt. They chatted for well over an hour with his family, then everyone headed home. "We'll see you for church and breakfast right Joe," his aunt said. "We'll do our best," Joe said. "You better." Joe hugged everyone goodbye, then they headed back to the hotel.

Joe and Ava came in, got changed, then curled up together in bed. "I can't forget," Joe said. "You have to let it go." "He kissed you. It's not like he said something stupid. He made a move." "And you've done a lot worse that I forgave you for," Ava said. "I get it." "I know. You can't hold onto a grudge against family." "Even . . ." "Even if family does something so stupid you could kick them for it." "I love you," Joe said. "I know. I love you too." "I'm sorry for freaking out." "It's fine. Just try to relax okay? You know he's going to be there tomorrow." "Although I wish he wasn't," Joe said. "He's your brother. Stop it." "Just until

I calm down." "No. We go to bed calm or not at all." "New theory," Joe asked. "Lowering stress." He kissed Ava's neck. "Okay. For you." "Get some sleep. No more stupid dreams," Ava said. "Only good ones about us." He linked his fingers with hers and wrapped his arms around her.

The next day went perfectly. Brunch was great, Grace actually sat through church quietly. They had a quick coffee together after church, then everyone headed home. Grace was asleep most of the flight and Ava and Joe were curled up together. They landed then headed home. Ava took Grace and tucked her into her bed, and Joe went through voicemail. She came downstairs and he was sitting at the table. "What's wrong," Ava asked. "Who's John?" "A friend of mine who was helping me with your guitar for your birthday." "Why would he need to talk to you," Joe asked. "To make sure you liked it." "Ava." "Don't you dare even think what I think you are." He pressed play on the voicemail. "Ava, it's Jon. Need to talk to you when you get a sec." "I talked to him. He wanted to make sure I grabbed the guitar pics that you ordered to go with it. Stop getting all upset over nothing," Ava said. "It wasn't nothing." "You need to relax." "Ava, he kissed you in my house. Under my roof." "And I walked away. I wouldn't do that and you know it." She walked off and went upstairs, unpacking and putting things away. "Babe." "No. Don't accuse me of doing something like that." "I was over-reacting," Joe said. "You know John. You've known him for years." "I've known my brother for 35 years. Doesn't make what he did any less painful." "Stop. Just stop. What he did was wrong. What he did was completely stupid and dumb. It happened. It's not happening ever again," Ava said. Ava finished unpacking her bag, then went and headed downstairs to do writing. "Where are you going?" "To do some writing."

An hour later, he'd unpacked, started laundry, cleaned, and was still pissed off. He worked out, then finally put all the anger into a song. He played it back to himself and it was good. No details were given, no calling out of people. Just a 'fighting for my woman' type of a song. He shot it over to Ryan via email, then headed upstairs. Ava was curled up on the sofa doing her writing. "Back sore," Joe asked. Ava nodded. "Scooch." He rubbed her back for her and curled up with her. "Feeling better," Ava asked. He nodded. "And managed to even get part of a song done." "See." "I know. I promise no more cranky," Joe said. "Good." Ava kissed him. "What are you writing?" "Continuing with an idea I had the other day." "And?" "Up to chapter ten." "Then you can take a break." Ava saved her work, closed the laptop and put it on the table. "What did you have in mind?" "Movie, snuggling on the sofa, then dinner." "Good plan for a Sunday," Ava said. "I thought so too." They snuggled up together, turned on a movie, then Grace woke up. "So much for the movie," Joe said. She came downstairs, curled up with Joe and Ava and asked if they could watch the wedding video again.

After another viewing of the wedding video, they had dinner, played with Grace, then gave her a bubble bath and put her to bed. "Daddy." "Yes baby." "When Mama has baby, me still baby?" "Always." She hugged him and after a kiss on the head, Grace was out like a light. Joe came into the bedroom and heard the bathtub water running. He walked in and Ava was surrounded in bubbles. "Hey." "Hey yourself." "Grace asleep?" "Out like a light." He walked over to Ava and kissed her. "You coming in?" He nodded and within a few minutes was sliding in behind her. "You still mad," Ava asked. "Trying not to be." "Good." "Why?" "They asked us to be at the wedding," Ava said. "What wedding?" "Wednesday. They're getting married in Jamaica." "You're kidding right?" Ava shook her head. "I don't know if . . ." "I'm going for Cat," Ava said. "Do I have to go?" "Unless you want me walking down the beach alone." "Just for the day," Joe asked. Ava nodded. "Fine. We're coming home that night then." She kissed him. "Babe." "What?" "I love you." "I know. I love you even more than you think." "Enough for," Joe asked. "You don't want to know." "Oh really. Now that could be interesting." The baby started kicking again. "Maybe you shouldn't be flying," Joe said. "I'm going to the doctor tomorrow. You can ask her for an excuse then." He kissed Ava's neck. "Promises, promises." They relaxed a while until the water went cool, then slid out and went to bed. Ava was almost cramping. "You okay?" Ava nodded. They curled up and went to sleep.

Around 4am, Ava woke up. Yep. Definitely cramping. She called the doctor and was told to come straight into the hospital. Joe woke up the minute he realized Ava wasn't in bed. "What?" "Hospital." He called Ryan as they got changed. Ryan showed up and Ava and Joe were out the door.

After an ultrasound and a few tests, the doctor came back in. "What?" "Few weeks further than I thought." "Meaning?" "You're two." Joe looked at Ava. "Which means," Ava asked. "You two are camping out." "But I'm early." "Only by 3 or 4 weeks," the doctor said. "What?" "If you have to call anyone, call." Joe called Ryan and Brad and let them know. "I'll take care of Grace. Let me know when the coast is clear," Ryan said. "Babe," Joe said. "I know."

After a few hours, Joe was getting impatient. So was Ava. By noon, the baby was born. "Well?" "Blake," Ava asked. Joe nodded. "Blake what?" "Blake Christopher." "Sounds good to me," Joe said. They curled up on the bed with him and Joe couldn't help but get emotional. "How in the world," Joe asked. "That's why I didn't want to know." He kissed Ava. "He's perfect." "Think he has your silly sense of humor. You know he's gonna be a night owl like you are," Ava said. Joe kissed her again. "Something tells me the Jamaica trip isn't gonna happen." They laughed. Ava fed him while Joe called the guys.

"Well," Ryan asked. "Blake Christopher." "A boy?" "How's Ava," Brad asked. "Smiling." "We'll be down with Grace and the kids in a half-hour," Brad said. The nurse came and cleaned Blake up and Joe came in with a blue teddy bear and roses. "Babe." "I can't believe we had a boy." "As long as he turns out like you we're good," Ava joked. "Wild and crazy? No. If he's like you we're better off," Joe said. "Stubborn from me, determination from you." "That works." When the guys showed, Joe was asleep beside Ava with his arms around her. "Congratulations," Ryan said. "Mama." Grace jumped onto the bed. "Shh. Let Daddy sleep," Ava said. "Who that?" "This is your little brother," Ava said. "Mine?" Ava nodded. "His name is Blake." "I'm your sister," Grace said. The baby yawned. "He like me?" "Think he loves you already baby." Ava handed Blake to Ryan. "Old pro," Ava said. "I can't believe he came so soon," Ryan said. "They were a few weeks off with the due date I guess." "We have a concert this weekend," Ryan said. "I know. I can handle it." "No. We'll postpone it." "Ryan, you guys are going." "Whatever you do Blake, don't get the stubbornness from her," Ryan joked. Brad came in with Danielle a few minutes later. "Can't believe you finally had a boy," Brad said. "Didn't want Joe to be outnumbered." He kissed Ava's cheek. "Hey guys," Danielle said. "Oh look. Sleeping beauty woke up," Ryan joked. They all joked around a while, Ava got flowers and baby gifts, then the guys headed home. "Mama, I stay," Grace said. "I'll take her home," Joe said. Grace jumped into Joe's arms. "So what do you think baby girl?" "He looks like dolly." "I know. He isn't though," Joe said. Grace kissed Blake's head. "He smell good."

After an hour or two, Joe took Grace to Ryan's for the night then came back over to the hospital with Ava's bag that she'd packed. "He sleeping," Joe asked. Ava nodded. Joe curled back up on the bed with her. "I want you to go this weekend," Ava said. "We just had a baby. I'm not going anywhere." "You're going." "Ava, I'm staying home with you. No fighting me on this." "Joe, I'm going to be fine." "I know, because I'm staying," he said. Joe kissed her. "Who's stubborn now?"

Ava came home the Wednesday morning with Blake. "Hi Mama," Grace said. "Hi baby girl." "Hi Blake." "He's sleeping Grace. I'm just gonna take him upstairs," Ava said. "Okay." Joe went and played with Grace. Ava walked into the nursery, turned the monitor on and saw the flowers and the teddy bears. She laid Blake down for a nap, then quietly snuck out. She came downstairs and Grace was singing with Joe. Ava handed him the monitor and went and grabbed some juice. "Mama, what wrong?" "Just tired baby." She climbed into Ava's lap in the chair and kissed her. "All better," Grace said. "Thank you Grace." She giggled and ran back into the TV room. "You okay," Joe asked. Ava nodded. "Come on," Joe said. "What?" "Upstairs." Grace ran off to play with Emily and Joe and Ava went upstairs.

They curled up together and had a nap for a while, then Joe went downstairs and made dinner. "Daddy, where Mama?" "She's with Blake," Joe said. "Daddy, why?" "He was hungry for dinner too." "Mama come down?" "She will baby." Grace hugged Joe. He knew just what Grace needed. "I have an idea." "What?" "Why don't we have a picnic on the bed with Mama." "Okay." Joe made a few of Grace's favorites, then they headed upstairs and brought Ava dinner.

He walked in and Grace ran over to Ava. "Hi Mama." "Hey baby girl. What were you and Daddy up to downstairs?" "Picnic." She looked over at Joe. "Thought you'd rather relax," he said. He kissed Ava. Grace slid onto the bed. "Where Blake?" "Sleeping." "Mama, why?" "He's just like you when you were a baby Grace. You slept all the time." "Really?" Ava nodded. "Mama, you love Blake like me?" "I love you and Daddy and Blake." "Really?" Ava nodded. Grace curled up with Ava. "Think she was feeling a little left out," Joe said. "I know how to fix that." Ava gave her kisses and raspberries on her cheeks and her tummy until Grace was giggling. They had dinner, then Ava gave Grace a bubble bath. "Mama, I missed you." "I missed you too." Grace splashed around for a while, then after being snuggled into a big towel, Ava got Grace changed into her pajamas. Just as she was about to grab a book to read, Grace hopped out of bed and went into Blake's room. He was awake. Ava changed him and Grace sat down on the rocker. "Up," Ava said. She sat down with Blake in her arm, then told Grace to hop into her lap. Joe snuck around the corner and saw them. After a few pictures, he heard Ava telling them both a bedtime story. He sat down by the door and listened. It was a G-rated version of their story. How he swept Ava off her feet and she loved him forever and ever and they lived happily ever after. "I like that story," Grace said. "Me too," Joe replied. Grace kissed Ava's cheek and Joe took her to bed. Ava got up and played with Blake a little while, then took Blake in to listen to Joe sing.

Once Grace was asleep, Joe noticed Ava with Blake. He got up and they snuck out. They went into the bedroom and played with Blake on the bed. "He looks like you," Ava said. "Babe, I think you might be right," Joe said. "Your mom showed me the baby pictures. Spitting image." "How did I know she would," Joe asked. They played with him a bit until Ava started yawning. "Get some sleep." "I can't." "Yeah you can," Joe said. He kissed Ava with one of his cure all kisses and he took Blake downstairs for some quality Dad and son time.

They sat downstairs, talked, played, then Blake fell asleep in Joe's arms. Within a few minutes, he was asleep too. Ava came downstairs around 3, and Blake was just waking up. Ava slid him out of Joe's arms covered Joe in a blanket and fed Blake in the rocker chair, then put him down. She came downstairs and slid onto the sofa with Joe, sliding the monitor onto the table. "Hey beautiful." "Lonely up there all alone," Ava said. He kissed her, then picked her up and carried her back up to their bedroom. They curled up together for a few hours until Blake was up again. "I got him," Joe said. "Joe." "I'll go get him." He slid in to Blake's room and scooped him out of his crib, then brought him in to Ava. She fed him, then Joe took him back into the bedroom and changed him while Ava fell back asleep. He came back in after Blake was back asleep and slid back into bed with Ava.

After another week of feedings, diapers, playtime with the kids, and being superdad, Joe finally went back to the stage. They did 3 concerts, then headed home. Ava met him at the airport with the kids in hand and he was running into her arms in seconds. Joe kissed her and Grace jumped into his arms. "Hi Daddy." "Hi baby girl. Did you take good care of Mama for me?" Grace nodded. They headed out and hopped into the SUV and headed back to the house. "So?" "What?" "How was it?" "Went well babe." By the time they pulled in, Blake and Grace were both asleep in the back seat. They put Grace down for a nap, put Blake down, then curled up in bed together.

"I missed you," Joe said. "I bet you did." Within a few minutes, he was making out with her. "Joe." "Don't," he said. "What happened?" "Nothing." "Tell me the truth." He kissed her. "I want you so bad I can taste it." "Joe." He kissed her again and had her pinned to the bed in minutes. "Tell me." "I missed you. That's all." He kissed her again and tried to distract her. She broke the kiss. "Now I know something's up," Ava said. "I'm not allowed to miss you?" "You are, but something is up with you." "Honestly, we got a lot of writing done. We came back to the hotel and hung out jamming all three nights." "And?" "You'll hear them when they're done." "I missed you too." "So what time are we supposed to go for his checkup," Joe asked. "Three." "Two hours with nothing to do." He smirked. Ava curled up with him. "You shrunk," Joe said. "Running around with Grace plus working out with Rose." "Babe, stop overdoing it." "I'm not. Just miss being able to wear the little dresses." "Always liked you better out of them anyway," Joe said. He kissed her and they curled up together talking, teasing, flirting and laughing. When Ava heard Blake wake up, she snuck in, fed him, changed him and brought him into Joe. They played a while on the bed until Grace woke up. "Mama, I hungry." "Grilled cheese?" Grace nodded. Ava kissed Joe and headed downstairs with Grace. She turned the TV on and TMZ was just starting.

"We ran into Joe Morgan this weekend minus his wife Ava. 'Where's Ava tonight?' 'Looking after the new baby.' 'She doing alright?' 'I definitely hope so.' I think he might have given up being a bad boy. Normally, when he was single, we'd always see him out at a night spot after a show. This time, we caught him running from the hotel to a Starbucks." Ava laughed. "That was Daddy," Grace said. "That it was." Ava flipped it off and finished making Grace's sandwich. He came downstairs with Blake a few minutes later. "Had to put the football shirt on him," Ava asked. Joe kissed Ava. "Game is on." "Daddy, you on TV." He looked at Ava. "Reformed bad boy." She kissed him then cut Grace's sandwich for her and poured her some milk. Grace curled up with Ava on the sofa and had her sandwich, then played with her dolls and then came over to give Blake a kiss. "Grace," Joe said. "Yes Daddy." "You love your little brother don't you?" She nodded. "Can we keep him," Grace asked. Ava laughed. "Think we're stuck with him." "Yay!" Grace kissed Blake again then played with Joe a while. "Daddy, Cinderella." "Doctor first, then Cinderella." "Okay." Joe helped Ava get the kids ready, then they headed to the doctor.

"He's a healthy little boy," the doctor said. "Good." The doctor checked Ava over. "You feeling alright?" Ava nodded. "Tired, but good." "Try to get some more rest. Looks like these two are going to zap every ounce of energy." "Three," Ava joked. The doctor laughed. After a good checkup and a lollipop for Grace, they headed home. The kids were out cold in the backseat by the time they got on the highway. "More rest. Think I could assist," Joe said. Ava laughed. "He said sleep." "Oh." He kissed Ava's hand.

Joe and Ava pulled in and put the kids down for a nap, then curled up together on the bed. "When's the last time you talked to your brother," Ava asked. "Before they . . . . shit." Ava called Cat. "Hey stranger." "Hey. I'm sorry we couldn't make it down there," Ava said. "For what?" "Well, Will asked," Ava said. "We aren't doing a beach wedding whether he wanted to or not. Not without you there." "Think you might need to get another tux for it anyway." "Why?" "The day we were supposed to fly down, I went into labor." "Ava." "Blake." "I'm so coming over there. I need to snuggle little man," Cat said. "Dinner?" "Definitely. Was beginning to think you were mad at me or something," Cat said. "No. Tired and lack of sleep, but we're still good." "I'll see you for dinner then." Cat hung up and Joe slid the phone out of Ava's hand. "What?" He kissed her. "Did I tell you I love you today," Joe asked. Ava shook her head. He kissed her with a kiss that made her toes curl and her body ache for him. "I love you." One kiss turned into a lot more. "I missed you." "When do you have to leave for this week," Ava asked. "Thursday night. You're coming with me." "Joe, I'm not going on stage like this." "You're still coming." He kissed her again. "Missed me that much?" He nodded. She leaned her head on his chest and curled up with him. "It doesn't matter to me if you come out and sing with us, or if you're just there. I just want you with me," Joe said. "I missed you too." "Babe." "Emily going to come," Ava asked. "She said she would. Something happened with her man." "Did you talk to her?" "She said he was acting a little weird. He was giving her the 'using her for the fame' thing." "Did you talk to her though?" Joe nodded. "She's feeling better." "As long as she's alright with looking after them," Ava said. He kissed her. "Babe, I'd do anything as long as you were there." "Better when I'm there," Ava asked. He nodded. "Where's the concert?" "By your old place," Joe said. "Seriously?" "Thought we could take Grace and Blake to your old house." "It's sold." "Nope." "What?" "Unsold," Joe replied. "Meaning?" He kissed her. "Meaning we're in that area for a few days. No hotels." "My old house," Ava asked. He kissed her. They relaxed and talked, then fell asleep together.

An hour or two later, Grace hopped onto the bed and curled up with Ava and Joe. "What you doing princess?" "Cuddling," Grace said. She snuggled between Joe and Ava. "Daddy, why Mama sleeping?" "Blake woke Mama up last night." "Oh." "Cinderella," Joe asked. She nodded. She hopped off the bed and ran down the steps. He kissed Ava, then headed downstairs to turn the movie on for Grace. Ava woke up then went and checked on Blake. He was just waking up. Ava changed him, then went downstairs. Ava kissed Joe when she came in. Grace was playing with her Cinderella dolls re-enacting the movie. Ava curled up in Joe's arms with Blake. She watched Grace and something finally felt right. There wasn't any more stress. They had the perfect life. Only problem was Joe being away on tour, but they always figured it out. Finally.

Once the movie was done, Ava got up and started putting dinner together. Cat and Will showed up a little while later. Within minutes, Cat was in love with Blake. They had dinner, then Grace played with Cat while Joe and Will talked outside.

"I shouldn't have done that Joe," Will said. "I know you were upset, but seriously. Hitting on Ava was wrong and you know it," Joe said. "I know. I'm sorry." "Just do me a favor okay?" "Name it." "No more hitting on her, drunk or not." "Joe, I'm sorry." Joe came back inside and walked over and saw Ava with Cat.

"What do you think," Cat asked. "We could." "I know the scheduling thing is going to be the hard part." "For what," Joe asked kissing Ava. "We're going to the Dominican," Cat said. "I thought you two already went away." "We didn't go," Will said. "So the beach thing?" "If we go to the Dominican, then I will," Cat said. Will was standing in the doorway. He looked over at Ava. "Did you find a dress," Ava asked. Cat nodded and handed Blake back to Ava. Joe slid onto the sofa behind Ava. "Daddy, look." Grace handed him a picture. "This is beautiful." "It's Mama and Cat." "You did so good baby," Joe said. Blake started crying. "I'll take him," Joe said. He kissed Ava then got up. He took Blake upstairs, calmed him down and put him to bed. Cat went to tuck Grace in, leaving Ava and Will alone.

Ava was cleaning up. "I need to talk to you." "Will, enough." "Outside." They walked outside and Ava slid her bare feet into the pool. "What did you need to talk to me about?" He sat down beside her and slid his shoes off, sliding his feet into the pool with her. "I can't help how I felt." "I love Joe. You know that." "I know. I guess I kind of wished that I had it that good for a while." "Things look perfect but they aren't. Nothing is. It's work. You have to stick to it," Ava said. "Think that we could make it work?" "Think you two might be pretty happy if you make it work." "One thing I have to do," Will said. "No." Ava got up and went to walk back inside. Will went to kiss her and Ava went inside. She saw Joe. "Hey," Ava said. She kissed him and wrapped her arms around him. "Babe." "Mmm." "Go." "No," Ava said. "Ava." "No." "Babe, what did he do now?" "Nothing. We were talking." He kissed Ava again. They went and sat down and Cat came down after tucking Grace in. Ava curled up on the sofa with Joe. "You know she's an amazing girl," Cat said.

"She loves you too," Ava replied. Will came in and sat down in the chair behind Cat. "So when were you thinking," Ava asked. "A month," Cat said. "You going to have time to plan it all," Ava asked. "Think we will." "Then let me know what day. We'll figure something out," Ava said. Joe kissed Ava again. After another hour of gabbing, Will and Cat headed out. Joe picked Ava up, wrapping her legs around him and carried her upstairs.

Chapter 41

The next concert, Ava, as promised, came with Grace and Blake. She even managed to find a dress she loved to sing a song or two as a surprise. The minute Joe walked off stage, he was in her arms. "Wasn't the same without you," Joe said. He kissed her leaning her against the concrete wall in the hallway to the dressing room. "You are hilarious." "God I missed this," Joe said. He kissed her again. "Joe." "Two more weeks?" Ava nodded. "Damn." He kissed her again and security walked towards them. "Joe, the car's ready for you." "Where are Grace and Blake and Emily?" "At the hotel for tonight." "Oh really." Joe nodded. "And why is that," Ava asked. He kissed her, grabbed her purse and his wallet, then left. "The suitcase," Ava asked. "At the house." "Keys?" He kissed her and they left.

They pulled into her old driveway and Joe kissed her. "It looks different," Ava said. He kissed her and they went inside. She saw the candles on the mantel. She saw the roses, the champagne and their picture. "And what's all this?" "Nothing," Joe said. "Sneaky." They sat down on the sofa, just where she'd had it. "How did you manage to get the house for a few days," Ava asked. "Talked the agent into it." "Joe." He kissed her and leaned her onto the sofa. "You gonna tell me," Ava asked. "Nope." He kissed her. The rest of the night they were kissing on the sofa, then curled up in the blanket by the fire. "Just wanted to relive a memory," Joe said. "I somehow remember Rose asleep upstairs in those memories." "Or the look on her face when I walked in with you," Joe joked. "Why the house?" "This is where we started." "Very true." "This is where every good memory we ever had started." "Babe, you know there's no point in worrying about anything," Ava said. "I know. I love you." "I love you too." They were asleep on the sofa a little while later.

The next morning, Emily showed up with the kids just as Ava was finishing getting dressed. "Hi Mama," Grace said as Ava picked her up in her arms. "How was your morning?" "We went to the park." "And did you have fun?" "Yep. Why here?" "This is my old house," Ava said as Joe came down the stairs. "Really," Grace said. "Come on Grace. I'll show you around." Joe took Grace all around the house. "You lived here," Emily said. Ava nodded. "This is where I was living when Joe and I met," Ava said as Emily slid Blake into her arms. "It's a beautiful house." "I wonder what the price is now on it," Emily said. "There wasn't a sale sign?" Ava shook her head. "What?" "Your cousin is up to something," Ava said. "When isn't he?" Ava showed Emily around. They were sitting on the porch when Joe came out with Grace. "How was Blake," Joe asked. "He was fine. Only woke up at 3am and 6am like Ava said." "I'm glad he wasn't too much trouble," Ava said. "Ava, I'm family. It's not trouble," Emily said. "I just don't want you to feel like you have to." "Daddy, come." Grace ran onto the lawn to play with her toys.

"So what happened with the boyfriend," Ava asked. "He was acting weird. He went from wanting to be with me, to wanting to come to concerts. Then he'd be staring at other women all night. He came with me one night with one of his friends and they pretty much took off on me." "I'm sorry Emily." "Like Joe told me. The right one is out there," Emily said. "Pretty smart guy." "Sometimes. Others he needs a swift kick in the bum." Ava laughed. Joe looked over at Ava. "And sometimes he needs a reminder of what he has," Ava said. "Just remember if you need me, I'll be there," Emily said. "As long as we aren't taking advantage of it." "You aren't. I love Grace and Blake. Plus, you two are a good influence on me. Not going to settle for anything less than what I want just like you did," Emily said. "You mean Joe?" Emily nodded. "I met him way before that night." "I know. He told me the day he met you." "When?" "He had the picture from the day you two met in his suitcase Ava," Emily said. "Seriously?" "He kept talking about it. Someday he'd bump into you again and he'd do something to win your heart." "Doesn't sound like him to me," Ava said. "He loved you a long time ago. You know he's never going to let go." "I know," Ava said.

They spent another hour out showing the kids around, then headed to the venue. "You gonna sing with us," Joe asked. "Don't know." "I brought the dress," Joe said. "So that's where it went." Grace was asleep in Emily's arms, and Ava was talking to Joe when Ryan and Brad showed. "Hey you guys. How was the house," Brad asked. "Good. You telling me that he planned it?" "100%. Something about starting over," Ryan said. Joe kissed her, then kissed Blake and hopped on the stage to start sound check. Ava sat and watched them. Grace slept through it. "I should take them and get them some lunch," Emily said. "Emm, relax." Ava grabbed lunch from her bag for Grace, something for Emily and something for her and Joe. "Where did all of this come from," Emily asked. "My favorite sandwich place." "This place is amazing. I don't know why you would leave," Emily said. "The one on stage with the guitar staring at me," Ava said. "Oh. Him," Emily joked. They worked out the lineup for the night, then Joe hopped off the stage and came and sat with Ava. She handed a sandwich to Ryan and Brad. "The sandwich place," Joe asked. Ava nodded. "You've been talking about it so long . . . ." After one bite, they were speechless. After lunch, the guys tried talking Ava into singing with them. "Guys, really," Ava said. "One or two songs. We're in your damn hometown woman," Brad said. "Exactly why I'd rather not." Joe nuzzled her neck. "One song," he asked. "First off, totally unfair. Secondly, I don't know," Ava said. "Ava, we had 50 people post that they wanted to hear love letter." "Fine. Two or three songs tops. Nothing else," Joe said. He slid his arms around Ava.

They headed back to the house to have dinner, got changed, got the kids settled, then went to leave. "Mama, I wanna go." "Grace." "Please," she asked. Joe picked Grace up. "You really want to come?" Grace nodded. "You can come with us, but who's gonna take care of Blake," Joe asked. "Please?" Emily nodded. "I guess you can come with us," Joe said. Grace hugged Joe. Emily took her upstairs and got her changed. "Couldn't resist," Ava asked. He kissed Ava. "Sucker," she teased. "Not going to say no if she wants to come." He kissed Ava again. Grace came running downstairs a little while later. Emily followed with the baby bag and Blake wrapped up in his snuggly. "Come on baby girl," Joe said carrying her to the car. Ava locked up and slid Blake into his car seat.

They pulled back in and headed in for the concert. Ava got her hair and makeup done, then the guys went to do the meet and greet. "Mama, where Daddy," Grace asked. "He's with the guys." "Can we go?" "He'll be back in a little while. Why don't you draw a picture for Uncle Ryan and Uncle Brad." "Okay." Grace ran off and started coloring. The guys came back in a little while later. Grace jumped into Joe's arms. "What you doing in here baby girl," Joe asked. "Coloring." "Where's Mama?" Grace pointed to the other room. He kissed her, then put her down to finish her coloring and went in to Ava. "You look beautiful babe," Joe said. "Thank you. Pretty handsome yourself." "Wow," Ryan said coming in. "Would you stop," Ava said. "You look amazing," Ryan said. "I'm not singing more than 3." Ryan kissed her cheek and laughed, going in and playing with Grace. Brad sat down with Ryan and Grace, and saw Blake asleep in Emily's arms.

"Babe," Joe said. "Mm." "Come with me for a minute." He slid his hand in Ava's and led her into the hallway. "Now what did you need me for?" He kissed her, leaning her into the wall. "Just like old times," Ava said. "Was wondering if you would remember." She slipped away from him and went into the change room. "This I remember," Ava said. He picked her up, leaning her onto the counter and kissed her. "Now there's the memory." "Still just as sexy as you were then," Joe said. "So are you." "So what am I gonna do with this sexy woman in front of me," Ava asked. "Hmm." He kissed her again. "Guys, 5 minutes," the manager said. "Go see Grace," Ava said. "She wants to watch it." "I know." "What about Blake," Joe asked. "He'll be fine." "Ava." "Emily's staying with him. Jesse's going to watch Grace while I'm on." He kissed her again and they went in to see Grace. "Thank you Grace," Ryan said as she handed him a picture. She gave one to Brad and he hugged her, then ran over to Joe. "Daddy." "We're going on stage in a few minutes." "Can I come," Grace asked. "You have to stay with Mama okay?" Grace nodded.

After another quick lucky kiss from Ava, and a kiss on the cheek from Ryan and Brad, the guys hit the stage. Grace sat with Ava. Three or four songs in, the stage manager came over and handed Ava a mic. Grace sat with Jesse and Ava slid on stage with the guys. "Thought you'd like a little something different tonight. You know, love letters are the best way to tell someone you love them." The song started and Ava slid on stage for her part. The crowd went crazy. Another song or two and Ava slid back off the stage. Joe kissed her, kissed Grace, grabbed his guitar and went back on with Brad and Ryan. "Mama, you sing," Grace said. Ava nodded. Grace hugged her, then watched a little more. When Ava noticed Grace asleep in her arms, she took her back to the sitting room. An hour later, Joe and the guys came down and noticed the kids asleep. Joe kissed Ava. "She fell asleep when Ryan sang the song you sing her before bed," Ava said. "You were amazing tonight Ava," Brad said. "Thanks. You guys were pretty great too." "Something was different out there tonight," Ryan said. "It was awesome," Brad said. "So where we headed next," Ava asked. "Home. We're flying back tonight. You guys are flying back tomorrow," Ryan said. "We are, are we," Ava asked. Joe nodded grabbing the baby bag and Grace's toy bag.

The guys headed home, and Joe, Ava, Blake, Grace and Emily headed back to the house. "So you gonna tell me what you're up to," Ava asked. "Nope." They got back to the house, put the kids to bed after Ava fed Blake, then Emily went to sleep. Joe walked back downstairs with Ava. "I know the house wasn't up for sale," Ava said. "Well, it was," Joe said. "Was?" He kissed her. "What is goin on in that head of yours?" "Our memories," Joe said. "Joe." "Can't just relax can you?" She kissed him. "Tell me." "Just thought the kids would be happier here," Joe said. "Joe." "We hold onto history right?" Ava nodded. "This place is part of our history." "Meaning?" "Just wanted to be here for a few days. Remember the happy memories." "For a second I thought you were going to say you bought it," Ava said. "Was tempted." "We have the other two houses." "I know. Just for this weekend, it's ours." He kissed Ava and they curled up together. "Kinda missed it here," Ava said. "I know. This is where I found the love of my life. Never letting her go." "Good." He kissed Ava.

The next morning, they locked up and dropped off the keys, then headed home with the kids. They pulled in and saw cars. "Okay, now I know something's up," Ava said. Joe smirked. They pulled in and Grace ran inside. Ava slid Blake out of his car seat and Joe came in behind her. "Surprise," Rose said. "See I knew you were up to something," Ava said. Joe kissed her. "We didn't get to do one before Blake came." Grace ran off playing with Jacob. Ava visited with everyone and Joe brought everything in and took it upstairs.

An hour or two later and after a pile of presents, everyone started heading home. Ava went and put Blake down, after feeding him, and came downstairs to sit with Joe. "I knew you were up to something," Ava said. "Rose made me promise." They curled up together on the sofa. "Thank goodness we're home."

A few more weeks passed and they were heading to the Dominican with the guys for Cat and Will's wedding. Grace was asleep on the plane in Emily's lap. Blake was playing on the floor with Ryan. Joe grabbed Ava's hand and pulled her away from everyone. "What?" He kissed her. "I know what you're thinking Joe. Stop worrying," Ava said. "I just hope it's out of his system." "For Cat's sake, so do I." He kissed her again. "I love you." "I love you too." "If something happens, you'll tell me right," Joe asked. "Joe, nothing will. Only other man who's kissing me is still in diapers." He laughed then kissed her again. "We're not staying on the same floor as them. We're down the beach," Joe said. "And who planned that?" "For my own piece of mind." "Guess that means we can do whatever we want," Ava teased. He went to kiss her again and Ryan walked over. "You know that's how you two got the two of them right," he joked. Ava laughed. "And?" "Rose was wondering where you two went." Ava kissed Joe then went and sat with her. "Why are you so edgy today," Ryan asked. "It's nothing." "Joe, I've known you ten years. Speak." "He made a move on Ava," Joe said. "Who?" "Will. He was loaded but I'm kind of worried he's gonna do something stupid and try again." "Considering she loves you more than anything, I don't think you need to worry Joe." "I know. Just gets to me." "You have two kids with her and she still looks like she could be a supermodel. Consider yourself lucky and hold on with both hands. She'll never stop loving you. Stop worrying." "Thanks." "No prob." "Daddy." "Yes Jacob," Ryan said. "Come." Ryan got dragged off and Joe sat and looked at all of this.

The guys had gone from single bachelors to fathers and husbands. Things had changed from back in the days. The days where they got the hot girls, the attention and whatever they wanted in a heartbeat. Now, Ryan had Rose and Jacob and a baby on the way. Joe had never seen him happier. Rose grounded him. She made him realize just what home was. It wasn't the house, the cars, the money, the fame and the high life. It was having someone to come home to. It was the sound of Jacob saying 'Daddy's home'.

Brad was finally a dad. He had family around him whether he was away or not. The guys were like his extended family. Danielle had new friends who really were more like family to her. They had their son Chris, plus had their own family. There was no stress, no drama, no screaming and yelling. They were the calmest of the group. Sure they had their fights, but they were always the picture of perfection to Joe. They'd known each other so long that they knew every movement. Joe watched Brad with Chris and then looked over at Ava with Blake.

The day he'd met Ava, he'd been dreaming of her and what he'd do if he won her over. Now, he had Ava, Blake and Grace. He knew somehow somewhere he'd done something good to deserve them. Sure they fought, but it only meant they got to make up. She's exactly what he'd always needed. Someone who wouldn't take his attitude or mistakes and make him be responsible. He fell asleep with her in his arms, and woke up happier than the day before. Somehow everything had changed so much, but it was all for the better. There was no way he was letting his brother mess all of it up now. Even if he had to hold on for dear life for the rest of his life, he would if it meant having Ava. She looked over at him. He went and sat down with her, curling up with her in the seat.

"What are you up to," Ava asked. "Thinking." "About?" "Everything we're lucky to have." "In one of those moods again?" "No. Was just thinking about how everything has changed so much," Joe said. "You are happy about that right?" "Always." "Good." Blake fussed in her arms and Ava put him in his car seat. "I'm not letting him get to me either. We're going to be together forever," Joe said. "Whether you like it or not." Ava leaned her head on his shoulder. The flight was over an hour or so later and they headed to the hotel. Blake got settled, Grace went down for a nap and so did Emily. Joe and Ava went for a walk by the water.

"What's wrong," Ava asked. "Nothing." "Joe, just say it." "We're not here for him. We're here because Cat wants you here." "I know. Stop worrying that something's going to happen," Ava said. "I know." "I don't want to be with anyone else." "Me either." They sat down and just watched the sun set. "I love you." "I love you too." Once the sun went down, they headed back and went to dinner with Will and Cat and the guys. All the way through dinner, Joe either had his arm around Ava, his hand in Ava's or was flirting with her. Will knew what his brother was getting at. Once dinner was done, the guys headed off to go to the bachelor party, and Joe went to the suite with Ava. "You should go with them," Ava said. "No." "Joe, I'm fine. I'm going to bed. I'll be here when you get back." "I'm not going." "Why?" "Because if I have a few, I'm going to snap on him and do something stupid." "Joe, he's marrying Cat. You and I aren't going anywhere," Ava said. He kissed Ava. "Go." "Fine. I'm coming back after a drink or two." "Try to have fun alright? Stop worrying." He slid his arms around her and kissed her again as his hands slid to her backside. "You're going." He kissed her again, then left to meet up with the guys. Ava had a hot bath, then slid into bed.

"Was wondering if you were gonna show," Ryan said as Joe came in. "Figured I'd come join you guys for a while. What's going on?" "Just telling him about what married life is about." Joe laughed. "What words of wisdom do you have," Will asked. Joe took two shots and grabbed a drink. "Hold onto what you have with both hands. Make sure you always remind yourselves how lucky you are to have found each other. Don't ever take a second for granted," Joe said. "I would've figured something a little more down to earth." "Such as?" "Always keep her guessing." "Okay. How about surprising her just because. Don't wait for a holiday. Make every day Valentine's Day." "Really," Will asked. "Don't start a fight unless you're willing to lose everything." Will backed off. He knew one more step and he was getting one hell of a fight. After things calmed down a bit, they were all cracking jokes and laughing. That is until Will took one step too far. "So how's Ava," Will asked. "Good. Better now." "I still don't know how you managed to marry a woman like that." "Meaning what," Joe asked. "Joe, I'm not trying to pick a fight with you." "Then say what you were gonna say." "After the shit you've done, I don't know how she's still with you." "Because we love each other. Because I grew the hell up the minute I even thought I would lose her." "She must really care about you." "Will, enough," Ryan said. "Because I know if I ever did any of that shit, I'd be damn lucky if my woman didn't cheat on me to get revenge," Will said. "There's the difference. Ava's not that person. That's why we're married and you're just getting the hell around to it." "I wouldn't be surprised though," Will said instigating a fight. Joe had another shot then went to leave. "Don't let him piss you off," Brad said. "Too fucking late." Joe walked out and went back to the beach. He sat down and tried to cool off before he went back.

Ryan came out a little while later. "Why do you let him piss you off?" "He made a move on Ava." "And he's marrying Cat. He's an idiot." "I want to nail the man." "He's your family. Brothers do stupid crap. We call them on it and drop it," Ryan said. "I don't want to ever lose her." "You won't." "He keeps pushing, he's going to get a fist to the head." "Remember something. Every time you start worrying that Will's going to do something remember this. She married you because she loves you. She's stayed because she loves you. Grace and Blake love you. Stop worrying that Will's going to take it away. One word and you can wipe Cat clear out of his life. He has no leverage," Ryan said. "I'm not that person." "I know. Just trust that Ava's not going to let anything happen. She loves you something fierce and she isn't letting it go without a fight," Ryan said. "Thanks." Ryan gave him a man hug, then Joe headed back to the suite.

He came in and saw Ava curled up in the blankets in a black satin and lace teddy. He washed up, then slid into bed with her. "How was it?" "Missed you." "Managed to not fight with him," Ava asked. He kissed her shoulder, then her neck. "I'll take that as a yes." "Blake?" "Went down 20 minutes before you came back." His hand slid down her side. "Teasing me with the satin. Nice touch," Joe teased. "Was at the doctor before we left." "Oh really," he said sliding the strap off her shoulder. "Hence why I packed this." "Oh really," Joe said. He kissed her shoulder. She turned towards him. "So everything okay?" He nodded. "Only one problem." "Which is?" He kissed her, taking her breath away and literally making her light-headed. Her body ached for him. "I think I missed you," Ava said. He kissed her again. They made love and it was like a tornado had hit them. It was more intense, more passionate, more everything than anything before. After, she leaned her head on his chest. "We should go away more often," Ava said. He kissed her. "I love you." "I love you too." He fell asleep that night remembering what Ryan had told him. He had to admit that the guy was pretty smart at these things. He was like the big brother he wished he had.

Ryan came back to his room and found Rose curled up on the bed. He sat down beside her. "How was the party?" "Good." "What's wrong," Rose asked. He kissed her. "Don't ever forget how much I love you." "Never will." "If I ever do something that pisses you off and makes you want to leave, then tell me," Ryan said. "Where is all this coming from?" "Rose." "Okay. You know I'd never leave you." He kissed her again and she slid his shirt off. "Come lay down." He curled up with her holding her close. "What has got into you?" "Just talking to Joe," Ryan said. "And you drank what?" He kissed her cheek. "Get some sleep." "I love you." "I love you too."

Brad went back and saw Danielle wide awake with Chris. "Hey beautiful." "Hey yourself. How did the party go?" He kissed her. "That good?" "How was your night," he asked getting changed for bed. "Quiet. We hung out a while, then the kids went to bed, then we decided to head to bed while we could." "You know we're pretty lucky," Brad said. "That we are." "We don't have the stress that everyone else does. We knew a million years ago we were meant to be." "Knew you were stuck with me the minute you kissed me." "And why is Chris up," Brad asked. "Hungry I assume." Danielle finished feeding him, then put him back down to sleep. She slid into the bed with Brad. "So what happened," Danielle asked. "Joe's brother was trying to piss Joe off." "So same old thing?" "He walked away." "Even better."

The next morning, Ava went for a run after feeding Blake. "Babe." "I'll be back in an hour." "Better idea." "I know. I'm going," Ava said. She slid her earphones in, kissed Joe, then took off for her run. About half way through she noticed Will on the beach. Ten minutes later, he was beside her. Ava slid her iPod off. "How was your night," Will asked. "Good. I see you're still trying to push his buttons." "Ava, I'm just saying." "Don't bother. You want a relationship with him at all you'll stop this crap." "I just think you can do a lot better," Will said. "And I think that I have what I want whether you like it or not." "Ava, he's gonna go back to the stupid crap he's pulled before." "Then that's for me to figure out Will. Not for you to throw in his face." Ava ran ahead and headed back to the room.

"Where Mama," Grace said. "Out for a run." The kids were playing in the sand when Ava came back. "Well what do you know. The sleepy heads are awake," Ava said. "Hi Mama." "Hey baby girl." "Fed and ready for the beach," Emily said. "Just going to grab a quick shower." Emily was making sandcastles with Grace and Blake was in her arms. "Be back out in a minute," Joe said following Ava inside. "How was . . ." Ava kissed him. He picked her up, carrying her into their bathroom and locking the door behind them. He peeled her workout gear off and they slid into a hot shower together. After making love in the shower, and slipping into their beach gear, they headed to the beach. Brad and Danielle and Chris joined them, then Ryan showed up with Rose and Jacob. The guys were playing in the water with the kids, splashing around while Ava sat with Blake and the girls.

"Anyone notice they've been acting weird since last night," Rose asked. "Blame it on Will and his crappy timing," Ava said. "What happened with those two? They used to be best friends." "Long story." "Ava." "Let's just say Will can be an idiot when he's been drinking." "He didn't," Danielle said. "He kissed me. Joe's wanted to rip a switch off him ever since." "No wonder." "It's done and over. Will keeps throwing things in his face which isn't helping." "Why did we come then," Rose asked. "Because without you he would've snapped on him already. Worse if he knew what happened when I went for my run." "Ava." "He said I deserved better, meaning him, and I told him I have what I always wanted. It managed to give a verbal slap to Will." "Just like it's nothing," Rose said. "It is nothing. He's acting like an idiot. At least Joe's not freaking out anymore."

Joe came walking back chasing after Grace and Jacob. "How was the water," Ava asked. "Rose, can you look after Blake for a few minutes," Joe asked. Rose nodded. Joe flipped Ava over his shoulder and ran for the water diving in. "You're so grounded," Ava said. He kissed her, holding her in his arms.

"Nice to see you're back to your normal silly self," Ava said. "I'm sorry." "For what?" "Acting like a goof with the whole Will stuff," Joe said. "Don't apologize for how you felt Joe. Just remember that you're stuck with me for good. Nobody's separating us ever." He kissed her again and dunked her. Then Ava slid underneath him and knocked him over. They chased each other back to the beach. Grace and Jacob chased them around on the beach, then Ava took off to the water with Grace. "Mama, Daddy coming," Grace said. "I know. We'll hide under the towel." Ava ran back in and Grace grabbed her towel, hiding under it. Joe sat down behind Ava, wrapping his arms around her. "You two are hilarious," Rose said. "And you two are sitting up here. Get your butts in the water." Ryan and Brad came back in and sat down with them. Blake started getting fussy. Ava fed him, then they all decided to head over for lunch.

Cat came running towards Ava. "What's wrong?" "My cousins are here. Rachel and Carrie showed and I'm losing it." "Deep breath. What do you need me to do," Ava asked. "I haven't confirmed the reservation for dinner." "Done. Next." "I have to make sure the florist has the flowers." "Cat, chill." "We're doing the rehearsal in 2 hours," Cat said. "Okay. I'll take the kids for a nap, then we'll be back." "Thank you." "No problem." "Did you get the dress," Danielle asked. "Have it in the room." "The guys have their shirts and pants?" "Cat, relax. Everyone has everything. It's fine." She hugged Ava. "I'll meet you back here in two." Ava nodded as Cat ran off. "She's wound tighter than a top," Joe said. "You forget what our wedding was like." "It was a heck of a lot calmer than that," Joe said. "You didn't see Ava the day of," Rose joked. "You weren't nervous." "Yeah I was," Ava said. "Like that?" "Not that bad, but nervous. So was Rose," Ava said. "Who wouldn't be," Rose replied. "I never understood why everyone got so nervous," Brad said. "I seem to remember you being nervous Brad," Ryan teased. "I was more excited than nervous. I couldn't wait to start forever." Ryan looked at Joe. "Back in a minute," Ryan said. He grabbed his notebook from the room and came back. "You two are hilarious," Ava said. Joe was holding Blake and they started on lyrics. "You three have two hours. I'll be back," Ava said. Joe kissed her.

Joe came back to the room with Blake asleep in his arms an hour and a half later. He put Blake down and saw Grace coloring with Emily. Ava slid the sundress on. "Hey handsome," Ava said. "Hey yourself." He slid his arms around her and kissed her. "How was the writing?" "Got the lyrics and part of the tune," Joe said. "You guys come up with the weirdest inspirations." "Your fault." "And why is that?" He kissed her. "Remembered the Vegas thing," Joe said. "The part where you couldn't wait two weeks." He laughed. "All I wanted was for forever to start." "And?" "Kinda glad it did." He kissed her again. "You have to get changed," Ava said. He kissed Ava, walking her backwards to the bed. "Joe." He kissed her again then hopped in the shower. He came out and saw Ava trying to put makeup on. "You don't need it," Joe said. "Says who?" She turned to face him and he kissed her, leaning her against the counter. "We have to be there in 15 minutes," Ava said. "And?" He had that look that Ava never could resist. He kissed her and they did it on the counter, then rushed to finish getting ready and Ava noticed Grace was asleep. "Let her sleep," Emily said. "We'll be back in an hour," Joe said. They headed to the rehearsal.

CHAPTER 42

The rehearsal went perfectly. Joe went back to the room and got the kids and Emily for dinner. They all headed to the restaurant and Will pulled Ava aside. "What?" "If you ever change your mind . . ." "You'll be married to one of my best friends ever. I'm happy with Joe. I'm not talking with you about this again," Ava said. "Ava, I'm just warning you." "And I'm warning you. One more stupid move or thought about provoking Joe and I'm telling her." Ava walked over and sat down with the guys. Joe came in and Grace sat down with Jacob. Blake was in his arms. "She calm down yet," Joe asked. Ava shook her head. "She'll be fine after tonight though." "What's tonight?" "Spa night," Ava said. "Oh really." Ava nodded. "You're coming back tonight right?" "Was supposed to be girl night." He kissed Ava. Grace giggled. "What you giggling for giggle puss," Joe asked. "Nothing." Grace giggled and kept coloring with Jacob. "Might be able to duck out." "Might," Joe asked. Ava smirked.

Cat and Will got up and did a little thank you to everyone. "I never thought the day would come where everyone was here for our wedding. I know a lot of you thought we'd never get married, but thanks to Joe and Ava, I met the man of my dreams. Thank you for coming all this distance to be with us. I know you all think that we're a little crazy to be rushing into this so fast, but I guess the spontaneous thing must be hereditary. I don't think I ever loved someone so much in my life." "Again everyone, thanks for coming all this way for the wedding. It wouldn't be the same without you here. I guess my brother rubbed off on me with the wedding bug. The day I met Cat, I knew I wanted to be with her. Couldn't wait another minute. Now we just have to wait until tomorrow morning." He raised his glass. "To good friends, family, and love." Joe kissed Ava.

Cat came over a few minutes later. "I got a little something for you and Rose." "Cat." "I know. It's just a little something." Ava opened the gift and saw a necklace with a single diamond pendant. Ava hugged her and so did Rose. "You still worried about tomorrow," Rose asked. "Now that this is out of the way, not so much." "Good. We have some more relaxation planned for you." "Meaning?" "You'll see," Ava said. Cat went back and sat with Will, talking with everyone. Joe's mom walked over. "What's going on with you two," Joe's mom asked him. "Nothing Mom." "Don't lie to me." "He's just being his normal self. Nothing to worry about. How was your flight," Joe asked. "Good. Tell me you two aren't at each other's throats again." "Mom, it's fine. I promise." Grace ran over and hugged his mom. "Well hello Ms. Grace." "Hi Gram." His mom watched Joe. Ava knew why. The rest of the dinner was pretty quiet. After, Ava took Blake and put him to bed, and after a long kiss goodbye, left for the spa with the girls.

"I think I really needed this," Cat said after her massage. "You need to stop stressing about all the details. The wedding isn't even the hard part," Ava said. "You have a point." "Of course I do." They all laughed. "The hard part is keeping the magic alive," Danielle said. "I don't know how you guys do it when they're on tour all the time." "You make it work," Rose said. "How?" "I used to be with them all the time. It was dresses he said he didn't want me going on stage in," Ava said. "Or him coming home to candles in the living room and the lights out," Danielle said. "Or walking in and seeing you asleep on the sofa in lingerie waiting for him," Rose joked. "You guys." "You do what you have to. We may have rushed the wedding, but he's still my best friend," Ava said. They relaxed a while longer, then Cat headed to her room with Rose and Danielle. "You coming," Cat asked. "I'll come up first thing tomorrow. I have to take care of Blake," Ava said. "Love you." "You too Cat." Ava hugged her goodbye and headed to the suite.

Half way back, Ava bumped into Will. "Ava," he said. "Not now." "I need to talk to you." "Will, you need to talk to Cat." "Why?" "If you don't stop this crap, I'm telling her." "I just think . . ." "Will, enough." He grabbed her hand. "Let go." He pulled her towards him. "One last time." Ava pushed him away and he fell to the ground. She went back to the room and saw Joe with Blake curled up on his chest. "Hey handsome," Ava said. "Hey yourself." "What's he doing up?" "He was hungry. He's just settling back down. How was the spa?" "Good. Cat finally calmed down." She kissed him. Ava took Blake and slid him into the crib, then came back into their room, closing the door.

"So what happened," Joe asked. "What do you mean?" "You look like you're ready to kick someone's shins in." "Nothing." "Ava, just say it." "I think you're brother's just as stubborn as you are." "What did he do now?" "He has to decide whether he's going to marry her or not." "Tell me he didn't do what I think he did." "Didn't get a chance since I pushed him into the garden." "What?" "It was either that or crack a nail kicking his butt," Ava said. Joe laughed then pulled her into his arms on the bed and kissed her. "See, no reason to get mad at him," Ava said. "I love you." "I know. I told you I'd deal with it." "That you did babe." He kissed her again. "So what did you do tonight," Ava asked. "Worked on the song a bit with the guys, put Grace to bed, then took care of Blake." "My Mr.Mom." He kissed her. "Missed you." "I bet." "So how did you get her calmed down," Joe asked. "Told her what

Danielle told me." "Which was?" "The wedding doesn't have to be perfect. The hard part is the marriage. The wedding's just the icing on the cake." "Well aren't you just Ms. Fix it." "That's what calmed me down when I was nervous." "You weren't nervous," Joe said. "Yeah I was." "Why?" "Jumping into it after only being together a few months." "Was it worth it?" Ava nodded and he kissed her. "Was hoping you'd say that," Joe said as he kissed her neck.

The next morning Ava got up, went for her run then headed back to the room. She saw Grace by the beach playing in the sand with Emily and Blake. "Hi Mama." "Hey baby girl. You having fun?" Grace nodded. Ava gave her a kiss, then went inside. "How was the run," Joe asked guitar in hand. "Good. How's the song coming?" "Got a little more done," Joe said. Ava kissed him, then went to hop into the shower. He slid in behind her. "What are you up to?" He kissed her, leaning her into the wall of the shower. "Missed you," Joe said. "I bet." He kissed her again and soaked them under the water. After a long hot shower, and making love in the shower, they got dressed. Grace came running in. Ava gave her a quick shower, then did her hair and slid her dress on for the wedding. Just as she was about to leave, Cat called. "What's up?" "You coming," Cat asked. "On my way now. What's wrong?" "Just hurry up."

15 minutes later, Ava was at her door with Grace. Joe kissed her and left with Blake. "What's wrong?" "I got in a fight with him," Cat said. "About what?" "I keep thinking there's something he's not telling me." "Cat, stop freaking out." "I'm right," Cat said. "What did he say?" "That he loves me." "Cat, you're nervous." "What if I'm right?" "You aren't." "Ava, you'd tell me if there's something you knew right," Cat asked. "Yes." She didn't want to lie to her, but it was her wedding day. "Now let's get you dressed woman." "Auntie Cat pretty," Grace said. "Thank you baby." The hairdresser came in and did Ava, Grace and Cat's hair, then finished Danielle and Rose's. The flowers showed up right on time, and they headed downstairs.

"You should get ready," Ryan said as he walked in and saw Will in just his pants. "I'm doing the right thing, right," Will asked. "Do you love her?" "Of course." "Enough to want to see her face every morning for the rest of your life," Ryan asked. "Yeah." "Then?" "I just wonder." "What,' Brad asked. Joe looked at Will. "Is she going to make me happy," Ryan asked. "What the hell changed with you two? I thought you were so happy," Joe asked. "We are. It's just . . ." "Will, you either marry her and stick to it, or don't, but don't think what I know you are," Joe said. "I'm just saying Joe . . ." "I know what you're saying. Concentrate on your own relationship." Joe handed him his shirt and they headed down towards the wedding.

They came down just as everyone was being seated. Everyone quieted when they heard the music start. The guys came down, then everyone turned to see Grace come down the aisle with Jacob. Then Ava, Rose and Danielle walked down the aisle. Ava looked right at Joe. Grace sat down with Emily. Cat came to the end of the aisle and everyone started snapping pictures. By the time she got to Will's side, her eyes were welling up. "You look beautiful," he whispered. She linked fingers with him. The ceremony was simple, traditional and to the point. Once or twice during the ceremony, Will looked at Ava. Ava's eyes were locked with Joe's. "I now pronounce you husband and wife." They kissed, then walked back down the aisle and down towards the party area. They did pictures, then everyone headed to the party area. Joe pulled Ava to the side on the way down.

"Hey," Ava said. "Hey yourself." Joe kissed her. "I love you too." "I was kinda worried there for a while." "Why?" "Just some stuff that happened before we headed down," Joe said. "You didn't fight with him again did you?" "No. I just told him to be sure he wanted to marry her. That it wasn't fair to her if he didn't love her 100%." "Still pushing your buttons." He kissed Ava again. "Just like you said last night. We married each other. There isn't anyone that can get between us," Joe said. "Pretty much surgically attached." "Just the way I wanted it." He kissed her again as Grace came running towards them. "Mama, what doing?" "Talking to Daddy." "Come." Grace grabbed her hand and they all headed down to the party area.

Joe grabbed them a drink and Ava sat down with Grace. Emily slipped Blake into Ava's arms. "He's just fussy," Emily said. "Well mister. What are you fussing for?" Blake looked at Ava. "Just what I thought." Ava gave him a bottle. "Mama, can I play with Jacob," Grace asked. Ava nodded. Joe sat down with Ava. He kissed her neck. "Everything okay?" "Grace is playing with Jacob." "And what's this one doing," Joe asked. "Demanding dinner." The rest of the night went well. Emily took Blake and Grace to the room around 8 and put them to bed. Ava danced a while with Joe, then they went to head back and Will grabbed Ava's hand. "What?" "One dance," Will said. "We're tired. We're heading back." "Ava, one song." She kissed Joe, then Will pulled her to the dance floor.

"What," Ava asked. "Not allowed to dance?" "If you're trying to cause a problem, then no." "He wouldn't be so nervous if there wasn't a reason," Will said. "You pushing his buttons is enough reason for me." "If he hadn't . . ." "I'm not playing the stupid game. Either act like a grown adult or I'm walking out." "And what if I . . ." Ava pushed him away and she walked out with Joe. "I'm gonna kick his . . . ," Joe said. Ava could see his blood starting to boil. "Let's just go."

They got back to the room and the walk hadn't cooled Joe off at all. "I can't believe him. What makes him think he isn't gonna get his butt kicked," Joe asked. "Because he's being an idiot. We're here. You and me. Calm down." "He was trying . . ." "I know. He was trying to push your buttons." "He managed to," Joe said. "I know. Remember what we said." "I know. Still." Ava kissed him. He slid his arms around her. "What is wrong with him," Joe asked. "No idea." He kissed her again and looked in her eyes. "I don't think I could ever let you go." "Good thing you don't have to then," Ava said. "I want to wake up every morning with you in my arms." "Deal." He kissed her and she wrapped her arms around him, leaning her head on his shoulder. "You know how happy I was the day we got married," Joe asked. "Think I might." "Forever right?" Ava nodded. "You and me and the kids."

The next morning, Ava got up and went for a run, then came back and showered and got ready for breakfast. Just as Ava was stepping out of the shower, there was a knock at the door. "Cat," Ava asked looking through the peep hole. "Can I come in?" "What's wrong," Ava said letting her in. "He was a jackass all night," Cat said. Ava slid her sundress on. "What happened?" "He walked off. He didn't come back until almost 2." "When did you go back to the room," Ava asked. "Midnight." "Did you ask him where he went?" "He said he needed to blow off steam." "Cat, are you okay?" "Just wasn't what I hoped it would be." "Nothing ever is. I can ask Ryan to talk to him." "We shouldn't have gone through with it." "Meaning what?" "Meaning I know I was right. That there's something he isn't telling me," Cat said. Joe came in with Blake. "Hey Cat. What you doing down here?" She looked at Joe and he saw her eyes filled with tears. Ava went in and slid her jeans and t-shirt on with her sandals. "Where you going?" "Stay here with Joe. I'll be back," Ava said. Joe ran over to Ava. "Where are you going?" "To tell the fucker off." He kissed her. "I'll go," Joe said. "No. I'll deal with it. You stay here." "Ava, I don't want you to . . ." "Your mom's already suspicious. Stay here." He kissed her again. "Ten minutes." Ava ducked out and headed straight to their room.

"Hey Ava," Will said. "Don't hey Ava me." "What?" "You took off on her on your wedding night? What the hell Will." "I needed to clear my head." "How about this for clearing it?" Ava smacked him upside the head. "What the hell?" "I told you once Will. I told you if you weren't honest with her than I was going to step in. Stop being an idiot. You married her. You don't want to be married, then you should've stayed single when you had the chance. Grow the hell up," Ava said. "I know who I want." "The answer better be Cat or you're getting your butt kicked." "I was feeling that way towards you because you're safe. I was scared," Will said. "Then get un-fucking scared." "You know how sexy you are mad?" She slapped Will and walked out. Ava was halfway down the hall when he caught up with her. "Where are you going?" "Back to my room to calm her the hell down and try to tell her something to make her less upset. She should've kicked your butt when she had the chance," Ava said. "Meaning what?" "Meaning you can't make up your damn mind. One minute you're in love with her, the next you're running for anyone other than her." "I love her." "Then tell her that," Ava said. Ava went down the elevator and went back to her suite.

She came back in and Cat was playing with Grace while Joe was changing Blake. "Hey," Ava said kissing Joe. "You okay?" Ava nodded. "Gave him hell didn't you," Joe asked. "And didn't break a nail." He laughed and got Blake re-dressed. He kissed Ava. "Nothing," Joe asked. Ava shook her head. His arm wrapped around her and Ava went outside to talk to Cat. "What did you do?" "Told him to grow up or I was kicking his butt to next century," Ava said. "Ava." "I told him to make a decision and stick to it. He married the love of his life. There's nothing he needs to clear his head over." Cat hugged Ava. "I told you years ago. I have your back," Ava said. "I know. I'm sorry I brought this to you." "It's something I could help with. All it is, is nerves." "I know. I just feel silly now." "Remember one thing okay? You can always come to me or Joe. You're family," Ava said. Cat hugged Ava and Joe, then Grace and left to go talk to Will.

Ava and Joe took the kids down for breakfast, then one last run around the beach before they headed home with the guys. Rose and Ryan were walking by the water while the kids ran around. "So what time we leaving," Joe asked. "Can't get out of here fast enough can you," Ryan asked. "Nope." "Around 1. What happened?" "Nothing." Rose looked at Ava. Joe's hand slid into Ava's and linked fingers as they headed back to their room. Within a half-hour they were packed. "I still can't believe him," Joe said. "Joe, enough," Ava said. "All he's doing is trying to cause problems." "And he can't if we don't let him." Grace came in with a handful of seashells. "Mama." Ava handed her a bag from the drawer and she put the shells into it, packing them into the carry-on. "I'm going to go check out," Joe said. "I'll meet you up there." Ava got the kids together, then headed up towards the front desk to meet Ryan, Rose, Emily, Brad and Danielle and the kids. "You guys ready," Ryan asked as he and Brad paid for their rooms. "Definitely," Joe said. They all piled into the car to head back to the airport. Just as Ava was stepping in, Cat came running out. "You weren't even gonna say goodbye," Cat said. "You're supposed to be honeymooning." Cat hugged Ava. "Everything okay?" "Getting there. Thank you." "That's what best friends are for." Cat hugged everyone and thanked them for coming, then they headed to the airport.

Within a few hours, they were all home. The guys were working on some music most of the way back. The kids were playing and Danielle and Rose were playing along with them. Ava managed to finish up some writing while flirting with Joe over the edge of the computer. They left the airport and got back to the house and the kids had a quick lunch, then went down for a nap. "So what exactly did you do this morning," Joe asked. "I told him to grow up and honor his commitment. He married her. If he was changing his mind to tell her now. That I wasn't an option for him, and never would be." "Babe." "Smacked him upside the head." "He didn't try anything did he?" "I think the slap across the face prevented that one. That and the fact that I walked out before he could." "I love you," Joe said. "I know. You'd better after that." They both laughed. He wrapped his arms around her. "Nothing's ever going to come between us," Joe said. "I promised that a long time ago Joe." "I know. That's why I love you even more than I did yesterday."

After a few days of downtime, they were off for another concert. The guys worked on the song after sound check, and Ava took care of Grace and Blake. "You singing tonight Ava," Brad asked. "No." "Babe," Joe said. "No." "Not even one song," Ryan begged. "No. It's never one song with you guys." Ryan smirked. "I'll think about it, but the answer's no." Joe slid his arms around her while Grace jumped into Ryan's lap. "Mama sing." "See, even Grace wants to hear it," Joe said. "Don't you even think about using her to get your way." "Grace, do you wanna hear Mama sing again," Ryan asked. Grace nodded and curled up to Ryan. "You guys are impossible. No. I'm not doing it." "Ava," Joe asked. "Grace, come on. We have to go have lunch," Emily said. "I wanna stay here." "I'll grab her lunch Ava." "Thanks. No talking her into getting me to sing either," Ava said. Joe kissed Ava's cheek. "That goes double for him." Ava went and fed Blake, then put him down for a nap. Emily was working on her online course and sat with him. Ava sat down and tried to get some writing in.

"You know the navy blue satin dress got packed by mistake," Joe said. "I bet the black one did too," Ava said. "Surprisingly it did." "I'm not singing tonight," Ava said. "Babe, come on." "Suck up all you want. I'm not doing it." He kissed her with one of his could make you do anything kisses. "Ava." "No," she replied. She got up and walked, with Joe chasing after her. Finally after 15 minutes of tag, he had her pinned to the RV. "Please," Joe asked. "No." "Why not?" "I just don't feel like it." "Not a good enough reason," he said. Joe kissed her again, picking her up and wrapping her legs around him. "I know you're going to." "No." "I know what to do to make you do what I want Ava," Joe said. "Blake's sleeping." "Hotel." "I'm not . . ." He kissed her again. He took her hand, letting her down, went and told Emily and the guys that they'd be back, and headed to the hotel.

The minute they got into the room, he was walking her backwards towards their bedroom. "I'm not doing it." "You will." "What makes you think so," Ava asked. He slid her jeans off. "You are so not winning this one." "Watch me." Within a few minutes, their clothes were in a pile on the floor and he was teasing and taunting her body. "I'm not doing it." A nibble, a lick, a kiss. "Babe." "No." Another lick, a tease, a kiss in just the right spot. "You know I could do this all night," Joe said. "And I'm still saying no." Her leg twitched. A kiss, the feel of his breath on her skin, then a nibble and her body covered in goose bumps. "Ava." "This is so not fair," Ava said. He moved up her torso, kissing her breast, then her collar bone. "Say yes." "One song," Ava said. He kissed her and made love to her. He couldn't resist her for another second. It was so right, so intense that she didn't want it to stop. When the kisses turned primal need, she was done for. He came so hard they both shook. "Fine. Two songs," Ava said. He kissed her again as they curled up together and her legs finally stopped shaking. "Told you so." "You sure you can handle the concert tonight," Ava asked. "If you're there, hell yes."

Two more concerts later, and 9 songs, they headed home. Joe and Ava were curled up together as usual, and the kids were asleep. All of a sudden Ryan's phone went off when they touched down. "Rose." "Baby. Now." He took off like a flash, with Brad behind him. Ava and Joe dropped the kids off with Emily, then headed to the hospital. Just as they were walking in, Angel Grace was born. "It's a girl," Ryan said. He kissed Rose. "About time you guys showed up," Rose joked. Ava heard Danielle down the hall. "It's a girl," Ava said. Ava hugged Rose. "Congratulations Rose," Ava said. Rose started crying. "Everything together." Ava laughed. Ryan was showing Angel off to the guys. "This is your Uncle Brad, and this is Uncle Joe. They're family baby girl. Get used to seeing those crazy faces," Ryan said. After a visit, and flowers and teddy bears, Ava and Joe headed home to the kids, and Brad and Danielle took Chris home.

The minute they walked in, the house was quiet. Emily was working on her laptop and the kids were still asleep. Joe and Ava went upstairs and started unpacking. Once that was done, they curled up on the bed to relax. "I'm glad you came with us this weekend," Joe said. "Me too, but I think I may stay in town next time." "Why?" "So I don't get talked into singing again." "But the convincing was the fun part," Joe said. "I know. I think that I might stay and help Rose with the baby." "We're not going back out for another 2 weeks." "I know. I don't want Grace to spend too much time on the road. The only friend she has is Jacob." "Ava." "She needs to make new friends." "If you're sure," Joe said. "You aren't convincing me into going again." "Oh really." "Don't you even think it," Ava said. "Ava." "I love being on the road with you guys but they have to have some normal parts of life." "Such as?" "Play dates without paparazzi," Ava said. Joe smirked. "Swimming lessons, friends, the park." "Babe, they have all of that." "Grace only plays with Jacob." "Soon she can play with Chris too," Joe said. "You know what I mean." "I know. Still would rather have you there." He pulled her into his arms. "I don't want Blake growing up spending more time with Emily than with us." He kissed Ava. "I know. You would rather be the super mom," Joe said. "Sorta." He kissed her again. "You're still going to come once in a while right?" "Once a month." "Babe." "It's that or nothing." "If you came but didn't go on?" "Stubborn as usual," Ava said. "Determined." Ava kissed him and got up. "Where you going?" "To make dinner."

The kids got up and were playing until dinner was ready. All Joe could smell was roasted chicken. He slid into the kitchen behind Ava. "Babe." "It's done." He kissed her neck. "Go get Grace." They had dinner, then played with the kids a while before bed. After a bubble bath for two, for the kids, they were out like a light. Joe slid into the bedroom behind Ava. "What you up to?" "Putting the laundry away." "You know they have as much fun on tour as we do," Joe said, still determined to convince her. "And they spend most of the time with Emily." "Babe." "I know she's family." "It's not going to be the same without you." "It'll be like old times. Just the guys." "Not the same," Joe said. "I know you want your way." He kissed her neck. "You're not getting it." Then kissed her shoulder. "Joe." He slid the strap of her shirt off her shoulder. "You're not winning this," Ava said. He undid her jeans. "I'm not winning right," Joe teased. "No you aren't." He slid her shirt off. "Now?" Ava shook her head. She felt the heat of his hands on her skin. "You know you're not going to convince me." He turned her towards him and kissed her. She peeled his shirt off. "Not winning at all right," Joe asked. Ava shook her head. He leaned her onto the bed.

Her legs tangled with his. "Ava." "What?" "Twice a month," Joe begged. Ava shook her head. "Please?" She shook her head. "You're sticking to it aren't you." Ava nodded. He kissed her again. His resistance was lowering. "Babe," Joe said. "Mm?" "Come with us twice and go on one weekend." "You aren't negotiating this." She slid his jeans off then peeled hers off. "Right. I'm supposed to negotiate when you have on the pink lace," Joe said. "Told you that you weren't gonna win." He kissed her again and hormones took over. An hour later, they were tangled together, under the covers. "Fine you win," he said. They made love for what felt like forever, then curled up together, still tangled together. "You know I'm gonna win at some point," Joe said. "Keep trying to negotiate." He kissed her again. "I'll win before we go back out." She leaned her head on his shoulder. "You can try." "Nice." "Told you a long time ago I wasn't that easy to convince," Ava said. "Seemed to convince you into something once." "Let you win." "Right," he said laughing. "Besides. Thought it was worth a try then," Ava said. "Oh I remember." "I bet you do." He kissed her again then finally let her get some sleep. Blake woke up an hour later. Ava got up with him, fed him, then changed him and put him back to bed. She came back into their bedroom and slid back into bed with Joe and within seconds, his arms were back around her.

After a week or two, the guys were back in the studio, then headed off to do the weekend concerts. "Couldn't talk her into it," Brad teased. "Tough negotiator," Joe replied. "Haven't seen you happy like this in weeks," Ryan said. "She told me to have a fun guys weekend." "So that mean we're going out after the show tonight," Brad asked. "We could if Ryan's up for it." "Meaning," Ryan asked. "Oh so you are up for a night out." "We're flying back out at 8am tomorrow. You two are probably going to sleep the whole flight again," Ryan said. "Probably," Brad joked. Ryan laughed. They worked on the song and finally finished it. The day went by fast, the concert even faster. After, they headed to a bar for a while. They were surrounded by fans most of the night. Joe's phone went off at 2am. He headed outside to the car with the guys behind him. "Hey beautiful." "How'd the show go," Ava asked. "Good. Not the same without you." "I'll be there tonight." "What?" "I have to go do a reading. Last minute thing," Ava said. "Oh really." "Stop gloating." He had a grin ear to ear. "I'm not gloating. I was right, but I'm not gloating." "Guy night out?" "Just a drink or two. We're headed back now." "I'll see you tomorrow." "What time?" "It's a 10am reading. Probably around 12:30." "Where?" "Barnes." "Love you." "Love you too." Joe hung up and laughed. "Knew I'd get my way."

CHAPTER 43

Ava came with the kids, and Emily, for the reading and book signing. She was handed a single red rose part way through the signing. There was a small note attached:

Turn around

She looked behind her and saw Joe. She was smiling the rest of the morning. After, she walked straight over to him. "What are you doing here," Ava asked. "Watching this super sexy mom I know." She slid her arms around him and kissed him. "Missed you." Ava smirked. "I bet you did." "Hi Daddy." Grace wrapped her arm around his leg. "Hey baby girl." He picked her up and kissed her. "You take care of Mama for me?" Grace nodded and hugged him. Emily came out with Blake. "He asleep again," Ava asked. "Just." They hopped into the car, then headed to the hotel.

They got to the room and Grace curled up with Ava. "Grace, there's something on the table for you," Emily said. It was a plate with a silver dome. Under it—grilled cheese and fries. "Mama, grilled cheese." She had lunch and Ava gave Blake his bottle. After, Grace hopped into Joe's arms. "Daddy, color." She handed him a few crayons. He played with her a while, then they went to sound check. They played the new song for Ava. He looked at her part way through and she had tears in her eyes. Ava walked over to him after. "So," Joe asked. "You should do it tonight." "Seriously?" Ava nodded. Joe kissed her. "You going to sing with me," Joe asked. Ava shook her head. "Babe." "No and you aren't convincing me." Ryan started laughing. "What you laughing at," Ava asked. "You two are hilarious." "You aren't going to convince me either," Ava said. "I know Joe could." "Leave her alone Ryan. She'll need her energy to negotiate," Brad teased. "I'm so telling Danielle on you." They all laughed. "Mama sing." "See, even Grace wants you to," Ryan teased. "You don't want to hear Uncle Ryan sing?" Grace shook her head. "I thought you were on my side Grace," Ryan teased as he picked her up and tickled her. Grace ran around with Brad and Ryan and Ava sat down with Joe, with Blake in her arms. "I'm not going to try to convince you," Joe said. "Good." "I promise." She leaned into his arms and he kissed her neck. "I'm just glad

400

you came." "Nice touch with the rose," Ava said. "You're always there for me. Figured it was only right." "So where you headed tomorrow," Ava asked. "Buffalo." "I'm going to head home tomorrow then." "Nope." "What do you mean nope?" "You're staying with us." "Oh I am, am I?" He nibbled her ear. "You and me and a king sized bed," Joe said. "And what would we need that for?" He kissed down her neck then her shoulder. "Have a few ideas." "I bet," Ava replied.

That night, the kids went to bed and stayed with Emily and Ava slid on the black, backless, short dress that always had Joe drooling and headed to the show with him and the guys. "Nice dress," Ryan said. "Thanks." Brad laughed. "What," Joe asked. "Convinced her?" "I tried. Trust me. I tried." Ryan laughed. "One song," Ava said. "Three." "Joe." "Three." "Then tomorrow . . ." He kissed her. "Tough cookie my butt," Ryan said. They pulled in, the guys did the meet and greet, then the opening act started. Joe came in and pulled Ava into the change room. "What?" He kissed her. "You get two songs. That's it," Ava said. "Good. Think I might be able to remember the words if you keep the jacket on. Ava smirked. "Guess you're forgetting the words then," Ava said. His arms slid around her. "Remember something." "What?" "You started this." Ava kissed him.

The guys went on, sang a few songs, Ava sang her three, then she slipped back off stage, and came around to watch them. The next song was the new one they'd started writing at the wedding. "This is a new one. It'll be on the next CD. It's called 'Forever in your arms'." The lighters went up in the air, and some of the female fans were tearing up like Ava had. They sang a few more, then finished up. As soon as they were done, Joe walked straight into Ava's arms and kissed her, spinning her around. "Told you so," Ava said. He laughed and kissed her again as they headed to the sitting room. "Ava, you know you're a lucky charm now right," Brad said. "Funny," Ava replied as Joe kissed her temple. "I haven't seen that kind of reaction in a while," Brad said. "I told you guys it was good." "So we need to go celebrate," Ryan said. "And I need to go take care of Blake." "One drink," Ryan teased. "You guys have fun." "Not the same without the lucky charm." "Then it can wait until tomorrow," Ava said.

They headed back to the hotel and everyone went to sleep. Ava was up 2 hours later with Blake. She slid back into bed with Joe after putting Blake back to sleep. "He okay?" "Just hungry," Ava said. His arm wrapped around her. "Still wired are you," Ava asked. "Can't help it." He kissed her neck. "Blake's going to be up in 4 hours." He nibbled her ear. She turned towards him. "Now that I'm awake," Ava said. "So that's how to wake you up." She slid her arm around him and he slid into her arms kissing her. "I'm glad you came," Joe said. "Couldn't just do all of it without me." "Never." He kissed her again. One kiss turned into two, then into four, then he slid her satin teddy off. He made love to her, kissing her from head to toe. After, they curled up together and fell asleep.

The next morning, Ava got up and Joe was playing with the kids in the living room. "Hi Mama," Grace said. "Hey baby girl. What are you guys up to?" "Puzzle." Ava kissed Joe good morning and he pulled her into his lap. "What time do we have to leave," Ava asked. "10." "Mama, we going home?" "Nope," Joe said. "Yay," Grace said. Blake giggled and reached for Joe. "What's up little man?' Blake gurgled. "Did you have breakfast," Ava asked. "Pancakes," Grace said. "Ordered something for her earlier. Decided to wait for you." Ava kissed him. "Mama, you like Daddy?" Ava nodded. "Me too." Joe smirked. "Grace, why don't we go get you and Blake dressed." "Okay." Grace got up and ran into the other room. Joe kissed Ava and took Blake to get dressed. Ava called for breakfast, then showered and got dressed. Just as she was finishing, breakfast showed up. They had breakfast, then they packed up, got Emily off the laptop, and headed for the plane.

Grace played with Ryan and Brad most of the flight. They landed and headed to the hotel. They walked in and unpacked, then headed to the venue to do sound check and an interview or two. Once they were done, Joe walked up to where Ava and the kids were with Emily and kissed Ava. "What was that for?" "Need your assistance," Joe said. "For?" He pulled her to her feet and they headed down to the stage. The makeup lady touched up Ava's makeup. "What did you need me for?" "You're part of the group babe. You're in the interview," Joe said. He kissed her and they sat down to do the interview.

"So we have to ask. Is Ava a permanent part of the group now?" "She's our lucky charm. She better be," Ryan joked. "I'll be popping in to do a song or two once in a while, but not every show,' Ava said. "Until we can talk her into it," Brad said. "So now that you all have kids, how have things changed?" "A lot less sleep," Ryan joked. "We all have grown up a bit. We're still the same guys, but just a little more mature. No more crazy parties," Brad said. "What about you and Ava? What's changed?" "Just makes me miss them more. Sometimes I can't wait to get home and hear my daughter say 'Daddy's home.' Just means some of the priorities change," Joe said. "Do you bring the family with you for the shows?" "Whenever I can. It's kind of nice to walk off stage and have Ava there," Joe said. "So what's next for you? New CD?" "We're working on a new one. Once the tour finishes up in September, we're heading back into the studio," Brad said. "Is Forever in your Arms going to be on it?" "If that's what the fans want, that's what they get," Ryan said. "So Ava, what's it like being the token woman in the group?" "It's kind of nice being the only girl. Plus being able to be out here with three of my best friends is pretty nice. We're like a family," Ava said. "Always have been," Ryan said. "Anything new for you on the writing front?" "Working on a new one now between shows and baby duty." "We have a fan question for you. We know you aren't always on tour with the guys. Isn't it hard having a semi long distance relationship?" "Honestly, we're closer than ever. Most of the time, they're home during the week. When they leave, I'm either with them or I have alone time with the kids.

It's kind of nice having time to myself, but I still miss Joe when they're gone. He normally tries talking me into coming most shows," Ava said. "So you're the one that talked her into singing?" "We were working on a song one day together, then was awestruck when I heard her sing. From then, it was history," Joe said. "So it's all because of you?" "Well, it's because of all of them. Ryan was the one who finally talked me into it," Ava said.

They finally finished the interview, then headed to the hotel for a quick nap before dinner. The kids were asleep and Emily went down to the gym. Ava and Joe curled up together. "Thanks for the warning about the interview," Ava said. "Didn't know they wanted you in it. Besides. You were amazing." "Was kind of nice." "You know you're stuck with us for life." "Something told me I would be." He kissed her. "What you wearing tonight," Joe asked. "The dark blue." "You would." Ava nodded and kissed him. "Don't know why you're always trying to get me all hot and bothered." "You bought it. Besides, that's what girls do," Ava teased. "Oh really." He leaned her onto her back, pinning her to the bed, and kissed her. "Beware of the piano," Joe said. Ava laughed. "Think I was kidding?" "Nope." He kissed her again and Ava slid his shirt off. "This is never gonna get old is it," Joe asked. Ava shook her head and kissed him. He slid his arms around her. They were curled up together until Grace came running into their room. "Mama." "Yes Grace." She climbed onto the bed with Ava and Joe and curled up beside Ava. "Bad dream?" Grace nodded. Joe kissed Ava and laid down beside her, with his arm still around her. Just as Grace was falling back asleep, Blake woke up. Joe kissed Ava's cheek and got up to take care of him. He came in a little while later, with Blake wrapped in his blanket and sat down on the bed beside Ava. Joe laughed. Ava kissed him. They didn't have to say a thing. They knew.

They met up with the guys for dinner, then they all went and got changed. "Still can't believe you're wearing that," Joe said. Ava slid the sexy lace bra from her suitcase. He looked over and saw her. Grace came running in a few minutes later. "Daddy, can I watch a movie?" "Sure baby girl." He took her into the living room and turned one of her movies on. Emily came back all giggles. "Hey giggles," Ava said. "Hey." "Might as well tell me," Ava said. "Met a guy downstairs at the gym earlier." "Um hm." "We had dinner." "Noticed. And," Ava asked. "He kissed me." "So that's what the giggles were for," Joe said. She threw a pillow at him. She sat down and played with Blake. Ava came out a few minutes later in the dress and her heels. Joe gulped. "What?" He walked towards Ava, sliding his arm around her waist. "Need you for a minute," Joe said. "I bet you do." Just as he was trying to talk her into the bedroom, Ryan and Brad showed up. "You two ready," Brad asked. "5 minutes," Joe said. "Buddy." "Don't even say it." Ava kissed him, then gave Grace a huge hug. "Mama, you sing tonight?" Ava nodded. "You look like my Barbie." "Thank you baby." Ava gave her a kiss, then kissed Blake and they were off.

The guys headed into the meet and greet and Ava got her hair and makeup finished. Joe came in after the meet and greet and Ava was on her laptop going through email. "Hello beautiful." "Hey yourself." He kissed her. "What are you doing here? I haven't seen you in forever," Ryan said. Ryan walked in with an old friend. Brad was cracking jokes with her. "You must be Ava," she said. Ava looked at her and had an odd feeling she'd met her before. "Nice to meet you," Ava replied. "Ava, this is Cassie. She used to date Rob." "I knew I'd seen that face before." "He told me come down tonight," Cassie said. "You two have been together forever." "Was hoping you three would rub off on him,' Cassie joked. "Ava." Rob motioned for her to come with him. "What's up?" "What do you think of this?" He showed her an engagement ring. "It's beautiful." "You think she'll like it," Rob asked. Ava nodded. "Was going to do it during the show." "During love letter." He hugged Ava and slid the ring box in his pocket. They went back in and sat down until the guys headed on stage. Cassie went and sat with her friends in their front-row seats.

The concert started. The guys did a few songs, then Ava came out and got Rob to join them. "There's something we have to do now, before any more songs tonight," Ava said. "I need Cassie to come up here," Ryan said. The security guy helped her onto the stage. "Rob and Cassie have been dating forever," Ryan said. "Thinking that she might get sick of waiting for me," Rob said. "Never," Cassie joked. "Just in case she was thinking about it, I have a little something for her. Yes in front of everyone," Rob joked. He slid the ring on her finger. Cassie cried and they started Love Letters. Two more songs and Ava headed off seeing Cassie side stage. Ava walked down to the sitting room with her. "You knew didn't you," Cassie asked. Ava nodded as she had a bottle of water. Ava handed Cassie a bottle of water and they went and watched the end of the concert.

The minute the curtain went down, Joe walked towards Ava and kissed her. They all headed down to the sitting room, Ava kicked her heels off and they relaxed. "I can't believe you finally did it," Ryan said. "What's he talking about," Cassie asked. "I've had the ring for weeks," Rob said. "Had to wait until I was at the concert?" "You deserve the grand gesture." Cassie kissed Rob. "We are seriously rubbing off on the guys," Joe teased. "That's a good thing," Ava said. "All your fault. You two started this," Ryan said. "Actually, Brad did," Joe replied. "Nice," Ryan joked. "It's true. Danielle was the one that told me that if I loved her so much I should do something about it." Brad laughed. "She just wanted you to quit with the girlfriend rotation," Ryan said. "Definitely glad I did." "Nice save," Ava said. They relaxed a while, then headed back to the hotel.

"We're having a drink to celebrate," Ryan said. "Fine. One." They went down to the hotel lounge and had a drink, the guys had 2 or 3, then everyone headed to their rooms. Joe had Ava leaned against the door the minute they got to their room. "Sleep," Ava said. He shook his head. "Not when you have that on, plus teasing me all night." "I could just keep teasing," Ava said. She walked into the room and saw Emily asleep on the sofa with Blake. Ava took Blake and put him down in the crib, then wrapped Emily in a blanket and headed into the bedroom with Joe. He closed the door and pulled her into his arms. "You know the piano is still there," Joe teased. "What has got into you?" "I'm just happy you're here with me." Ava smiled and he kissed her. "Hate sleeping alone don't you?" He nodded. "Good thing I don't have to." He pulled her close, picking her up in his arms. Ava kicked her heels off, then he leaned her onto the bed.

"What are you all smiles for?" "Why did Rob tell you but not us," Joe asked. "He wanted to surprise her. You guys aren't the best at keeping secrets." "So not fair." "He wanted my opinion on the ring. He was going to ask her before, then I told him to do it before the Love Letter song," Ava said. "You do know romance I tell ya." "I know. Another reason why you love me." "One of the millions." He kissed her. "I never should have let you get this dress," Joe said. "Why's that?" "Like you don't already know." Ava teased. He slid the zipper down her back. "Thanks for the assistance with that." He kissed her and slid the dress off. Ava pulled his shirt off, then he kicked his jeans off. Within a few minutes, there was a pile of clothes on the floor and they were snuggled underneath the covers. "What am I going to do with you," Joe asked. "Just too much woman to handle?" He laughed, shook his head and kissed her. Her legs slid around his. He made love to her, then, still a mess of arms and legs, they fell asleep.

Ava went to get up the next morning and Joe was still wrapped around her. She managed to sneak out of bed, throwing on her sweater and leggings, and went and checked on Blake. He was just waking up. Ava took him into the living room and fed him. Emily was just waking up. "Morning." "Morning to you too. What are you doing up so early," Emily asked. "Didn't want him waking Grace up. How was your night?" "We had coffee here. The kids were out cold at 8." "And?" "I like him." "What does he do?" "He works with the record company." "Not Jeff?" She nodded. "How did I know you'd like him," Ava asked. "He's a sweetheart." "Joe's going to laugh when he hears this." "Why?" "I told him we should've set you two up. He's the one that said no." "Go figure." Blake fell back asleep and Ava put him back down, then came out and tried to get some of Grace's toys packed up. "So are you going to breakfast?" "I'll be back before you guys are ready to head home." "I'll do your hair." Emily showered, then got dressed and Ava put the finishing touches on her hair and makeup. She hugged Ava, then headed to meet him. Ava slid back into bed with Joe and he pulled her back into his arms. "Where'd you go," Joe asked. "Fed Blake, got Emily ready for her breakfast date . . ." "With who?" "You won't believe me if I tell you." "Who?" "Jeff." His eyes opened. "Emily?" Ava nodded. "Where?" "Joe, leave them alone." "He's not dating my cousin." "Why?" "You thought I was bad before we met, he brings new meaning to the term." "You turned out to be a good man." "Ava, trust me." "You're leaving her alone. Let her have some fun." "I don't want to see her crying again."

"Stop." "Fine, but if she . . ." Ava kissed him. He peeled her leggings and sweater off and curled back up with her.

They left around 11, with a giggling Emily, and met up with the guys, then headed to the airport. "What are you all giggly about," Ryan asked. "Breakfast date," Emily said. "With?" Joe was about to say and Ava covered his mouth. "A friend." "You're giggly over a friend," Brad asked. "You know it's like having 3 brothers being over-protective. Yes a friend." "We know this friend," Ryan asked. Joe nodded. Grace hopped into Emily's lap. "Who," Ryan asked. "Doesn't matter." "Oh yeah it does. Watch it be Jeff." Emily smirked. Ryan and Brad both laughed. "Seriously? Was wondering why he wasn't there last night," Ryan said. "We had coffee last night, then met up for breakfast." "Just be careful Emily," Brad said. "He couldn't be any worse than Joe was," Emily joked. "Nice." "I'm just saying." "Who do you think was out with me when I was single," Joe said. "Still." "Nice." "I know you mean well, but I like him," Emily said. Joe was going to say something and Ava said not to. "As long as he treats you right and makes you happy, he's fine with me. The second he gets out of line, he's getting a butt kicking," Ava said. "Trust me. She'll do it," Ryan said. Emily laughed and Joe kissed Ava.

They finally landed, then everyone headed home. The minute the plane touched down, Emily was on the phone with Jeff. "Sure I can." Joe looked at Ava. "What?" "Big mistake," Joe said. "Let her live her own life," Ava said. "Huge mistake." Ava shook her head and leaned back as Joe took them home. They pulled in and the kids were asleep. Ava tucked Grace in, and Joe put Blake down. They unpacked—again—and relaxed. "Ava, can you help me do my hair," Emily asked. She smirked. "Let me know when you're ready." "Ava," Joe said. "What?" "He's not a good guy." "Joe, let her make her own decision. Even though everyone told me you were a playboy, I still married you," Ava said. "That was just dumb luck on my part." "Very very true." "Nice." "She's an adult. She gets to make her own choices whether we like them or not," Ava said. "Babe." "She's not our daughter. When it is, I give you permission to guard her with a shotgun." "Deal." He pulled Ava into his arms. "Was pretty lucky to have found you." "You mean all those years ago?" "Been dreaming about you ever since." He kissed her. They were kissing and cuddling when Emily came downstairs.

Ava looked at Emily and shook her head. "What?" "Better idea. We'll raid my closet," Ava said. Ava took Emily upstairs and found something for her to wear, that Ava knew Joe would agree to. She fixed her hair and added an umph to her makeup, then Emily headed off to meet Jeff. "Better," Ava asked. He nodded. "I still think she shouldn't be going out with him." Ava kissed him. "Now where were we?" He pulled her into his arms and had her pinned to the sofa. "You know I'm gonna win that fight someday," Joe said. "No you won't. Joe, he can't be that bad." "He can. He's the one that used to go out to the bars with me to meet girls. The things he's done." "And you were just as bad for going along with it. You changed. Why can't he?" "He's the one that gave Jess the meet and greet passes," Joe said. "And why would he do that?" "In case I felt like a night out." "Then he needs a butt kicking." "Every event, he knew the guest list. He gave passes to two or three of my ex's." "Then he's causing crap. Doesn't mean he'd dare pull that crap on Emily." "Unless I talk her out of dating him, he's going to hurt her. You don't even wanna know the places he's taken me," Joe said. "Well now that you opened that can of beans." "Ava." "Speak." "Sex clubs, swinger bars, singles nights." "I'm sure she can handle telling him where to go all on her own." "Babe." "If it happens that he tries it, I'll deal with him like I did with your brother." "I haven't heard from them in a while," Ava said. "Nice change of topic." "I'm just a lot happier with you than I ever could have been." "Nice save." He went to kiss her and she turned her head. "Babe, I'm allowed to worry about her," Joe said. "I know . . . . Seriously though. Swinger bars and sex clubs?" "That was when a drink or two got me tipsy." "Right. Last week," Ava joked. He tickled her then kissed her. "Seriously, I'm happier being with you. Even if you do intentionally tease me." "Oh you haven't seen teasing yet mister."

The kids got up a while later. Ava put dinner together, and Joe barbecued, then after another Disney marathon, Grace went to bed. After a quick bubble bath, Ava put Blake to bed. She walked past the bedroom and Joe was texting someone. "What are you up to," Ava asked. "Making sure she's alright." "Starting to feel sorry for the first guy that Grace dates." "She's not replying." Ava grabbed her phone and called Emily. "Hi Ava." "Everything okay?" "Was going to stay," Emily said. "I'll be there in 20." "You think?" "Yep." "I'll text you the directions. Tell Joe to stop worrying." Ava hung up, pulled her sweater on and grabbed her purse. "Where you going?" "To pick her up." Ava kissed Joe, then left.

"Hey Ava." "Hey. How are you," Ava said. "Good. Better now that Emily's around." "Where is she?" "Washroom. Come in." "I need to talk to you for a minute." They went into the office and Jeff closed the door. "What's up?" "No more of his ex's at the shows," Ava said. "They're friends." "Not mine and not his. End of discussion." "Ava, fans are fans." "And causing shit intentionally doesn't fly with me." "Fine." "Any of them on the meet and greet I get told before the show." "Fine." "You actually like Emily," Ava asked. "I kinda do." "One step out of line you know he's going to kick your butt." "Trust me. I know." "No stupid crap. No pulling her into something then dumping her after using her." "Ava." "And don't tell me you don't do that." "If I wanted that, I wouldn't be going after her." "And stop with the innocent act. I know better Jeff." "He told you did he," Jeff said. "He did. You even think about taking her anywhere near those places, and I'm kicking your butt to the next century." "Tell Joe you did a good job. I don't fall for it though." "Don't test me," Ava said. "Now I know why Will has such a thing for you," Jeff said. Ava walked out and took Emily back to the house. "What was that about?" "Balance of power." "Okay," Emily replied a little confused.

Ava slid into bed beside Joe in a black satin and cream lace teddy. "Tease." She turned and looked at him. "What?" "Nothing." "She okay?" Ava nodded. "You told him off didn't you," Joe asked. "Nope. Just put him in his place." "Meaning?" "One more of your ex's show up at the show, he's getting his butt kicked." "You know they're his ex's too." "Figured that much. He knows I'm not a pushover." "Miss Tough Guy." "He wants to be a dick, Emily will see it for herself." He slid her leg around him and slid his hand up her silky smooth leg. "What?" "Smooth." Joe kissed her. She could feel her body aching for him. He slid one strap off her shoulder and she slid it back up. He kissed her, nibbling her neck, her ear, her collar bone. "All mine." "Maybe," Ava said. He kissed her again with one of those, you can feel your heart racing and pounding at the same time, kisses. It seemed to go on forever. They made love and still hadn't come up for air. Finally, as her body gave into his, he finally let her up for air. "I love you." "Oh . . . I love . . . you . . . too." Her legs tightened around him. They fell asleep curled up together a little while later.

Ava got up with Blake an hour or two later, her legs still a little shaky. She changed him and put him back down then curled back up in bed with Joe. He slid his leg over hers and pulled her in close. They were both back asleep in minutes.

The next morning, Grace came into their room and woke Ava up. "Morning baby." "Where's Emily?" "In bed." "No." "I'll come in in a minute. Go put your slippers on." "Okay Mama." Ava slid her leggings and sweater back on, pulled her hair into a ponytail, then grabbed her phone and went downstairs. There was a note on the kitchen table that Emily went for a morning run with Jeff and she'd be back around lunch. Ava looked at the clock. It was almost ten. She went upstairs and put Grace's track suit on then got Blake dressed. "Where we going," Grace asked. "For a drive." "Okay." Ava gave Grace her breakfast and fed Blake. While Grace was putting her boots on, Ava went upstairs. "Where are you going," Joe asked. "She's out with Jeff." "It's like 10:30." "I know." "I can look after Blake." "You sure?" He nodded. Blake was asleep in Ava's arms. "I'll put him in the crib." "Call me and let me know," Joe said. Ava put Blake down then came into the bedroom. Joe pulled her onto the bed and kissed her. "You know I'll know," Ava said. He kissed her again. Ava went downstairs and left with Grace. They went to drive past Jeff's place and Ava saw his car parked on the street. The engine was cold. She saw Emily's bag in the backseat. She got in the SUV and called Emily. "Hi Ava," Jeff said. "Jeff. Emily around?" "We're kinda in the middle of something." "Baseball bat wants to meet your car," Ava said. "Hi Ava," Emily said. "Hey. Everything okay?" "Can I call you back after?" "Emily." She hung up. Ava headed back to the house stopping to get a Starbucks for her and Joe. She walked in and Blake was asleep on Joe's chest on the sofa.

Ava set Grace up with her crayons and she sat the coffee behind Joe's head. She kissed him. "Hey." "Hey yourself." "He got fussy after you left. This calmed him down," Joe said. Ava took Blake back up to his crib and set him down, then came back downstairs, baby monitor in hand. "And?" Ava looked at him. "Are you kidding me?" Ava shook her head. "I'll . . ." "She knows I know." The phone rang. "Hey Ava. Joe around," Ryan asked. "Yep." Ava handed the phone to him. "Hey . . . . seriously? Fine. I'll meet you there in an hour," Joe said. "Studio?" He nodded. "I'm gonna see if I can get some writing done today anyway." "Call me when she gets back," Joe said. "Joe, she's already done whatever she's gonna do." "Still." Ava kissed him. "I'll be back downstairs in a minute," Ava said to Grace. "Okay Mama." Ava went upstairs with Joe. They showered, then Ava got dressed and threw her hair into a ponytail. Joe finished getting changed, grabbed his coffee and headed to the studio. "Come by at dinner," Joe said. Ava kissed him again, and he had her leaned into the wall. One more super intense kiss that almost had her knees going numb and he went and kissed Grace goodbye and left for the studio.

"Where Emily," Grace asked. "She's visiting a friend." "Mama, need snuggle." She hopped into Ava's lap and snuggled her. "What do you feel like doing today?" "Play at the park." "Now there's an idea." Ava snuggled with Grace until Blake woke up. She fed the kids, then called Rose. "I'll meet you there," Rose said. Grace ran around with Jacob and Ava and Rose sat with Blake and Angel. "Thought you might be needing some grownup time," Ava said. "If you can call it that." "Closest we're getting. How are things going," Rose asked. "Better when he's home. How are you two doing?" "Good. Really good actually." "You know how long I wanted to hear that?" "It's hilarious having Emily. Totally seeing the over-protective side of him." "Why," Rose asked. "She met Jeff." "And they're all against it." "Understatement." "Tell me she hasn't done anything." "Not sure, but yeah." "Ava, the girl's going to get massacred." "She has to figure it all out on her own. We did," Ava said. "And you had me to fall back on remember?" "She has me and she knows that." Ava's phone went off. "Hi Emily." "Sorry about that earlier," she said. "We're down at the park. Should be home in a little while." "I'll get Jeff to drop me off." "See you in a few then." Ava laughed. "You know I'm getting details." Grace came running over to Ava. "Mama, we saw your tree." "You have a tree," Rose asked. Ava nodded and walked over with Grace, Jacob, Rose and the little ones to show them. "The day I got here he did this," Ava said. "You two are too cute." "We try." "See, I told you Jacob." "Why he do that?" "Because he loves Auntie Ava," Rose said. "Oh." "You two hungry for a snack?" Grace nodded. Ava handed her a drink box and one for Jacob, then some goldfish crackers. Emily showed up 15 minutes later. He even walked her over to Ava and Rose. Ava set Blake in his car seat. "Was wondering if you two were going to come up for air," Ava said. "Funny," Jeff said. He had his arms wrapped around Emily like Joe always did after he'd been with

Ava. "I have to grab something from the car. Jeff, can you help me," Ava asked. "Sure." He followed Ava to the SUV.

"Completely ignored me as usual," Ava said. "She's hot." "And?" "For now." "You're still a jackass," Ava said. "Ava, she's fun to be around. We have fun together. What's wrong with that?" "You use her and you have me and Joe to deal with." "Right. That's such a threat." Ava shook her head. "The woman I want is taken," Jeff said. "Good. Hopefully they all are." "Ouch." "How many girlfriends can you actually manage at one time," Ava asked. "Right now, three." Ava looked at him. "Gotta say though, I'd do her any day of the week." Ava kicked him, then pushed him into the SUV. "You touch her again, you're in serious shit. This was a pat compared to what I'm going to do," Ava said. "We were just having fun." "Unless you're taking it seriously, leave her the hell alone. Got me?" "Fine," Jeff said still wincing. "Get the hell out of here before I get out the tire iron." He left and headed home.

Ava came back over to Rose and Emily and the kids. "Where's Jeff," Emily asked. "He got a call. Had to head into work." "He didn't even say goodbye." Ava had to bite her tongue. Either what she said was going to make a difference to Jeff or it wouldn't. Either way, Emily was in deep and it was going to hurt like hell. "Emm, we need to talk," Ava said. "I'll watch them. Blake and Angel are sleeping anyway," Rose said. Ava walked with Emily down by the river.

CHAPTER 44

"What's the problem," Emily asked. "Remember when Joe and I were fighting all the time?" "Yeah." "We kept bumping into his old girlfriends," Ava said. "I remember how pissed you were." "It was because of Jeff." "What did he do?" "He invited them to the shows to 'entertain' Joe," Ava said. "Are you serious?" Ava nodded. "They have history. It's not pretty history either." "Ava, he's a good man," Emily said. "No he isn't. He's still the same jackass he has always been." "How would you know?" "Because he has two other girlfriends Emily." "What?" "I told him unless he was going to treat you right, he needed to step back. That you weren't some toy for him to play with." "Two other girlfriends," Emily asked. "Emily, trust me. That's why Joe and I were trying to stop you." "But, he said . . ." "I know. Rose and I have been through a million guys like Jeff. They say what they have to, to get what they want," Ava said. "I thought he really liked me." "He did, but not seriously." "So it was just a fuck to him." "I know you're mad. Remember one thing. You deserve a hell of a lot better than that. You always will," Ava said. "But." "I know. Just try to remember that not all guys are like him. Some of them are, but some aren't." "Joe used to have a million girlfriends." "All because of Jeff." "But if Joe was like that . . ." "He used to be Emily. When we met, there weren't any other girls. There was me and Joe. That's it. He proposed after two weeks." She hugged Ava. "We'll find you the right guy Emily. Just listen to what we tell you," Ava said. "I'm sick of being the third wheel." "I'll help you alright?" Emily nodded and hugged Ava. "Come on. We'll go have a girlie day." Emily wiped the tears and walked back hand in hand with Ava. "You're going to be an amazing mom," Emily said. "Thank you."

They headed off and went shopping, then Ava took the kids home and made them dinner, ran a hot bath for Emily, then headed to the studio to see Joe. She walked in and he had a grin ear to ear. Ava handed him dinner. "It isn't," Joe asked. Ava nodded. He kissed her. "Smells like quesadillas." "I am so not sharing with you guys," Joe said curling up with Ava on the sofa. Ava handed something to Brad and Ryan. "Your fried chicken," Ryan asked. Ava nodded. "I love this stuff," Brad said. "So what happened," Brad asked. "What?" "You never go to all this trouble. What happened," Ryan asked. "Nothing." Joe

411

looked at Ava. She had a smirk. "You kicked his butt didn't you," Joe asked. "Sorta." He kissed Ava. "Emily helped me make dinner." "You two have to give us a decoder ring for your conversations," Brad said. "Emily was dating Jeff." "He has like a million girlfriends," Ryan said. "Hence why they're no longer dating." "You kicked Jeff's butt," Brad asked. "If that's what you want to call it." "Remind me not to piss her off," Ryan joked. "Ryan," Brad joked. "Not funny." "So how's the music going," Ava asked. "We have one for you," Ryan said. "Of course you do." "Two actually," Brad said. "So that's why you wanted me to come down." "Nope. Wanted to see your beautiful face," Joe said. "Liar." The guys laughed. "Fine. When you're done dinner, play them for me," Ava said. "Babe. You seriously outdid yourself," Joe said. "Was in a cooking mood." He kissed her. "Aww," Ryan joked. Everyone finished dinner, then they got to work on the two songs they had for Ava. They actually got one song recorded before they left for the night.

Joe and Ava got home around 11. Blake was asleep. Grace was asleep, and Emily was doing her work on the computer. "Hey Emm," Joe said. "Hi." "We're going to head to bed. How was the bath," Ava asked. "Quiet. Thank you." Ava hugged her. "Remember what I said." Emily nodded and wiped a tear away. Ava gave her another hug then they headed to bed.

"You gonna tell me what you told her," Joe asked. "I told her that she deserved a lot better than him." "That she does." "And I told her that we'd help her find a good man. One that's going to treat her right and love her as much as you love me," Ava said. "That's gonna be hard to do." "Why's that?" "We're forever." "And she'll find it when the time's right." "True." "Hopefully she won't have the drama we've had." "I want her so happy she oozes it," Joe said. Ava smiled. "She'll find the right one." "We just have to keep her away from all those musicians. They're all bad news," Ava said. "You didn't say that last night." He kissed Ava. "You're different." "Oh really," Joe teased. "The hot one that tells women he's married is a good guy." "Good thing I'm telling people that then." Ava wrapped her legs around him and they curled up on the bed together. "She's closer to you than she is her mom," Joe said. "I know. She told me Grace and Blake were lucky to have me as their mom." "They are." "Pretty lucky to have superdad too," Ava said. Joe kissed her. "I remember the first time you sang Grace to sleep." "Knocked her right out," Joe said. "I wish I'd videotaped it." "It's the only thing that got her to sleep." "You know I have pictures of you two when she was little." "Oh really." "The two of you snuggling on the sofa, both sleeping away," Ava said. "My heartbeat calmed her. It works on Blake too." "I know. That's the only thing I remembered from helping my other friends with their kids." "Now that you're done being super mom for the day, you deserve some you time," Joe said. "What were you suggesting?" He got up, grabbing her hand and pulled her into the bathroom, drawing them a hot bath.

"There was an offer on the other house." "Really?" "What do you think?" "It was the dream house," Ava said. "I had a better idea for the break from reality." "What?" He looked at her then smirked. "You're thinking my old place aren't you?" "It's more home than that place was." "Joe." "Why not," he asked. "You're serious?" He nodded and rubbed her feet. "We loved the house." "Babe, it was our getaway house. The other one is more of a getaway than anything else." "Who's going to stay when we aren't there," Ava asked. "Doesn't matter. We'll figure that out." "You're serious." He nodded. "It's so far away." "Which means no getting called into the studio or anything else." Ava smirked. "Yes?" "We'll figure out the details first." He kissed her as Ava slid into his lap in the tub. She slid her legs around him. "You know you come up with good ideas when we're in the tub," Ava said. "And your old place now has a hot tub." Ava smirked. "You know where everything is. I love that house." "We can take them to the stadium where we met," Ava said. "Ava." "We'd have more babysitters available." "Emily can meet descent guys," Joe said. "They don't exist there." "Babe." "We'll call in the morning." He kissed her. "Besides. You wrote some amazing stuff there." "Oh really." "Couldn't sleep. Read the e-book versions," Joe said. Ava kissed him then got up. "Right behind you."

They curled up together in bed, kissing and talking, then kissing and snuggling. Just as Ava was falling asleep, Blake woke up. "I got it." "Babe." "Bottles in the fridge." Joe got up, warmed up a bottle and went into Blake's room. "Hey buddy. What's all this noise for?" Joe changed him, then gave him the bottle. Ava grabbed her camera and recorded them. He sang to him. After his bottle, Blake was just nodding off. He sang another song he'd been working on with the guys. Ava sniffled. He looked at Blake after and he was back asleep. He rocked him until he knew he was out cold, then tucked him in. Ava slipped back into bed and turned the camera off.

"Think you're so sneaky," Joe said. Ava laughed. "I wanted to be able to show it to him when he gets to be Grace's age." "He was so cute. Trying to fight off falling asleep." "Stubborn just like his dad." He kissed her. "You know, I still don't know why you don't sing that one in concert." "Trying to weasel out," Joe asked. "Just saying," "You're stuck with us." "Oh darn." He kissed her again. "There's only a month or so left anyway." "Then what?" "A few months at the other house." "It's so far away." "We need to be here, we fly back." "It will definitely be different." "You still thinking it's a bad idea?" "Somewhere a few hours from here is a better idea." "We looking?" Ava nodded. "Don't want to move back do you," Joe asked. "Memories were packed from that place a long time ago." "Plus the James thing." "Exactly." "One to build memories in." Ava nodded. "Sounds good to me." They curled up together and fell asleep.

The next morning, Ava got up and heard Joe in with Blake. He was giggling. Ava slid her robe on and peeked her head in. "Morning," Joe said kissing her. "Morning Blake." "Hi

413

Mama," Grace said running in and wrapping her arms around Ava's leg. "Morning baby girl," Ava said picking her up and giving her a hug. "Well now that we're all up," Joe said. He kissed Ava and they went downstairs and made breakfast. "What do you feel like doing today Grace," Joe asked. "Swimming." "Sounds good to me." "Yay." Grace had her breakfast and Ava fed Blake, then Joe and Ava had their breakfast while Grace played. "I called Kate to help us look for a place," Joe said. "When is she coming?" "Around 1." "You're excited aren't you?" "Wouldn't you be babe? New house, new everything." "Why new house," Grace asked. "Just for fun when Mama and I aren't working." "Can Jacob come," Grace asked. "Sure," Joe said. "Okay." Grace ran back in and had a tea party with her teddy bears. Ava went upstairs and got changed into her bikini, put Blake in a bathing suit, and put Grace in hers. Joe changed and grabbed the towels and they headed outside.

The minute they went to hop into the water, Ava's phone went off. She grabbed it, handing Blake to Joe. "What's up," Ava asked. "You were serious weren't you," Jeff asked. "You think I wasn't?" "I like her." "You can't have her in your life unless it's just her. You're not going to use her Jeff." "Why are you so intent on not letting me see her," he asked. "Because. A broken heart isn't a good feeling. If you're just going to lie, cheat and treat her like a piece of meat, then she's better off without you." "But." "But nothing." Emily came outside with her laptop and sat down to do some work. "I miss her." "Only because you can't have what you want," Ava said. "Ava." "Get used to it. Any woman with half a brain is going to turn you down. You sweet talked her." "Can I talk to her," Jeff asked. "No." Ava hung up. Emily looked over at her. "It was him wasn't it?" Ava nodded. She saw Emily getting all teary-eyed again. "He knows if he wants something bad enough, he has to fight for it. If he can snap out of the playboy crap and thinking he can do whatever he wants with whoever, then he might just grow up," Ava said. "Does he at least miss me?" "He said he does." "You sure he was dating those other girls," Emily asked. Ava nodded. Emily went back to her laptop and Ava slid into the pool with Joe and the kids.

"She okay," Joe asked. Ava shook her head and kissed him, then slid Blake out of his arms. They played around until Grace started getting tired. Ava hopped out and wrapped herself in a towel. Just as she did, the doorbell rang. Ava opened the door to see Jeff. "What?" "I need to talk to her." "If you're going to feed her some line, don't bother," Ava said. "You were right." "Meaning?" "I don't know why, but I miss her." "If you aren't going to treat her right, then you aren't going in." "If I say I'll try, is that enough?" "If you hurt her or do something stupid, I'm gonna know," Ava said. "I know." "What about the other girlfriends?" "I miss her." "Jeff, she's not going to be part of your gaggle of women." "They weren't right for me anyway," Jeff said. "If you do anything, I'm seriously going to find you." "I know." Ava walked Jeff in and talked Joe and the kids into coming inside and letting them talk.

"What are you doing here," Emily asked. "I need to talk to you," Jeff said. "Why? Your other girlfriends dump you?" "I broke it off." "And you think it's going to be that easy to win me back?" "No, but I'll do whatever it takes." "You really thought you could play that game on me?" "I realized something after Ava told me off yesterday." "Which was?" "You're worth fighting for." "Meaning what?" "Meaning give me another chance to do it right." "Prove you're worth giving a chance to and I'll think about it," Emily said.

"Whatever you said to her must have worked," Joe said. "Why?" "It's like the hard time you gave me times ten." Ava smirked. "You turned her into a tough cookie didn't you?" "Just reminded her that she was worth fighting for. That he was lucky to have had her around at all," Ava said. Joe gave Blake his bottle, then they had lunch. Ava went outside and brought them some sweet iced tea, then came back in. "Joe, stop snooping on them," Ava said. "What did you say to him," Joe asked. "Gave him the speech that I gave you a long time ago." "He's still standing? Wow." "Leave them be." Ava closed the shutter and gave them some privacy.

"You know I'm not going to be easy to convince," Emily said. "Worth it. Can you come with me for a while," Jeff asked. "I have homework to finish," Emily said. "Tonight." "Maybe." He kissed her and she was putty in his hands. "Fine." "I'll come get you at 7." "And I'm coming home before midnight," Emily said. "Okay." He kissed her again and Emily walked him out. "I'll see you tonight," Jeff said. He left and Emily walked into the kitchen. She looked at Ava and smiled. "Ladies and gentlemen, she's back," Ava joked. She hugged Ava. "What are you all smiles for now," Joe asked. "Ava was right." "Oh really." She hugged Joe. "What was that for," Joe asked. "For being the exception." "What?" Emily went upstairs and started trying to find something to wear.

"What was that about," Joe asked. Ava walked over and kissed Joe. "Just proved that I was right." "About what?" "Some guys who are notoriously bad boys, can grow up when it comes down to the right woman," Ava said. "Huh?" "You stopped the crazy partying and hundreds of girlfriends when we started dating." "That's because I had the woman I wanted in my arms," Joe said. "Exactly." "Ava, I need your help," Emily said. "You okay to stay with the kids for an hour or two," Ava asked. "Kate's coming." "After Kate goes." "Yeah. Why," Joe asked. "Going to take her to the mall." "Need to get jeans," Emily said. "Fine." Ava kissed him then went to go upstairs. She looked in on Grace and she was curled up on the sofa. "Baby, you tired," Ava asked. Grace nodded. "Come to Mama." Grace got up and walked over to Ava, then snuggled her. Ava took her and put her down for a nap, while Joe put Blake down. Joe kissed her as she was heading to Emily's room.

"What's up," Ava asked. "Can't decide." She held up two outfits. "We need to go shopping," Ava said. "Ava." "Black jeans with the pink top and the black boots." "Ooh." "And you can wear my bracelet," Ava said. She hugged Ava. "I'm going to get dressed. The agent should be here in a few." "Ava." She looked back at Emily. "Thank you," Emily said. "You're welcome."

Ava went into the bedroom, then went to slide into the shower and Joe slid in with her. She slid underneath the hot water and he kissed her. "Hey." "Think you have us all figured out don't you," Joe asked. Ava nodded. She washed her hair and then he kissed her. "She's going to be here in 15 minutes," Ava said. He kissed her again. The heat from the shower steamed up the mirrors. "Thank you for helping her," Joe said. "It was either that or you hurt yourself kicking his butt." "You managed to do it so that she didn't get hurt. She loves you like a mom. You know that right," Joe said. Ava nodded and kissed him then put the shampoo in his hair.

Just as she stepped out, Ava got a call from the security gate. "You have a guest. Kate Francis." "Let her through," Ava said. Ava pulled her jeans on and her tank top, pulled her hair back into a ponytail, then headed downstairs. Just as Kate got to the door, Ava was there to meet her. "Long time no see Ava," Kate said. "Hey. Joe's just getting changed. Was a perfect pool day." They sat down and chatted and Kate took a few notes about things Ava wanted in the house they were looking for. Joe heard Kate downstairs. He pulled his jeans and a t-shirt on, then went downstairs.

"Hey Kate," Joe said. "Hey stranger. How you been?" "Good. Busy as usual. How are you?" "Good. Just talking to Ava about the new place you two are lookin' for." They chatted and Kate showed them one or two listings. "It's a gated area. They have security on staff 24/7. It's smaller, and feels cozy." Joe looked. "See what we can find in that area," Joe said. "I'll give you a shout Thursday. You guys leave Friday for the next show right?" Joe nodded. "I'm staying home this one, so I can take a look over the weekend," Ava said. "No you aren't," Joe replied. Ava laughed. "Give me a shout and let me know." "Anything else on the must have list," Kate asked. "Big back porch. Quiet. Lots of privacy between the houses," Joe said. "I'll see what I find." They showed Kate out. After she pulled out, Ava thought of something. "You didn't give her a price range," Ava said. "Did when I emailed her last night." "Oh really." He nodded and slid his arms around Ava. "You ready," Emily asked. "Makeup, then we're ready." "Ava," Joe said. She kissed him. They went upstairs and finished getting ready. Grace came into the bathroom and wrapped her arms around Ava's leg. "Hey sleepyhead. What's wrong? Bad dream?" Grace nodded. "What happened?" "You didn't come home." "We always do baby," Ava said. "You didn't." Ava picked her up. "No matter what, we always will." Grace hugged her. "Wanna come with Daddy and I?" She nodded. Ava sat her down and put her shoes on. Joe snuck in and slid Blake into his car seat.

Joe and Ava, the kids, and Emily all got to the mall and were swarmed. Ava took Emily to a few stores, they went with Joe to one or two, then they headed home. "Seriously? I haven't seen a crowd like that in forever," Joe said. "We also haven't publicized any pictures of us with Blake." "That was just ridiculous." "You looked great in those jeans Em," Joe said. "Now I just have to do my hair and makeup." "You seriously are going to all this trouble for him," Joe asked. "I used to do it for you Joe. Stop," Ava said. "Did not." "The night we met." "You seriously went all out," Joe asked. Ava nodded. "Manicure and pedicure and made a whole day out of it." "Babe, I loved you the second I saw you," Joe said. "All the more reason." Emily laughed. "You two are hilarious," Emily said. "I'll help you with the hair and makeup." "Thank you for all of this." "You deserve a pamper day anyway," Ava said. Joe shook his head laughing. "What?" "Not gonna say it." They pulled back in and headed inside. Grace played while Ava helped Emily.

Joe made dinner and just as he was about to tell them dinner was done, Ava came downstairs with Grace, Emily and Blake. "Whoa," Joe said. "Told you." "Now I know we're related," Joe teased. "Great." "You look beautiful," Joe said. Emily felt like a million. They had dinner with the kids, then Emily headed out with Jeff. When Jeff saw her at the door he did a double-take. "You look amazing." "Thank you." Emily turned and smiled at Ava. Joe wrapped his arm around Ava. "Good dinner handsome," Ava said. "Thank you." "Daddy, yummy," Grace said. "Thanks baby girl." Blake giggled. "I will never figure this out. How did I get two giggle pusses instead of kids," Ava asked. "Hereditary on your side," Joe joked. Ava threw a towel at him. Grace giggled. "What you giggling about," Joe asked walking over to her. "You and Mama are funny." Joe cleaned her up and Ava cleaned Blake up, then the kids went into the TV room. "I'll finish these. You go," Joe said. Ava kissed him. Grace put another Disney movie in and Blake played with his teddy bear on the blanket. "Mama," Grace said. "Yes baby." "Are we going away?" Joe answered 'Yes' from the kitchen. "We'll see," Ava said. "Can we bring Jacob?" "You miss him don't you?" Grace nodded. Ava called Rose and put the kids on the phone.

"Ava." Joe motioned for her to follow him. "You rang." He kissed her. "What was that for?" "For getting dressed up," Joe said. "You can thank me later." He kissed her again with one of those kisses that could melt an iceberg. "Mama," Grace said walking over and handing her the phone. "Hi Rose." "So, what if she stays here this weekend while you guys are gone?" "Who says I'm going," Ava asked. "Ryan and Brad." "They think they know everything." "I know. So what do you think?" "You have two already," Ava said. "Ava, she's no trouble." "What if Emily comes and helps?" "She's staying in town," Rose asked. "What do you think?" "Even better." "I'll talk to her when she gets back tonight. She sleeping through the night yet," Ava asked. "Almost. Ryan was up with her twice last night." "Think she just likes the smell of his cologne." Rose laughed. "Probably." "I'll let you know. Give the kids a kiss for me," Rose said. "I will. Give yours a hug for me." Ava hung up. "So you are coming," Joe asked. "Sneaky. Very sneaky." He kissed her again.

"Did you want to come back to my place," Jeff asked. "Not really. Think I should get back," Emily said. "Emily." "What?" "I'm sorry." "It's not that easy Jeff." "What do I have to do? Just tell me." "Stop pretending you can handle something you probably can't. The only reason why guys do that is because they're scared of a real relationship," Emily said. "I just got caught up in the partying." "You want to be with me, then it's just us. I'm not about to try to compete with your other toys." "Emily." "Just take me home then." He kissed her. She kept repeating what Ava had told her over and over in her head. "Just for a little while," Jeff asked. "I'm going home." "I thought we could go out dancing or something." "Not in a crowd mood." "Walk?" She nodded. They headed down to the park by the water. They walked and talked, then walked some more.

Ava and Joe put the kids down to bed, then curled up together on the sofa downstairs. His phone went off. "Hey Kate." "I sent you the listing for a few. Let me know what you think." "Sounds good," Joe said. He hung up and grabbed Ava's laptop. "What?" He went into his email and into the links that Kate had sent. "You still have my emails," Ava asked. "Never got around to cleaning up my email." Ava giggled. "Back on topic," Joe said. She slid into his arms. "Babe, don't you want to see what she sent," Joe asked. Ava closed the laptop and kissed him. "What?" "Nothing." "You don't want to see the houses?" "They're not going anywhere." She kissed him and slid the laptop onto the table. He pulled her in close. "You have a point," Joe said. Ava nodded. "We could just look in the morning." "Or in an hour or two." He kissed her. "Or we could just take it upstairs and look at them in bed," Joe said. "Not tired." "Me either." He kissed her again, picked her up, kissing her she grabbed the laptop, and he carried her up the steps.

An hour or two later, Joe couldn't stand the wait. He curled up with Ava and started looking through the listings. House after house, something was missing. They were beautiful houses, but they weren't right. There was always something that was off. The carpet where there should be hardwood, three bedrooms instead of four, small kitchens. "I have an idea," Joe said. "What?" "We go look ourselves." "You're leaving Friday." "We're leaving Friday. We can go look in our spare time," Joe said. "You sure?" He nodded. "That way, we know we find it. Kate keeps looking but we look too." "Sounds like a good idea, but we don't have a heck of a lot of spare time," Ava said. "Oh yes we do." "You mean you letting me get up before 9?" He kissed her neck. "Could make it earlier." "Some sleep is important," Ava said. "Hmm." Ava laughed. She curled back up with him. "We'll go tomorrow," Joe said. Ava nodded. "Ryan postponed the studio tomorrow anyway." "Ooh." He kissed her again and they curled up together and tried to get some sleep before Blake woke up. "I love you Ava." "Love you forever."

Ava got up with Blake a few hours later. She fed him, rocked him a while, changed him then rocked him back to sleep. Joe came in an hour later and he was asleep in Ava's arms. "What you doin," Joe asked. "Thinking." "About what?" Ava put him back in his crib, then they snuck out. "Just thinking about everything before us." "Babe." "All the things I went through. All the millions of times that Rose and I helped each other. All the times that Cat and I went and did outrageous things just to get over guys." "Why would you be thinking about that," Joe asked. "If that's what it took to get here, I wouldn't trade it for the world." "And Grace is never going to have to go through any of that if I have anything to say about it," Joe said. "Every woman does Joe." She looked in and saw Emily asleep with her cell phone in hand. Ava went in and turned it off, plugged in the charger, and slipped out. "I think having Rose and Cat around was the best thing for me back then. My parents were pretty great too," Ava said. "You started thinking about Grace all grown up didn't you?" Ava nodded. "And Blake. What he's going to be like when he's all grown up." "One thing I know." "What's that?" "He's totally gonna be a mama's boy," Joe said. "And why do you say that?" "Who wouldn't with a Mom like you?" She kissed Joe. "Pictured Grace on her first date and you with a shotgun at the door," Ava joked. "Already picking one out." Ava laughed. They went back to bed and were out cold a little while later.

The next morning, Joe got up with the kids. Ava came downstairs and saw him making them breakfast. "Hey beautiful." "Hey handsome." "Hi Mama," Grace said. "Good morning Grace. Good morning Blake." Ava kissed the kids good morning. Emily came in 15 minutes later from her run. "So how was last night," Ava asked. "You were right. Feels amazing," Emily said. She hugged Ava, kissed Joe's cheek then went upstairs to shower. "Who was that," Joe asked. "Just reminded her that the chase is the best part." "Oh really." Ava nodded. He kissed her, then brought Grace her breakfast and fed Blake his bottle. Ava grabbed a coffee for her and Joe, and they had breakfast together. "Mama, we're going to the zoo." "You are," Ava asked. "Auntie Emily is taking us." Joe smirked. "Well, that sounds like lots of fun." "I get to see the lions." "Wow." The kids finished eating. Ava cleaned them up. Emily got them dressed and took them. Joe and Ava showered, got changed, then left to look for houses.

They talked the entire way. They wanted the big back deck, a pool, dream kitchen, room for the kids to run around, and it to feel like a home. They drove past one, and Joe laughed. "What," Ava asked. "Something like that one?" Ava nodded. Six hours later, they'd found a few, wrote down the info and sent it to Kate. They got home and Grace was playing with Jacob. Blake was playing with his toys. "Hi Mama." "Hi baby girl." "Hi Daddy." Grace wrapped her arms around his leg. "Hi baby. You have fun with Blake and Emily at the zoo?" "Yeah. Jacob came too." Emily looked over at Ava. "Thought Grace would have fun if he was there," Emily said. "So they weren't too much of a handful?" "Nope. They wouldn't go down for a nap, but other than that they were fine." "How's Blake," Joe asked. "Needs Ava." Ava took him upstairs. "Now what's all this fussing for," Ava asked. "Ba." "Hungry?" He looked at Ava. She saw the time. She fed him, then took him downstairs. Ava could smell the quesadillas from the steps.

She went in and Joe was teaching Grace to cook. He looked over at her. "Daddy cooking Mama." "I know. You going to help?" Grace nodded. Ava wrapped her arm around Joe. "Smells good." He kissed her. Ava set the table. Emily came in and got Ava's attention. "What's up?" "He wants me to come to a concert," Emily said. "Up to you." "But if I don't go . . ." "Never worry about the if's," Ava said. "He'll change his mind." "Then he's not worthy," Ava said. "I do have work to do for my class." "If you want to go, then go. If not, then tell him you don't feel like it." "Thanks Ava." "You're welcome." She messaged Jeff back that she couldn't go. Ava came in and Grace was carrying dinner to the table. "You made all those," Ava asked. Grace giggled. "Pretty good helper I tell ya," Joe said. He kissed Grace's head. She jumped into her chair. Ava sat down with Blake in her arms. They said grace, then had dinner.

They went out again the next day, then Friday left for the concerts. "Still can't believe you talked me into this," Ava said. "Ava, you have to wear the black one tonight," Brad said. "Now you guys are telling me what I should wear?" "And I'm taking you out to dinner," Joe said. "Okay, you guys are up to something." "Why do you say that," Ryan asked. "First talking me into the concerts, then the dress, then dinner. What are you up to?" "Nothing," Brad said. Joe looked guilty. "Fine. Then it won't matter if I just stay at the hotel in my pajamas all night." "Ava, you have to," Joe said. "Why?" Joe looked at her. "Either you say it, or I'm staying," Ava said. "We'll talk about it later," Joe teased. Ava logged into her computer. "Kate found a few more." Ava and Joe went through them. "You're telling me or I am seriously not going," Ava said. He kissed her. "That isn't changing my mind either." "Now this one I like," Joe said.

They stopped on a house that was beautiful. 5 bedrooms, 3 bathrooms, big kitchen, media room, pool, big deck, and surrounded by trees for privacy. "Wow," Ava said. "Babe." "We can't go this weekend." "We're going Monday." He emailed Kate back and said yes to the listing. Then they saw the others. There was no comparison.

They landed, got settled in at the hotel, then went over for sound check. "I'm not doing sound check until you tell me," Ava said. "I'll tell you after." "No." "Ava, just go with it." "I know you guys are up to something." They did sound check, went through the song list, then headed back to the hotel. "You're telling me or I'm seriously staying here." Ryan laughed. "Fine. Have a good show guys," Ava said. Ava headed for the elevator. "Babe." "What?" He kissed her and they got in the elevator. Ryan and Brad went the other way.

"You're telling me." "Can't just trust me on this," Joe asked. Ava shook her head. "Please." They got into the room and he slid his arms around her. "Babe." "Either say it or I'm staying." "It's a good surprise," Joe said. "What are you up to?" "I promise." He kissed her and walked her into the bedroom. There were sterling roses by the bed. "Flowers?" "What?" "Fine. I'll go, but I still want to know what's going on." He kissed her again and they curled up in bed together.

An hour or so later, Ava and Joe got up and started getting ready. Ava was in her satin robe when there was a knock at the door. "Hey guys. She's in there," Joe said. The hairstylist and makeup artist came in. "Do I at least get to know where we're going?" "Dinner," Joe said. Ava threw a sofa pillow at him. "Trust me." He kissed her then finished getting changed. When he came out, Ava's hair was in rollers and she looked like a supermodel. "Nice dress." Ava kissed him. "Look pretty handsome yourself." 15 minutes later they were done. Ava looked amazing. "So do I get to know now?" He kissed her. He handed her purse to her, along with her phone and slid his leather jacket over her shoulders. They went through the lobby and hopped into the car. "Joe." He kissed her. "One hint." He shook his head and had that grin like his plan was working perfectly.

They pulled up to the restaurant and were swarmed by fans. They signed an autograph or two, then went inside. "Okay. Fans know and I don't," Ava asked. He wrapped his arm around her. They walked into the private dining room and Ava saw roses. "Sit." "Joe, what are you up to?" "Forgot what day today is didn't you?" "Nope. Was wondering if you remembered." "Three years." "I know. That's why I bought you something." Ava handed him the card and box that she'd hid in her purse. He opened it and saw the poem Ava had written. "This is beautiful." Ava smirked. "You really want to know that badly?" Ava nodded. He kissed her. "This is part of it," he teased. "Joe, seriously." He kissed her. "Stop worrying. You'll love it." "You know I'm going to figure it out." "Nope." They brought dinner in, then once dinner was done they headed down to the show. He opened the gift on the way. "Babe." "To remind you." It was a bracelet that looked like rings. Subtle enough, and meant more than anything.

They walked in and the guys were laughing. "Seriously, I want to know," Ava said. Joe kissed her then they headed to the meet and greet. Ava touched her makeup up, then the guys came back in. They were laughing. "Someone is telling me or I'm going," Ava said. "Happy anniversary," Ryan and Brad said as they hugged them. "Seriously." "Just let the man do his thing," Brad whispered. They chilled a while and had a drink, then Joe pulled Ava into the dressing room. "Where are we going?" He closed the door and kissed her. "Still no hint?" He kissed her again. "You'll know soon enough."

The guys went on. They sang one or two they hadn't sung in a while, then Ava came out. "So just so y'all know, it's Joe and Ava's anniversary today." The crowd roared. "So we decided she needed a little surprise." Ava looked at Joe and he was smiling a huge smile. "Can you believe these guys won't give me a hint," Ava said. "Hint number one," Brad said. The spotlight hit the front row. The security man handed her a single red rose with a note:

Where you were when I first saw you.

Ava smirked. "Everyone knows I have the most romantic husband in the planet right," Ava said. The girls in the crowd screamed. "We all know Ava used to be a big fan. That's the exact seat she was in when he first saw her." "Guys, can we get back to the music," Ava asked. They sang a song or two, then Joe slid his hand in hers. He put a note in her hand and kissed her. They sang one last song, then Ava slid off stage. She looked at the note:

Where we had our first kiss.

CHAPTER 45

She looked at him, still smiling. She watched another song or two, and he kissed her when he grabbed his other guitar. "Guess." He kissed her and Ava went down to the dressing room. She saw a small box with a note. She opened the box and found diamond earrings. She put them on, then looked at the note:

> I've loved you since the day 8 years ago when we first met. I looked in those eyes and knew that somehow, someday, you were going to make me the happiest man in the world. Now we have Grace and Blake, a home, and each other. There's nothing else we could ask for. I'll love you today, tomorrow, and every day for the rest of our lives. I've never loved anyone more. You're surprise is where you belong. No it's not the house, and it isn't in your office. The one place you belong forever.

Ava wiped a tear away and walked back to side stage. He looked over at her. Ava blew him a kiss. He smiled. Ava watched the rest of the concert. When they came off the stage, Joe kissed Ava and they headed down to the sitting room. "Well?" Ava motioned for him to follow her. "What?" She wrapped her arms around him and kissed him. "First guess?" Ava nodded. Joe kissed her. "You're good." "I know." "Figure out what the present was," Joe asked. Ava nodded. She kissed him. "And it's the right size and everything," Ava teased. He slid an envelope out of his back pocket and handed it to her. "What's this?" "Something." Ava smirked. She opened it. It was the picture of the two of them from the day she first met him. Ava looked at him. "Where did you find this?" "One of the guys from the website helped the guys and I find it," Joe said. Ava wrapped her arms around him. "You were in my arms then and I didn't know what I had. Now, I'm never letting you go."

They went back into the sitting room and Ryan handed them each a glass of champagne. "You two knew about this," Ava asked. "See, I told you she was gonna cry," Brad teased. "You guys knew all along?" "Ava, he was so excited when they found the picture, he could barely contain himself." "I can't believe they found this," Ava said. "I'm surprised you didn't have it." "I do." "What?" "I have it." Ava pulled her wallet out and handed him a faded version of the picture, folded to just show the two of them. "You had this and never told me," Joe said. "Everyone has secrets Joe." Ryan laughed. "You two seriously are too funny for words," Brad said. They curled up together on the sofa and finished their champagne, then headed back to the hotel.

"So this is why I was going this weekend," Ava asked. "And why Rose said she'd look after the kids." "You had this all planned out." Joe nodded. "It was a good surprise." "See why I couldn't tell you," he said. "Do you like the bracelet," Ava asked. He kissed her. "One ring for every time I've kissed you." "This month." They laughed. "This was the perfect way to celebrate," Joe said. "So you're not mad I dragged you this weekend?" They hopped out and headed inside. "Ava." They walked down the hall and into their room. "You can't actually be mad," Joe said. Ava kissed him. It was so hot, they both started over-heating. He had her in the bedroom minutes later. She kicked her heels off. "Guess you're not mad," Joe said. "Not for this." He kissed her. "Babe." "Mm." "Happy Anniversary." "Happy Anniversary Joe." He kissed her again. He motioned towards the side table. There was a bottle of champagne with two glasses, strawberries and whipped cream. "And who's idea was that," Ava asked. "That one wasn't me." "The hotel probably." "I still can't believe you had that picture." "What do you think I used to help me write the other books," Ava asked. "Seriously?" Ava nodded. "Always had it close by." "Tired," Joe asked. Ava shook her head. "Still can't believe you wore the dress." "You thought I'd wear the less revealing one didn't you," Ava asked. He nodded. "This one was just for you." "And I love every inch of the woman in it." He kissed her and they curled up together on the bed.

"Still wired aren't you?" Ava nodded. "I know you are, and I know you can think of a million things to do to zap what's left of your energy," Ava teased. He laughed. "No wonder we got married. You can practically read my mind," Joe said. "Truth be told, I miss the kids already." "You and me both. Did sort of miss the crazy stuff we used to do when it was just us." "Like what?" "Like when we'd take off for a few days and had nothing to worry about at home." "And?" "Stay in bed all day." Ava smirked. "We still can't do that." "You have a point," Joe said. "Joe, not that much has changed. Only difference is, we have two adorable little kids that love us unconditionally. Someone to tuck into bed instead of each other." "We have to put this dress to good use," Joe said. "What are you suggesting?" He pulled her into his arms. "We're going out." "Where?" "Don't care. I'm showing my wife off." Ava laughed. He kissed her. They got up and he kissed her again. Ava slid her heels on and they took off.

An hour later, they were dancing on the dance floor with nobody bothering them. They had a drink or two, then a slower jam came on. "Ava." She looked at him with the eyes that had him wanting to carry her out the door. He kissed her. "What?" "Had enough sharing for the night." She kissed him, then took his hand and led him outside. They got back to the hotel, and he had the dress off before they even made it to the bed. Ava peeled his shirt off, and he picked her up, while she wrapped her legs around him. "Now this is how we should've spent our anniversary," Joe said. Ava kissed him and he leaned her onto the bed. He slid his jeans off and slid into her arms. She loved him something fierce. They'd always had the magnetism. The passion had always been there since they'd first met. She'd felt it, and so had he. The first time he'd kissed her, it had rocked him to his soul. The first time they were together, it was fireworks, and it had been every day since. Tonight was no different, except that it was better, more intense, more passionate, more everything than back in the beginning.

"Tell me we're going to be like this forever," Joe said. "You don't need me to say it." "And tell me why it took us so long to get together?" "You and you're playing the field thing. We met. We knew then. We just weren't ready for it," Ava said. "You mean back in the days when I was blind?" Ava laughed and nodded. "Back in the days where we were different people." "If I'd known them what I know now, I would've married you the day of that first concert," Joe said. "Probably still would've given you a hard time." "Nah. Would've talked you out of that." "Nope." "Still stubborn." "Still sexy." "Mm." Ava kissed him and slid her leg over his hip. "Ava." "What?" "I wouldn't do that if I were you," Joe said. "Do what?" She nuzzled his ear. "You want sleep or not?" "Have tomorrow for that." "Funny." She kissed his neck. "You are so in for it," Joe said. He pinned her to the bed and kissed her. "What?" "Tease." "That's why you love me." He kissed her again as their tongues wrestled, and their hearts raced.

The next morning, Ava and Joe got up, Starbucks in hand, showered, refilled their coffee, then got changed and went down to meet the guys. "So how was your night," Brad asked. "Awesome as always." Ryan laughed. "What?" "You got the extra bold Starbucks didn't you," Ryan teased. Joe nodded. They headed for the airport. "How much sleep you two actually get," Brad asked. "Enough," Joe joked. Ava was yawning. "Where we off to?" "Toronto." "Great." "You two have 3 hours," Brad said. Joe laughed. "What are you two giggly about," Ryan asked. "Nothing." "Well, one thing's for sure. You two had a good night." Ava cuddled up to Joe. "So I had an idea about that other song we were working on," Ryan said. "Which one," Joe asked. "The one Ava's singing on." "You volunteering me for something else," Ava asked. "Of course. Good inspiration having a sexy blonde on stage with us," Joe said as he kissed her. Ava laughed. They pulled into the airport. They went through security quickly, then hopped on the plane.

"So what you think Ava. You up for another song?" "I'd wait." "Could work on it on the plane." Ava curled up with Joe. He pulled his guitar out, and they started playing around with it. Brad grabbed his guitar. "Here's the deal. I sing that, Joe sings Like Me." Ryan looked at him. "Negotiator," Brad said. "And I always win." "Fine. Deal but you have to sit on stage with me while I sing it. Ava nodded. The guys started playing and they went over the song a few times. Joe was teary-eyed by the end of the song. "Wow," Ryan said. Joe wiped the tears from his eyes. "So here's my next question. What have you decided I'm wearing tonight," Ava asked. Ryan looked at Joe and so did Brad. "The white one," Ryan said. "Did I pack it?" Joe nodded. "Tell me you didn't plan any other surprises." Joe smirked. "Are you serious?" He laughed. "Full of surprises remember?" Ryan and Brad laughed. "I have to say, I'm glad you two are so happy. After everything, I'm glad you two found each other," Ryan said. "Me too," Joe said kissing Ava's temple. "I remember when he told me that you were coming to the show. It was like Christmas morning to a kid. He was so excited." "We had to make him call you," Brad said. "Oh really." "I dialed and handed him the phone," Ryan said. "Thought I'd say no," Ava asked. ""All I knew was that if you said yes, I was going to be the happiest man in the entire arena." "Good thing I said yes then." He wrapped his arm around Ava pulling her close and kissed her.

They relaxed the rest of the flight. Joe and Ava napped. As soon as the plane landed, Ava was awake. "We have to go through customs again," Ryan said. The officer came on board and did their checks, then they headed to the hotel. "I'm calling the kids," Ava said. "Party pooper." Ava laughed. "Hi Mama," Grace said. "Hey baby girl. I miss you. How are you?" "We playing." "What you playing?" "House." "You having fun?" "Miss you and Daddy." "We miss you too baby. Is Auntie Rose there?" "Hi Ava," Rose said. "Hey. How's Mama?" "Good. Just put Blake down for his nap." "I hope they aren't being any trouble." "Blake is the easiest baby in the planet. Grace and Jacob are having a blast." "Rose." "Yep." "Thank you for everything." "For what?" "You know what," Ava said. "It was totally him." "I know." "Wait until you see what he planned for tonight." "Another night of little sleep I assume," Ava joked. "Ava, enjoy every second of it. After what you've gone through with him, you two deserve it."

Ava and Joe got settled in, they all had lunch, then headed down to the arena for sound check. Ava laughed when they pulled in. "What?" "Nothing," Ava said. "Ava." Ava looked at Joe. "What?" "Remember when you did the tour from the third CD?" Joe nodded. "You did a show here." "And how would you have . . . ." Ava sat down in the seat that she had that night. Joe looked at her. "Seriously?" Ava nodded. "I saw you that night," Joe said. Ava nodded. "Came back to see you guys," Ava said. "That's when you handed me your phone number. You stuck it in my pocket." "And you never called," Ava said. "See, if you'd done it back then, you'd be the old married guy," Ryan teased. "I barely remember it. I just remember staring at you," Joe said. "Most of the concert. Oddly enough, I still have the shirt," Ava said. Brad laughed. "It was definitely fate when you walked in that night," Joe said. "Tell me about it," Ryan said.

They did sound check, ran through the new song again, then got changed to do an interview or two. After, they headed back to the hotel and Joe and Ava had a nap. Around 4, there was a knock at the door. Joe walked in with a box and handed it to Ava. "What's this?" "Don't know," Joe teased kissing her. She opened it and saw a small blue box with white ribbon. "Joe." "What?" "What did you do?" "I had to." Ava opened the box. Inside was a diamond bracelet with a white gold heart hanging from it. "It's beautiful," Ava said. "See, that's why I had to." "I already got what I wanted you know." "Which was?" "You." "I saw it and I had to." "It's beautiful." "You're wearing it tonight." "Whatever you want." "Mm. Now that I could use to my advantage," Joe said. "Good." "Babe." "Yes I meant it." "Tease." "Nope." Ava kissed him, then got into the shower. Within minutes he had his arms wrapped around her under the hot water.

They finally headed back to meet the guys. They had dinner, followed by flowers, then got changed. Joe snuck in to sit with Ava while she was getting her makeup done. "What?" "Nothin." "I love you too." He smiled. "Do I get to see the dress on," Joe asked. "When I come on stage." "Ava." "Mr. Surprises has to wait." They finished makeup and Ava went in and sat with Joe before the meet and greet. "We're staying home tonight," Joe said. Ava nodded. "Don't think you're getting all that beauty sleep. You don't need it," Joe said. "And just what else have you planned?" He smiled. "Fine. Then I'm not telling you what your surprise is either," Ava said. "What surprise?" Ava stuck her tongue out at him. "I told you once not to stick it out unless you're gonna use it." Ava kissed him. "You two still at it," Ryan teased. "She's planning something." Ryan smirked. "It's only fair," Brad said. "See," Ava replied. "Guys, time to go." He kissed Ava and they headed off to the meet and Greet. Ava went and did her hair, with a little help, then put her surprise into action.

Ava came out when it came to do her songs. "So I have a surprise for you ladies. I talked someone into a song or two. Anyone remember the song Like Me," Ava asked. The crowd went nuts. "You know the louder you cheer, the easier it'll be to talk him into it." The crowd was screaming. "Well?" "Nice negotiation," Joe teased. The ladies went crazy and Ryan was laughing. Once the song was done, he walked over towards Ava. "So now that you heard me, you get our new song. One of Ava's favorites. It's called Forever in your arms." The crowd went crazy. They made it through another song. "So I guess you all know it's our anniversary this weekend. The last one for you means you have to hold someone close. Come on ladies. Pull that handsome man close. This was our wedding song," Joe said. Ava and Joe sang 'You' then Ava slipped off the stage sliding something in his pocket. He kissed her and Ava walked to the back. She left him a note in his guitar case that he never made a move without. Then left and headed back to the hotel.

They came off stage and she was gone. He looked at the note in his pocket:

Remember the look in my eyes the moment I met you? What's the one thing that you hold almost as close as me?

Joe laughed. "She playing the game now," Brad teased. "She's going to drive me nuts."

He walked over and saw the note on the edge of his guitar case.

The one thing you love more than music, more than the guys. Come get it.

He laughed. "What?" "Nothing." He called her. No answer. "Guys," Joe said. "Go." Joe took off for the hotel. He walked into the room and saw the candles. He looked into the bedroom and saw her heels. There was a note on the bed:

When you light those candles, up there on the mantel setting the mood.

He slid his shirt off and heard a door. He turned and saw Ava in the black lace teddy he loved. She handed him a cold beer. "Babe." "What?" "How did you know?" "Better than champagne." He put it down and slid his arms around her pulling her close to him.

"Figure it out?" "What?" "Remember the look?" He nodded. Ava handed him an envelope. "What's this?" "Your anniversary gift." "You gave me the bracelet." "That was part of it." He slid the paper from the envelope and saw pictures. They were soft, sexy, and had a smile across his face in seconds. "So that's what you've been up to." Ava nodded. "Wow." "For when I'm not here," Ava said. "You're always going to be here." "In your heart." "Babe." "When I'm not with you in bed." "Definitely not letting the guys see these," Joe joked. "For you. Look in the bottom of the envelope." He grabbed something from the bottom. There was a picture of Joe with Blake, one of Ava and Grace, one of Ava with the kids, and one of Grace and Blake, along with wallet size of the sexy shots. "Damn." "So you remember why you need to come home," Ava asked. "You know Grace has your eyes." "That's why I said it." "We make beautiful kids." Ava nodded. He kissed her.

"Now as for this," he said as his hands slid down her back and cupped her backside. "Mm?" "You can't just walk around in this. We have to make good use of it." "Thought you'd never ask," Ava teased. He kissed her and leaned her onto their bed. His phone rang 5 minutes later. He threw it onto the pillow and made love to Ava. When his phone went off again, Ava grabbed it and looked at the caller. He pulled it out of her hand and kissed her.

They curled up together on the bed after, surrounded by candles. "Who called," Ava asked. He grabbed the phone. "Cat." "Why would she be calling your cell?" "Good point," Joe said. Ava grabbed the phone and Joe spooned her. "Hey Cat." "Hey honeymooner." "Funny.

How are you?" "Good. Happy anniversary." "Thanks. What you two up to," Ava asked. "Waiting for you two to come down for a drink." "What?" "Get your butt downstairs. We're going out."

A half-hour later, Ava and Joe came back downstairs. "About time. Let's go," Cat said. "Where?" They headed off to a dance club. They walked in and went straight to the VIP. Will bought Ava and Joe a drink and they sat down. "What are you doing here," Joe asked. "We decided to surprise you. You two were great tonight by the way," Cat said. "You were there?" Will nodded. "Second row." "You should've told us." Cat pulled Ava off to the ladies room. "What's the real reason," Ava teased. "He wanted to talk to Joe." "For what?" "He said you'd know. You filling me in or are you letting my imagination make a decision," Cat asked. "It's nothing. They got in a fight at the bachelor party." "Oh." "So how are you two doing," Cat asked. "Better. Still love him." "That's a good sign." "Remember when you told me about the numb knees?" Ava nodded. "Definitely hereditary," Cat joked. They both laughed. "I missed you," Ava said. "I missed you too." They came out and Joe and Will looked pissed off. "Come on," Ava said. "What?" "Dance floor," Ava said pulling Joe to his feet.

They headed to the crowded dance floor, danced until they got tired, then went back to the table. "You still being cranky," Ava asked. "We'll talk about it when we get back." "What now?" "He starts this shit on our damn anniversary." Ava kissed him. "Remember one thing. You're the only man I want to kiss. All yours forever." He kissed her again. Will and Cat came back over to the table. "Could spot you two a mile off," Cat joked. "What do you want from us? It is our anniversary remember," Joe said. Cat handed something to Ava. "What?" "For you two." "Cat." "No I didn't get it at the adult shop," Cat teased. Ava opened it and saw two keychains with pictures of the kids that Cat had taken. "These are beautiful." "I took them a while ago. That day where I looked after them for you." "Thanks Cat," Ava said. Joe hugged her. They hung out a while longer, then Joe and Ava headed back. "What time you guys heading out tomorrow," Will asked. "Heading home at 8am." "Ava, call me tomorrow once you're settled," Cat asked. Ava nodded and hugged Cat goodbye. "Ava." Will walked towards her. "What?" "I'm sorry," Will said. "Thanks." "I mean it. I shouldn't have been such a jackass." "Got that right," Joe said. "Friends?" "We'll see," Ava replied. He hugged Ava. Just the look on Will's face told Joe it was all just a façade. He still wanted her, but Joe knew that he was the only man she loved. They headed back to the hotel then straight into the elevator.

The minute they got back in the room, they were back to normal. Joe had his arms around Ava, trying to tease her and she was joking around with him. "Babe." "Mm." "You realize in six hours, we're back to being grownups." Ava laughed. "I know. Kinda miss those people." "We should get something for Rose on the way home." "Already taken care of,"

Ava said. "What?" "A massage. Mommy time." "Good idea." "Thought you'd think so." "So what we doing before we turn back into grownups?" Ava turned towards him. "Hmm." He kissed her. The look on his face said he knew what she was thinking. "You know, this dress looks sexy as hell on you," Joe said. "I know what you're hinting at." "I still can't believe you did that." "You know it was for you," Ava said. "If he'd noticed, you would've been in trouble." "Didn't want the line." "If Ryan had known." Just the thought that she was on stage in nothing but the dress, shoes and bra had him hot and bothered all over again. He kissed her and picked her up, peeling her heels off, and leaning her onto their bed. Ava helped him with his shirt and she threw it into the suitcase. His phone went off again. "We are so totally turning them off," Joe said. Ava slid her arms around him and slid the phone from his pocket. "And why would she be calling?" "Who," he asked kissing her neck. Ava pushed him away. She handed the phone to him.

"Hey Jodi." "You come into town and you don't even tell me," Jodi said. "We're busy." "Doing? Joe, she really have you on that short of a leash?" "Why the hell are you always causing shit?" "Because. You need a reality slap." "We're celebrating our anniversary." "You mean you two are still together?" "Never going to be apart ever." "Figured you'd be tired of the playing house by now." "I have to go." "I'll meet you for breakfast," Jodi said. "We're leaving at 8am. Maybe never." Joe hung up and walked over to Ava. "Just go to bed," Ava said. "No. She's not ruining our night." "Already did." Ava washed her face and went to slide on her pajamas when Joe slid up behind her. "What?" "Don't need them," he said. "Joe, just go." He kissed her neck. "What?" He walked her back into the bedroom. "Joe, moment was ruined." "Nope." She shook her head. "Phones are off. Only way anyone can call us is if it's the guys or Rose," Joe said. "Joe." He slid the shoulder of the dress off. "One last night of us. No fighting allowed," he said. His arms held her close. He kissed from her shoulder, up her neck to her ear. "Ava." "Yes." "Still mad?" "Depends." She turned to face him. "Depends on what?" "What time is it," Ava asked. "Doesn't matter." "Good answer." He kissed her and they curled up together on the bed. "You know, you're wearing too many clothes for bed," Ava said. He kicked his jeans off. He slid Ava's dress off. "So are you."

The next morning, after a few hours of sleep, they grabbed breakfast to go and they headed for the plane. They all slept the entire way back. Ava and Joe hopped off, packed up the SUV, then the guys headed off. They went and grabbed something for the kids, then called Emily. "Grace and Blake are asleep at home. You guys heading back," she asked. "See you soon," Ava said.

CHAPTER 46

"How did it go," Emily asked. "It went great. How were the kids?" "They were good. Blake was a little fussy, but I put on the CD you told me to and he calmed right down." "And what CD was that," Joe asked. "The one of the song you always sing to them." "Thought of everything." Ava nodded and he kissed her. "Looks like you two had a good weekend." "It went pretty good," Ava said. "Ava, I need your advice on something." Joe kissed Ava. He went and unpacked, throwing in laundry and Ava sat down and made some tea for her and Emily.

"What's up?" "I was out with him." "And?" "If I'm over-reacting tell me." "Where did you go?" "It was a party with some of the people from the record label." "And?" "I met someone." "Who?" "His name is Mike." "Not Mike Andrews." "He's such a nice guy." "I know Mike. You're better off with Jeff." "What's wrong with him?" "Remember what your auntie said about Joe?" She nodded. "Multiply it by ten." "But you and Joe." "We're the fluke," Ava said. "He's hot." "I know. Trust me. He may look like a gentleman, but he's a dog." "We went out last night." "Were you trying to piss Jeff off?" "I admit it. I kind of liked him begging." "Whatever you do, think about what you're doing before you do it. Don't get into something you know is going to get you hurt." "He kissed me. I still have butterflies." "So you like him?" Emily nodded. "Make sure you make the right decision okay? I don't want to have to come save you." "I still like Jeff too." "It's hereditary," Ava said. Joe came into the TV room and slid onto the sofa behind Ava. "What's hereditary?" "Nothing." "Liar," Joe said. "She has a thing for two guys." "It's the Morgan genes." "Thank god you grew out of them then," Ava teased. He kissed her cheek and wrapped her arms around her.

They chatted a while, and Emily refused to tell Joe who the other guy was. The kids woke up a half-hour later. Grace came walking down the stairs rubbing her eyes. Joe snuck up behind her. "Grace." "Daddy!" She wrapped her arms tight around his neck and leaned her head on his shoulder. "How was your sleepover?" "I missed you." "We found something for you." "What?" Joe handed her a stuffed animal that she'd been talking about for days.

"Thank you Daddy." She kissed his cheek. "Thank Mama. She found it." She ran to Ava and jumped into her lap. "Hi Mama." "Hi baby girl. You like the frog?" She nodded and hugged Ava. "I missed you too baby." Joe slid onto the sofa behind Ava. "Mama." "Yes baby." "Happy Avinersary." Joe laughed. "Thanks baby girl." She kissed Joe and Ava, then curled up in Ava's lap. "You have fun with Jacob." Grace nodded hugging her frog.

They relaxed with Grace a bit, then Jacob woke up. "I'll get him," Ava said. Grace curled up with Joe and Ava went to get Blake. "Well hello there handsome." Ava changed him, made him giggle, then came downstairs with him. "He can sit up by himself for a few minutes now," Emily said. "I noticed. He's growing up." Just as Ava went to sit down, the phone rang.

"Hi Kate." "How was the show?" "Good. How goes the house hunt?" "I have some good news. Remember that house you two looked at that you fell in love with?" "The one that we saw when we were driving through?" "It's up for sale. They just posted it today." "Are you serious?" "You have an appointment at 10 tomorrow morning." "And?" "What you just saw is just the icing." "Kate." "Exactly what you wanted and more." "Who's house was it?" "A record producer. It was his summer place." "Wow." "And the view is amazing," Kate said. "We'll meet you there at quarter to." "See you tomorrow."

"What," Joe asked. "Nothing." "You are so full of it." "Later." "Ava, you know the suspense will kill me." "Good." "Where going," Grace asked. "Daddy and I are house shopping." "Why?" "So that we can take care of you and your little brother." "I like my room." "I know. So do I. Daddy did good." Grace nodded. Joe wrapped his arms around her. "Where is it," Emily asked. "A few hours from here. It's quiet, and has a lot more privacy." "Wow." "Bigger room for you and your own bathroom." "Don't worry about me," Emily said. "You're family," Joe said. She looked at her watch. "Why are you watching the clock," Ava asked. "I'm meeting him." "Where?" "We're going to a movie." "Who," Joe asked. Emily looked at Ava. "Black top and blue jeans with the black boots." "Can you help with the hair?" Ava nodded. Emily ran off to get changed.

They played with the kids a bit, then Ava went upstairs and did Emily's hair. "Emm," Ava said. "I know." "Remember what I told you about Jeff?" She nodded. "Goes double for Mike." "Ava, he's a good man." "I'm saying, just don't rush it." "I know. If he kisses me like that again, I think my knees may give." "Just take your time." Ava added an umph to Emily's makeup, then finished her hair and Emily took off to dinner and a movie with Mike.

Ava made dinner for them, then fed the kids. Grace played with her frog all the way through dinner, then for a while after dinner while they were cleaning up. "I didn't think she'd love it that much," Joe said. "One of her favorite shows." "You gonna tell me who she is out with," Joe asked. Ava shook her head. "You know I have ways of getting the info out of you." He leaned against her at the sink. "Go sit with the kids," Ava said. "8:30 you're mine." Ava laughed. He kissed her neck, then went into the TV room with Blake. The kids played a while. Ava took Grace upstairs for her bath, then after she splashed around a while, Ava tucked her in. "Mama." "Yes baby." "I glad you home." "Me too. I missed you." "Me missed you too." Ava kissed Grace and hugged her. "Daddy song?" Grace nodded. Joe came in. "You sure," he asked. She nodded. He sang to her a bit while Ava gave Blake a bath then fed him and put him down for the night. Joe snuck out a little while later and came into their bedroom.

"Hey," he said sliding his arms around Ava. "Hey yourself." "Tell me." "Tell you what?" "Ava." "You'll see tomorrow," she said. "Tell me it isn't about that house you loved." "It isn't," Ava said. "Liar." "We're going to see it tomorrow," Ava said. "Seriously?" Ava nodded. He kissed her. "Like a kid at Christmas I tell you." "Only one present I want," Joe said. "I bet." He kissed her and pulled her close. "Only one thing I want more than that house." "Which is?" He kissed her again. "Good thing I like you too." He laughed and hugged her. "Couldn't get rid of me if you tried," Joe said. "Oh darn." He kissed her again. Ava heard a car. "Stay here for a second." "Babe." "Shh." Ava snuck downstairs and heard her at the door with Mike.

"You sure you don't want company?" "I'm sure. You have to get up early tomorrow." He kissed her. "Mike, seriously. I have to go in." "Better idea." He kissed her again and pinned her to the brick at the front door. "Mike." "Just come back to my place." "Not tonight," Emily said. "Pack a bag for tomorrow night then." He kissed her again. "I have to be back in the morning. I can't stay." "Emm, they can take care of the kids themselves." "Those kids are my family." "I'll bring you back by six o'clock." "I'll let you know. That's all I can do," Emily said. He kissed her again. "I have to go in." "Intentionally teasing me now." "Good at it." "Damn right you are. Fine. I'll come get you tomorrow after dinner. Then I'm getting you all to myself." He kissed her and she slid inside.

"Ava," Emily said coming inside. Ava came out of the kitchen, vitamin water in hand. "Hey. How was the date?" "You were right." "Thought so." "And I saw a note at the door for Joe." She handed it to Ava. "You going out with him again," Ava asked. "Might need pepper spray." Ava laughed. "There's some industry party thing tomorrow. Joe's supposed to go," Emily said. "Hadn't heard anything about it." "They said the guys were playing there tomorrow." "Okay." Emily ran up to her room and Ava looked at the note:

Joe,

I'll talk to you at the party tomorrow night. We really need to talk. You told me not to call, so I won't. When you can get a few minutes, call me. Please. It's important. I swear I am not trying to cause another fight between you two.

Tiff.

Ava walked upstairs and changed for bed, then slid into bed and turned her light off. "Ava." "What?" "You okay," Joe asked. "Fine." "Why do I get the feeling you're pissed off?" Ava handed the note to him, then went downstairs into her office and locked the door. She curled up on the sofa with her laptop and did some writing, then turned it off and went to sleep. A few hours later, Ava heard the office door open. He walked in and sat down on the floor beside the sofa, leaning his back onto it. "What?" "I forgot about the party," Joe said. "Joe, just go to bed." "I can't sleep." "What did she want?" "It's her daughter's fourth birthday this weekend." "So?" "She wanted me to come to the party." "Have fun then." "Ava. Stop." "You can go by yourself. Have a blast." She went to get up and Joe pinned her to the sofa. "Let go." "Ava, stop thinking what I know you are. I'm not going." "Fine. Don't." She managed to get up and she walked off.

Ava grabbed an ice water from the kitchen. "You know, at some point, you have to stop assuming that I'm going to walk out." "Didn't say you were. Just said have fun at the party. I'm not going." "You have to." "Says who? I'm staying home with my kids," Ava said. "You're seriously starting this now?" Ava nodded. She heard Blake wake up. She walked upstairs, then rocked him in the rocking chair and fed him. "Ava, seriously. Stop this." "I would if the crap would stop," she said. "She said it was important that I was there." "Then you better go running." Blake fussed and could tell there was tension. He sat down on the chair beside her. Blake finally calmed down, and Ava got him back to sleep. She tucked him back into his crib, then went back to head downstairs. Joe picked her up and walked into their bedroom, locking the door behind him. "Put me down," Ava said. He put her on the bed. He leaned into her. "Joe, stop." "You going to stop thinking that I'm going to walk out?" "Prove me wrong then." He kissed her. Every time they were fighting he wanted her even more. Something about the fire in her eyes. Now was no different. Ava got away and walked back downstairs.

The next morning, Ava woke up, showered, then made sure Emily was up with the kids and left. Joe came walking downstairs as she was pulling out of the street. "Where's Ava," Joe asked. "She just left." "To go where?" "She said she was meeting Kate." He poured himself a coffee, then went upstairs and showered and changed. He called Ava, but she refused to answer.

"I thought Joe was coming with you," Kate asked. "Long story." "Well, come on in then." She showed Ava around. Everything they asked for was under one roof. "And, there's a recording studio downstairs which I know Joe and the guys will make good use of." There was even a workout room. There was a huge downstairs living room, and a play area for the kids. They went upstairs and Ava saw the master bedroom. It had a balcony that was the full length of the back of the house. Everything was beautiful. Lots of room for the kids, plus, there was a big bedroom and private bathroom for Emily. It really was perfect. "So?" "He's going to love this house," Ava said. Kate's phone went off. "Hey Joe. We were just talking about you." "Can I talk to Ava for a minute? Her phone battery's probably dead again," Joe said. She handed the phone to Ava. "Yep." "I'm half way there." "Good." "It's what we thought isn't it." "Better." "Wait for me." "Can't." "Ava, please." "I'll meet you at home." She handed the phone back to Kate. "She loves the house doesn't she," Joe said. "Think so." "I'll be there in a half-hour. Just keep her there." "Okay."

A half-hour later of chatting with Kate and Joe was walking in. Ava walked outside. Kate showed Joe around. "Give us a few minutes," Joe asked. Kate nodded and went into the office to make a call or two. He walked outside and sat down beside Ava. "Well?" Ava got up and went to walk back inside. He pulled her into his lap. "Let go." "We letting it go or keeping it Ava," Joe asked. "I'll stay here. You stay there." She got up and walked out the front door. She saw her car but not his. She got in. She called Cat. "Hey." "Girls night," Ava said. "Can't. We're going to that party tonight. Aren't you guys supposed to be there?" "I'm not going." "Ava." "Cat." "Just go. We'll leave from there," Cat said. "No." "That bad?" Silence. "I'll meet you at your place." "Three hours." "Looking at the dream house," Cat asked. "It's perfect." "See you at 1:30." Ava hung up as Joe walked towards the SUV. He hopped in and pulled out, heading to the park nearby.

"We're talking," Joe said. "No we aren't." "Ava, I'm not going to that party if we're fighting." "Fine." She got out and walked. He hopped out and went after her. "Ava." "What?" "Stop." "Have fun at the party Joe. Go. Even better, why don't you take Tiffany as your date," Ava said. He pulled her to him and kissed her. "Let go." He kissed her again and leaned her against a tree. "Stop fighting with me," Joe said. "You want to go with her then go." "I want to go with you. Nobody else." "Just go with her." Ava tried to get away but he wouldn't let her. "I'm going with you. End of discussion." "I'm not going." "Yes you are." "Let me go." "No," he said. "Joe, let go." "I'm not letting you go until you get it through your head." "I did. You called her before you came downstairs. It's crystal clear." Ava got away and walked off and went and got back into the SUV. They drove back to the house and Ava was silent.

They got back to the house and he leaned over to try and talk to her and she got out. She went inside. He took a deep breath, then went to go inside when his phone went off. "We have sound check at 5," Ryan said. "I'll meet you there." "You okay?" "Fine." Joe hung up. He walked inside and saw Ava walking into her office. "I'm just taking the kids to the pool," Emily said. "Thanks Emm," Joe said. "You two alright?" "Working on it." "You going to the party tonight," Emily asked. "We're performing." "Joe, talk to her," Emily said. "I'm trying." He unlocked the door and walked into the office. "We're talking until this is done." "It is done." "Ava." "What? You're going with Tiffany. I'm staying here with the kids so Emily can go with Mike. Have fun," Ava said. "You're being ridiculous." "No I'm not. Go." Ava went to walk out and he pulled her back to him. "There's only one woman I am going to that party with and she's right in front of me." "I'm not going," Ava said. "Ava, I want you to come with me." "I'm not going." "Ava, I need you there." "Oh well." Ava walked off. Cat was at the door. Ava went to walk out. "You're not going anywhere." "I'm going out to the gym," she said. "Ava." "What?" "I'll meet you here at six." "We'll see." "Cat, she isn't back by six, then you know I'll figure out where you are," Joe said. "I'll get her home. She needs chill time." Ava left with Cat, gym bags in hand.

"What are you two fighting about now," Cat asked. "Tiffany left him a note last night. When he realized I'd read it, he called her, then came down to me." "Ooh." "Exactly." "Ava, you can't let him go without you." "I'm not going. I'm not competing with someone who's practically a damn wet dream to the male population," Ava said. "Then we need to find you a dress that will make his knees give way." "No." "Ava, you have to. I know you don't want to lose him." "Whatever." "Don't you dare whatever me." They went to the gym, worked out, showered and changed, then Cat dragged Ava to the mall. They went through a few stores, then Cat spotted a dress. "I'm not even trying that on," Ava said. "Yeah you are." "Cat." She pushed her into the change room. Ava came out a few minutes later. "Holy shit," Cat said. "Cat, it's too much." "Trust me. It's perfect." It was short, sheer through the torso except for the sparkles, showed off the curves, low in the right places, with two strings of Swarovski crystal on the base of the back. "What's the point," Ava said. "You're going. He can drool over you all night like all the other guys in the room will be." Cat was hinting. "Good point." "Exactly," Cat said. Ava found a pair of silver sparkle stilettos to go with it. Ava called Jacquie. "What's up?" "Party." "Come on by." They left and Ava got ready. Cat went back to the house and dropped off her gym bag. "Where is she," Joe asked. "At our place." "Cat." "I'll get her to go." "Blake," Joe said. "Two bottles in the bag." "Cat, I need her there." "I'll get her there."

Joe got changed and tucked the kids in. "Where's Mama," Grace asked. "She's with Auntie Cat." "Mama coming home?" "We'll be home in a few hours." Grace hugged him. "Sweet dreams baby." Grace was asleep when he left. He got down to the party and met up with the guys. "Where's Ava?" "She's coming with Cat," Joe said. "Cat's here," Brad said. He walked down towards Cat. "Hey. How are you," Cat said. "Where is she?" "She's here. I saw her talking to Jeff a minute or two ago." Joe looked around then saw a woman in a dress that seriously had him turned on.

The dress was white and silver, and showed off her legs. It was almost backless, shy of the two miniscule straps barely holding it up. He couldn't take his eyes off her. He saw someone wrap their arm around her. She shrugged them off. She was obviously a tough as nails girl. Cat walked over to her and handed her a martini. Joe walked back over to Cat. "Who's that," Joe aked. "Who?" "The chick that you just handed the drink to." Cat smirked and walked off. Joe looked back over and saw her face. She was surrounded by men and had on Ava's wedding ring. He looked and realized it was Ava. He walked over.

"Excuse me guys. I need to talk to my wife for a minute," Joe said. He slid his hand in Ava's and pulled her away. "What?" "You look amazing." "You done," Ava asked. "No." He kissed her. "I love you." "Where's Tiffany?" "Don't care." He kissed her again. "Stop it," Ava said. "Ava." She walked off. Ryan walked over to him. "Tell me that was Ava." "She's still pissed." "She's about to get more pissed off." Tiffany walked over to him. "What," Joe asked. "I need to talk to you." "Then talk." "Somewhere quieter." "Not gonna happen." "I think she may be yours," Tiffany said. "What?" She handed him a picture. "She looks just like you." "Are you kidding me?" She shook her head.

Ava looked back and saw him with Tiffany. "Ava." Ryan walked up behind her. "What?" "You need to come with me," Ryan said. "No." "Ava, you need to." He grabbed her hand and walked back to the stage area. "Ryan, I need to go." "No. You're staying." "What for?" "Ava, you need to." "Why? He can just hang out with her for the night." "Ava, stop being so damn stubborn. He needs you." "And I need to be in a drama-free relationship." "Stop being a pain in the butt. Sit." "And do what? Watch them," Ava asked. "Look at me. Stop freaking out. He wants you. Stop being ridiculous." "I'm not sitting here and watching that." Ava walked off. Joe saw her heading towards the door and took off after her. Ava got in the car and left.

Ava called Rose. "Thought you were at the party." "Need out." "Where are you," Rose asked. "I'm coming to get you." "Ava." "We're going out." A little while later, Emily was with the kids and Ava and Rose were on their way to a party. They walked in and the guys flocked to Ava. A few hours later, and a few drinks on Ava's part, Ryan called Rose. "Where are you two?" "Zone." "I'll be there in a few with Joe." "She's snapped," Rose said. "I bet. She has a reason this time." Ava's phone went off. "Ava, it's Kate. I thought you should know, they accepted the offer. The house is yours." "Thanks Kate." "And I can drop off the keys on Sunday." "I'll meet you there," Ava said. "Everything okay," Kate asked. "Yep." "I'll see you Sunday. Let me know when you two are back." "I will." Ava hung up. Rose was looking at her. "What?" "Nothing." "You're so completely full of it." "Do you want to go," Rose asked. "Rose." "I'll take you back to the house." "What's going on?" They walked towards the door and left. "We're not moving until you tell me," Ava said. "You need to talk to Joe." "No I don't." "Yeah you do." "What aren't you saying?" "I'm taking you home."

Joe walked into the house. He went upstairs to the bedroom and saw Ava sitting on the bed in her black jeans and black sweater with her boots. "Ava." "We need to talk," she said. "Babe." "Don't touch me." "Ava, please." "What did she have to tell you?" "She's completely full of it." "Speak." "She isn't sure. She thinks that her daughter could be mine. I know she's wrong." Ava got up, grabbed her bag and went for the stairs. "Ava." "Don't," she said. "Ava." She walked down the stairs and out the front door. He went into Grace's bedroom to check on her and she was gone, so was Blake. He saw Ava pulling out of the driveway. He closed the gate. Ava got out and he walked towards her. "What is your problem," Ava asked. "Where are the kids?" "Emily is looking after them at Ryan and Rose's." "You're not leaving. We're talking." He grabbed her hand and the keys and went back inside the house. "Let go of my damn hand," Ava said. "No." "I'm not going to sit here and pretend that all of this is alright Joe." "Her daughter is 4." "A year older than Grace." "Exactly." "And your point is what," Ava asked. "Ava." "What? You have another daughter. Better go make sure that Tiffany is alright." Ava went to walk back out. "I get that you're hurt. I need you right now. I need my best friend. I need the woman I love," Joe said. "What if I can't do it?" He pulled her to him and kissed her, then picked her up with her legs around him and carried her upstairs. He leaned her onto their bed. "Babe." "What?" "You are the only one that matters to me." "Just let me go." "No. I love you." "I can't just sit here and deal with this," Ava said. "We're doing it together." "I'm not." "Ava." "I can't do this. I can't sit here and pretend that this doesn't hurt like hell. The one woman who's itching to get with you just happens to drop this bomb on you? No. I am not sitting here." She tried to get up and Joe pinned her. "Joe." "I'm scared too. I know damn well she's wrong. The only thing I know is that I'm not letting you walk away from me. I love you." "I'm not going to sit here while she injects herself into our lives." "Ava." "No." He kissed her and pulled her close. "Joe."

"Stay with me." Ava shook her head. "Ava." "I can't." "Ava." "Let go." "Babe." He kissed her again. Fine. She wanted him, but not if that was the price. "I can't do this." "Ava, we're doing it together. She's not going to be part of our lives. I know it's not mine. I know it isn't." "I am not going to be part of this," Ava said. "I love you. I need you right now. Please." "Joe." "I know it's not fair. I know it sucks. I love you. Please Ava." He wrapped his arms around her. "You promise me that the answer is no and that nobody is hearing a single thing about this. No news no nothing." He kissed her. "When do you get the test back," Ava asked. "They can do it in 24 hours." "Fine." "Babe." "Joe, I'm not going to sit here and let her in this house." "Fine." "I don't want the kids knowing." "Okay." "Anyone finds out, I'm leaving," Ava said. "Okay." "Let go." He let go and Ava got up and walked out the front door. She pulled the SUV back in and brought her bag in, then grabbed a drink and went and sat down outside.

Joe came out a little while later, giving her time to cool off. He walked outside and saw her crying. "Ava." "Just go back inside." "No." She wiped the tears away. "Ava." "Leave me alone." "No." He sat down beside her. "I know it's hard babe." "Joe, just leave me alone." Ava walked back inside and went and laid down on the sofa and turned a movie on. He walked inside, then went downstairs to his studio room and tried to work on some music. A few hours later, he heard footsteps. Ava walked in. "Hey." "Promise me it's not yours," Ava said. He kissed her, pulling her into his lap. "Joe." "I know it isn't. I promise you." "If it is . . ." "Ava, it's not. There's no way it could be." "Why?" "I may have been an idiot, but never went without protection." "Joe, don't just say what I want to hear." "Ava, I love you. The only person I haven't used anything with was you. I love you," he said. "I don't want to be blindsided." "Babe, you won't. I swear." "I mean it." He kissed her and slid his arms tight around her. She straddled him in the chair. "I love you. I don't want you crying," he said. "Joe, do you even know what this feels like? The one chick that's tried to break us up for years figured out a way in." He kissed Ava. "Nobody will ever break us Ava." "I really hope not." He kissed her again and a little while later, her shirt and his were on the floor. They were on the sofa, then his jeans hit the floor, then hers.

They were curled up together, hot, sweaty, and shivering. Ava slid the blanket from the back of the sofa on top of them. "Ava." "Mm." "You know you did look beautiful tonight," Joe said. "Thought you'd like it." "I barely even recognized you." "Hence why I got my hair done." "Tell me you're wearing that dress this weekend," he said. "For what?" He kissed her neck. "No I'm not." He kissed her again, then nibbled his way down her neck. "Joe, no." He kissed her again. "You have to." "Why?" "Because we are releasing the new song." "Joe, no." She felt his hand slide across her leg. "Don't you even think it." "Think what?" He teased Ava. "Joe." He kissed her again. "This is so not fair," Ava said. Her leg shook. "Joe, come on." One touch and literally he was as turned on as she was. They did it again, then Ava curled up with him with her leg around him. "I promised Grace I'd be home this weekend," Joe said. "Then we can bring her." "Joe." "What?" "I can't make Emily come with us." "She wants to." "Joe." "Don't make me pull out the big guns," he said. Ava tried to get up. "Where you going?" "Getting out while I can." He kissed her. "Bed." He slid his jeans on, wrapped her in the blanket and carried her to the bedroom.

They curled up in bed together and were out cold a little while later. At 9am, Grace came upstairs and jumped onto their bed. "Good morning baby girl," Joe said. "Hi Daddy." "How was your sleepover," he asked. "We had fun. Why are you in bed?" "Mama and I were up late." "Can we pool?" Joe nodded. "Hey. How did the show go," Emily asked. "Long story." "I'll take them out. Mike's popping by if that's okay." Ava looked at her. "It's fine." "We'll be down in a couple," Joe said. Ava got up and hopped into the shower, then freshened up and pulled her string bikini on. "Ava." "What?" "You know that's coming off faster than you think," Joe said. "No it isn't." "Intentionally trying to get me all hot and bothered again?" Ava shook her head. She slid her shorts on and he slid his arms around her, backing her into the bathroom counter. "Joe." "What?" "We're going down there." "The tech is coming at ten," Joe said. "With?" "I want to make sure the guy's doing things right." "I don't want her here," Ava said. "Babe." "I'm not coming inside." "I need you to do this with me." He kissed her. "Shower. I'll do my makeup." He kissed her again. "It's 9:30." "Fine," Joe said. He got in the shower and Ava did her minimal makeup, then put on the black bikini that was more tempting to Joe than the other one. Ava went downstairs with her phone just as Mike was showing up.

"Hi Ava," Mike said. "Hi. Come on in." "Nice bikini," he said. "If you watch my ass, I'm kicking yours." They came outside and Emily came over to him. "Hey." "Hey yourself," Mike said. Emily kissed him. Joe walked outside and saw her with Mike. "Hey Joe," Mike said backing right off. "And what might you be doing in our backyard?" "I invited him," Emily said. "I didn't know you two knew each other," Joe said. "We met a week or so ago at a party." "Really." "Joe, chill out. We're just hanging out." Ava played with the kids in the pool, then heard the doorbell. "Ava." "Go." "Ava." She hopped out then dried off and slid her shorts on.

"Hi Ava," Tiffany said. "Just get it overwith." "I'm sorry," she said, "Tiffany, don't talk," Joe said. The doctor did the test. "No results will be released without both of you present." "When," Ava asked. "Tomorrow." "Fine. Come back here tomorrow and we'll do this," Joe said. "Joe," Ava said. "Let me walk you both out," Joe said. Ava stood at the office door watching Joe with Tiffany. "Joe, I didn't mean to get her upset," Tiffany said. "Just go. She's gonna be pissed off until she finds out that I'm right." "There's only one other person I was with Joe." "Then you better tell him that he's a daddy." "I'm sorry," she said. "Tiff, if you think in any way this is getting you back in my life, you know you seriously need help." "What if she is?" "She isn't." "Joe." "Go." She left. He walked back towards where Ava was and she was gone. She walked outside and dove into the pool. She played with the kids a bit, then she noticed that Mike had Emily cornered.

"Yes or no?" "Mike, you're not pressuring me into anything. That's what you want, then forget it." "Yes or no?" Ava walked up behind him. "Mike, either back off or you're leaving." "Ava, this has nothing to do with you." "You're in my house. Yes it does." "You the one that told her how to be a damn tease," Mike asked. "Pissing off the wrong damn person today," Ava said. "Why don't you go take care of your husband?" Ava was itching to kick his ass. Joe walked over, grabbed Mike's shoulder. "What?" "You're gone," Joe said. "Who's going to stop me?" Joe walked him out. "Don't call her again," Joe said. "That's her choice." "No it isn't. You're gone." "Joe, you can't make me leave." "The hell I can't." Joe called the security gate and walked him outside. "There a problem Mr. Morgan?" "I want him permanently removed." "No problem sir." Mike left and Joe came back inside.

He walked out to the back and Grace and Blake were in the pool with Emily. "Where's Ava," he asked. "Inside." He came inside and Ava was upstairs in the bedroom. "Babe." "I'm going until you find out," she said. "Ava." "I need to." "You can't leave." "I'm going to take Grace and Blake with me," Ava said. "Ava." "Joe, I can't deal with this." He wrapped his arms around her. "I don't want to do this alone," he said. "I'm so mad I wanted to rip a piece off him." "Ava." "I'll go to the gym and get the stress out." "Ava, running off isn't going to fix this," Joe said. "It'll get my mind off it." He kissed her. "I have to." "I know. Just do me one favor." "What?" "Remember something. Remember what you said the other night." "Joe." "Ava, I'll be here with the kids." Ava pulled on her workout gear and left for the gym with her purse and her iPod.

After an hour workout, Ava headed home. She came in and Grace and Blake were asleep. Emily was doing homework. "How was the gym," Emily asked. "Good. Where is everyone?" "The kids are napping and Joe's downstairs. He told me to tell you to come down when you got back." "I'm just going to shower," Ava said. She went upstairs and slid into a hot shower. She came out and Joe handed her a towel. "Thought you were downstairs." "Em told me you were home," he said. Ava wrapped the towel around her and went into the bedroom. "I'm losing it," Joe said. "Thought you were so sure." "I am. I am petrified I'm gonna lose you." "Why?" "Ava, I can't lose you." "Then tell me why," Ava said. "I dated her before us." "And?" "We hung out once or twice. I told you about it." "And?" "Ava." "Tell me you didn't sleep with her again." "I didn't." "Joe." "I swear I didn't." "Then what's the problem," Ava asked. "I thought I wanted to be with her." "Joe." "There might have been once." Ava grabbed her things and locked herself in the bathroom. She got dressed, then did her hair, then put her things in the travel case and walked out of the bathroom. "Ava." She grabbed her bag from under the bed and started putting things in it. "Ava," Joe said. She put the dresses for the weekend, jeans, bathing suits, lingerie, perfume. "Ava, please." She walked down the steps and put the things in the SUV, then walked back upstairs. "Ava." She grabbed some clothes for Grace and Blake, then put them in the car. "Ava, you're not going," Joe said. She walked past him and went into Blake's room, sliding him into the car seat, then grabbed the baby bag. She walked downstairs and put the bag in the car. Blake was still out cold. "Mama, where going," Grace said. "Come on baby. We're going for a ride." Ava put Grace and Blake in the SUV. "Ava," Joe said. She pulled out and left.

CHAPTER 47

An hour later, Ava pulled into her favorite hotel. She brought the kids and the suitcases in and checked in for the night. "No phone calls and privacy," Ava said. "Yes ma'am." She got them settled, then sat down and played with them. "Mama, where's Daddy?" "At home." "Why for," Grace asked. "Thought we could have a day just us." "Okay." After dinner with the kids, she gave them a bath and tucked them in. "Mama, can I call Daddy," Grace asked. Ava nodded and handed her phone to Grace. "Hi Daddy." "Hey baby girl. What you doing?" "Going to bed. Can you sing me?" "Mama will put the CD on. I love you baby girl." "I love you too Daddy." "Give the phone to Mama okay," he said. She handed it to Ava and she hung up. She put the CD on then went and sat in the bedroom.

The next morning, Ava's phone was ringing off the hook. "Ava, where are you," Ryan asked. "Why?" "You know Joe's losing it." "Good." "What the hell happened," Ryan asked. "I just want to be alone alright?" "Where are you?" Ava hung up. A half-hour later, Ryan was at the door. "What," Ava asked. "Fine. You're mad. You don't walk away." "Ryan, leave me alone." He looked in her eyes and saw the redness and the tears. "Come here," he said. "Ryan." He pulled her into his arms and hugged her. "I know you're mad," he said. "You don't get it." "Yeah I do. I know what's going on. He needs you there." "And I can't do it. I'm not going to sit there while he finds out he's a dad," Ava said. "You really think that's going to happen?" "Yeah I do." "You need to take them home and be there." "Ryan." "Ava, get dressed and go," he said. "Why?" "Because you'll kick yourself if you don't." "Where are the kids," Ava asked. "With Emily. Get dressed." He handed her a pair of jeans and a tank top from her bag and got the bellman to carry the other bags down to the car. She had a quick shower, put some makeup on to cover the puffiness, then got dressed and left with Ryan.

Joe was on his third cup of Starbucks. He'd barely slept. He went upstairs and showered, tried to snap out of it, then came downstairs as Ryan and Ava were pulling in with the kids. Grace ran into the house and straight into his arms. "Hi Daddy." "Hey baby girl." She hugged him and kissed his cheek, then ran into the TV room. Emily came in with Blake and the kids suitcases. "Where's Ava," Joe asked. "With Ryan." He sat down on the front step. "I'm not getting out of the car," Ava said. "Ava, stop being a stubborn pain in the ass and go." "What if it turns out he is?" "It won't." "Ryan." "Ava, have a little faith," Ryan said. "Ryan." "Don't. Ava, go in that house." "Then what?" He hugged her. Ava went to get out and Ryan brought the bags inside. "Ryan," Joe said. "You better hope and pray Joe." He looked at him. "The two of you have both been miserable all damn night. Go and fix this," Ryan said. Ryan pulled out in his car. "Sent out the artillery," Ava asked. "I had to find you." "Did they show up?" "20 minutes." Ava leaned against the SUV. They pulled in 5 minutes later. Joe walked over and grabbed Ava's hand. "Come on in," he said. They went into the office and Joe wouldn't let go of the vice grip he had on Ava's hand. "I re-did the test twice to be sure." "And?" "Amanda and Joe aren't a match." "What about," Tiffany asked. "The other test you did was positive." "I'm sorry," Tiffany said. "Thank you doctor," Joe said. Joe walked them both out and Ava went upstairs.

Once they were gone, Joe walked upstairs. "Ava." He heard water running. A few minutes later, Ava walked past him in a bikini and went outside. He followed her and walked outside, then saw her with the kids. He knew. Her answer to anything he would ask would be 'Not now'. "Daddy, you coming?" Grace had her arms around his leg. He picked her up and hugged her. "Thought you would never ask." Grace hugged him and kissed his cheek then went and jumped into the pool. He changed into a bathing suit and jumped in with Ava and Grace. Blake was in Ava's arms giggling. "Mama, can we live in the pool," Grace asked. "No. You'd get all wrinkly like you do when you're in the tub too long." "Eww," Grace said. Joe laughed. Ava got out with Blake and changed him, then sat by the pool's edge while Blake played with his toys. Joe splashed around with Grace for a while, and Ava made everyone lunch. Grace curled up in Joe's lap. "I missed you Daddy," Grace said. "I missed you too." After lunch, Grace played with Blake a while until she started yawning. "Grace." She snuggled up to Joe. "Do you want to come curl up with me for a nap," Joe asked. Grace nodded and he carried her upstairs to bed. Ava fed Blake, then put him down for a nap. She went in and slid on her jeans and a t-shirt, then came back downstairs and sat down at her laptop.

Joe came in a little while later. "You can stop wondering," Ava said. "I love you." "Joe, tell me that I never have to hear it again," Ava said. "Trust me on that one." "Good." Ava went back to her writing. He wrapped his arms around her. "I know you aren't gonna say it." "I don't want to see her in this house ever again." "And she's back," Joe teased. "Funny." "I'm sorry we had to go through all of it at all." "If I ever find out that you . . ." He kissed her. "I promise to never put either one of us through that again," Joe said. "You know why I had to go." He nodded. "Still wish you hadn't." "I didn't want the kids seeing us upset." "I know. Come sit with me." He took her hand and curled up on the sofa with her. "It's over right?" He nodded. "Good." "I missed you Ava. I couldn't sleep last night." "I didn't either. The things running around my head kept me up." "Like what?" "If she was yours. Dealing with Tiffany being a permanent part of our lives." "Babe, like it or not, you're stuck with me." "As long as I'm not stuck with her, we're fine." "So you going to tell me some good news? I know Kate called you." "You'll find out Sunday." "Ava." "After we get back." "You're killing me with suspense." "And I can keep a secret," Ava said. "Give me a hint." Ava shook her head. Her phone went off. "No phones." She grabbed it and answered. "Hey Ava." "Hey yourself." "You two okay," Rose asked. "We will be." "At least you're talking we again." "It's fine." "See, I told you." "I have to go." "I'll pick you up for the massage at 2." "See you then." "Where you going," Joe asked. "To de-stress." "Babe." "What?" "Promise me something." "What?" "That from now on we don't sleep alone." "Joe." "Ava, I can't sleep when you're mad." "You're going without me this weekend." He shook his head. "I'm staying here with the kids," Ava said. "Then we bring them." "Joe, I'm staying home." He kissed her. "Don't even try." "Come with me," he said. "I have writing to get finished." "Then finish it. I want you there." He kissed her again.

Ava finally left with Rose and headed to the spa. The minute they walked in, they were pampered. They had an hour massage, a manicure and pedicure, then relaxed a while. "Feeling better?" Ava nodded. "Good idea." "How's Joe," she asked. "Fine." "Ava." "He's just glad I'm home." "I can't believe you walked out of the house. What the hell were you thinking," Rose asked. "That I wasn't going to let her be part of my life." "So if it had come back that he was?" "I wouldn't have a choice." "Ava." "What? You telling me that in the same situation you wouldn't walk as fast as you could the other way," Ava asked. "You know you would've come back." "Rose, there's things you can handle, and there's things you can't. This would be a can't." "You don't mean that." "I love him so much it hurts. He's a part of me. Fact is, the kids come first," Ava said. "So you'd let them be without their dad?" "Away from her." "You know how much you've changed," Rose asked. Ava nodded. "I grew up. I love him Rose, but I wouldn't let those kids have to go through it." They hugged, then got changed and headed back to the house.

Ava came in and saw roses at the front door. She looked around for the kids and the house was quiet. She followed the roses into the kitchen. She could smell the dinner from the front door. "Hey." "Hey yourself," Joe said. "Where are the kids?" "Movies with Emily." "Really." He kissed her. "What's the occasion?" "Just because." He slid his arms around her. "What are you cooking?" "Your fave." "Joe." "After the crap we've been through in the last few days, I thought dinner just us was called for." Her hands cupped his face. "You know you were right." "About what?" "I couldn't leave," Ava said. "I know. That's why when you left . . ." Ava kissed him. He held her close and hugged her. "I never want to lose you." "You won't," Ava said. She wiped away the tears from his eyes and they had a quiet dinner together. After dinner, they were curled up together on the sofa watching TV when Grace came running in. "How was the movie Grace?" "We had fun." She jumped into Ava's lap and hugged her and Joe. "What watching?" "Nothing exciting. Emily handed Blake to Ava. "How were they," Joe asked. "Grace had a blast. Blake watched part of it and played the rest of it." Blake was yawning. Ava took him upstairs, fed him, put him in pajamas and put him to bed. She came down and Grace was curled up with Joe on the sofa. "Grace." She looked at Ava. "Lavender bubbles?" She nodded and ran up the steps.

Ava gave her a bath then she hopped into her pajamas and went back downstairs. "What you doin," Joe asked. "Nothing," Grace said. "Bedtime song?" Grace nodded. He carried her upstairs, tucked her in and sang to her a bit. Once she was asleep, he walked into the bedroom and saw Ava on her laptop. "What you doing," Joe teased mocking Grace. "Writing." He got an email 2 minutes later. It was lyrics. Then he saw who'd sent them. "Aren't you supposed to be working on the new book," Joe asked. "Got distracted." He closed the laptop and slid it on the side table. "What?" He pulled her into his arms and kissed her. "What?" "I'm just glad you're here." "I bet," Ava said. "You wouldn't believe the thoughts I had running through my head." "Such as?" "You leaving for good. Never seeing the kids again." "I'd never prevent you from seeing them." "I was more scared that I'd lost you." "I assumed the worst," Ava said. "So did I. When she told me, I was scared as hell." "Joe." "Then I come home to tell you and you try to walk out." "A little hint. When I need space, I need space. Just give me time to cool off." "You know I'm going to fight you every time." "I know. Just remember I will come back once I've cooled off." "Just do me a favor and stay here next time," Joe said. "When you know I need to cool off, then just let me cool off." "I will. I promise that nothing like this is happening ever again." "Good." "I hate fighting with you." "I know. I don't like it either." "We should just be crazy-glued together." Ava laughed. "Oh really?" He smirked and kissed her. "You have to come with me this weekend." "Never going to stop are you?" "Ava." "I'll think about it." He kissed her. "It doesn't mean yes." "It will be."

Emily sat in her room trying to make sense of what had happened. Mike had been freaking out for as long as Ava and Joe had. Something was up. The question was, what was it? She called Mike. "What?" "I don't think we should hang out anymore." "Emily." "You think you're strong arming me into sleeping with you, then you need a brain replacement." "Can't just have fun can you?" "Not when it means getting used." "Emily." "I'm not just some chick you can screw and walk out on." "Why do you have to be such a hard ass?" "Because. You either take all of me, good and bad, or nothing. You don't get a taste Mike." "I bet I could change your mind." "And I know you won't." "You going back to him?" "I don't know. What I do know, is unless I am being treated right, you can forget it." "Doesn't mean we can't . . . ." "Yeah it does." "You know you've been hanging with Ava too long." "I see that as a good thing." She hung up and almost felt like patting herself on the back. It felt way too good.

Joe and Ava watched a movie and curled up together in bed. "Not even one hint?" "Joe, stop asking." "It's not my birthday." "Trust me. You'll be happy." "Ava." "No." "One hint." "Fine." "What's the hint?" "Trees." "Funny." "That's the only hint you're getting." "Ava." "Nope." Her phone went off. "Hey Kate." "I can drop them off to you Thursday," she said. "Even better." "See you tomorrow." Ava hung up. "Come on." "Fine. You get the surprise tomorrow." "Just a hint." "Grass." "Ava." "I'm not telling." "I have ways you know." "Yep." "Going to taunt me all night?" "Just until tomorrow," Ava said. "Ava, come on." "I'm not going this weekend because of it." "You're not pregnant. The kids are fine. I know we totally didn't get the house, what is it?" "It's a delivery." "New car?" Ava shook her head. "Is it something for the kids?" "Sort of." "You know you are intentionally throwing me." "I know." "Not even one non-riddle hint," Joe asked. "You've had a few hints Joe." "What time tomorrow?" "Probably in the morning." "You know we're leaving Friday morning right?" Ava nodded. "You should probably pack tomorrow," Ava said. "You mean we." "Trust me. I'm not going this time." He nodded. She went to say no and he kissed her. "You're coming." "Joe." "I'm not taking no for an answer Mrs. Morgan." "And he pulls out the big guns," Ava joked. "Once you find out what the surprise is, you'll know why." "You're still coming." They laughed and played around then finally slid into bed. "Ava." "No." "I love you." "I love you too crazy man." They fell asleep and he was tossing and turning all night trying to figure it out.

Ava got up the next morning with the kids. "Em, I need you to help me with something," Ava said. "What?" "Gimme a half-hour head start, then give this to Joe." "What are you doing?" "It's a surprise for him." "Call me when you want me to wake him up." Ava hugged her, then she snuck upstairs and grabbed her mini sundress. She got the keys from Kate, then called Emily.

"What do you mean she left," Joe said. "She told me to give you this."

> Joe. I didn't leave for the reason you thought. I'm the treasure at the end of the treasure hunt. You wanted a hint, here it is. Your GPS is programmed. Follow it.

He pulled his jeans on, kissed the kids then ran out. There was a hot Starbucks coffee in the cup holder and a warm bagel. He turned the car on and followed like she asked. Two and a half-hours later, he pulled into the park. He saw a note on the bench:

> Look to your left. Anything look familiar? See if you can find the SUV.

He drove towards the house they'd been staring at. He went to go past it and saw a balloon attached to the gate. He saw her SUV in the driveway. "How the hell?" He pulled in. Cat left and drove the SUV back to the house. "Ava," Joe said. She opened the front door. "What are you up to?" "Hint." He nodded. Ava put house keys in his hand. "What's this?" "Thought you'd want a front door key," Ava said. "We didn't get the house." Ava nodded. "This house?" She nodded. "Ava." "Sign the papers," she said. He went and signed under Ava's signature. "Congrats you two." Kate hugged Ava, then left. "Tell me we didn't just get this house," Joe said. "You said it was perfect." "I lowballed the offer." "And they threw in the appliances and the flat screen in the media room." "Ava." She wrapped her arms around him. "It's ours," Joe said. Ava nodded. "What about the cheque?" "Done." "Babe." "Starting fresh," Ava said. He kissed her pulling her into his arms. "Welcome home." "You were seriously going to hold out until Sunday?" "Was going to get some of my furniture and set it up this weekend." "You're too much." "Know what this means right," Ava teased. He nodded and pulled her tight to him. He picked her up, wrapping her legs around him. "I meant paint color." "Liar," Joe said. Ava laughed. "Like the surprise?" "What about the kids?" "Emily's on her way." "So we have an hour or two?" He picked her up and carried her into the kitchen. "What are you up to?" "Christening our kitchen." He kissed her and leaned her onto the countertop.

The kids showed up with Emily an hour and a half later. "Ava?" Ava came out of the kitchen as they were both laughing. "I thought you were kidding," Emily said. "What doing Mama?" "Something I want to show you," Ava said. "What?" Ava walked Grace upstairs. "What do you think of this?" "Big room." "Think you like it?" "My room?" Ava nodded. "Why?" "You can still see Jacob." "I like Mama. Purple?" Ava nodded. "We can pick it out together." She hugged Ava. "Emily, come up." She walked upstairs. "This is your room." Emily walked in and saw a bay window, a killer view and a bathroom all her own. "Ava." "For everything you do to help Joe and I. You deserve a spot of your own." "This is too much," Emily said. "That way you can have bubble baths without the kids." She hugged Ava. "What do you think," Joe asked. "This place is unbelievable," Emily said. "You haven't seen the whole thing," Ava said. Blake started getting fussy. Ava slid him out of Joe's arms while he showed the kids around.

Ava called Rose. "Hey." "You sound better." "Much better," Ava said. "Where are you? I saw Joe take off." "We found a house." "Where?" "A couple hours away. It's beautiful." "You're still going to be here right," Rose asked. "Don't worry. You didn't lose your neighbor." "More home?" "It's better. More cozy." "That where he took off to?" "I didn't tell him we had it. If things hadn't worked the way I hoped . . ." "Ava." "I would've." "You know you wouldn't." "Rose." "So tell me about the house." Ava told her about it. The yard, the privacy, the open space and that it was their clean slate. "Which means the guys are going to come record there. You know they will," Rose said. "I know. Plus there's room for the kids to run around." "Sounds beautiful." "And, it means away from the drama." "Ava, it follows you." "This is home. No more stress, or drama, or ex-girlfriends. Just me, Joe and the kids," Ava said. "Sounds like an oasis." "It is." Joe came back to the steps with Emily and the kids. "You know I want the grand tour," Rose said. "Once it's put together, you'll be one of the first ones." Ava got off the phone with her. "You know what this means," Joe asked. "Shopping?" He laughed. "This means Grace can have a big girl bed." "You're right." "They left the stuff in the media room." "I know. It was built in." "Mama, is that my room?" Ava nodded. "I like it." Emily's phone rang.

"It's me." "Hey." "Can you come by?" "Gimme an hour or so." "Okay." She hung up. "Emily?" "I'll put the car seats in the car. Can you two do without me?" "See you at dinner," Ava said. "Em." She turned to look at Joe. He walked over to her. "What?" "Thank you." She smirked, then left. "So what do you think about going to the park," Joe asked as Grace jumped up and down. "Now?" He nodded. Grace ran out and got in the car, Ava put Blake in his car seat, then they headed to the park. Grace ran around with Joe for a while, then they headed back to the house. He held Ava's hand the entire way back. "You're still coming." She laughed. "Then so are they." "Wouldn't want it any other way." They stopped at a light and he kissed her. Grace giggled. "What you giggling about giggle puss?" "Nothing." By the time they pulled back in, Grace was asleep and Blake was just waking up. Joe got Grace and took her and put her down for a nap, and Ava fed Blake, changed him and brought him downstairs to play for a while.

Joe came down and saw Ava on the sofa with Blake. He was giggling away. He kissed Ava. "She sleeping?" Joe nodded. "And as for you little man. What you doing down here with Mama?" Blake giggled. "Babe." She looked up at him. "This is what we should be like." "I know. Too much to ask for a few more weeks of no stress?" He slid onto the sofa behind her. "Depends." "On what?" "Studio. Stress?" "Depends." "How about we hold up at the new house with the kids." "We have to paint and get furniture." "You have the leather sofa from your place." "And tables." "We need beds." "True." He smirked. "I know what you're thinking." "What," Joe asked. "Don't think it." "Can't blame me." "You know Blake, your Daddy has a one-track mind." "Always around you." "Guess that's a good thing," Ava said. He tickled Ava and Blake giggled. "You know you are completely hilarious." "Wait until tonight." "What's tonight?" "Negotiations," Joe said. "There's no negotiating." "Oh yes there is." "Joe." "You're coming. I want to see that sexy dress again." "Can't just wear it around the house?" "If you did, I wouldn't make it to the tour bus." "Must make a mental note of that." He wrapped his arms around her and tickled her neck with his kisses.

Ava finally put Blake down for a nap, and the minute she closed the door, Joe carried her to their bedroom. "What are you up to?" He kissed her and leaned her back onto the bed. "Didn't get to say good morning." "Definitely important." He curled up in her arms and held her close. "Thank you for being an amazing mom, and the most beautiful and loving and amazing wife in the world." "Joe." "I mean it. You're amazing." "Even if I think I could, I couldn't do this without you." "Never going to have to." He kissed her. "You are the best thing that ever happened to me. No matter what, I'm never letting go." "Good." "Now as for the negotiations." Ava laughed. "Please." "If Emily doesn't have plans, then fine." "You gonna wear the dress?" "Maybe." "With?" "My wedding ring." "Very sexy Mrs. Morgan." "Just for you though." "Mm. Even better." He kissed Ava. "But I'm not singing." "Ava." "No. Joe, I just want a weekend to relax." "You have to." "Why?" "Babe." "Joe." "You know the guys will talk you into it." "Nope." "Be a shame for you to not be able to show that dress off." "No." He kissed her again. "You know I'll talk you into it." "No you won't." He kissed her. "Mama." "Yes baby." "What doing?" "Snuggling with Daddy." Grace jumped onto the bed and curled up with them. "I thought you were tired." Grace shook her head and snuggled up to Ava. "You coming with Daddy this weekend Grace?" "Where?" "Daddy is going with Uncle Ryan and Uncle Brad." "Okay." "Nice." "Think we should bring Mama and Blake?" She nodded. "Outvoted Ava." "Totally unfair voting." "Daddy." "Yes baby girl." "Sing." "For you and Mama?" Grace nodded. He kissed her nose, then grabbed his guitar and played something for Grace. He stared right at Ava. "I like that one Daddy." "Your mom's favorite." She kissed Joe. "Thank you Daddy." "You're welcome baby girl." "Daddy." "Yes baby." "Can we bring Jacob?" Ava laughed. "I'll call Uncle Ryan and ask." "Okay." She snuggled back up to Ava. "You are like a toaster oven," Ava said as she felt how hot Grace was. She took her temperature, then gave her something to get rid of the fever. "You feeling okay baby girl?" Grace shook her head. "Tummy hurts."

Ava went downstairs and got Grace some ginger ale and crackers, then laid her down on their bed. "Mama, can we watch a movie?" "I'll grab one from downstairs." Joe wrapped Grace up in her fuzzy blanket. Ava came in and put one of Grace's movies on. A half-hour later, Grace was asleep and her fever had gone down. Joe carried her into her room and put her in bed with a sippy cup of ginger ale by the bed. Joe came back into the bedroom and curled up with Ava. "So back to what we were talking about." "If she's sick, I'm not going." "Deal." An hour or so later, Grace woke up. She came back in and snuggled up to Ava. "Still not feeling good?" She shook her head. Grace was definitely sick. Joe crossed his fingers it was a 24 hour bug.

The next morning, Grace woke up and felt better. "You sure," Joe asked. Grace nodded. Ava checked and the fever was gone. "Better pack," Joe teased. Grace ran into her room and grabbed her frog and her teddy bear. "I ready," Grace said. Joe laughed. "What about pajamas?" She went back into her room and Joe grabbed her bag. He helped Grace pack, then they packed for Blake. Joe walked back into the bedroom with the kids and Ava was sliding the dress in her bag. A grin came across his face. "Don't you start," Ava said. He kissed her. "Daddy, is Jacob coming?" "Uncle Ryan said yes." "Yay!" They loaded up the SUV, then headed to the airport. Ava got writing done while the kids played with Emily. Joe and the guys worked on a song, Rose napped.

They landed and headed to the hotel. Grace went down for a nap with Jacob, Blake and Angel slept. Joe talked Ava into doing sound check. "Joe." "You're coming," he said, "I'll look after them," Emily said. Ava left with the guys. They showed up, did sound check, then two interviews later, they headed back to the hotel. Ava and Joe came in and saw the kids playing. Blake was playing with Angel. "So," Ava asked. "Perfect as usual. Seriously, how do people get by without an Emily," Rose joked. Emily laughed. "I have more energy than the kids do some days." "Plus Grace loves her to bits," Ava said. "How was sound check," Rose asked. "Good. Ava, you have to sing tonight," Emily asked. "Still trying to convince her," Joe joked. "Funny," Ava said. Ryan just laughed. "Where's Brad?" "Talking to Danielle and Chris in the hallway." "And they didn't come because," Rose asked. "Chris is sick." Brad came in a few minutes later and Grace ran over to hug him. "Hey princess Grace. You having fun," Brad asked. She nodded. "So what are we all doing for dinner," Brad asked. "Other than talking Ava into coming on with us tonight?" "Ryan, I said I'd come. That's it." "And she brought the dress," Joe said. "You're coming on." "No." "Ava." "No." Joe pulled her into his lap. "Man, talk her into it," Ryan said, "Intend to," Joe said. "Seriously, I just want a night to relax," Ava said. "Ava," Ryan said. "You aren't going to stop pestering me until I say yes." "True," Ryan said. "Doing the new song," Brad said. "Of course." "Babe," Joe asked. "Fine. If I do this tonight, I'm chilling tomorrow no badgering permitted." "We'll see," Ryan joked. Ava threw a sofa pillow at him. "You starting," Ryan asked. The kids were having a blast. "We going to do dinner," Ava asked. Joe nodded. They headed down to the private dining room at the hotel and had dinner, then everyone went to get ready.

Joe slid his arms around Ava's waist. "What?" "You're wearing it right," Joe asked. Ava shook her head. "You sure?" Ava nodded. "Babe." "Something else instead." "What color," Joe asked. "Just put the black on." "Tell me you aren't making this a surprise." She smirked. "You're killing me." She kissed him, then went into the bedroom. He started getting changed and noticed her unwrapping something from her suitcase. He went back to getting ready, then turned and saw her doing up a wrap dress. "What you doing," Joe asked. "Nothing." "Ava." "I'm changing there." "Give me one hint." "No." He slid his arms around her. "I knew we were gonna talk you into it." "I'm staying home next weekend," Ava said. "You sure?" Ava nodded. He kissed her. Ryan knocked at the door. "There in two," Joe said. Ava grabbed her purse, a bag, then kissed the kids goodnight and left.

Joe and the guys went off to do the meet and greet while Ava got changed. By the time they came back, she was changed. Joe walked in and saw her in a black and silver version of the dress he drooled over at that party. "Whoa," Ryan said. "Understatement," Brad said. Joe stood there. "What," Ava asked. Joe motioned for her to come closer. Ava shook her head. "Babe." She shook her head. "Guys, ten minutes," the stage manager said. Ava went and grabbed her phone. He slid it out of her hands. "What," Ava said. Ryan started laughing. Ava saw the fire in Joe's eyes. He walked towards her, grabbing her hand and they walked off into the hall. "What?" He pinned her to the wall and kissed her. "Joe." "Intentionally taunting me," he asked. Ava smirked. "You are so in trouble." "Why's that?" He pulled her close and kissed her again. "Joe." "See, if you'd had this on in the room . . ." "We wouldn't have made it to dinner," Ava said. He kissed her again. "Joe, you're on." One more kiss and he headed to the stage with the guys. Ava fixed up her lipstick, then stood side stage until she had to go on.

The entire time on stage, Joe was staring at her. The dress was almost the same as the other, except that this one was black with silver straps covered in crystal. It skimmed every curve, and she looked so tempting, that Joe wanted her. After the two songs, Ava made it off the stage. She went back and slid her heels off, then went and stood side stage with Joe's leather jacket around her. As soon as the show was done, he walked towards her and slid his arms around her and kissed her. "You know, I think we should go out for a drink," Ava said. "Nope," Joe replied. "Walk?" His head shook. "Bubble bath?" "Ava." "Bed," she asked. "Warmer." He kissed Ava and they headed back to the hotel. They walked in and Ava saw Jeff and Emily asleep on the sofa. "What the hell," Joe said. "Shh." Ava grabbed a blanket from her bed and covered them up. "Ava." "Let them sleep." "Oh hell no." Ava dragged him into the bedroom and closed the door. "Blake will be up in a half-hour. Relax." "I'm not leaving him out there with my cousin." Ava kissed him. "Babe." "Fine." Ava went in and checked on the kids. Joe scared Jeff to death.

"Hey. How was the show," Jeff asked. "Great. What you doing here?" "Wanted to see Emily," Jeff said. "I gather that." "Joe, quit freaking out," Ava said. "It's fine. I should've told him," Emily said. "More like asked." "Joe, you forget who's paying for the room," Jeff asked. "You start that, you're out of here." "I asked him to come Joe," Emily said. "Why?" "Because I like him." "Emily." "I'm not putting this up for debate," Emily said. "I should get back to my room anyway," Jeff said. "Don't leave because of him." "Seriously. You guys have an early flight tomorrow," Jeff said. "Fine. I'll come hang out down there then." "Em," Ava said. She came walking over. "He was stunned. I'll work on him. Just don't do something stupid to get back at him ok," Ava said. She hugged Ava. "Blake ok?" Ava nodded. "Sleeping like angels." "Thank you." Ava nodded. Emily walked out with Jeff.

"You're not stopping her," Joe asked. "Not if you're going to act all huffy." "He just walked out with my cousin." "Who's getting all over-protective Dad on her now," Ava asked. "Ava." "She is a grown up. She can handle it. If not, she knows where we are." "You sure?" Ava nodded. She slid the jacket off. "Tease," Joe said. Ava threw him the jacket. "I still can't believe you walked out on stage like that." "You like?" He nodded. The dress was the perfect distraction.

Ava walked over to him. "Now what were you saying about coming back here?" He slid one arm around her and pulled her to him. "And you playing all cool. We'll just go for a drink. You thought you'd get away with that," Joe asked. Ava nodded. "Never." "And what are you gonna do to stop me?" "Don't even think of teasing." Ava kissed him, then broke away and went into the bedroom, washing the makeup off. "Much better," Joe said. "You are so full of it." He wrapped his arms around her. "Always will be." "Say that when we're old," Ava said. "Every minute of every day." "Babe," Ava said. He kissed her neck. "What if I wanted to stay at the hotel with the kids tomorrow night," Ava asked. "Ava." "I have to finish planning Grace's birthday." "Can't do anything after 8 anyway," Joe said. "Someday I'll find an excuse you know." He kissed her shoulder, sliding the practically nothing strap off her shoulder. "Joe." His arms wrapped around her. "You know how sexy you look," he asked. "Enough that you couldn't play?" She turned to face him and he kissed her. She slid his jacket off and he picked her up, carrying her to bed.

The next morning, they all got up, had breakfast with Emily, then headed to New York. They got there, checked in, then they took the kids out for a day at the toy store. Grace ran around with Jacob and the guys, and Ava and Rose got a few things for the kids and for Chris. They headed back to the hotel and Rose napped with them. "You sure," Ava asked. Rose nodded. She left with Joe and did a little shopping, then they headed to sound check. They walked into Ava and Joe's room and the guys were running around with the kids. "Daddy," Grace said running at him. "Saved by the super hug." Grace giggled. "Hi Mama." "Hey baby. Were they chasing you?" Grace nodded and giggled. "Where's Jacob?" "Uncle Ryan ate him." Jacob ran up behind Ryan. "Mama found something for you." Ava handed her the princess crown that went with her frog. "See, I'm a princess." "Way to over-inflate her head," Brad teased. They got on with the sound check, then had an interview or two, then headed back to the hotel. Ava and Joe relaxed with the kids a bit, then they headed to dinner.

By the time they got back, Ava was itching to get home and start on the new house. "So what exactly are we changing," Joe asked. "Paint color." And?" "Putting in the furniture." "I called Devon to take measurements," Joe said. "And?" "What?" "You never call just for her to take measurements. What are you up to," Ava asked. "She put some of your stuff in." "Sneak." "We can figure out the rest when we get to it." They spent the day relaxing with the kids. Devon showed around 8.

"So what do you think," she asked. "I didn't know you could do that on the computer," Joe said. "Joe," Ava replied. "I like." "I can get them in this weekend," Devon said. "What about the furniture," Ava asked. "Not much that you need for the main level." "Just stuff for the bedrooms?" Devon nodded. Joe smirked. "Well," Ava asked. "Grace will love the bedroom, and the color is perfect for Blake." "Emily's room?" "You'd have to ask her." She emailed the shots to Emily. "It'll be done by the time you guys get back next weekend," Devon said. "I'll be home," Ava said. "I'll call you when we land," Joe replied. He wrapped his arm around Ava's shoulders. Joe walked her out, then came back in to Ava cleaning up the TV room. "We," Ava asked. He smirked. "No." He nodded. "Joe." "Have to." "I have to breathe, eat, drink water and take care of the kids. I don't have to go on stage," Ava said. "Yes you do." "And why is that?" He walked towards her. "Because you're the most beautiful, amazing, wife in the entire planet." "Nice try." He slid his arms around her. "Because I'd miss you," Joe said. "You just want someone to flirt with on stage." "That too." "I'll think about it." He kissed her. "Not gonna work." He laughed and she hugged him. "I still can't believe you kept the house a secret," Joe said. "Gave you something to look forward to." "You are so darn sneaky aren't you?" Ava kissed him then finished cleaning up.

A while later, Ava heard Joe downstairs working on a song. She slid her satin nightie on and walked downstairs. "Hey." "Hey yourself. What are you up to down here," Ava asked. "Song stuck in my head." "And?" "A few lines. Nothing else." She sat down on the chair beside his. He played a bit of it for her, then stopped. "What?" He kissed her, then played the rest that he'd written. "Always a charmer aren't you," Ava asked. "That's why you love me." "One of the million reasons." "Had another idea for a song for you and Ryan," Joe said. "No more. Y'all should be writing like I'm not singing with you." "Party pooper." Ava nodded.

A while later, she went upstairs to bed and Joe kept going on the song. Around 1, he slid into bed beside her and wrapped his arms around her. "Hey." "Hey yourself." He kissed her neck. "How is the writing going," Ava asked. "Need sleep." He snuggled up closer to her. "I love you," he whispered. "Forever," Ava replied.

The rest of the week was a blur of studio time, writing, kids playing and Joe taunting Ava into performing. "Babe." "No. I'm not doing it. We have too much to get done," Ava said. "Where's the house going? Never Never Land?" "Funny." "You know the fans want you there." "If the fans means you, then I know," Ava said. "Babe." "I need to stay home with the kids. I don't want to lug them off every time you're performing." "Ava." "Afraid you'll miss me too much?" He nodded. "Joe." "Then just come Saturday," he said. "Where's the show?" "Memphis." "That I can do." "The other one's downtown." "Which means?" "Home both nights." "So well planned." He nodded and kissed her.

CHAPTER 48

The last two concerts came up quick. They were both close to home, and Ava couldn't wait for a break. Grace always wanted to come and watch the show, and never made it through it without falling asleep in Emily's arms. Blake was crawling, and starting to chase Grace around. "Mama, you singing with Daddy tonight," Grace asked. Ava nodded as she tried to figure out what to wear. "Mama." "Yes baby girl." "I like the pink one." "I know." "Or the white one." Ava laughed. "Joe, if you are coaching her . . . ," Ava said. She came walking out and Joe was tickling her on the bed. "Where's Blake," Ava asked. She felt a tug at her leg. "Well, there you are." He tried to stand up, and almost fell when Ava caught him. "You want to be part of the party," Ava asked. He giggled. "Still think you should wear the white one," Joe said. "And I know why." He laughed and snuggled with Grace. "Mama looks like a princess," Grace said. "Think you're right Grace," Joe said. "Thank you baby girl." "Blake agrees," Joe joked. "Good to know you're telepathic now." He got up and came into the bathroom behind her. "Babe." "I know." "You should." "Either that or the black backless one," Ava teased. "White." "Some reason in particular?" "Nope." He kissed her then took the kids downstairs.

Ava grabbed the red, black and the white with the sparkly shoes, throwing them into the bag to take with them. "Daddy, when you coming home," Grace asked. "Tonight." "Can we have pancakes," she asked. "In the morning." "Can we keep Emily," Grace asked. Ava started laughing. Grace was full of a million questions. Joe finally got her calmed down and they headed off to the stadium.

"Ava." "What?" "Tell me you aren't doing the surprise again," Joe begged. "Eenie meenie miny mo." Joe laughed. He kissed her then headed off with the guys for the meet and greet. Ava did her hair, fixed up her makeup and slid on the white dress. Just as she was finishing up, Joe slid into the dressing room behind her. "Nice dress sexy lady," he said. "Thanks handsome." Ava kissed him, then they relaxed a bit before heading on stage. "So you telling me why you wanted me to wear the white dress so badly," Ava asked. "Nope." He wrapped his arm around her. They chatted a bit, then the guys headed on stage. Ava came on when her song started. The crowd roared. "So Ava, you like surprises," Brad asked. "Depends what kind of surprises," Ava replied. "Two years ago today, Ava was singing along with something we were working on. From then on, she was part of the group. Lots of things have changed, but they only got better," Brad said. "They couldn't live without me," Ava joked. "We thought it only right that she sings the song she started with," Ryan said. Ava sang two more songs with them, then headed back stage. She stood side stage and one of the stage guys handed her a bouquet of flowers. There was a note attached:

You'll be needing these.

Ava looked at Joe and he had a grin ear to ear. Her phone went off. "Ava." "Hey Cat. What's up?" "Tell them to let me back." Ava blew Joe a kiss, then went down and got security to let her by. "What's going on?" "I've been calling you for days," Cat said. "Was getting the new place together." "How do you feel about being a godmother?" "Cat." "Almost six weeks." Ava hugged her. "When did you find out?" "I was trying to get you to come to the doctor with me. I found out today." "Mama Cat. Sounds good," Ava teased. "Will wants Joe to be the godfather." "He's not going to say no," Ava said. "You know you're walking me through this." "You're amazing with Grace and Blake. You're going to be great Cat."

The guys came off stage and Joe saw Ava with Cat. "Hey Cat. What you doing here," Joe asked wrapping his arm around Ava and kissing her. "Just wanted to talk to Ava about something." "What'd he do now," Joe asked. "Asked you to be the godfather," Cat said. Joe looked at her. "She's pregnant.," Ava said. "Seriously?" He hugged Cat. "Finally he's going to be a Dad," Cat said. "So that's a yes?" Joe nodded. "I'd be honored." "For what," Ryan asked. "Cat and Will are having a baby," Ava said. Ryan and Brad hugged her and said their congrats. "So what's with the cryptic note," Ava asked. Joe excused him and Ava.

"What are you up to mister," Ava asked. Joe kissed her. His hands slid down her bare back. "You'll see." "Joe." He kissed her again." "Spill." He shook his head. "Joe." "You'll find out soon enough." The guys walked towards them with Cat. "Ready," Ryan asked. "For," Ava asked. Joe kissed her. They left and headed off. "Where are we headed," Ava asked. "I'm not telling," Joe said. "Joe, don't pull the secret thing." "You could." "We're headed towards the new place," Ava said. "Memorized the highways?" "As a matter of fact . . ." Joe kissed her. Ryan was sending text messages, so was Brad. "This is the quietest you guys have been in months," Ava said. A half-hour later, they pulled into the driveway. "When did we get driveway lights," Ava asked. Joe kissed her. The guys got out with Cat and went inside. Joe pulled Ava towards him.

"Now I know you're up to something." "Nope," Joe said. "Liar." "Remember what you said about being somewhere new," Joe said. "Fresh start. Clean slate." "I know I've made a million mistakes. Fact is, we learned a lot more than we thought we would," Joe said. "Very true." "I also remember something you said that literally caused chest pain," Joe said. "Joe." "I know you were upset. Fact is, I never want us to ever regret one second, one minute, one hour." "I know we would have been miserable without each other," Ava said. "And we wouldn't have the kids." "True." "So." "What did you plan," Ava asked. "Remember one thing." "Okay." "Our wedding song." He kissed her, then they got out. Ava touched up her lipstick and Joe handed her the flowers.

They walked in and Ava could smell the flowers. Rose and Danielle were there with Ryan and Brad. Cat was there with Will. "Okay, if we're all here, who's looking after the kids," Ava asked. "Emily has the kids at the house," Joe said. "So since you're here, what do you guys think of the house," Ava asked. "It's beautiful." Rose smirked. "You know something," Ava said. Rose shook her head. Ryan slid his arm around her. Cat hinted for her to look behind her. It was the minister that had married them. "Hi Ava." "Oh my goodness. How are you," Ava hugged him. "Very well." "Okay, seriously you guys. What's going on?" He handed Ava a note from Joe.

Babe,

Three years ago, you made me the happiest man in the world, and verified that I am way too spontaneous for my own good. In three years, I've fallen for you more every day. You give me a reason to wake up in the morning, a reason to smile, laugh and be happy. Now, we have two amazing kids, and you're more beautiful than the day I met you (even without your makeup). Three years ago I made you a promise that I would love you forever, never hurt you, that I'd honor you, protect you and always be there. That I promised to be yours forever. That you would be the only woman I ever loved, and I would spend the rest of my life with you. We both changed during the years, but the love only grew. Only one thing I have to ask you . . .

That was the end of the note. Ava looked at him. "Joe." He got down on bended knee. "See, I missed the bended knee thing the first time. Ava, will you marry me again," Joe asked. "In a heartbeat." He got up and kissed her. "So, now that you agreed," Joe said. Ava looked at Joe.

"Dearly beloved., . . . we are gathered here today to renew the vows between Joe and Ava." She smirked and so did he. "The day I met you all those years ago, my life changed. No matter how much I wanted to be wrong back then, my heart set me straight. When I saw you again, I refused to let go. I still do. I promise to hold you in my arms every night, kiss you at least 25 times a day, be a good Dad, and remind you how much I love you every minute of every day of every year for the rest of our lives."

"When we first met, I knew there was something different about you. Then three years ago when we saw each other again, we were drawn together. The day you talked me into running away to Nashville with you, I knew that I was hooked. We've gone through our share of growing pains. We always found our way back to each other. Then came Grace and Blake. You stole my heart. It's yours forever. I promise to be your best friend, to love you down to the core of my soul, to be a great Mom to the kids. I promise to always hear you out, to give you a hug whenever you need one, to never go to bed mad, to love you for every minute, day, hour, year and decade of the rest of our lives, and to always be your biggest fan."

Joe slid an eternity band on with her wedding band, then kissed her hand. "By the power vested in my by the state of Tennessee, I pronounce you husband and wife . . . . again." Joe kissed her. They cheered. "Hence why you needed the flowers," he whispered. She smirked and he kissed her again. The minister snuck out after talking to Ryan. "This is why I had to wear the white dress," Ava asked. He nodded. Joe had his arm around her and refused to let go. "So when did you plan this?" "The second you said a fresh start," Joe said. "Who knew you were so sneaky?" Ryan and Brad both laughed. "You mean Mr. Super Spy," Ryan teased. "I am not," Joe said. "You are so full of it," Brad said. "Okay, this is a story I have to hear."

They went and sat down in the TV room on the new black leather furniture that Devon had chosen. Joe wrapped his arm around Ava and she slid her heels off and leaned into Joe. "I am not a super spy," Joe said. "You tell the story or I am," Ryan said. He glared at Ryan. "Back when he first met Ava . . ." "Ryan." "Yes or no?" "When we first met, I kept trying to find a clue as to your full name," Joe said. "Oh really?" "Trust me, the man searched everywhere," Brad said. "Oh really?" "I called the people that set up the meet and greets and I would always come up a dead end," Joe said. "Miss smarty pants deleted her email address after the concert," Ryan teased. "Was getting crazy junk mail," Ava said. "I bet," Brad joked. "Anyway, every time we came back into town, I asked them to get in touch with you. Eventually, I sorta put it on the back burner," Joe said. "All those girls and so little time," Ava teased. "Funny," Joe said. "I was at the concert every time you know," Ava said. "Seriously?" "I saw Ryan and he laughed. Never did figure out why," Ava said. Joe threw a pillow at him. "Every time you showed up, you looked different. What do you want from me," Ryan teased. "I'll give you that one," Ava said.

"Then when you showed up that night with James, my heart jumped. I saw you walk in and knew you in a second. When you came and sat down, I was so excited I could barely hold myself back. Then I realized you were with James. That I had no chance in hell," Joe said. "Big mistake he was," Ava teased. His arm slid tighter. "After you two left after the concert, I finally had a name," Joe said. "Then he went nuts," Ryan said. Ava laughed. "Ryan," Joe said. "You did," Brad replied. "So I was up half the night trying to get info," Joe said. "Borderline stalker," Ryan joked. "Was trying to find out information to see how long you two had been together and if I had any chance at all," Joe said. "And?" "Was still nervous when I finally came across your address and phone number," Joe said. "Which was unlisted," Ava said. "Got in touch with your agent," Joe said. "And she blabbed the info. Remind me to give her a talking to," Ava joked. He kissed Ava. "Anyway, then I spent like a week and a half trying to figure out how to get you here. Took me a week to figure out what to say to you when I saw you." "Then I came to my senses and told James to screw off," Ava joked. "Especially when I found out what he'd done before you knew," Joe said. "What?" "One of my old buddies is friends with him too." "And how did you know," Ava asked. "The man sent Joe pictures," Brad said. "Then I finally got the guts to actually call you," Joe said. "And how convenient that Rose wasn't there." "I was out front," Joe said. "Definitely stalkerish." The guys laughed.

"Then I asked you to come to the concert." "What if I'd said no?" "I would've stood at your door with flowers until you said yes," Joe said. "And who's idea was that?" Brad laughed. "That's how he won me over. Every hour on the hour," Danielle said. "Good thing it only took 3 or 4 hours," Brad joked. They laughed. "I told him that flowers are a good way for him to get your attention," Brad teased. "Bad influence," Ava teased. "Then I showed." "No. Then I was so nervous before you showed, I changed 4 times," Joe said. "Seriously?" "He was like a teenager going to a dance. Had to pick the right shirt," Ryan teased. "You picked the right one," Ava said. "I paced most of the day. Then you finally showed up," Joe said. "Still can't believe the look on your face when I walked in." "Then I saw this sexy woman in one hell of a dress, walking in and right towards me." "Then I told him that James and I had broken it off. He was like a kid on a sugar high," Ava said. "All the things I wanted to say flew out of my head." "Still can't believe I agreed to that," Ava said. "What did you agree to," Cat asked. "He told me to come on tour with them for a few weeks." "And you went?" "Took a little negotiating, but she did," Joe said. "Still remember Ava walking in, packing then trying to sneak out. When I saw you I almost passed out," Rose said. "I wanted to get away. Definitely managed to do that," Ava said. "That the only reason you came with me?" "Yep," Ava teased. Ava giggled and Joe pulled her close and kissed her. "At the time it was."

"Still remember the look on your face when I asked you to marry me the first time," Joe said. "How long did you manage to wait," Cat asked. "A few weeks," Joe said. "Still can't believe that miss predictable said yes," Cat said. "She didn't have a choice," Joe said. "Oh really?" "Tough negotiator." "You two are hilarious," Danielle said. "Fell for him day one didn't you," Brad asked. Ava nodded. "One kiss and I was totally and completely hooked." "Still can't believe you," Joe said. "You think you were shocked? Seeing him wave goodbye when he left with her stunned me," Rose said. "That is until you met Ryan." "See, if you hadn't finally been with Ava after waiting all that damn time of us teasing you constantly, I wouldn't have met Rose," Ryan said. "And I wouldn't have met Will," Cat said. "She knows she was stuck the second we met each other the first time," Joe said. "Surprised you remembered who I was after all your million and one girlfriends," Ava teased. Will laughed. "Just knew when to hold on to the right one." "Nice save," Will teased. "Meaning," Cat asked. "I don't intend on getting my butt kicked. I'm pleading the fifth." "Good move Will," Joe said.

"It's not like you were all innocent before you met him," Cat said. "Shh." "Ooh, juicy stories. Speak on girl," Brad said. "I knew there was a reason we needed a muzzle," Ava said. "Funny. I seem to remember you when you were in your wild and crazy phase. "You mean pre-Derrick," Rose said. "And Kevin." "That was a bad nightmare," Ava said. "We used to laugh when Ava made it past the 3 month mark with a guy." "Why," Brad asked. "Because I would make them wait then leave when they thought they had won me over." "Intentionally," Joe asked. "No. I'd just realize that I didn't want to wake up the next morning beside an idiot." "Besides. You'd already seen what you wanted," Rose said. "What me and every other woman in the city wanted," Ava teased. "Think you dated them all didn't you," Ryan teased. "No. I just figured there was no point. Unless it was a real relationship, there was no point in getting attached to anyone," Ava said. "And Derrick," Joe asked. "A friend for years. We were drinking one night and boom." "And?" "A year and a half." "Ava." "He's still a good friend," Ava said. "Then there was the oh so wrong, dickhead in armor, idiot and a half, scrawny ass Kevin," Rose said. "So what happened there," Joe asked.

"We dated a while, then he figured he didn't need his place and moved in with me," Ava said. "Okay," Joe replied. "He had a handful of girlfriends on the side he didn't think I'd find out about. We broke up a few times, then finally he got scared of watching over his shoulder for me to find him." "What happened," Ryan asked. "He used me one too many times. I started getting fed up. He walked in and non-chalantly dumped me. No feeling, no emotion. Told him to get out and never come back," Ava said. "Tell me he didn't try," Joe said. "Locks can be changed." "Then there was psycho," Rose said. "Guess he finally got the hint after this long," Ava said. "Why did you two break it off anyway," Ryan asked. "One minute he was begging me to be with him. The next he was demanding that I stay. Then he was asking me to marry him. I remember asking him 'What is it that you love so much you don't want to ever lose me'. He told me that I gave him butterflies." "James," Joe asked. Ava nodded. "And he really thought that would work?" "Then he tried to schmooze me. Introduced me to these crazy guys he knew," Ava said. "Didn't work," Brad joked. "Nope. Did meet a hot guy out of it though," Ava said as Joe leaned over and kissed her. "So what happened? Why'd you break up with him," Ryan asked. "Truthfully, After I'd tried to dump him the first few times, I caught him with someone else." "Where," Ryan asked. "At a bar." "It was a strip club," Rose said. "He was with one of the dancers," Ava said. "Not Dare," Brad asked. Ava nodded. "James and Jackie at it as usual," Ryan teased. "What?" "They were always like that. He brought her to a show and she was trying to hit on Joe," Brad said. "When," Ava asked. Joe pulled her close. "A few months ago," Ryan said. Ava looked at Joe and he kissed her. "Nice save," Brad teased. "Told her I didn't like the stripper type. Only had eyes for you," Joe said. Ryan and Brad both laughed.

"So you walked away that easily," Ryan asked, "Got a pretty good distraction." "Am I allowed to say that we're pretty grateful you're here," Brad said. "I am too Brad." They all chatted a while longer, then headed home, leaving Ava and Joe in the new house. "Babe." "Mm." "We're staying here," Joe said. "And how are we doing that?" He pulled her close and kissed her. "Joe." "Your things are upstairs," he said. "What things?" "Plus Cat told me she got you something," Joe said. "Seriously, you planned this out to the end didn't you?" He nodded. "I wanted us to start right. No fighting, no stress, no bad karma," Joe said. "You know me so well don't you?" He nodded. "That's why you'll never get rid of me." "Think so," Ava asked. He cupped her face in his hands and kissed her with a kiss so passionate, so love-filled that her entire body was covered in goose bumps. After this many years, he still knew just what to do to cause the goose bumps he did the first day. He took her hand and walked upstairs.

They walked into the bedroom and Ava's mouth dropped. "Where," Ava asked. "Remember that magazine you have in your office where you have pages marked," Joe asked. She nodded. "Joe, this is beautiful." The four poster bed, the sheer draping, the sateen sheets, and white rose petals on the bed. It was exactly like the picture. "You didn't think I was actually downstairs all that time the other night," Joe said. She kissed him and curled into his arms. He grabbed something off the counter. The fireplace lit. "That was my favorite part," Joe said. Ava smirked. He kissed her. "I love you." "I love you too." He kissed her again and held her close. "What's wrong," Ava asked. "Never thought we'd make it to this." "Got news for you Mr. Morgan." "What's that?" "You're stuck with me too." He kissed her. Ava looked over to the counter and saw a bag that Cat left her. "What did she leave here?" He slid his arms around her and they walked over to it. She saw the Frederick's of Hollywood paper. "One of my favorite stores," Joe teased kissing her neck. Ava looked in the bag. "Well?" She laughed. "What?" "Sit." "Ava." "Sit." He kissed the back of her neck. His hands slid under the dress, sliding it off her shoulders. She turned towards him and he kissed her as the dress slid down her torso to the floor. She undid his shirt, then slid her arms around him. "The present can wait," Ava said. She kissed him, then walked towards the bed and he saw the white lace g-string. "And when did you get that?" "Girl has to have secrets." He followed her and leaned onto the bed beside her.

"Where would I be without you," Joe asked. "Probably searching on Google still," Ava joked. He kissed her again. He kicked his pants off and slid into her arms. "Don't think I could've done any of this without you," Joe said. "I love you." "Never going to be apart again. You know that right?" Ava nodded. He kissed her and they made love. The feel of her silky skin on his was one of his favorite things now. The feel of her body holding his. The feel of her kiss, even the smell of her hair had him past happy. He knew he would never lose it. He'd never be without her ever again.

They curled up under the covers of their new bed, still entangled together. "Joe." "Yes Mrs. Morgan." She smirked. "The New York thing." "That's where you came with us for the first time." "And you didn't say a thing," Ava said. "I know." "You are amazing. You know that?" "Especially for you." "Ever wonder what would have happened if we hadn't met up that day?" "No. I told him to bring you. When I realized who you were, I almost didn't want you to leave the room," Joe said. "You're hilarious." "Babe, if he hadn't brought you there, I would've taken you permanent hostage myself." "That would've gone over well." "The second I saw you," Joe said. "What makes you think I would've gone along with it?" He kissed her, curling up in her arms holding her so close she could hear his heart pounding in unison with hers. "I know one way I could've convinced you." "Oh really. You think that would've worked." He nibbled her ear. He nibbled down her neck, then kissed her. "Right. Like that would've worked," Ava said. She laughed. He kissed down her chest, then she felt his warm breath on her right hip. "Joe." He slid up to meet her gaze and pinned her arms to the bed. "Fine. It would've worked." "Better," he said. "Things would have been so different." "Still would've been trying to find out who you were." "And I still would have been front row," Ava said. "You know I would've found you eventually." "You never know." "Babe, I would have found you in a heartbeat." "Think so?" "Tell me you aren't testing the theory." She smirked. "Ava." She managed to sneak away from him.

Joe's phone went off first thing the next morning. "Brad, this better be good." "We have a show Friday." "Where?" "Downtown." "I thought we were getting a break for a while." "I wasn't going to turn them down," Brad said. "What days are we in the studio this week?" "Tuesday and Thursday. Sound check Friday at 3." "And?" "If you can talk her into it," Brad said. "I'll see what I can do." Ava came out of the bathroom. "I have to go." "Joe." He hung up. "Whoa." Ava came out in a black satin teddy with a plunging neckline and one strap across the back. "Had a feeling you'd like this," Ava said. He walked towards her. "We have to drive back," Ava said. She grabbed her sweater. "Not yet." "Yes now," Ava said. She managed to slip her leggings on and made it to the top of the steps when he pinned her to them. "Where do you think we're going?" "Home."

The doorbell rang. "Come on in Em," Joe said. He kissed Ava, then went into the bedroom. She walked downstairs. "Hi Mama," Grace said. "Hi baby girl." "I grabbed the bags Joe put in the closet. This place looks great," Emily said. Grace ran into the TV room. "Why does she sound like she's in heaven," Ava asked. Ava came downstairs and saw the teddy bear that Joe had bought her. She looked upstairs and he was leaning over the railing with a grin ear to ear. Ava walked up the steps, kissed him, then walked back downstairs. "And how is Blake," Ava asked. "Hungry." Ava slid him out of Emily's arms. "Well hello handsome." He was getting fussy. "I'll show you to your bedroom," Ava said. Ava walked upstairs then sat down in the glider chair. She saw the note by the speaker that said—press play. She pressed it and it was a few of the quiet songs that the guys had done. She fed Blake, then rocked him a while. She changed him, then he fell asleep in her arms. She tucked him into the crib. She saw the monitor on the counter. She turned it on then went into the bedroom. "Sneaky," Ava said. He nodded. He wrapped his legs around hers and pulled her on top of him on the bed. "Just thought of everything didn't you?" "Only forgot one thing." "What's that?" He kissed her. "And what did you forget?" "To disconnect the phones." Ava laughed.

They came downstairs and played with Grace while Emily got settled. "Daddy, where my room?" "We're going to get you a bed today." "Really?" "A big girl bed." He looked at Ava. "I can stay with Blake," Emily said. "Guess we're going to find you a bed then." "Don't we need one for Emily's room?" He shook his head. "Already done?" He nodded. "We need one for our room though." "My old bed?" He kissed her. They left with Grace after grabbing a coffee and some juice for Grace.

After an hour or so, they found one, bought it, got Grace's bed and had them delivered. "Not even a crowd." He kissed Ava. "Daddy, who that?" He looked over and saw Tiffany. "Hey." Ava picked Grace up. "I'll meet you in the car." He kissed Ava and she left before she said something in front of Grace that she would no doubt remember and repeat.

"What are you doing here," Joe said. "Heard you moved down here." "Tiff, if you're trying to cause shit, you succeeded." "Just reminding you of what you could have." "We renewed our vows last night." "Her decision or yours?" "Mine." "Still miss the party," Tiffany asked. "I have Ava. The party can kiss my ass." "I know you miss it." "Just let it be alright? I don't need to be fighting with her again." "Bet I could still convince you." He turned and walked off. "You know I'm right." He hopped in the car, kissed Ava, then pulled out. "Daddy, can we have ice cream?" "Sure." Ava slid her hand in his and they headed to the store. They got a few treats for the kids, groceries, and a few movies. They pulled back in and the delivery from the furniture store was coming down the street. The groceries came in, and Joe showed the delivery guys where the beds needed to go. Ava came upstairs with Grace and Joe was making the bed in Grace's room. "I like them Daddy," Grace said. "Could it be because they have your frog on them?" She hugged him. Blake was waking up. Ava went in and got him, slid him into his t-shirt and pants, then brought him downstairs. Ava made some lunch while Blake played on the floor.

They came downstairs and Ava handed Grace her veggie pizza and her and Joe had their lunch. After, Grace was determined to get in the pool. "Fine. Come with me and we'll get our suits on," Ava said walking upstairs with Grace. She slid her bathing suit on, and Grace ran downstairs. She found her black bikini, that Joe had made sure was packed, and he came in behind her. "What are you doing up here," Ava asked. "Emily took them into the pool." "And you're up here because?" He kissed her and tried to untie her bikini top. "It's a damn shame to waste this." "Joe." He kissed her again and picked her up. She wrapped her legs around him. He leaned her onto the bathroom counter. She slid her leggings off and he wrapped his arms around her. They had sex on the counter. It was hot. So hot it could have melted the marble countertop. "Really not allowed to wear that anymore." "Unless." He smirked. "So what did Tiffany want," Ava asked. "Doesn't matter." "Joe." "Tried to cause shit." "Just say it." "She asked if I missed the party." "And?" "Told her all I wanted was you." "And?" "Doesn't matter." "Joe. Do you?" "Sometimes I miss it, then I come home and I see you and I see the kids and I don't miss it anymore." "Why?" "Because all that time, I was looking for something I didn't think existed. Then I found you. After all that time trying to hunt you down, I found you. I love you. Always have." "Very sweet." "I mean it. I've spent so much time running away from being an adult, and trying to be the player, that I looked past the one thing I always wanted. I'm not backing one inch away from it." She motioned for him to come closer. "I love you. Always will." He kissed her.

She slid her bikini back on, he slid his swimsuit on, then they went outside. Grace was splashing around and so was Blake. Emily was playing with them. "Everything okay," Emily asked. Ava nodded. Ava dove into the pool with Joe one step behind her. She came up under Grace and tickled her feet. "Mama." "You having fun?" She nodded. Joe had Blake in his arms. "Em." She turned towards Ava. Grace splashed her. They played around in the pool for a while, then they hopped out. Grace played with her toys, Blake played with his toys and Joe and Ava curled up on the chaise together. Emily went through her emails, then did some more homework. "So how is the course coming," Ava asked. "Finished the first 4 classes. Have another ten to go." "So what did you decide to take anyway," Joe asked. "Child psychology." "You knew I minored in psychology at school," Ava said. "Really?" "Hence why I can make characters in the stories everyone can get involved in." "Then you can help when I have stuff I don't understand," Emily said. Ava nodded. "Emily, can you watch princess with me," Grace said. "Come on short stuff." Grace ran inside and Blake started getting upset. Ava walked over to him. "What is up with you?" Grace came back out and he stopped. Joe laughed. "Can Blake come," Joe asked. Ava brought him in and Emily sat with them while they watched the movie. Joe and Ava curled up on the chaise and relaxed.

"What," Joe asked. Ava kissed him. "What was that for?" "Being a good man." "Oh really." Ava nodded. He leaned her onto her back and she slid a leg around his and he kissed her. It was a make your body stand up at attention and melt into his kind of kiss. His arms slid around her and she felt him undoing the top of her bikini. "Joe." "Party pooper." He kissed her again. "You know we haven't tried the hot tub out yet," Joe said. He smirked, kissed her, then got up and pulled her to her feet. He turned it on and they slid into it. "Devon made it salt water," Joe said. "Mm." He sat opposite her. She slid her legs across his lap. "I wouldn't if I were you," Joe said. "And why is that?" "Mama," Grace said. "Over here baby." "Can we watch in the movie room?" "Sure." Ava heard them head down the steps. Joe stared at her. She slid across the tub and into his lap. "Hey." "Hey yourself," Joe said. "So what were you saying?" "Unless . . ." "Ava, I'm making Grace popcorn. Did you two want any," Emily asked. "No but thanks." Ava slid back over to her side. He smirked. "What?" He heard the microwave, then heard them go downstairs. He slid over to Ava and pulled her into his lap. He kissed her and pulled her close. "Now where were we," Joe asked. "You know we're going to get . . . ." He kissed her and his hands slid down to her backside. "Joe." "What?" She heard his phone. "It can wait whoever it is." Ava kissed him then got up. He watched the water slide down her body.

"Is Joe there?" "Can I ask who's calling?" "Callie." "And you'd be calling my husband because?" "He asked." Ava walked over and handed the phone to him, then went inside. She went upstairs and showered, then slid her leggings and sweater on and went downstairs. She heard him come inside, then walk downstairs. Grace was in Ava's lap and Blake was asleep in the chair beside her. Emily was out cold on the other side. "Babe." "Shh." Grace was just drifting off. He took Blake upstairs and put him down for a nap, then came back down and Ava was turning the TV off. She slid a blanket over Emily and took Grace upstairs to her bed. She walked back downstairs and went into the kitchen, pouring herself a large glass of iced tea. "Babe." She walked past him and into the office. "You seriously going to get mad," Joe asked. Ava sat down and logged into her laptop. He walked over and snapped it shut. "Do you know who that was?" "Callie. As in 'if it means seeing you again, I won't tell anyone'." "Babe." "Don't try telling me I'm taking it out of proportion." "She works for the awards. We were nominated for three shows." "Fine." Ava opened her laptop back up. He closed the office door. "If it's fine then why do you look pissed off," Joe asked. "Gee. After all this time, a girl you fucked calls your cell phone. Funny enough, the same day, we bump into Tiffany at the grocery store." "Ava." She got up and he stopped her. "Let go." "Ava." "I'm going for a drive." "Babe." She grabbed her purse and phone and walked out.

Ava drove for a while, then stopped and walked through the park. She sat down by the tree he'd carved their initials in when he'd first found out who she was. She relaxed and tried to cool off. Her phone went off. "Yep." "Tell me I didn't see your car at the park," Cat said. "Just taking a breather." "Ava, what happened?" "Just needed quiet." "You don't sit like that unless you're upset." "Meaning?" "Meaning something is wrong," Cat said standing in front of her. Ava hung up and put the phone in her bag. "Talk." "It's nothing." "You suck at lying, especially when I know you better than you think I do," Cat said. "We bumped into Tiffany when we were out." "Doing?" "New bed for Grace and a new mattress for us." "And?" "I kissed him, then took Grace to the car." "Then?" "Callie." "She is the rep for the awards. Think it's just two of them though," Cat said. "Not the point. Why would she call Joe directly?" "You have a good point." "After what he did last night, I don't want to get pissed off, but I can't help it," Ava said. "I know what you need," Cat said.

An hour later, they were having a drink and something to eat at one of Ava's new favorite places. After the snack and a hug, Ava took her time heading back. She made a stop or two, then pulled into the driveway. Ava walked in, then went straight upstairs. Joe came in with Blake in his arms. "You okay," Joe asked. Ava slid Blake out of Joe's arms and took him into the bedroom and rocked him in the glider. She fed him, then put him to bed. She came back in and Joe was finishing giving Grace her bath. "Hi Mama," Grace said. "Hey baby." She hopped out of the tub, slid on her little robe and ran into Ava. "How was your bath?" "Lots of bubbles." "Good." "Mama, can you and Daddy sing," Grace asked. "Daddy will." "Mama." She picked her up and carried her into her new bedroom. She helped Grace into her pajamas, handed her the frog, then tucked her in. "You mad at Daddy?" "No. I went to go see Auntie Cat. She's having a baby." "Mama." Ava looked at her. "I love you." "I love you too baby." She heard Joe. "Daddy will sing you a song, then sleep time okay," Ava said. Grace nodded and hugged Ava. Joe grabbed her hand as she was walking past him. She pulled it back. She went into the bedroom and he sat down to sing Grace to sleep.

Ava slid on her new bathing suit, then her robe and walked back downstairs. She grabbed herself a lemonade then went outside and sat in the hot tub. Her phone rang two minutes later. "Hey Emily." "I'll be back in a half-hour. Just went out with Jeff." "Okay." "Ava." "What?" "You alright," Emily asked. "I will." She hung up, then put the phone down. Ava leaned back in the tub. A little while later, she saw the kitchen lights go out and Joe came outside. He slid into the hot tub with her. He slid her legs across his lap. He slid his hand in hers. She looked at him. Her eyes were welling up. "Stop thinking it," Joe said. She didn't say a word. His phone rang. She got up, grabbed a towel and sat down on the chaise. "Yep." "There's a party tonight. Come." "No." "Joe, come on. Stop being all stuffy." He hung up. He walked over to Ava and she got up and dove into the pool. "You do realize that you can't run forever," Joe said. Ava leaned onto the edge. He jumped in and slid up behind her wrapping his arms around her. "Who now?" "Doesn't matter." She went to move and he pinned her to the edge. "You can't keep walking away." "And I'm supposed to do what?" "Trust me." "Joe." "You promised me." "And you promised me that shit was over." "It is."

"Then why is she calling you?" He tried to turn her to face him and she slipped out of his grasp, swam to the other side and got out.

He sat there and watched her. "Do you believe me?" "You get a phone call from who I can only guess was Tiffany, then you think that I'm not going to be pissed off?" He got out of the pool and walked towards her. "She asked me to come party. I said no." "I told you before. I'm done with the drama Joe. Why don't you just go to the damn party." Ava got up and pulled on her sweater and he pulled her towards him. "Let go." He kissed her. He picked her up and carried her to the double chaise. "Put me down." He kissed her again, then had her pinned. "Joe." "You think I want to be at that party?" "Don't know." "I do." "See." "I want to be here, with my wife and my kids. I want to curl up in bed with one woman, every night for the rest of my life." "Let go." He kissed her. "You gonna stop getting all mad?" She managed to get up. She walked into the house and closed the door.

She went upstairs, then slid on her nightgown, washed up and climbed into bed. A half-hour later, he came upstairs, then sat on the edge of the bed. "Ava." "Just go. Have a blast." "Stop being a child." "Go." She heard him walk into the bathroom, heard water running, then he walked back into the bedroom. He sat down beside her. "I'm not going to the party." "Just go." "No." "Don't let me stop you," Ava said. "Ava, I'm staying in this house with you. I'm not going to the damn party." "Joe." "Not going unless you're there with me. I'm not putting you through that." "Just go. Then they'll stop asking." "Not without you." "I can't." "Then I'm not going." Before she could start again, he kissed her. "I love the sexy woman in my arms. I don't need the damn party." He kissed her again and slid his arms around her. "Joe." "Wanna know what those parties are? Girls who think if they sleep with me, they'll be somebody. Girls who want to be known as the girl that fucked that guitar guy." "So have a blast." Ava tried to move, but his arm was around her. "Why are you so mad?" "We move here to get away from them and they follow us. That's why." She got away and went to walk off when he stopped her at the door. "You made me a promise," Joe said. "And?" "Never going to bed mad." "I'm not mad. I'm just sick of them always in our faces." He kissed her sliding his fingers through her hair. "There always will be something. Difference is, you know I love you, and I know you love me. That the ring on our hands means that the stupid party shit is over." "If you go . . ." He kissed her. As he was doing that, Emily came home. "Em, you in the rest of tonight?" "Yep." "We're going out," Joe said.

He handed Ava the black dress, then got changed. "Where are we going?" "You want me to go, then you're coming with me." "Joe." He pulled his shirt and his blue jeans on, then fixed up his hair as she was doing her makeup. He noticed her put on the black satin dress instead that had a daringly low back and the front showed off just enough to make him not want to take her anywhere. He grabbed her hand, she grabbed her purse and her phone, then they left. She slid her heels on in the SUV.

Chapter 49

Joe walked in and Tiffany walked right towards him. "I knew you'd change your mind." She went to kiss him when she saw Ava as he white knuckled her hand. "Didn't." "You are such a party pooper," Tiffany said. "And why is that," Ava asked. "You know Callie's here." "And," Ava said. "You'll see." Ava tried to let go, but he wouldn't. "I'm getting a drink," Ava said. He followed her. "Same old," the bartender asked Joe. He nodded. "And for you?" "Vodka Martini," Ava said. He looked at Ava. "Soda," Joe saie. They grabbed their drinks, then he walked over towards the group of girls. "So Tiff talked you into it did she," a girl said. "Ava, Kitty," Joe said. "As in your wife Ava?" They kept walking. Finally he got to Callie. "Hey stranger." "Callie." "Missed you." "I bet. You remember Ava right," Joe said. "Nice meeting you." Callie saw the ring on Ava's finger. They went over to the empty table and sat down. "See," Joe said. "And the reason we had to be here was?" He kissed her. "You wanted to know. This is the reason why I'm not going to the parties." She saw the girls falling all over the guys. "Then why did you even go in the first place," Ava asked. "Because there was no you." Ava looked over and Tiffany was heading towards them. "Joe, can I talk to you for a minute," Tiffany asked. "We're heading home in a few." "Joe." Ava nodded and he went to talk to her.

"What?" "Why," Tiffany asked. "Because she's my wife. You were going to annoy me until I showed. I'm here." "Still." "I told you the parties were done. She is the best thing that ever happened to me. I'm not messing it up because you feel like trying to talk me into coming to this stupid thing." "I know you missed this," Tiffany said. "Not really." "Joe." "All I wanted all that time was to find Ava. I found her and I'm not messing it up to make you happy." He walked back towards where they'd been sitting and Ava wasn't there.

He looked around for her, then saw her talking to someone by the bar. He slid up behind her and slid his arms around her. "Hey Joe," Jeff said. He looked at the man standing beside her and realized who it was. "What are you doing here?" "Wanted to make an appearance, then I'm heading home," he said. Ava walked off. He took off after her. "Ava." She went and sat back down. She finished her drink. He sat down with her. "Tell me we're leaving," Ava asked. "Think we should." "And why is that," Ava asked. "Because I know by the look on your face that you're either going to kick Jeff's butt, or you're going to go after Tiffany." Ava put the glass down and walked towards the door. "Ava." She walked out. Tiffany grabbed him as he was about to go after her. "What?" She kissed him. He broke the kiss, then took off after Ava. He saw the cab pull out as he made it out the door. He had another drink then headed home.

Joe walked in and the lights were off. He walked upstairs and she was in bed. He got changed, then slid into bed with her. He slid his arms around her. "Wipe off her lipstick," Ava said. "Ava." She went to get up and he pulled her back towards him. "You aren't starting this." "I'm tired alright." "Ava." "What?" "I love you. You wanted to see the parties that I used to go to. That's what they were. I sat off by myself then ended up leaving with some nameless person." "And tonight?" He turned her towards him. He kissed her. "I love you. To me, there was nobody else in that room." "Joe." He kissed her again. It was one of those toe-curling kisses. When they finally came up for air, he pulled her leg around him. "You finally going to give up," he asked. "No." "Why did you take off?" "I didn't want to sit around and wait for something to happen." "Such as?" Before she could answer, he kissed her. "Don't even say what I think you are." "Her to cause a scene . . . again." "If I had to ravage you in front of her to make her buzz off I would have," Joe said. "Joe." "I'm just saying." "We allowed to just avoid her from now on?" He kissed Ava. "Blocked her cell number. You have to remember something." "What?" "That ring that I put on your finger yesterday means something to me. All of the stupid crap I did 4 and 5 years ago is done. There's only one woman for me." "Still." "I'm never going to another party like that. I'd much rather be here, curled up with you, and reminding you every second that I love you," Joe said. "And how were you planning to do that?" His hand slid the satin nightgown up her leg. "Have an idea or two." "Joe, seriously." "If I have to tell you every minute of every day I will." "Joe." "I love you. Nothing she does is going to stop that." "Why can't we just erase her from our lives?" "Don't think there is one big enough."

He curled up with her and tried to make up for things that had happened. He knew there was no erasing it. It was part of his past. The one thing he knew, and Ava knew, was that she was his future. There would be no more parties like that. No more running off and playing playboy. No more groupies, and no more partying until all hours. This was where he'd always wanted to be, and there was no more giving it up. She was the only woman he ever wanted. No matter what happened next, he wasn't going to ever let her go.

Ava and Joe curled up together and she fell asleep in his arms. The next morning she woke up to an empty bed. She got up and went downstairs and the kids were gone. She checked in the driveway and the SUV was gone and so was Emily's car. Ava made herself coffee, then sat down and did some writing. 'Why not make the best of the silence.' She got a few chapters in when she heard the SUV pulling in blaring a song that Ava knew had to be one of Joe's favorites. She saved her work, then refilled her coffee cup.

Joe came in and walked into the kitchen. "Morning beautiful." He kissed Ava. "Where are Blake and Grace?" "With Em. They're at the park." "Why are you so perky mister non-morning person?" He slid his arms around her and sat her on the counter. "What are you up to?" He kissed her again. "Joe, spill it." "You needed sleep," Joe said. "Blake?" "Fed. Grace has decided she now loves pancakes with strawberries." "What time is it?" "9:30." "Joe." "And I got fresh croissants and some fruit from the store." "What else happened last night?" "Nothing." "Then why . . ." He kissed her. "We get to relax. I have to go to the studio tomorrow. I wanted to spend the morning with you." "And just what were you planning?" He held her closer. "Thinking that you need to get dressed." "Where are we going?" He kissed her. "You should eat something first though." "Such as?" He handed her a plate with pancakes and strawberries. "Oh you think this is going to work on me do you," Ava asked. He kissed her again. They had something to eat, then she got changed and they left. "Where are we going?" "You'll see."

They pulled into the photo studio a while later. Ava looked at him. "Pictures for the new CD." "Joe." "And a few for us." They got changed, did the photo shoot, then the guys showed and they did a few more shots. "Found a couple good ones. Thanks." Ava and Joe left. "What are you up to," Ava asked. Joe smirked then pulled into the house. "Joe." He hopped out and came around to her door. "What are you up to?" He picked her up and carried her. Put me down. "Nope." "What are you up to," Ava said. He kissed her. They went inside and walked upstairs. He walked into the bedroom and leaned her onto the bed. "Joe." Within an hour, the proofs were in his email. They looked through them and Ava saw why Joe had done it. They were pictures of the two of them. Laughing, him flirting with her. Ava smirking as he went to nibble her ear. Him leaning in to kiss her. "That's the reason why," Joe said. "That's what I see every time you get mad." "I love you." "I know. And if you'd stop getting mad over nothing, we'd be fine," he said. "So the pictures were because?" "You have to stop worrying. If seeing the look in my eyes that I have every time you're around is going to do it, then so be it." "Joe." "I love you. Nothing and nobody is ever going to change any of it."

That Friday, they showed up at the venue. Joe came in hand in hand with Ava. "I see you two are still just as bad as newlyweds," Ryan joked. Joe smirked. They got set up for sound check, then they had dinner. Ava went and changed, then came out and walked over to Joe. "So we're doing the new mix of the my gang song, forever in my arms, and love letter," Ryan said. "We have to do that other one," Joe said. Ryan motioned for Joe to turn around. She walked towards him in the black satin dress and heels. Backless, plunging neckline and fit so well it was like it was sewn onto her. "Whoa," Joe said. "Thanks," Ava said. She slid her arm around Joe. His arm wrapped around her and all he could feel was her soft skin. Then he realized there was no back to the dress. He nuzzled her ear. "You know, you guys should get changed," Joe said. "Guess we're wearing whatever tonight then." "Black and red," Ava said. "Well okay then miss stylist." Ryan kissed her cheek. Brad gave her a hug then left with Ryan. "Nice dress," Joe said. "Got it to impress this hot guy I know." "I know him?" Ava nodded. "Think I might need your help getting changed," Joe said. "Funny." He kissed her, then grabbed her hand and they went to go get changed.

An hour or so later, the place was starting to fill up. Ava went to talk to someone leaving Joe with the guys. "Where'd she take off to," Joe asked. "No idea," Brad said. "Buddy, you sure you want her out there in that dress," Ryan joked. "Not like I can run out and get her." He called her cell, then heard the phone ringing. "Damn it." "Joe, Ava told me to hand you this," Brad said. He handed him a note:

Can spot me from a crowd? Prove it. XO

He laughed. "You're on guys," the stage manager said. They walked out, sang a song or two and he looked over towards the first row. "We need some help on this next one. Anyone seen Ava," Joe asked. Joe stared straight at her. The fans started going nuts. "Well gee, if you can't do it without me," Ava joked. He kissed her. The crowd screamed again. They sang the two or three songs with Ava, then Joe had to do something. "So, I know all of you know the words to this song. It means a lot to me and the guys. I know you know what song I'm talking about," Joe said. "Every road that I've been down . . ." Ava sang with the guys, then they finished up. She slipped backstage. The second they got back there, Joe kissed her. "Will always be able to," Joe said. "What are you two talkin' about," Ryan asked. "Thought I wouldn't be able to find her in the crowd." "In that dress? Just look for the guys that were drooling," Brad teased. "Funny." Joe's arms wrapped around her. "You have a point." She went to slip out of his arms and he pulled her back. "Going to have to be a bodyguard tonight," Joe said. Her back was to him, but he was tight up against her. "So where's Rose and Danielle," Ava asked. "They're out there. You ready?" Ava nodded. Ryan and Brad went out and Joe pulled Ava to him and kissed her. "You think I wouldn't find you?" "Knew you would." He kissed her. They headed out and went and grabbed a drink, then found the guys and Rose and Danielle.

"Seriously, I don't know how the hell you look that good after two kids," Rose said. "We work out," Joe joked. "Seriously Ava, you look amazing." "Sorta helps when Grace can outrun both of us most of the time," Ava said. "I would never have pictured you in a dress like that," Danielle said. "I would've," Cat said sneaking up behind Ava. She hugged her, then saw Will at the bar. "Didn't know you two were coming," Ava said. "He said he needed to talk to Joe." "Everything okay?" Cat nodded. Joe kissed Ava, then walked over.

Within a few minutes, a calm conversation had turned into another fight with Will. Joe felt someone lean against him, then saw Ava's ring. "Hey beautiful." He kissed Ava. "You two are way too serious over here," Ava said. "Just talkin." "Well, I think you need to stop pouting and come dance," Ava said. She kissed Joe and led him to the dance floor. They put on Like Me for them then he pulled her close.

He sang it in her ear. She smirked. "I love you." He kissed her neck. She felt his fingers slide under her dress at the base of her back. "Joe." He kissed her. "Home?" He nodded. They grabbed their things, then walked over to the guys. "We're heading home," Joe said. "You know you two can't hide away forever in that house." "That's why we got it. To get away from everything," Joe said. "You need to have a party." "Nope." "Ava," Rose said. "Remember a long time ago when you wanted a space to yourself with no noise and you could just relax?" Rose nodded. "Still." "Party at the other house. This one's our little getaway." "I get it," Brad said. Ava hugged the girls goodbye then left with Joe.

They walked into the house and all was quiet. Ava heard Emily on the phone with who could only be Jeff. Joe leaned Ava into the wall. "What?" He kissed her with a kiss that had her knees turning to Jell-o. "Joe." He kissed down her neck. "Not here." They were walking up the stairs when Ava heard Blake wake up. He kissed her as she slid into Blake's room. She settled him back down, then gave him his bottle and put him back to sleep. She walked into the bedroom and slid her arms around Joe. "Hey." She undid his belt. He turned towards her. "What you doing?" "Nothing." He closed the bedroom doors. "Now back to where we were," he said. His hands slid down her bare back. "This is my new favorite dress," Joe said. "Uh oh." He kissed her. "So now that we're home, now what?" He turned the music on quietly and sang to her as they danced. "Think that's gonna work do you?" He kissed her and backed her into the wall. "I know something that will." He kissed her again and slid the straps of her dress off her shoulders, dropping the dress to the ground. He slid her arms above her head, linking his fingers with hers then pinned her arms to the wall. "You know how sexy you are," Joe asked. Goose bumps grew across her skin. "Joe." He kissed her again and her knees went weak. He picked her up, carrying her to the bed. He slid off the last of her clothes then she went to help him with his shirt and he kissed her. His shirt was on the floor with her dress in minutes. He leaned against her. She craved him. Every inch of her wanted him.

Ava played with the kids for the better part of the early afternoon the next day, then put them down for a nap and came downstairs. Joe was on the phone. "I can't talk." "Joe, come on." "I'm not repeating myself." "So I'll meet you?" "Fine." He hung up. She looked at him, then walked back upstairs. "Ava." She walked upstairs, threw on her workout gear, then went for the door when he dove in front of her. "Babe." "What?" "Where are you going?" "The gym." "It wasn't what you think." "Whatever." She walked past him and hopped in the car and left. After an hour and a half workout, she came home, then went upstairs and showered. Just as she was stepping out, he walked in and slid his arms around her. "Hey." She said nothing. "Ava." "What?" "What's wrong?" "Say it." "What?" "What's this one's name Joe?" "Babe." "Don't play the stupid card. Just say it." "Ava." "Fine." She walked away, grabbed his phone and checked for herself. "Callie?" "Babe." She threw the phone at him. She got dressed then heard Grace waking up. He pulled Ava into his arms. "Let go." "You're coming with me." "No I am not." He went to kiss her and she broke away just as Grace was coming out of her room. "Hi Mama." "Hey baby girl." She walked over to Ava, and she picked her up. She curled up in Ava's arms. "Hungry?" She nodded. Ava walked downstairs with her and gave her some fruit, then curled up on the sofa with her.

Joe came down a little while later with Blake. "Mama, can we watch the movie?" "Pick something else." "Mama." Joe put the DVD of their wedding in. Ava got up and went and started dinner. Emily came in a few minutes later. "Thought you and Joe were going out to dinner," Emily said. "No." "We are," Joe said. He came in behind Ava. "No we aren't." "It's a restaurant opening." "Have fun then," Ava said. "I'll do this," Emily said. Ava walked towards her office and he grabbed her hand, walking downstairs towards the studio.

"What?" He closed the door. "Get it out of your system," Ava said. "I'm not going anywhere with you." "Done?" "No. I walk in here and you're having a conversation with another one of your damn girlfriends, then you actually think . . ." He kissed her, pinning her to the wall. "That she's the owner of the restaurant. She asked me to come and I told her I wouldn't. Only way I am going is if you are with me." "Like I'm . . ." He kissed her again and pulled her close. "Stop being a pain in the ass," Joe said. "And why should I believe you?" "Left hand. The finger beside your pinky." "You are a pain . . ." He kissed her again and picked her up, wrapping her legs around him and walked her to the sofa. They broke the kiss and he looked at her, brushing the hair from her face. "Always have to make things difficult don't you?" "What do you expect me to think when I hear a conversation like that," Ava said. "I love you. You're ridiculously in love with me and I couldn't even think of being with anyone else." She looked at him. "No more being mad and bringing up ancient history either," Joe said. "Didn't say a word." He kissed her. "You're coming with me." Ava shook her head. "Two hours max." "Why do we even have to go out," Ava asked. "Because I said so." "And if I said no?" "Then you'd still be there."

An hour later, they left. They showed up at the restaurant and walked in hand in hand. "Hey Joe." Callie walked straight to him and hugged him, practically falling out of her low cut cocktail dress. "You remember Ava right," Joe asked. "Yeah. Hi." Awkward silence. "Nice restaurant." "Thanks." "Joe, I have to show you around," she said. Ava walked over to the bar and grabbed herself a drink. Joe slid up behind her and ordered himself one. "Thought you were going on the grand tour." He kissed her neck. "Not interested." He grabbed their drinks and they headed to their quiet table. "Stop thinking what I know you are," Joe said. "She's staring over here." "Then give her a reason to." "What?" He kissed Ava. When they broke the kiss, Callie had walked off. They had dinner, then went to head out when Callie stopped them. "Can I borrow him for a few minutes," she asked. "Fine with me," Ava said. Joe kissed Ava.

"What," Joe asked as Callie pulled him away from everyone. "I thought you were coming just you." "We're married. Package deal." "Joe." "I told you no. You didn't want to hear it, then you need your ears cleaned." She pulled him into the office. "I miss you." "And you know better." "Please." "Callie, I married her because I love her. I know you want me, but it's not happening. I love her." She kissed him. A piece of him let him kiss her back, then he stopped himself. "Bet I could still tease you into it," Callie said. He walked out and grabbed Ava's hand and they left. He went to get in the car, and Ava tried not to cause a scene. "Ava." "I'm going to Starbucks," she said. She walked down the street with the paparazzi following her. He finally caught up to her. "Babe." She shook her head. He went to kiss her. "Wipe her lipstick off," Ava said. Ava grabbed her coffee and walked out. She went and got in the car, and they left and headed home.

They got to the house and he locked the car doors. "Talk." Ava unlocked her door and went to get out when he pulled her back into the car. "Ava." "I'm going to bed." "Stop it." "Tell me she didn't try something. Go ahead and tell me." "She did. I walked out." Ava got out of the car and went inside. He walked in and she was upstairs. Emily was asleep on the sofa. He walked upstairs and closed the bedroom door, then slid up behind her. "Don't." "Ava." "Give me 5 minutes to cool off." "Nothing else happened." "Am I going to find out a year from now that something did?" He shook his head and kissed her shoulder. "Babe." "Five minutes." "For what? Nothing happened." Ava turned towards him. "I want you to remember something." "What's that?" "That ring on my finger means something to both of us, and I am never ever risking losing you." "Good." Ava walked off. She slid into bed and grabbed her book. He slid it out of her hands and sat down on the bed beside her. "What?" He kissed her. Within minutes, one kiss turned into 20. She slid her legs around him and undid his shirt, never breaking the kiss for a second. "I love you." "I love you too," Ava said. "About time." He smirked and kissed her again as his shirt hit the floor. Ava heard Blake wake up. "Don't move." "Joe." He got up, gave Blake a bottle, then put him back down. He came into the bedroom and kicked his dress pants off, then slid into bed with Ava. She handed him his phone and got up.

1 missed call—Tiffany

She sat downstairs and dove into her writing. An hour or so later, she stopped. She grabbed a drink from the kitchen, then went back into the office. He was sitting on the edge of her sofa. Ava went back to writing, ignoring that he was in the room. "You have to talk to me at some point." "What did she want," Ava asked. "I don't know. I deleted the message and blocked the number." Ava kept going. "I can't stop the world from doing the things it does." "Never asked you to." "Babe." "I don't want to deal with this anymore." "Meaning what?" "Meaning we're changing the numbers. No more calls from your ex's, and the only ones that will have the numbers are the guys and family and our actual friends," Ava said. "Good idea." "And if one more call comes from one of your girlfriends, you're leaving." Ava got up and walked out of the office, then walked upstairs and went to bed. It was the first night that she hadn't fallen asleep in his arms, and the first night that he fell asleep worried since they renewed their vows.

The next morning, he woke up and the bed was empty. He heard Ava downstairs with the kids. He got up, cleaned up, then went downstairs. It wasn't Ava with them. "Hey. She left you a note on the counter." He went into the kitchen.

Gone shopping. Back at lunch.

He called her phone. "Where are you?" "I told you." "Ava." "I have to go." She hung up. He made a coffee, then went in and played with the kids.

CHAPTER 50

"Who was that," Cat asked. "Who do you think?" "Okay, something is going on." "Cat, it's nothing." "You know you suck at lying." "We got invited to Callie's restaurant opening and she made a move on him." "Shit." "Then we went home and Tiffany called him." "It's coincidence." Ava looked behind Cat and swore she saw Will. "Tell me that isn't who I think." Cat turned and saw exactly what Ava did.

Cat walked towards him and he kissed the woman he was with. "Will, can't you wait until we get back to my place?" "Yeah Will. Can't you," Cat said. He turned around and she slapped him so hard he fell. Ava dragged Cat the other way and towards the lingerie store. "I can't believe him," Cat said. Ava grabbed a few items and pulled Cat into the dressing room. "Deep breath." She sent a text. "What are you doing?" "Getting the locks changed."

2pm hit and Ava wasn't back. Joe called her cell. "Where are you?" "Taking care of Cat." "What's wrong?" "She caught Will." "Where are you?" "Joe." "Ava, where?" "Wyndham." An hour later, he was pulling into the hotel. He found out the room and went upstairs. "What is he doing here," Cat asked. "Cat." "Where was he," Joe asked. "The mall." He kissed Ava then took off to find Will.

He got down to the lobby and saw him with a blonde who he thought looked like Ava's twin. He walked over to him. "Hey. Joe, this is Eve. This is my baby brother Joe." "Talk. Now," Joe said. "Sorta in the middle . . ." Joe dragged him off. "What the hell?" "You do realize who you pissed off," Joe asked. "Life isn't perfect." "You married her. She's pregnant." "You two are the only ones who can act that well Joe." "Meaning?" "You two have to be fighting again. The bags under your eyes tell me I'm right." "They tell you that we have two kids, one of whom is still up at least once or twice a night." "Liar." "Did you sleep with her," Joe asked. "I don't kiss and tell." "Then you deserve what you're getting." "Meaning what?" Joe walked off. He headed for the elevator.

"We'll just go to the house and get your stuff. You can stay at the house with us." "Ava, you two are fighting too." "And you get the house to yourself." "Oh." "Just until you figure out what you want to do." "Meaning what? I'm not taking him back," Cat said. "Stop." "What?" "You married him. You don't get out that easily." "I'm not staying with him if this is what he's doing." Joe knocked. "Hey." "Grab her things," Joe said. "Joe." "I got an extra set of keys for the house."

They got Cat settled, then Ava went into the master bedroom. Joe pinned her to the closed door.

"What is up with you," Ava asked. He kissed her. "Joe." "I love you." "Joe, let go." He shook his head. He pulled her tight to him. "I never want you like that," he said. "Joe." "Never." It finally hit him that she'd been through what Cat was living right now because of him. He picked her up, leaning her onto the bed. "Joe." "I am never ever losing you." He kissed her again. "Joe." "I don't want him in this house," Joe said. "I know." He kissed her. He slid his arms tight around her. "Stop worrying." He kissed her again. "I want you home tonight," Joe said. Ava nodded. He kissed her again then pulled her to her feet. "Promise me something." "What?" "That if I ever do that to you, you kick my ass into the ground," Joe said. Ava kissed him. She walked him downstairs then to the car. After another long kiss goodbye, he left and headed home.

Ava walked inside and grabbed Cat a drink. "I didn't mean to get him all mad," Cat said. "Cat, it's fine." "It wasn't fair." "You can't use Joe and I as an example," Ava said. "But look what happened to you two." "We have been to hell and back and I still love him. That's what we've been through," Ava said. "I can't take him back." "You need time to figure it all out." Ava talked to her for a bit, then headed to Cat's house.

Will was sitting on the front step. She walked past him and grabbed the new keys and walked inside. "Ava." "Don't you even fucking think it. You don't get to fuck around on one of my best friends and think that I'm still going to talk to your stupid ass. You have a damn death wish right now," Ava said. "Where is she?" "As far away from you as she can get and I don't blame her one bit," Ava said. "You're right." "I know." "I shouldn't have married her," Will said. Ava looked at him. "Now you fucking think that? You already did Will. You don't get take backs," Ava said. "I should've been with the woman I wanted." Ava grabbed a few last things to bring to her. "Ava." She turned around and Will kissed her. He pinned her to the wall. "Get off me." "Not giving the chance away this time," Will said. Ava pushed him away and headed for the door. He grabbed her waist and pulled her back towards the bedroom. "Either you let the fuck go, or you are a dead man," Ava said. He didn't. Ava dropped him in one step. She walked out. She dropped the things off with Cat, told security not to let Will in under any circumstances, then headed back to the house.

Ava walked in. The kids were in bed and Ava saw candlelight from the TV room. She walked in and Joe had set up a late dinner for them. Her favorite Chinese food, her favorite wine, and sterling roses. He slid up behind her, wrapping his arms around her. "How is she," Joe asked. "Fine. Will has a death wish, but all is fine." "You saw him?" Ava nodded. He looked at her. "Ava." "I handled it." "What did he do," Joe asked. "Kissed me." She turned towards him. "Then I used a kickboxing move and dropped him to the floor and walked out." A smirk came across Joe's face. She kissed him. "Food." They went and sat down and had dinner together, then curled up and relaxed. "You seriously dropped him," Joe asked. Ava nodded. "Babe." "What?" "I love you." "I know." "Promise me that nothing's coming between us." "You're worried?" She turned towards him and leaned her body into his, wrapping her arms around his neck. "After all the stupid crap I've done." "Revenge isn't something I do," Ava said. "I love you." "I know. Going to remind you why every day." Joe smirked. "I don't know what I'd do without you." "I could guess," Ava teased. "Don't need to because it isn't happening." He pulled her tight to him and kissed her.

---

7 months passed. Ava and Joe were back and forth with the guys on tour, and Cat was at home. She'd eliminated Will from her life. He didn't exist to her anymore. She'd moved on, even to the point of sending divorce papers that he never sent back. Cat leaned back rubbing her stomach. The baby had been kicking up a storm, but this wasn't feeling like a kick. She called Ava. "What's up?" "Something's wrong." "Feels like a giant kick with aftershocks?" "Ava." "On my way." Ava left the studio and went to the house, picked Cat up and took her to the hospital. "How far apart?" "According to my watch, 3 minutes." "When did it start," the doctor asked. "Last night." "Why didn't you call me," Ava asked. "You had just got back with Joe from the shows." "You are ridiculous."

Within an hour or so, Joe showed up. He came running down the hall. "Hey." "Hey yourself." "How we doing Cat?" "I am kicking your brother's ass," Cat said. "8," Ava joked. He grabbed the glass and got her ice chips. Joe came back and handed them to her. Ava kissed him. The doctor came in and checked her. "The baby's crowning." An hour later, Joseph Andrew was born. Ava cut the cord. "He's adorable," Ava said. Cat started crying. Ava wiped her tears away. "So now you can stop kicking me," Cat teased. "Do you want me to call him," Joe asked. "No." "Cat." "No." "He's his son." "He didn't want me, and he didn't want the baby. I'm done." "Cat." "No." "We can talk about it later," Joe said. "You tell him, I will sick Ava on you." Joe laughed. "Fine. Not that I wouldn't love to see what happens." "In a few days I'll tell him. I want nothing to do with him." "Just as long as you tell him." She nodded. Ryan and Brad came in with flowers and teddy bears. "What did you two do? Buy out the toy store?" "Nope. Just the blue section," Ryan joked. Brad put the flowers by Cat's bed. Danielle and Rose came in. Ava went out into the hall, and Joe followed her. "What?" Ava kissed him. "What was that for," he asked wrapping his arms around her. "For taking care of her. Being there like your idiot brother should have been." "She needs us, then we're there." Ava kissed him. He hugged her and held her close.

Ava and Joe took the kids home. They played for a while, then once they went down for their after-lunch nap, Joe and Ava curled up together on the sofa. "Part of me wants to call and check on her." "Better idea," Joe said. She turned towards him. "Which would be?" She pressed her body to his and he pulled her close. He kissed her.

After everything, after all the fights, the stress, the screaming, there was one thing that remained that always grew stronger. So strong that neither of them worried anymore.

He flipped the CD player on one night after a long flight home. The kids were asleep. The house was quiet. "Dance with me," Joe said. He pulled her to her feet. He played the songs from their wedding and held her close. "Only one thing I can't live without . . . you."